Lincoln Peirce

BiG NATE

GENIUS MODE

HarperCollins *Children's Books*

Also by Lincoln Peirce

Big Nate: The Boy with the Biggest Head in the World
Big Nate Strikes Again
Big Nate on a Roll
Big Nate Goes for Broke
Big Nate: Boredom Buster
Big Nate: Fun Blaster
Big Nate: What Could Possibly Go Wrong?
Big Nate: Here Goes Nothing!
Big Nate Flips Out

First published in Great Britain by HarperCollins *Children's Books* in 2013
HarperCollins Children's Books is a division of HarperCollins*Publishers* Ltd,
77-85 Fulham Palace Road, Hammersmith, London, W6 8JB.

These comic strips first appeared in newspapers
from January 11, 2009 through August 9, 2009

www.harpercollins.co.uk

1

ISBN 978-0-00-751564-6

Printed and bound in England by Clays Ltd, St Ives plc.

MIX
Paper from
responsible sources
FSC
www.fsc.org
FSC C007454

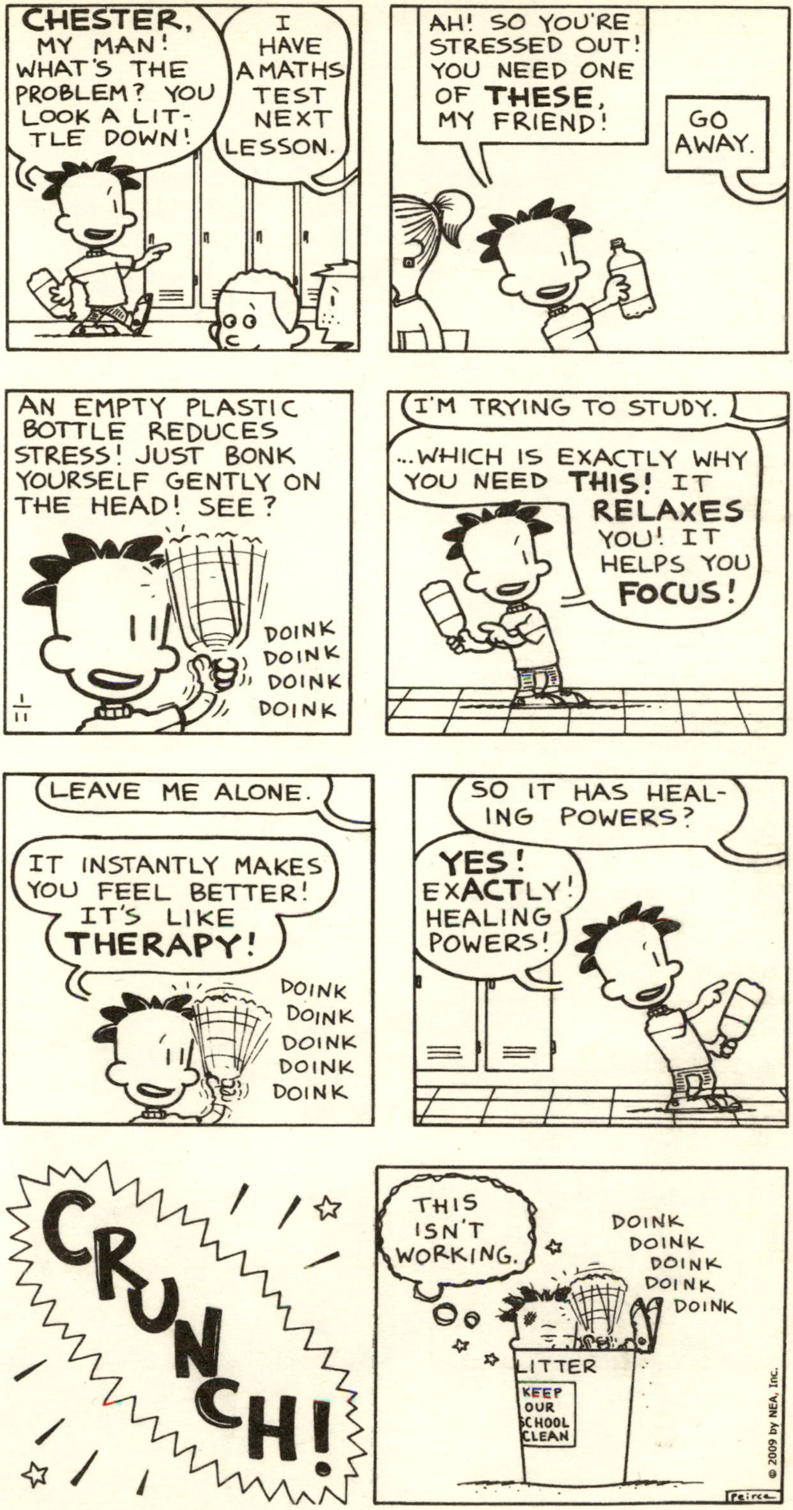
CHESTER, MY MAN! WHAT'S THE PROBLEM? YOU LOOK A LITTLE DOWN!
I HAVE A MATHS TEST NEXT LESSON.
AH! SO YOU'RE STRESSED OUT! YOU NEED ONE OF THESE, MY FRIEND!
GO AWAY.
AN EMPTY PLASTIC BOTTLE REDUCES STRESS! JUST BONK YOURSELF GENTLY ON THE HEAD! SEE?
DOINK DOINK DOINK DOINK
I'M TRYING TO STUDY.
...WHICH IS EXACTLY WHY YOU NEED THIS! IT RELAXES YOU! IT HELPS YOU FOCUS!
LEAVE ME ALONE.
IT INSTANTLY MAKES YOU FEEL BETTER! IT'S LIKE THERAPY!
DOINK DOINK DOINK DOINK DOINK
SO IT HAS HEALING POWERS?
YES! EXACTLY! HEALING POWERS!
CRUNCH!
THIS ISN'T WORKING.
DOINK DOINK DOINK DOINK DOINK
LITTER
KEEP OUR SCHOOL CLEAN
© 2009 by NEA, Inc.
Peirce

WHAT'S IN A NAME?

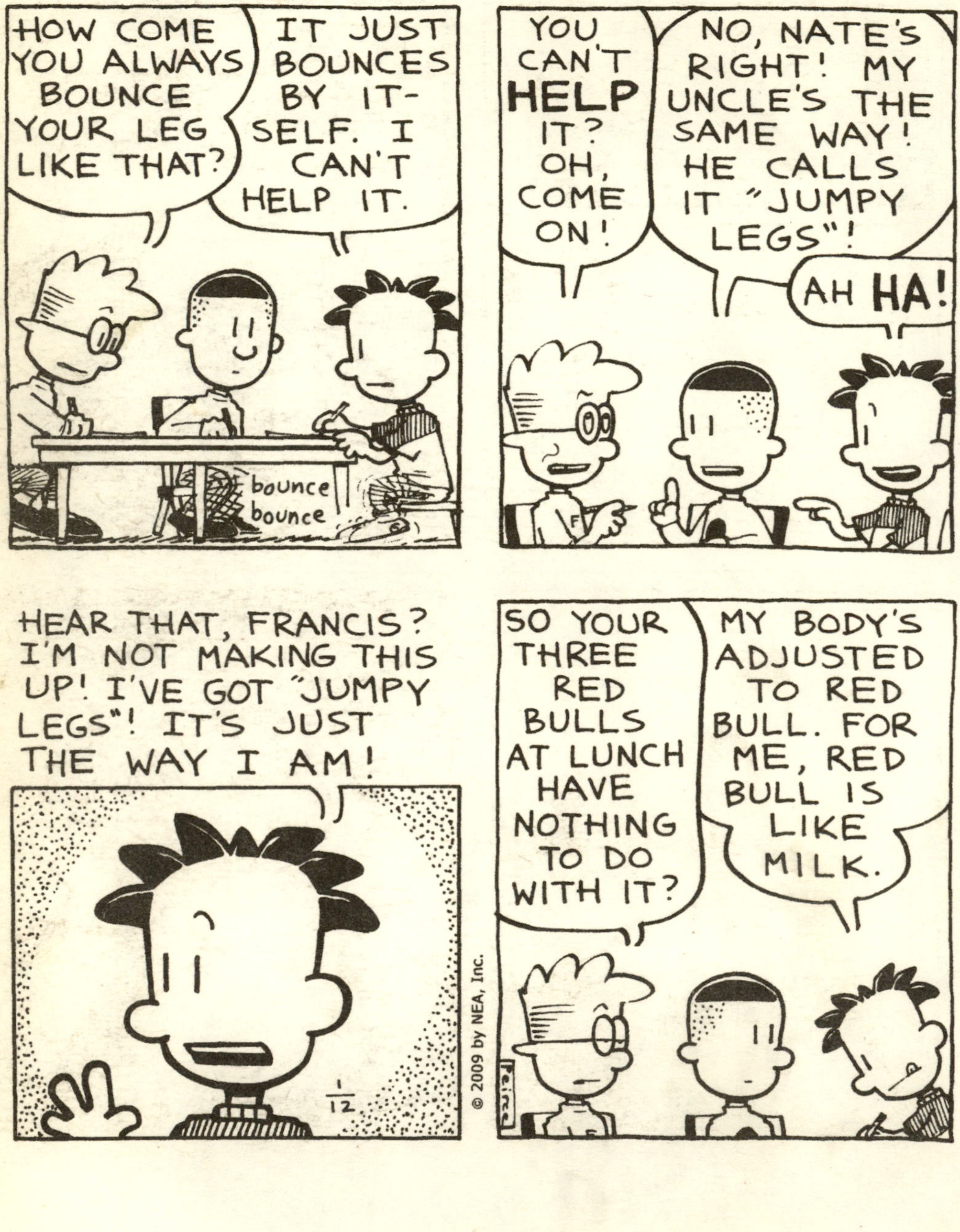
HOW COME YOU ALWAYS BOUNCE YOUR LEG LIKE THAT?
IT JUST BOUNCES BY IT-SELF. I CAN'T HELP IT.
bounce bounce
YOU CAN'T **HELP** IT? OH, COME ON!
NO, NATE'S RIGHT! MY UNCLE'S THE SAME WAY! HE CALLS IT "JUMPY LEGS"!
AH **HA**!
HEAR THAT, FRANCIS? I'M NOT MAKING THIS UP! I'VE GOT "JUMPY LEGS"! IT'S JUST THE WAY I AM!
1/12
© 2009 by NEA, Inc.
Peirce
SO YOUR THREE RED BULLS AT LUNCH HAVE NOTHING TO DO WITH IT?
MY BODY'S ADJUSTED TO RED BULL. FOR ME, RED BULL IS LIKE MILK.

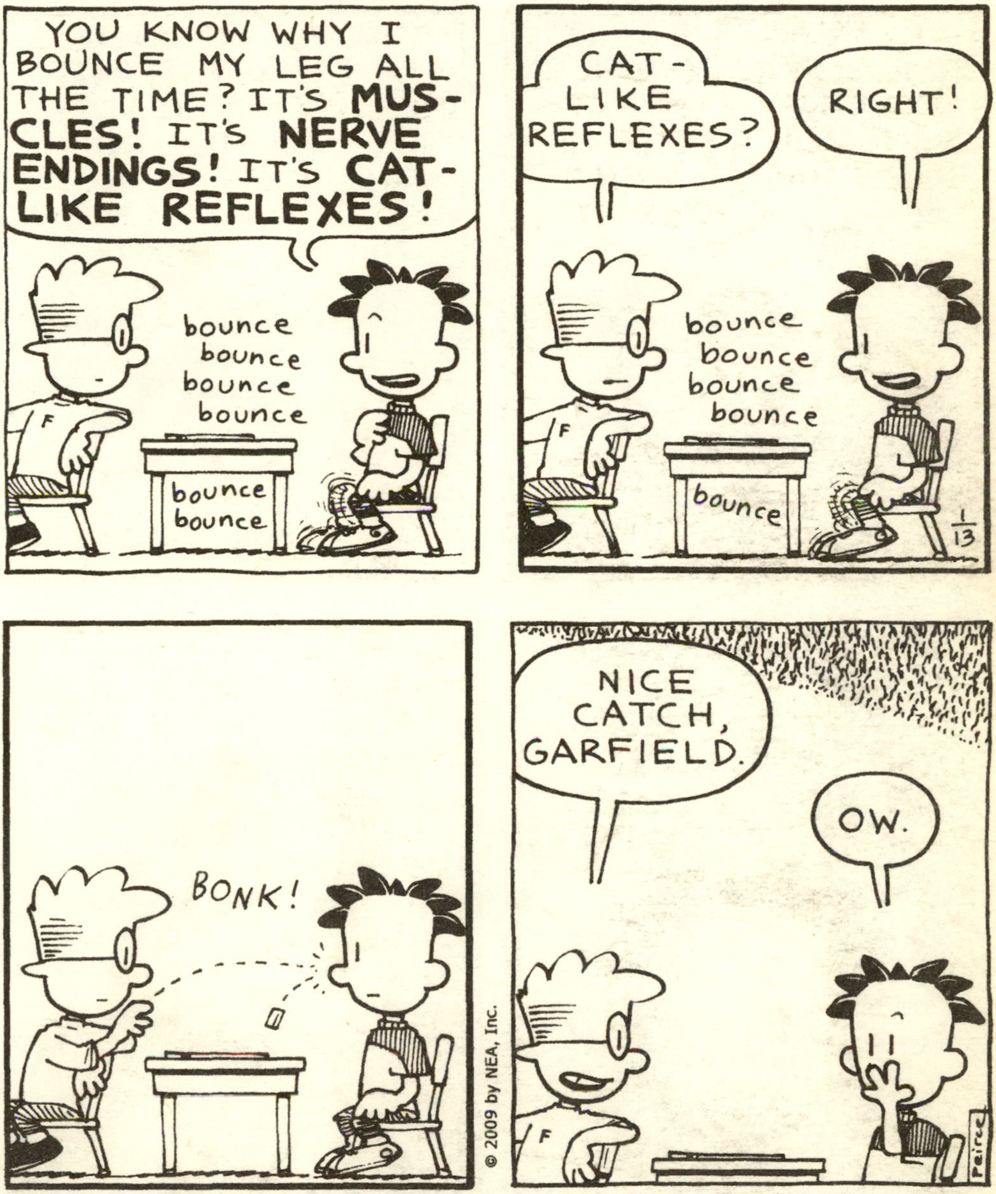
YOU KNOW WHY I BOUNCE MY LEG ALL THE TIME? IT'S MUSCLES! IT'S NERVE ENDINGS! IT'S CAT-LIKE REFLEXES!
bounce bounce bounce bounce
bounce bounce
CAT-LIKE REFLEXES?
RIGHT!
bounce bounce bounce bounce
bounce
1/13
BONK!
© 2009 by NEA, Inc.
NICE CATCH, GARFIELD.
OW.
Peirce

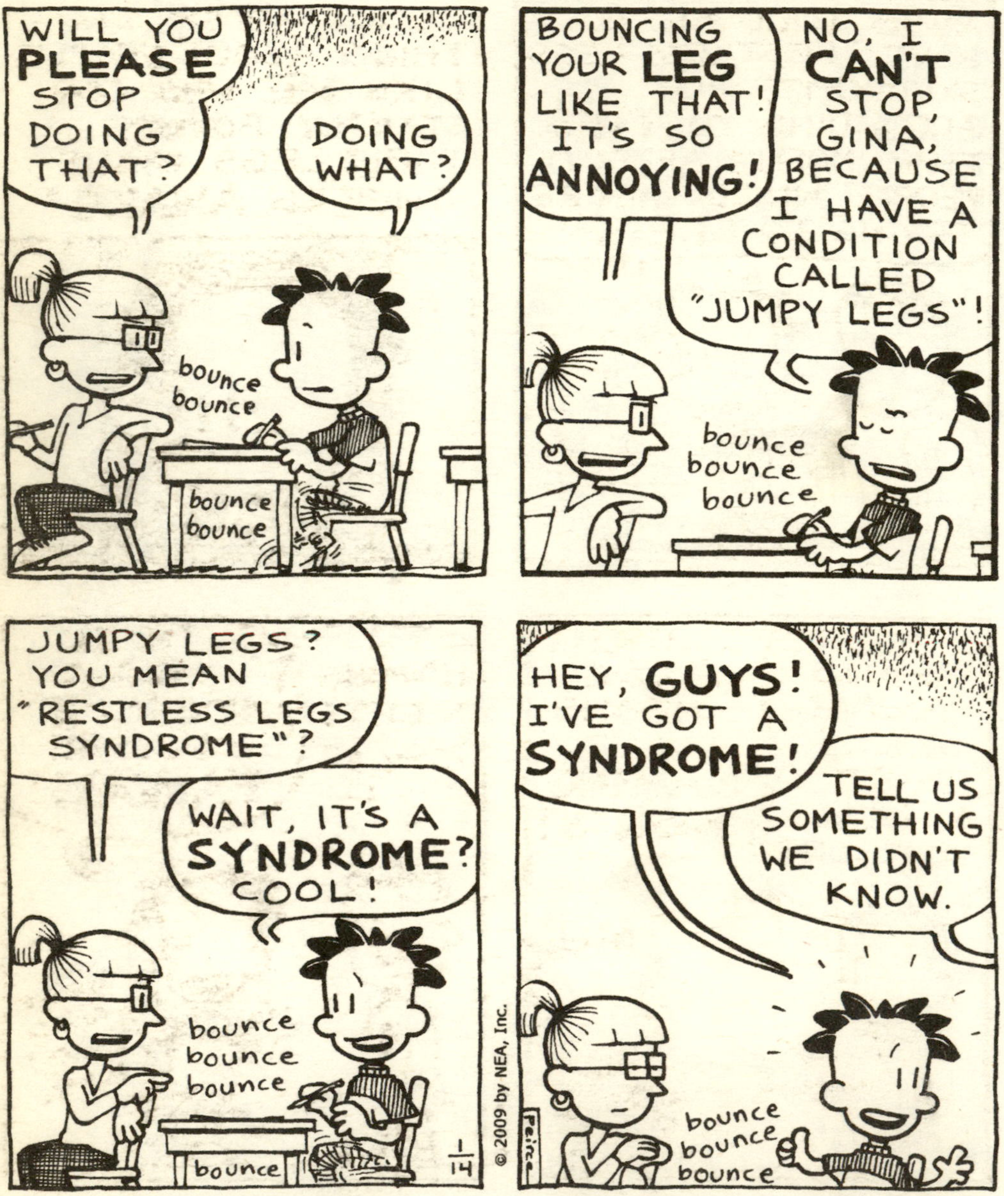
WILL YOU **PLEASE** STOP DOING THAT?
DOING WHAT?
bounce bounce
bounce bounce
BOUNCING YOUR **LEG** LIKE THAT! IT'S SO **ANNOYING!**
NO, I **CAN'T** STOP, GINA, BECAUSE I HAVE A CONDITION CALLED "JUMPY LEGS"!
bounce bounce bounce
JUMPY LEGS? YOU MEAN "RESTLESS LEGS SYNDROME"?
WAIT, IT'S A **SYNDROME**? COOL!
bounce bounce bounce
bounce
1/14
HEY, **GUYS!** I'VE GOT A **SYNDROME!**
TELL US SOMETHING WE DIDN'T KNOW.
bounce bounce bounce
Peirce
© 2009 by NEA, Inc.

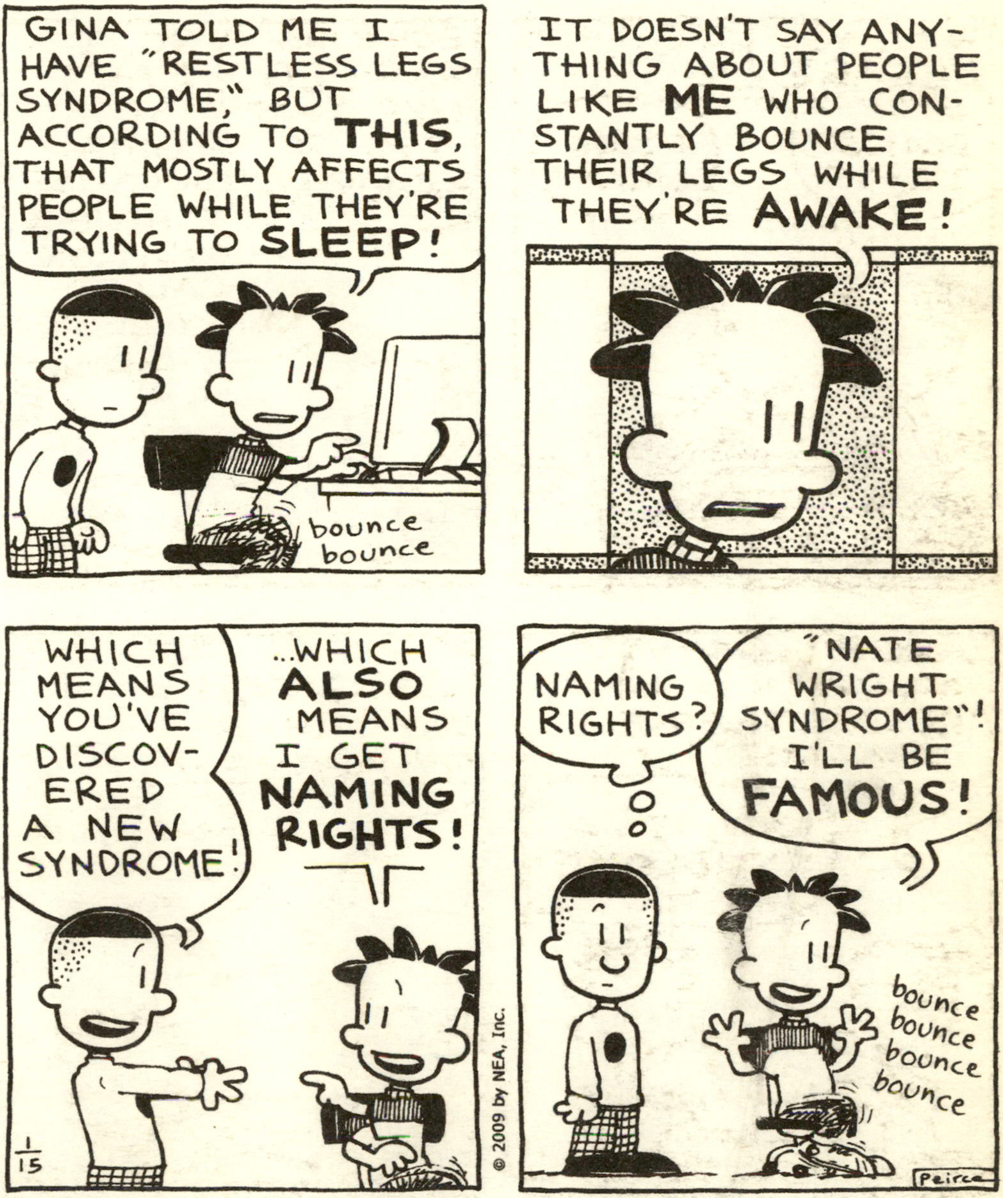
GINA TOLD ME I HAVE "RESTLESS LEGS SYNDROME," BUT ACCORDING TO THIS, THAT MOSTLY AFFECTS PEOPLE WHILE THEY'RE TRYING TO SLEEP!
bounce bounce
IT DOESN'T SAY ANYTHING ABOUT PEOPLE LIKE ME WHO CONSTANTLY BOUNCE THEIR LEGS WHILE THEY'RE AWAKE!
WHICH MEANS YOU'VE DISCOVERED A NEW SYNDROME!
...WHICH ALSO MEANS I GET NAMING RIGHTS!
1/15
© 2009 by NEA, Inc.
NAMING RIGHTS?
"NATE WRIGHT SYNDROME"! I'LL BE FAMOUS!
bounce bounce bounce bounce
Peirce

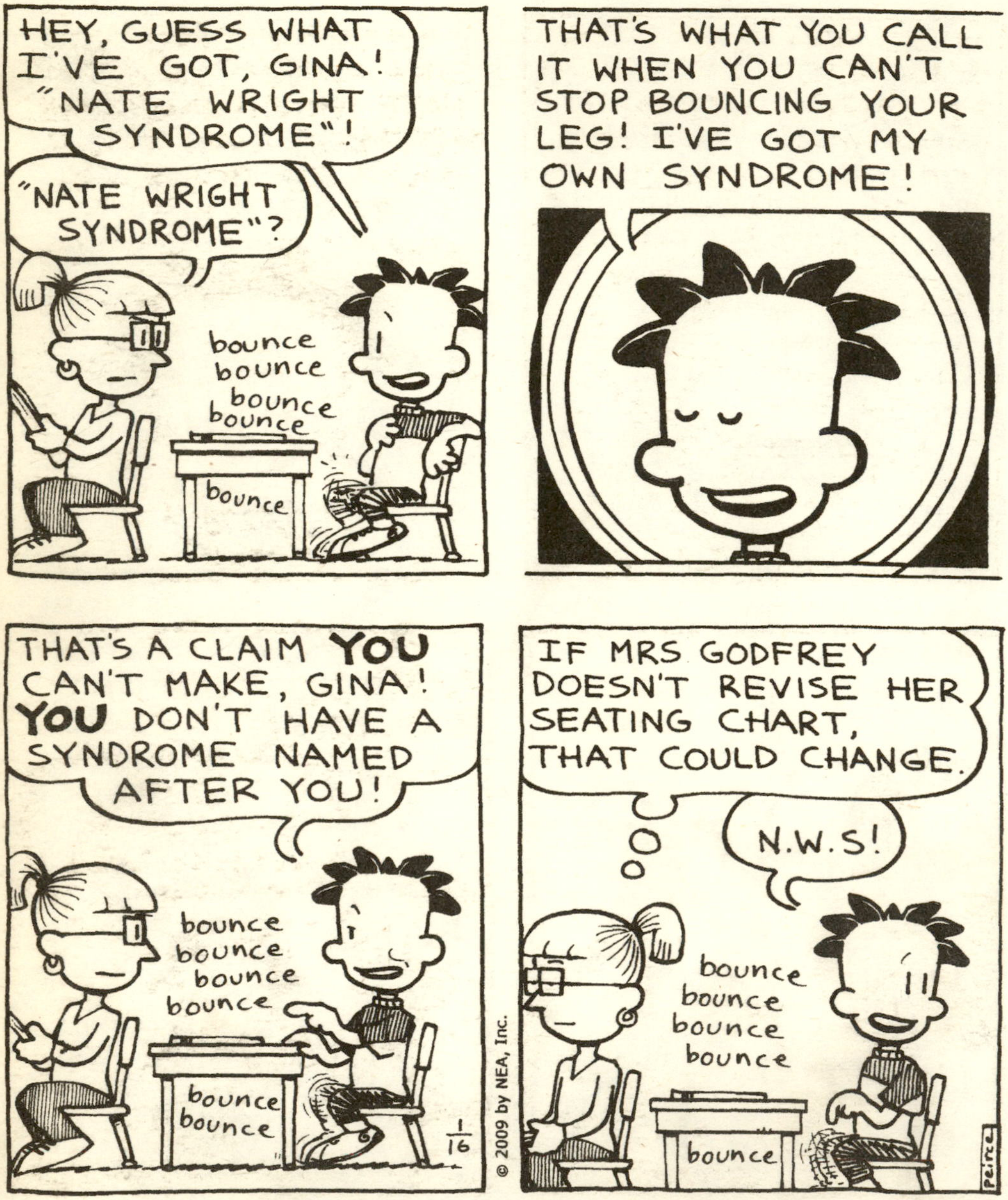
HEY, GUESS WHAT I'VE GOT, GINA! "NATE WRIGHT SYNDROME"!
"NATE WRIGHT SYNDROME"?
bounce bounce bounce bounce
bounce
THAT'S WHAT YOU CALL IT WHEN YOU CAN'T STOP BOUNCING YOUR LEG! I'VE GOT MY OWN SYNDROME!
THAT'S A CLAIM YOU CAN'T MAKE, GINA! YOU DON'T HAVE A SYNDROME NAMED AFTER YOU!
bounce bounce bounce bounce
bounce bounce
1/16
© 2009 by NEA, Inc.
IF MRS GODFREY DOESN'T REVISE HER SEATING CHART, THAT COULD CHANGE.
N.W.S!
bounce bounce bounce bounce
bounce
peirce

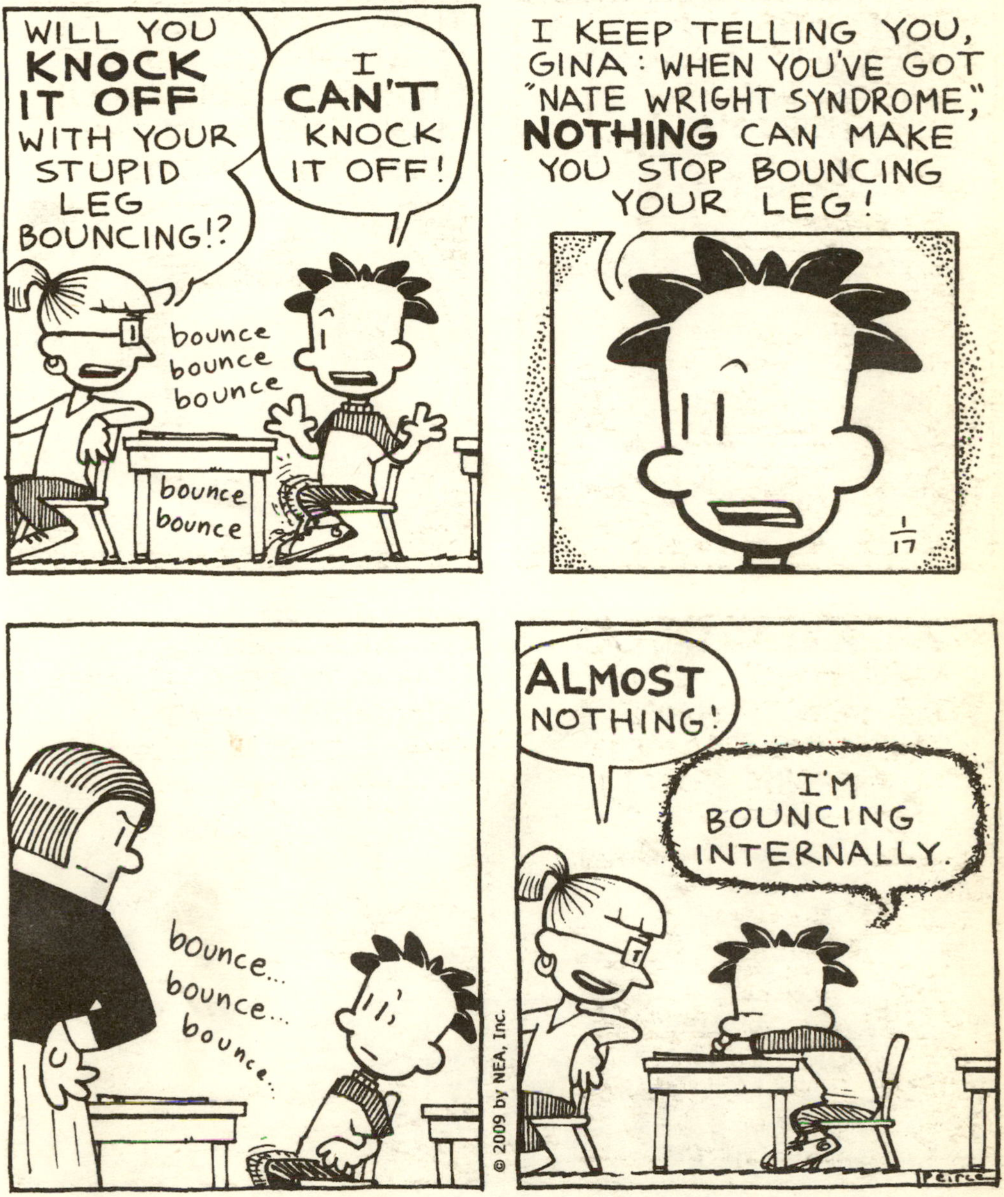

WILL YOU **KNOCK IT OFF** WITH YOUR STUPID LEG BOUNCING!?
I **CAN'T** KNOCK IT OFF!
bounce bounce bounce
bounce bounce
I KEEP TELLING YOU, GINA: WHEN YOU'VE GOT "NATE WRIGHT SYNDROME," **NOTHING** CAN MAKE YOU STOP BOUNCING YOUR LEG!
bounce... bounce... bounce...
ALMOST NOTHING!
I'M BOUNCING INTERNALLY.
Peirce

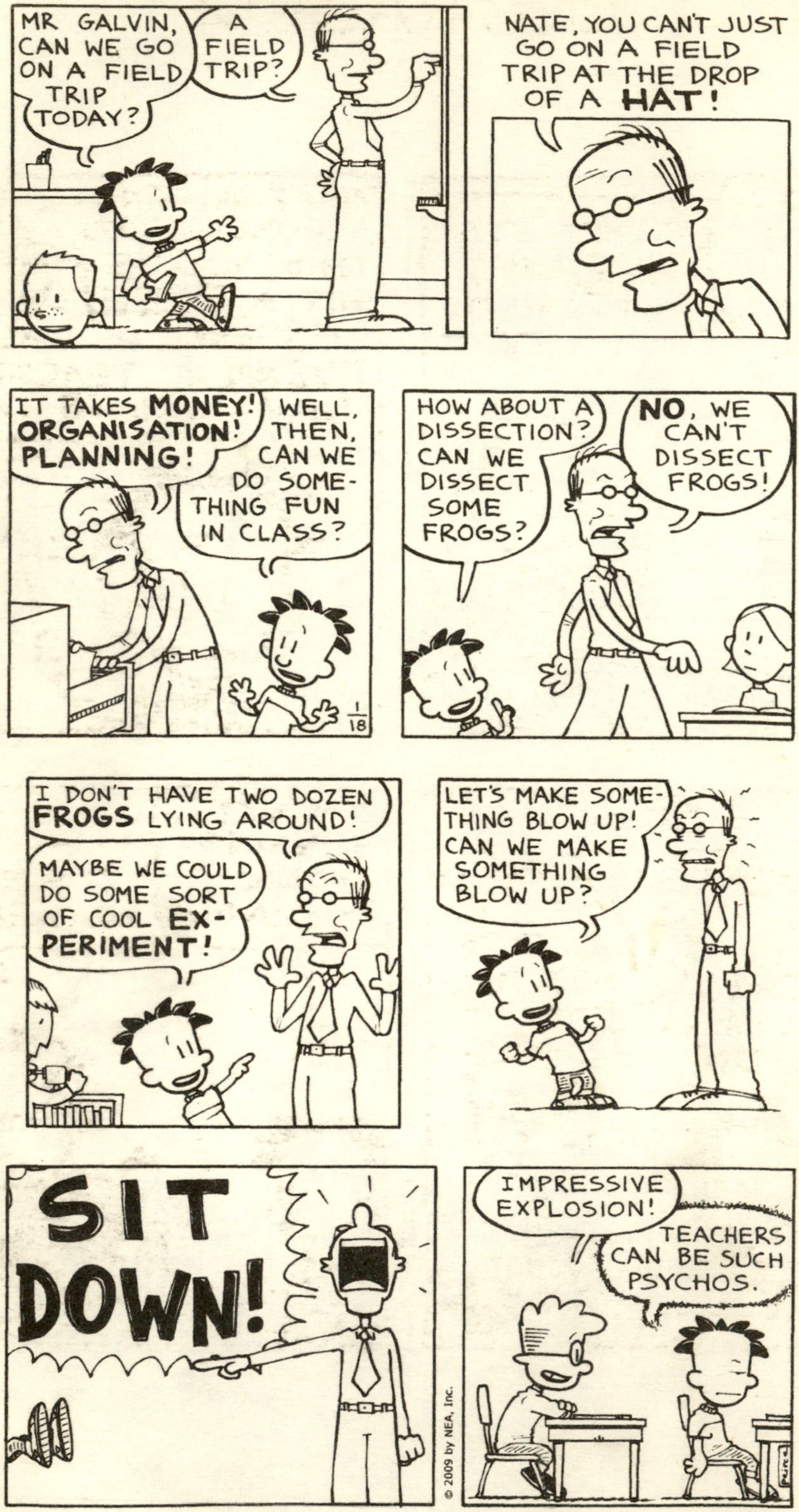
MR GALVIN, CAN WE GO ON A FIELD TRIP TODAY?
A FIELD TRIP?
NATE, YOU CAN'T JUST GO ON A FIELD TRIP AT THE DROP OF A HAT!
IT TAKES MONEY! ORGANISATION! PLANNING!
WELL, THEN, CAN WE DO SOMETHING FUN IN CLASS?
1/18
HOW ABOUT A DISSECTION? CAN WE DISSECT SOME FROGS?
NO, WE CAN'T DISSECT FROGS!
I DON'T HAVE TWO DOZEN FROGS LYING AROUND!
MAYBE WE COULD DO SOME SORT OF COOL EXPERIMENT!
LET'S MAKE SOMETHING BLOW UP! CAN WE MAKE SOMETHING BLOW UP?
SIT DOWN!
© 2009 by NEA, Inc.
IMPRESSIVE EXPLOSION!
TEACHERS CAN BE SUCH PSYCHOS.

OUTRAGED!

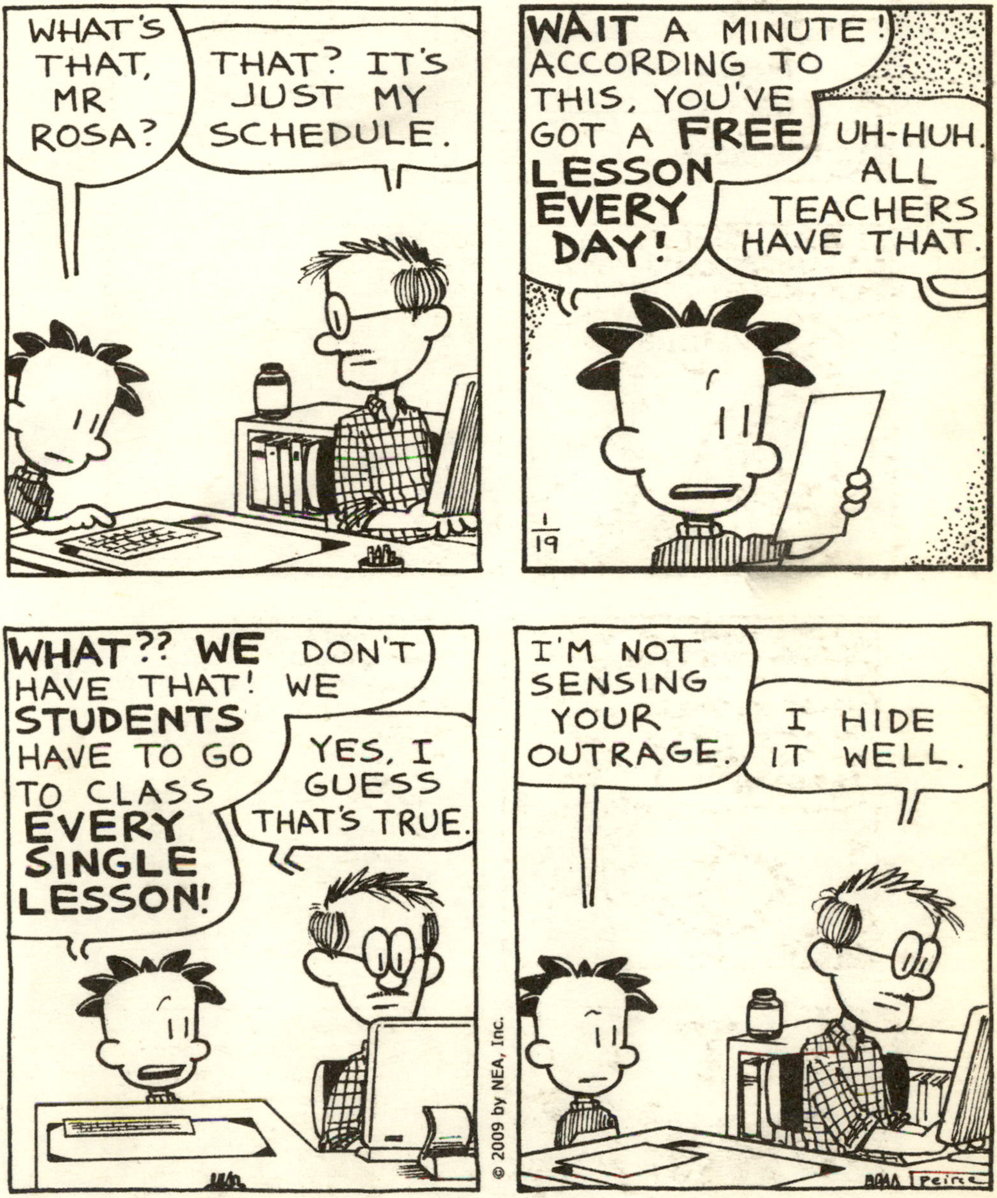
WHAT'S THAT, MR ROSA?
THAT? IT'S JUST MY SCHEDULE.
WAIT A MINUTE! ACCORDING TO THIS, YOU'VE GOT A FREE LESSON EVERY DAY!
UH-HUH. ALL TEACHERS HAVE THAT.
1/19
WHAT?? WE DON'T HAVE THAT! WE STUDENTS HAVE TO GO TO CLASS EVERY SINGLE LESSON!
YES, I GUESS THAT'S TRUE.
© 2009 by NEA, Inc.
I'M NOT SENSING YOUR OUTRAGE.
I HIDE IT WELL.
Peirce

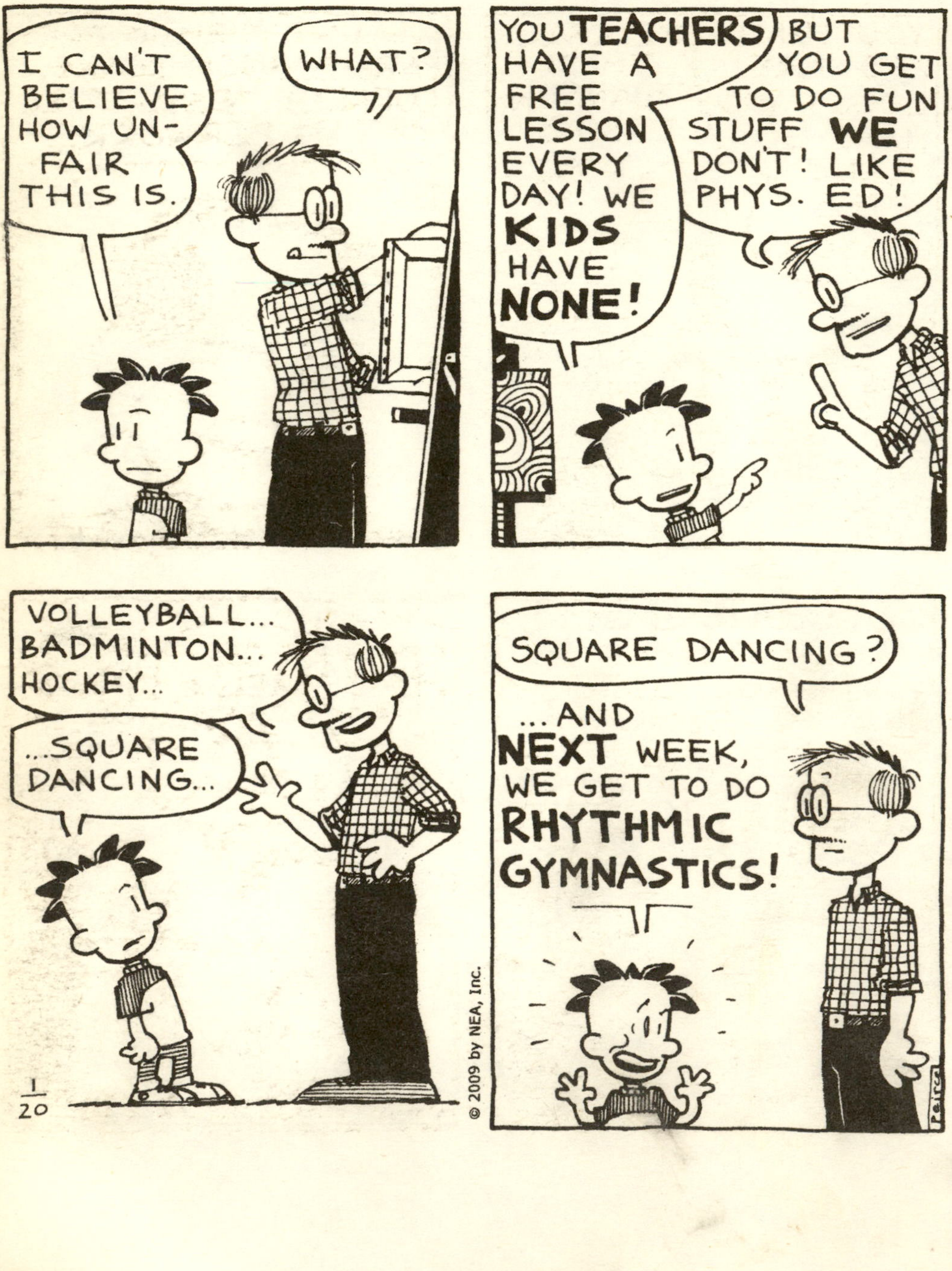
I CAN'T BELIEVE HOW UN-FAIR THIS IS.
WHAT?
YOU TEACHERS HAVE A FREE LESSON EVERY DAY! WE KIDS HAVE NONE!
BUT YOU GET TO DO FUN STUFF WE DON'T! LIKE PHYS. ED!
VOLLEYBALL... BADMINTON... HOCKEY...
...SQUARE DANCING...
SQUARE DANCING?
...AND NEXT WEEK, WE GET TO DO RHYTHMIC GYMNASTICS!
1/20
© 2009 by NEA, Inc.
Peirce

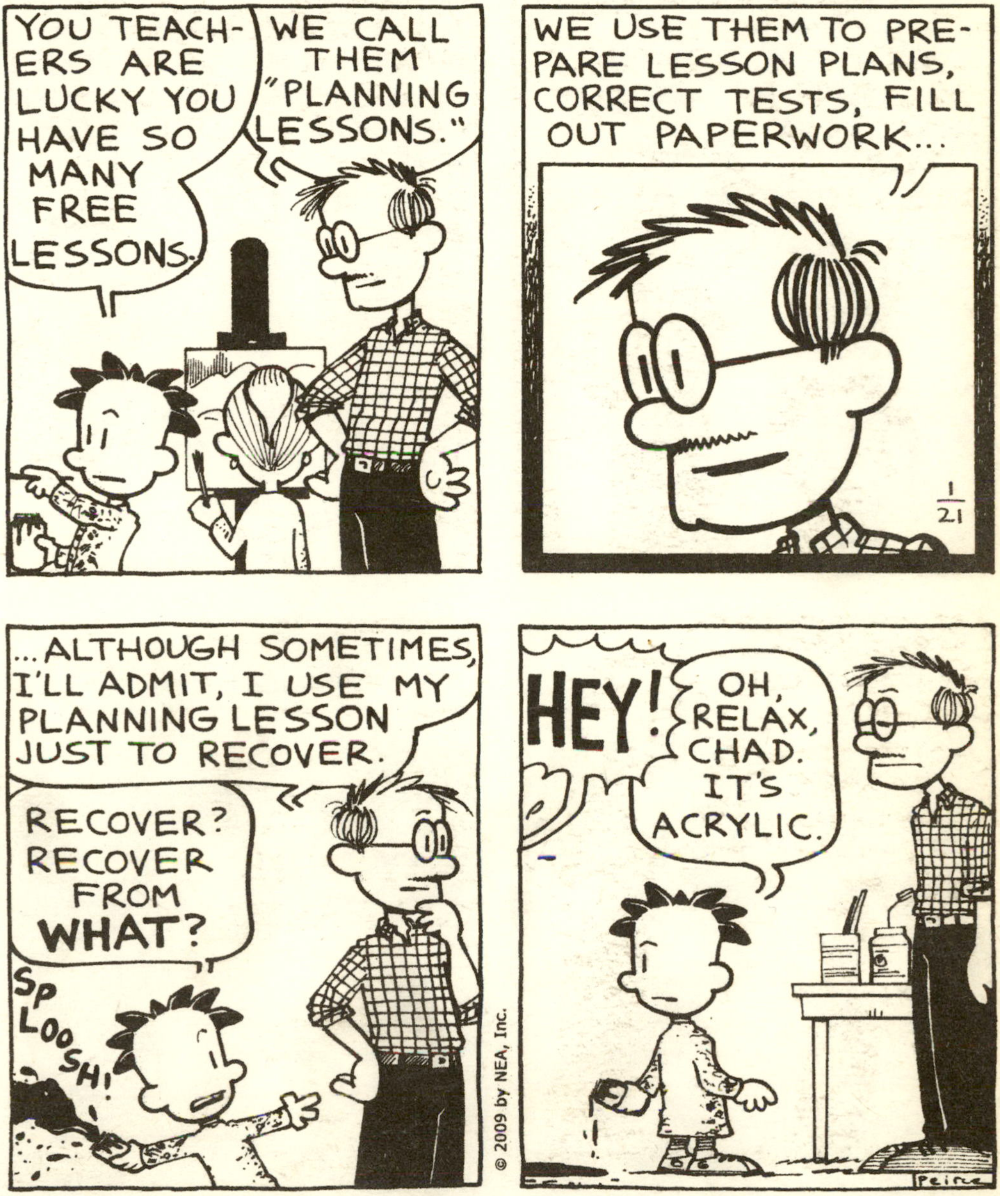
YOU TEACHERS ARE LUCKY YOU HAVE SO MANY FREE LESSONS.
WE CALL THEM "PLANNING LESSONS."
WE USE THEM TO PREPARE LESSON PLANS, CORRECT TESTS, FILL OUT PAPERWORK...
1/21
...ALTHOUGH SOMETIMES, I'LL ADMIT, I USE MY PLANNING LESSON JUST TO RECOVER.
RECOVER? RECOVER FROM WHAT?
SPLOOSH!
© 2009 by NEA, Inc.
HEY!
OH, RELAX, CHAD. IT'S ACRYLIC.
Peirce

ALL IN

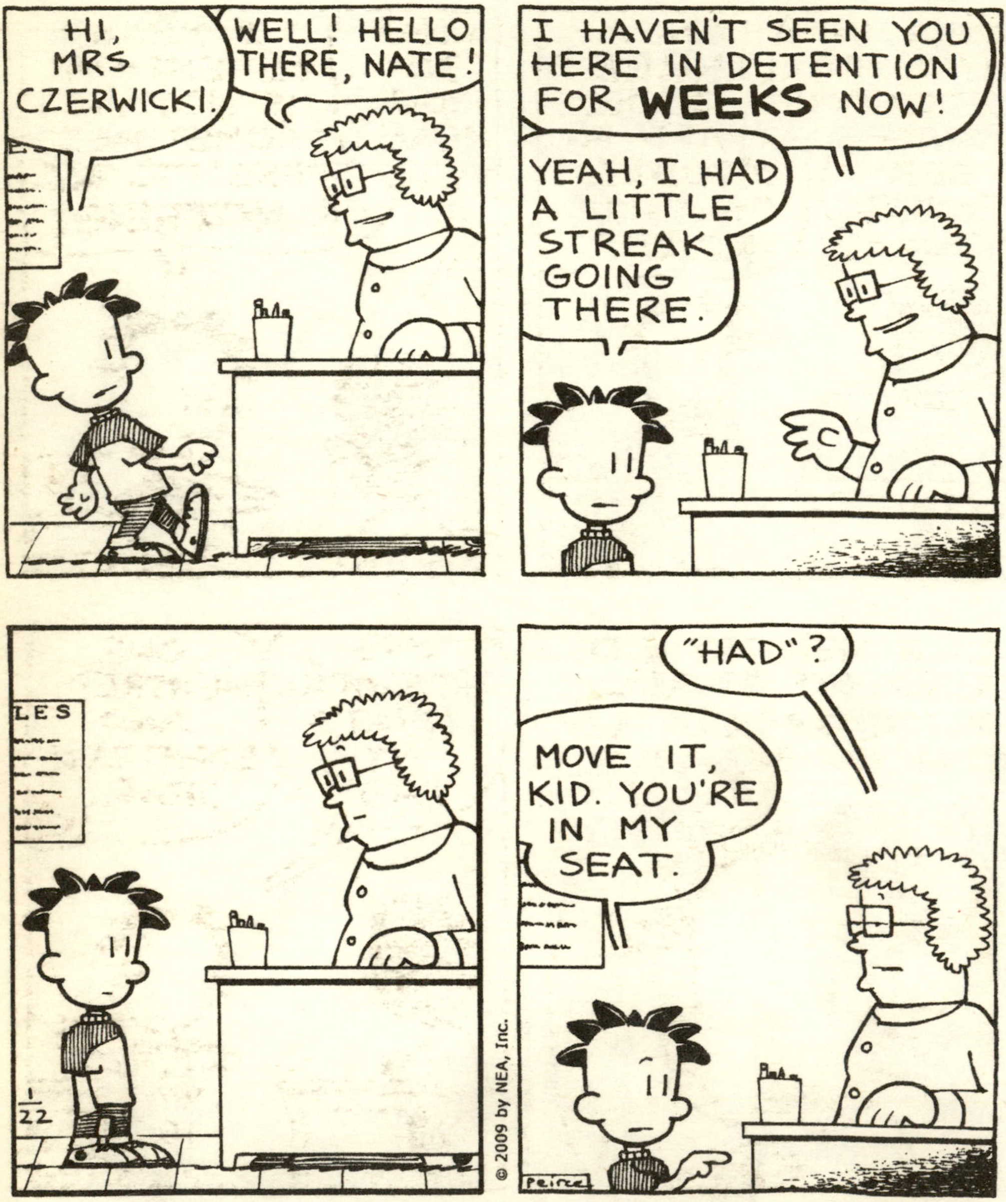
HI, MRS CZERWICKI.
WELL! HELLO THERE, NATE!
I HAVEN'T SEEN YOU HERE IN DETENTION FOR **WEEKS** NOW!
YEAH, I HAD A LITTLE STREAK GOING THERE.
LES
1/22
"HAD"?
MOVE IT, KID. YOU'RE IN MY SEAT.
© 2009 by NEA, Inc.
Peirce

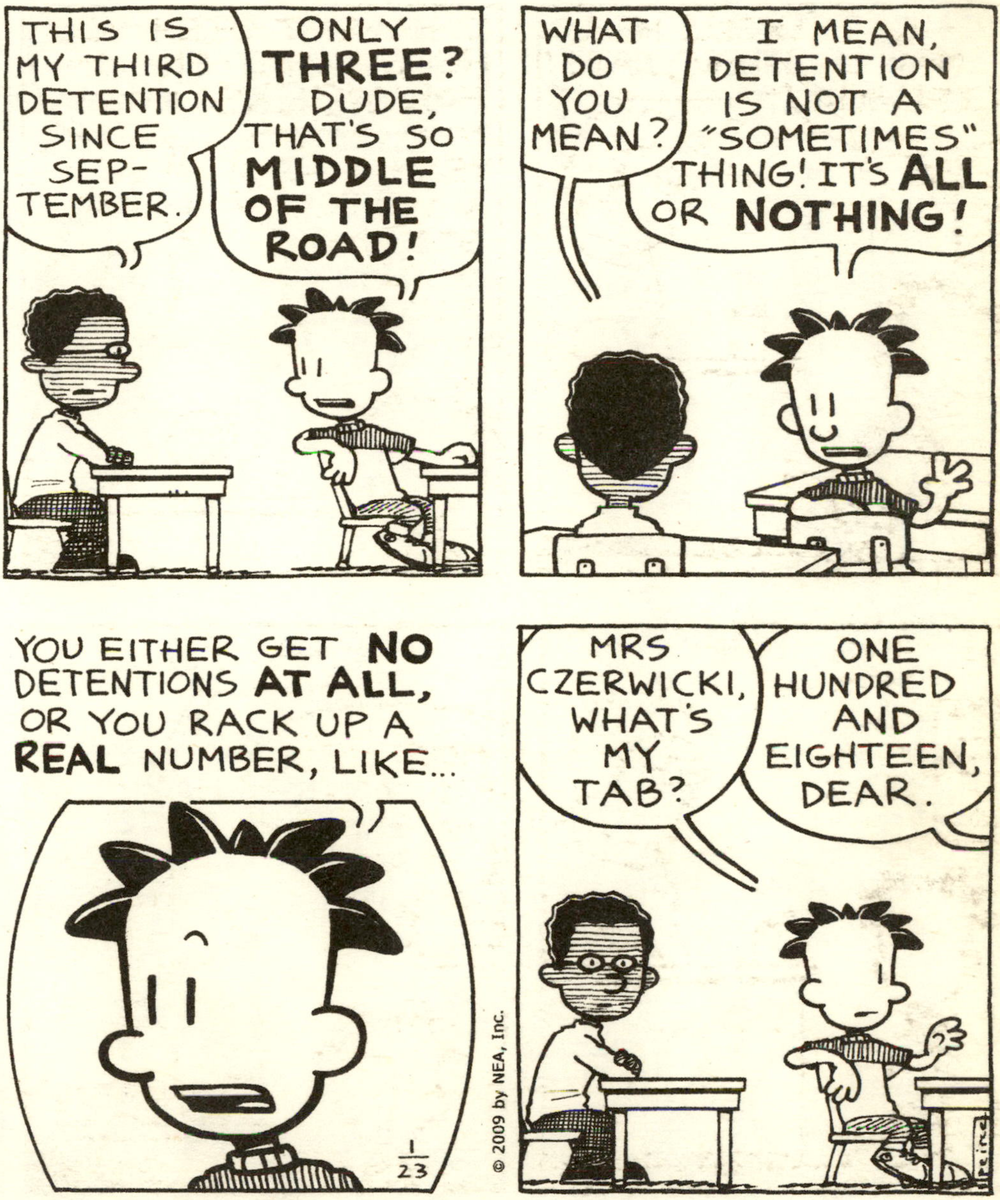
THIS IS MY THIRD DETENTION SINCE SEP- TEMBER.
ONLY THREE? DUDE, THAT'S SO MIDDLE OF THE ROAD!
WHAT DO YOU MEAN?
I MEAN, DETENTION IS NOT A "SOMETIMES" THING! IT'S ALL OR NOTHING!
YOU EITHER GET NO DETENTIONS AT ALL, OR YOU RACK UP A REAL NUMBER, LIKE...
1/23
© 2009 by NEA, Inc.
MRS CZERWICKI, WHAT'S MY TAB?
ONE HUNDRED AND EIGHTEEN, DEAR.
Peirce

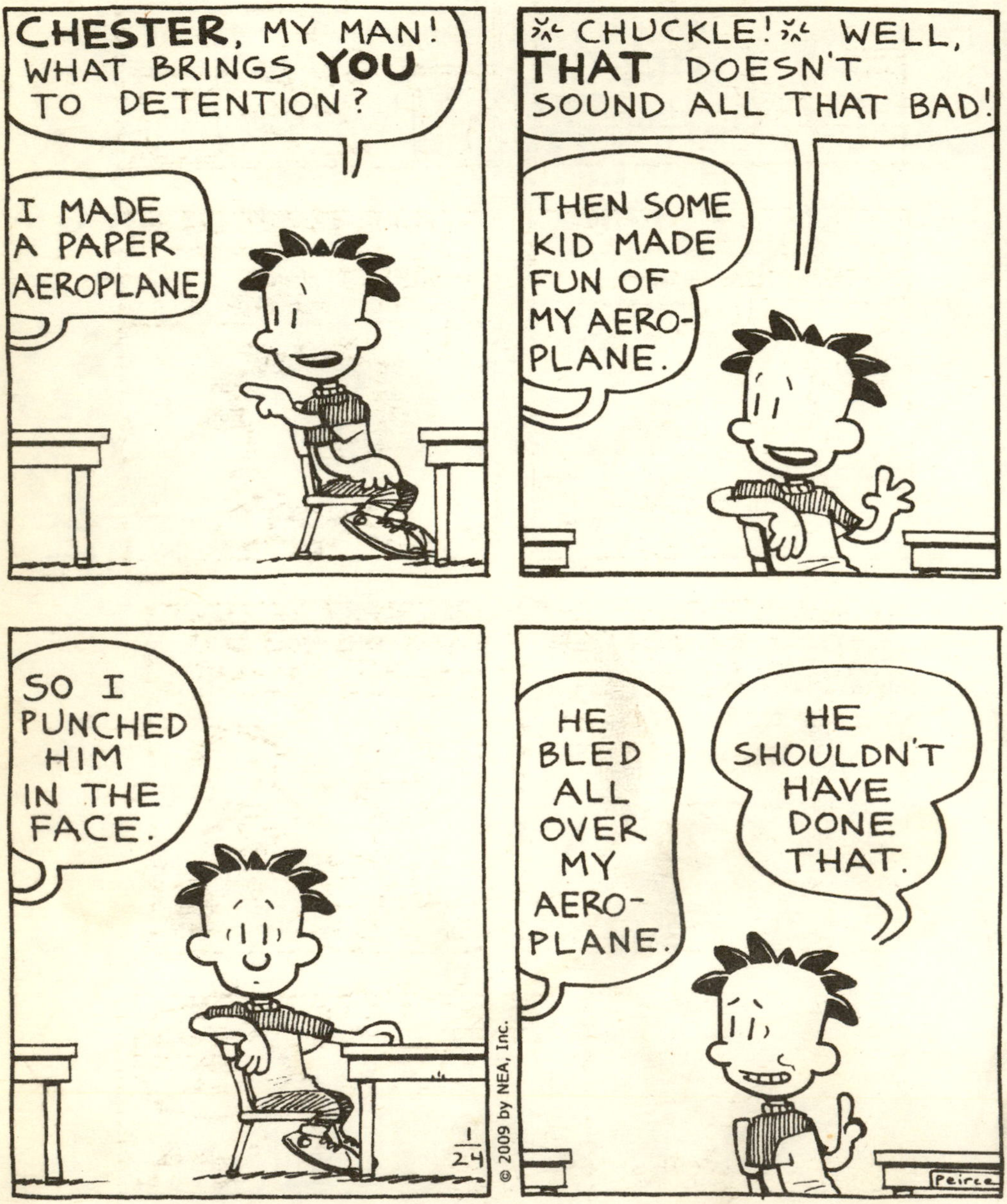
CHESTER, MY MAN! WHAT BRINGS YOU TO DETENTION?
I MADE A PAPER AEROPLANE
CHUCKLE! WELL, THAT DOESN'T SOUND ALL THAT BAD!
THEN SOME KID MADE FUN OF MY AERO-PLANE.
SO I PUNCHED HIM IN THE FACE.
HE BLED ALL OVER MY AERO-PLANE.
HE SHOULDN'T HAVE DONE THAT.
1/24
© 2009 by NEA, Inc.
Peirce

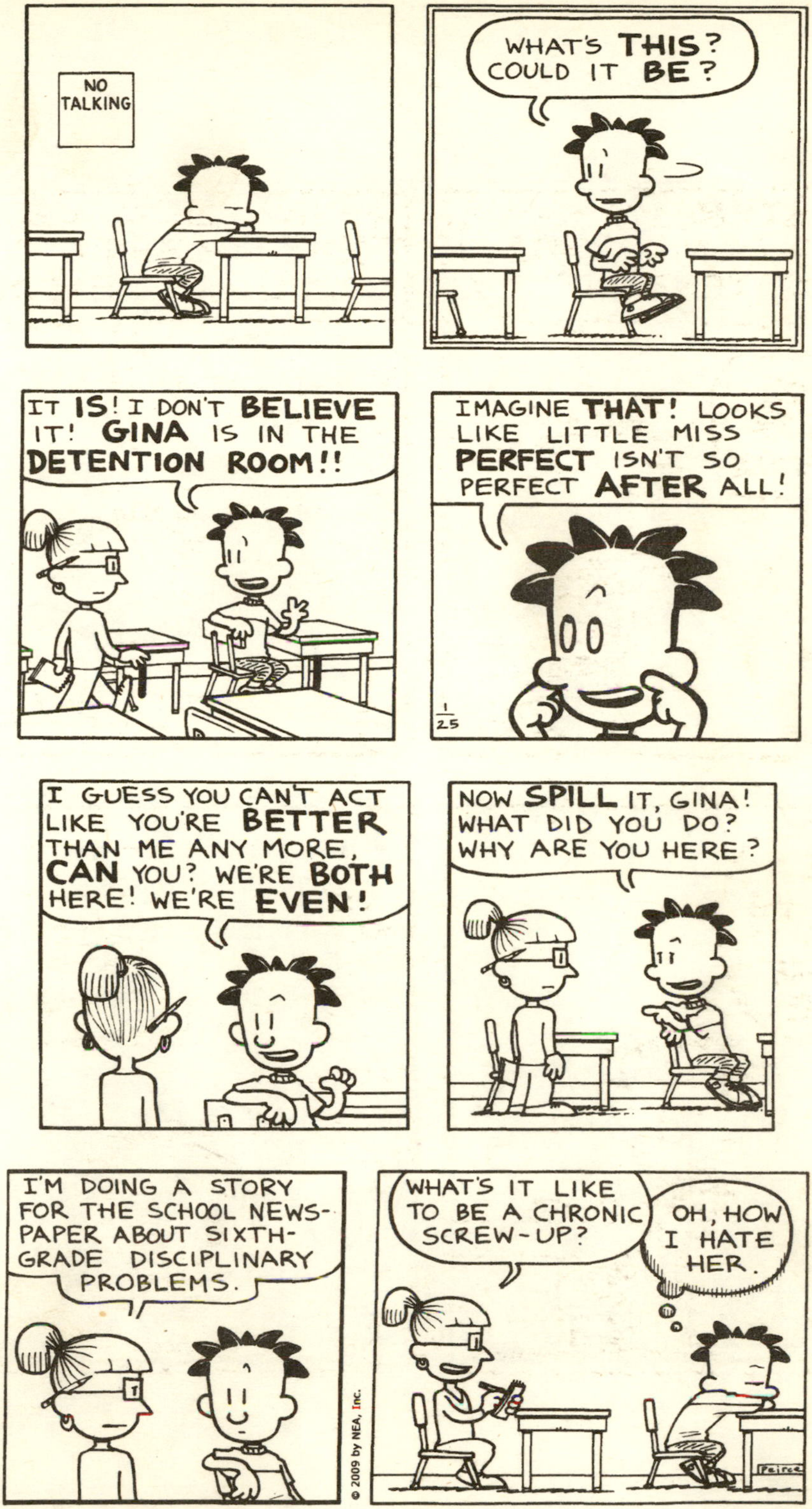
NO TALKING
WHAT'S THIS? COULD IT BE?
IT IS! I DON'T BELIEVE IT! GINA IS IN THE DETENTION ROOM!!
IMAGINE THAT! LOOKS LIKE LITTLE MISS PERFECT ISN'T SO PERFECT AFTER ALL!
1/25
I GUESS YOU CAN'T ACT LIKE YOU'RE BETTER THAN ME ANY MORE, CAN YOU? WE'RE BOTH HERE! WE'RE EVEN!
NOW SPILL IT, GINA! WHAT DID YOU DO? WHY ARE YOU HERE?
I'M DOING A STORY FOR THE SCHOOL NEWS-PAPER ABOUT SIXTH-GRADE DISCIPLINARY PROBLEMS.
© 2009 by NEA, Inc.
WHAT'S IT LIKE TO BE A CHRONIC SCREW-UP?
OH, HOW I HATE HER.
Peirce

SAY CHEESE!

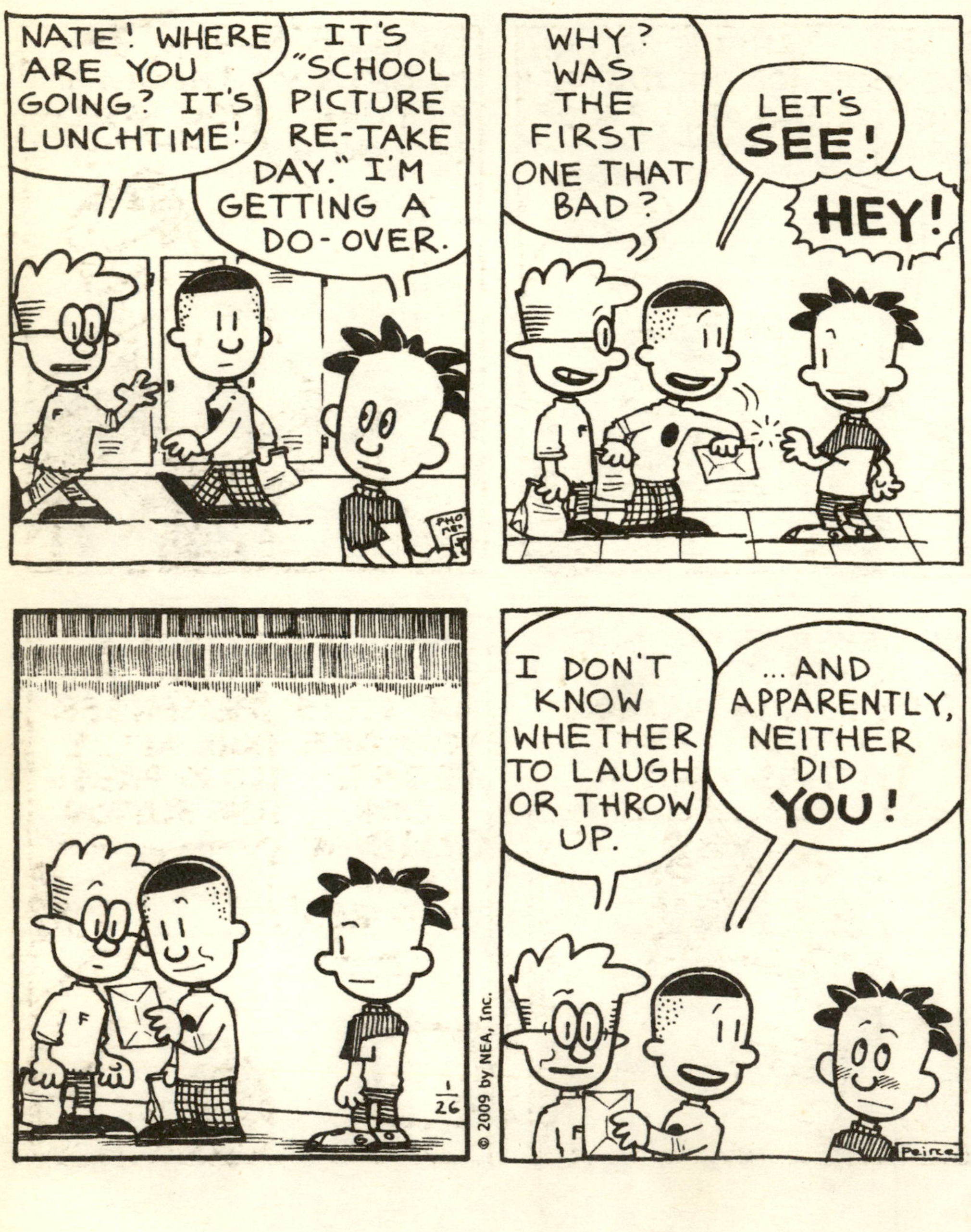
NATE! WHERE ARE YOU GOING? IT'S LUNCHTIME!
IT'S "SCHOOL PICTURE RE-TAKE DAY." I'M GETTING A DO-OVER.
WHY? WAS THE FIRST ONE THAT BAD?
LET'S SEE!
HEY!
I DON'T KNOW WHETHER TO LAUGH OR THROW UP.
...AND APPARENTLY, NEITHER DID YOU!
1/26
© 2009 by NEA, Inc.
Peirce

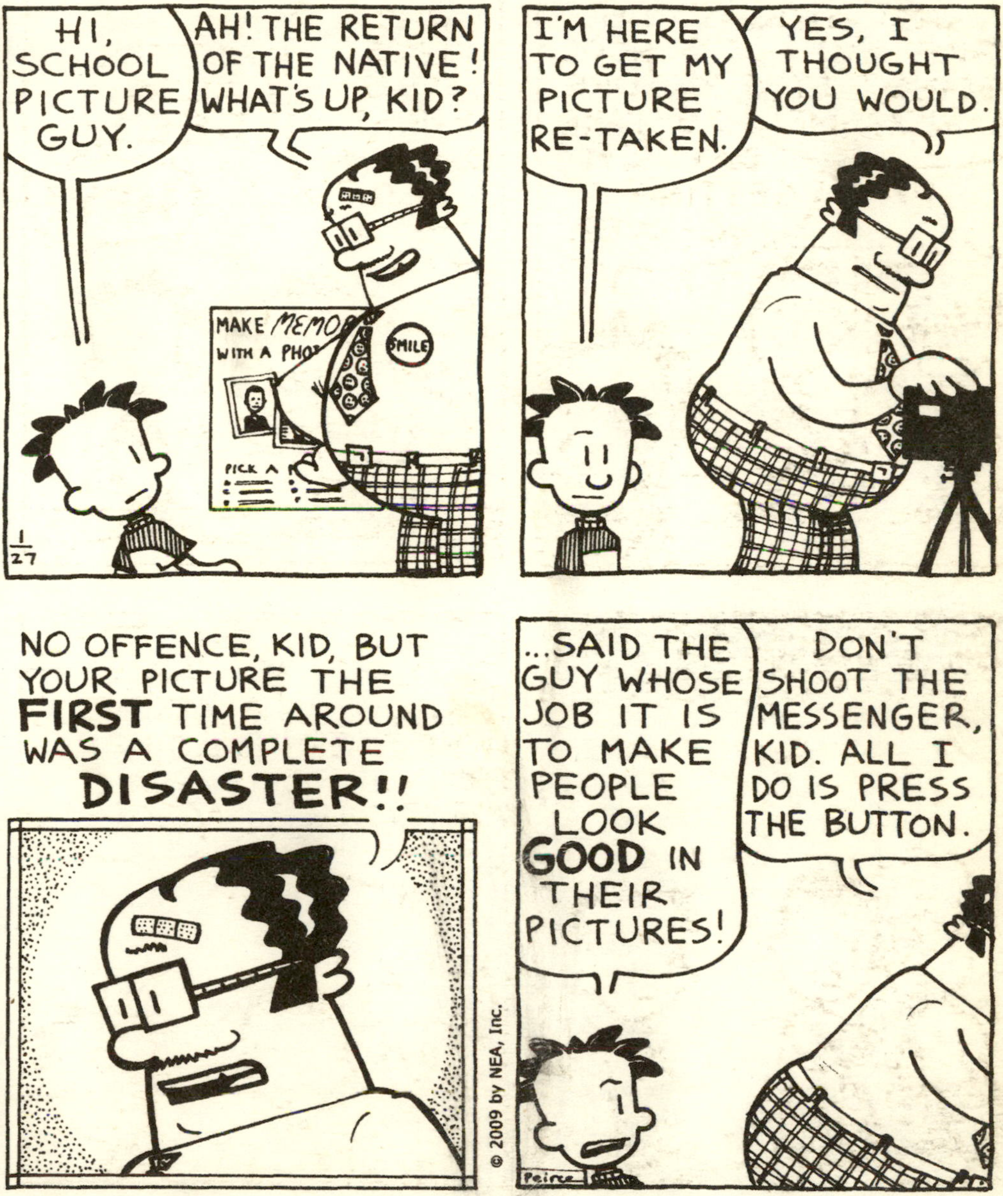
HI, SCHOOL PICTURE GUY.
AH! THE RETURN OF THE NATIVE! WHAT'S UP, KID?
MAKE MEMO
WITH A PHO
PICK A
SMILE
I'M HERE TO GET MY PICTURE RE-TAKEN.
YES, I THOUGHT YOU WOULD.
NO OFFENCE, KID, BUT YOUR PICTURE THE **FIRST** TIME AROUND WAS A COMPLETE **DISASTER!!**
DON'T SHOOT THE MESSENGER, KID. ALL I DO IS PRESS THE BUTTON.
...SAID THE GUY WHOSE JOB IT IS TO MAKE PEOPLE LOOK **GOOD** IN THEIR PICTURES!
© 2009 by NEA, Inc.
Peirce

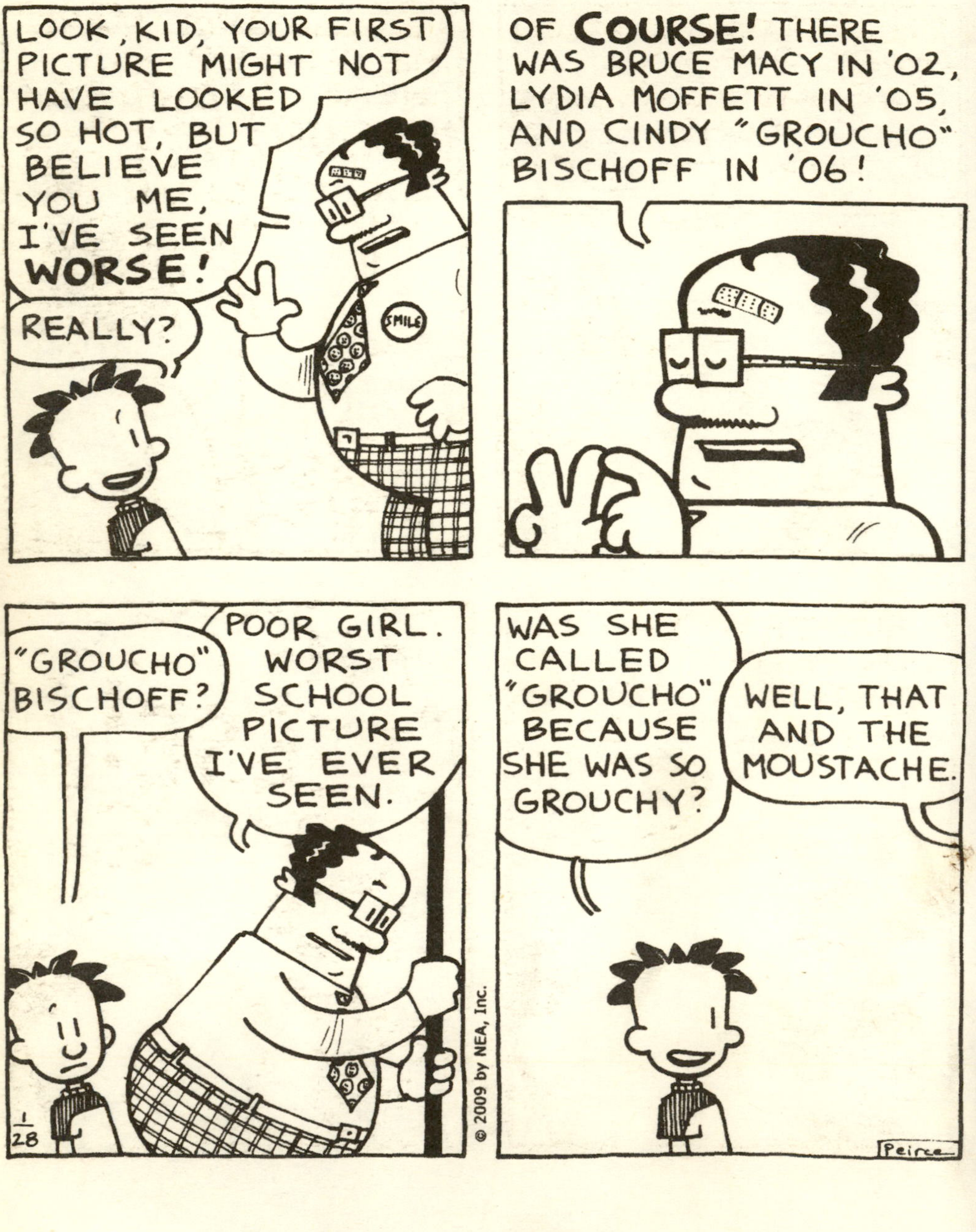
LOOK, KID, YOUR FIRST PICTURE MIGHT NOT HAVE LOOKED SO HOT, BUT BELIEVE YOU ME, I'VE SEEN WORSE!
REALLY?
OF COURSE! THERE WAS BRUCE MACY IN '02, LYDIA MOFFETT IN '05, AND CINDY "GROUCHO" BISCHOFF IN '06!
"GROUCHO" BISCHOFF?
POOR GIRL. WORST SCHOOL PICTURE I'VE EVER SEEN.
WAS SHE CALLED "GROUCHO" BECAUSE SHE WAS SO GROUCHY?
WELL, THAT AND THE MOUSTACHE.
1/28
© 2009 by NEA, Inc.
Peirce

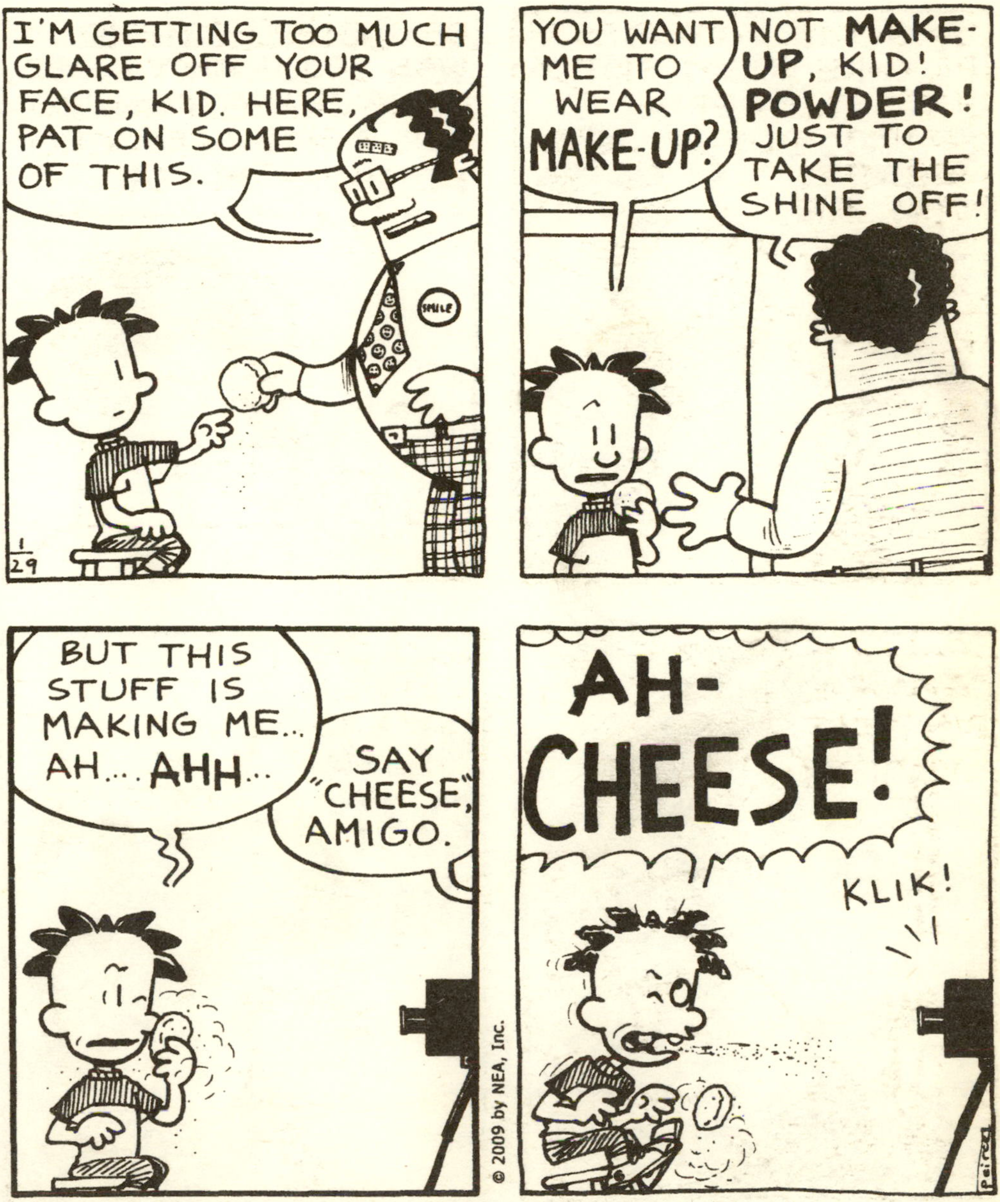
I'M GETTING TOO MUCH GLARE OFF YOUR FACE, KID. HERE, PAT ON SOME OF THIS.
1/29
YOU WANT ME TO WEAR MAKE-UP?
NOT MAKE-UP, KID! POWDER! JUST TO TAKE THE SHINE OFF!
BUT THIS STUFF IS MAKING ME... AH... AHH...
SAY "CHEESE," AMIGO.
© 2009 by NEA, Inc.
AH-CHEESE!
KLIK!
PEIRCE

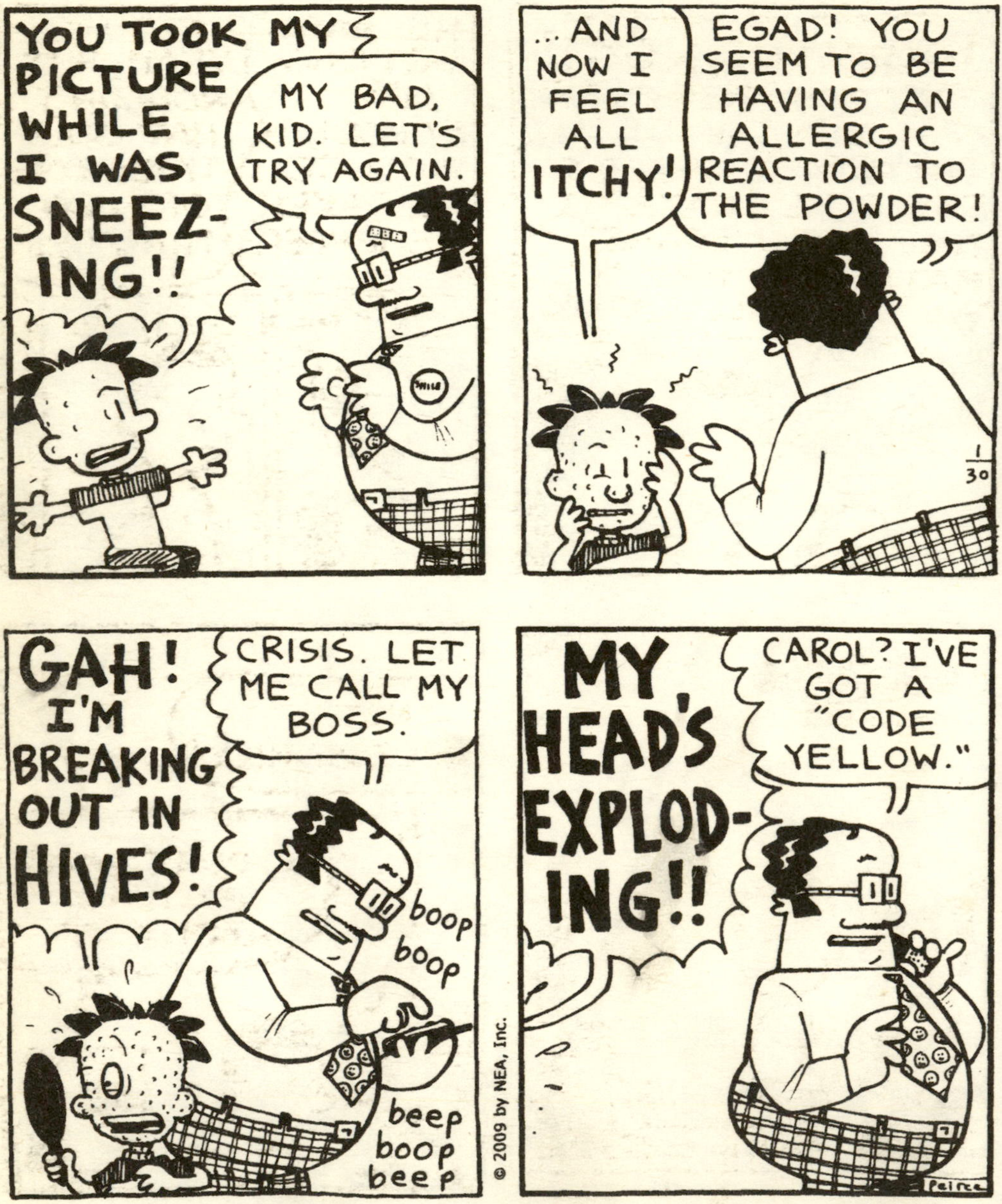
YOU TOOK MY PICTURE WHILE I WAS SNEEZ-ING!!
MY BAD, KID. LET'S TRY AGAIN.
...AND NOW I FEEL ALL ITCHY!
EGAD! YOU SEEM TO BE HAVING AN ALLERGIC REACTION TO THE POWDER!
1/30
GAH! I'M BREAKING OUT IN HIVES!
CRISIS. LET ME CALL MY BOSS.
boop boop
beep boop beep
© 2009 by NEA, Inc.
MY HEAD'S EXPLOD-ING!!
CAROL? I'VE GOT A "CODE YELLOW."
Peirce

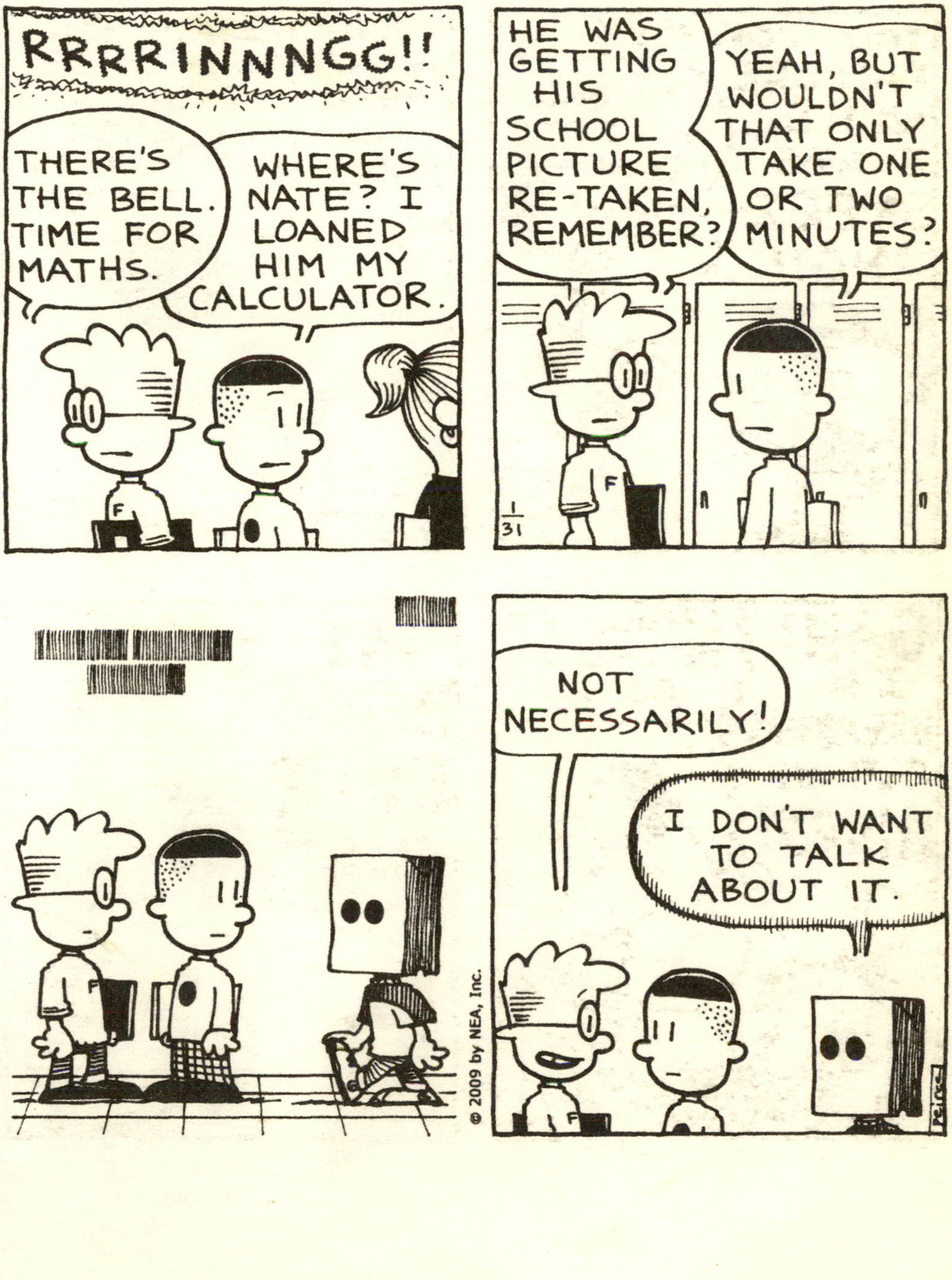
RRRRINNNGG!!
THERE'S THE BELL. TIME FOR MATHS.
WHERE'S NATE? I LOANED HIM MY CALCULATOR.
HE WAS GETTING HIS SCHOOL PICTURE RE-TAKEN, REMEMBER?
YEAH, BUT WOULDN'T THAT ONLY TAKE ONE OR TWO MINUTES?
1/31
[redacted]
[redacted]
NOT NECESSARILY!
I DON'T WANT TO TALK ABOUT IT.
Peirce

"AVOID MINOR ARGUMENTS WHICH COULD ESCALATE INTO MAJOR DISAGREEMENTS."

HM?

THAT'S MY **HOROSCOPE!** TALK ABOUT A **LOUSY** ONE!

WAIT A MINUTE, WHAT'S SO LOUSY ABOUT IT?

THAT'S A **GOOD** HOROSCOPE! IT'S SHOWING YOU HOW TO AVOID CONFLICT!

IT'S NOT **SHOW**ING ME HOW TO DO **ANY**THING!

IT'S JUST SAYING: HERE'S WHAT **COULD** HAPPEN! IT'S NOT GIVING ME ANY ACTUAL INFORMATION!

© 2009 by NEA, Inc.

BUT WHAT DO **YOU** CARE, FRANCIS? **YOU** DON'T EVEN **BELIEVE** IN HOROSCOPES!

SO?

SO YOU SHOULD **SHUT UP!**

LOOK, **I** DIDN'T BRING UP YOUR STUPID HOROSCOPE! **YOU** SHUT UP!

MAKE ME!

GLAD TO!

"DO NOT INVOLVE YOURSELF IN THE PETTY SQUABBLES OF OTHERS."

HEARD THAT.

22

GET A LIFE

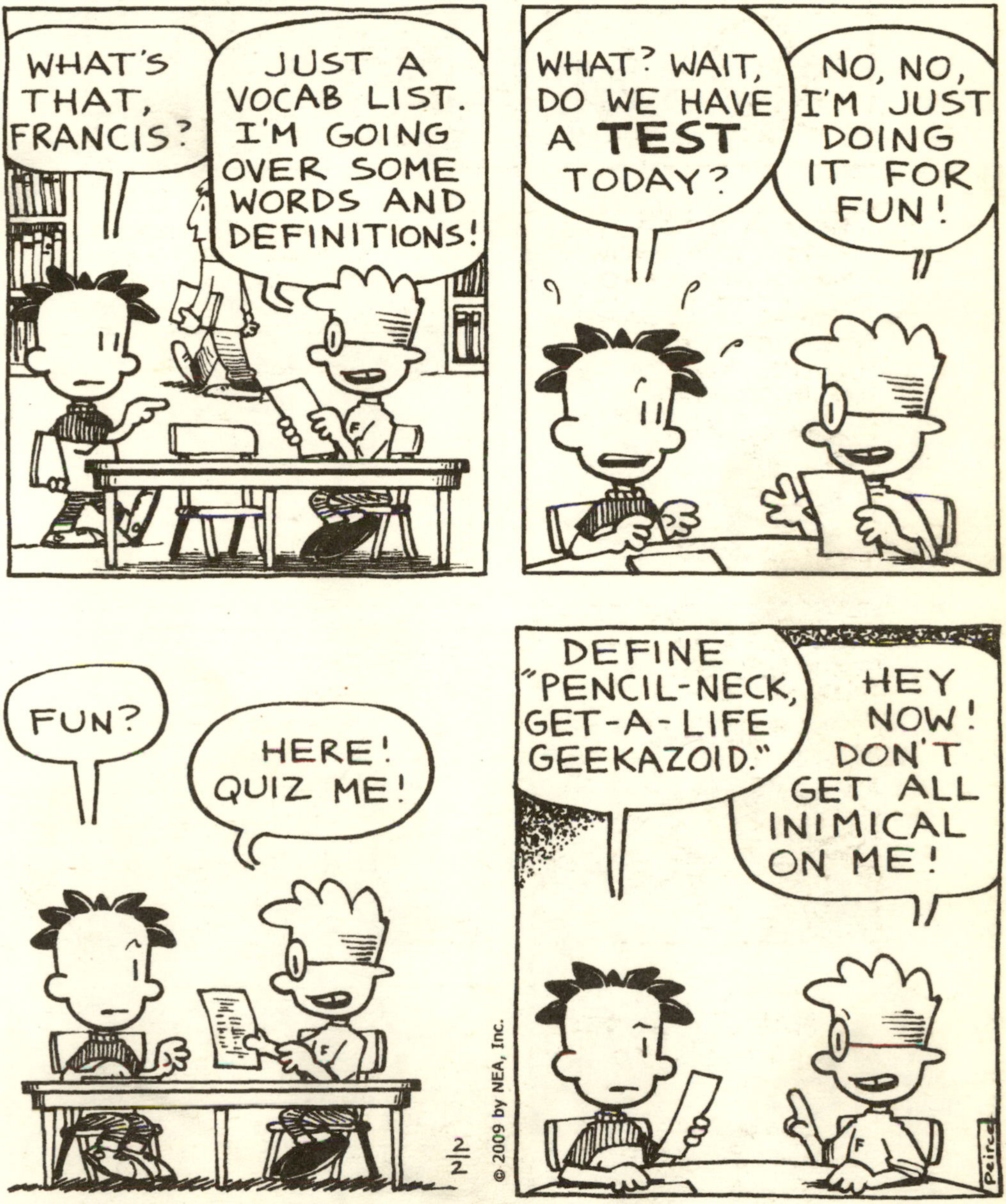
WHAT'S THAT, FRANCIS?
JUST A VOCAB LIST. I'M GOING OVER SOME WORDS AND DEFINITIONS!
WHAT? WAIT, DO WE HAVE A **TEST** TODAY?
NO, NO, I'M JUST DOING IT FOR FUN!
FUN?
HERE! QUIZ ME!
DEFINE "PENCIL-NECK, GET-A-LIFE GEEKAZOID."
HEY NOW! DON'T GET ALL INIMICAL ON ME!
2/2
© 2009 by NEA, Inc.
Peirce

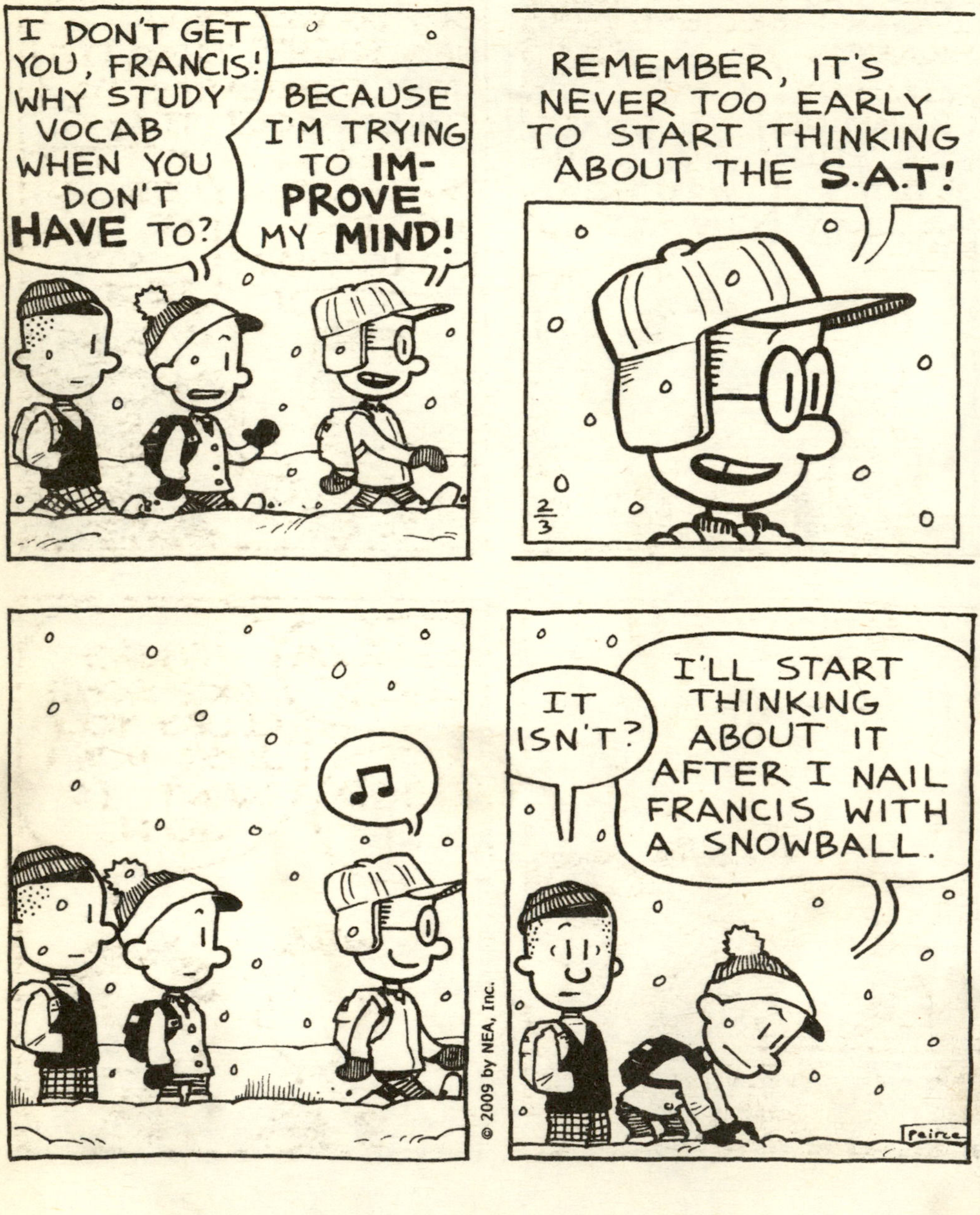
I DON'T GET YOU, FRANCIS! WHY STUDY VOCAB WHEN YOU DON'T **HAVE** TO?
BECAUSE I'M TRYING TO **IM-PROVE** MY **MIND**!
REMEMBER, IT'S NEVER TOO EARLY TO START THINKING ABOUT THE **S.A.T**!
♫
IT ISN'T?
I'LL START THINKING ABOUT IT AFTER I NAIL FRANCIS WITH A SNOWBALL.
Peirce

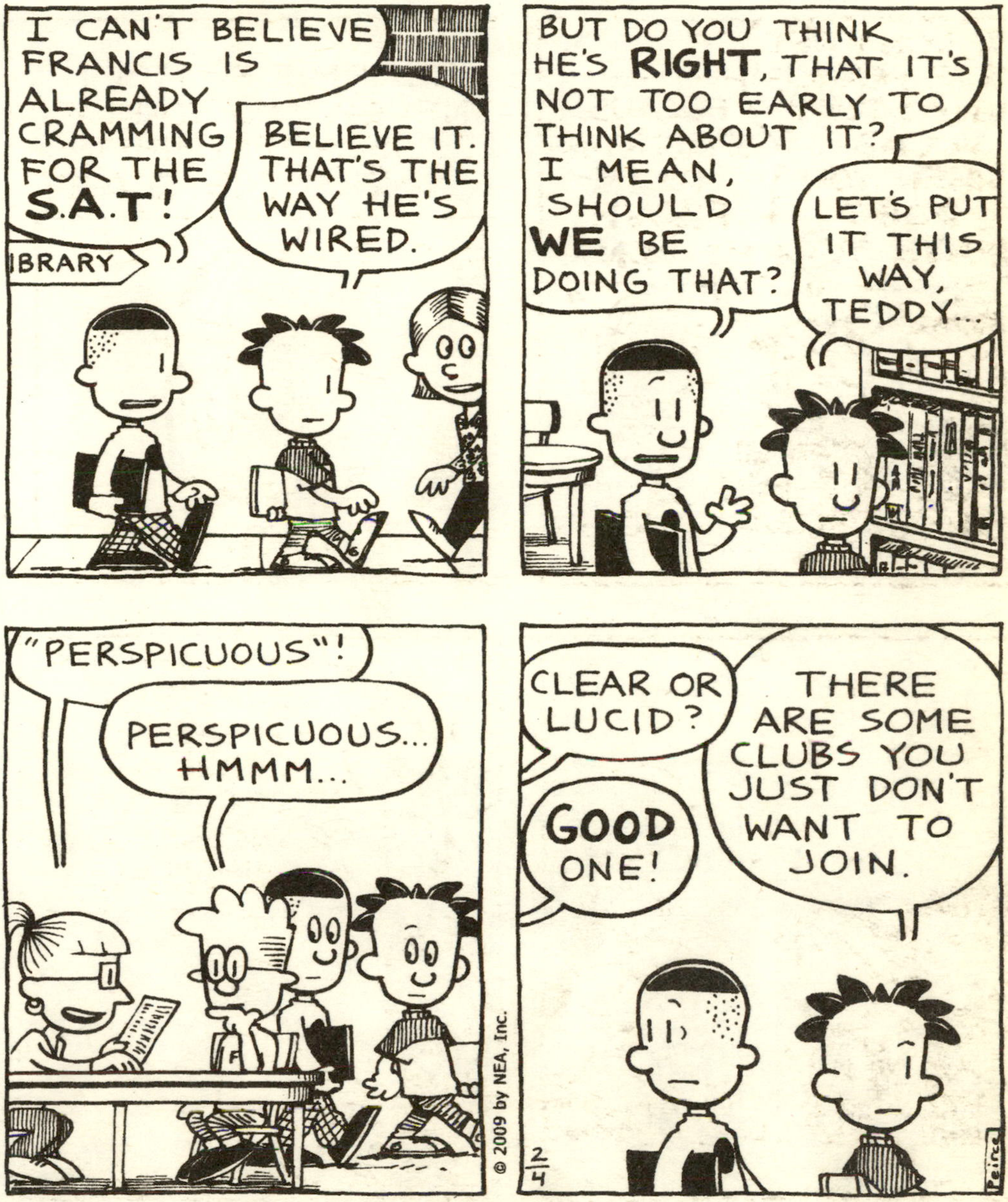
I CAN'T BELIEVE FRANCIS IS ALREADY CRAMMING FOR THE S.A.T!
BELIEVE IT. THAT'S THE WAY HE'S WIRED.
IBRARY
BUT DO YOU THINK HE'S RIGHT, THAT IT'S NOT TOO EARLY TO THINK ABOUT IT? I MEAN, SHOULD WE BE DOING THAT?
LET'S PUT IT THIS WAY, TEDDY...
"PERSPICUOUS"!
PERSPICUOUS... HMMM...
CLEAR OR LUCID?
THERE ARE SOME CLUBS YOU JUST DON'T WANT TO JOIN.
GOOD ONE!
2/4
Peirce

DAD ON ICE

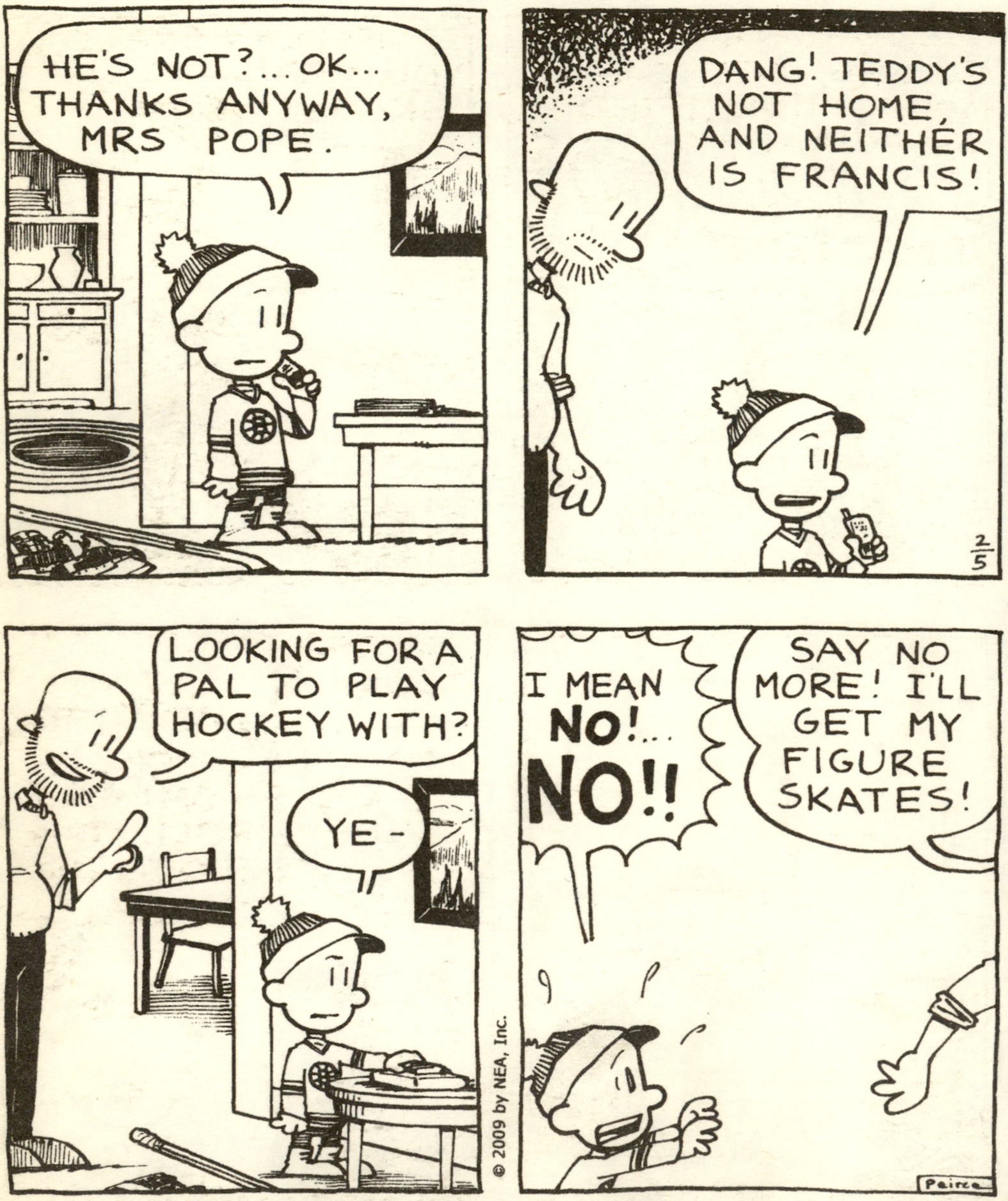
HE'S NOT? ... OK... THANKS ANYWAY, MRS POPE.
DANG! TEDDY'S NOT HOME, AND NEITHER IS FRANCIS!
2/5
LOOKING FOR A PAL TO PLAY HOCKEY WITH?
YE -
I MEAN NO! ... NO!!
SAY NO MORE! I'LL GET MY FIGURE SKATES!
© 2009 by NEA, Inc.
Peirce

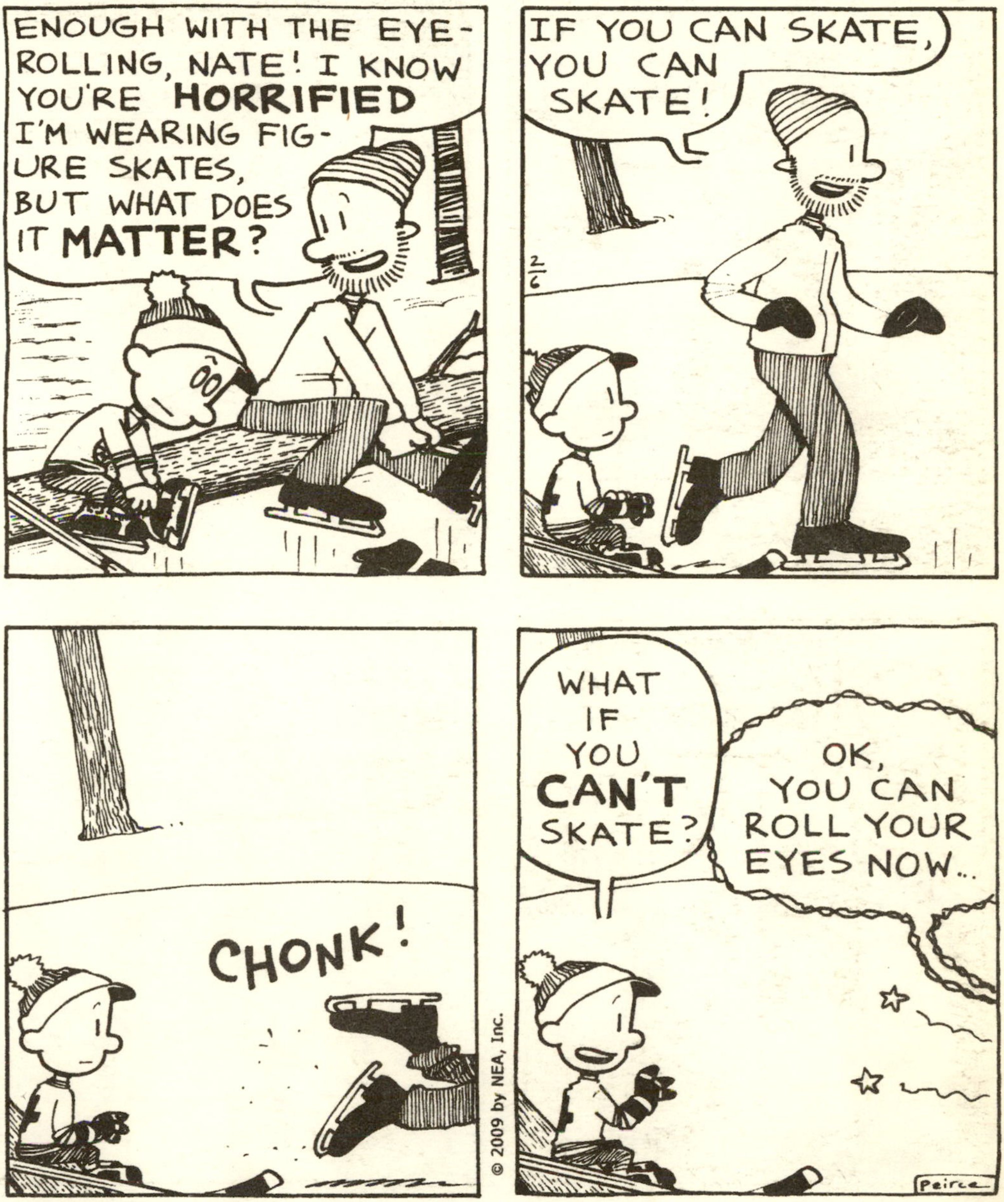
ENOUGH WITH THE EYE-ROLLING, NATE! I KNOW YOU'RE **HORRIFIED** I'M WEARING FIGURE SKATES, BUT WHAT DOES IT **MATTER**?
IF YOU CAN SKATE, YOU CAN SKATE!
2/6
CHONK!
WHAT IF YOU **CAN'T** SKATE?
OK, YOU CAN ROLL YOUR EYES NOW...
Peirce

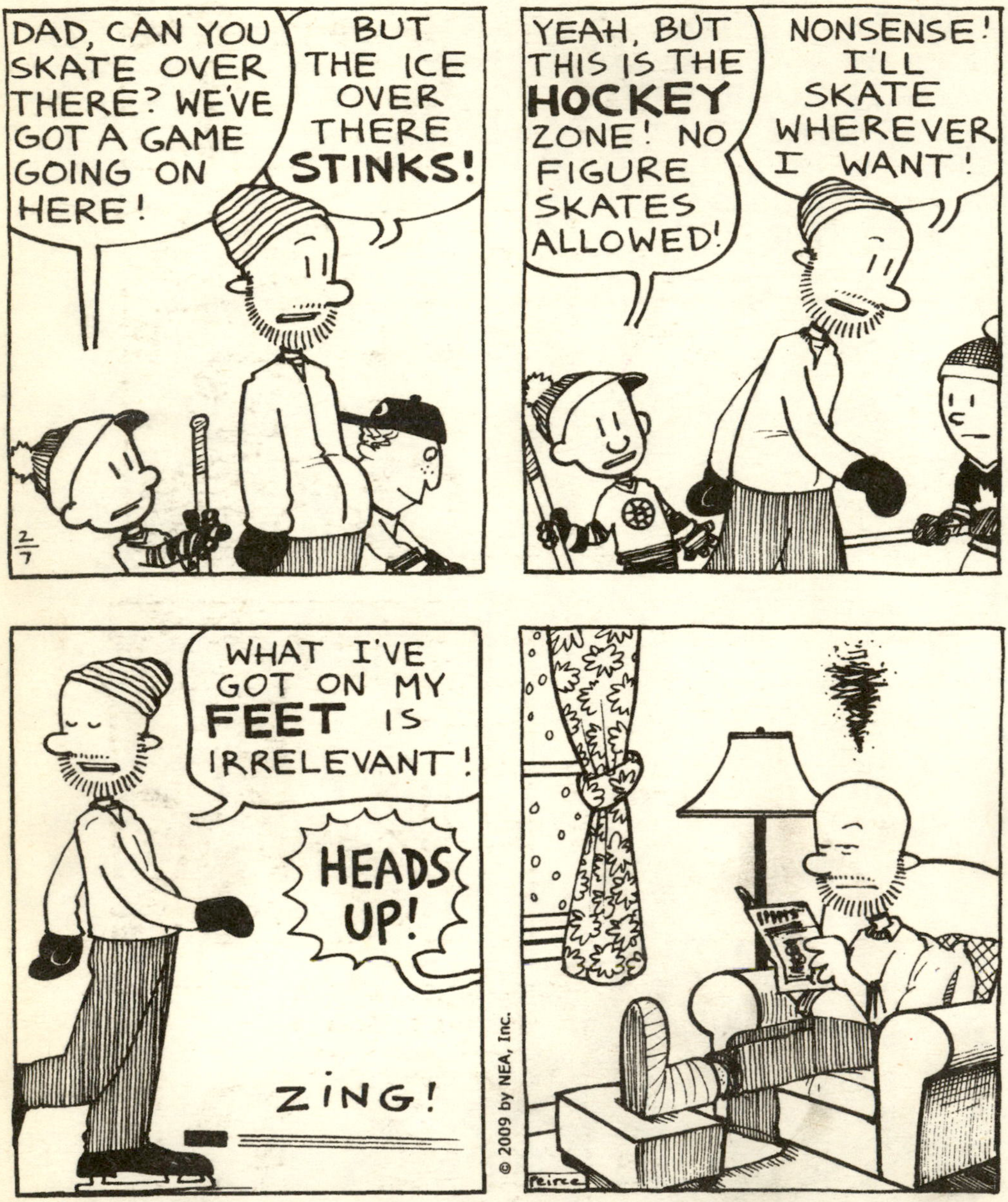
DAD, CAN YOU SKATE OVER THERE? WE'VE GOT A GAME GOING ON HERE!
BUT THE ICE OVER THERE **STINKS!**
2/7
YEAH, BUT THIS IS THE **HOCKEY** ZONE! NO FIGURE SKATES ALLOWED!
NONSENSE! I'LL SKATE WHEREVER I WANT!
WHAT I'VE GOT ON MY **FEET** IS IRRELEVANT!
HEADS UP!
ZING!
© 2009 by NEA, Inc.
Peirce

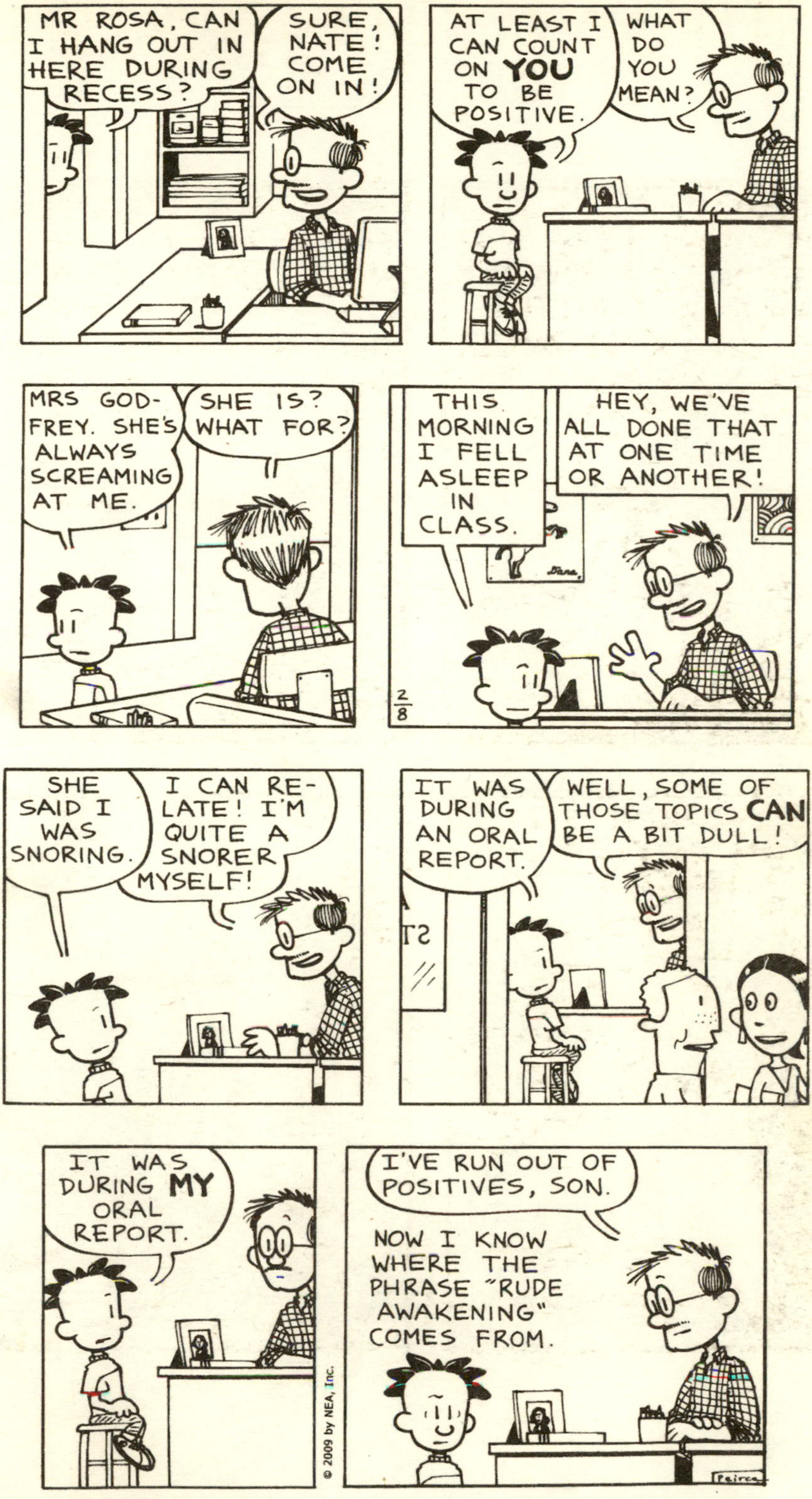
MR ROSA, CAN I HANG OUT IN HERE DURING RECESS?
SURE, NATE! COME ON IN!
AT LEAST I CAN COUNT ON YOU TO BE POSITIVE.
WHAT DO YOU MEAN?
MRS GODFREY. SHE'S ALWAYS SCREAMING AT ME.
SHE IS? WHAT FOR?
THIS MORNING I FELL ASLEEP IN CLASS.
HEY, WE'VE ALL DONE THAT AT ONE TIME OR ANOTHER!
2/8
SHE SAID I WAS SNORING.
I CAN RELATE! I'M QUITE A SNORER MYSELF!
IT WAS DURING AN ORAL REPORT.
WELL, SOME OF THOSE TOPICS CAN BE A BIT DULL!
IT WAS DURING MY ORAL REPORT.
I'VE RUN OUT OF POSITIVES, SON.
NOW I KNOW WHERE THE PHRASE "RUDE AWAKENING" COMES FROM.

THE WAY THE COOKIE CRUMBLES

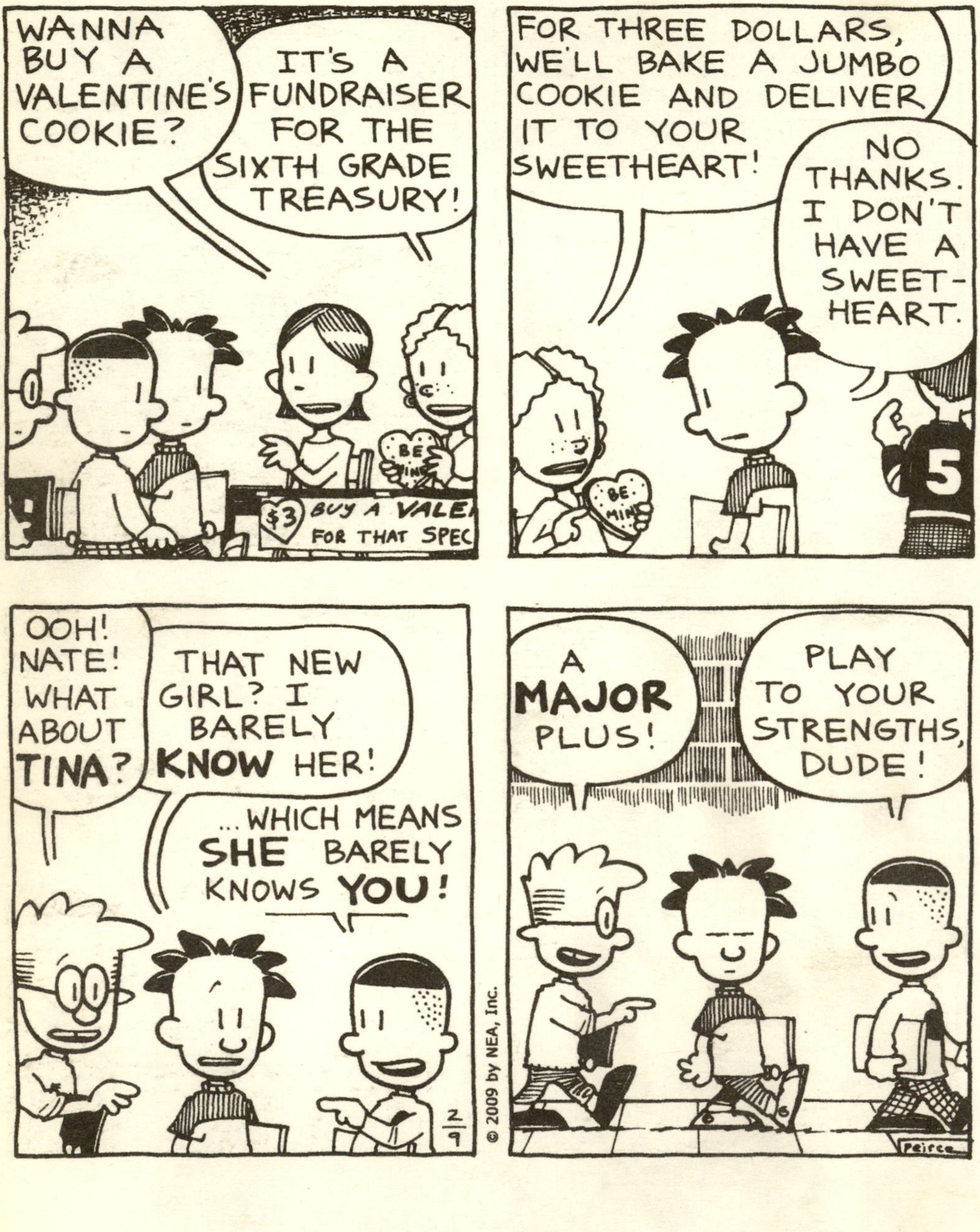
WANNA BUY A VALENTINE'S COOKIE?
IT'S A FUNDRAISER FOR THE SIXTH GRADE TREASURY!
$3
BUY A VALE
FOR THAT SPEC
BE MINE
FOR THREE DOLLARS, WE'LL BAKE A JUMBO COOKIE AND DELIVER IT TO YOUR SWEETHEART!
NO THANKS. I DON'T HAVE A SWEET-HEART.
BE MINE
5
OOH! NATE! WHAT ABOUT TINA?
THAT NEW GIRL? I BARELY KNOW HER!
...WHICH MEANS SHE BARELY KNOWS YOU!
2/9
© 2009 by NEA, Inc.
A MAJOR PLUS!
PLAY TO YOUR STRENGTHS, DUDE!
Peirce

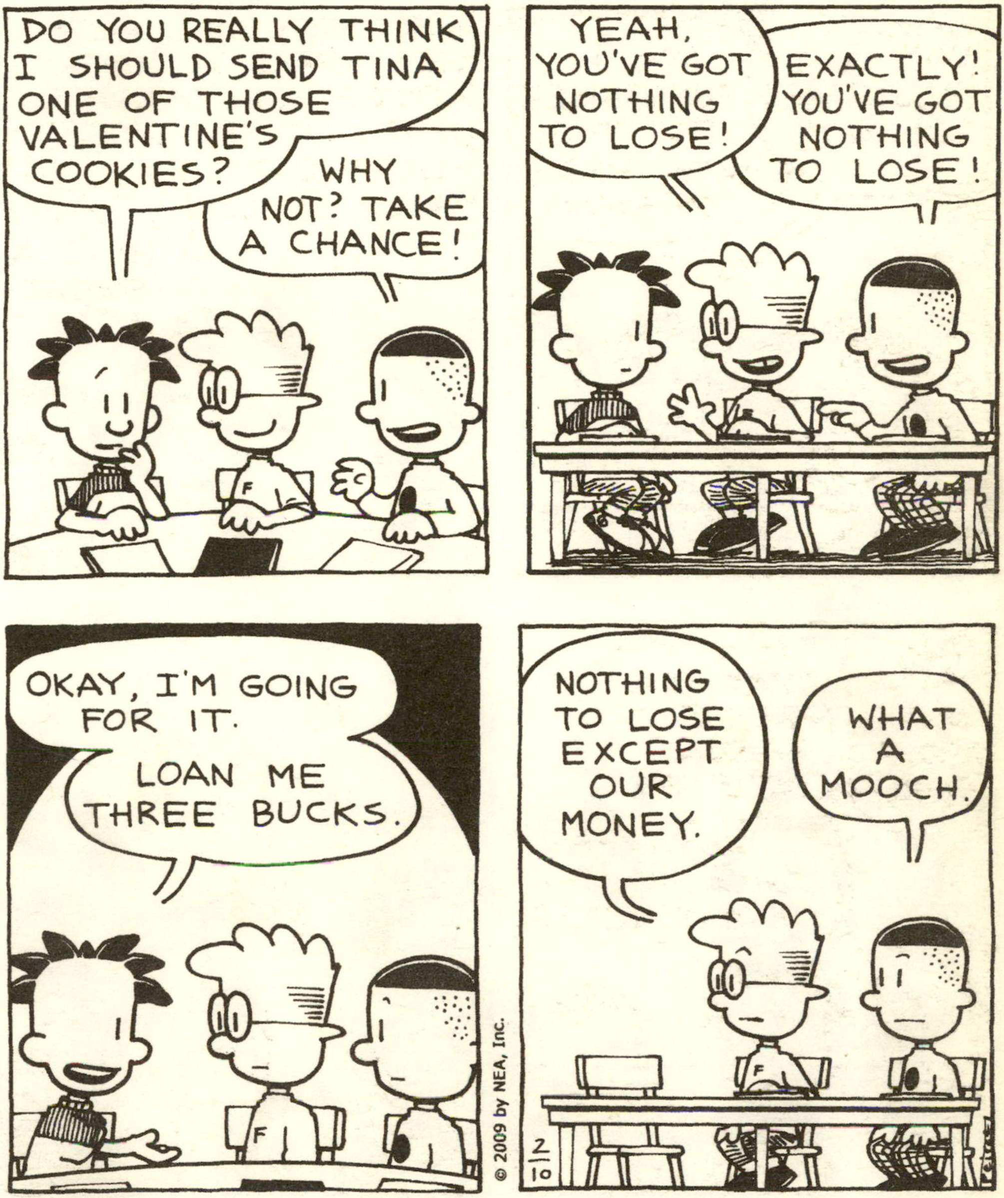
DO YOU REALLY THINK I SHOULD SEND TINA ONE OF THOSE VALENTINE'S COOKIES?
WHY NOT? TAKE A CHANCE!
YEAH, YOU'VE GOT NOTHING TO LOSE!
EXACTLY! YOU'VE GOT NOTHING TO LOSE!
OKAY, I'M GOING FOR IT.
LOAN ME THREE BUCKS.
© 2009 by NEA, Inc.
2/10
NOTHING TO LOSE EXCEPT OUR MONEY.
WHAT A MOOCH.

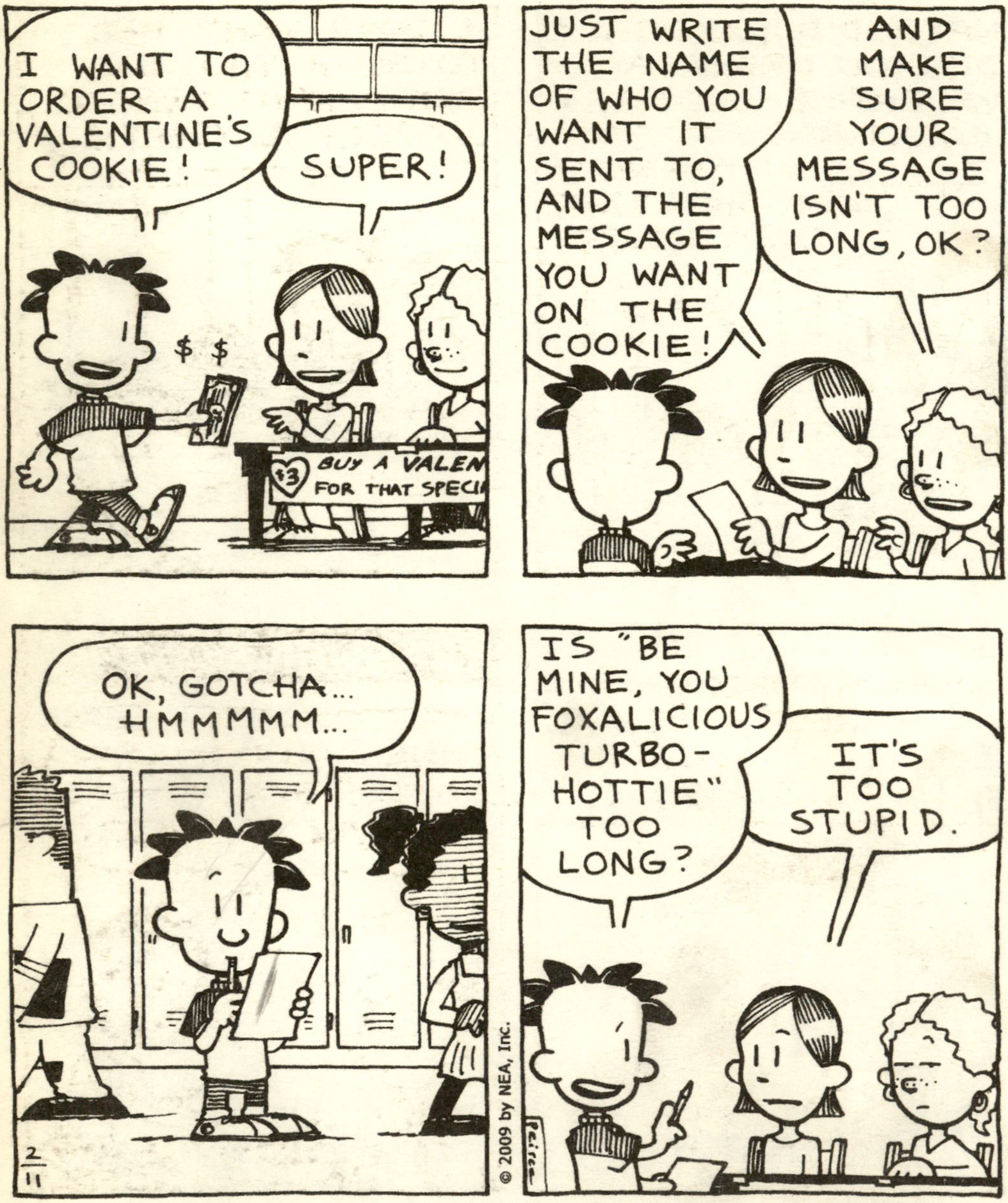
I WANT TO ORDER A VALENTINE'S COOKIE!
SUPER!
$3
BUY A VALEN
FOR THAT SPECI
JUST WRITE THE NAME OF WHO YOU WANT IT SENT TO, AND THE MESSAGE YOU WANT ON THE COOKIE!
AND MAKE SURE YOUR MESSAGE ISN'T TOO LONG, OK?
OK, GOTCHA... HMMMMM...
IS "BE MINE, YOU FOXALICIOUS TURBO-HOTTIE" TOO LONG?
IT'S TOO STUPID.
2/11
© 2009 by NEA, Inc.
Peirce

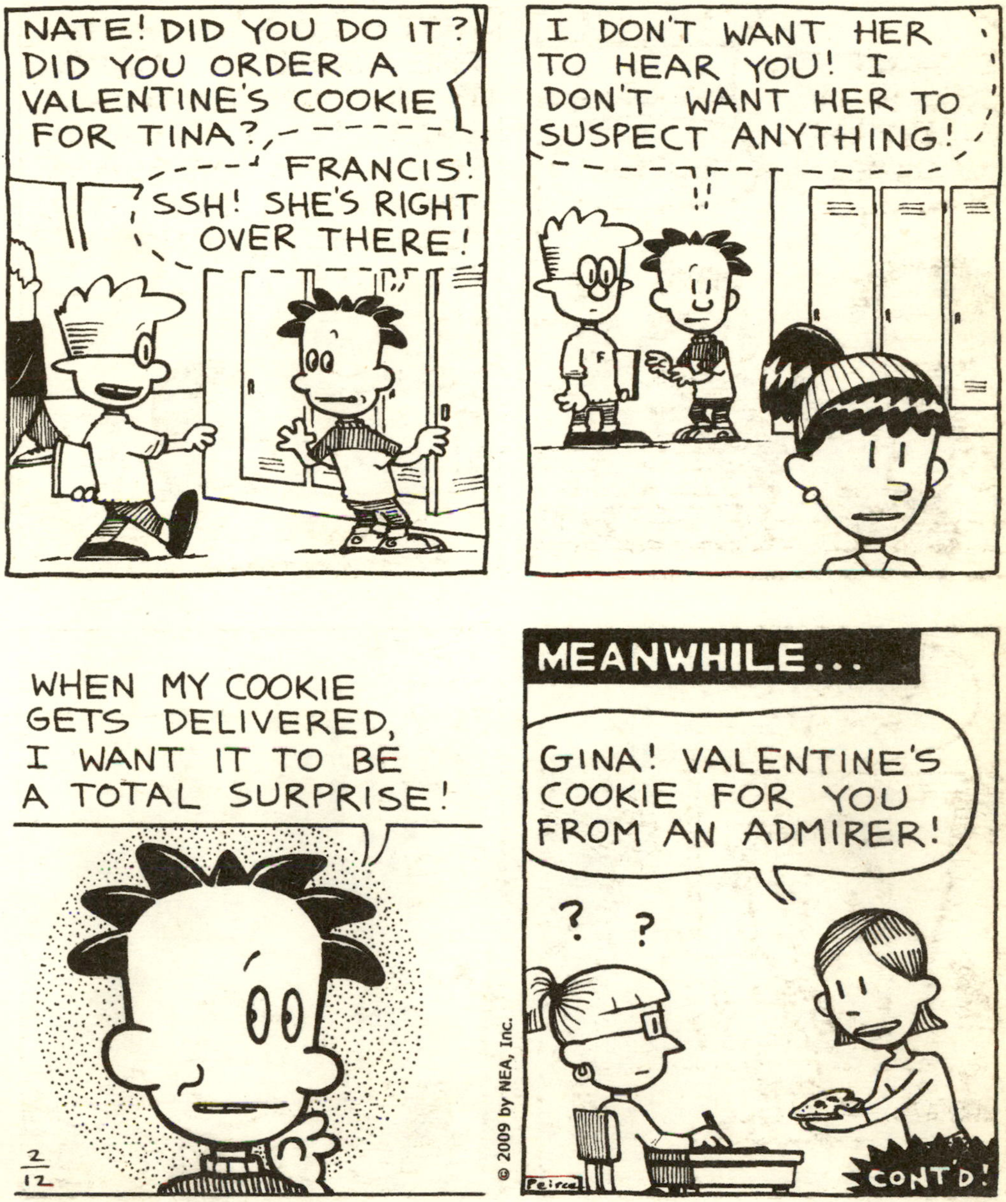
NATE! DID YOU DO IT? DID YOU ORDER A VALENTINE'S COOKIE FOR TINA?
FRANCIS! SSH! SHE'S RIGHT OVER THERE!
I DON'T WANT HER TO HEAR YOU! I DON'T WANT HER TO SUSPECT ANYTHING!
WHEN MY COOKIE GETS DELIVERED, I WANT IT TO BE A TOTAL SURPRISE!
2/12
© 2009 by NEA, Inc.
MEANWHILE...
GINA! VALENTINE'S COOKIE FOR YOU FROM AN ADMIRER!
? ?
Peirce
CONT'D!

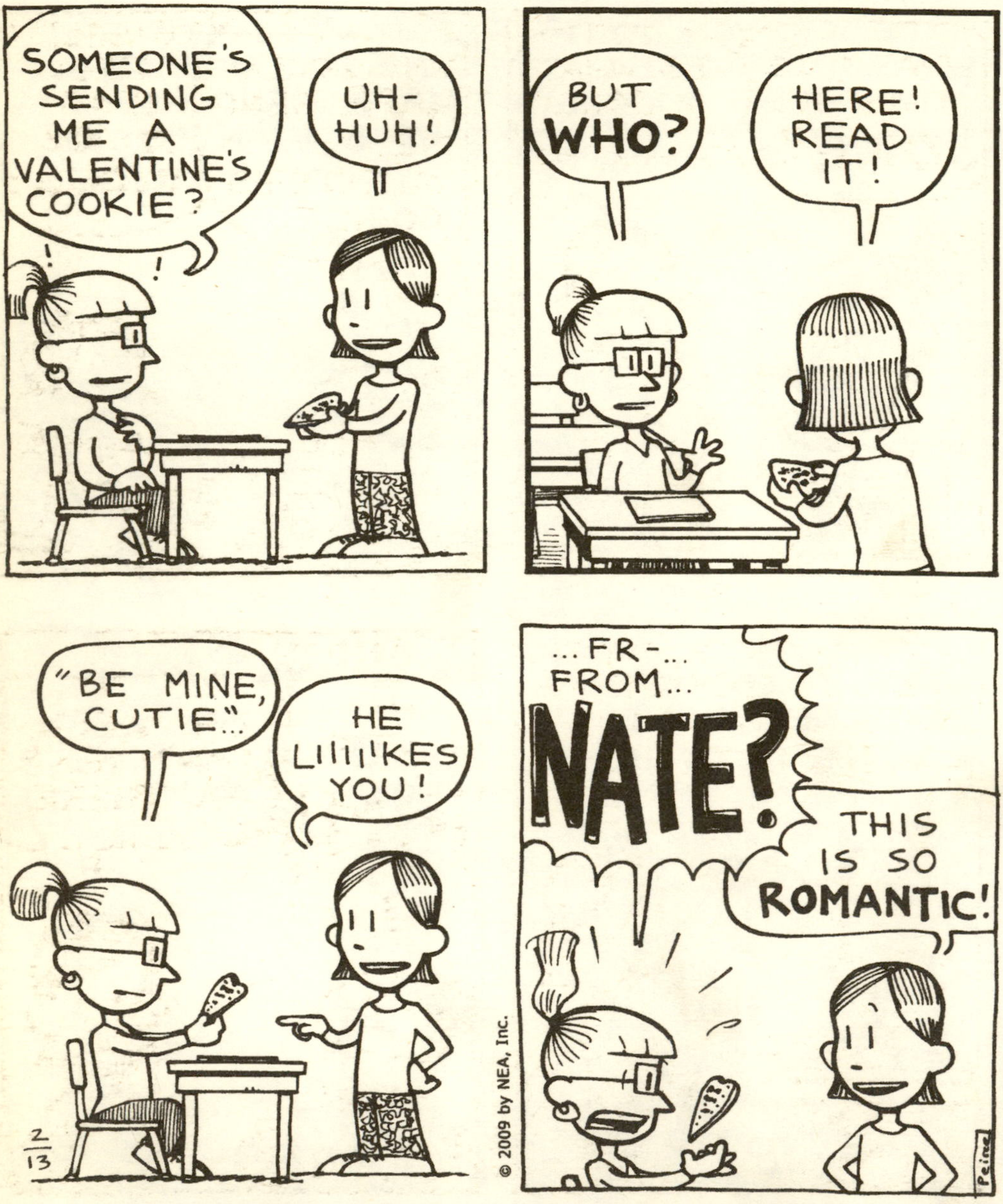
SOMEONE'S SENDING ME A VALENTINE'S COOKIE?
UH-HUH!
! !
BUT WHO?
HERE! READ IT!
"BE MINE, CUTIE"...
HE LIIIIKES YOU!
2/13
...FR-... FROM... NATE?
THIS IS SO ROMANTIC!
Peirce

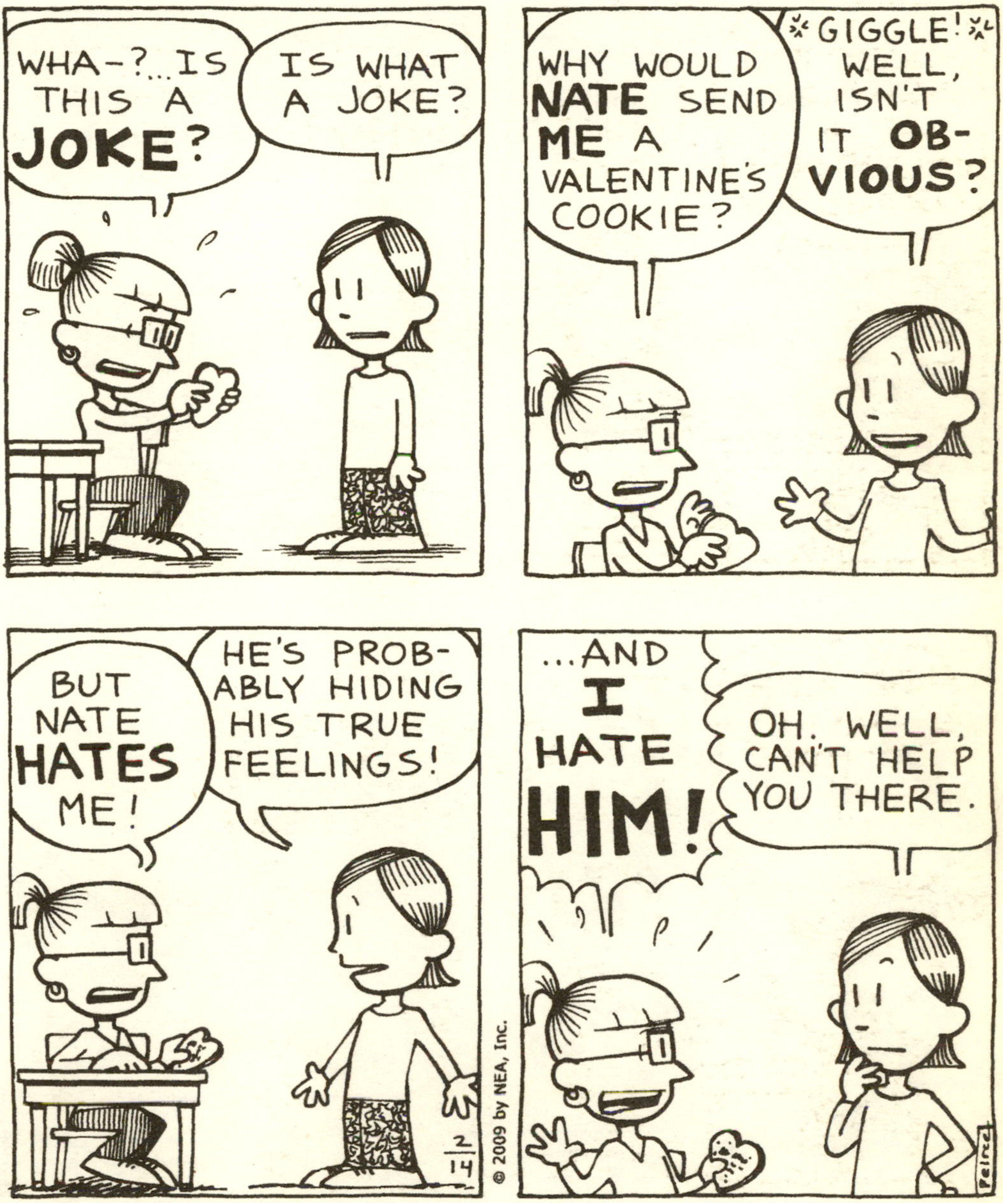
WHA-?...IS THIS A JOKE?
IS WHAT A JOKE?
WHY WOULD NATE SEND ME A VALENTINE'S COOKIE?
GIGGLE! WELL, ISN'T IT OB-VIOUS?
BUT NATE HATES ME!
HE'S PROB-ABLY HIDING HIS TRUE FEELINGS!
...AND I HATE HIM!
OH. WELL, CAN'T HELP YOU THERE.
2/14
Peirce

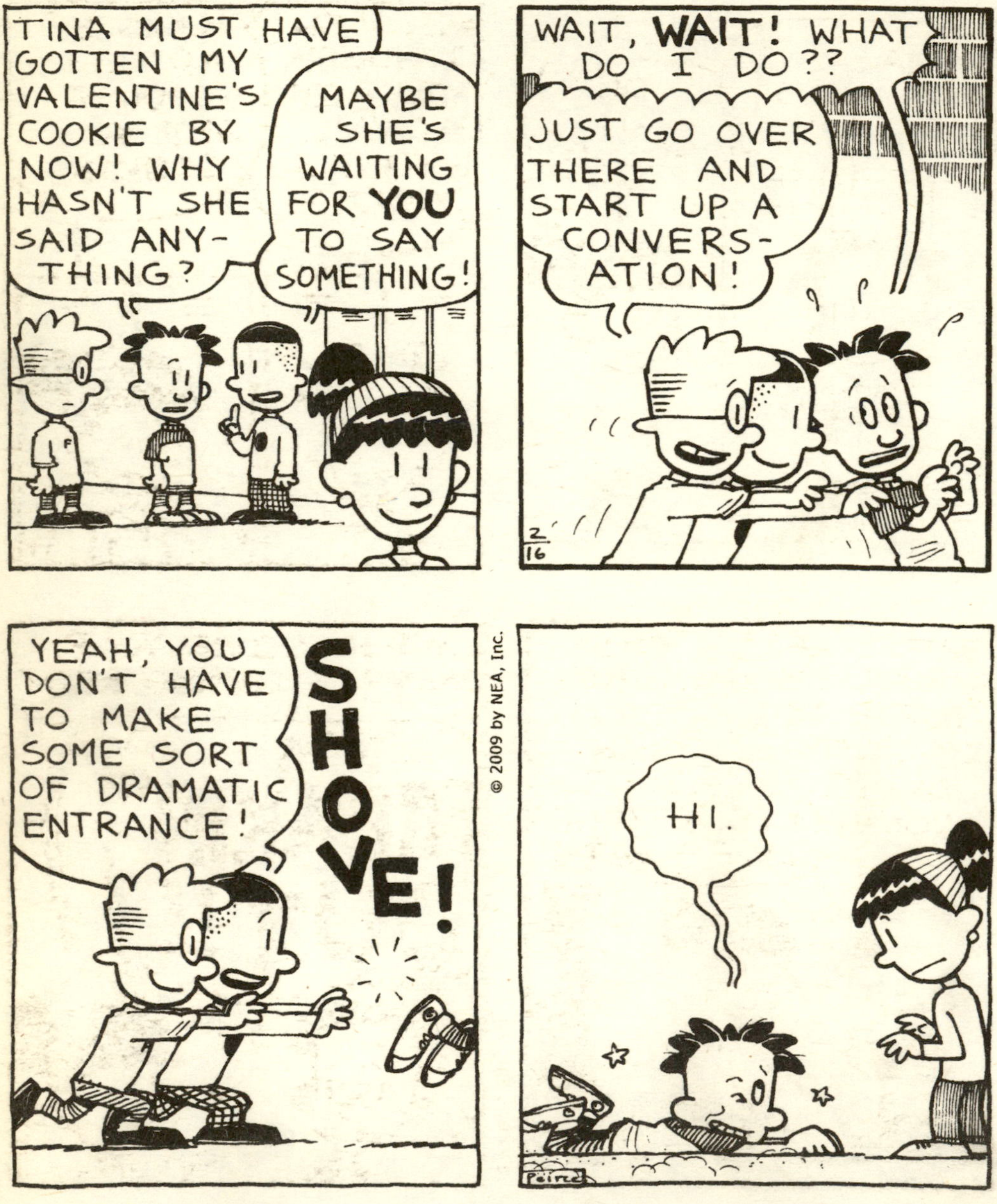
TINA MUST HAVE GOTTEN MY VALENTINE'S COOKIE BY NOW! WHY HASN'T SHE SAID ANYTHING?
MAYBE SHE'S WAITING FOR **YOU** TO SAY SOMETHING!
WAIT, **WAIT!** WHAT DO I DO??
JUST GO OVER THERE AND START UP A CONVERSATION!
2/16
YEAH, YOU DON'T HAVE TO MAKE SOME SORT OF DRAMATIC ENTRANCE!
SHOVE!
© 2009 by NEA, Inc.
HI.
Peirce

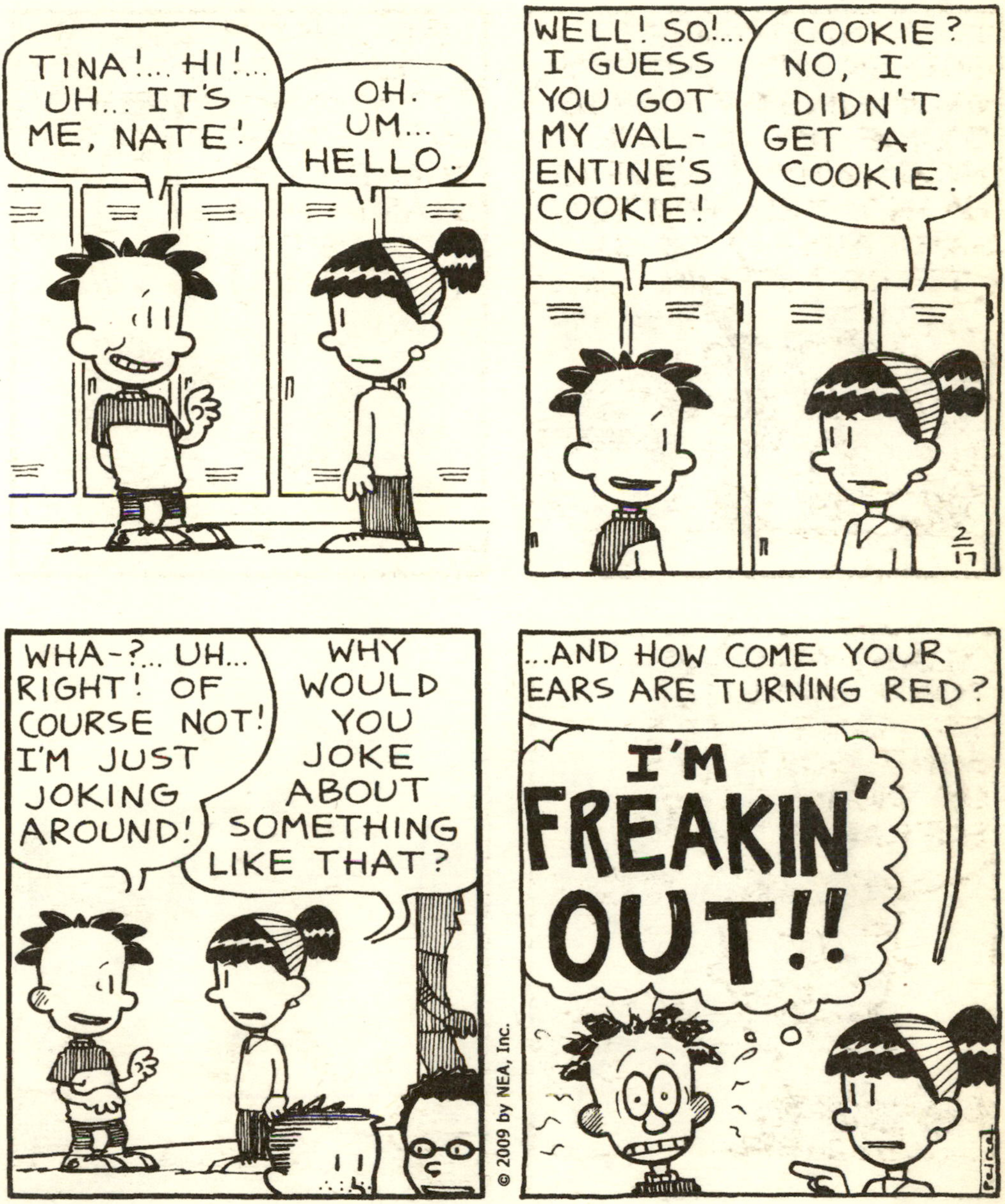
TINA!... HI!... UH... IT'S ME, NATE!
OH. UM... HELLO.
WELL! SO!... I GUESS YOU GOT MY VAL-ENTINE'S COOKIE!
COOKIE? NO, I DIDN'T GET A COOKIE.
2/17
WHA-?... UH... RIGHT! OF COURSE NOT! I'M JUST JOKING AROUND!
WHY WOULD YOU JOKE ABOUT SOMETHING LIKE THAT?
© 2009 by NEA, Inc.
...AND HOW COME YOUR EARS ARE TURNING RED?
I'M FREAKIN' OUT!!

HEY! HOW COME YOU TWO DIDN'T DELIVER MY VALENTINE'S COOKIE?
WHAT ARE YOU TALKING ABOUT?
I DELIVERED IT TO GINA RIGHT AFTER RECESS!
WHA-?... TO GINA?... TO GINA?
2/18
THAT COOKIE WAS FOR TINA!
TINA?
WITH A "T"!
Peirce

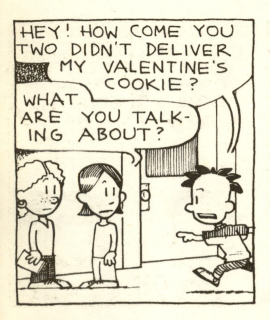

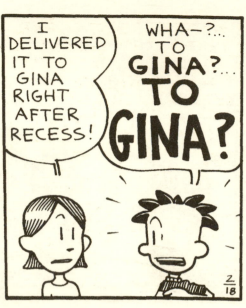

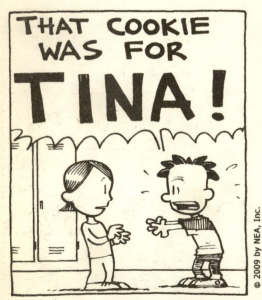

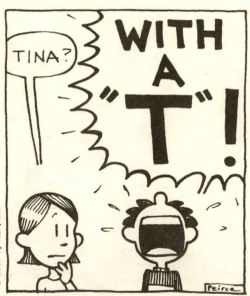

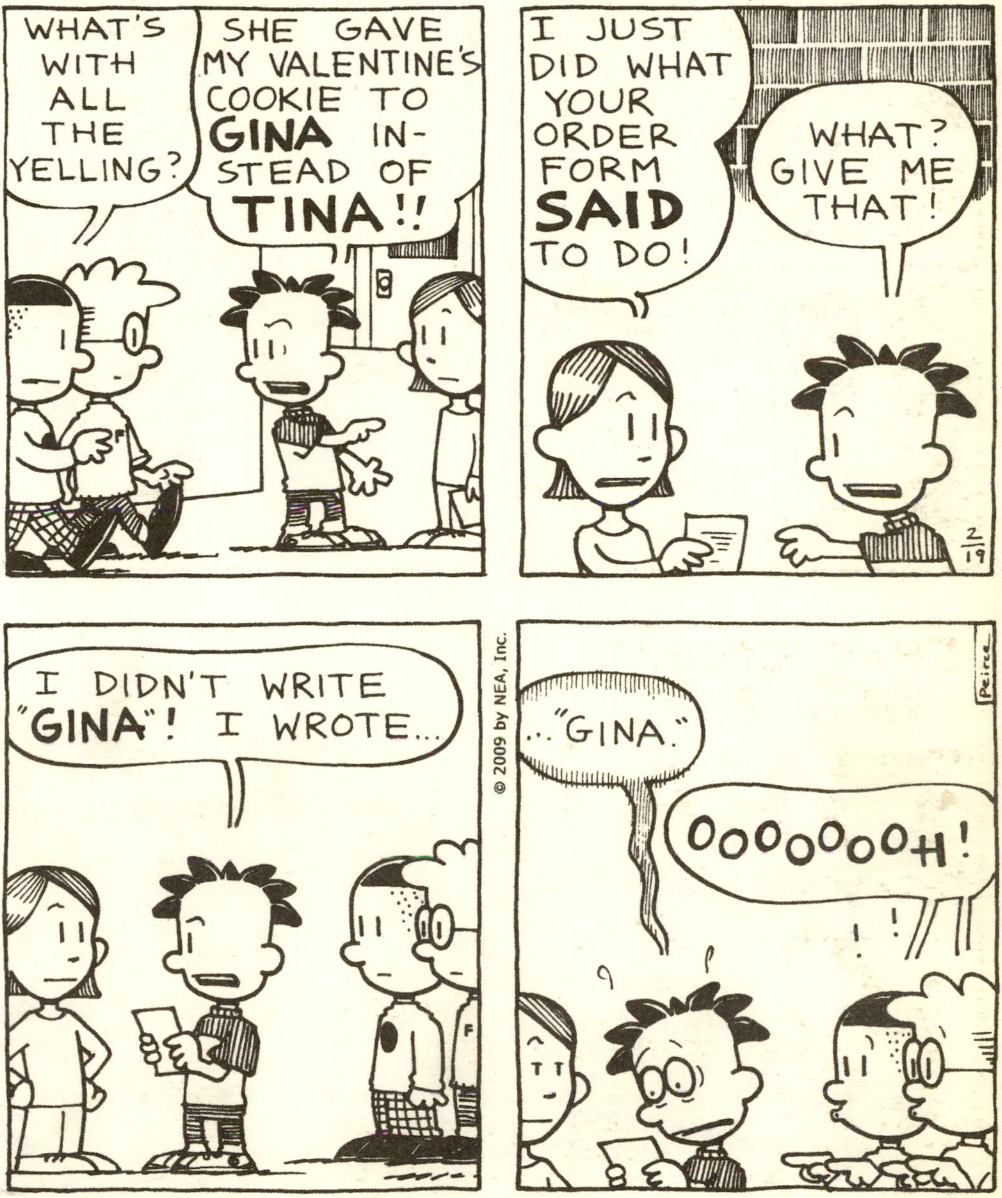
WHAT'S WITH ALL THE YELLING?
SHE GAVE MY VALENTINE'S COOKIE TO GINA INSTEAD OF TINA!!
I JUST DID WHAT YOUR ORDER FORM SAID TO DO!
WHAT? GIVE ME THAT!
2/19
© 2009 by NEA, Inc.
I DIDN'T WRITE "GINA"! I WROTE...
Peirce
..."GINA."
OOOOOOOH!

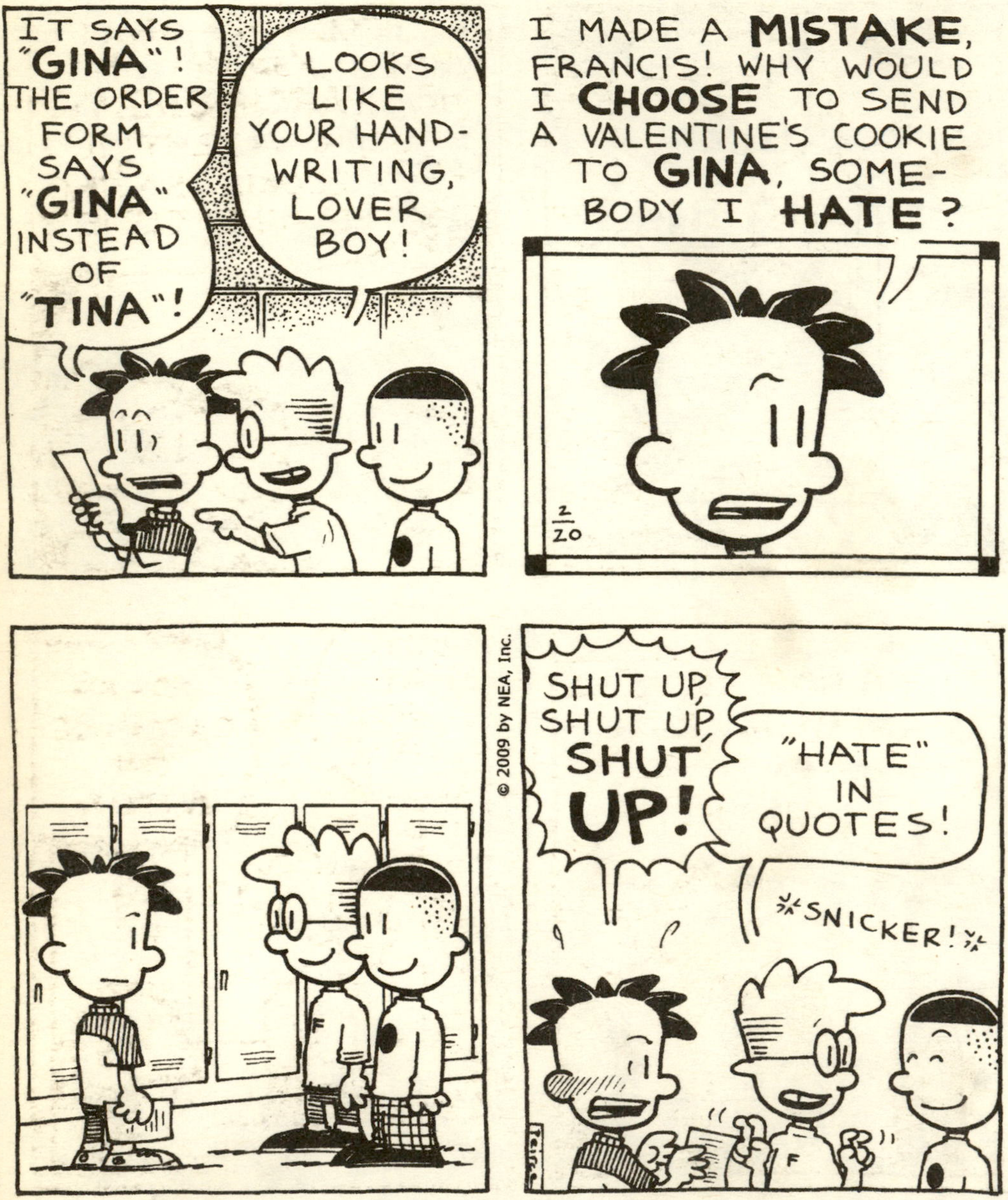
IT SAYS "GINA"! THE ORDER FORM SAYS "GINA" INSTEAD OF "TINA"!
LOOKS LIKE YOUR HAND-WRITING, LOVER BOY!
I MADE A MISTAKE, FRANCIS! WHY WOULD I CHOOSE TO SEND A VALENTINE'S COOKIE TO GINA, SOMEBODY I HATE?
2/20
© 2009 by NEA, Inc.
SHUT UP, SHUT UP, SHUT UP!
"HATE" IN QUOTES!
SNICKER!
Peirce

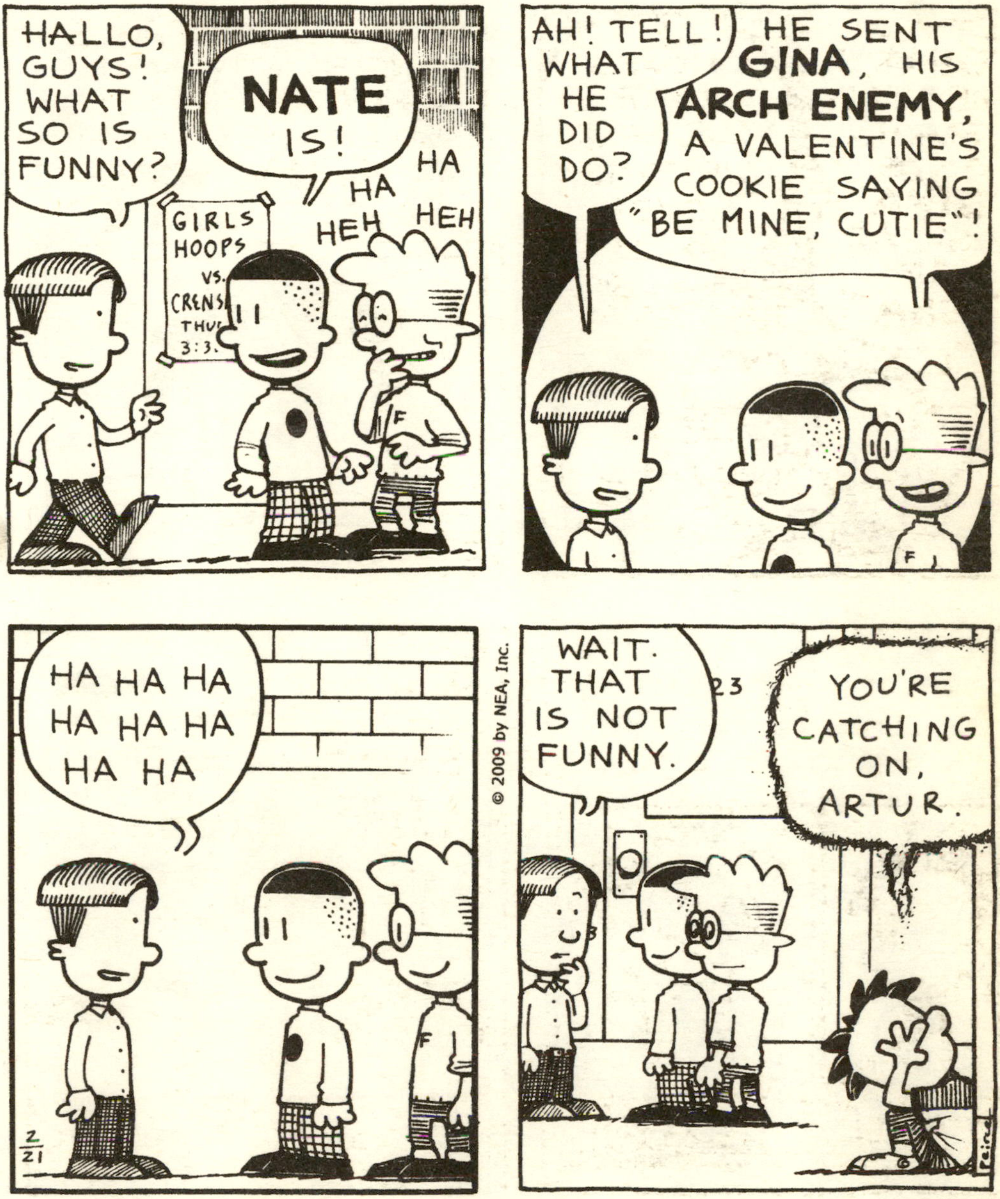
HALLO, GUYS! WHAT SO IS FUNNY?
NATE IS!
HA HA HEH HEH HA
GIRLS HOOPS VS.
AH! TELL! WHAT HE DID DO?
HE SENT GINA, HIS ARCH ENEMY, A VALENTINE'S COOKIE SAYING "BE MINE, CUTIE"!
HA HA HA HA HA HA HA HA
WAIT. THAT IS NOT FUNNY.
YOU'RE CATCHING ON, ARTUR.
© 2009 by NEA, Inc.

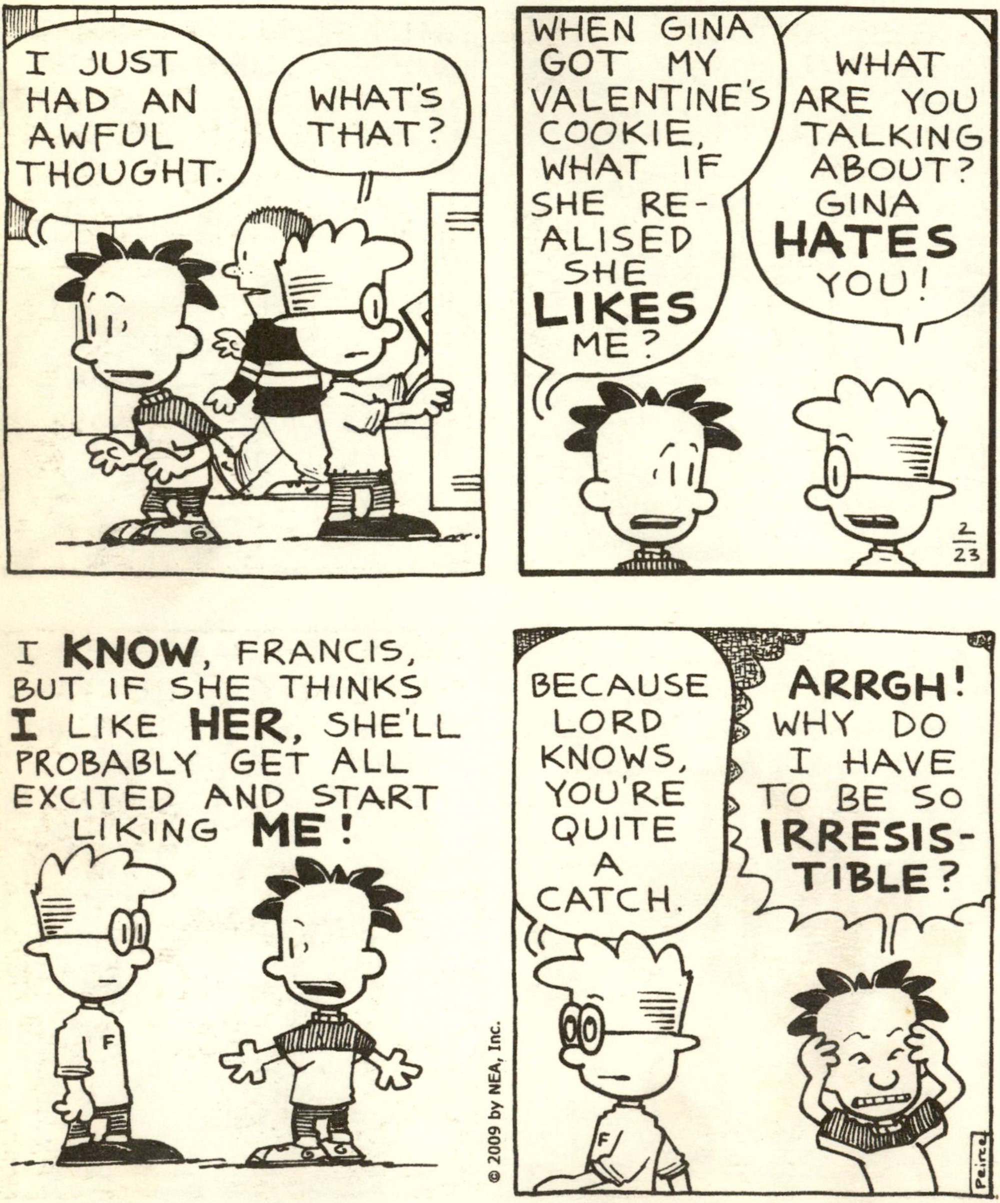
I JUST HAD AN AWFUL THOUGHT.
WHAT'S THAT?
WHEN GINA GOT MY VALENTINE'S COOKIE, WHAT IF SHE RE-ALISED SHE **LIKES** ME?
WHAT ARE YOU TALKING ABOUT? GINA **HATES** YOU!
2/23
I **KNOW**, FRANCIS, BUT IF SHE THINKS **I** LIKE **HER**, SHE'LL PROBABLY GET ALL EXCITED AND START LIKING **ME**!
© 2009 by NEA, Inc.
BECAUSE LORD KNOWS, YOU'RE QUITE A CATCH.
ARRGH! WHY DO I HAVE TO BE SO **IRRESIS-TIBLE?**
Peirce

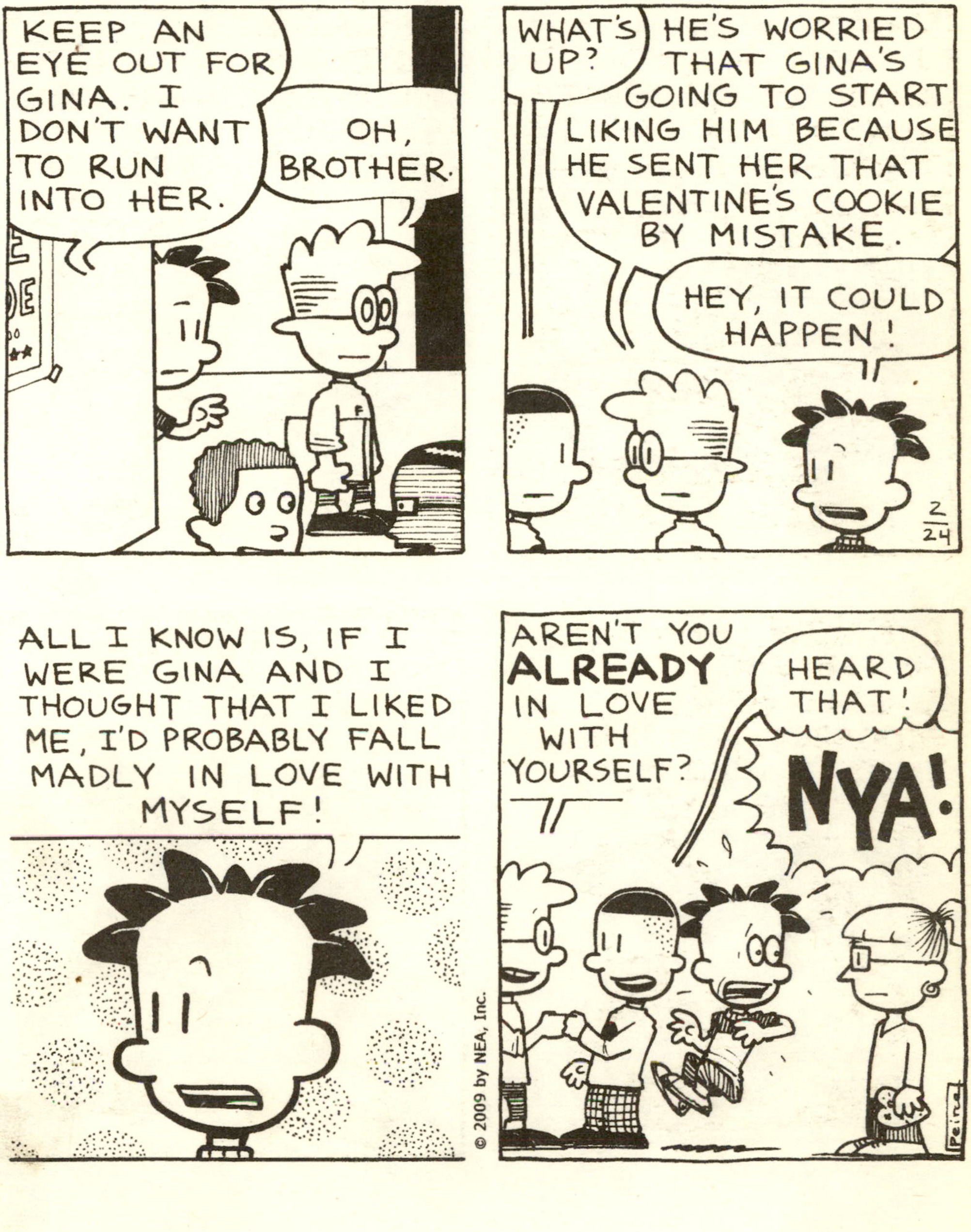
KEEP AN EYE OUT FOR GINA. I DON'T WANT TO RUN INTO HER.
OH, BROTHER.
WHAT'S UP?
HE'S WORRIED THAT GINA'S GOING TO START LIKING HIM BECAUSE HE SENT HER THAT VALENTINE'S COOKIE BY MISTAKE.
HEY, IT COULD HAPPEN!
2/24
ALL I KNOW IS, IF I WERE GINA AND I THOUGHT THAT I LIKED ME, I'D PROBABLY FALL MADLY IN LOVE WITH MYSELF!
AREN'T YOU **ALREADY** IN LOVE WITH YOURSELF?
HEARD THAT!
NYA!

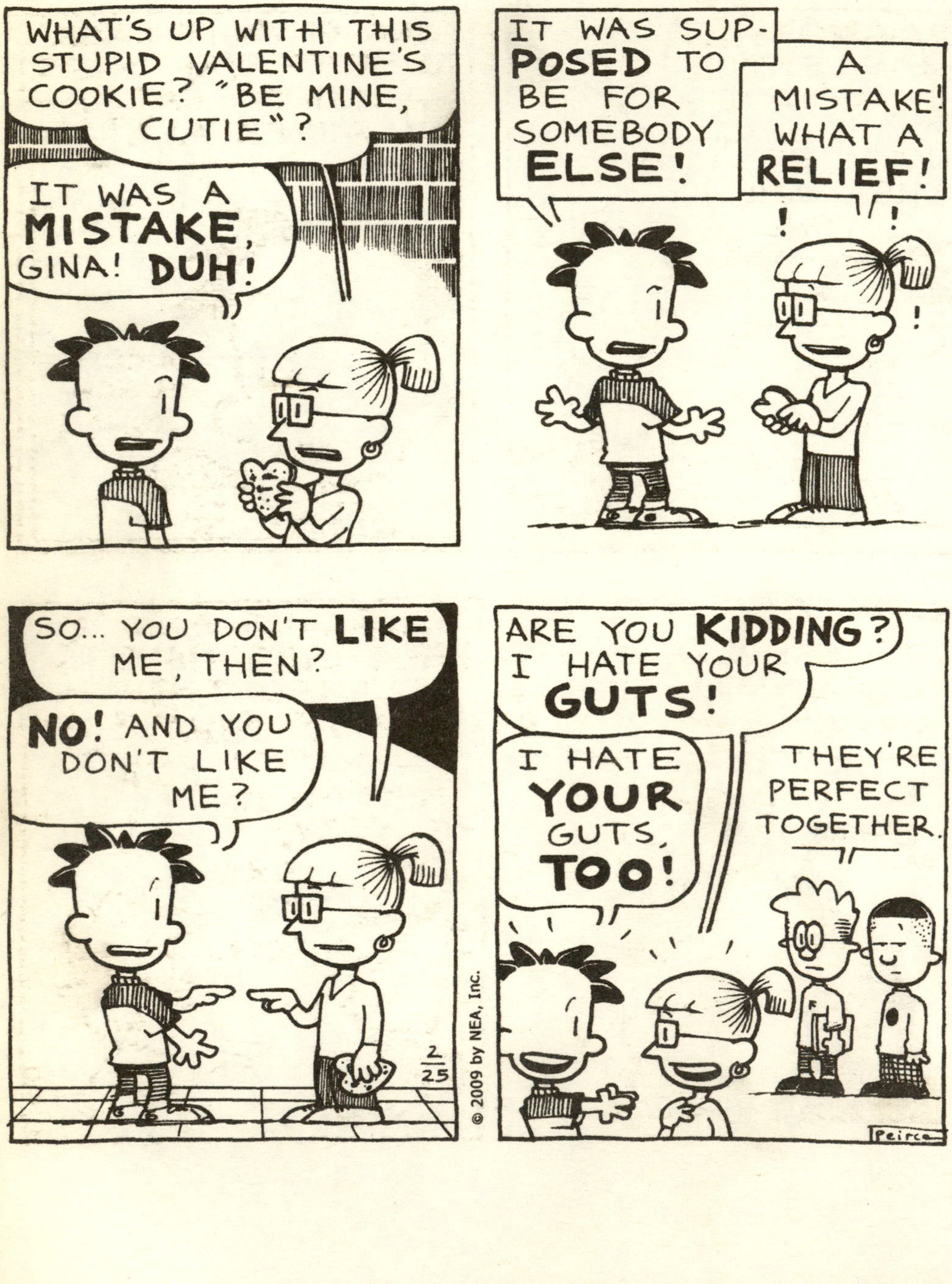
WHAT'S UP WITH THIS STUPID VALENTINE'S COOKIE? "BE MINE, CUTIE"?
IT WAS A **MISTAKE**, GINA! **DUH**!
IT WAS SUP-**POSED** TO BE FOR SOMEBODY **ELSE**!
A MISTAKE! WHAT A **RELIEF**!
SO... YOU DON'T **LIKE** ME, THEN?
NO! AND YOU DON'T LIKE ME?
ARE YOU **KIDDING**? I HATE YOUR **GUTS**!
I HATE **YOUR** GUTS, **TOO**!
THEY'RE PERFECT TOGETHER.
2/25
© 2009 by NEA, Inc.
Peirce

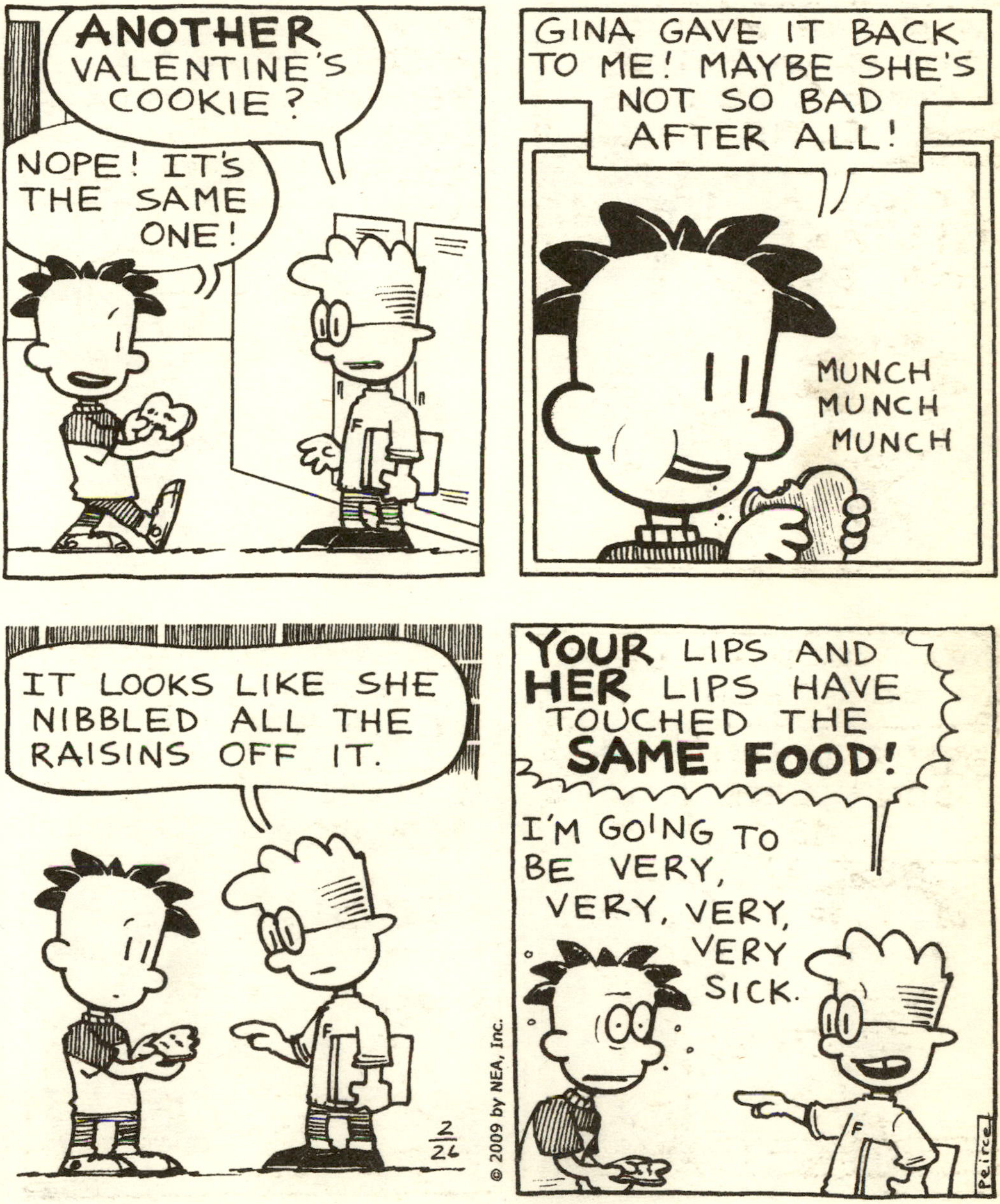
ANOTHER VALENTINE'S COOKIE?
NOPE! IT'S THE SAME ONE!
GINA GAVE IT BACK TO ME! MAYBE SHE'S NOT SO BAD AFTER ALL!
MUNCH MUNCH MUNCH
IT LOOKS LIKE SHE NIBBLED ALL THE RAISINS OFF IT.
YOUR LIPS AND HER LIPS HAVE TOUCHED THE SAME FOOD!
I'M GOING TO BE VERY, VERY, VERY, VERY SICK.
2/26
© 2009 by NEA, Inc.
Peirce

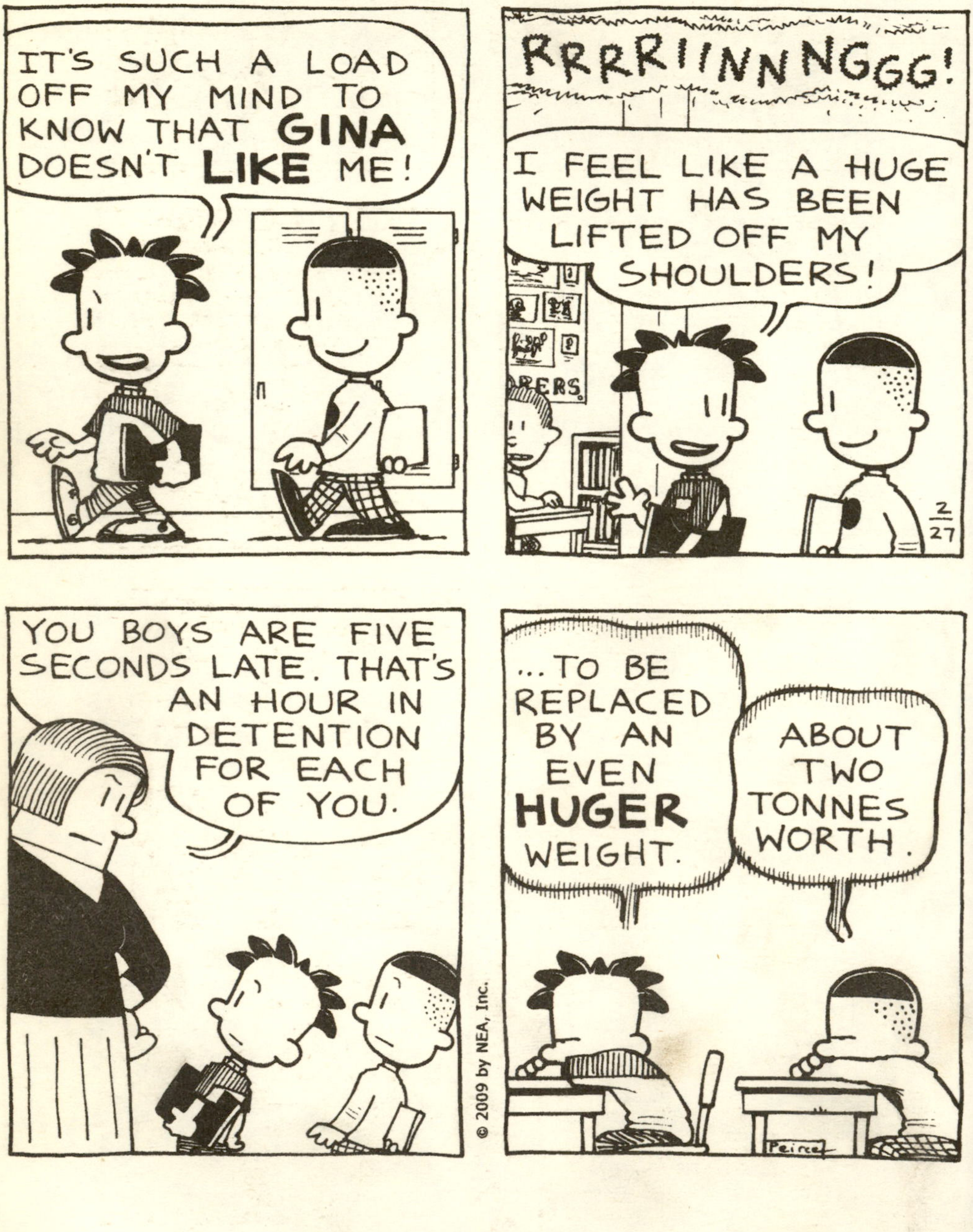
IT'S SUCH A LOAD OFF MY MIND TO KNOW THAT GINA DOESN'T LIKE ME!
RRRRIINNNGGG!
I FEEL LIKE A HUGE WEIGHT HAS BEEN LIFTED OFF MY SHOULDERS!
2/27
YOU BOYS ARE FIVE SECONDS LATE. THAT'S AN HOUR IN DETENTION FOR EACH OF YOU.
© 2009 by NEA, Inc.
...TO BE REPLACED BY AN EVEN HUGER WEIGHT.
ABOUT TWO TONNES WORTH.
Peirce

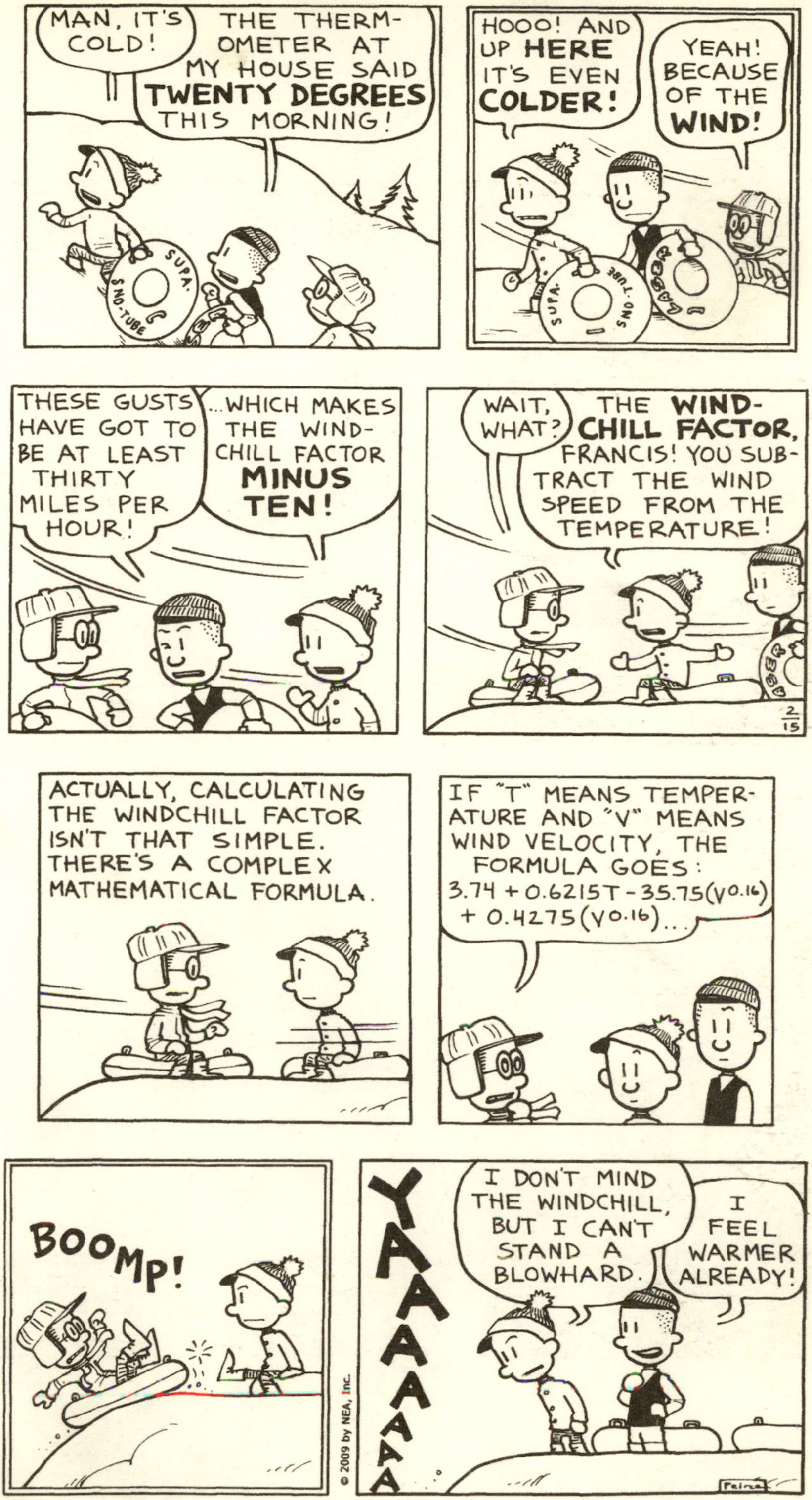
MAN, IT'S COLD!
THE THERMOMETER AT MY HOUSE SAID **TWENTY DEGREES** THIS MORNING!
HOOO! AND UP **HERE** IT'S EVEN **COLDER!**
YEAH! BECAUSE OF THE **WIND!**
SUPA SNO-TUBE
THESE GUSTS HAVE GOT TO BE AT LEAST THIRTY MILES PER HOUR!
...WHICH MAKES THE WIND-CHILL FACTOR **MINUS TEN!**
WAIT, WHAT?
THE **WIND-CHILL FACTOR,** FRANCIS! YOU SUBTRACT THE WIND SPEED FROM THE TEMPERATURE!
2/15
ACTUALLY, CALCULATING THE WINDCHILL FACTOR ISN'T THAT SIMPLE. THERE'S A COMPLEX MATHEMATICAL FORMULA.
IF "T" MEANS TEMPERATURE AND "V" MEANS WIND VELOCITY, THE FORMULA GOES:
3.74 + 0.6215T - 35.75(V0.16) + 0.4275(V0.16)...
BOOMP!
YAAAAAA
I DON'T MIND THE WINDCHILL, BUT I CAN'T STAND A BLOWHARD.
I FEEL WARMER ALREADY!
© 2009 by NEA, Inc.

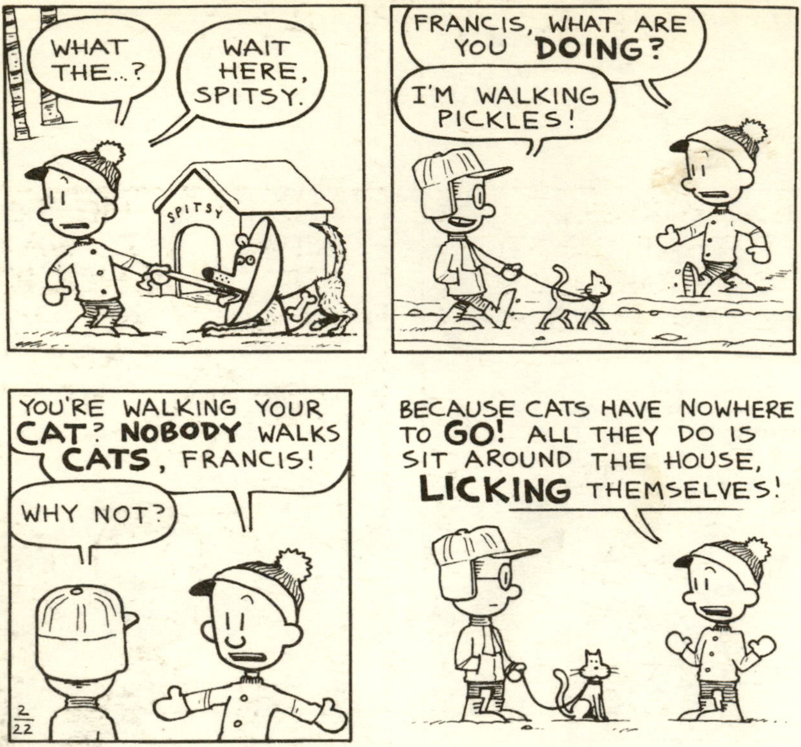
WHAT THE...?
WAIT HERE, SPITSY.
SPITSY
FRANCIS, WHAT ARE YOU **DOING**?
I'M WALKING PICKLES!
YOU'RE WALKING YOUR **CAT**? **NOBODY** WALKS **CATS**, FRANCIS!
WHY NOT?
2/22
BECAUSE CATS HAVE NOWHERE TO **GO**! ALL THEY DO IS SIT AROUND THE HOUSE, **LICKING** THEMSELVES!

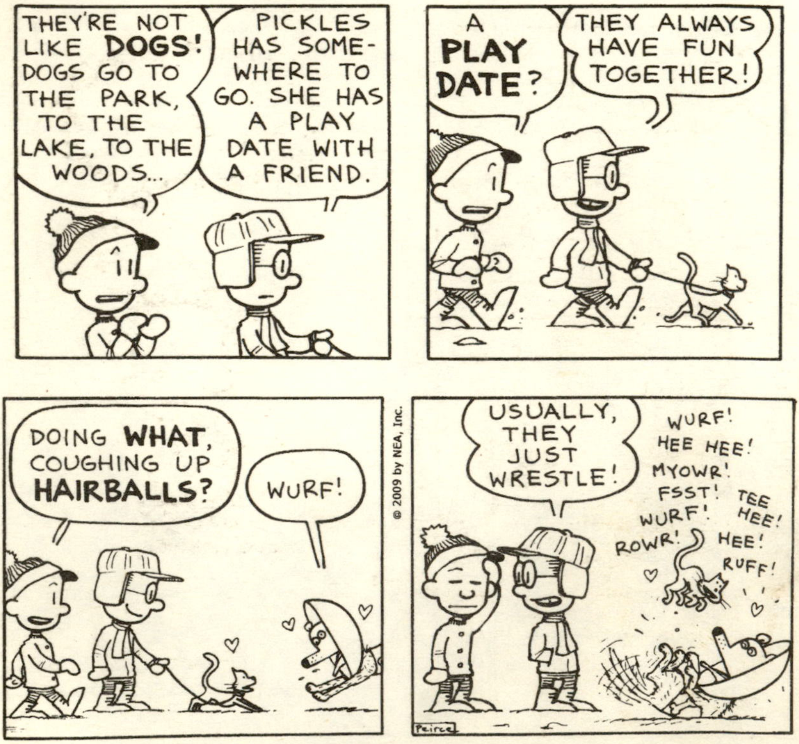
THEY'RE NOT LIKE **DOGS**! DOGS GO TO THE PARK, TO THE LAKE, TO THE WOODS...
PICKLES HAS SOME-WHERE TO GO. SHE HAS A PLAY DATE WITH A FRIEND.
A **PLAY DATE**?
THEY ALWAYS HAVE FUN TOGETHER!
DOING **WHAT**, COUGHING UP **HAIRBALLS**?
WURF!
USUALLY, THEY JUST WRESTLE!
WURF!
HEE HEE!
MYOWR!
FSST!
TEE HEE!
WURF!
HEE!
ROWR!
RUFF!
Peirce

EASY PEASY

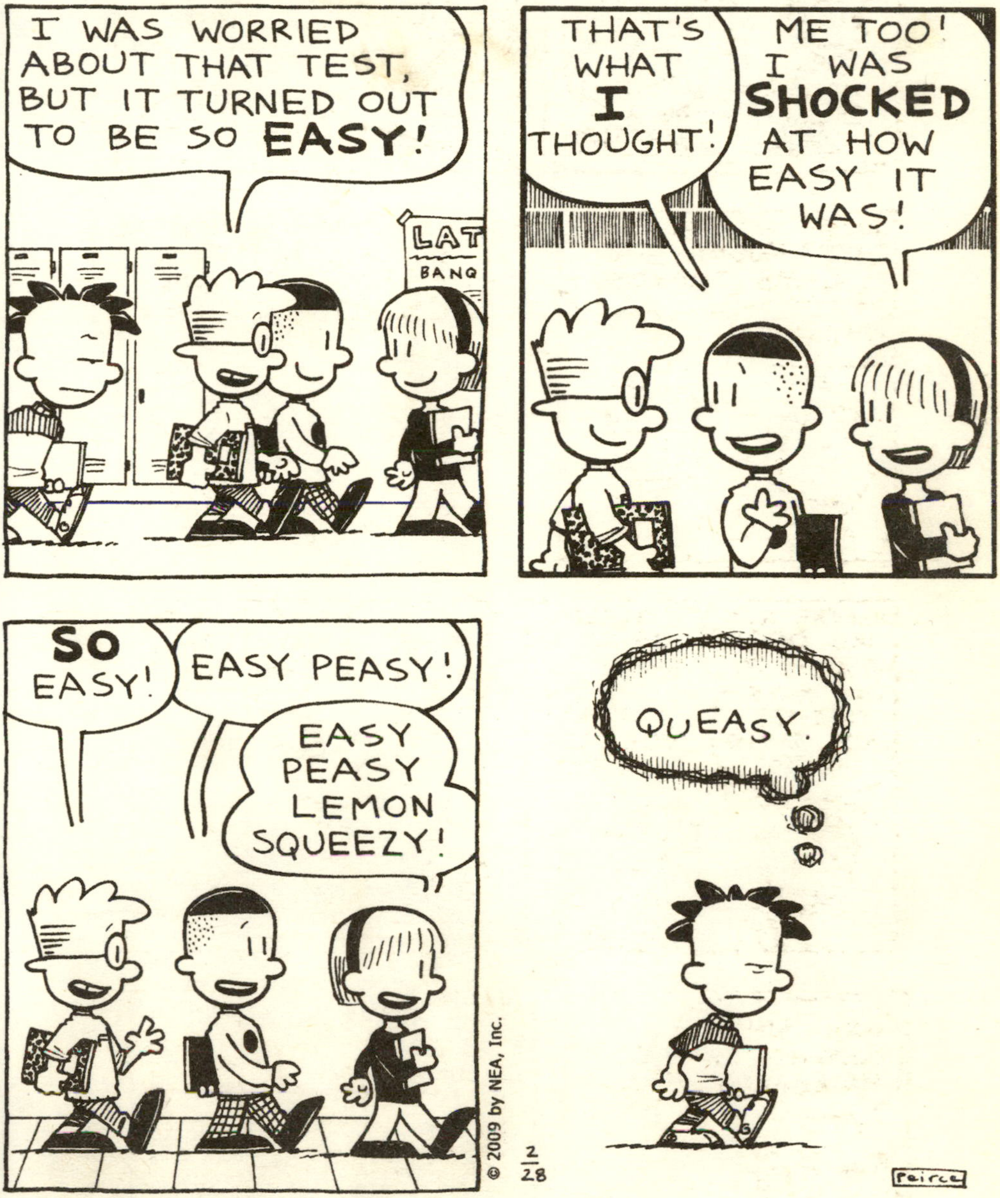
I WAS WORRIED ABOUT THAT TEST, BUT IT TURNED OUT TO BE SO **EASY**!
LAT
BANQ
THAT'S WHAT **I** THOUGHT!
ME TOO! I WAS **SHOCKED** AT HOW EASY IT WAS!
SO EASY!
EASY PEASY!
EASY PEASY LEMON SQUEEZY!
QUEASY.
© 2009 by NEA, Inc.
2/28
Peirce

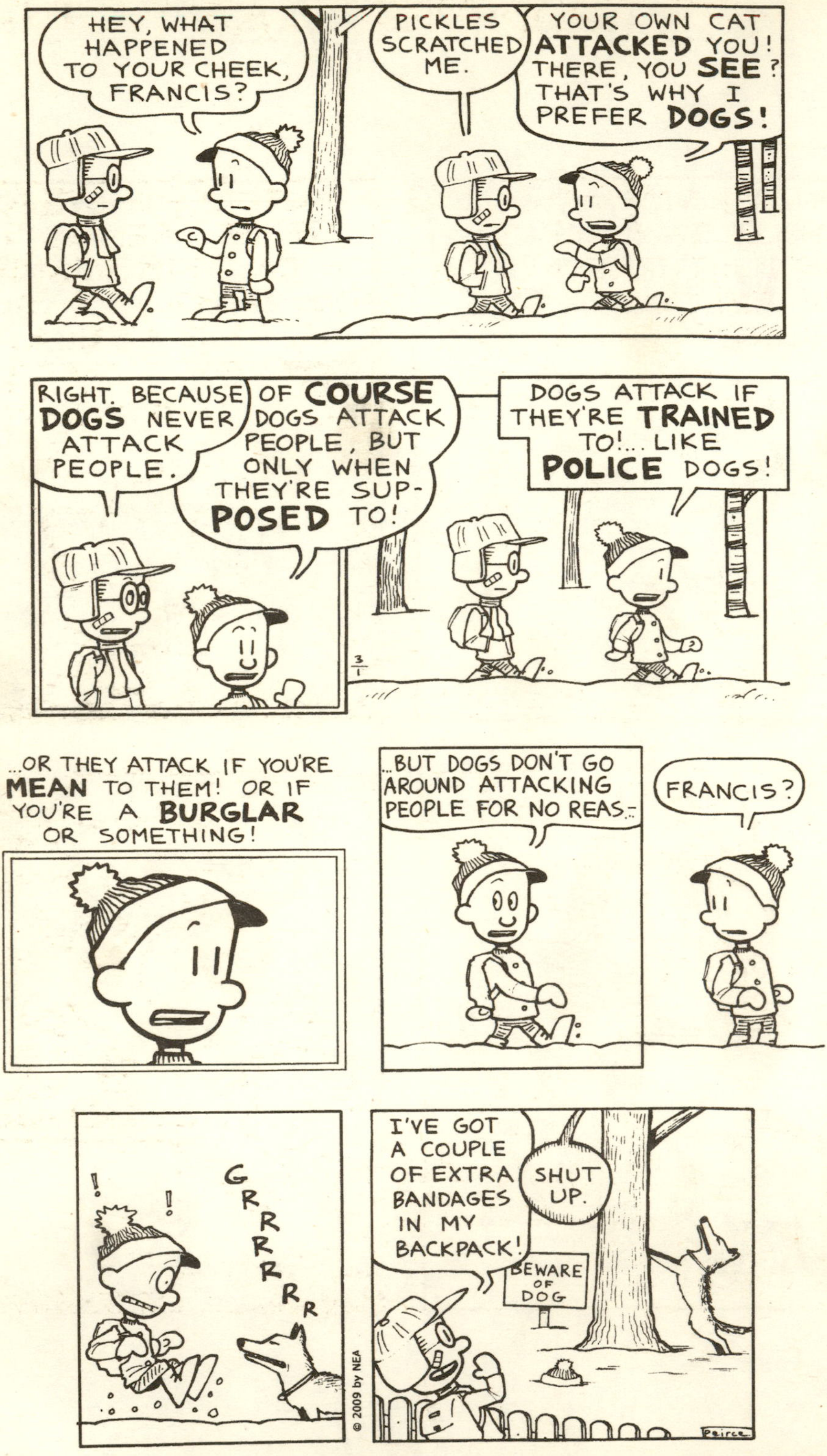
HEY, WHAT HAPPENED TO YOUR CHEEK, FRANCIS?
PICKLES SCRATCHED ME.
YOUR OWN CAT ATTACKED YOU! THERE, YOU SEE? THAT'S WHY I PREFER DOGS!
RIGHT. BECAUSE DOGS NEVER ATTACK PEOPLE.
OF COURSE DOGS ATTACK PEOPLE, BUT ONLY WHEN THEY'RE SUPPOSED TO!
DOGS ATTACK IF THEY'RE TRAINED TO!... LIKE POLICE DOGS!
...OR THEY ATTACK IF YOU'RE MEAN TO THEM! OR IF YOU'RE A BURGLAR OR SOMETHING!
...BUT DOGS DON'T GO AROUND ATTACKING PEOPLE FOR NO REAS–
FRANCIS?
! !
GRRRRRR
I'VE GOT A COUPLE OF EXTRA BANDAGES IN MY BACKPACK!
SHUT UP.
BEWARE OF DOG
© 2009 by NEA
Peirce

MRS GODFREY ACTS UP

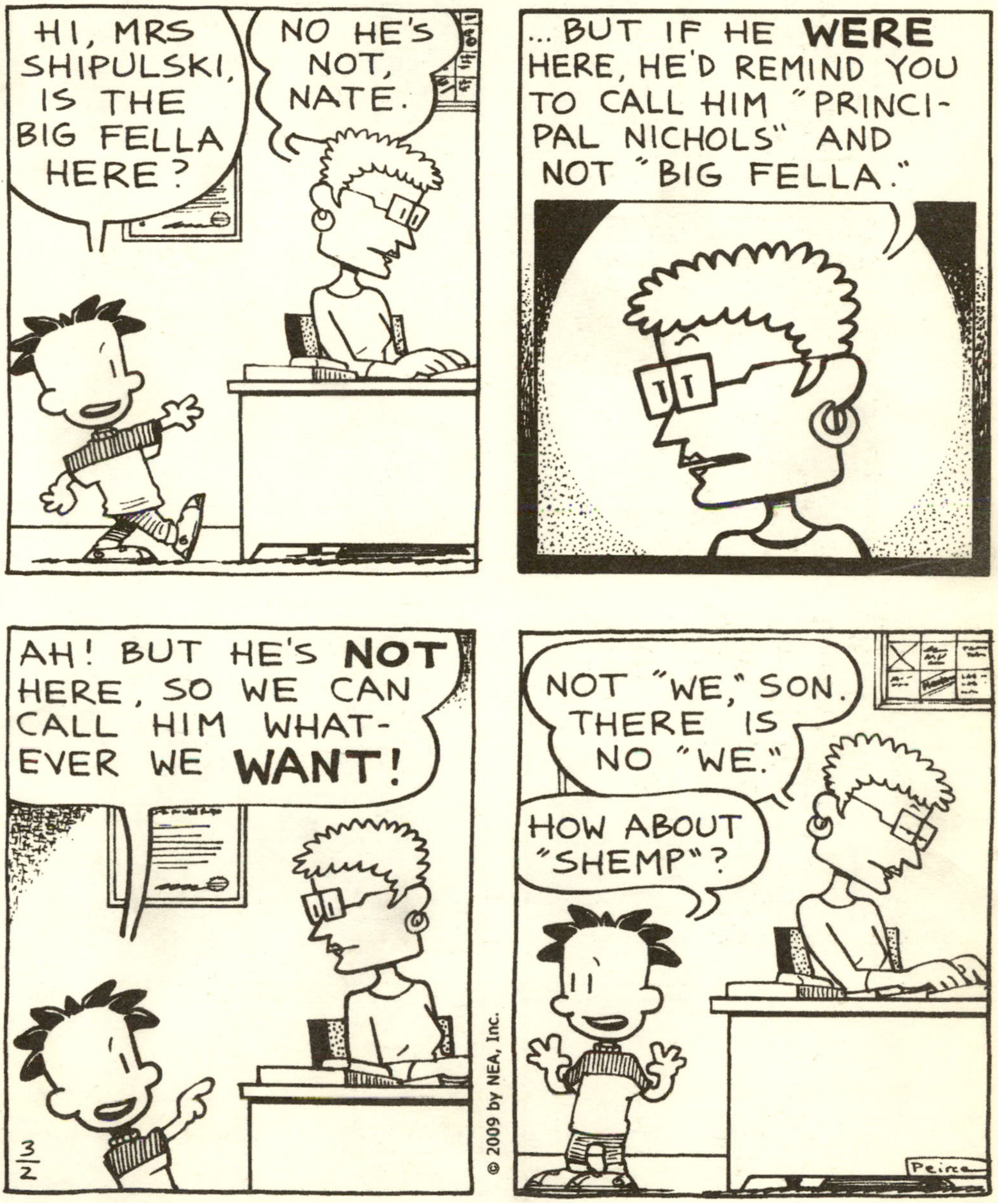
HI, MRS SHIPULSKI, IS THE BIG FELLA HERE?
NO HE'S NOT, NATE.
... BUT IF HE **WERE** HERE, HE'D REMIND YOU TO CALL HIM "PRINCIPAL NICHOLS" AND NOT "BIG FELLA."
AH! BUT HE'S **NOT** HERE, SO WE CAN CALL HIM WHATEVER WE **WANT**!
3/2
© 2009 by NEA, Inc.
NOT "WE," SON. THERE IS NO "WE."
HOW ABOUT "SHEMP"?
Peirce

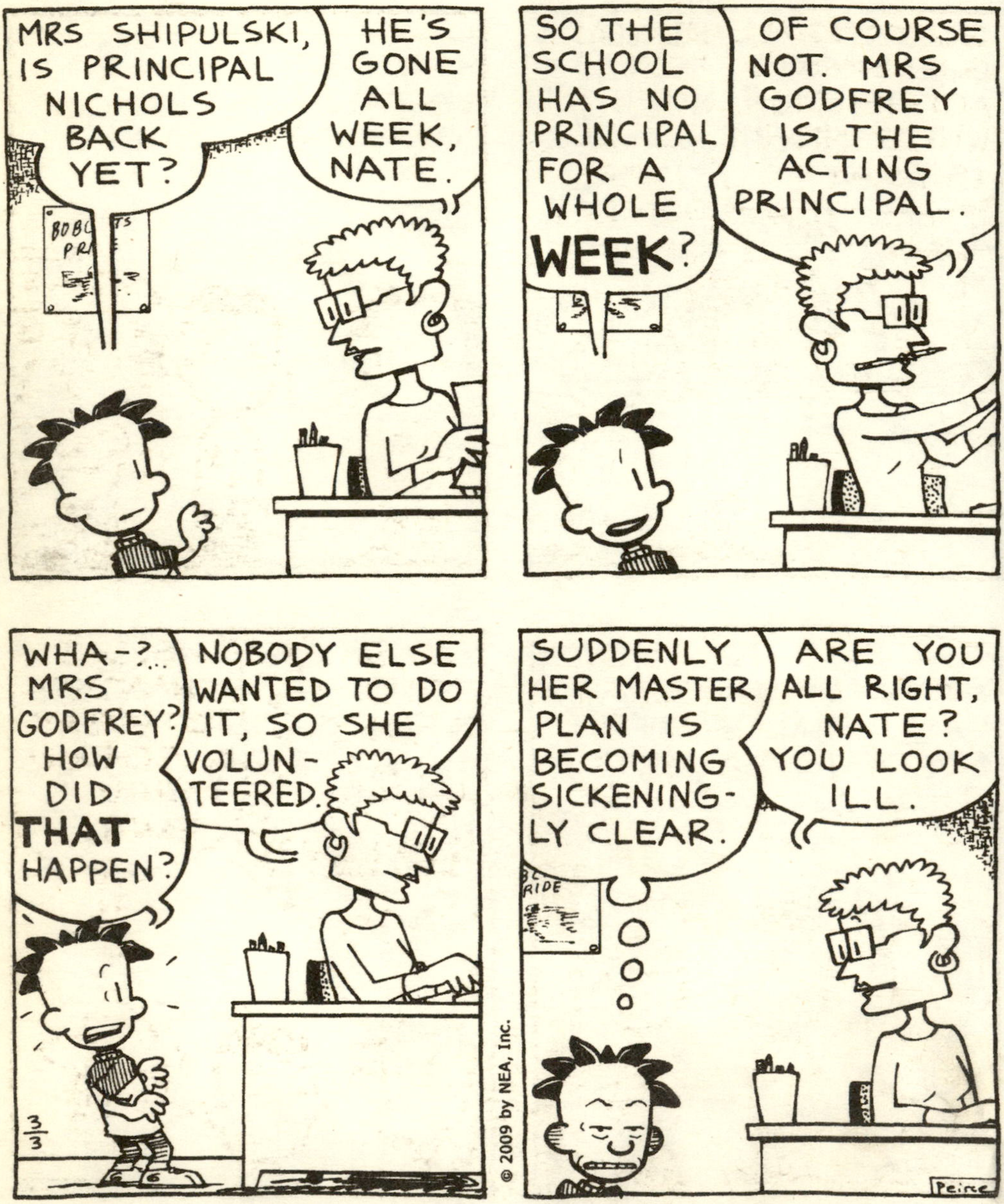
MRS SHIPULSKI, IS PRINCIPAL NICHOLS BACK YET?
HE'S GONE ALL WEEK, NATE.
SO THE SCHOOL HAS NO PRINCIPAL FOR A WHOLE **WEEK**?
OF COURSE NOT. MRS GODFREY IS THE ACTING PRINCIPAL.
WHA-?... MRS GODFREY? HOW DID **THAT** HAPPEN?
NOBODY ELSE WANTED TO DO IT, SO SHE VOLUNTEERED.
SUDDENLY HER MASTER PLAN IS BECOMING SICKENINGLY CLEAR.
ARE YOU ALL RIGHT, NATE? YOU LOOK ILL.
3/3
© 2009 by NEA, Inc.
Peirce

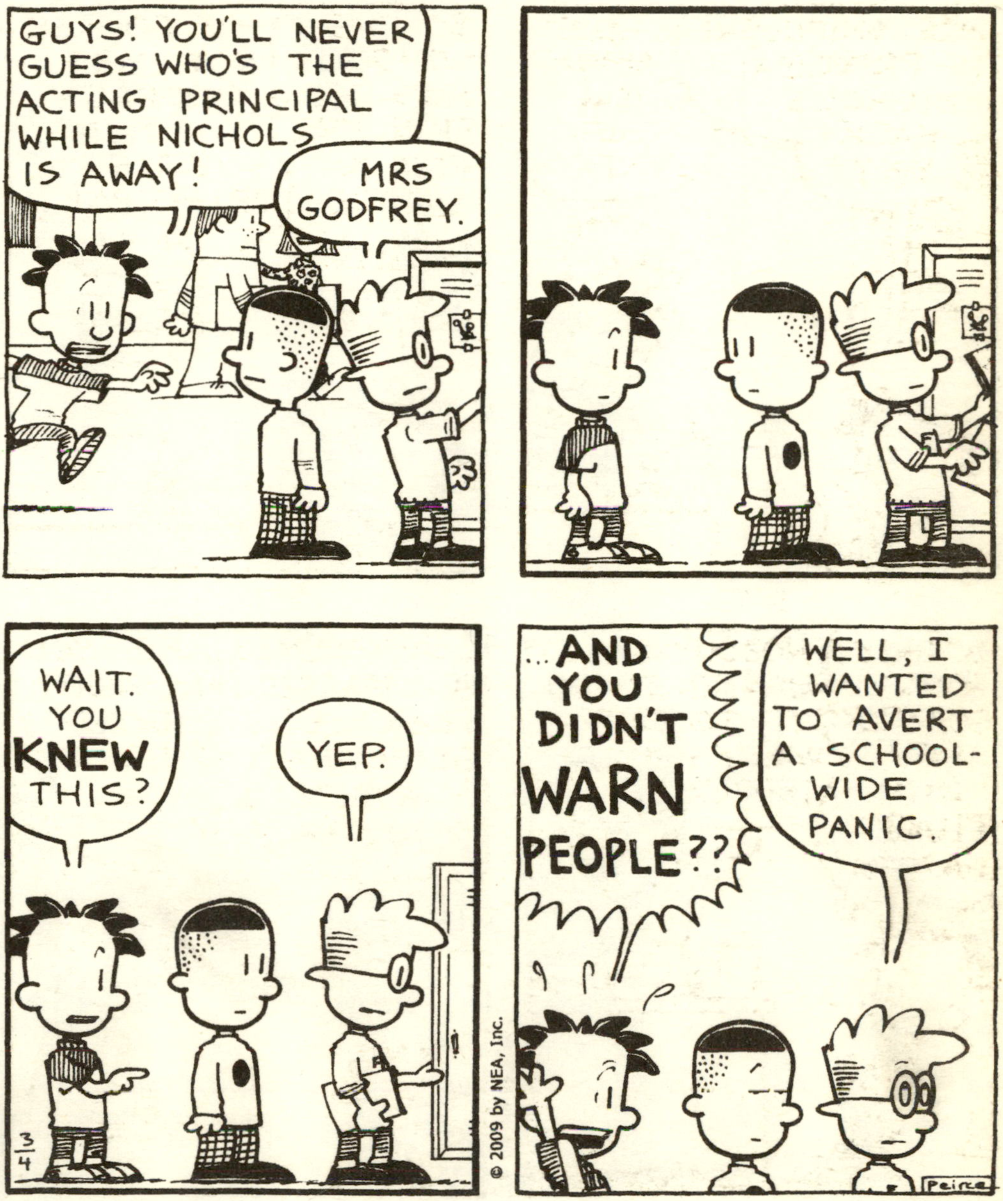
GUYS! YOU'LL NEVER GUESS WHO'S THE ACTING PRINCIPAL WHILE NICHOLS IS AWAY!
MRS GODFREY.
WAIT. YOU **KNEW** THIS?
YEP.
...**AND YOU DIDN'T WARN PEOPLE**??
WELL, I WANTED TO AVERT A SCHOOL-WIDE PANIC.
3/4
© 2009 by NEA, Inc.
Peirce

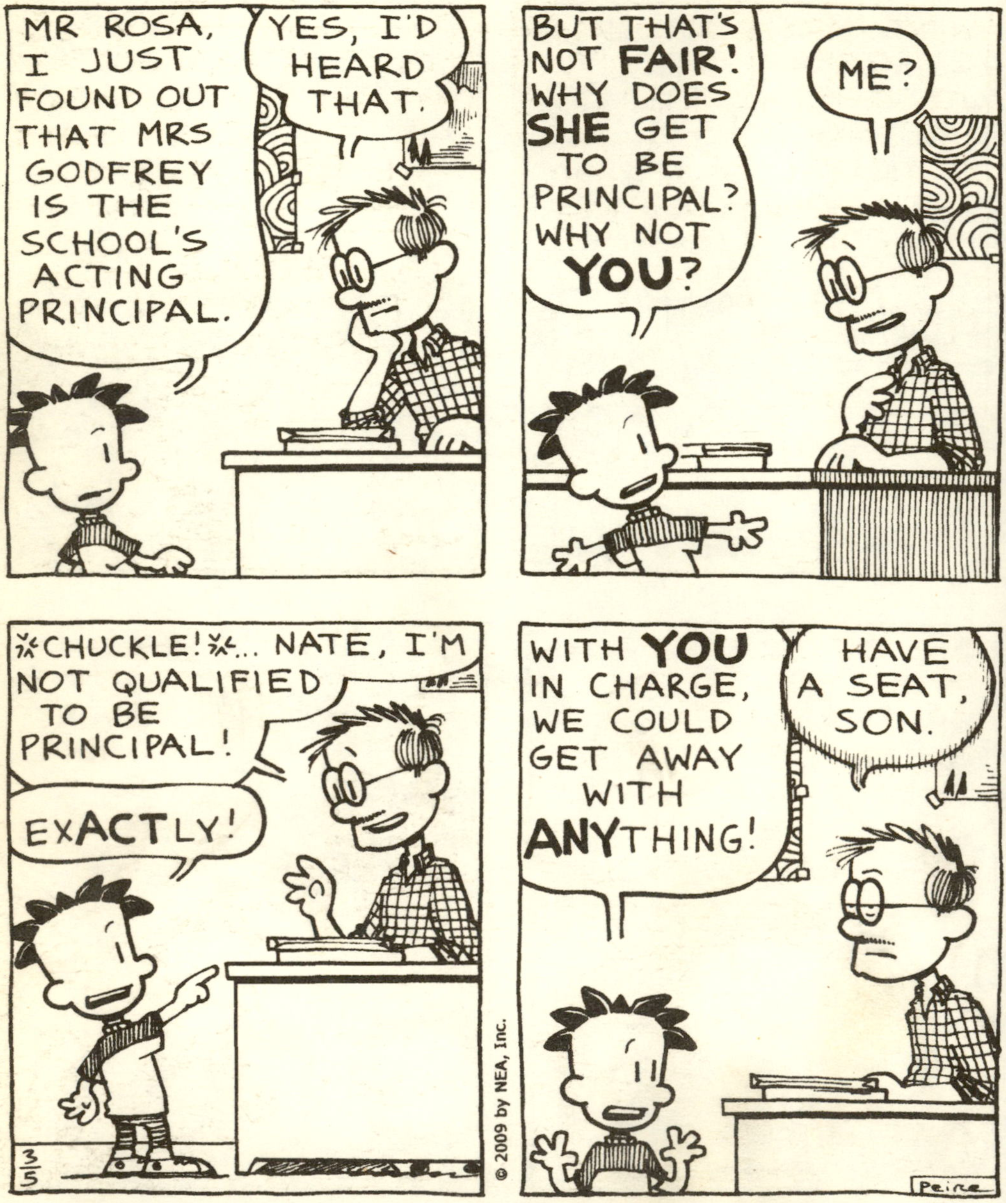
MR ROSA, I JUST FOUND OUT THAT MRS GODFREY IS THE SCHOOL'S ACTING PRINCIPAL.
YES, I'D HEARD THAT.
BUT THAT'S NOT FAIR! WHY DOES SHE GET TO BE PRINCIPAL? WHY NOT YOU?
ME?
CHUCKLE!... NATE, I'M NOT QUALIFIED TO BE PRINCIPAL!
EXACTLY!
WITH YOU IN CHARGE, WE COULD GET AWAY WITH ANYTHING!
HAVE A SEAT, SON.
3/5
© 2009 by NEA, Inc.
Peirce

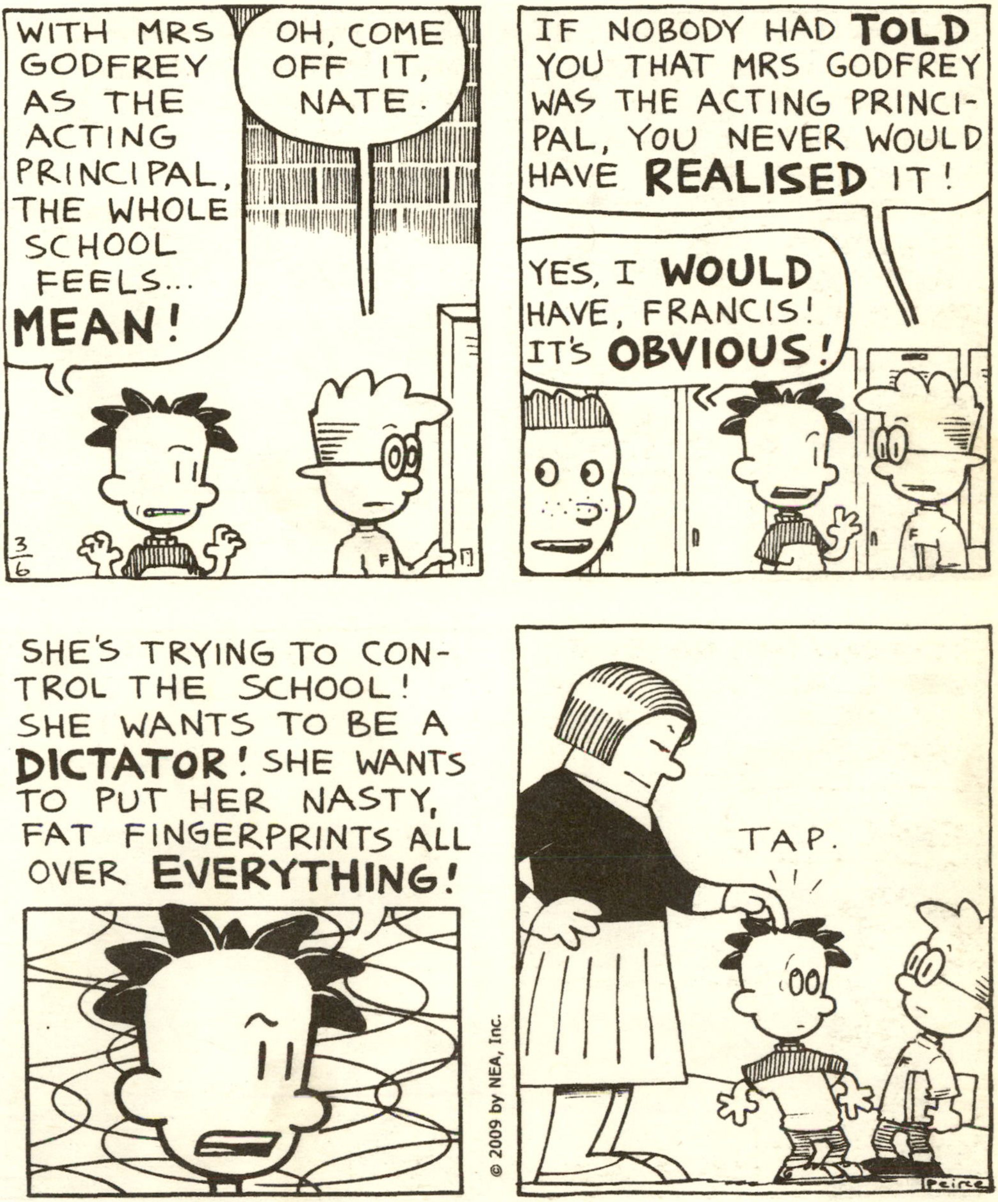
WITH MRS GODFREY AS THE ACTING PRINCIPAL, THE WHOLE SCHOOL FEELS... MEAN!
OH, COME OFF IT, NATE.
IF NOBODY HAD TOLD YOU THAT MRS GODFREY WAS THE ACTING PRINCIPAL, YOU NEVER WOULD HAVE REALISED IT!
YES, I WOULD HAVE, FRANCIS! IT'S OBVIOUS!
SHE'S TRYING TO CONTROL THE SCHOOL! SHE WANTS TO BE A DICTATOR! SHE WANTS TO PUT HER NASTY, FAT FINGERPRINTS ALL OVER EVERYTHING!
TAP.

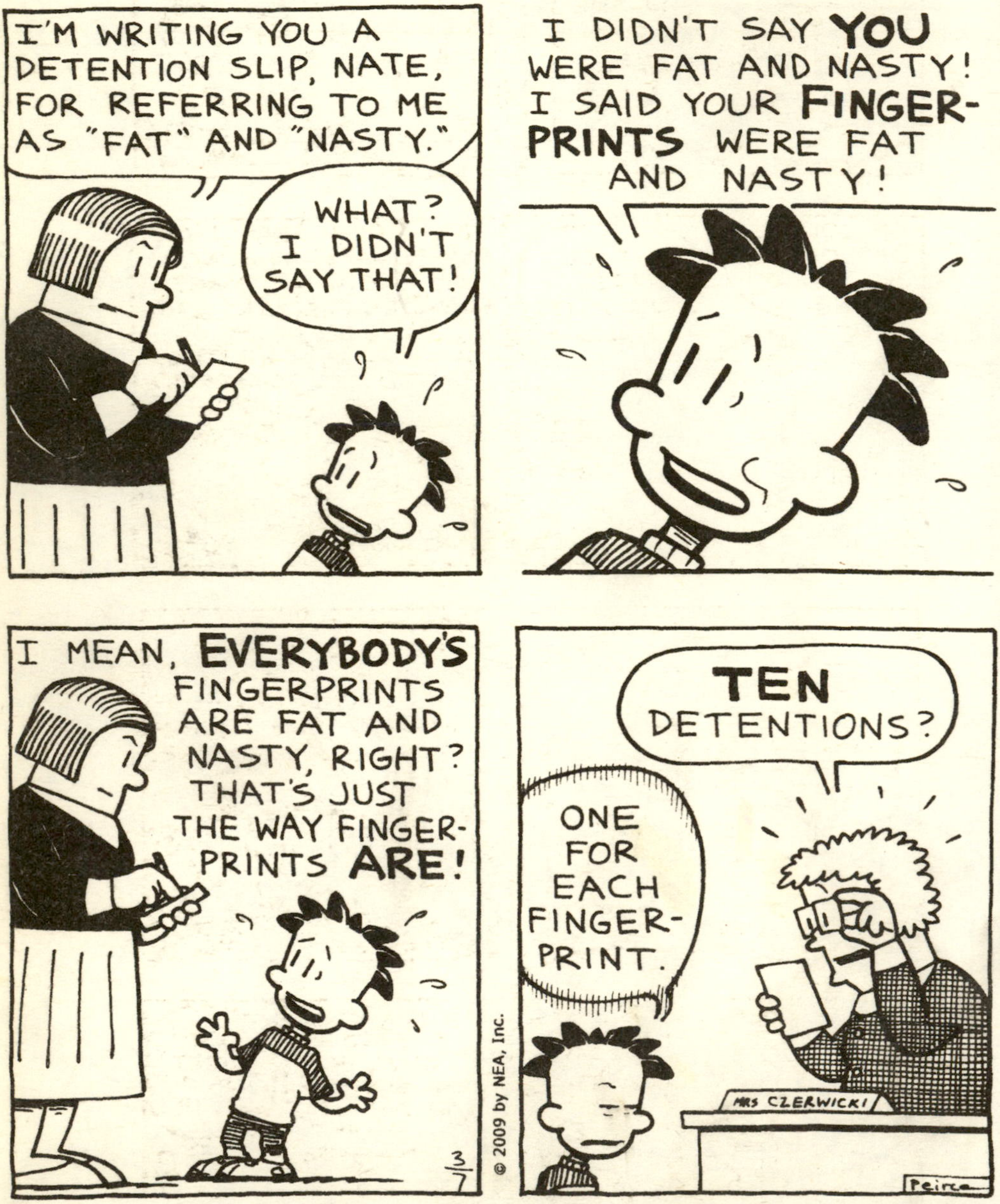
I'M WRITING YOU A DETENTION SLIP, NATE, FOR REFERRING TO ME AS "FAT" AND "NASTY."
WHAT? I DIDN'T SAY THAT!
I DIDN'T SAY YOU WERE FAT AND NASTY! I SAID YOUR FINGER-PRINTS WERE FAT AND NASTY!
I MEAN, EVERYBODY'S FINGERPRINTS ARE FAT AND NASTY, RIGHT? THAT'S JUST THE WAY FINGER-PRINTS ARE!
3/7
© 2009 by NEA, Inc.
TEN DETENTIONS?
ONE FOR EACH FINGER-PRINT.
MRS CZERWICKI
Peirce

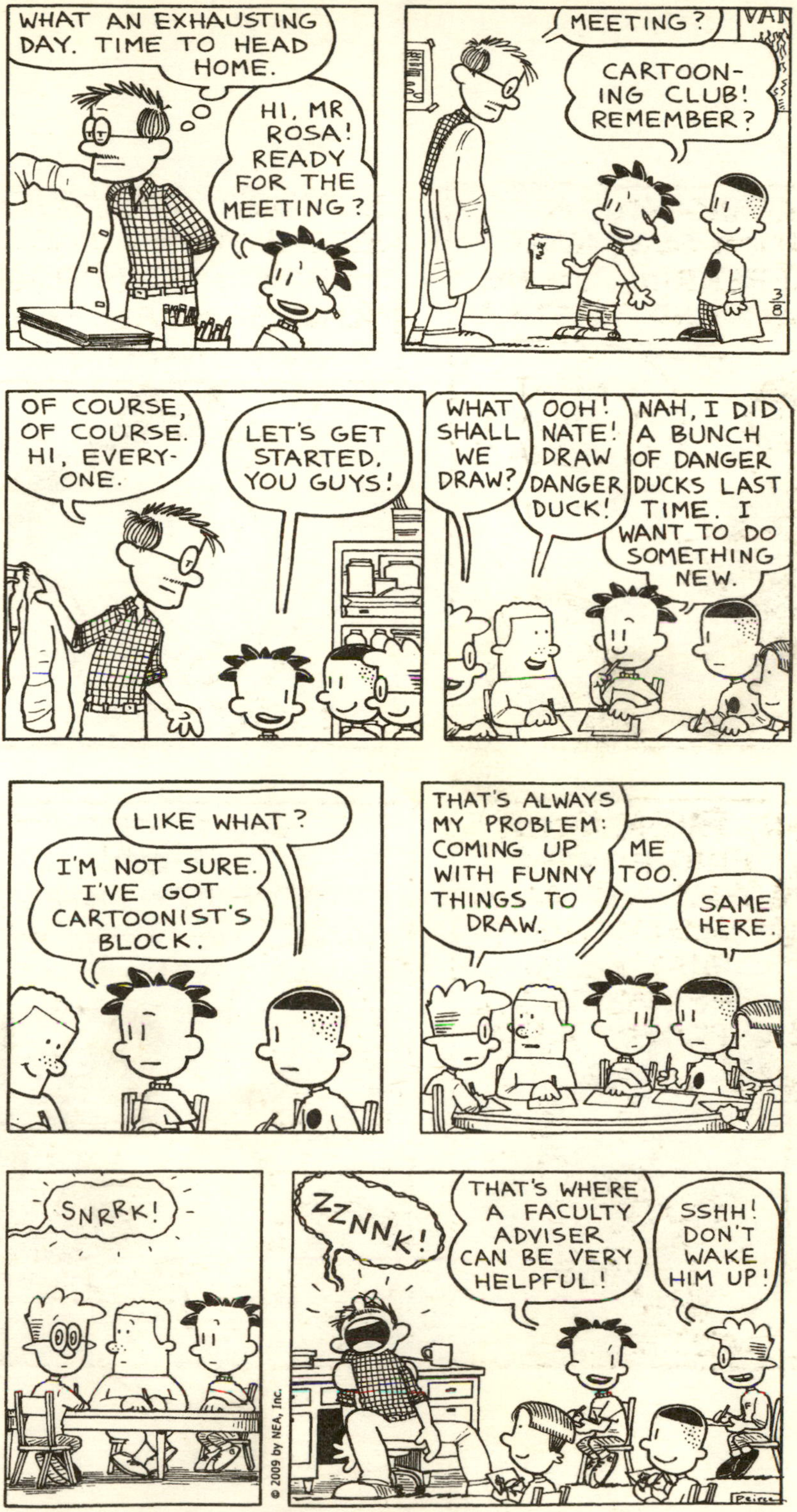
WHAT AN EXHAUSTING DAY. TIME TO HEAD HOME.
HI, MR ROSA! READY FOR THE MEETING?
MEETING?
CARTOON-ING CLUB! REMEMBER?
3/8
OF COURSE, OF COURSE. HI, EVERY-ONE.
LET'S GET STARTED, YOU GUYS!
WHAT SHALL WE DRAW?
OOH! NATE! DRAW DANGER DUCK!
NAH, I DID A BUNCH OF DANGER DUCKS LAST TIME. I WANT TO DO SOMETHING NEW.
LIKE WHAT?
I'M NOT SURE. I'VE GOT CARTOONIST'S BLOCK.
THAT'S ALWAYS MY PROBLEM: COMING UP WITH FUNNY THINGS TO DRAW.
ME TOO.
SAME HERE.
SNRRK!
ZZNNK!
THAT'S WHERE A FACULTY ADVISER CAN BE VERY HELPFUL!
SSHH! DON'T WAKE HIM UP!
© 2009 by NEA, Inc.
Peirce

FAME OR LAME?

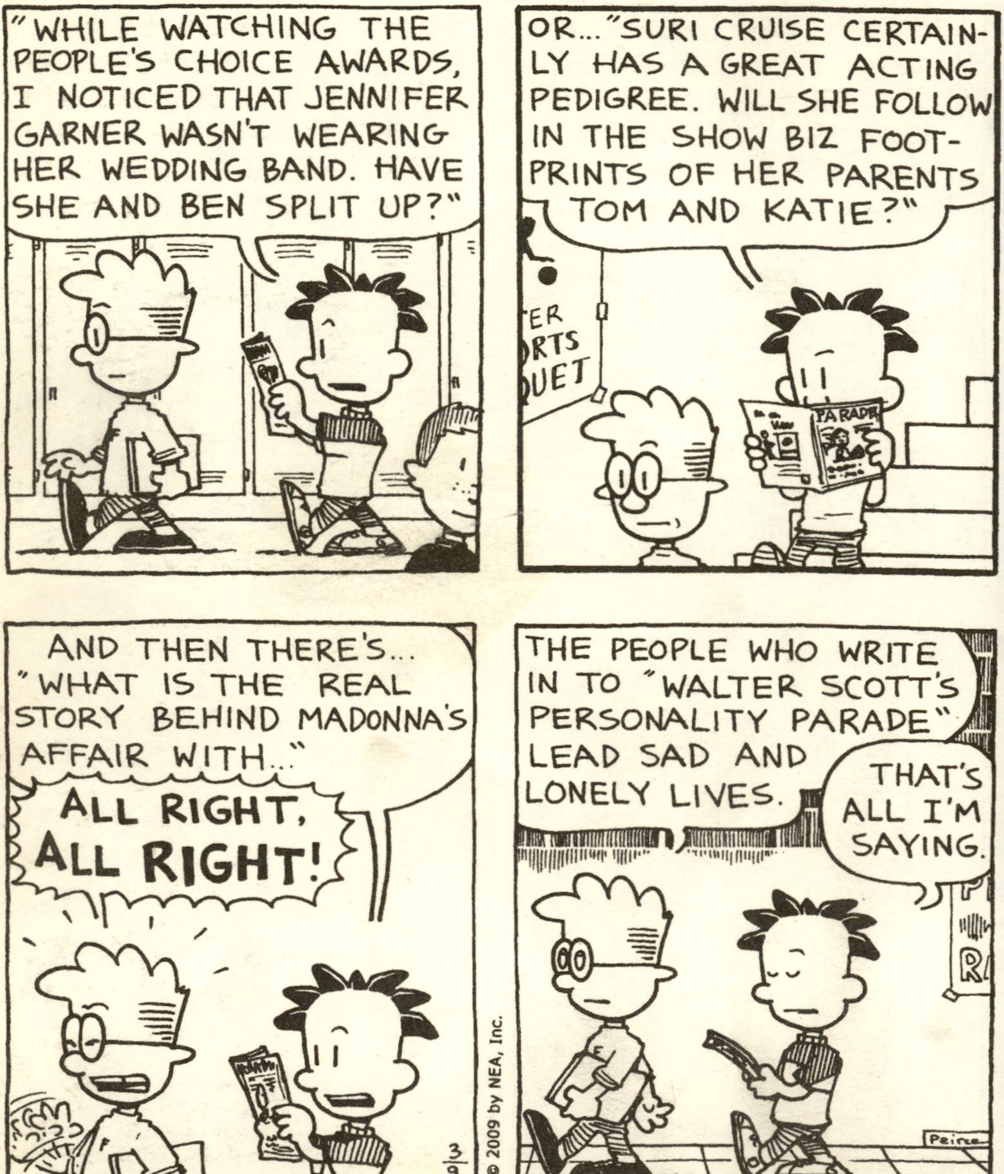
"WHILE WATCHING THE PEOPLE'S CHOICE AWARDS, I NOTICED THAT JENNIFER GARNER WASN'T WEARING HER WEDDING BAND. HAVE SHE AND BEN SPLIT UP?"
OR... "SURI CRUISE CERTAINLY HAS A GREAT ACTING PEDIGREE. WILL SHE FOLLOW IN THE SHOW BIZ FOOTPRINTS OF HER PARENTS TOM AND KATIE?"
PARADE
AND THEN THERE'S... "WHAT IS THE REAL STORY BEHIND MADONNA'S AFFAIR WITH..."
ALL RIGHT, ALL RIGHT!
3/9
THE PEOPLE WHO WRITE IN TO "WALTER SCOTT'S PERSONALITY PARADE" LEAD SAD AND LONELY LIVES.
THAT'S ALL I'M SAYING.
Peirce
© 2009 by NEA, Inc.

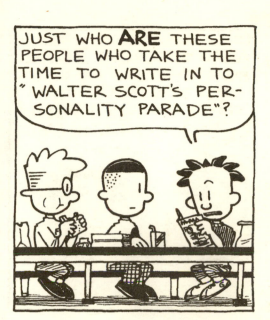

JUST WHO **ARE** THESE PEOPLE WHO TAKE THE TIME TO WRITE IN TO "WALTER SCOTT'S PERSONALITY PARADE"?

IS IT REALLY IMPORTANT TO THEM TO KNOW WHO'S DATING WHO IN HOLLYWOOD, OR WHICH OVER-THE-HILL ACTRESS HAS HAD PLASTIC SURGERY?

I MEAN, SOMEBODY ACTUALLY SPENT FIVE MINUTES WRITING A LETTER TO ASK ABOUT **PARIS HILTON'S HAIRSTYLIST!**

© 2009 by NEA, Inc.

3/10

AND THEN SOMEBODY ELSE SPENT FIFTEEN MINUTES COMPLAINING ABOUT IT.

TWENTY.

YAK YAK YAK YAK YAK YAK

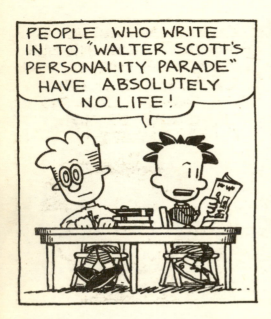

PEOPLE WHO WRITE IN TO "WALTER SCOTT'S PERSONALITY PARADE" HAVE ABSOLUTELY NO LIFE!

HOW WOULD **YOU** KNOW WHETHER THEY HAVE LIVES OR NOT?

I CAN **TELL** BY READING THEIR **LETTERS!**

SEE FOR YOURSELF, FRANCIS! READ ANY OF THESE LETTERS! PICK ONE AT RANDOM!

3/11

" PLEASE SETTLE A NICOLE KIDMAN ARGUMENT BETWEEN ME AND MY CAT.."

SEE?

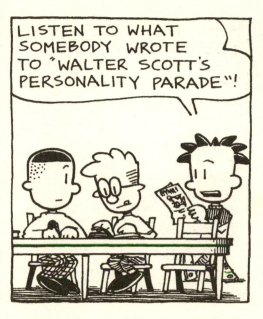

LISTEN TO WHAT SOMEBODY WROTE TO "WALTER SCOTT'S PERSONALITY PARADE"!

"I KEEP HEARING ABOUT ARGUMENTS ON THE SET OF 'GOSSIP GIRL.' **PLEASE** TELL ME THIS WON'T LEAD TO THE SHOW BEING **CANCELLED!**"

IS THAT PATHETIC OR **WHAT**? OH, **NO!** MY LIFE WILL BE DE-**STROYED** IF I CAN'T WATCH MY FAVOURITE **TV SHOW!**

© 2009 by NEA, Inc.

3/12

I'VE GOT TO LEARN TO IGNORE HIM.

IGNORE WHO?

THAT DOES IT. I'M TURNING TO "ASK MARILYN."

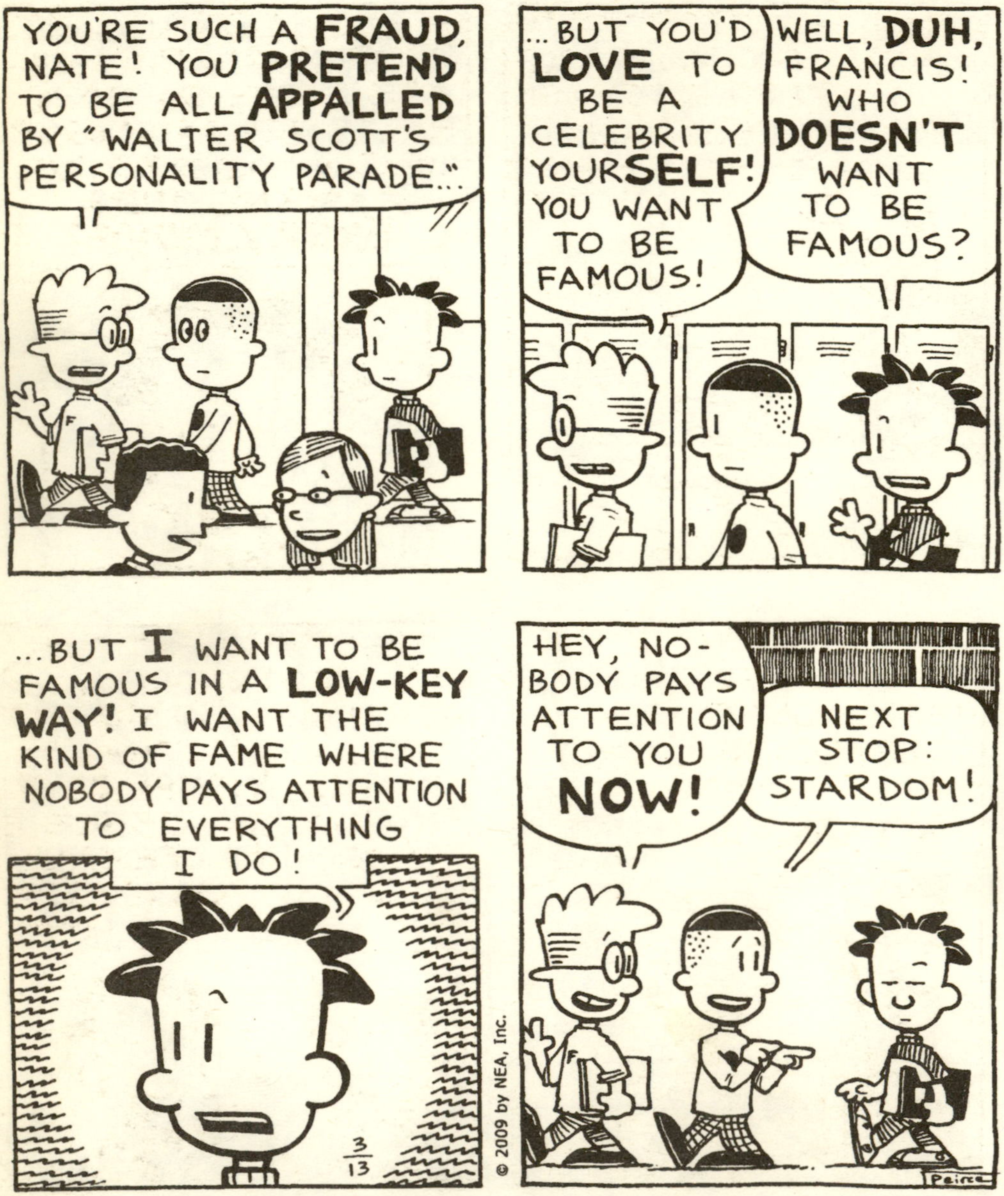
YOU'RE SUCH A FRAUD, NATE! YOU PRETEND TO BE ALL APPALLED BY "WALTER SCOTT'S PERSONALITY PARADE..."
...BUT YOU'D LOVE TO BE A CELEBRITY YOURSELF! YOU WANT TO BE FAMOUS!
WELL, DUH, FRANCIS! WHO DOESN'T WANT TO BE FAMOUS?
...BUT I WANT TO BE FAMOUS IN A LOW-KEY WAY! I WANT THE KIND OF FAME WHERE NOBODY PAYS ATTENTION TO EVERYTHING I DO!
3/13
© 2009 by NEA, Inc.
HEY, NO-BODY PAYS ATTENTION TO YOU NOW!
NEXT STOP: STARDOM!
Peirce

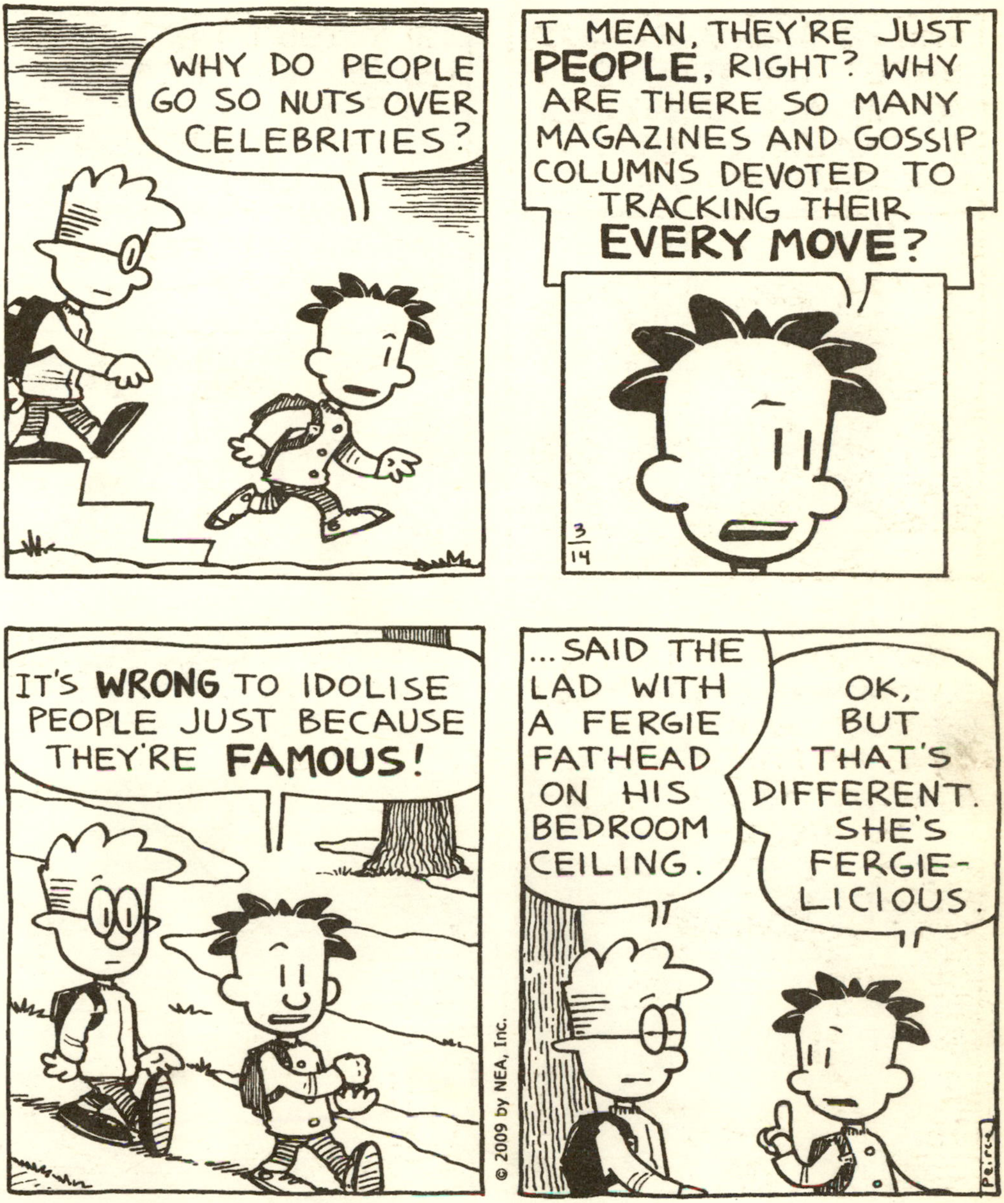
WHY DO PEOPLE GO SO NUTS OVER CELEBRITIES?
I MEAN, THEY'RE JUST **PEOPLE**, RIGHT? WHY ARE THERE SO MANY MAGAZINES AND GOSSIP COLUMNS DEVOTED TO TRACKING THEIR **EVERY MOVE**?
3/14
IT'S **WRONG** TO IDOLISE PEOPLE JUST BECAUSE THEY'RE **FAMOUS**!
...SAID THE LAD WITH A FERGIE FATHEAD ON HIS BEDROOM CEILING.
OK, BUT THAT'S DIFFERENT. SHE'S FERGIE-LICIOUS.
Peirce

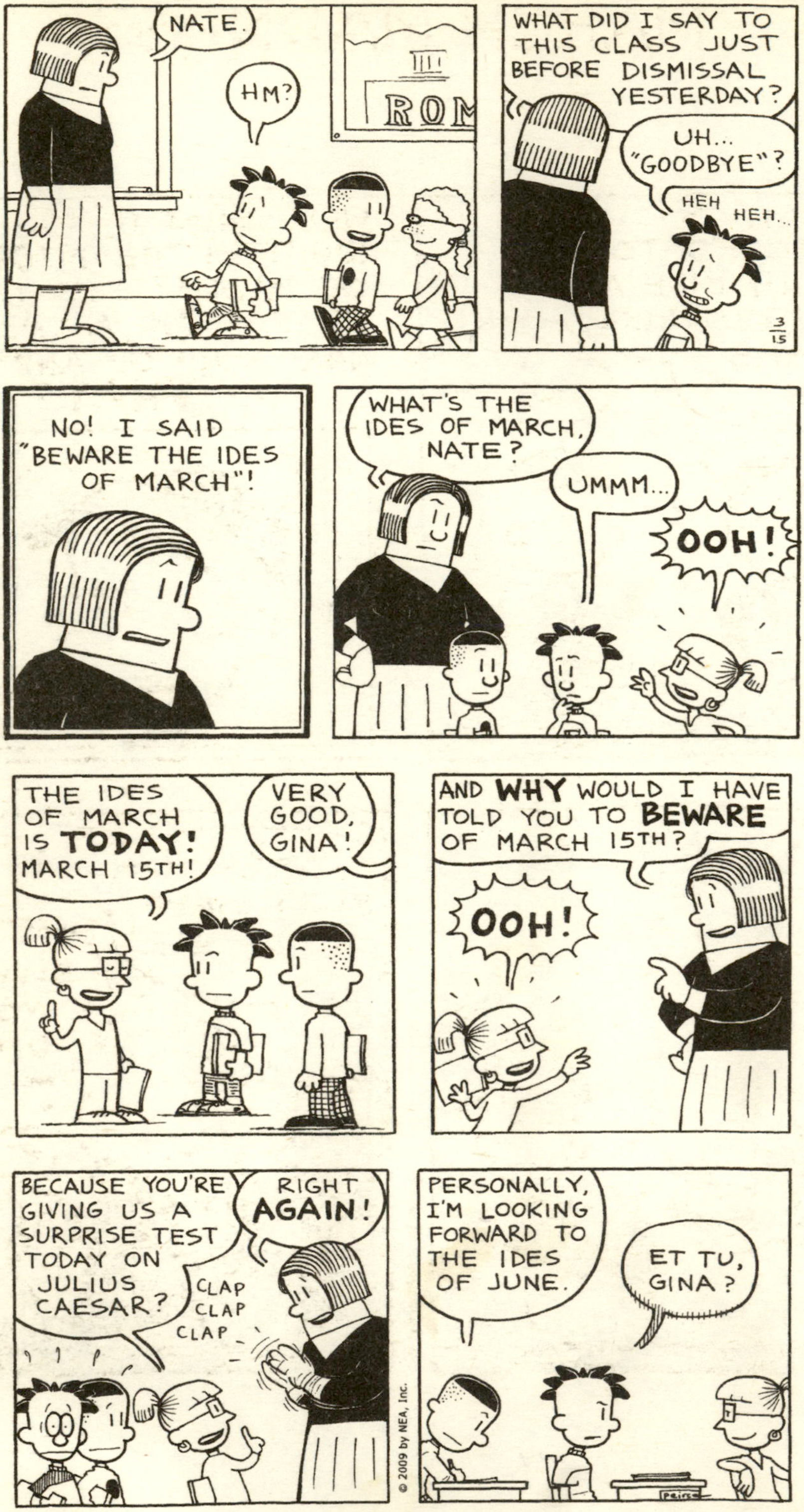
NATE.
HM?
ROM
WHAT DID I SAY TO THIS CLASS JUST BEFORE DISMISSAL YESTERDAY?
UH... "GOODBYE"?
HEH HEH...
3/15
NO! I SAID "BEWARE THE IDES OF MARCH"!
WHAT'S THE IDES OF MARCH, NATE?
UMMM...
OOH!
THE IDES OF MARCH IS TODAY! MARCH 15TH!
VERY GOOD, GINA!
AND WHY WOULD I HAVE TOLD YOU TO BEWARE OF MARCH 15TH?
OOH!
BECAUSE YOU'RE GIVING US A SURPRISE TEST TODAY ON JULIUS CAESAR?
RIGHT AGAIN!
CLAP CLAP CLAP
© 2009 by NEA, Inc.
PERSONALLY, I'M LOOKING FORWARD TO THE IDES OF JUNE.
ET TU, GINA?
Peirce

MARCH MADNESS

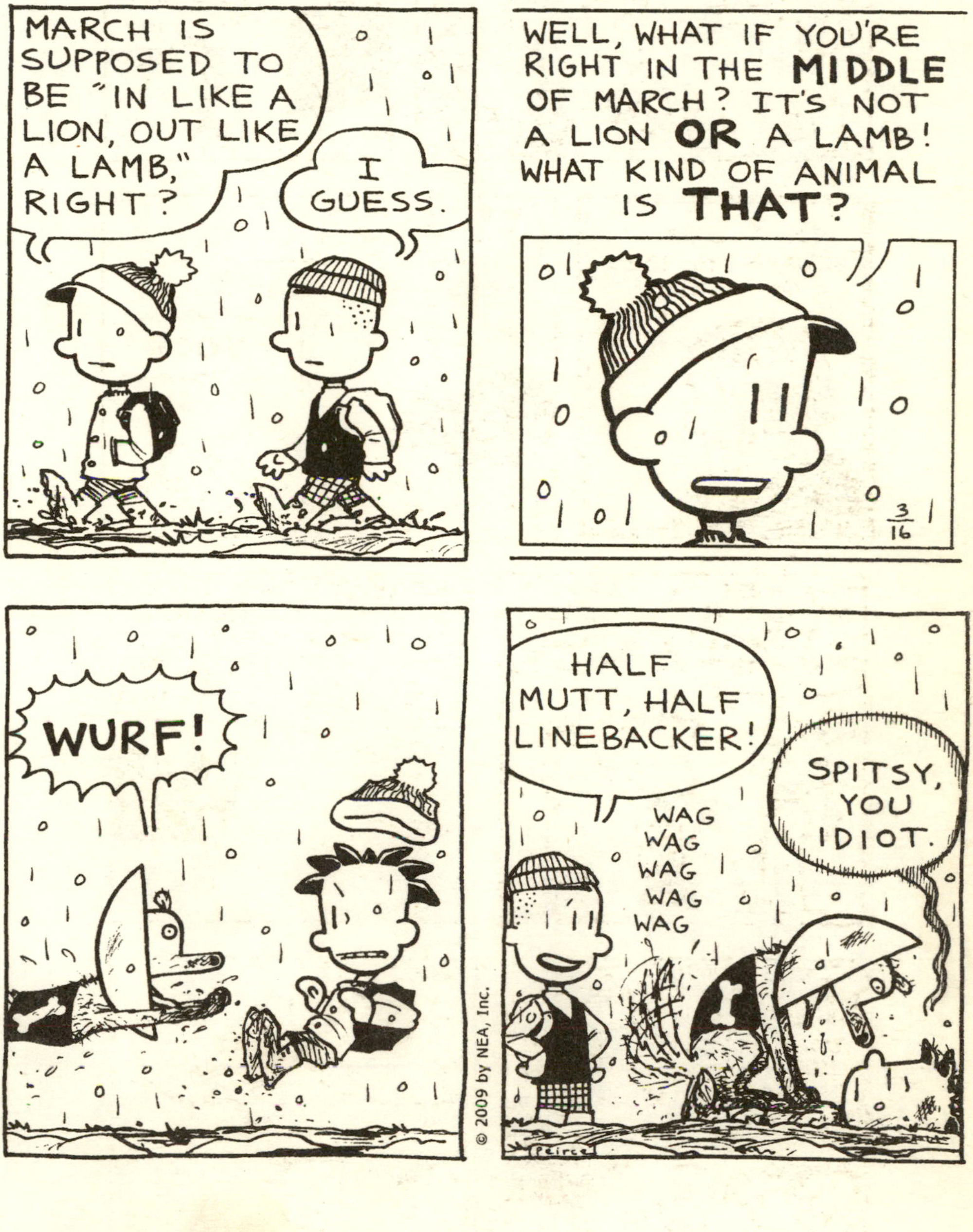

MARCH IS SUPPOSED TO BE "IN LIKE A LION, OUT LIKE A LAMB," RIGHT?
I GUESS.
WELL, WHAT IF YOU'RE RIGHT IN THE **MIDDLE** OF MARCH? IT'S NOT A LION **OR** A LAMB! WHAT KIND OF ANIMAL IS **THAT**?
3/16
WURF!
© 2009 by NEA, Inc.
HALF MUTT, HALF LINEBACKER!
WAG WAG WAG WAG WAG
SPITSY, YOU IDIOT.
Peirce

IS IT SPRING YET?

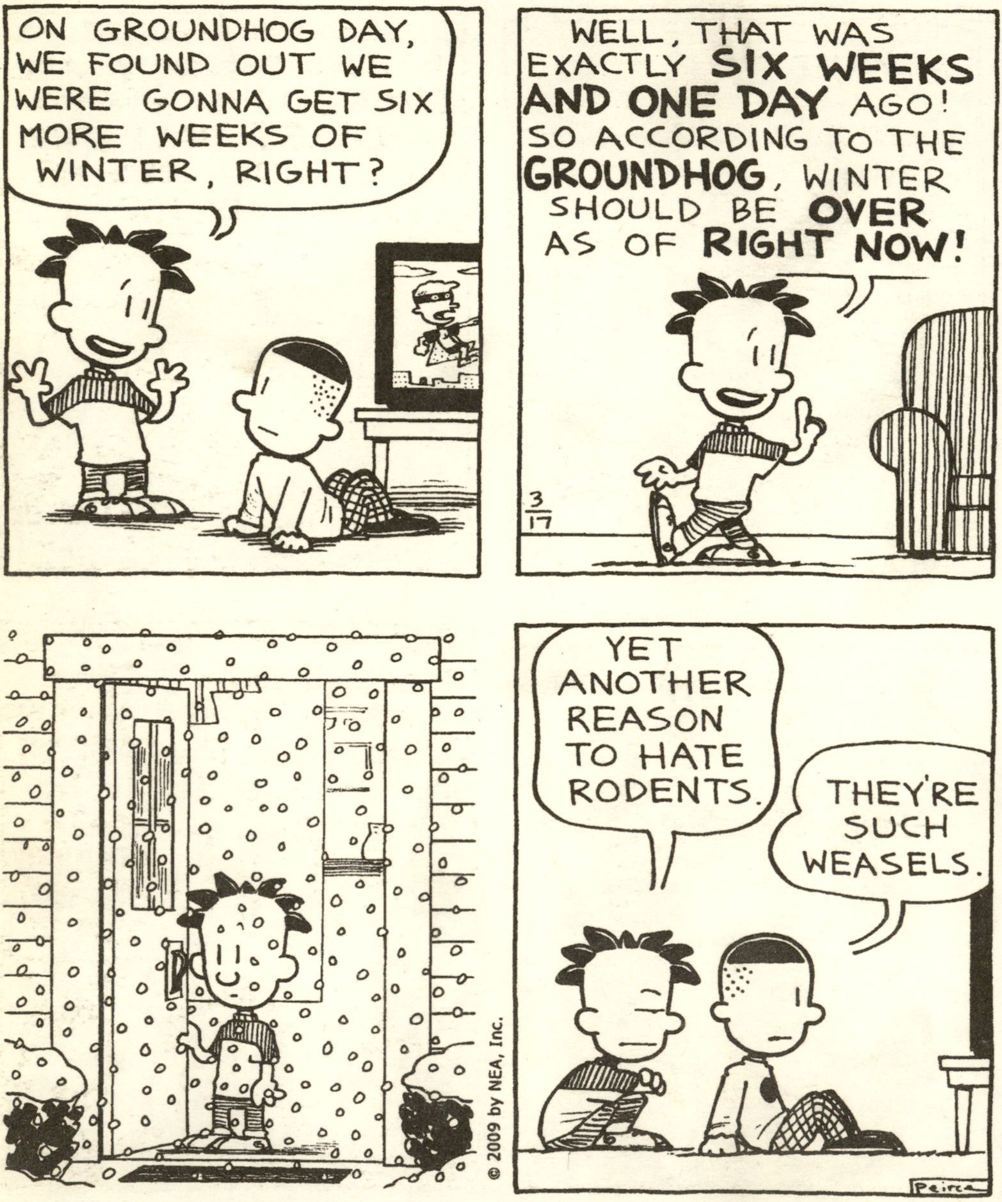
ON GROUNDHOG DAY, WE FOUND OUT WE WERE GONNA GET SIX MORE WEEKS OF WINTER, RIGHT?
WELL, THAT WAS EXACTLY **SIX WEEKS AND ONE DAY** AGO! SO ACCORDING TO THE **GROUNDHOG**, WINTER SHOULD BE **OVER** AS OF **RIGHT NOW!**
3/17
YET ANOTHER REASON TO HATE RODENTS.
THEY'RE SUCH WEASELS.
Peirce
© 2009 by NEA, Inc.

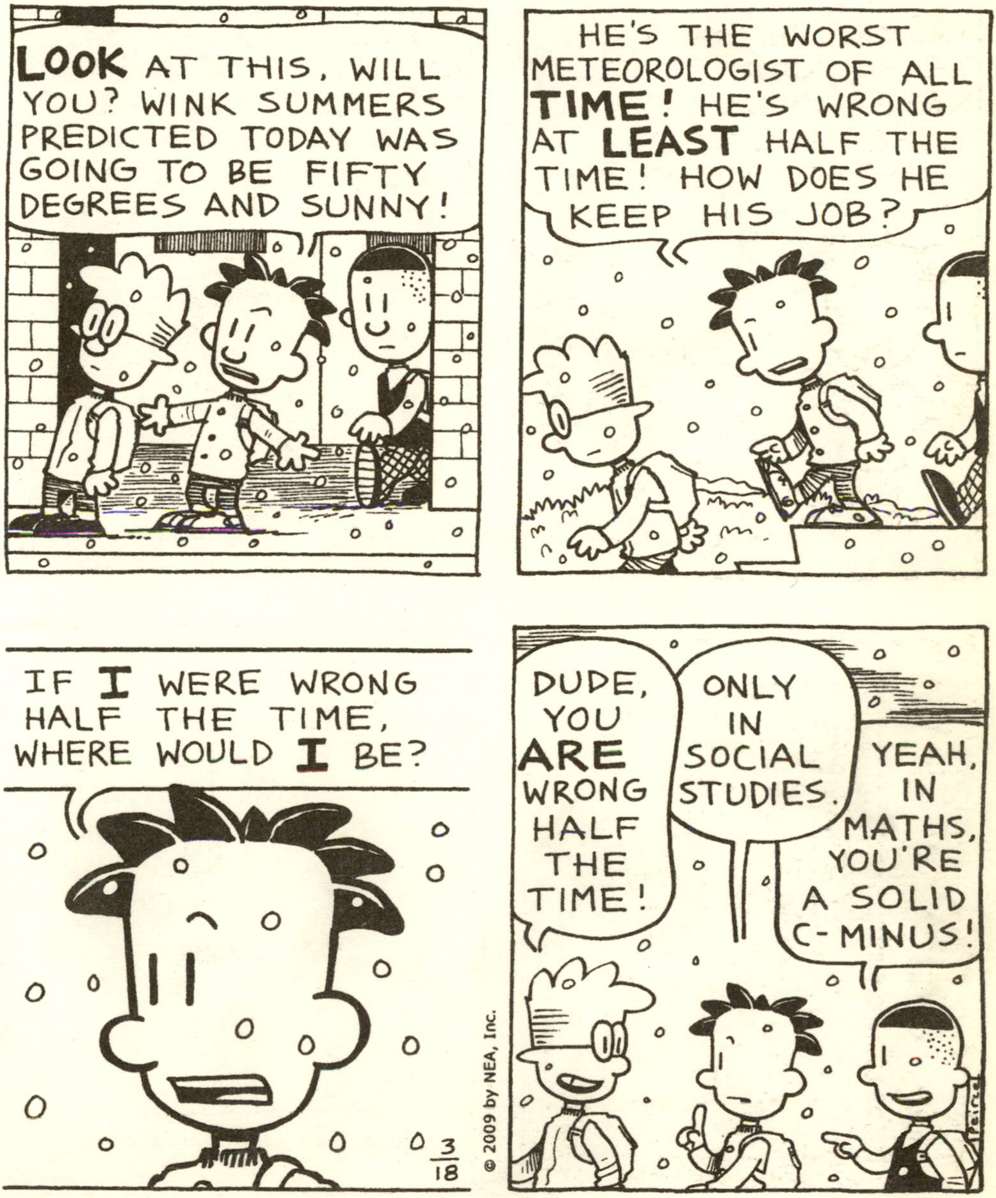

LOOK AT THIS, WILL YOU? WINK SUMMERS PREDICTED TODAY WAS GOING TO BE FIFTY DEGREES AND SUNNY!
HE'S THE WORST METEOROLOGIST OF ALL TIME! HE'S WRONG AT LEAST HALF THE TIME! HOW DOES HE KEEP HIS JOB?
IF I WERE WRONG HALF THE TIME, WHERE WOULD I BE?
3/18
DUDE, YOU ARE WRONG HALF THE TIME!
ONLY IN SOCIAL STUDIES.
YEAH, IN MATHS, YOU'RE A SOLID C-MINUS!
Peirce

TAKE OFF

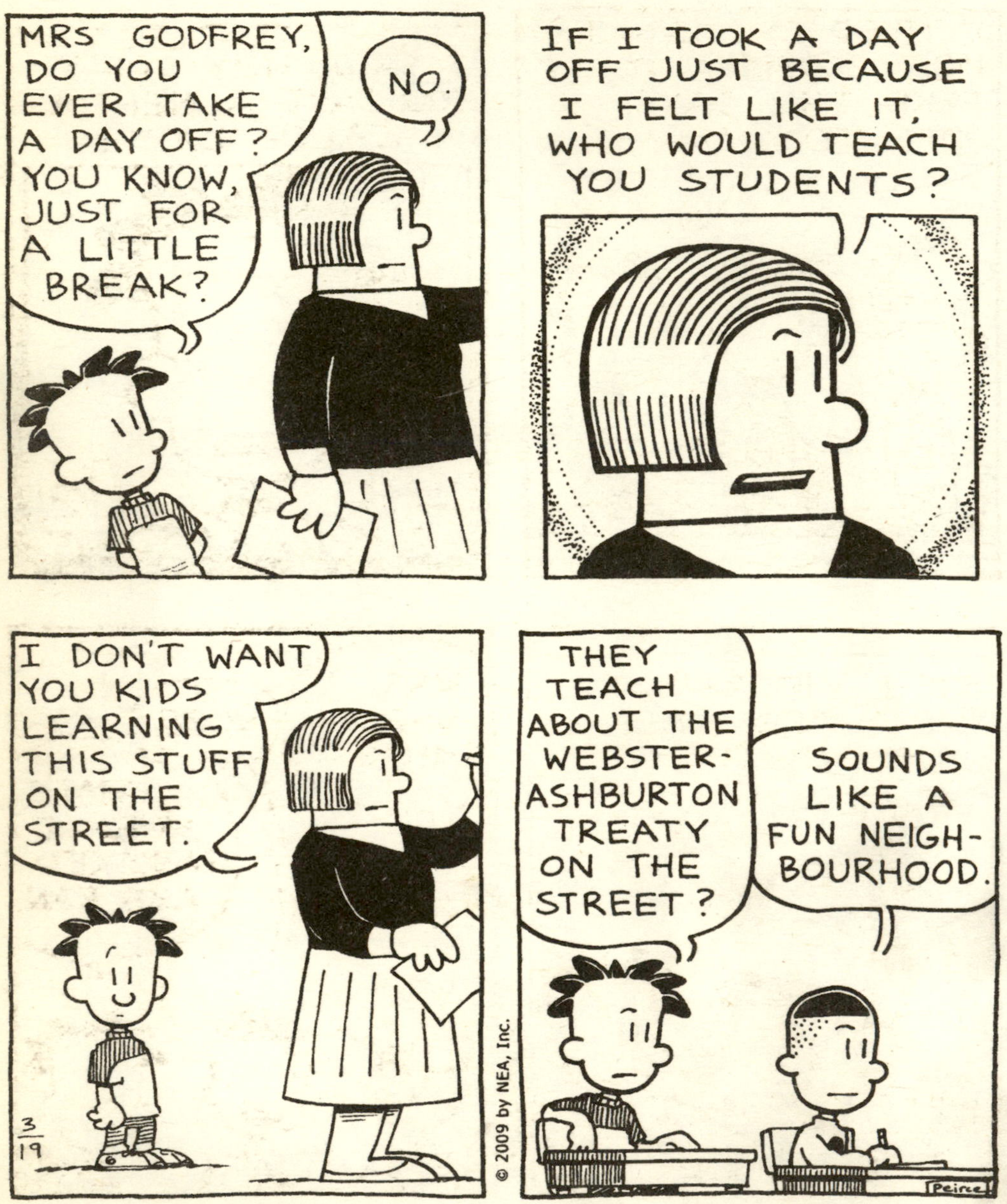
MRS GODFREY, DO YOU EVER TAKE A DAY OFF? YOU KNOW, JUST FOR A LITTLE BREAK?
NO.
IF I TOOK A DAY OFF JUST BECAUSE I FELT LIKE IT, WHO WOULD TEACH YOU STUDENTS?
I DON'T WANT YOU KIDS LEARNING THIS STUFF ON THE STREET.
3/19
© 2009 by NEA, Inc.
THEY TEACH ABOUT THE WEBSTER-ASHBURTON TREATY ON THE STREET?
SOUNDS LIKE A FUN NEIGH-BOURHOOD.
Peirce

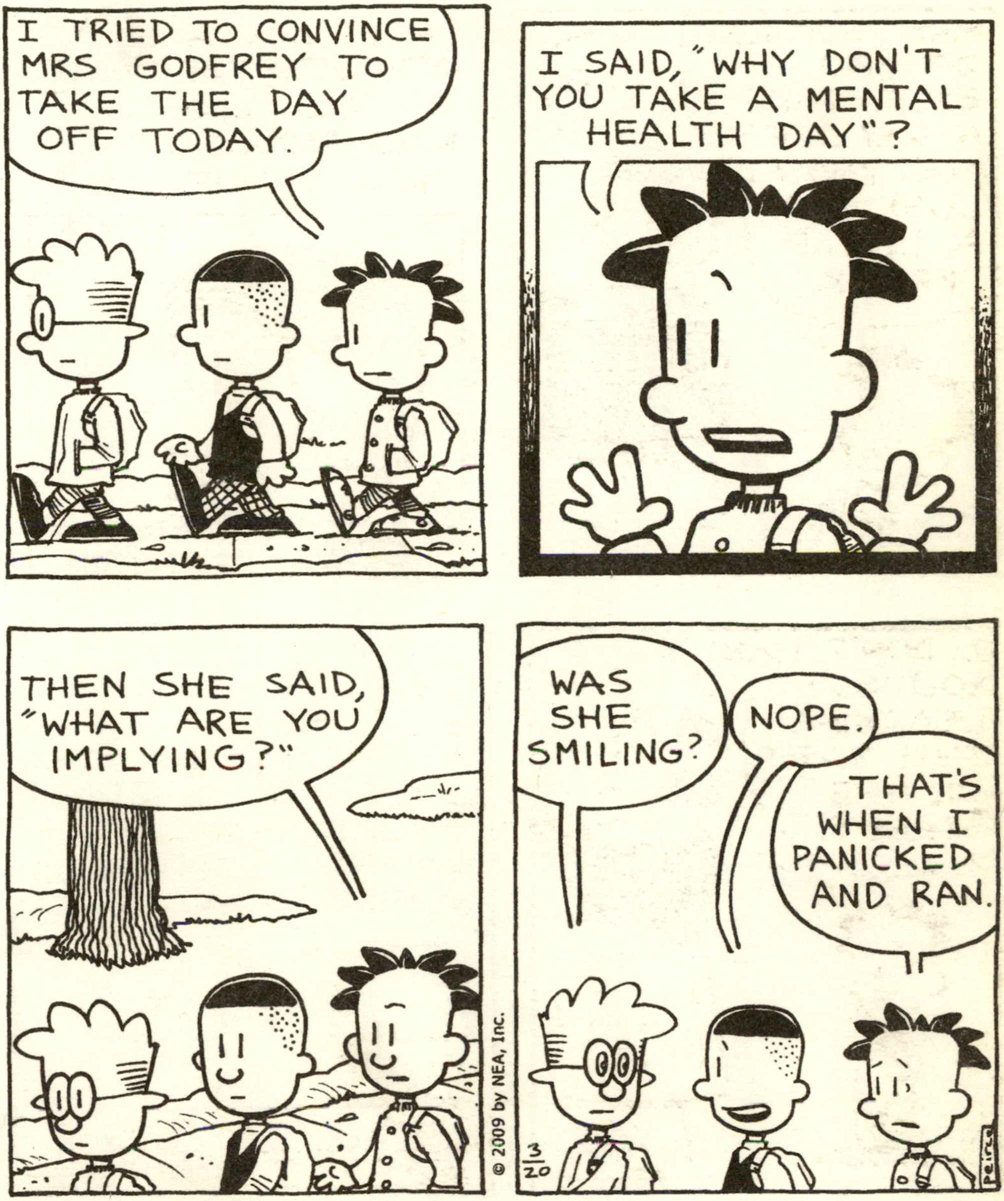
I TRIED TO CONVINCE MRS GODFREY TO TAKE THE DAY OFF TODAY.
I SAID, "WHY DON'T YOU TAKE A MENTAL HEALTH DAY"?
THEN SHE SAID, "WHAT ARE YOU IMPLYING?"
WAS SHE SMILING?
NOPE.
THAT'S WHEN I PANICKED AND RAN.
© 2009 by NEA, Inc.
3/20
peirce

WAIT 'TIL YOU SEE HIS MATHS GRADE

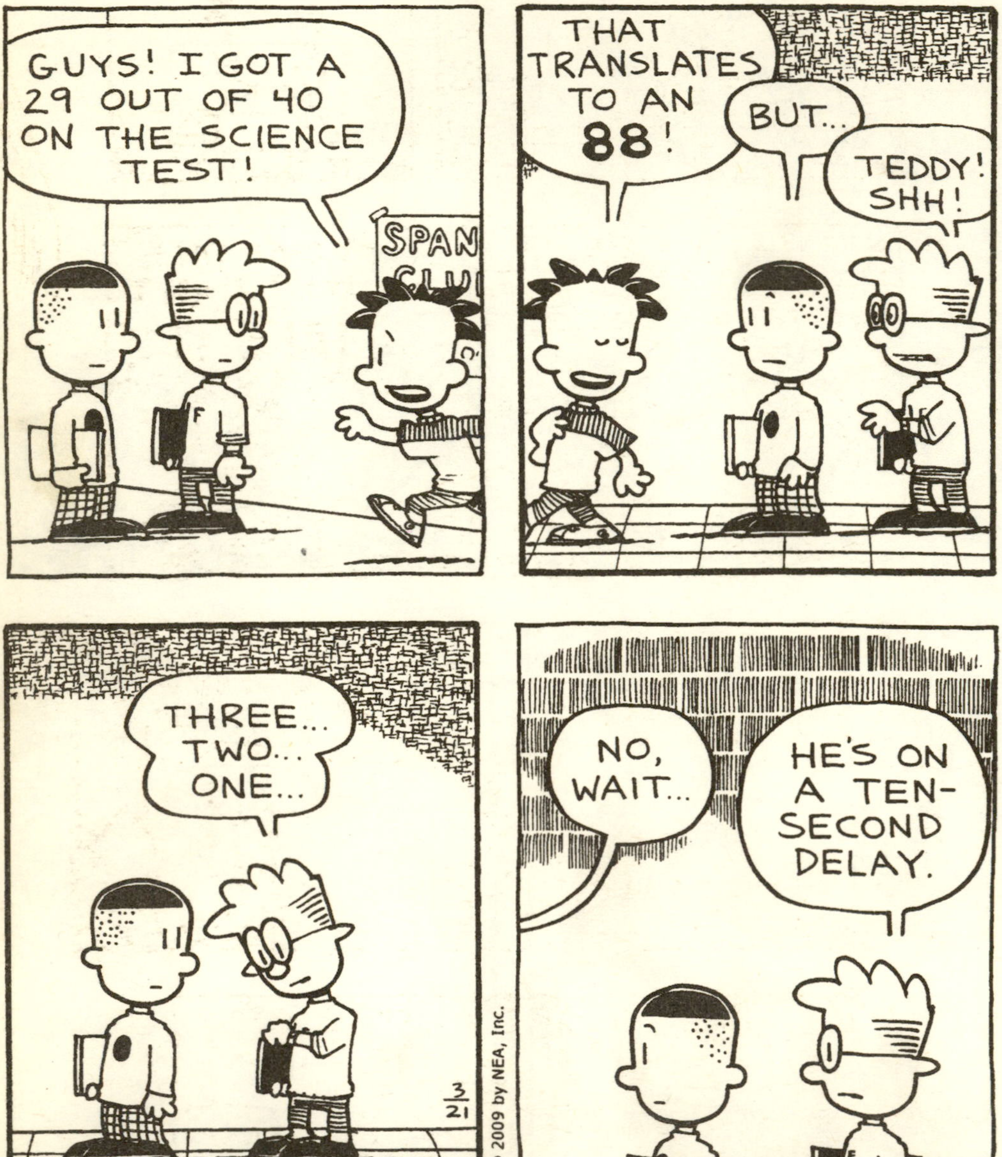

GUYS! I GOT A 29 OUT OF 40 ON THE SCIENCE TEST!
SPAN CLU
THAT TRANSLATES TO AN 88!
BUT...
TEDDY! SHH!
THREE... TWO... ONE...
NO, WAIT...
HE'S ON A TEN-SECOND DELAY.
3/21
© 2009 by NEA, Inc.
Peirce

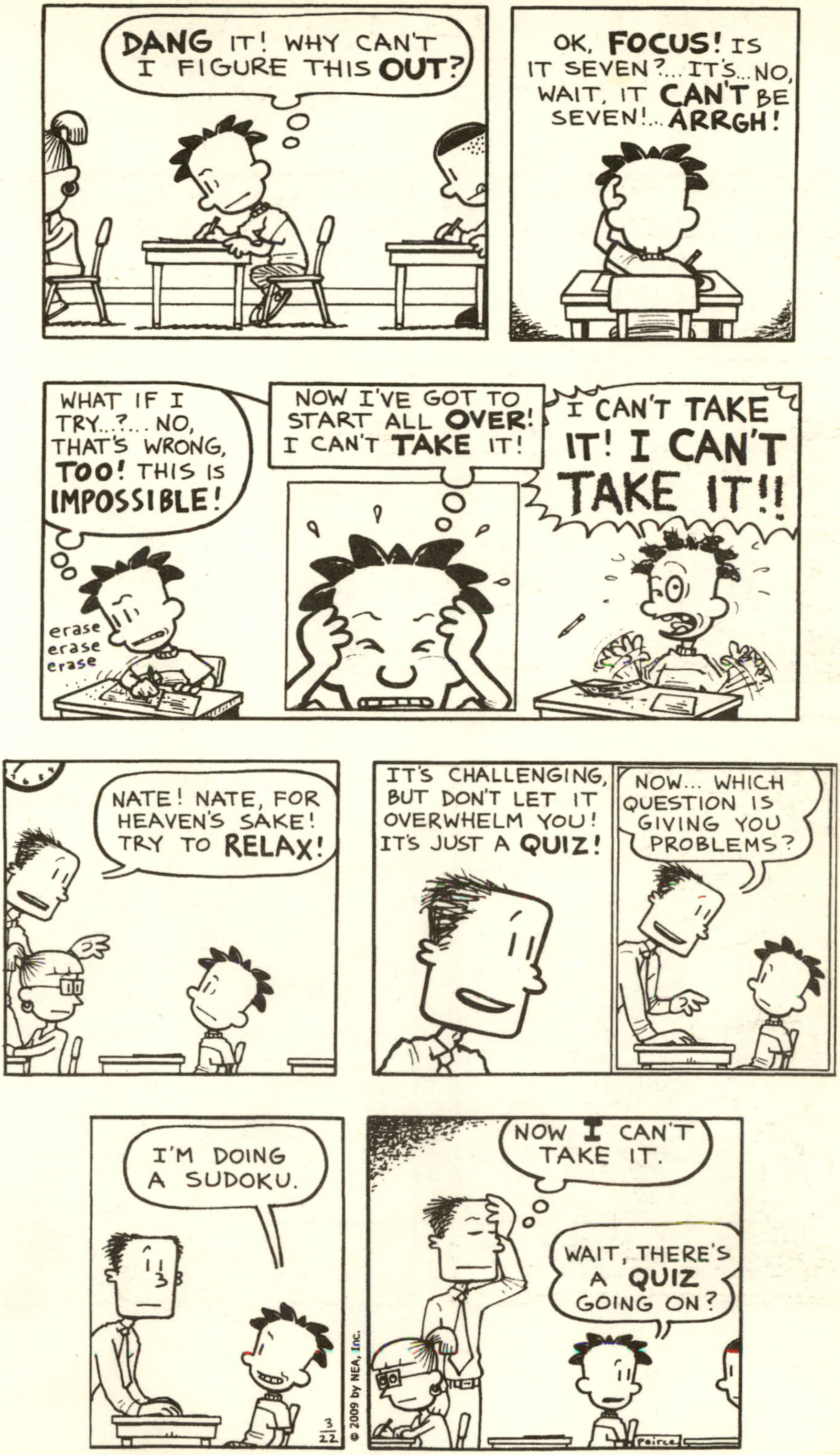
DANG IT! WHY CAN'T I FIGURE THIS OUT?
OK, FOCUS! IS IT SEVEN?... IT'S... NO, WAIT, IT CAN'T BE SEVEN!... ARRGH!
WHAT IF I TRY...?... NO, THAT'S WRONG, TOO! THIS IS IMPOSSIBLE!
erase erase erase
NOW I'VE GOT TO START ALL OVER! I CAN'T TAKE IT!
I CAN'T TAKE IT! I CAN'T TAKE IT!!
NATE! NATE, FOR HEAVEN'S SAKE! TRY TO RELAX!
IT'S CHALLENGING, BUT DON'T LET IT OVERWHELM YOU! IT'S JUST A QUIZ!
NOW... WHICH QUESTION IS GIVING YOU PROBLEMS?
I'M DOING A SUDOKU.
3/22
© 2009 by NEA, Inc.
NOW I CAN'T TAKE IT.
WAIT, THERE'S A QUIZ GOING ON?
Peirce

GOOD BREEDING

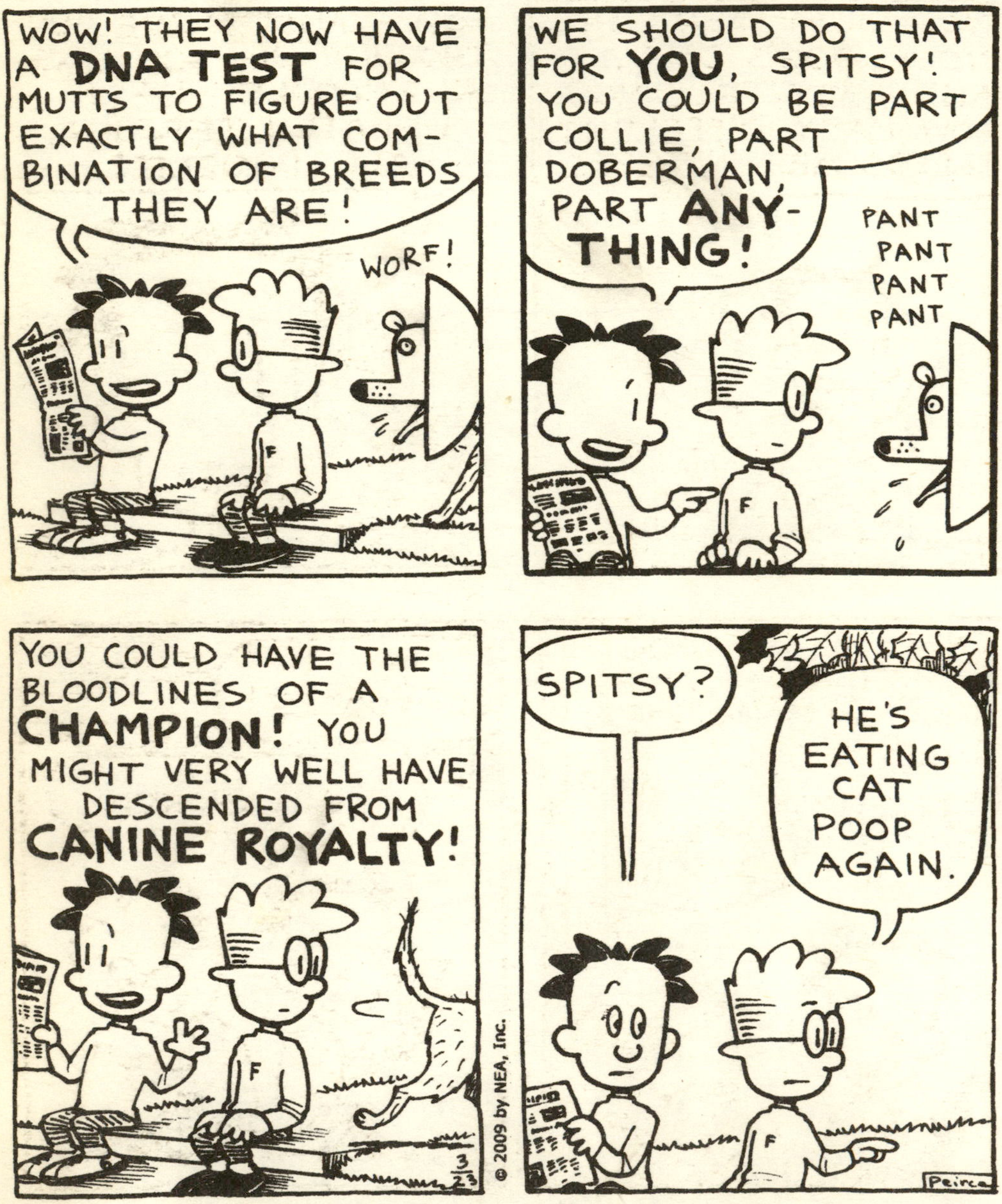
WOW! THEY NOW HAVE A DNA TEST FOR MUTTS TO FIGURE OUT EXACTLY WHAT COMBINATION OF BREEDS THEY ARE!
WORF!
WE SHOULD DO THAT FOR YOU, SPITSY! YOU COULD BE PART COLLIE, PART DOBERMAN, PART ANYTHING!
PANT PANT PANT PANT
YOU COULD HAVE THE BLOODLINES OF A CHAMPION! YOU MIGHT VERY WELL HAVE DESCENDED FROM CANINE ROYALTY!
3/23
© 2009 by NEA, Inc.
SPITSY?
HE'S EATING CAT POOP AGAIN.
Peirce

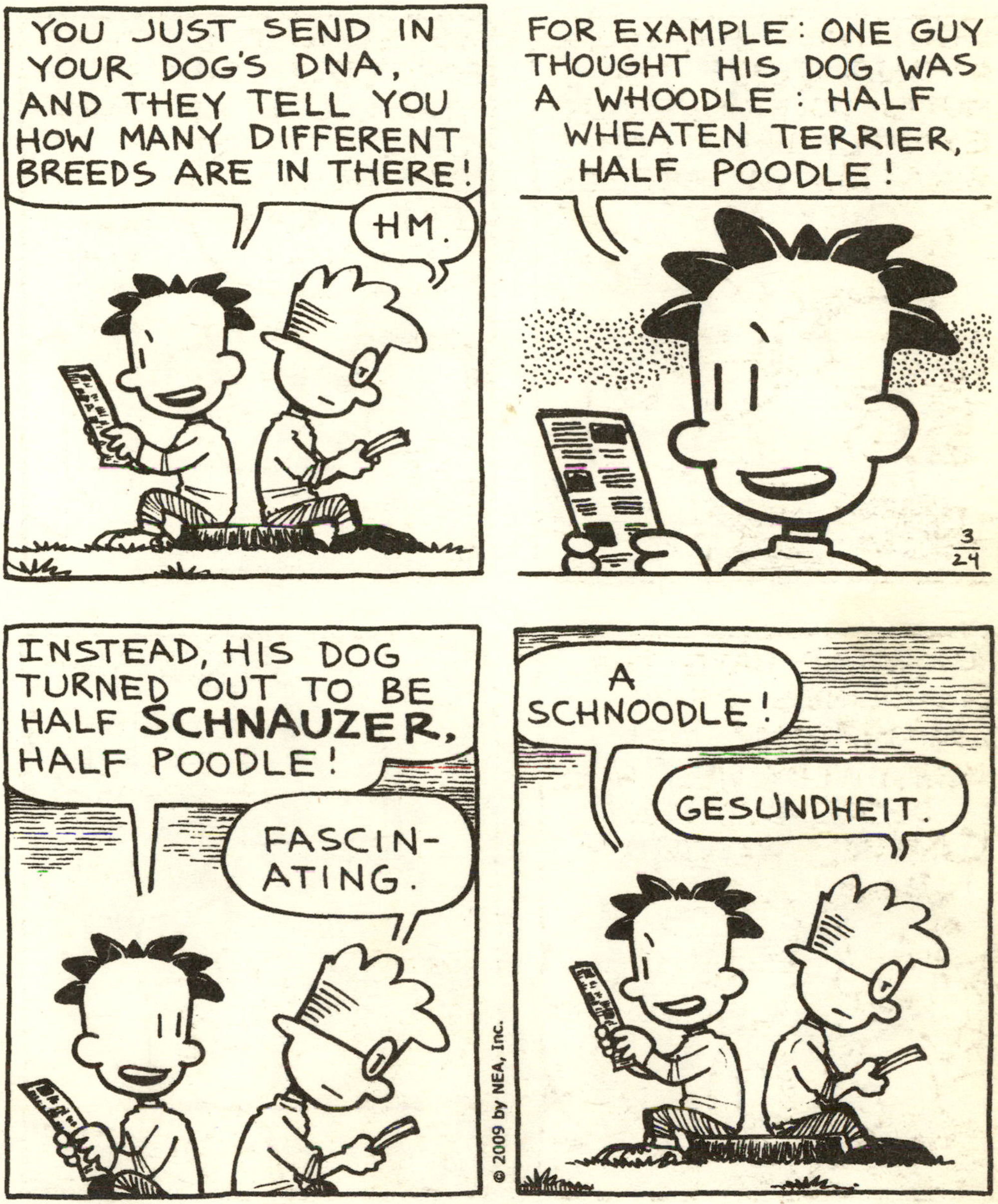
YOU JUST SEND IN YOUR DOG'S DNA, AND THEY TELL YOU HOW MANY DIFFERENT BREEDS ARE IN THERE!
HM.
FOR EXAMPLE: ONE GUY THOUGHT HIS DOG WAS A WHOODLE: HALF WHEATEN TERRIER, HALF POODLE!
3/24
INSTEAD, HIS DOG TURNED OUT TO BE HALF SCHNAUZER, HALF POODLE!
FASCIN-ATING.
© 2009 by NEA, Inc.
A SCHNOODLE!
GESUNDHEIT.

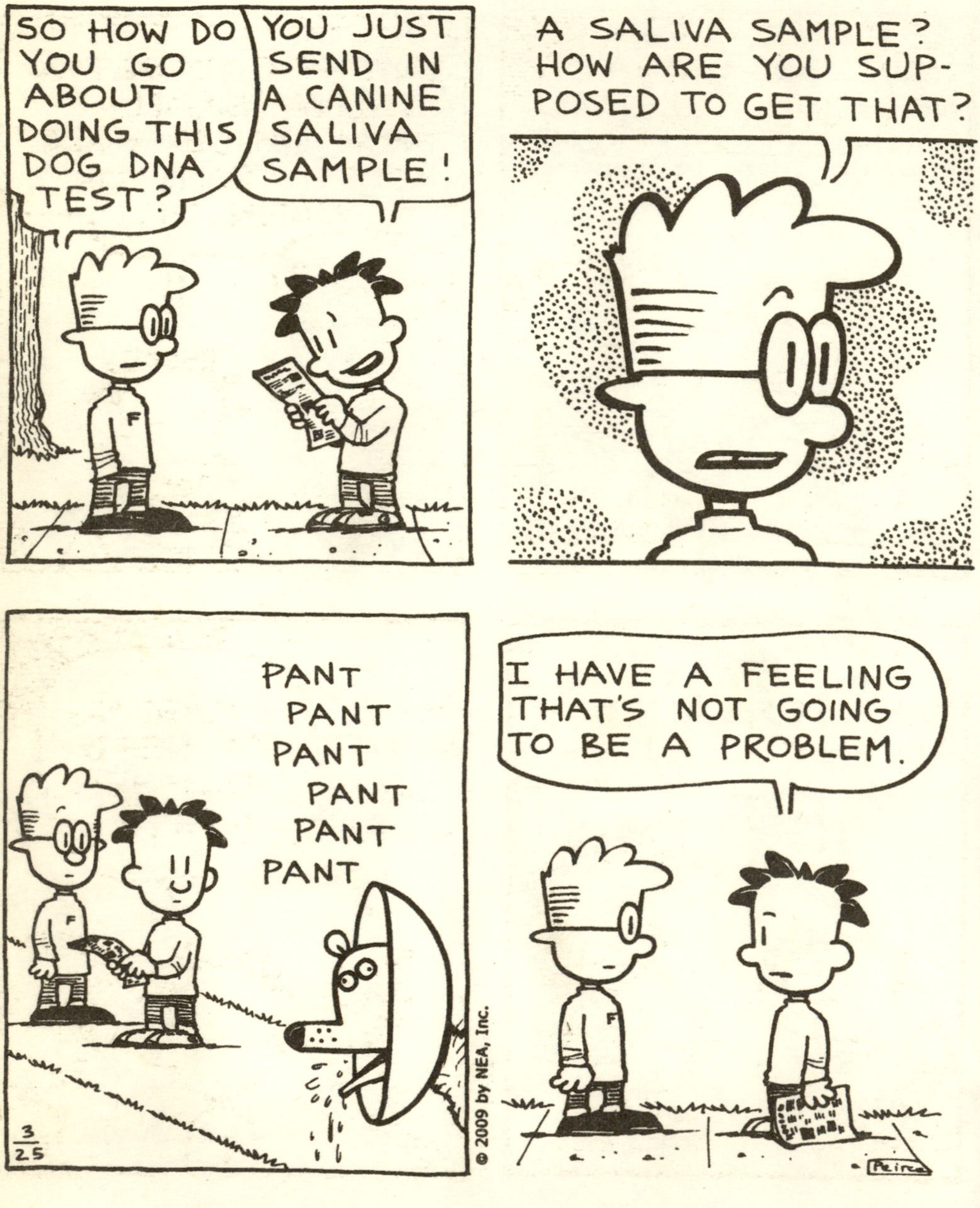
SO HOW DO YOU GO ABOUT DOING THIS DOG DNA TEST?
YOU JUST SEND IN A CANINE SALIVA SAMPLE!
A SALIVA SAMPLE? HOW ARE YOU SUPPOSED TO GET THAT?
PANT PANT PANT PANT PANT PANT
3/25
© 2009 by NEA, Inc.
I HAVE A FEELING THAT'S NOT GOING TO BE A PROBLEM.

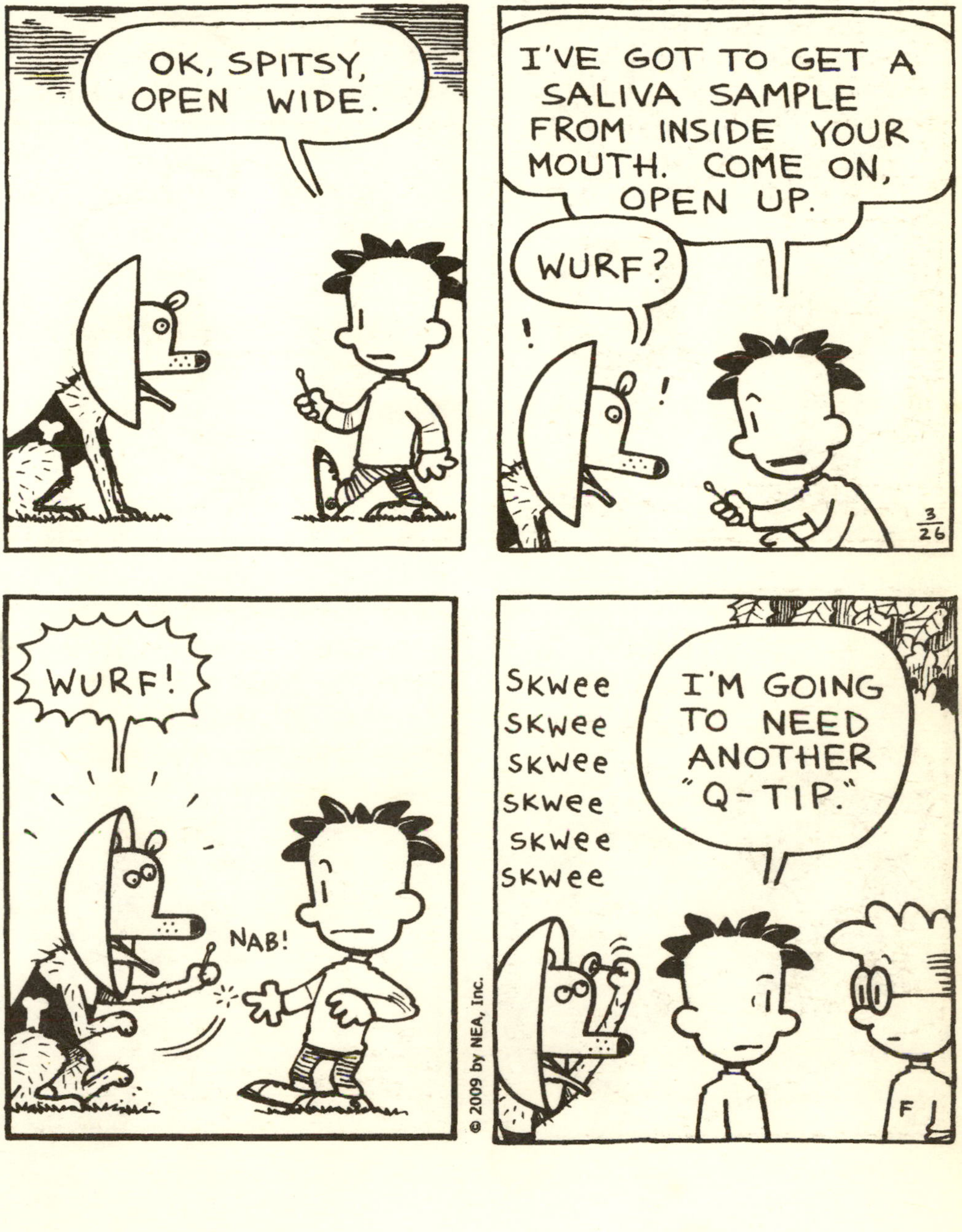
OK, SPITSY, OPEN WIDE.
I'VE GOT TO GET A SALIVA SAMPLE FROM INSIDE YOUR MOUTH. COME ON, OPEN UP.
WURF?
!
!
3/26
WURF!
NAB!
SKWEE
SKWEE
SKWEE
SKWEE
SKWEE
SKWEE
I'M GOING TO NEED ANOTHER "Q-TIP."
F

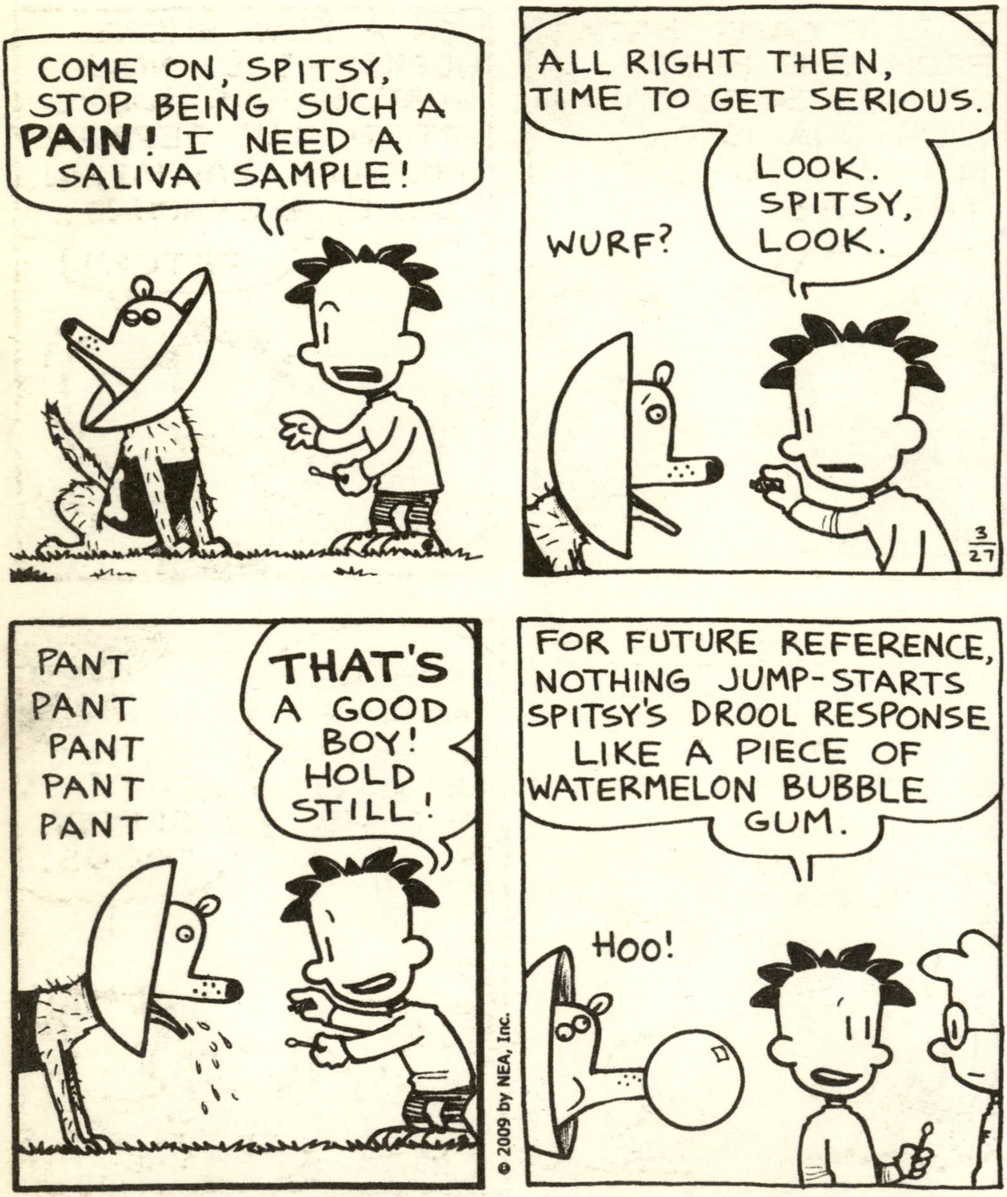
COME ON, SPITSY, STOP BEING SUCH A PAIN! I NEED A SALIVA SAMPLE!
ALL RIGHT THEN, TIME TO GET SERIOUS.
LOOK. SPITSY, LOOK.
WURF?
3/27
PANT PANT PANT PANT PANT
THAT'S A GOOD BOY! HOLD STILL!
© 2009 by NEA, Inc.
FOR FUTURE REFERENCE, NOTHING JUMP-STARTS SPITSY'S DROOL RESPONSE LIKE A PIECE OF WATERMELON BUBBLE GUM.
HOO!

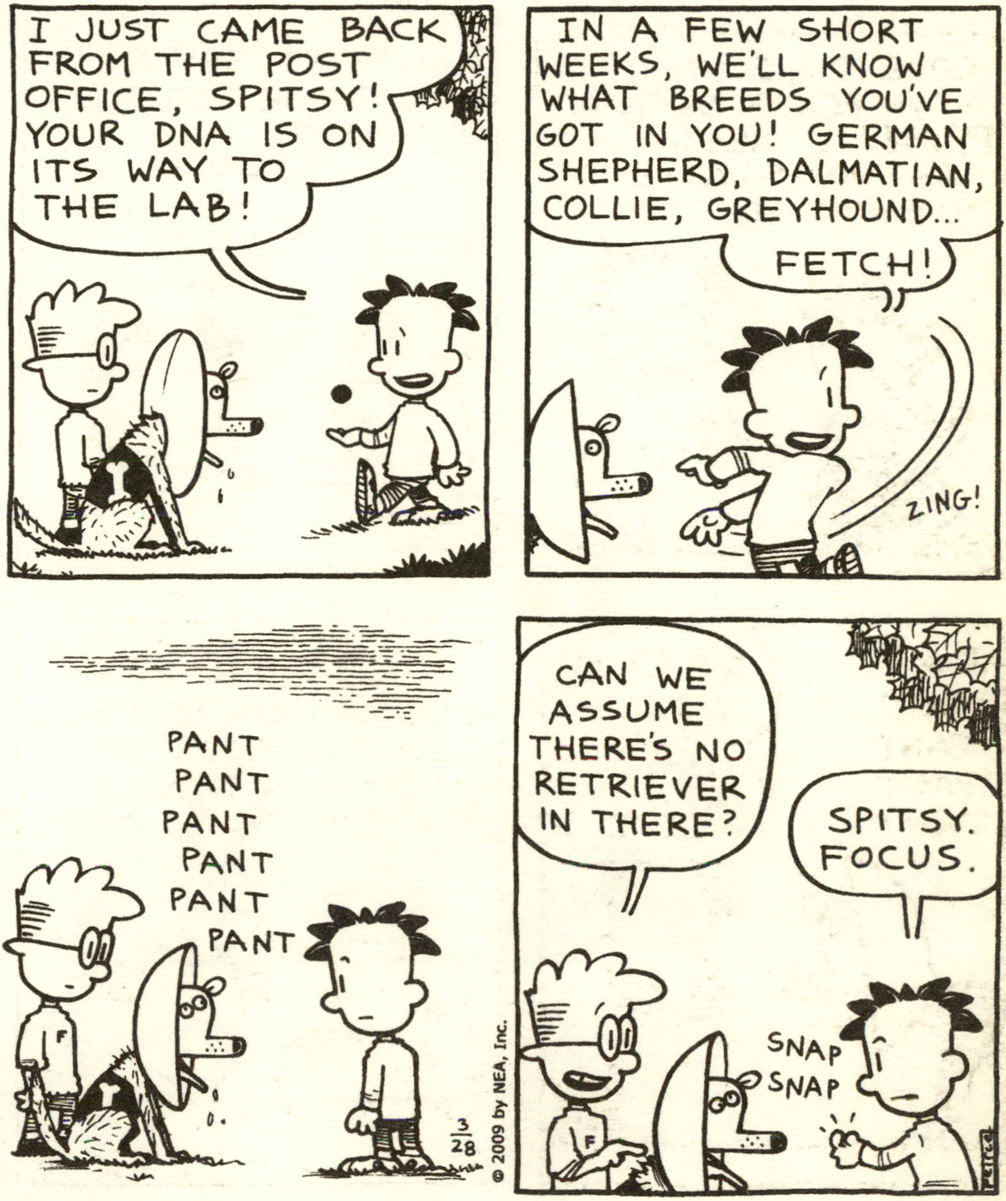
I JUST CAME BACK FROM THE POST OFFICE, SPITSY! YOUR DNA IS ON ITS WAY TO THE LAB!
IN A FEW SHORT WEEKS, WE'LL KNOW WHAT BREEDS YOU'VE GOT IN YOU! GERMAN SHEPHERD, DALMATIAN, COLLIE, GREYHOUND...
FETCH!
ZING!
PANT
PANT
PANT
PANT
PANT
PANT
© 2009 by NEA, Inc.
3/28
CAN WE ASSUME THERE'S NO RETRIEVER IN THERE?
SPITSY. FOCUS.
SNAP
SNAP

A LITTLE LIGHT READING?

"THE BOOK OF LISTS"!

RIGHT NOW I'M READING ABOUT THE TOP 100 MOVIES OF ALL TIME!

...OR HOW ABOUT THE TOP 500 ALBUMS OF THE ROCK 'N' ROLL ERA?

WANNA KNOW WHO THE FIFTY WINNINGEST PITCHERS IN BASE-BALL HISTORY ARE? IT'S IN HERE!

3/29

THE BESTSELLING BOARD GAMES EVER? THE MOST VALUABLE STAMPS IN THE WORLD? IF IT'S A LIST, IT'S IN THIS BOOK!

YOU LIKE LISTS, EH?

LOVE 'EM!

HERE YOU GO, THEN!

© 2009 by NEA, Inc.

1. Clean gutters
2. Trim hedge
3. Move boxes from g
Wash second floor
Replace fence post
Pull weeds from along
nge oil in lawnmower
n out recycling bins
and sweep driveway
pe and prime
two an prime

HARDY HAR **HAR**.

Peirce

LET'S REVIEW

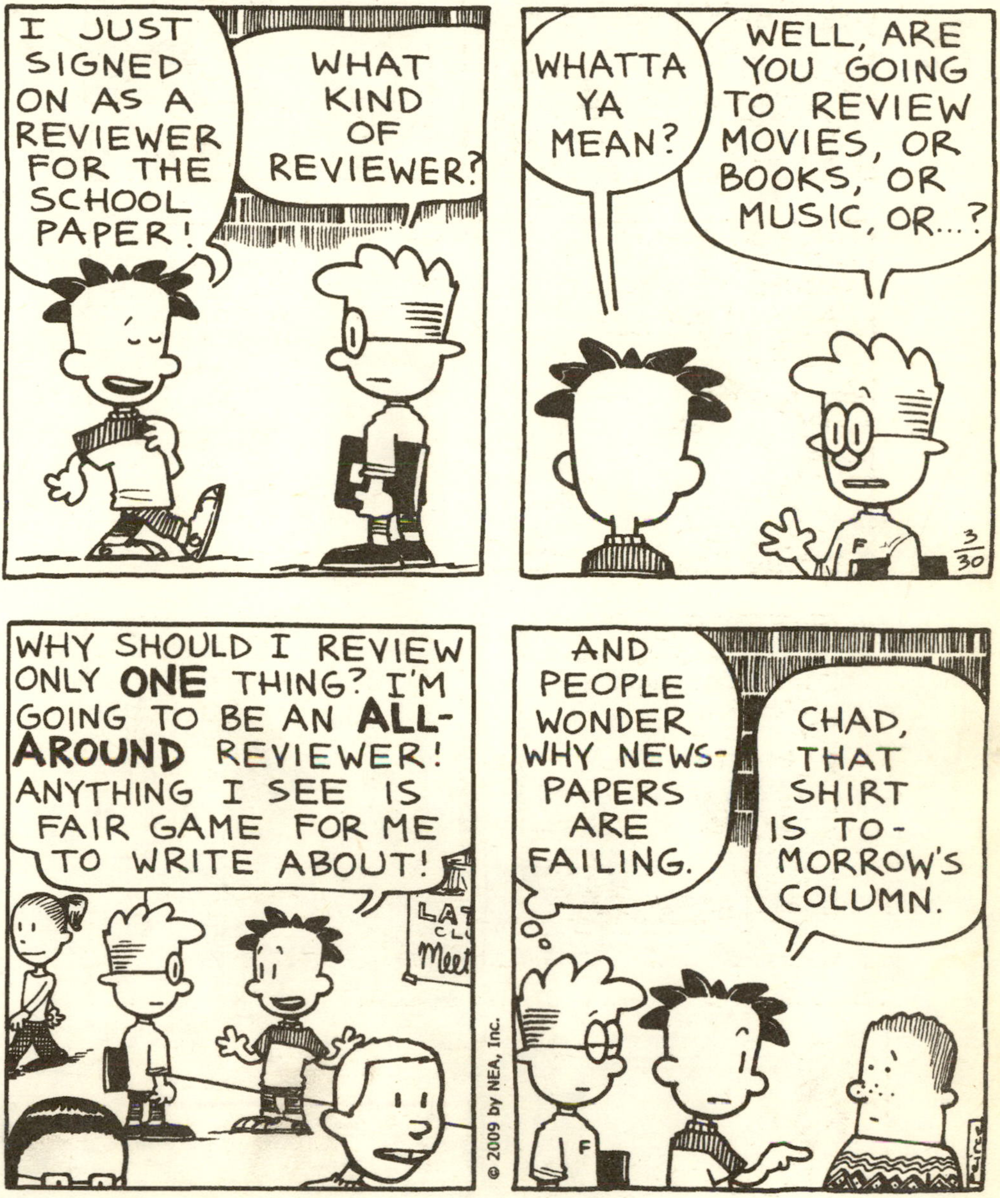
I JUST SIGNED ON AS A REVIEWER FOR THE SCHOOL PAPER!
WHAT KIND OF REVIEWER?
WHATTA YA MEAN?
WELL, ARE YOU GOING TO REVIEW MOVIES, OR BOOKS, OR MUSIC, OR...?
3/30
WHY SHOULD I REVIEW ONLY ONE THING? I'M GOING TO BE AN ALL-AROUND REVIEWER! ANYTHING I SEE IS FAIR GAME FOR ME TO WRITE ABOUT!
© 2009 by NEA, Inc.
AND PEOPLE WONDER WHY NEWS-PAPERS ARE FAILING.
CHAD, THAT SHIRT IS TO-MORROW'S COLUMN.

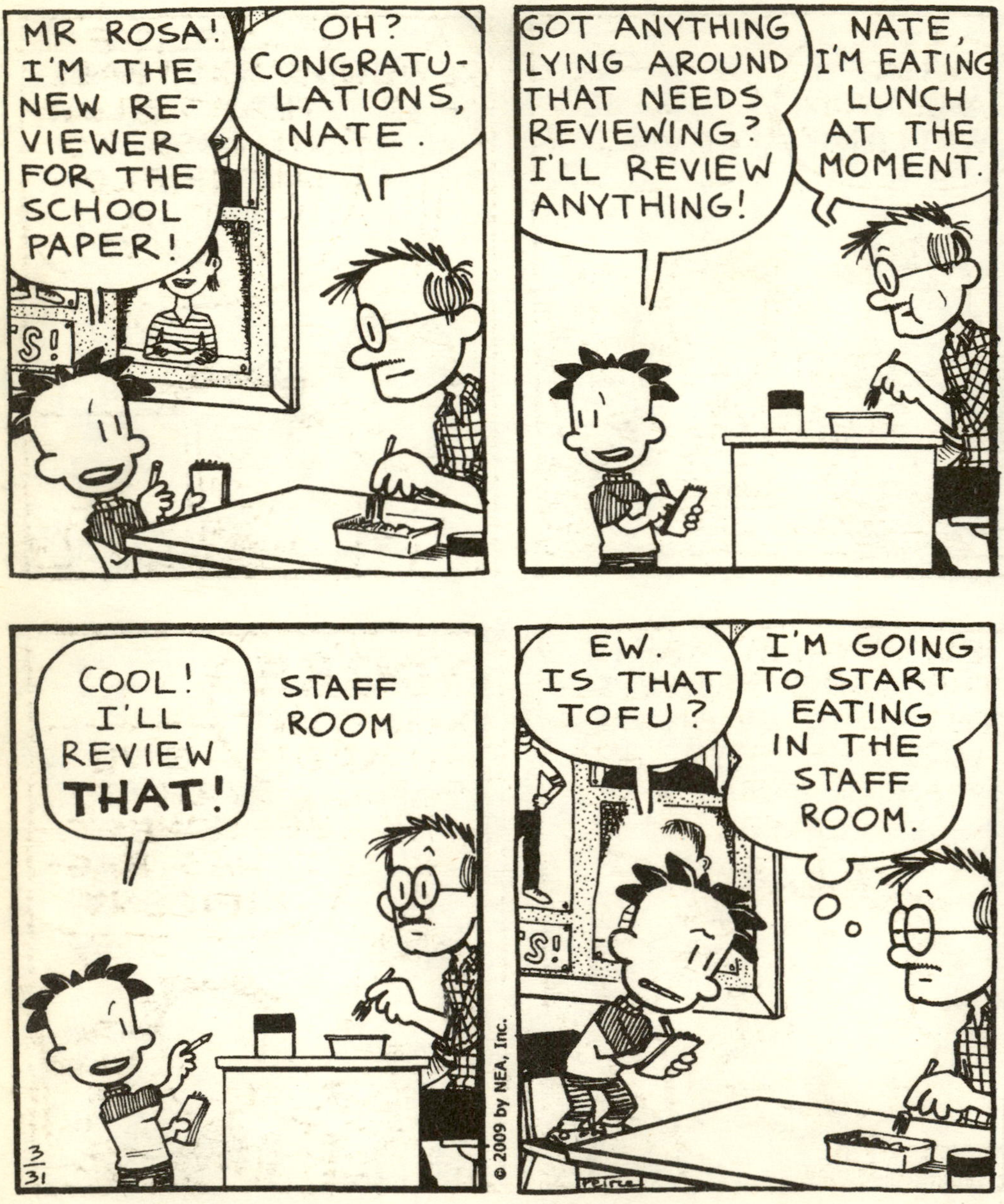
MR ROSA! I'M THE NEW RE-VIEWER FOR THE SCHOOL PAPER!
OH? CONGRATU-LATIONS, NATE.
GOT ANYTHING LYING AROUND THAT NEEDS REVIEWING? I'LL REVIEW ANYTHING!
NATE, I'M EATING LUNCH AT THE MOMENT.
COOL! I'LL REVIEW **THAT**!
STAFF ROOM
3/31
© 2009 by NEA, Inc.
EW. IS THAT TOFU?
I'M GOING TO START EATING IN THE STAFF ROOM.

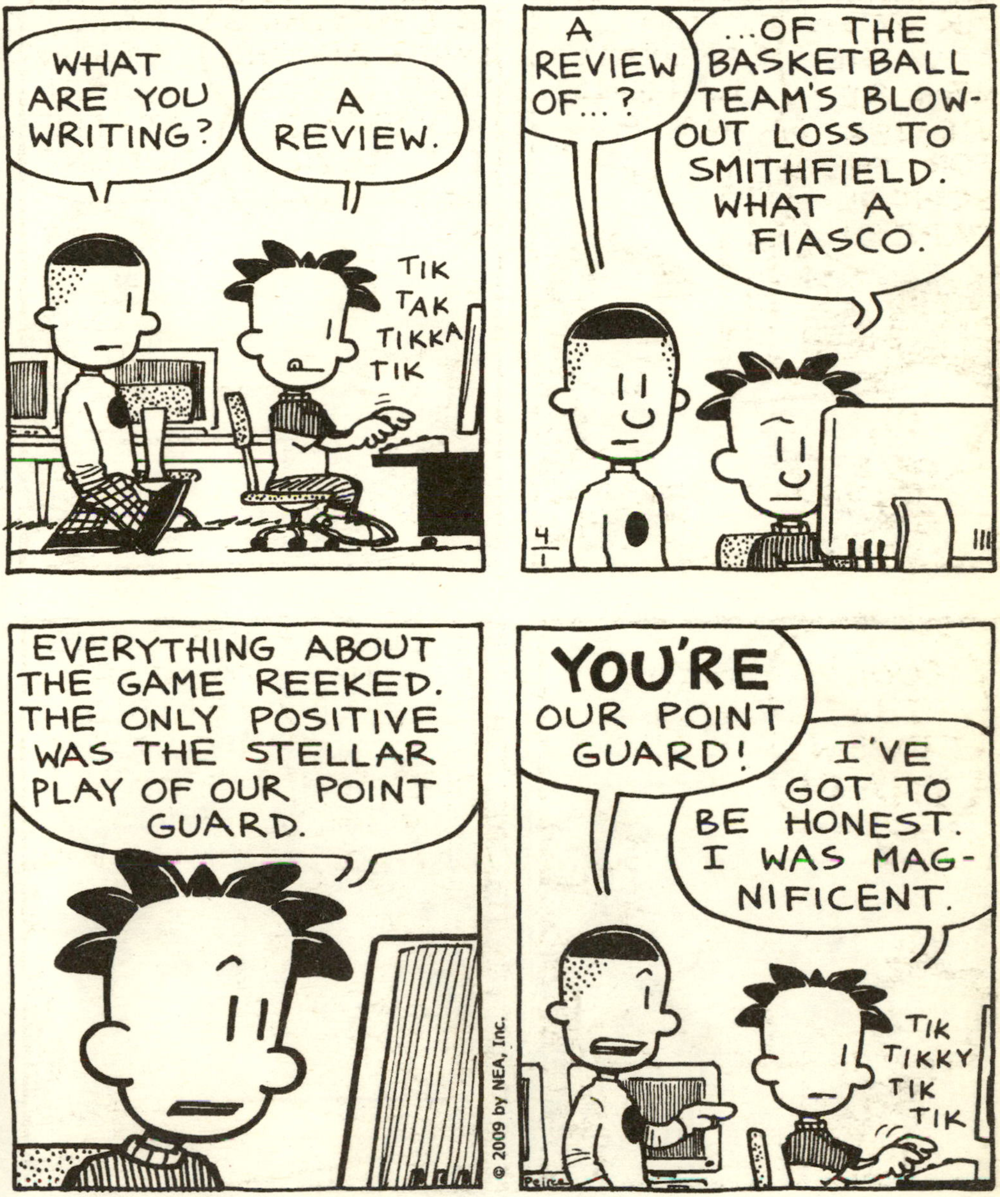
WHAT ARE YOU WRITING?
A REVIEW.
TIK TAK TIKKA TIK
A REVIEW OF...?
...OF THE BASKETBALL TEAM'S BLOW-OUT LOSS TO SMITHFIELD. WHAT A FIASCO.
EVERYTHING ABOUT THE GAME REEKED. THE ONLY POSITIVE WAS THE STELLAR PLAY OF OUR POINT GUARD.
YOU'RE OUR POINT GUARD!
I'VE GOT TO BE HONEST. I WAS MAG-NIFICENT.
TIK TIKKY TIK TIK

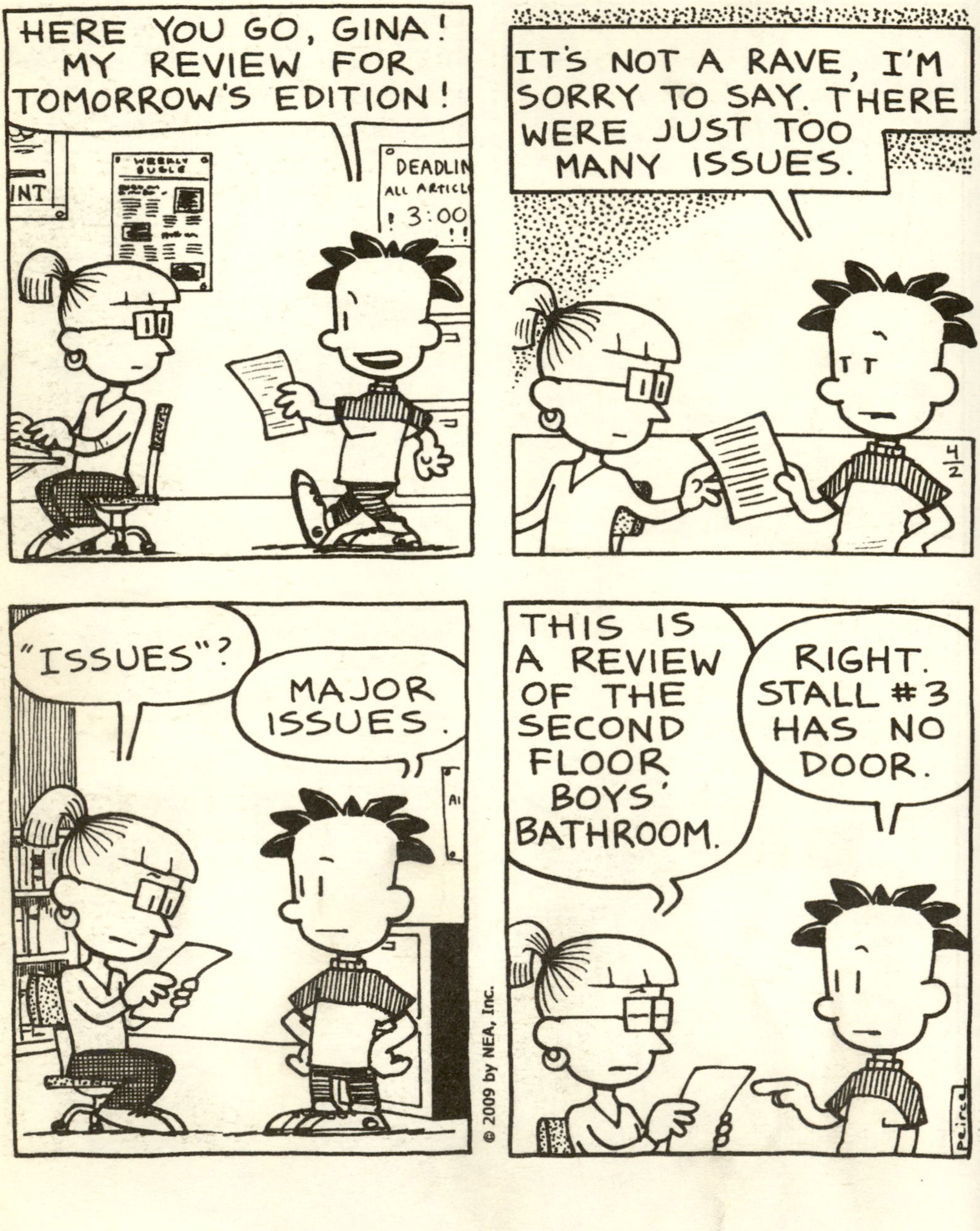
HERE YOU GO, GINA! MY REVIEW FOR TOMORROW'S EDITION!
DEADLIN
ALL ARTICL
3:00
IT'S NOT A RAVE, I'M SORRY TO SAY. THERE WERE JUST TOO MANY ISSUES.
"ISSUES"?
MAJOR ISSUES.
THIS IS A REVIEW OF THE SECOND FLOOR BOYS' BATHROOM.
RIGHT. STALL #3 HAS NO DOOR.

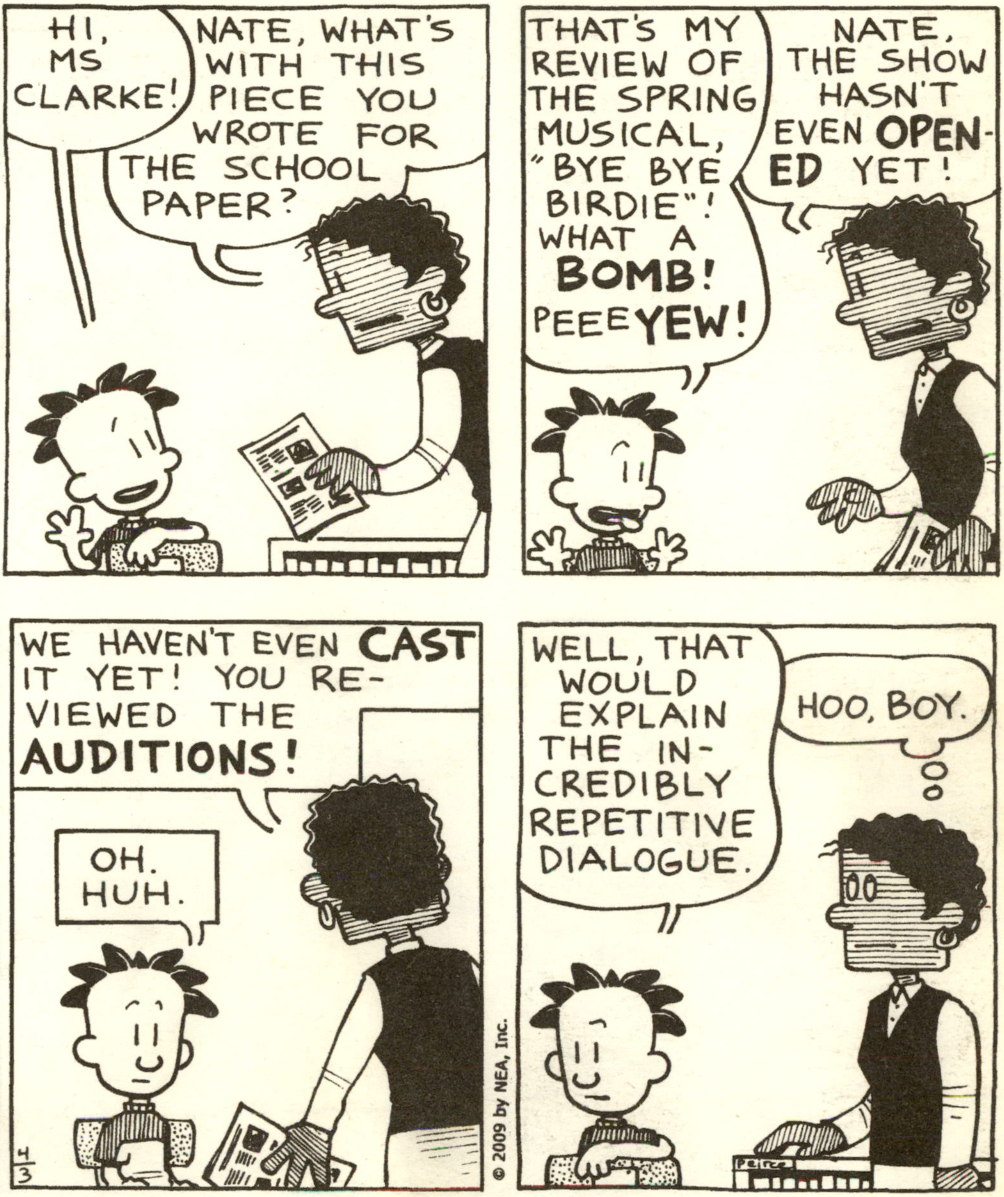
HI, MS CLARKE!
NATE, WHAT'S WITH THIS PIECE YOU WROTE FOR THE SCHOOL PAPER?
THAT'S MY REVIEW OF THE SPRING MUSICAL, "BYE BYE BIRDIE"! WHAT A BOMB! PEEEYEW!
NATE, THE SHOW HASN'T EVEN OPENED YET!
WE HAVEN'T EVEN CAST IT YET! YOU REVIEWED THE AUDITIONS!
OH. HUH.
WELL, THAT WOULD EXPLAIN THE INCREDIBLY REPETITIVE DIALOGUE.
HOO, BOY.
4/3
© 2009 by NEA, Inc.

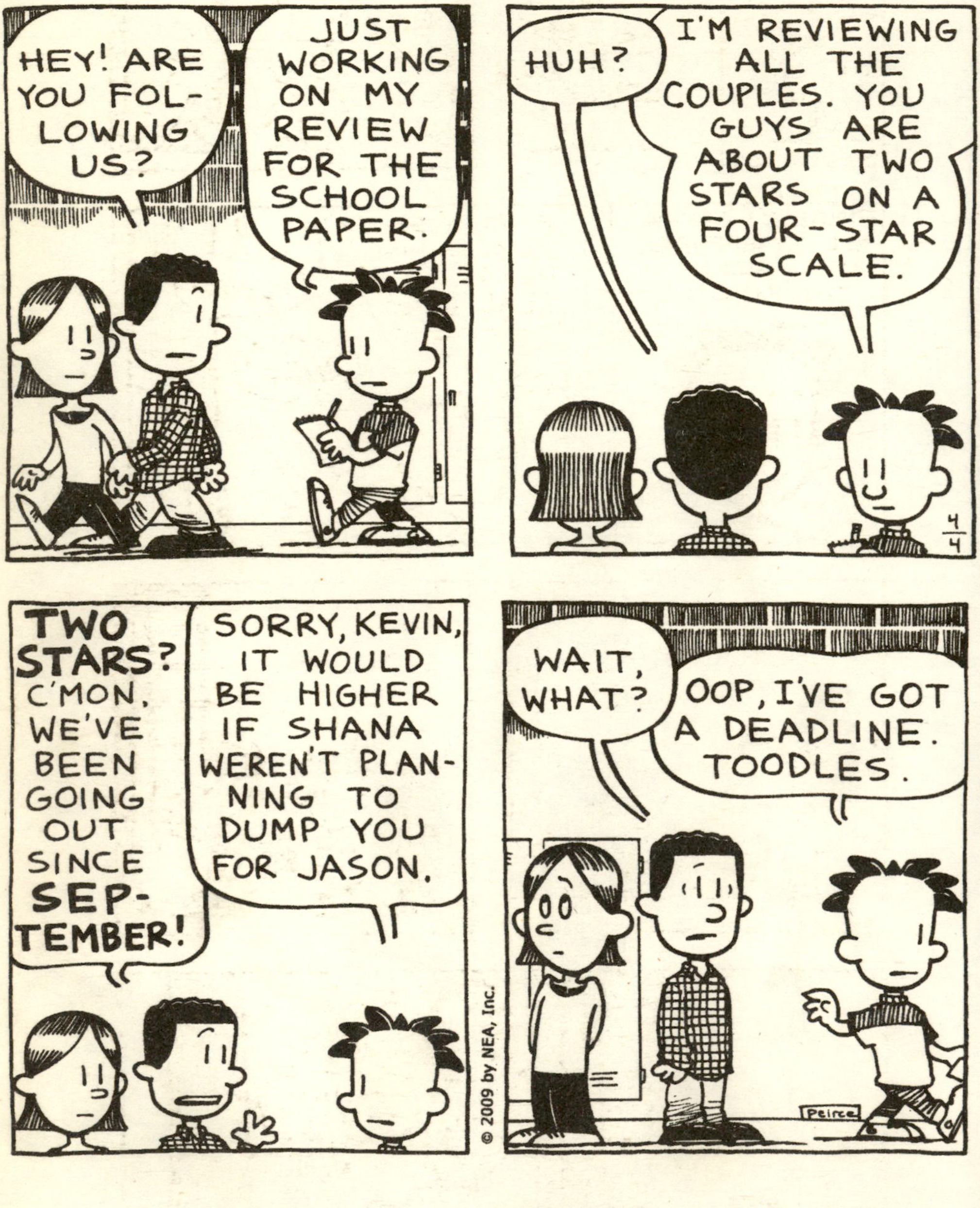
HEY! ARE YOU FOLLOWING US?
JUST WORKING ON MY REVIEW FOR THE SCHOOL PAPER.
HUH?
I'M REVIEWING ALL THE COUPLES. YOU GUYS ARE ABOUT TWO STARS ON A FOUR-STAR SCALE.
4/4
TWO STARS? C'MON, WE'VE BEEN GOING OUT SINCE SEPTEMBER!
SORRY, KEVIN, IT WOULD BE HIGHER IF SHANA WEREN'T PLANNING TO DUMP YOU FOR JASON.
© 2009 by NEA, Inc.
WAIT, WHAT?
OOP, I'VE GOT A DEADLINE. TOODLES.
Peirce

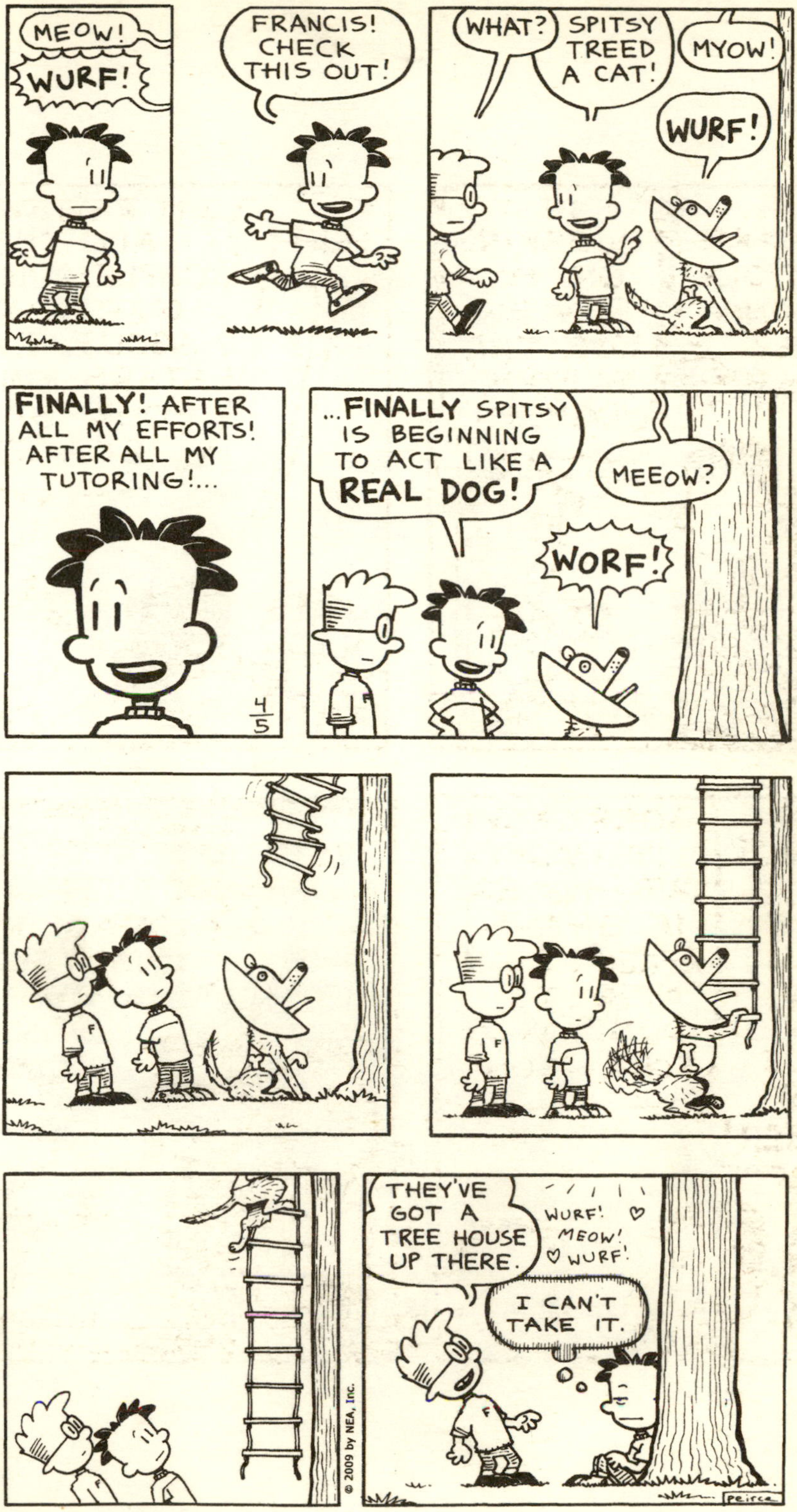
MEOW!
WURF!
FRANCIS! CHECK THIS OUT!
WHAT?
SPITSY TREED A CAT!
MYOW!
WURF!
FINALLY! AFTER ALL MY EFFORTS! AFTER ALL MY TUTORING!...
...FINALLY SPITSY IS BEGINNING TO ACT LIKE A REAL DOG!
MEEOW?
WORF!
THEY'VE GOT A TREE HOUSE UP THERE.
WURF!
MEOW!
WURF!
I CAN'T TAKE IT.
© 2009 by NEA, Inc.
peirce

LEGGO MY MOJO

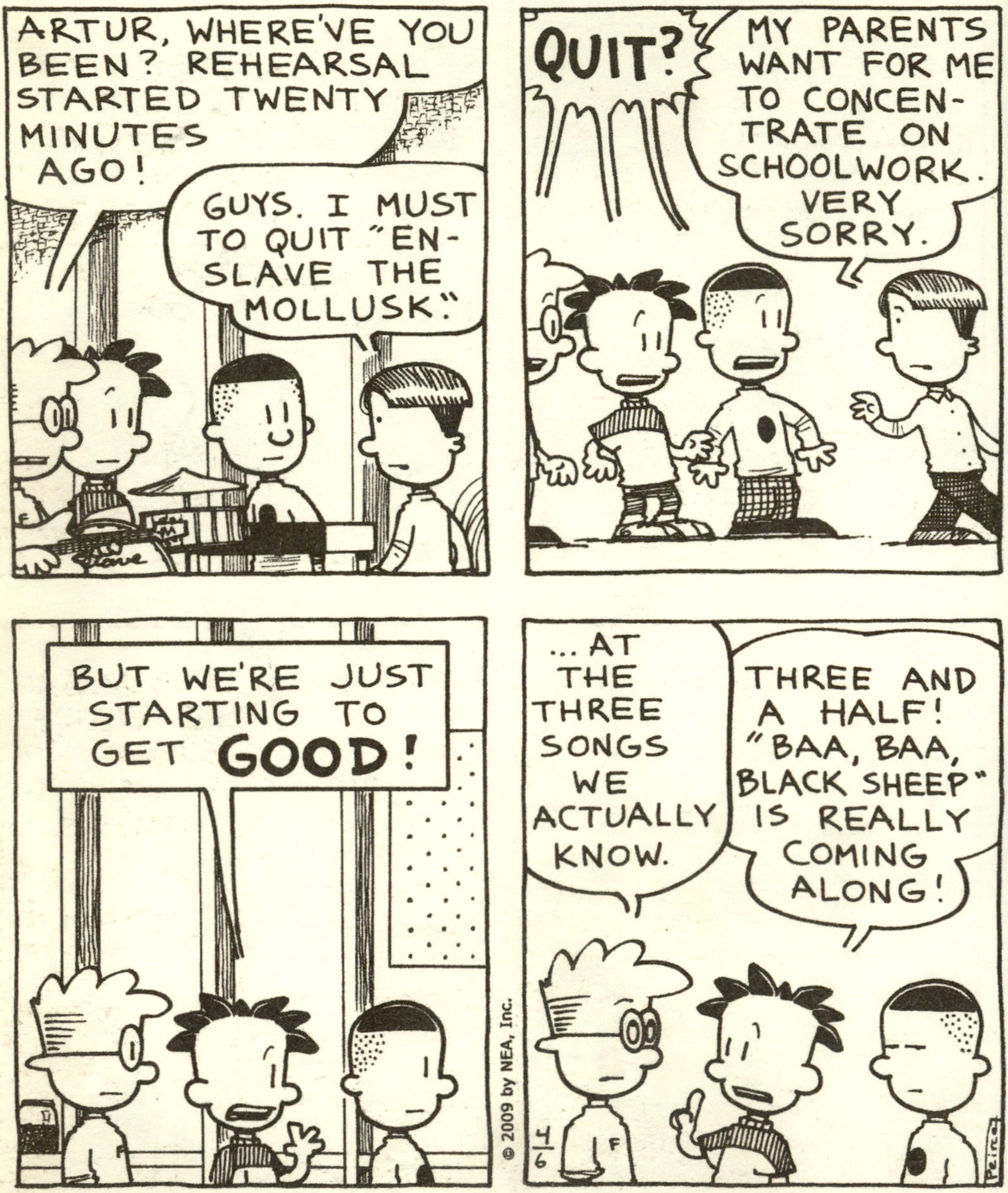
ARTUR, WHERE'VE YOU BEEN? REHEARSAL STARTED TWENTY MINUTES AGO!
GUYS. I MUST TO QUIT "ENSLAVE THE MOLLUSK."
QUIT?
MY PARENTS WANT FOR ME TO CONCENTRATE ON SCHOOLWORK. VERY SORRY.
BUT WE'RE JUST STARTING TO GET GOOD!
... AT THE THREE SONGS WE ACTUALLY KNOW.
THREE AND A HALF! "BAA, BAA, BLACK SHEEP" IS REALLY COMING ALONG!
© 2009 by NEA, Inc.
4/6
Peirce

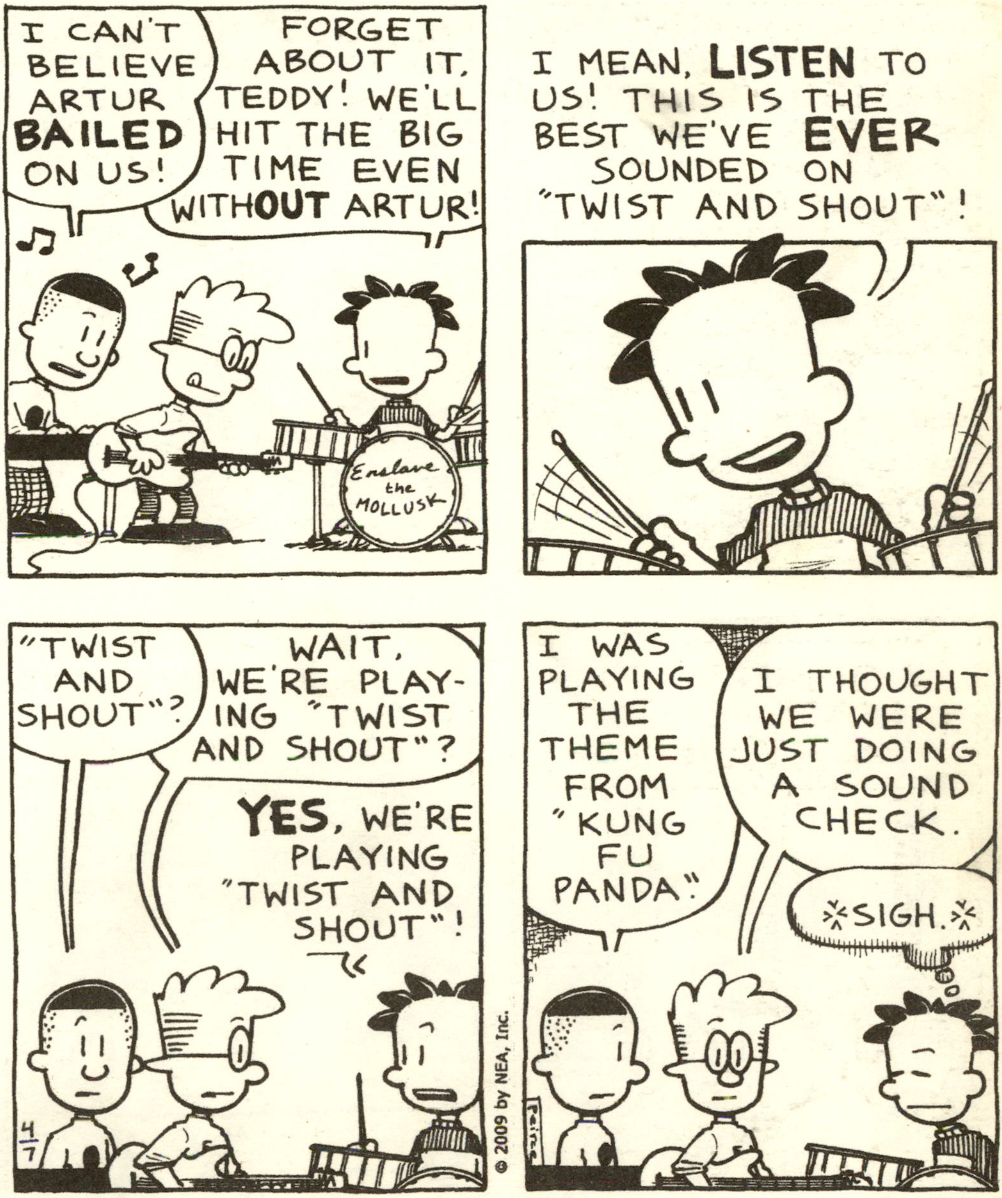
I CAN'T BELIEVE ARTUR **BAILED** ON US!
FORGET ABOUT IT, TEDDY! WE'LL HIT THE BIG TIME EVEN WITH**OUT** ARTUR!
Enslave the MOLLUSK
I MEAN, **LISTEN** TO US! THIS IS THE BEST WE'VE **EVER** SOUNDED ON "TWIST AND SHOUT"!
"TWIST AND SHOUT"?
WAIT, WE'RE PLAYING "TWIST AND SHOUT"?
YES, WE'RE PLAYING "TWIST AND SHOUT"!
I WAS PLAYING THE THEME FROM "KUNG FU PANDA."
I THOUGHT WE WERE JUST DOING A SOUND CHECK.
SIGH.
4/7
© 2009 by NEA, Inc.

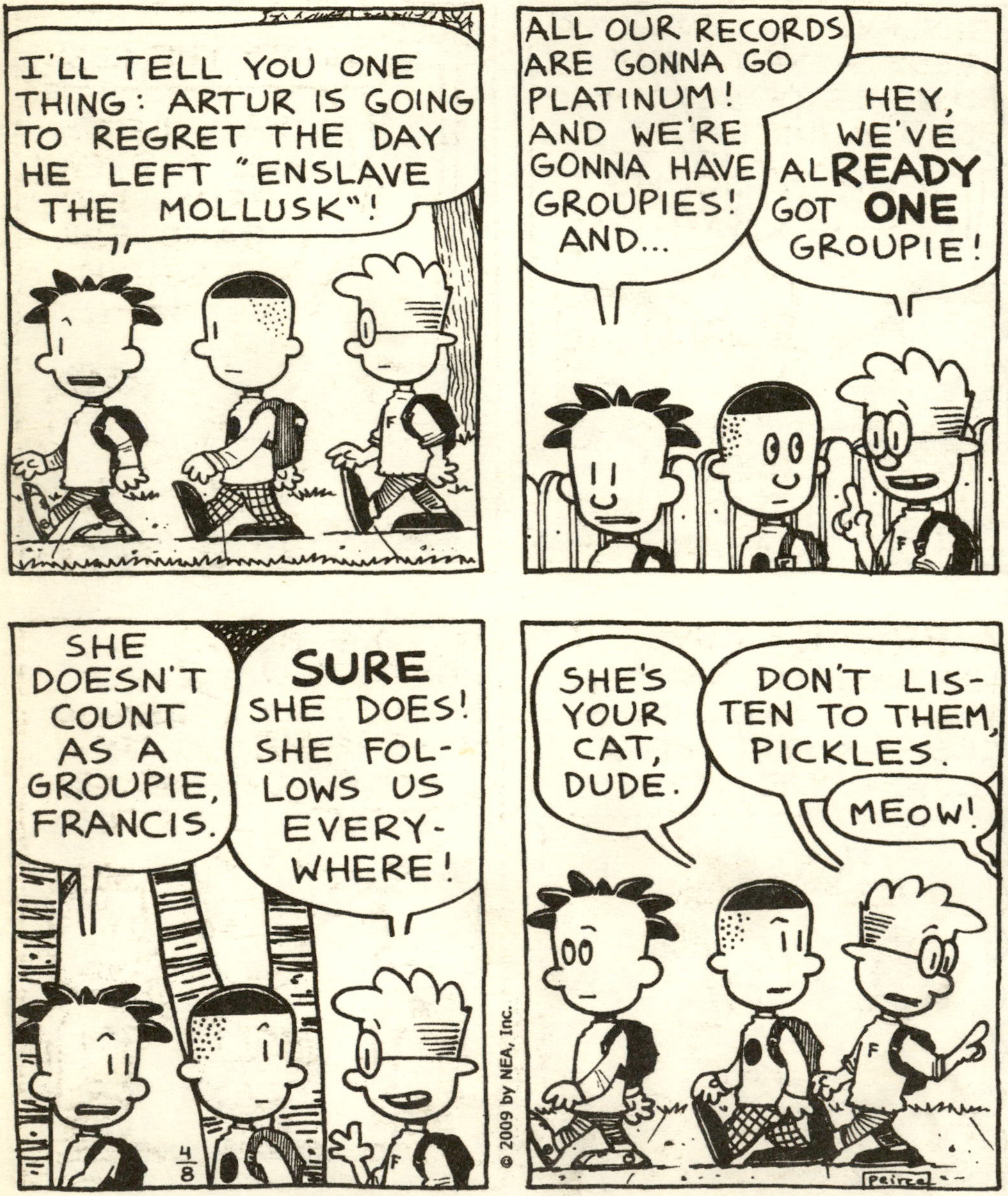
I'LL TELL YOU ONE THING: ARTUR IS GOING TO REGRET THE DAY HE LEFT "ENSLAVE THE MOLLUSK"!
ALL OUR RECORDS ARE GONNA GO PLATINUM! AND WE'RE GONNA HAVE GROUPIES! AND...
HEY, WE'VE ALREADY GOT ONE GROUPIE!
SHE DOESN'T COUNT AS A GROUPIE, FRANCIS.
SURE SHE DOES! SHE FOLLOWS US EVERYWHERE!
4/8
© 2009 by NEA, Inc.
SHE'S YOUR CAT, DUDE.
DON'T LISTEN TO THEM, PICKLES.
MEOW!
Peirce

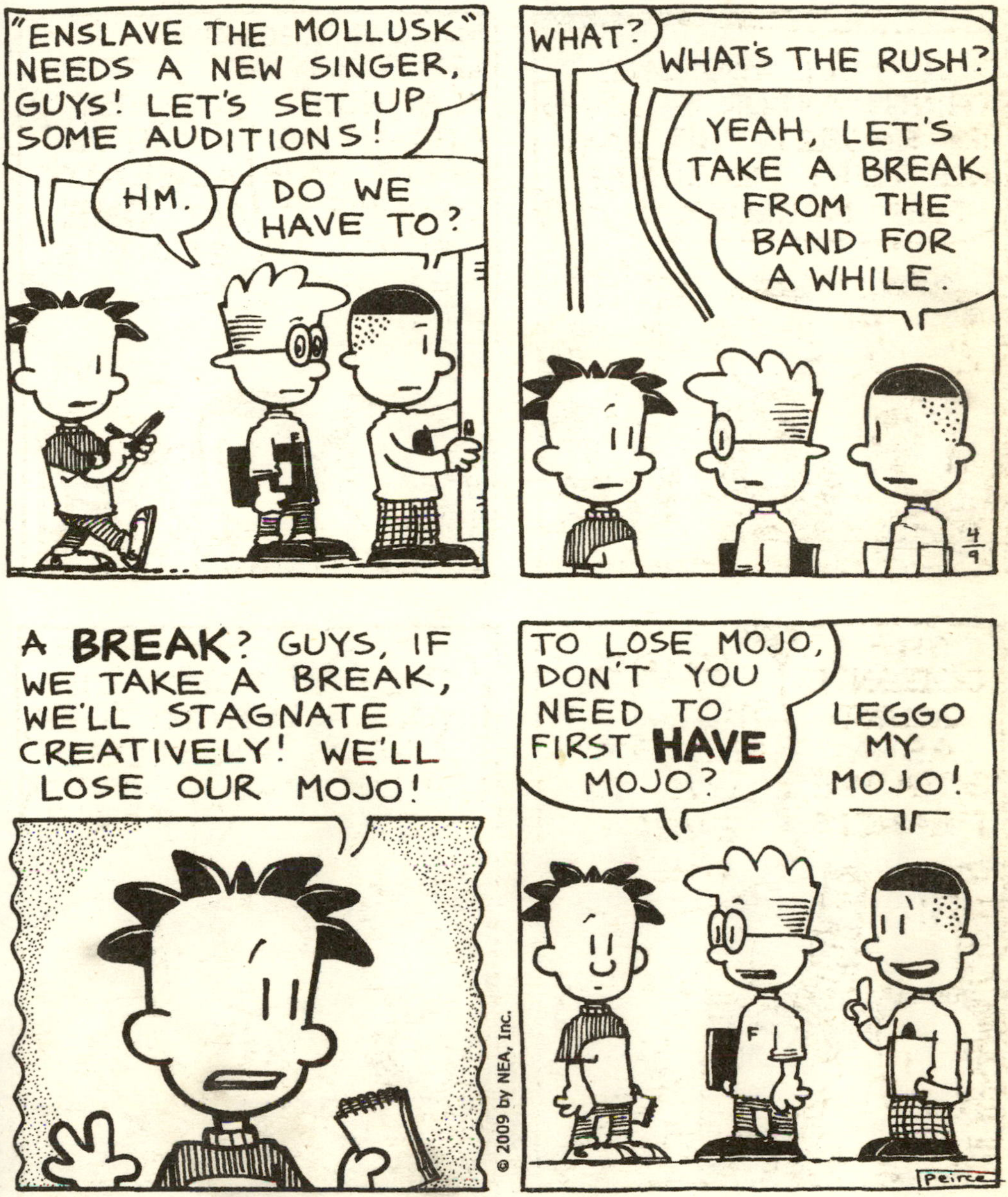
"ENSLAVE THE MOLLUSK" NEEDS A NEW SINGER, GUYS! LET'S SET UP SOME AUDITIONS!
HM.
DO WE HAVE TO?
WHAT?
WHAT'S THE RUSH?
YEAH, LET'S TAKE A BREAK FROM THE BAND FOR A WHILE.
4/9
A **BREAK**? GUYS, IF WE TAKE A BREAK, WE'LL STAGNATE CREATIVELY! WE'LL LOSE OUR MOJO!
© 2009 by NEA, Inc.
TO LOSE MOJO, DON'T YOU NEED TO FIRST **HAVE** MOJO?
LEGGO MY MOJO!
Peirce

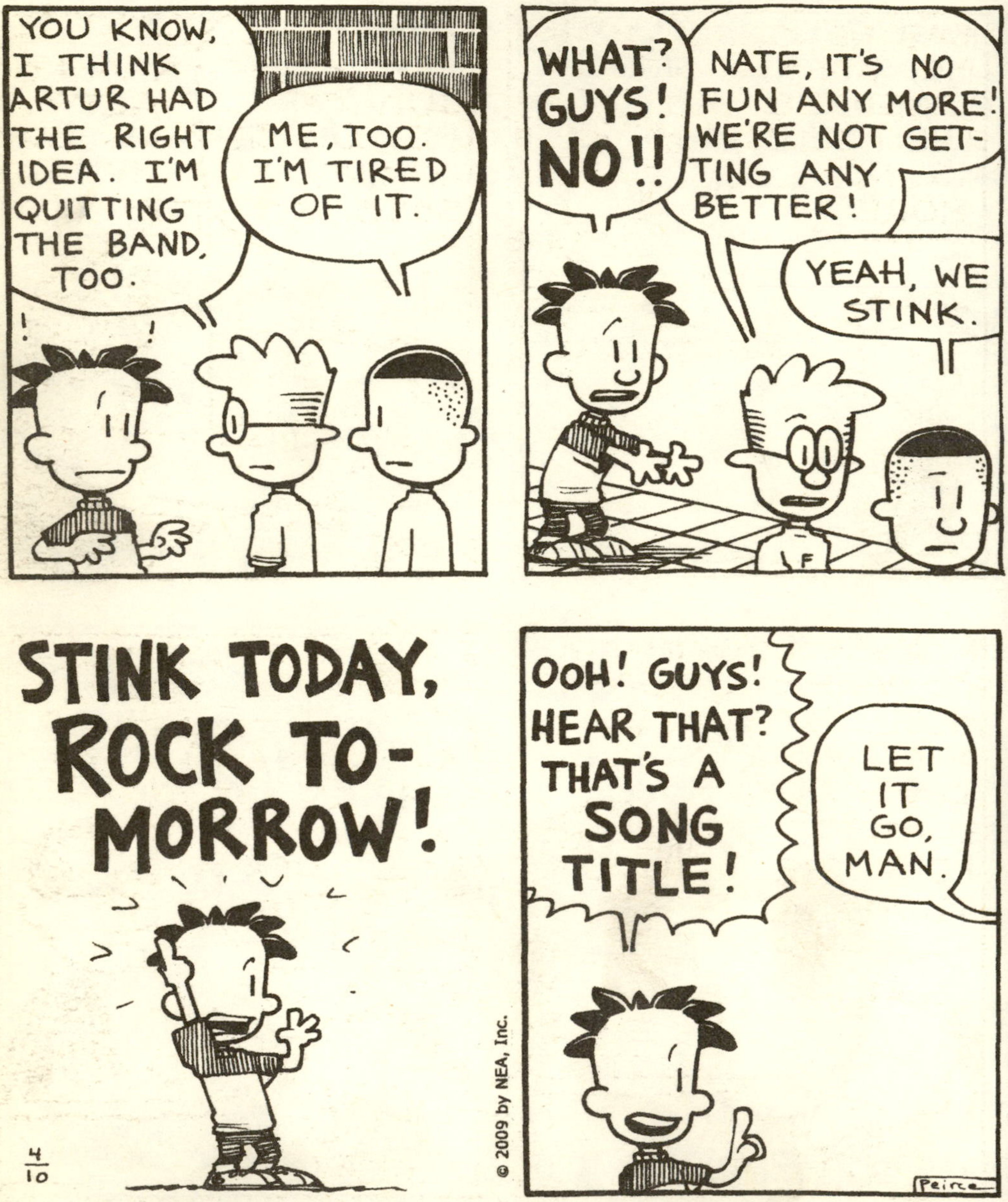
YOU KNOW, I THINK ARTUR HAD THE RIGHT IDEA. I'M QUITTING THE BAND, TOO.
ME, TOO. I'M TIRED OF IT.
! !
WHAT? GUYS! NO!!
NATE, IT'S NO FUN ANY MORE! WE'RE NOT GETTING ANY BETTER!
YEAH, WE STINK.
STINK TODAY, ROCK TOMORROW!
4/10
© 2009 by NEA, Inc.
OOH! GUYS! HEAR THAT? THAT'S A SONG TITLE!
LET IT GO, MAN.
Peirce

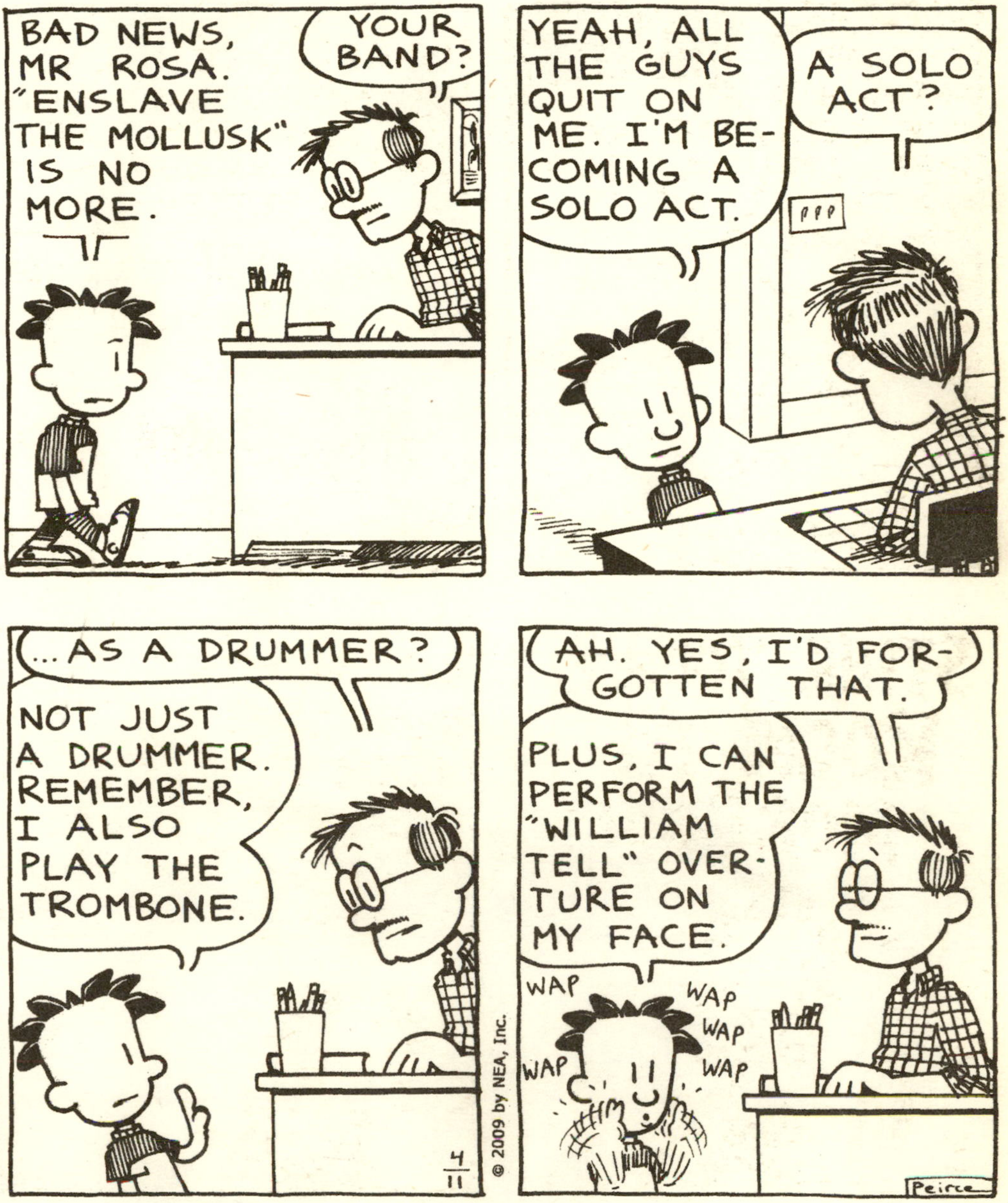
BAD NEWS, MR ROSA. "ENSLAVE THE MOLLUSK" IS NO MORE.
YOUR BAND?
YEAH, ALL THE GUYS QUIT ON ME. I'M BE-COMING A SOLO ACT.
A SOLO ACT?
...AS A DRUMMER?
NOT JUST A DRUMMER. REMEMBER, I ALSO PLAY THE TROMBONE.
4/11
© 2009 by NEA, Inc.
AH. YES, I'D FOR-GOTTEN THAT.
PLUS, I CAN PERFORM THE "WILLIAM TELL" OVER-TURE ON MY FACE.
WAP
WAP
WAP
WAP
WAP
Peirce

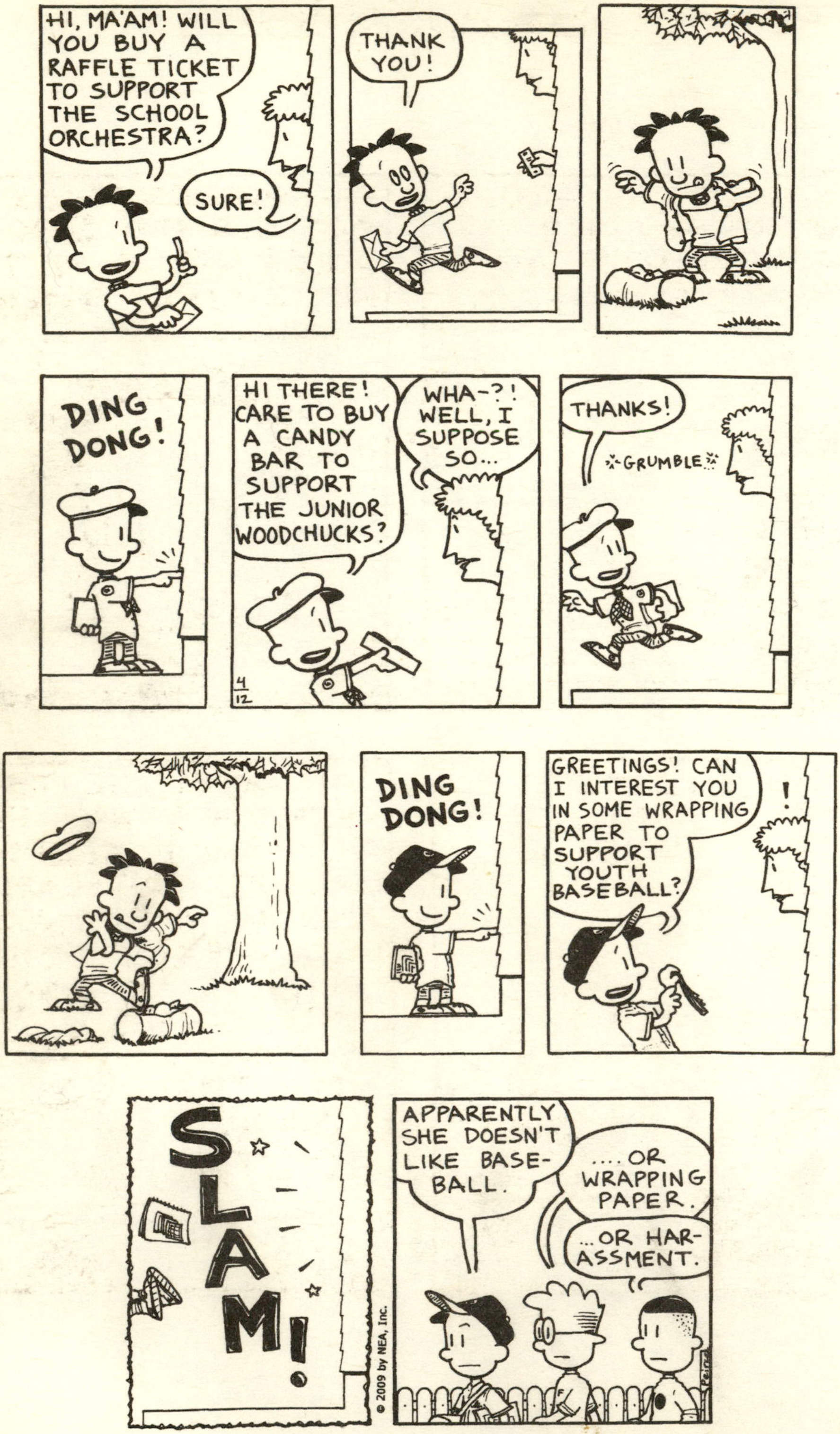
HI, MA'AM! WILL YOU BUY A RAFFLE TICKET TO SUPPORT THE SCHOOL ORCHESTRA?
SURE!
THANK YOU!
DING DONG!
HI THERE! CARE TO BUY A CANDY BAR TO SUPPORT THE JUNIOR WOODCHUCKS?
WHA-?! WELL, I SUPPOSE SO...
4/12
THANKS!
GRUMBLE
DING DONG!
GREETINGS! CAN I INTEREST YOU IN SOME WRAPPING PAPER TO SUPPORT YOUTH BASEBALL?
!
SLAM!
© 2009 by NEA, Inc.
APPARENTLY SHE DOESN'T LIKE BASE-BALL.
....OR WRAPPING PAPER.
...OR HAR-ASSMENT.

GENIUS MODE

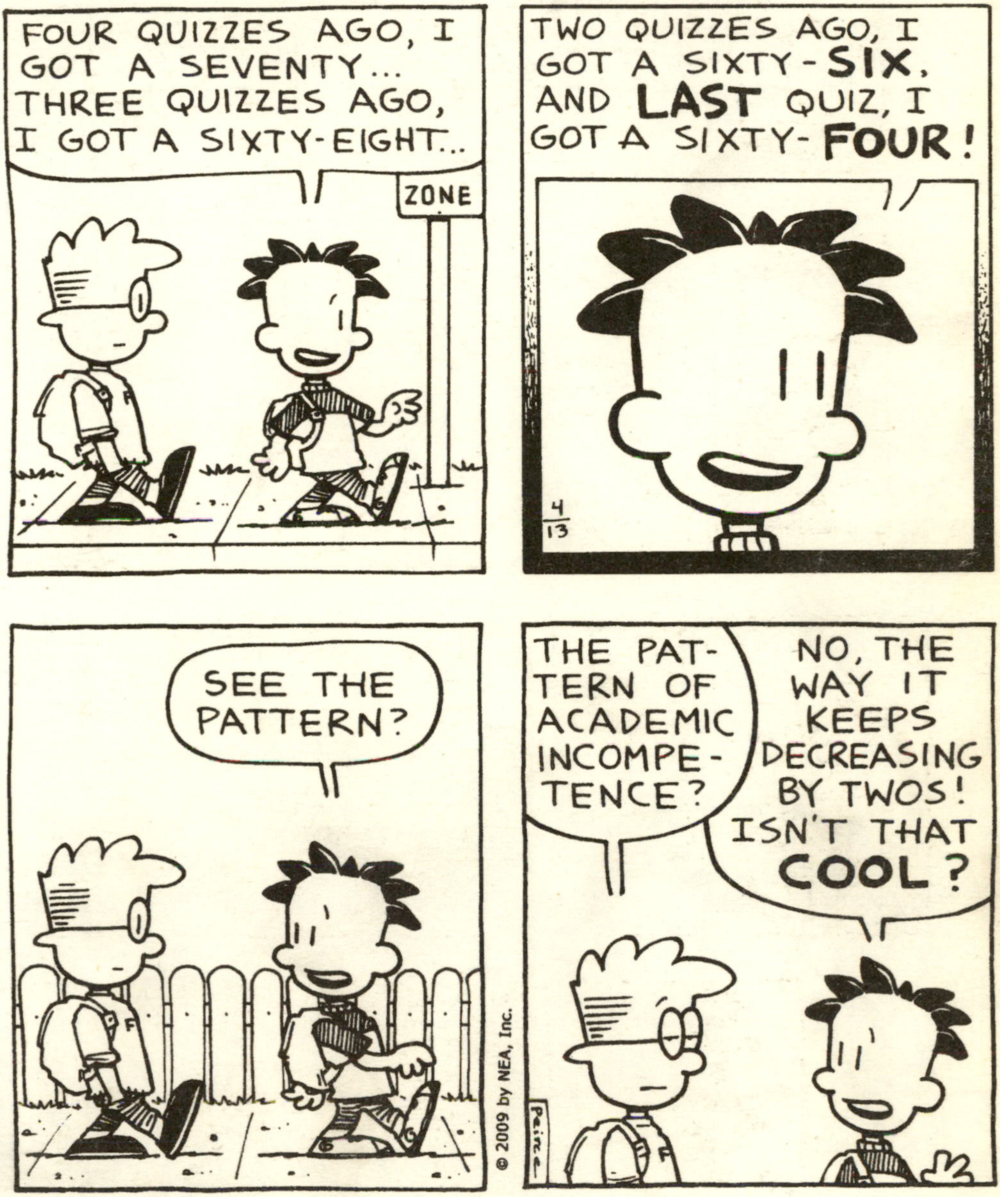

FOUR QUIZZES AGO, I GOT A SEVENTY... THREE QUIZZES AGO, I GOT A SIXTY-EIGHT...
ZONE
TWO QUIZZES AGO, I GOT A SIXTY-**SIX**. AND **LAST** QUIZ, I GOT A SIXTY-**FOUR**!
4/13
SEE THE PATTERN?
© 2009 by NEA, Inc.
THE PATTERN OF ACADEMIC INCOMPETENCE?
NO, THE WAY IT KEEPS DECREASING BY TWOS! ISN'T THAT **COOL**?

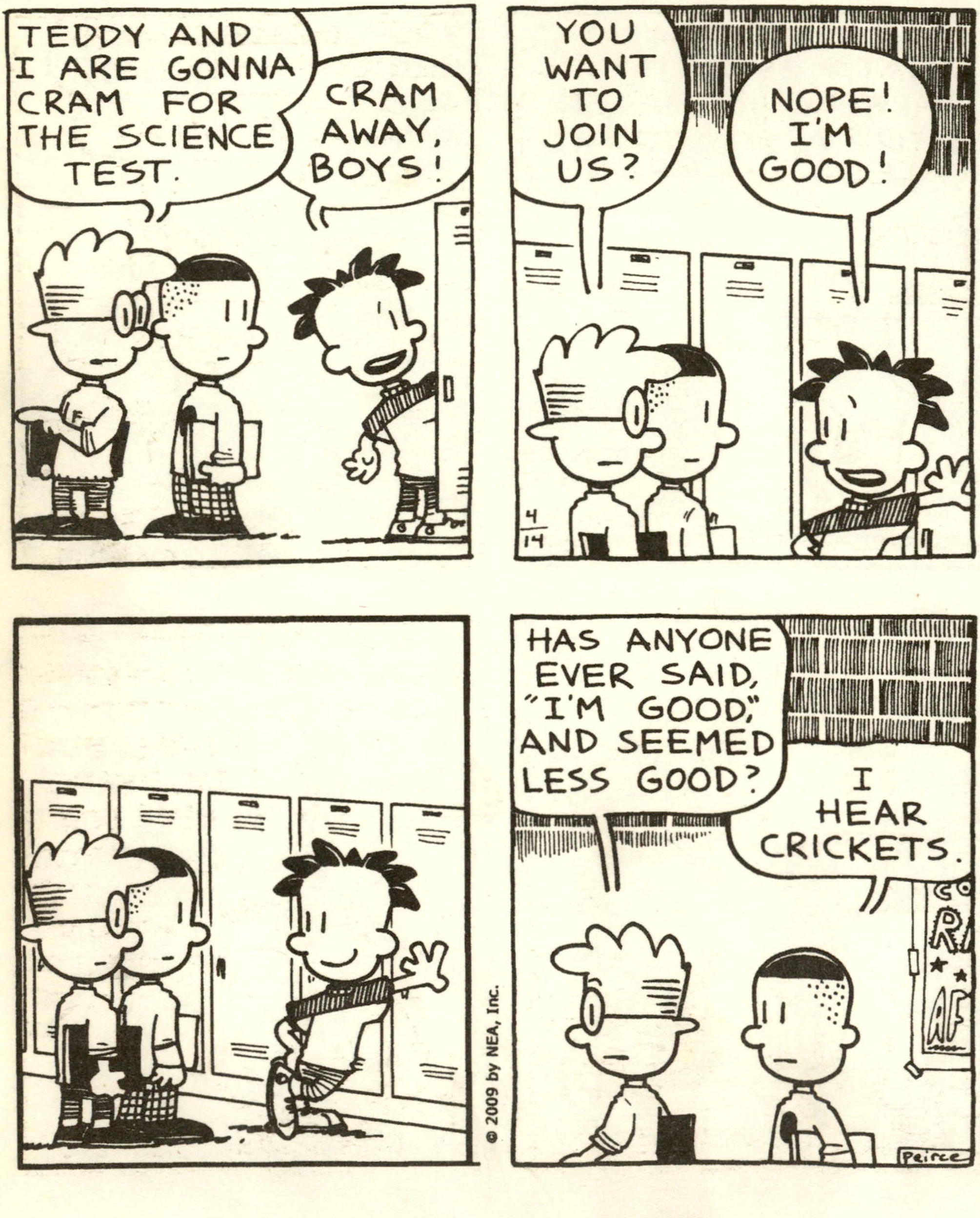
TEDDY AND I ARE GONNA CRAM FOR THE SCIENCE TEST.
CRAM AWAY, BOYS!
YOU WANT TO JOIN US?
NOPE! I'M GOOD!
4/14
HAS ANYONE EVER SAID, "I'M GOOD," AND SEEMED LESS GOOD?
I HEAR CRICKETS.
© 2009 by NEA, Inc.
Peirce

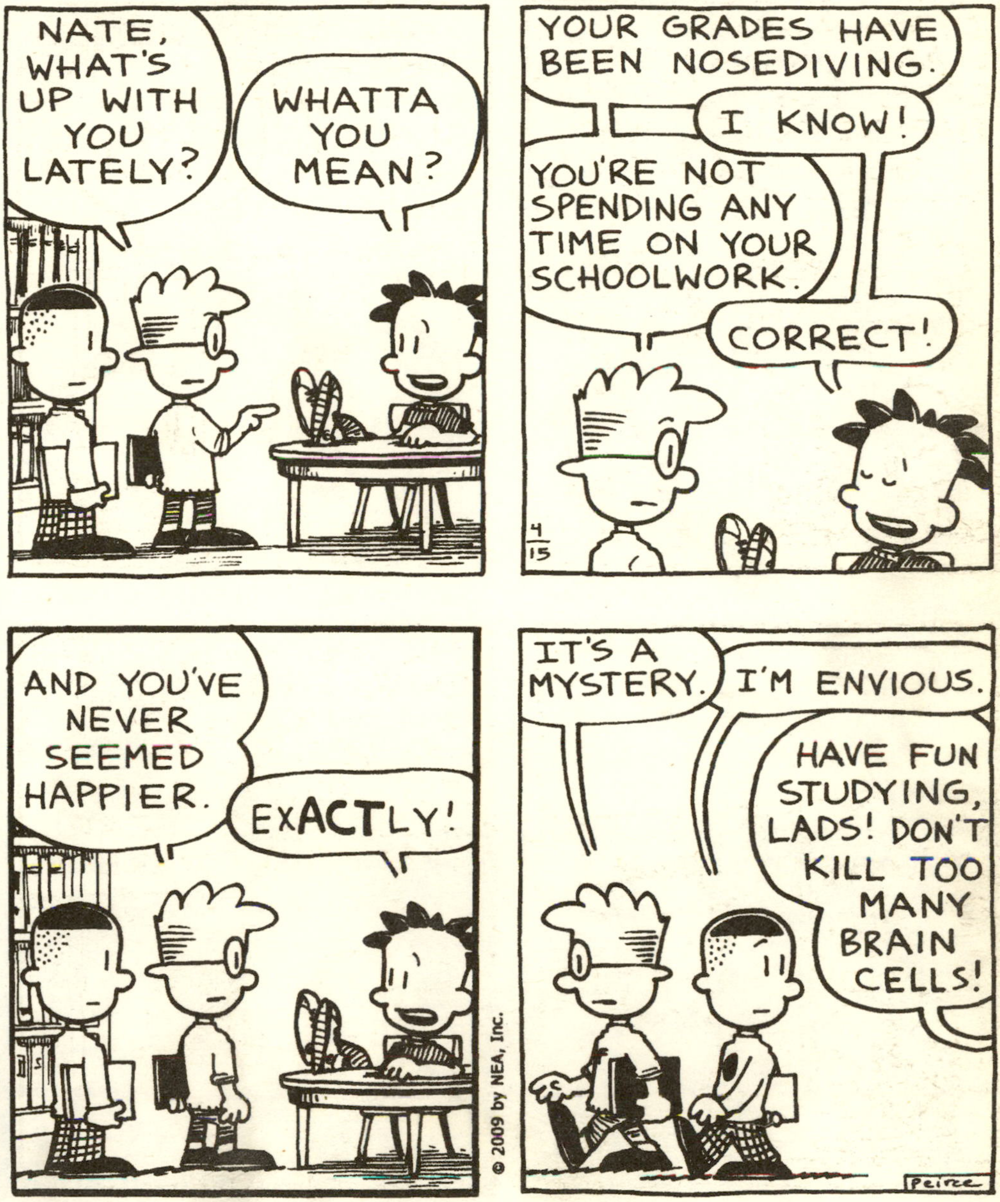
NATE, WHAT'S UP WITH YOU LATELY?
WHATTA YOU MEAN?
YOUR GRADES HAVE BEEN NOSEDIVING.
I KNOW!
YOU'RE NOT SPENDING ANY TIME ON YOUR SCHOOLWORK.
CORRECT!
4/15
AND YOU'VE NEVER SEEMED HAPPIER.
EXACTLY!
IT'S A MYSTERY.
I'M ENVIOUS.
HAVE FUN STUDYING, LADS! DON'T KILL TOO MANY BRAIN CELLS!
Peirce

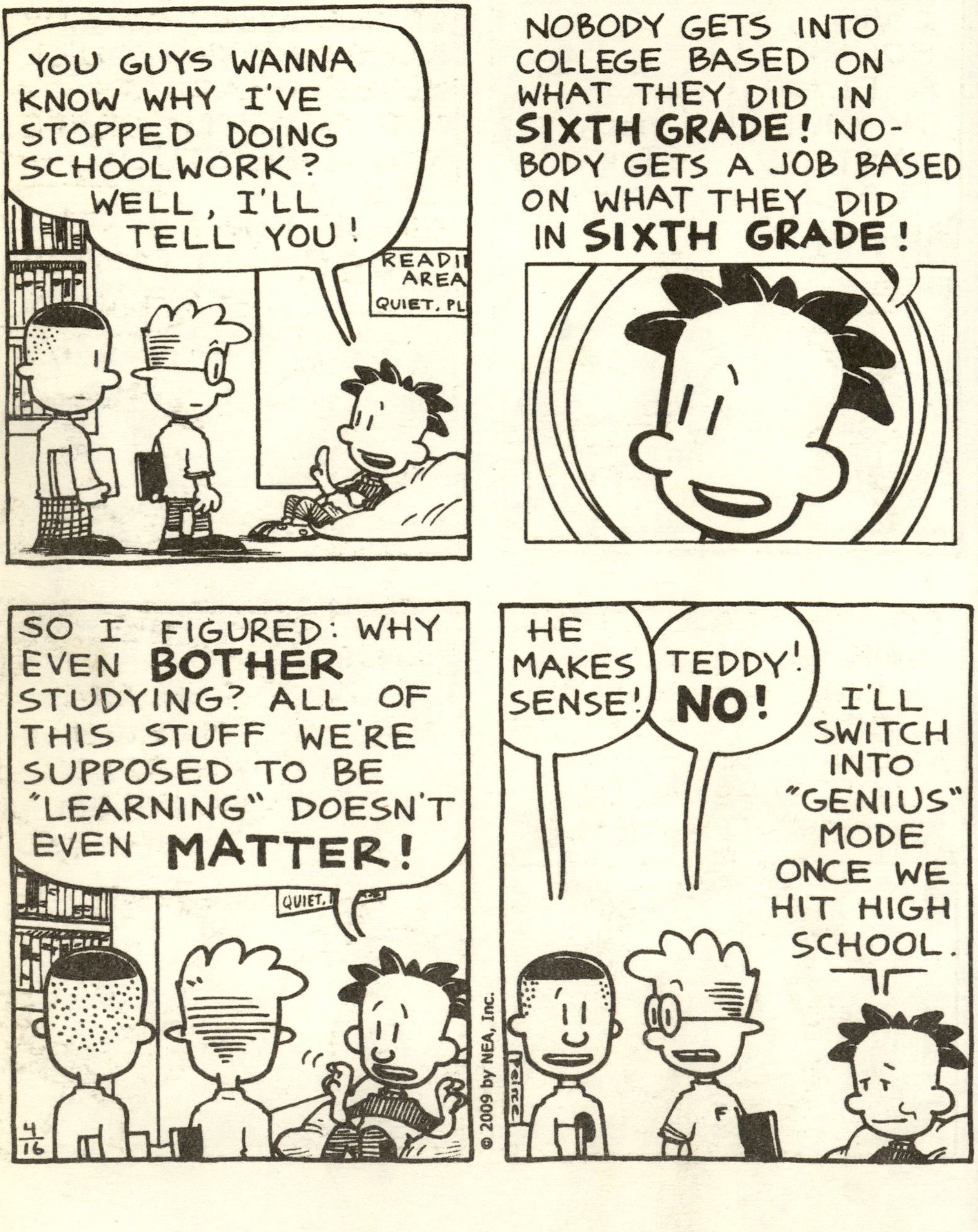
YOU GUYS WANNA KNOW WHY I'VE STOPPED DOING SCHOOLWORK? WELL, I'LL TELL YOU!
READI AREA QUIET. PL
NOBODY GETS INTO COLLEGE BASED ON WHAT THEY DID IN SIXTH GRADE! NOBODY GETS A JOB BASED ON WHAT THEY DID IN SIXTH GRADE!
SO I FIGURED: WHY EVEN BOTHER STUDYING? ALL OF THIS STUFF WE'RE SUPPOSED TO BE "LEARNING" DOESN'T EVEN MATTER!
QUIET.
4/16
© 2009 by NEA, Inc.
HE MAKES SENSE!
TEDDY! NO!
I'LL SWITCH INTO "GENIUS" MODE ONCE WE HIT HIGH SCHOOL.

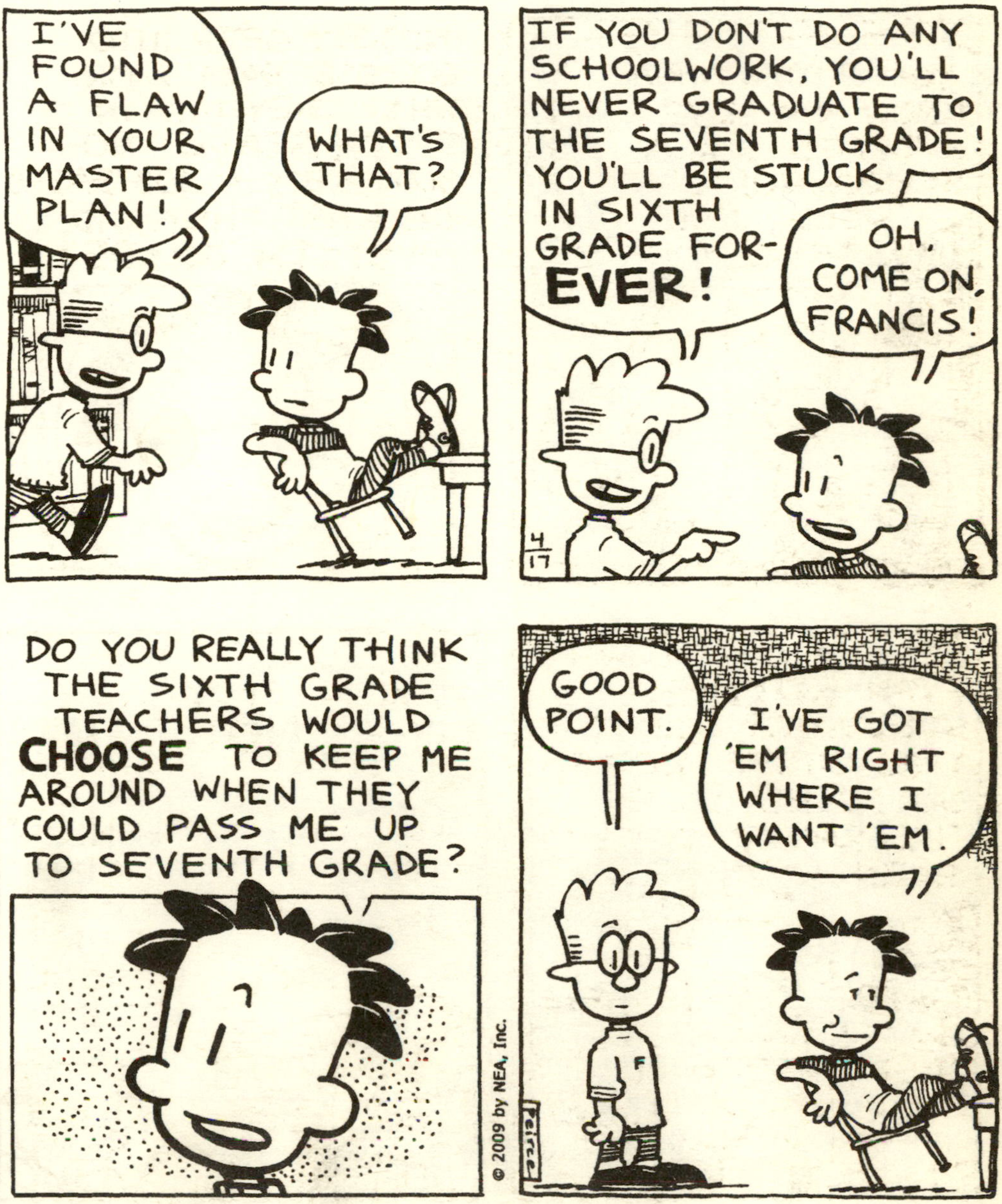
I'VE FOUND A FLAW IN YOUR MASTER PLAN!
WHAT'S THAT?
IF YOU DON'T DO ANY SCHOOLWORK, YOU'LL NEVER GRADUATE TO THE SEVENTH GRADE! YOU'LL BE STUCK IN SIXTH GRADE FOR-**EVER**!
OH, COME ON, FRANCIS!
4/17
DO YOU REALLY THINK THE SIXTH GRADE TEACHERS WOULD **CHOOSE** TO KEEP ME AROUND WHEN THEY COULD PASS ME UP TO SEVENTH GRADE?
GOOD POINT.
I'VE GOT 'EM RIGHT WHERE I WANT 'EM.
© 2009 by NEA, Inc.
Peirce

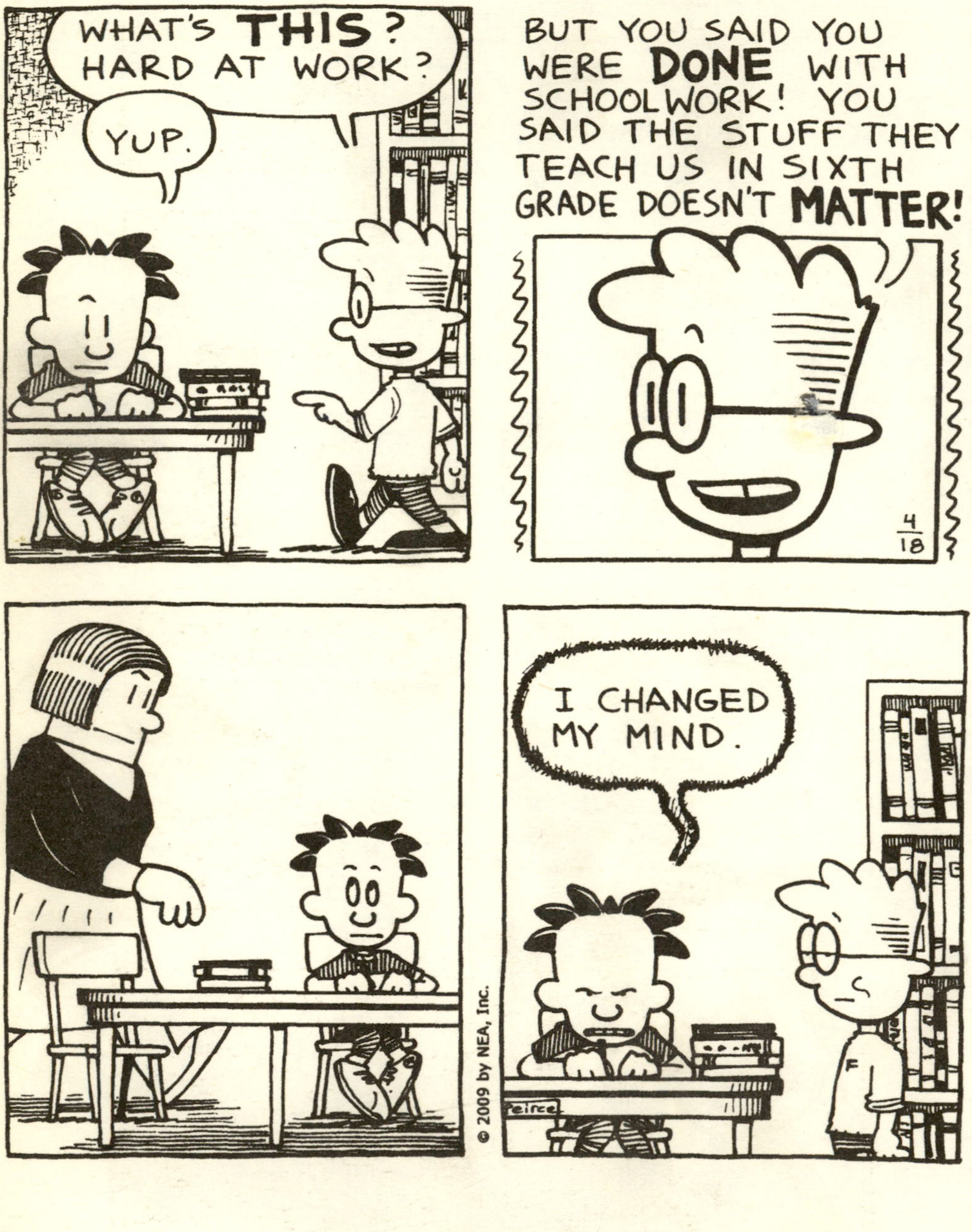
WHAT'S THIS? HARD AT WORK?
YUP.
BUT YOU SAID YOU WERE DONE WITH SCHOOLWORK! YOU SAID THE STUFF THEY TEACH US IN SIXTH GRADE DOESN'T MATTER!
4/18
© 2009 by NEA, Inc.
I CHANGED MY MIND.
Peirce

I WISH JUST ONCE I COULD MAKE AN AMAZING PLAY!

LIKE MAYBE THERE'S A LONG FLY BALL THAT LOOKS LIKE A SURE HOME RUN...

4/19

...BUT I SPRINT BACK AND GO DIVING INTO THE CROWD TO MAKE AN INCREDIBLE GRAB!

MAYBE I LAND IN THE LAP OF SOME CUTE GIRL WHO'S WATCHING THE GAME!

THAT WOULD BE AWESOME.

KRAK!

OOP! I CAN'T **BELIEVE** IT!

THIS COULD FINALLY BE MY CHANCE FOR AN AMAZING PLAY!

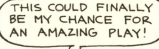

LEAP!

...OR NOT.

YOU MADE ME DROP MY CHIPS.

© 2009 by NEA, Inc.

OO, LA, LA!

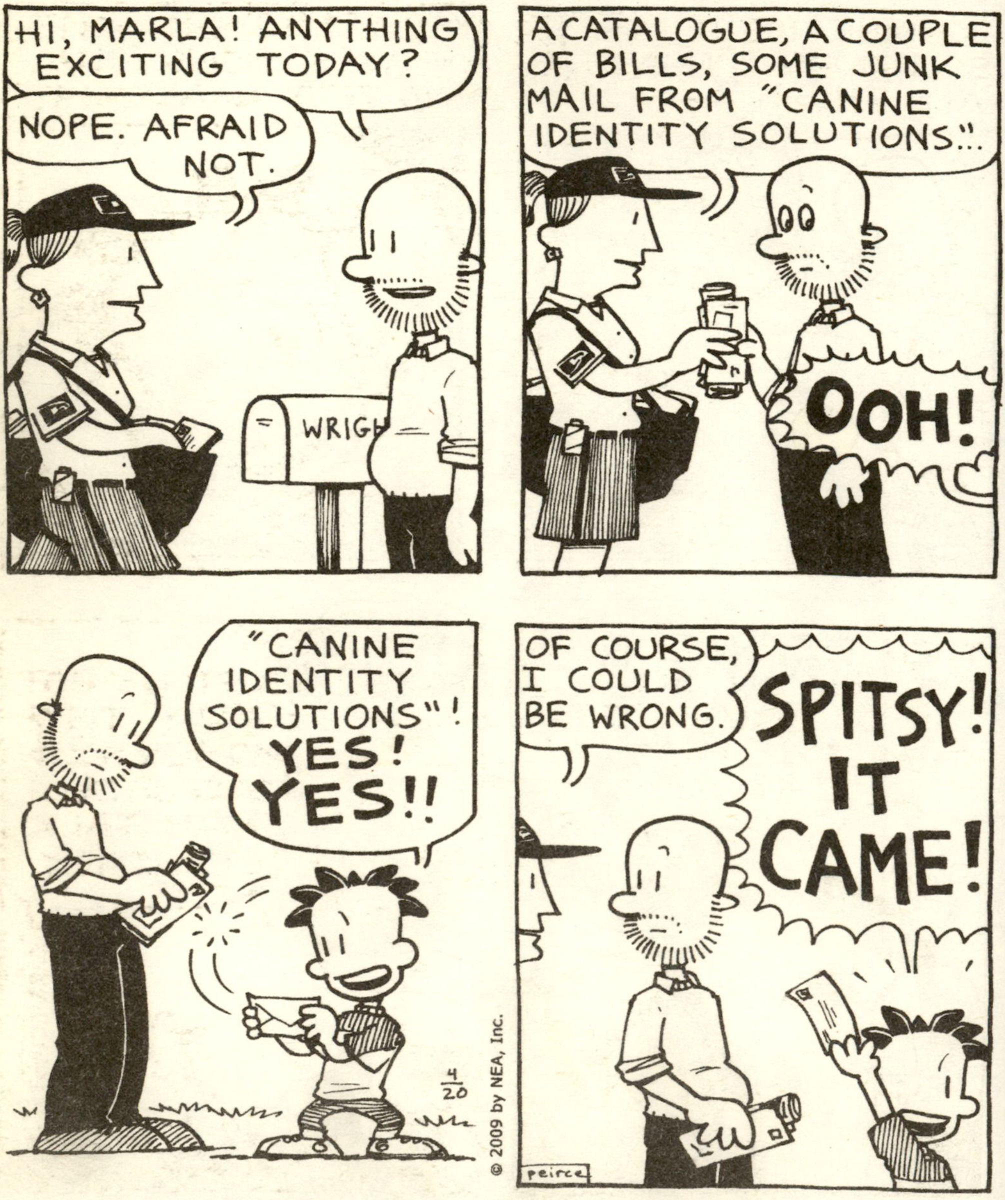

HI, MARLA! ANYTHING EXCITING TODAY?
NOPE. AFRAID NOT.
WRIGH
A CATALOGUE, A COUPLE OF BILLS, SOME JUNK MAIL FROM "CANINE IDENTITY SOLUTIONS"...
OOH!
"CANINE IDENTITY SOLUTIONS"! YES! YES!!
4/20
© 2009 by NEA, Inc.
OF COURSE, I COULD BE WRONG.
SPITSY! IT CAME!
peirce

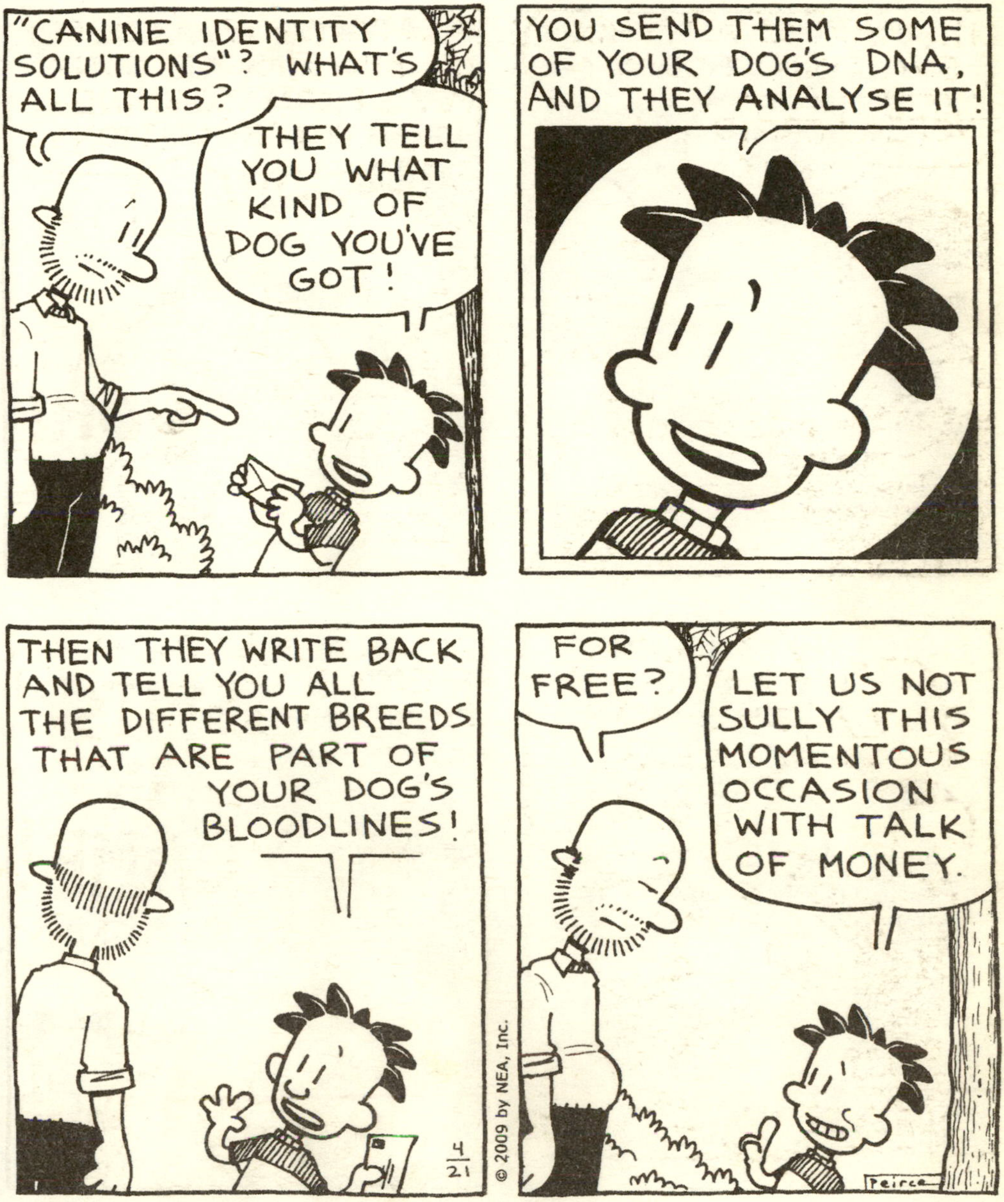
"CANINE IDENTITY SOLUTIONS"? WHAT'S ALL THIS?
THEY TELL YOU WHAT KIND OF DOG YOU'VE GOT!
YOU SEND THEM SOME OF YOUR DOG'S DNA, AND THEY ANALYSE IT!
THEN THEY WRITE BACK AND TELL YOU ALL THE DIFFERENT BREEDS THAT ARE PART OF YOUR DOG'S BLOODLINES!
FOR FREE?
LET US NOT SULLY THIS MOMENTOUS OCCASION WITH TALK OF MONEY.
4 21
© 2009 by NEA, Inc.
Peirce

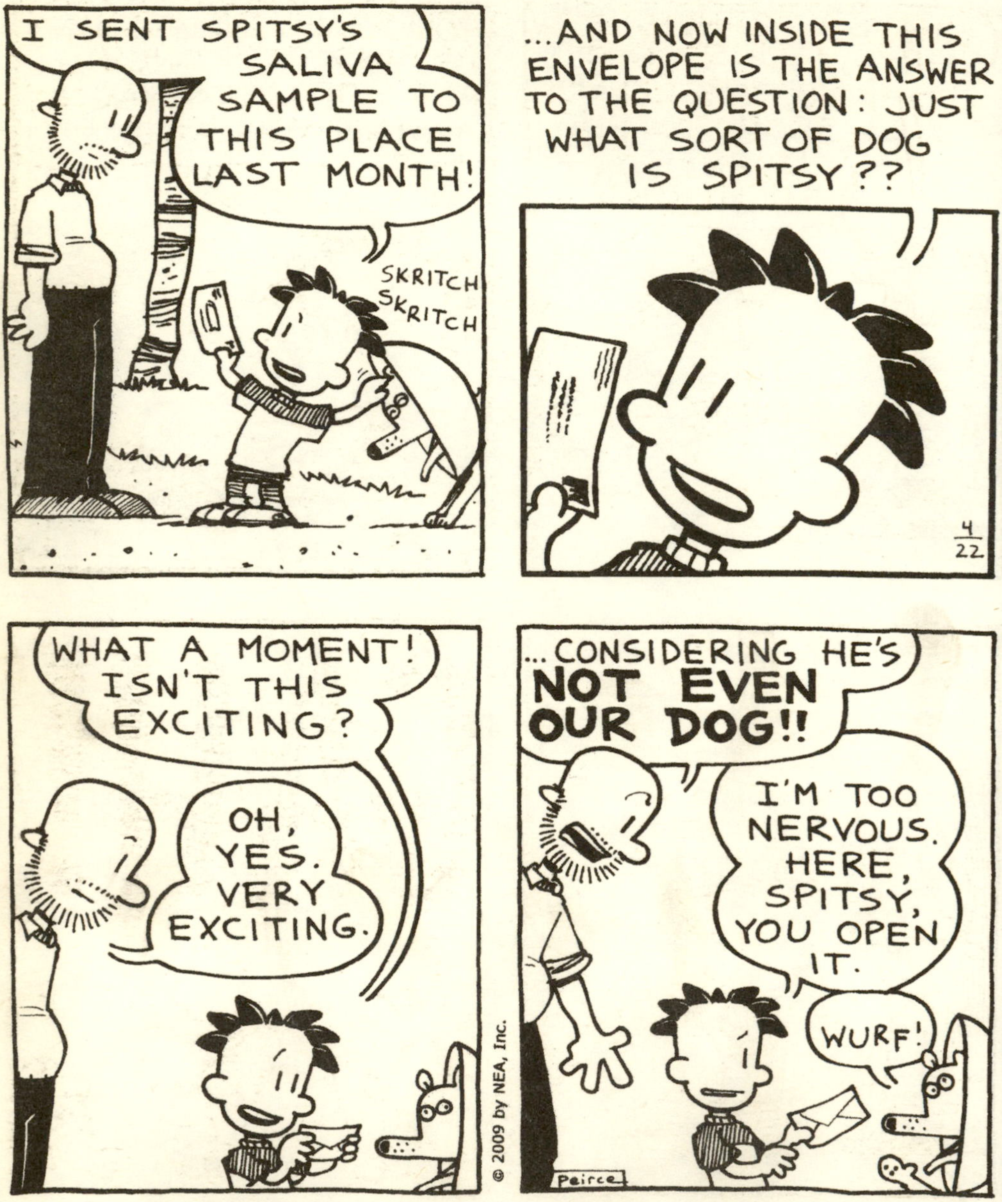
I SENT SPITSY'S SALIVA SAMPLE TO THIS PLACE LAST MONTH!
SKRITCH SKRITCH
...AND NOW INSIDE THIS ENVELOPE IS THE ANSWER TO THE QUESTION: JUST WHAT SORT OF DOG IS SPITSY??
4/22
WHAT A MOMENT! ISN'T THIS EXCITING?
OH, YES. VERY EXCITING.
© 2009 by NEA, Inc.
...CONSIDERING HE'S **NOT EVEN OUR DOG!!**
I'M TOO NERVOUS. HERE, SPITSY, YOU OPEN IT.
WURF!
Peirce

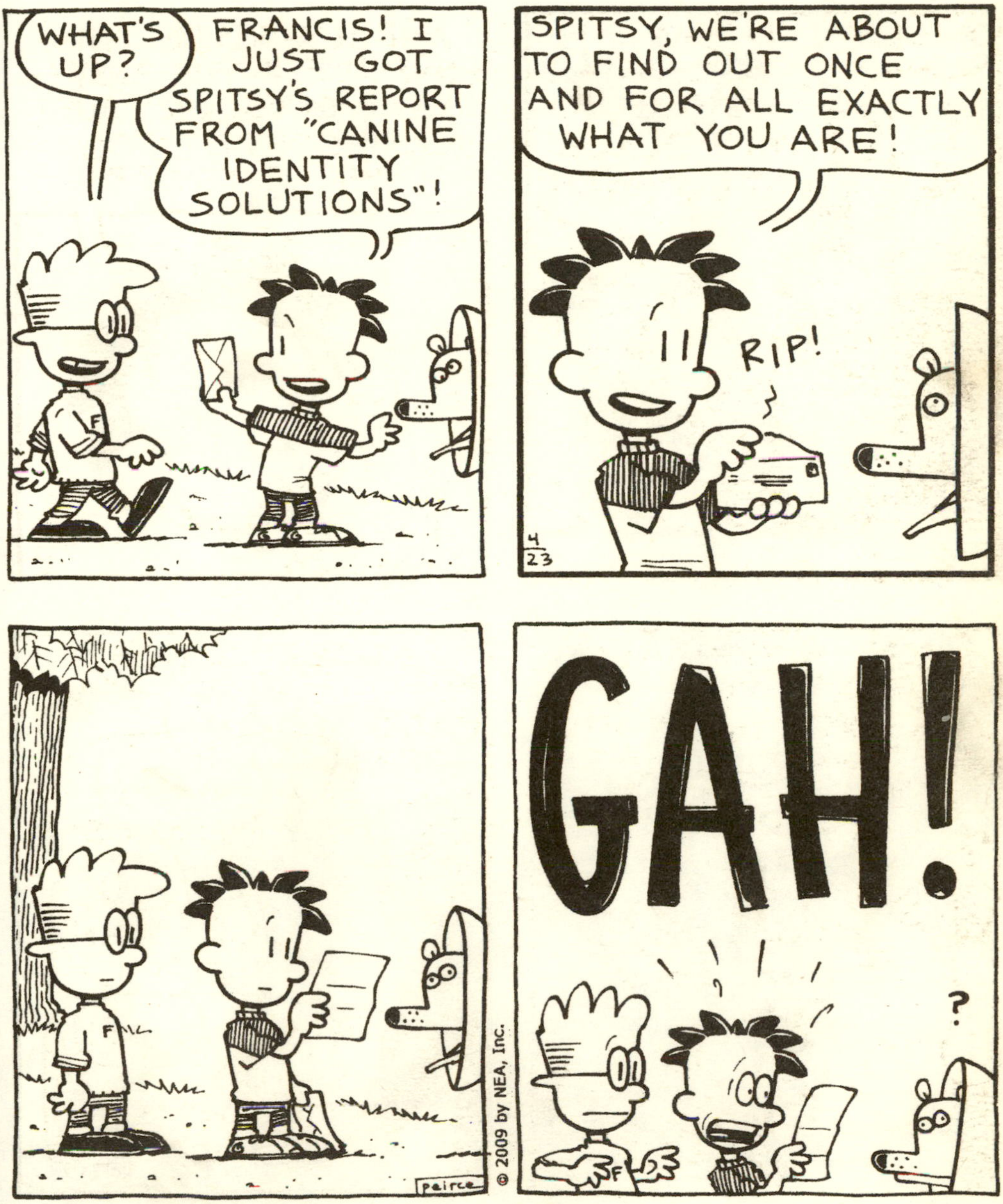
WHAT'S UP?
FRANCIS! I JUST GOT SPITSY'S REPORT FROM "CANINE IDENTITY SOLUTIONS"!
SPITSY, WE'RE ABOUT TO FIND OUT ONCE AND FOR ALL EXACTLY WHAT YOU ARE!
RIP!
4 23
peirce
© 2009 by NEA, Inc.
GAH!
?

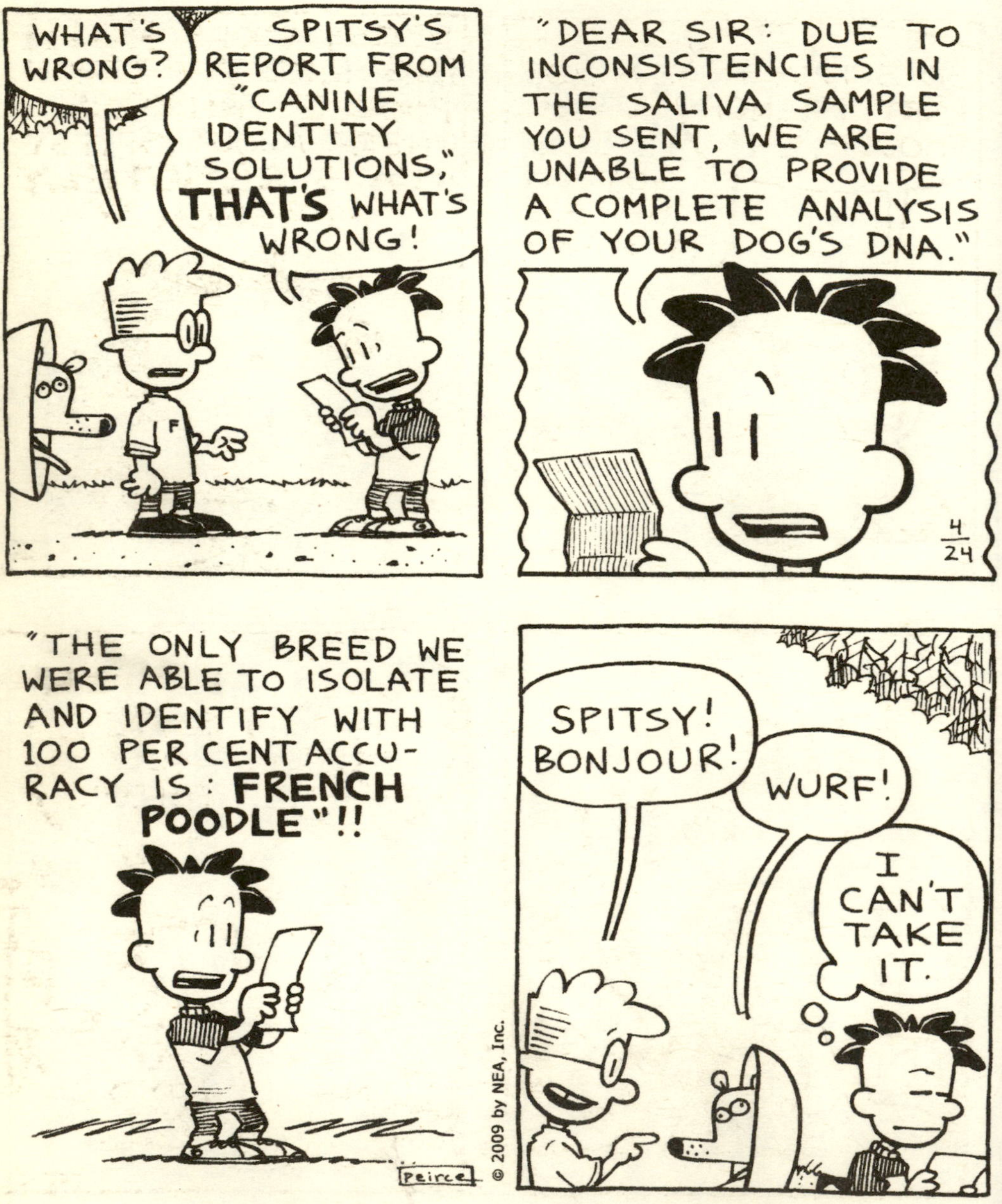
WHAT'S WRONG?
SPITSY'S REPORT FROM "CANINE IDENTITY SOLUTIONS," THAT'S WHAT'S WRONG!
"DEAR SIR: DUE TO INCONSISTENCIES IN THE SALIVA SAMPLE YOU SENT, WE ARE UNABLE TO PROVIDE A COMPLETE ANALYSIS OF YOUR DOG'S DNA."
4/24
"THE ONLY BREED WE WERE ABLE TO ISOLATE AND IDENTIFY WITH 100 PER CENT ACCURACY IS: FRENCH POODLE"!!
Peirce
© 2009 by NEA, Inc.
SPITSY! BONJOUR!
WURF!
I CAN'T TAKE IT.

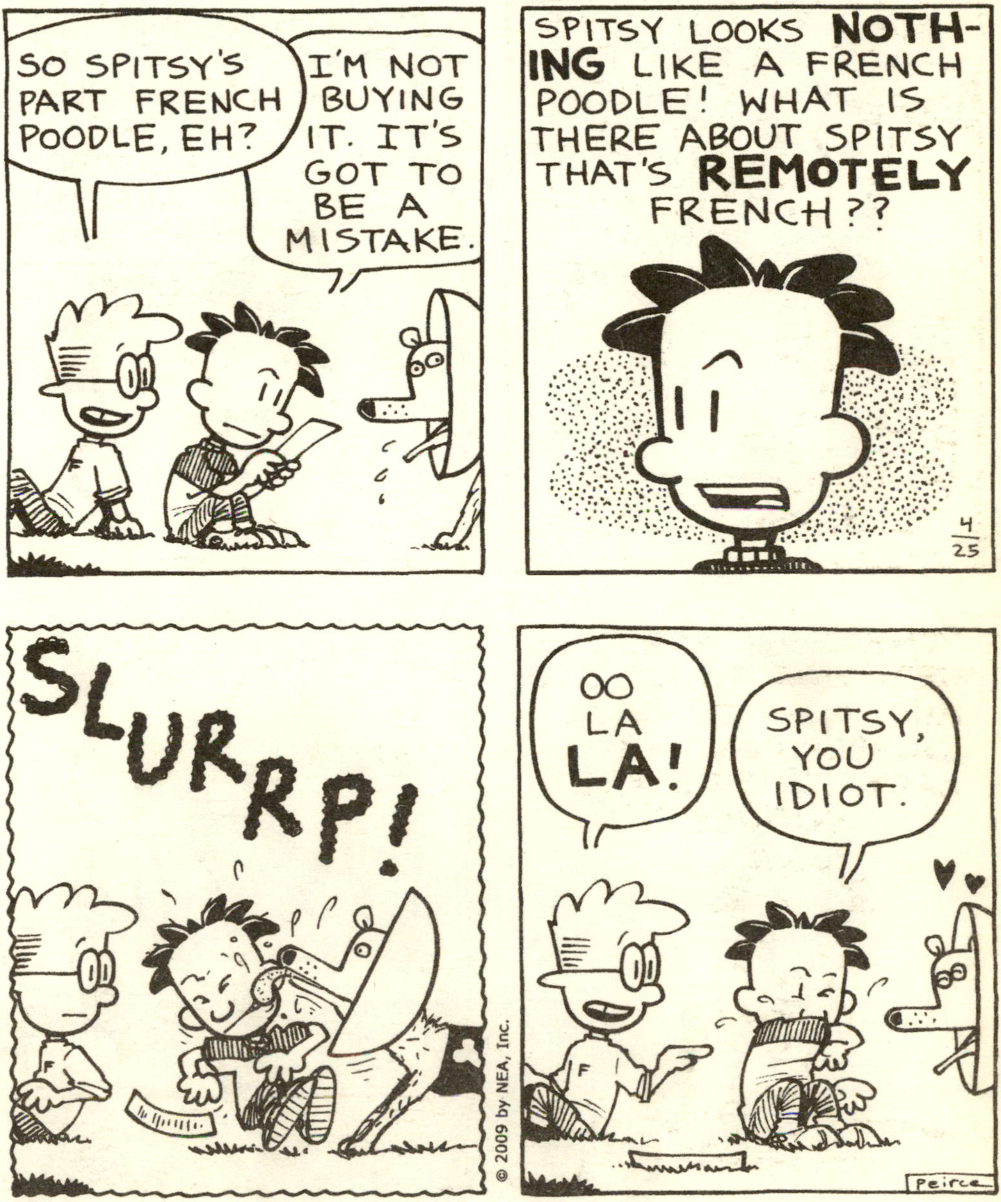
SO SPITSY'S PART FRENCH POODLE, EH?
I'M NOT BUYING IT. IT'S GOT TO BE A MISTAKE.
SPITSY LOOKS **NOTHING** LIKE A FRENCH POODLE! WHAT IS THERE ABOUT SPITSY THAT'S **REMOTELY** FRENCH??
4/25
SLURRP!
© 2009 by NEA, Inc.
OO LA **LA**!
SPITSY, YOU IDIOT.
peirce

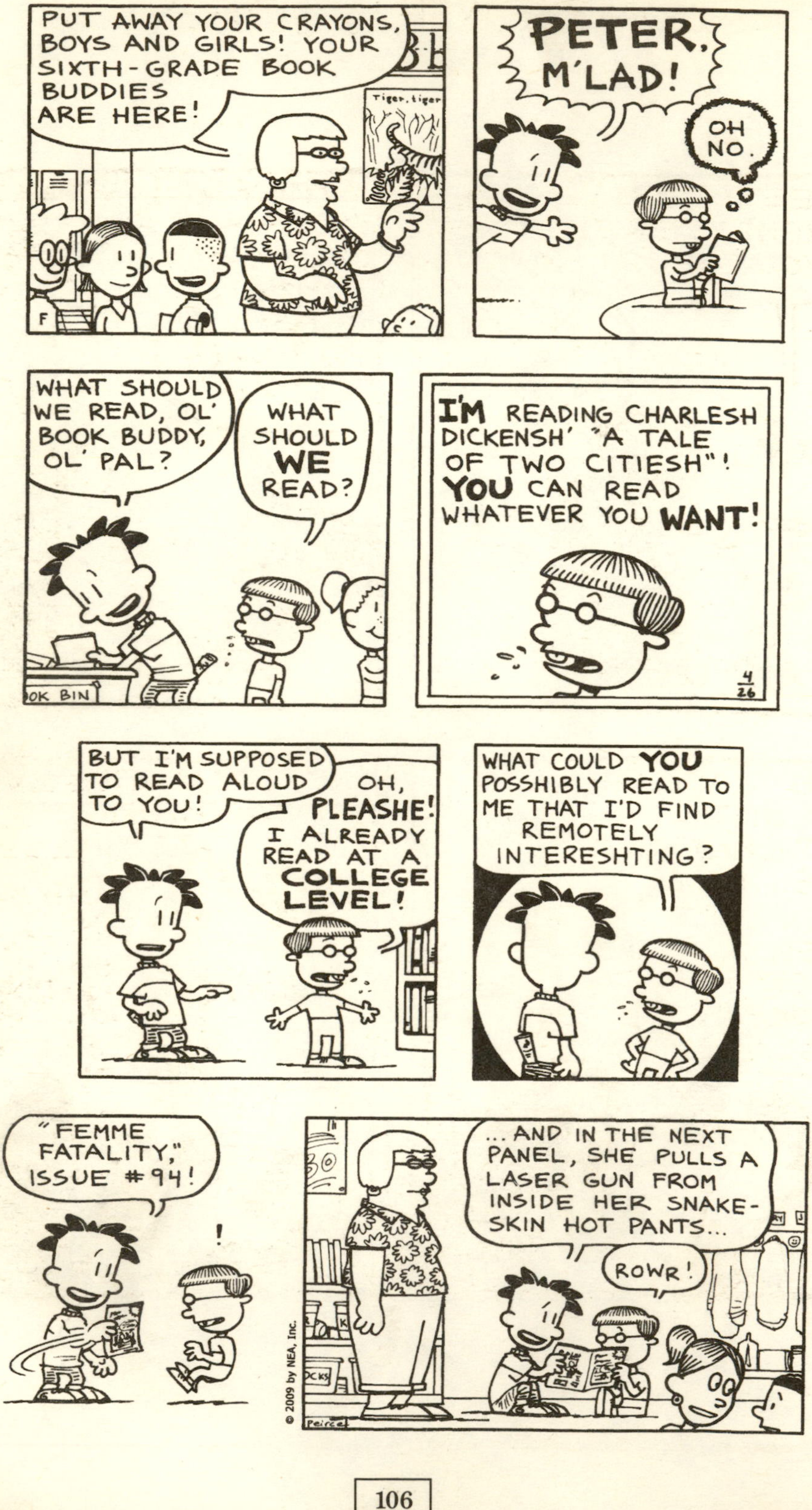
PUT AWAY YOUR CRAYONS, BOYS AND GIRLS! YOUR SIXTH-GRADE BOOK BUDDIES ARE HERE!
PETER, M'LAD!
OH NO.
WHAT SHOULD WE READ, OL' BOOK BUDDY, OL' PAL?
WHAT SHOULD WE READ?
I'M READING CHARLESH DICKENSH' "A TALE OF TWO CITIESH"! YOU CAN READ WHATEVER YOU WANT!
4/26
BUT I'M SUPPOSED TO READ ALOUD TO YOU!
OH, PLEASHE! I ALREADY READ AT A COLLEGE LEVEL!
WHAT COULD YOU POSSHIBLY READ TO ME THAT I'D FIND REMOTELY INTERESHTING?
"FEMME FATALITY," ISSUE #94!
!
... AND IN THE NEXT PANEL, SHE PULLS A LASER GUN FROM INSIDE HER SNAKE-SKIN HOT PANTS...
ROWR!
© 2009 by NEA, Inc.
Peirce

A NOVEL IDEA

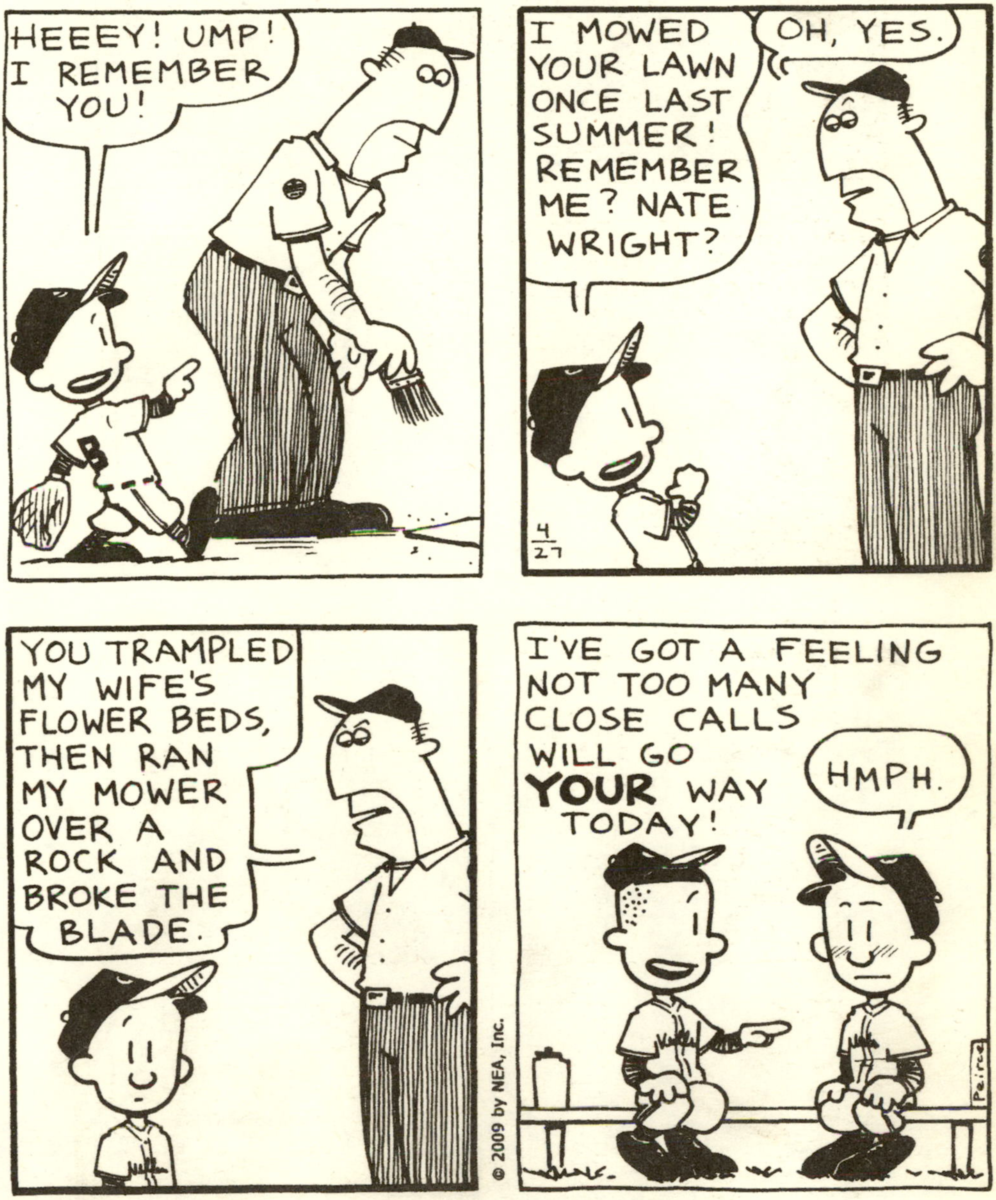
HEEEY! UMP! I REMEMBER YOU!
I MOWED YOUR LAWN ONCE LAST SUMMER! REMEMBER ME? NATE WRIGHT?
OH, YES.
4/27
YOU TRAMPLED MY WIFE'S FLOWER BEDS, THEN RAN MY MOWER OVER A ROCK AND BROKE THE BLADE.
© 2009 by NEA, Inc.
I'VE GOT A FEELING NOT TOO MANY CLOSE CALLS WILL GO **YOUR** WAY TODAY!
HMPH.
Peirce

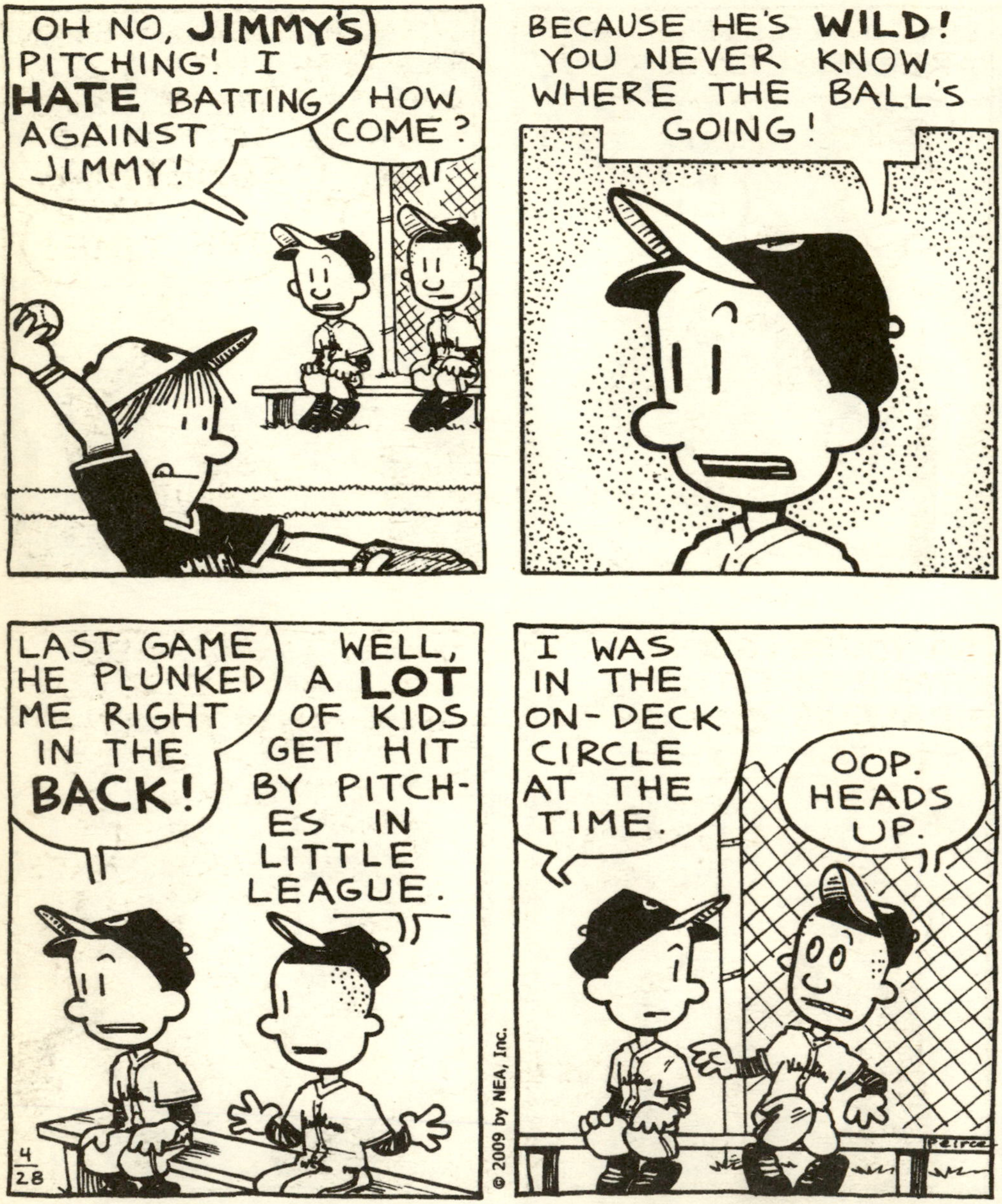
OH NO, **JIMMY'S** PITCHING! I **HATE** BATTING AGAINST JIMMY!
HOW COME?
BECAUSE HE'S **WILD!** YOU NEVER KNOW WHERE THE BALL'S GOING!
LAST GAME HE PLUNKED ME RIGHT IN THE **BACK!**
WELL, A **LOT** OF KIDS GET HIT BY PITCHES IN LITTLE LEAGUE.
I WAS IN THE ON-DECK CIRCLE AT THE TIME.
OOP. HEADS UP.
4/28
© 2009 by NEA, Inc.
Peirce

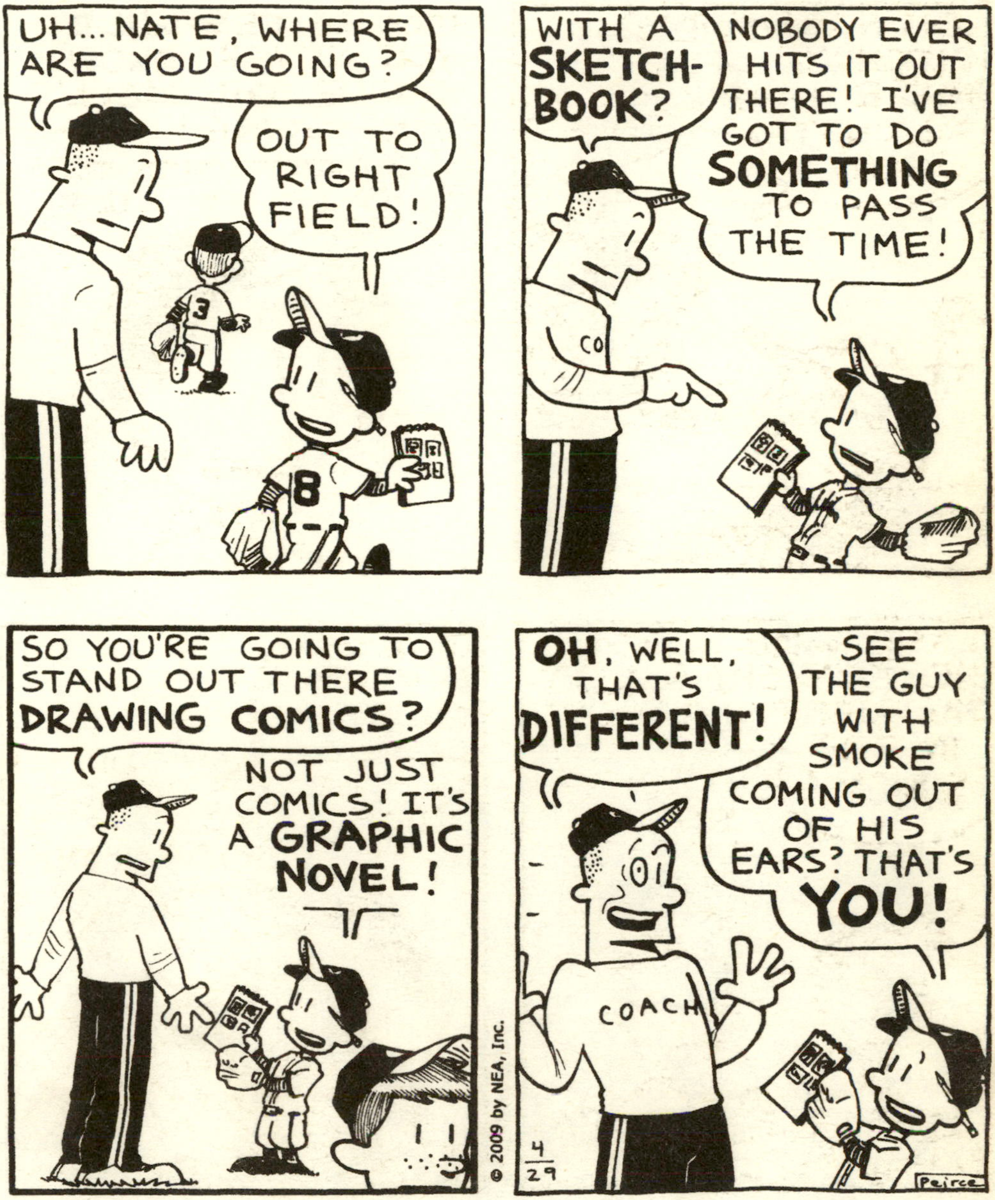
UH... NATE, WHERE ARE YOU GOING?
OUT TO RIGHT FIELD!
WITH A SKETCH-BOOK?
NOBODY EVER HITS IT OUT THERE! I'VE GOT TO DO SOMETHING TO PASS THE TIME!
SO YOU'RE GOING TO STAND OUT THERE DRAWING COMICS?
NOT JUST COMICS! IT'S A GRAPHIC NOVEL!
OH, WELL, THAT'S DIFFERENT!
SEE THE GUY WITH SMOKE COMING OUT OF HIS EARS? THAT'S YOU!
COACH
4/29
Peirce

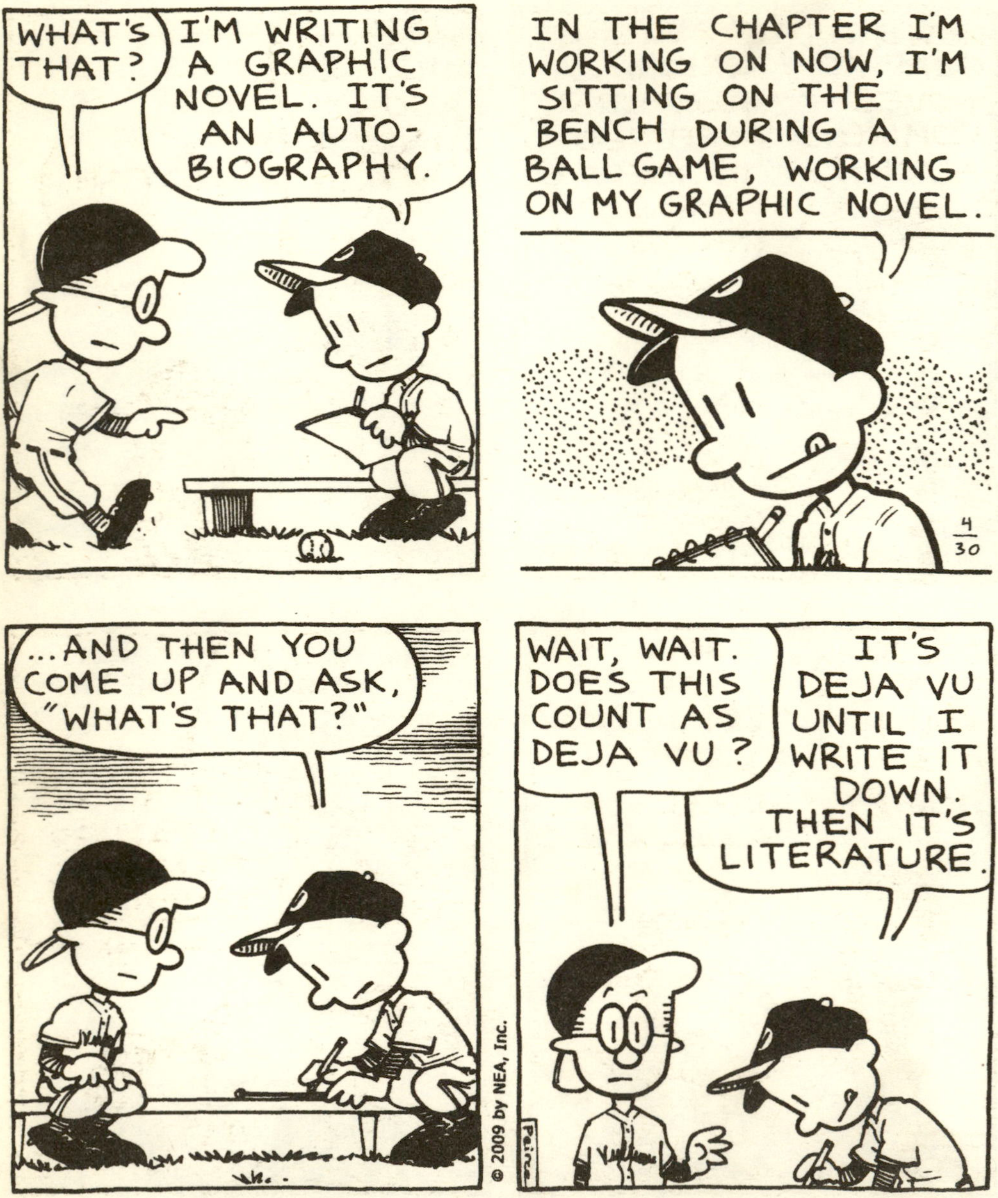
WHAT'S THAT?
I'M WRITING A GRAPHIC NOVEL. IT'S AN AUTO-BIOGRAPHY.
IN THE CHAPTER I'M WORKING ON NOW, I'M SITTING ON THE BENCH DURING A BALL GAME, WORKING ON MY GRAPHIC NOVEL.
4/30
...AND THEN YOU COME UP AND ASK, "WHAT'S THAT?"
© 2009 by NEA, Inc.
Peirce
WAIT, WAIT. DOES THIS COUNT AS DEJA VU?
IT'S DEJA VU UNTIL I WRITE IT DOWN. THEN IT'S LITERATURE.

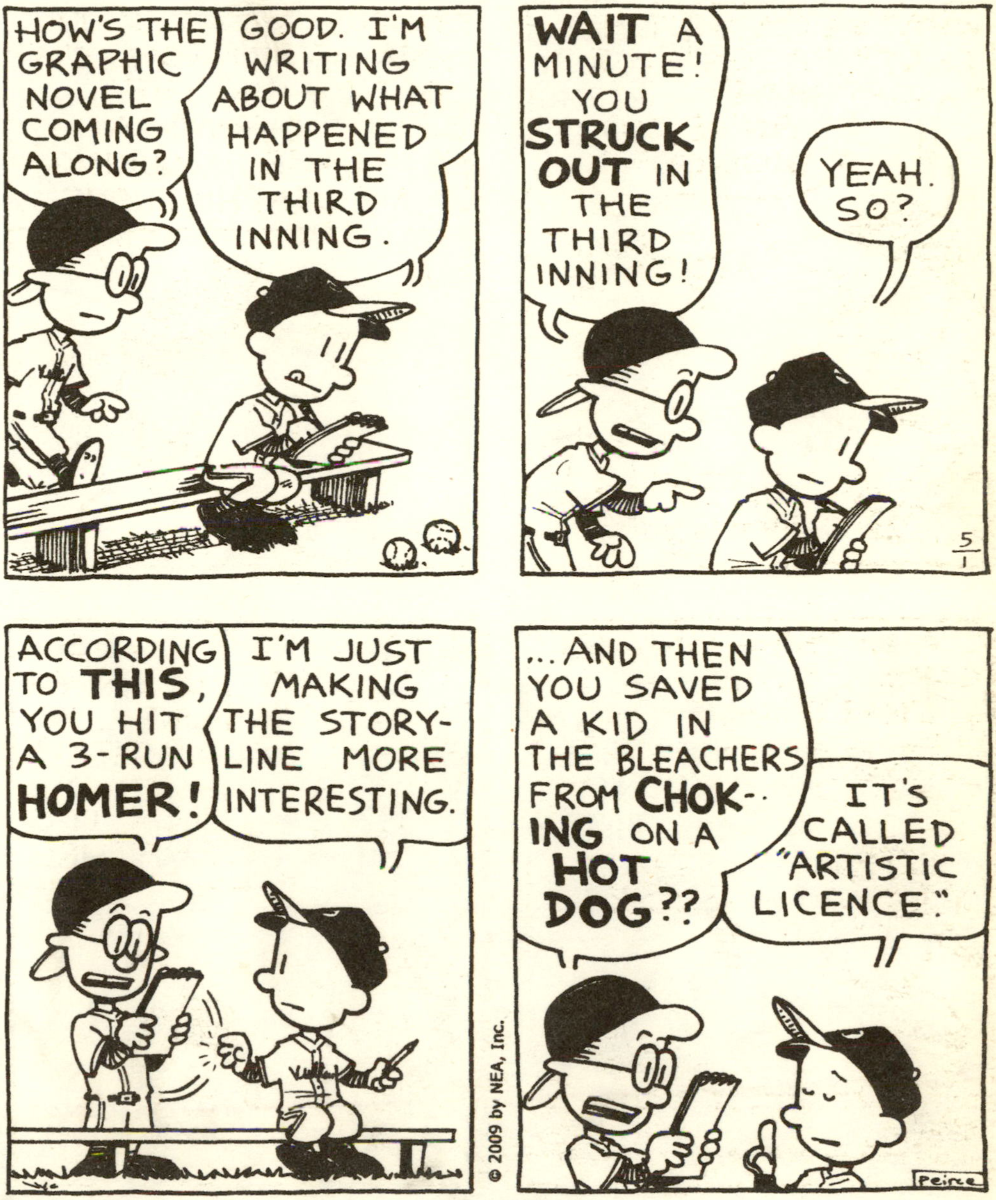
HOW'S THE GRAPHIC NOVEL COMING ALONG?
GOOD. I'M WRITING ABOUT WHAT HAPPENED IN THE THIRD INNING.
WAIT A MINUTE! YOU STRUCK OUT IN THE THIRD INNING!
YEAH. SO?
5/1
ACCORDING TO THIS, YOU HIT A 3-RUN HOMER!
I'M JUST MAKING THE STORY-LINE MORE INTERESTING.
...AND THEN YOU SAVED A KID IN THE BLEACHERS FROM CHOK-ING ON A HOT DOG??
IT'S CALLED "ARTISTIC LICENCE."
Peirce

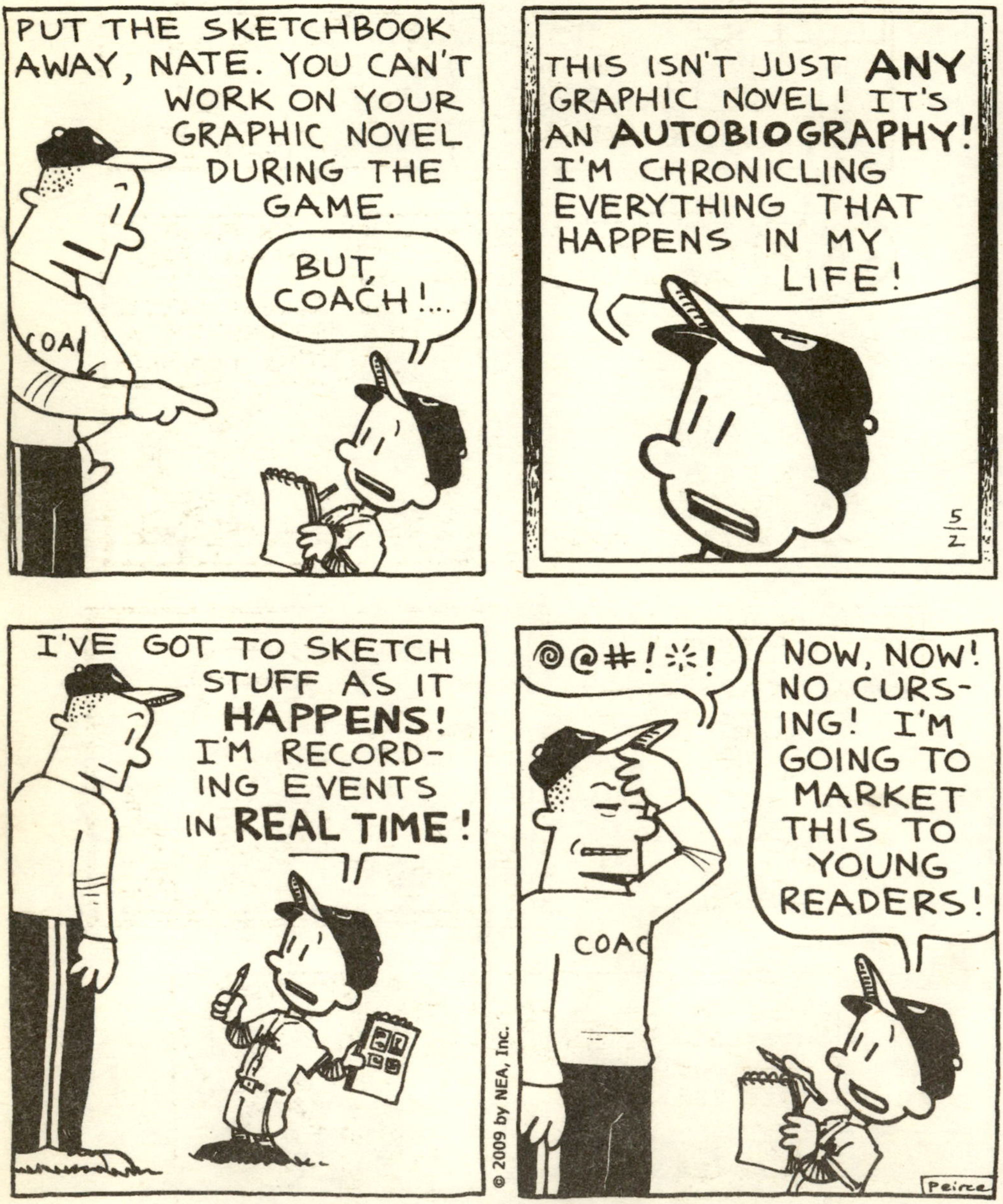
PUT THE SKETCHBOOK AWAY, NATE. YOU CAN'T WORK ON YOUR GRAPHIC NOVEL DURING THE GAME.
BUT, COACH!...
COA
THIS ISN'T JUST **ANY** GRAPHIC NOVEL! IT'S AN **AUTOBIOGRAPHY!** I'M CHRONICLING EVERYTHING THAT HAPPENS IN MY LIFE!
5/2
I'VE GOT TO SKETCH STUFF AS IT **HAPPENS!** I'M RECORDING EVENTS IN **REAL TIME!**
© 2009 by NEA, Inc.
@@#!*!
NOW, NOW! NO CURSING! I'M GOING TO MARKET THIS TO YOUNG READERS!
COA
Peirce

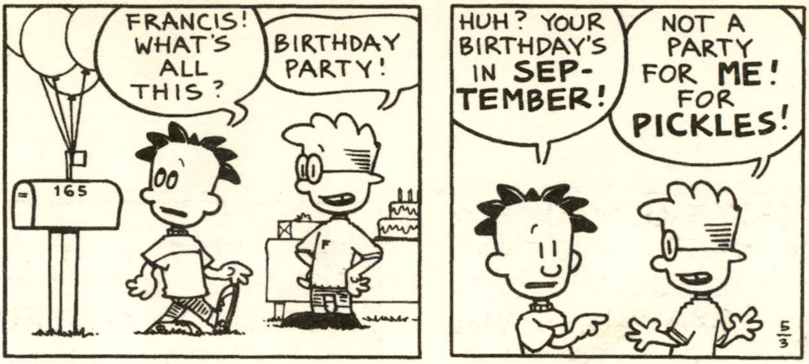
FRANCIS! WHAT'S ALL THIS?
BIRTHDAY PARTY!
165
HUH? YOUR BIRTHDAY'S IN SEP-TEMBER!
NOT A PARTY FOR ME! FOR PICKLES!
5/3

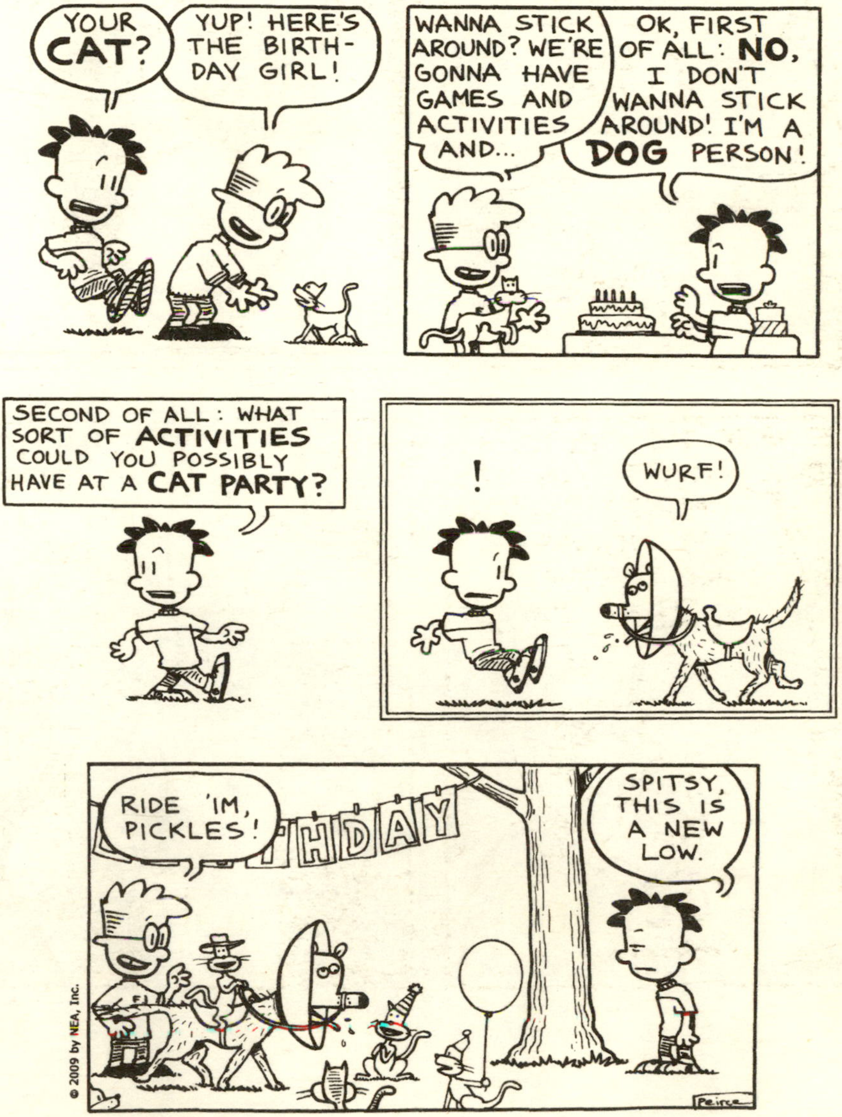
YOUR CAT?
YUP! HERE'S THE BIRTH-DAY GIRL!
WANNA STICK AROUND? WE'RE GONNA HAVE GAMES AND ACTIVITIES AND...
OK, FIRST OF ALL: NO, I DON'T WANNA STICK AROUND! I'M A DOG PERSON!
SECOND OF ALL: WHAT SORT OF ACTIVITIES COULD YOU POSSIBLY HAVE AT A CAT PARTY?
!
WURF!
RIDE 'IM, PICKLES!
HDAY
SPITSY, THIS IS A NEW LOW.
© 2009 by NEA, Inc.
Peirce

SUGAR BUZZ

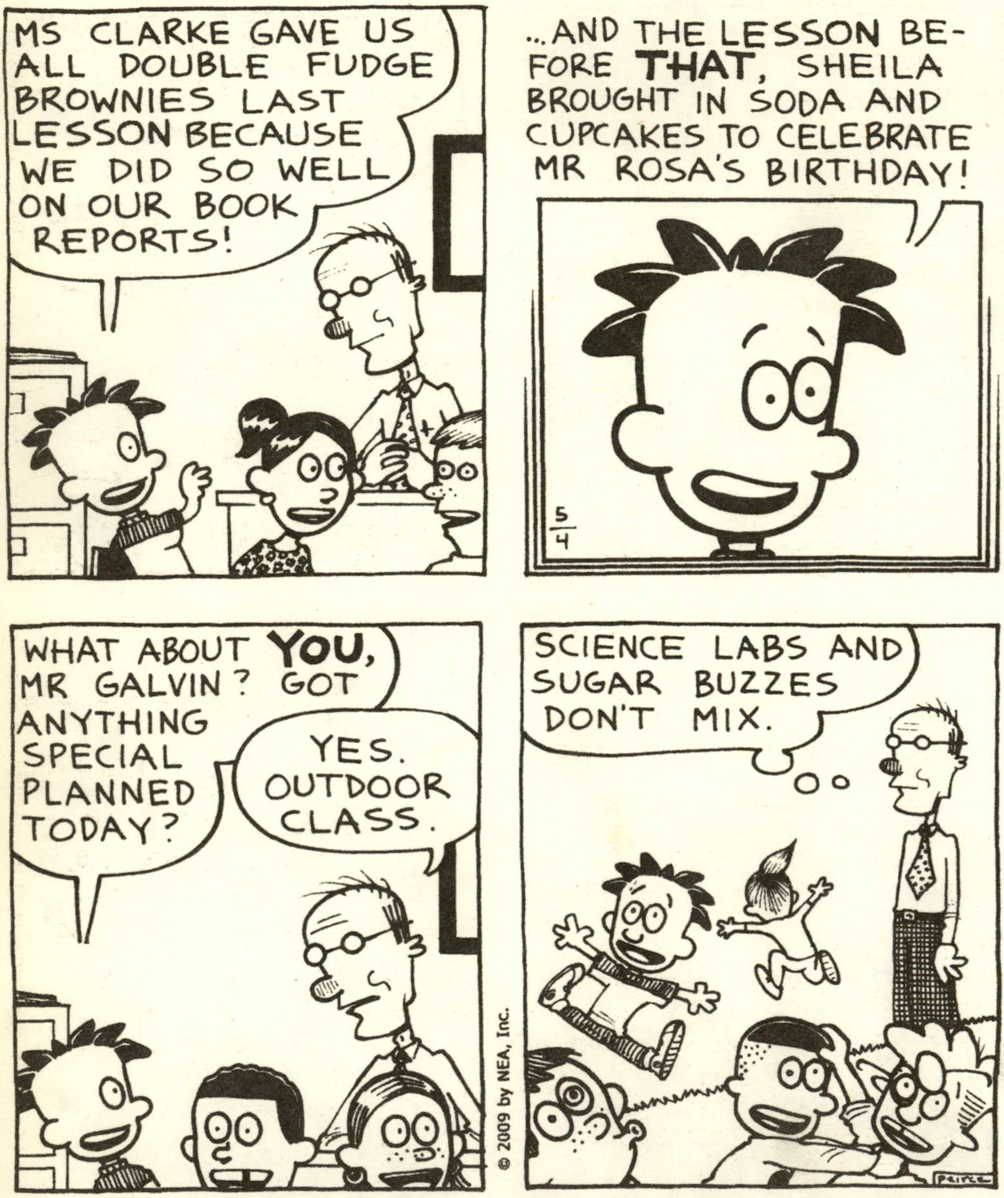
MS CLARKE GAVE US ALL DOUBLE FUDGE BROWNIES LAST LESSON BECAUSE WE DID SO WELL ON OUR BOOK REPORTS!
...AND THE LESSON BEFORE THAT, SHEILA BROUGHT IN SODA AND CUPCAKES TO CELEBRATE MR ROSA'S BIRTHDAY!
WHAT ABOUT YOU, MR GALVIN? GOT ANYTHING SPECIAL PLANNED TODAY?
YES. OUTDOOR CLASS.
SCIENCE LABS AND SUGAR BUZZES DON'T MIX.
© 2009 by NEA, Inc.

NATE MAKES THE GRADE

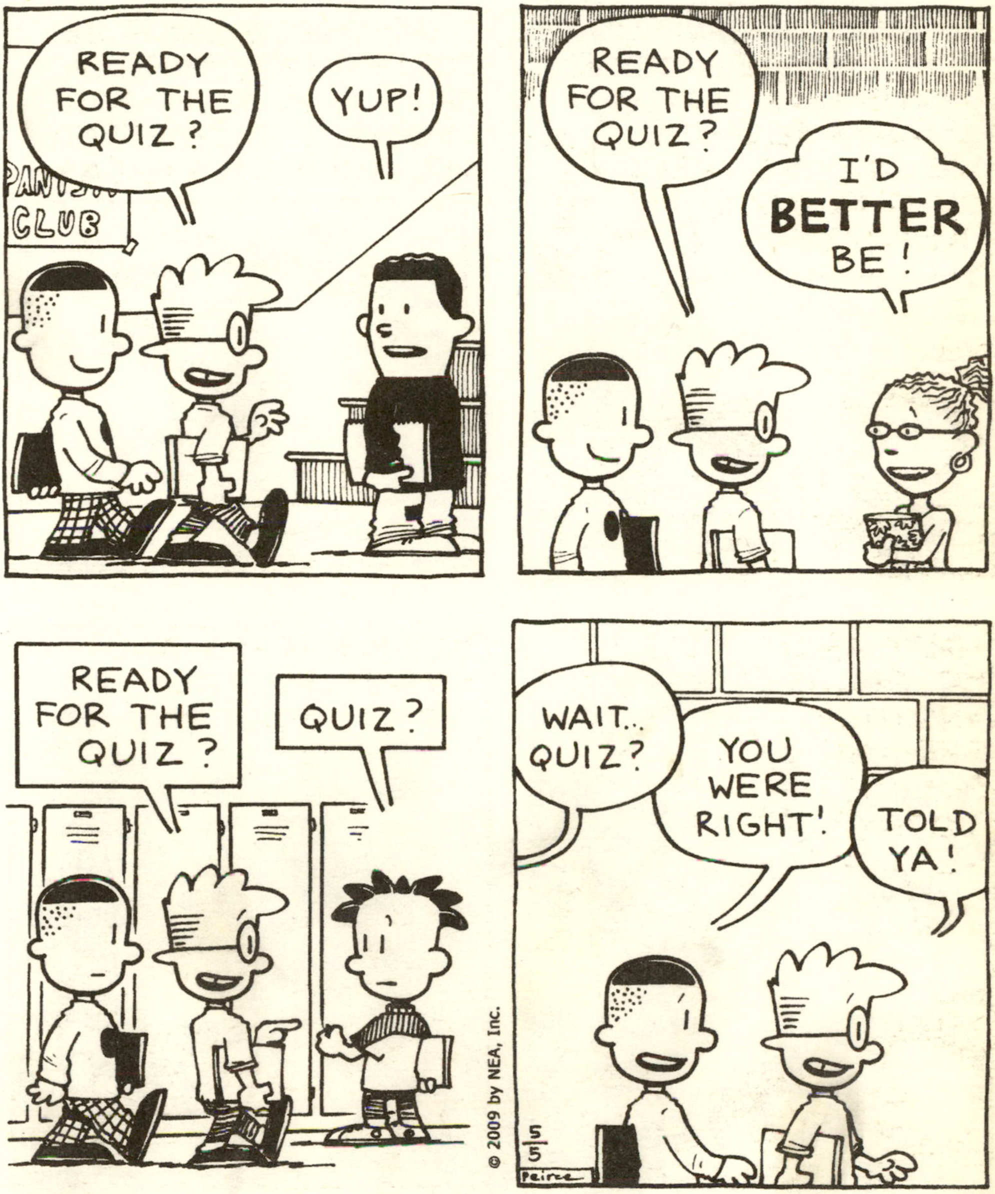

READY FOR THE QUIZ?
YUP!
PANISH CLUB
READY FOR THE QUIZ?
I'D BETTER BE!
READY FOR THE QUIZ?
QUIZ?
WAIT.. QUIZ?
YOU WERE RIGHT!
TOLD YA!
5/5
Peirce

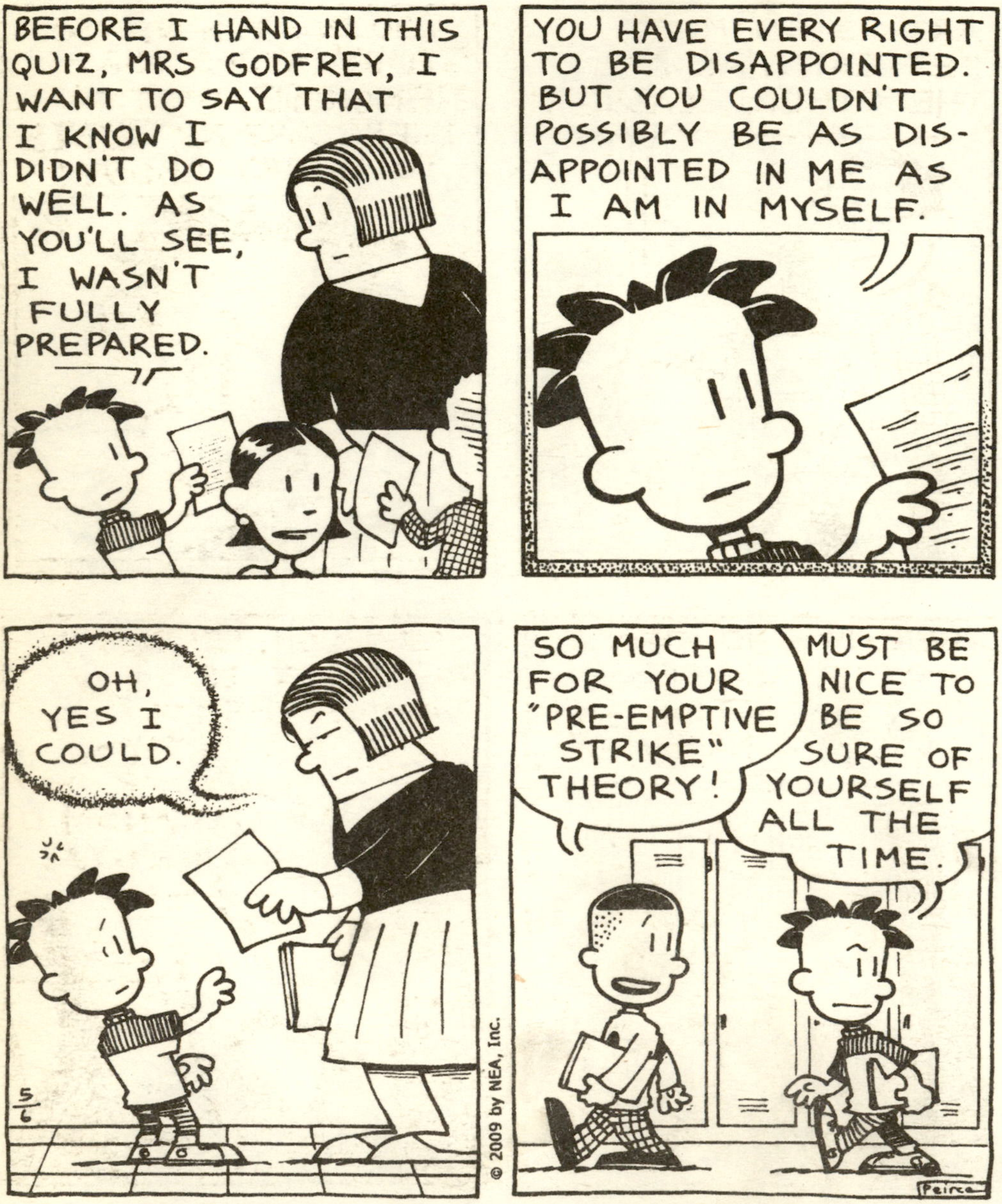
BEFORE I HAND IN THIS QUIZ, MRS GODFREY, I WANT TO SAY THAT I KNOW I DIDN'T DO WELL. AS YOU'LL SEE, I WASN'T FULLY PREPARED.
YOU HAVE EVERY RIGHT TO BE DISAPPOINTED. BUT YOU COULDN'T POSSIBLY BE AS DIS-APPOINTED IN ME AS I AM IN MYSELF.
OH, YES I COULD.
SO MUCH FOR YOUR "PRE-EMPTIVE STRIKE" THEORY!
MUST BE NICE TO BE SO SURE OF YOURSELF ALL THE TIME.
5/6
© 2009 by NEA, Inc.
Peirce

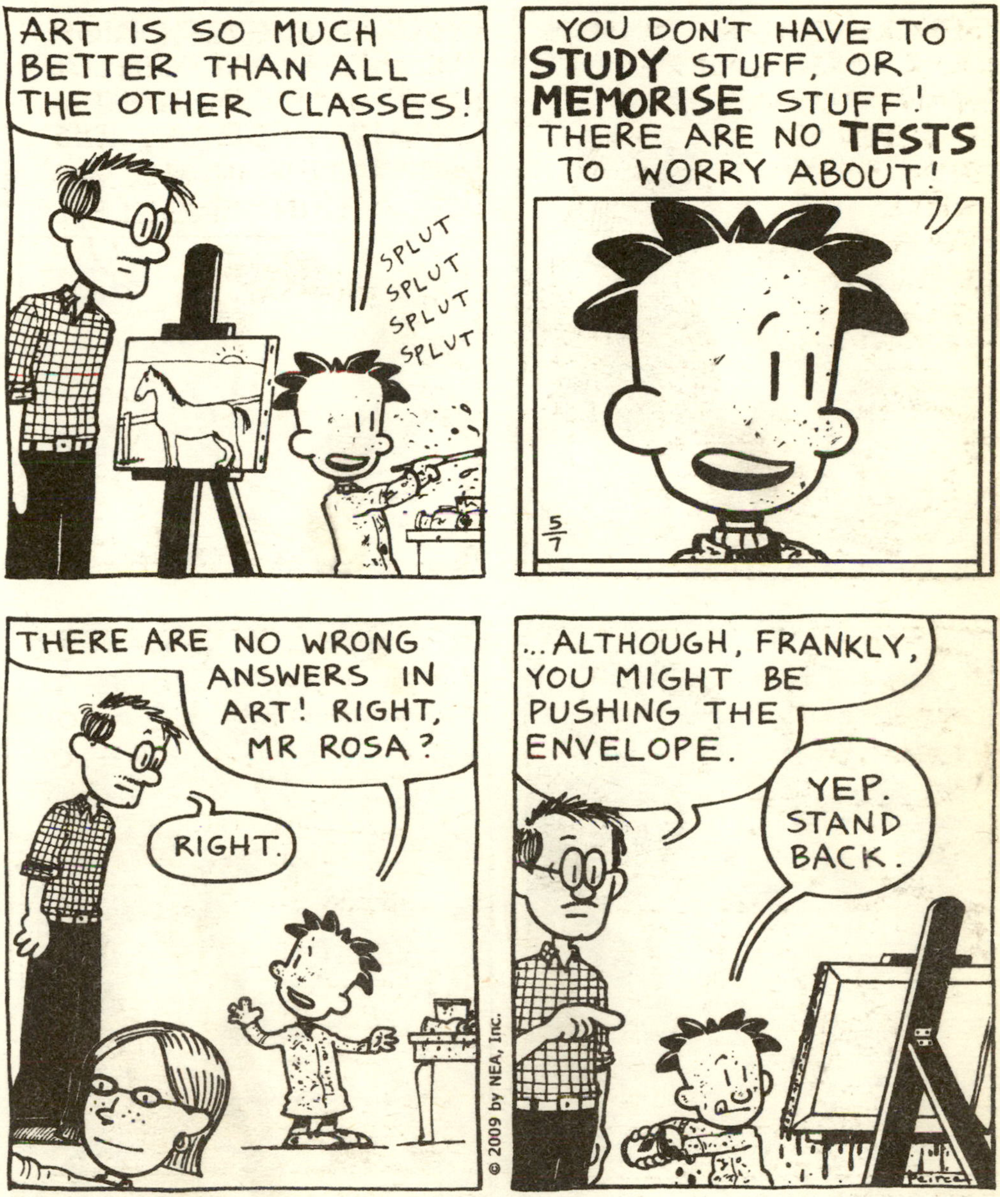
ART IS SO MUCH BETTER THAN ALL THE OTHER CLASSES!
SPLUT SPLUT SPLUT SPLUT
YOU DON'T HAVE TO **STUDY** STUFF, OR **MEMORISE** STUFF! THERE ARE NO **TESTS** TO WORRY ABOUT!
5/7
THERE ARE NO WRONG ANSWERS IN ART! RIGHT, MR ROSA?
RIGHT.
...ALTHOUGH, FRANKLY, YOU MIGHT BE PUSHING THE ENVELOPE.
YEP. STAND BACK.
Peirce

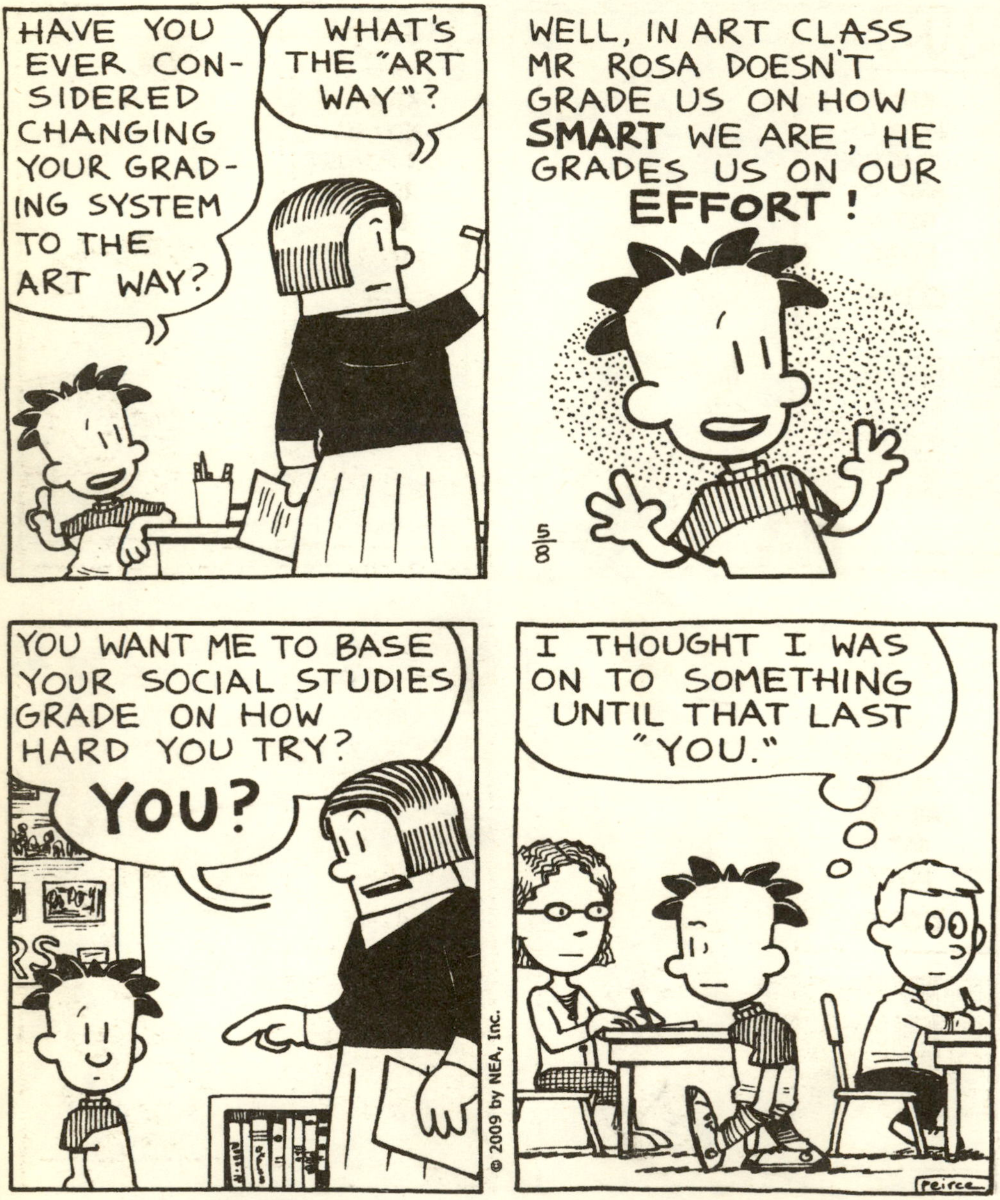
HAVE YOU EVER CONSIDERED CHANGING YOUR GRADING SYSTEM TO THE ART WAY?
WHAT'S THE "ART WAY"?
WELL, IN ART CLASS MR ROSA DOESN'T GRADE US ON HOW **SMART** WE ARE, HE GRADES US ON OUR **EFFORT**!
5/8
YOU WANT ME TO BASE YOUR SOCIAL STUDIES GRADE ON HOW HARD YOU TRY?
YOU?
© 2009 by NEA, Inc.
I THOUGHT I WAS ON TO SOMETHING UNTIL THAT LAST "YOU."
peirce

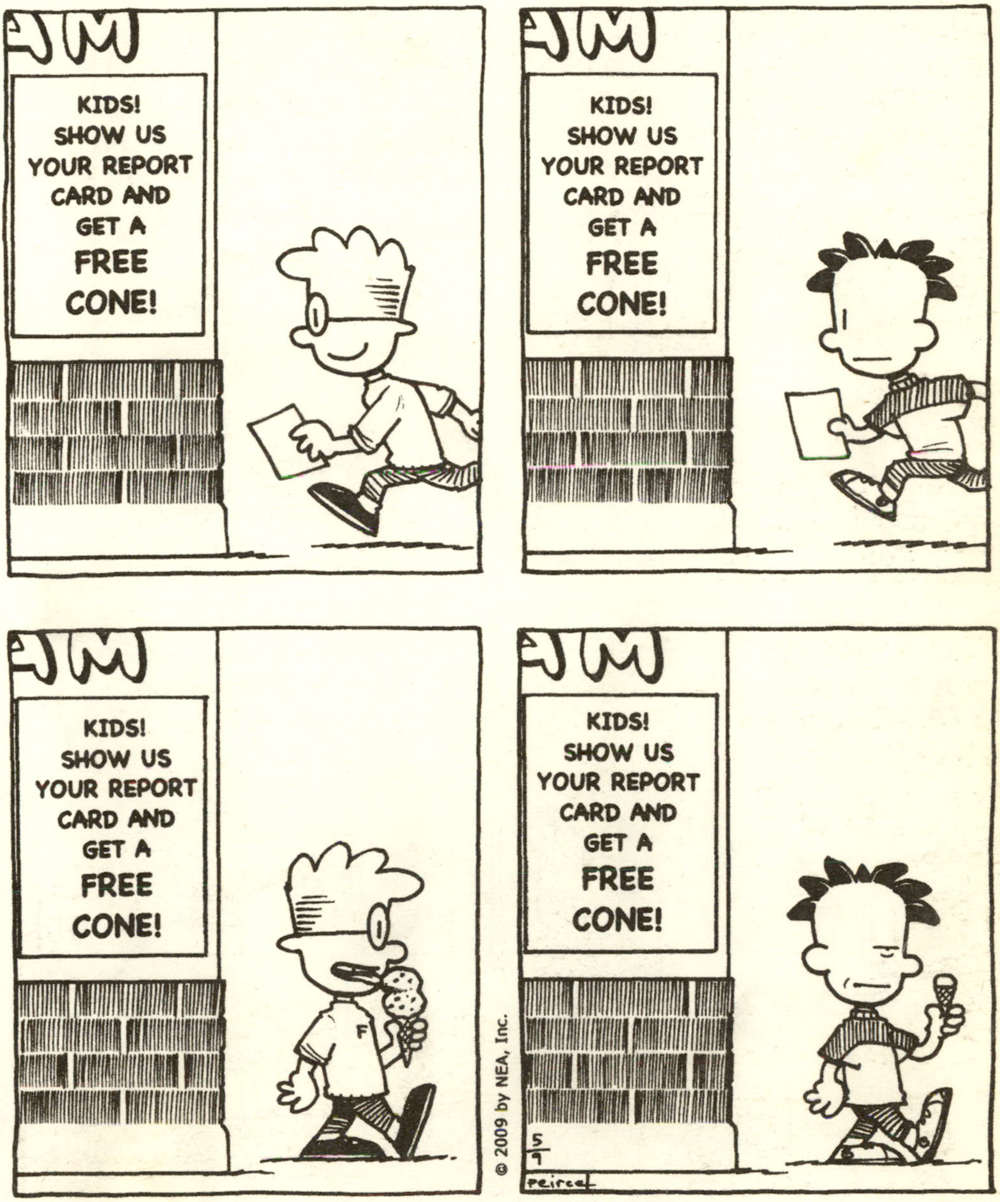
KIDS! SHOW US YOUR REPORT CARD AND GET A FREE CONE!
KIDS! SHOW US YOUR REPORT CARD AND GET A FREE CONE!
KIDS! SHOW US YOUR REPORT CARD AND GET A FREE CONE!
KIDS! SHOW US YOUR REPORT CARD AND GET A FREE CONE!
© 2009 by NEA, Inc.
5/9
peirce

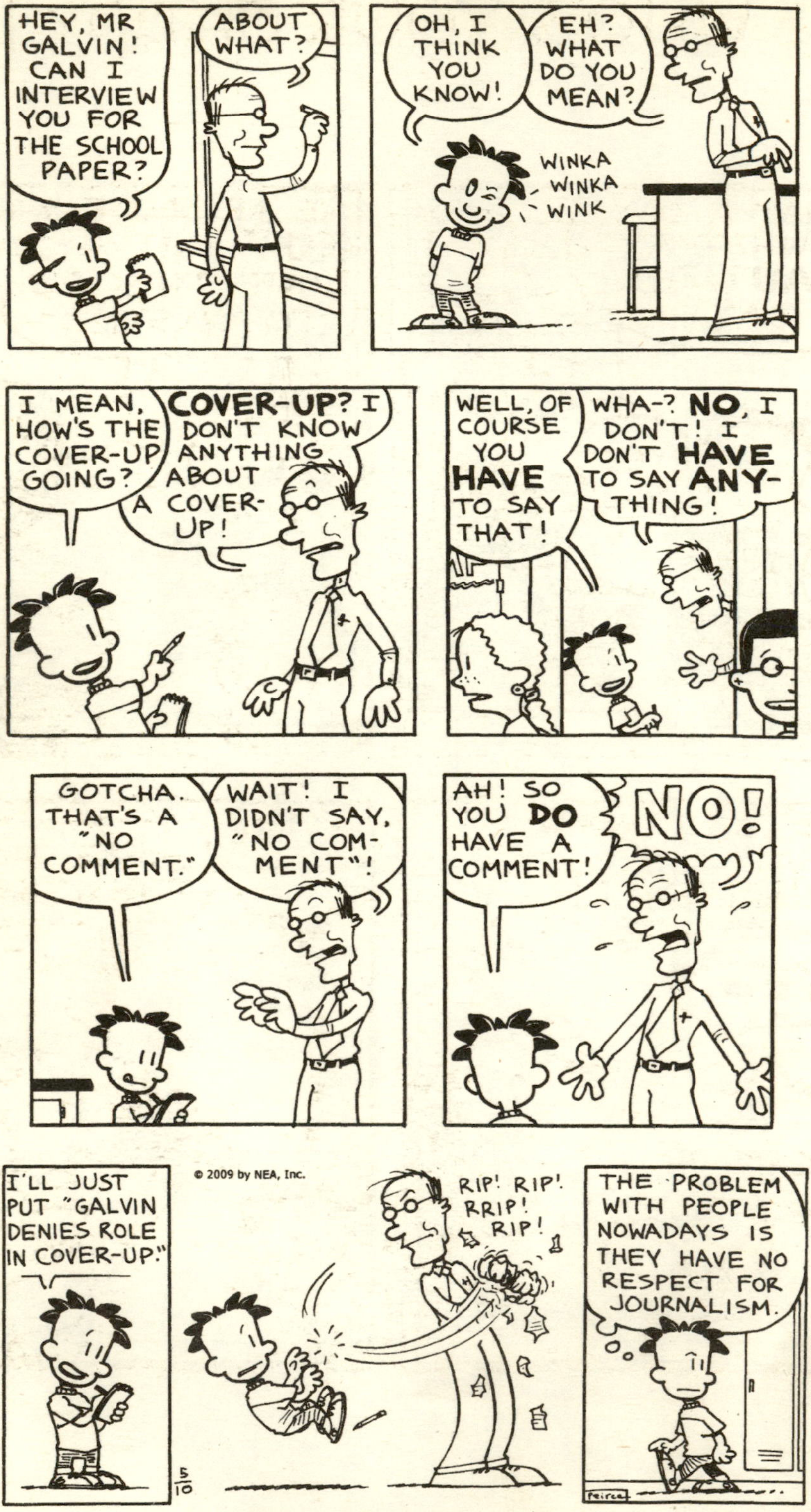
HEY, MR GALVIN! CAN I INTERVIEW YOU FOR THE SCHOOL PAPER?
ABOUT WHAT?
OH, I THINK YOU KNOW!
EH? WHAT DO YOU MEAN?
WINKA WINKA WINK
I MEAN, HOW'S THE COVER-UP GOING?
COVER-UP? I DON'T KNOW ANYTHING ABOUT A COVER-UP!
WELL, OF COURSE YOU **HAVE** TO SAY THAT!
WHA-? **NO**, I DON'T! I DON'T **HAVE** TO SAY **ANY**-THING!
GOTCHA. THAT'S A "NO COMMENT."
WAIT! I DIDN'T SAY, "NO COMMENT"!
AH! SO YOU **DO** HAVE A COMMENT!
NO!
I'LL JUST PUT "GALVIN DENIES ROLE IN COVER-UP."
© 2009 by NEA, Inc.
RIP! RIP! RRIP! RIP!
THE PROBLEM WITH PEOPLE NOWADAYS IS THEY HAVE NO RESPECT FOR JOURNALISM.
5/10
Peirce

WHO'S YOUR CADDY?

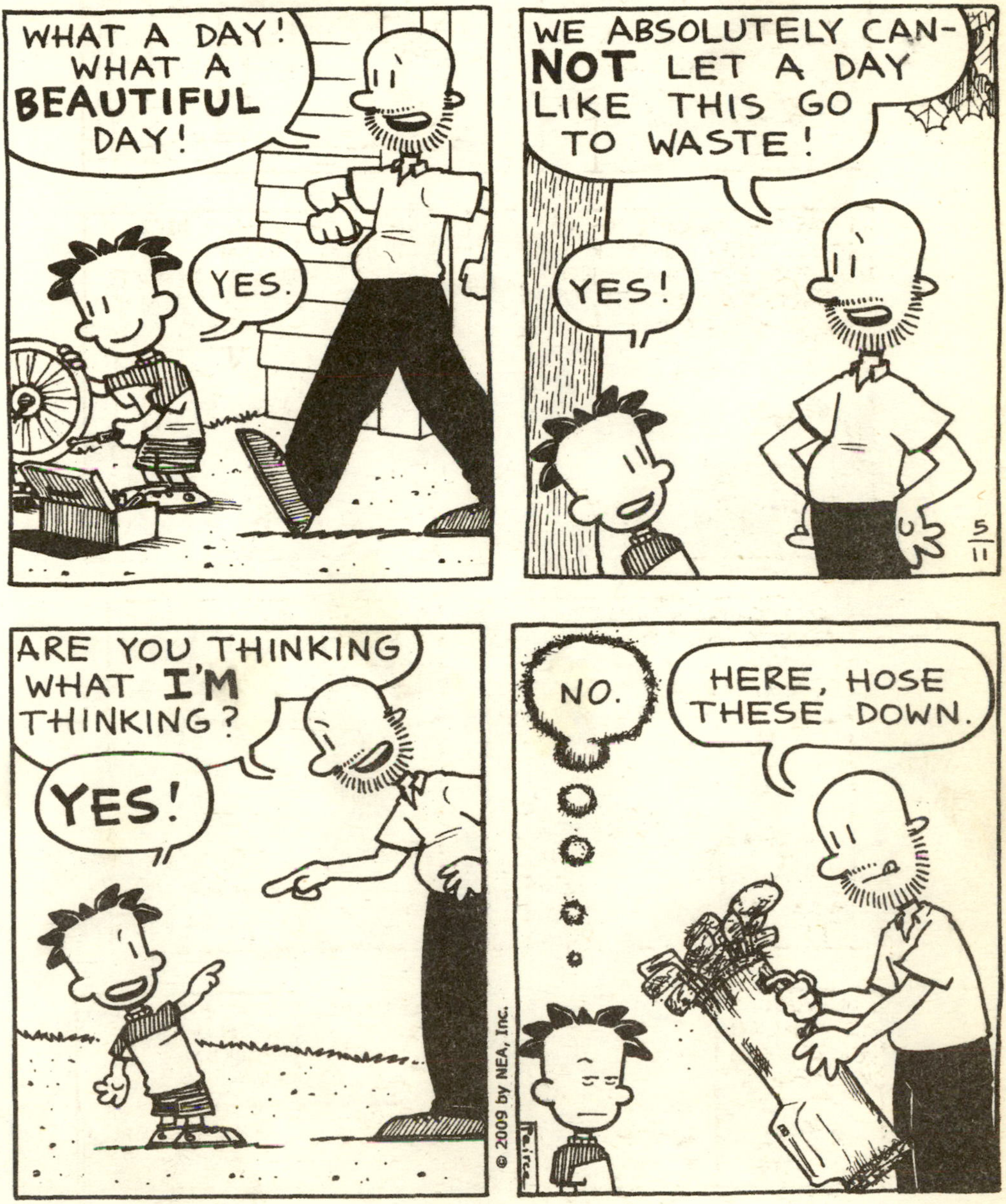
WHAT A DAY! WHAT A BEAUTIFUL DAY!
YES.
WE ABSOLUTELY CAN-NOT LET A DAY LIKE THIS GO TO WASTE!
YES!
5/11
ARE YOU THINKING WHAT I'M THINKING?
YES!
© 2009 by NEA, Inc.
NO.
HERE, HOSE THESE DOWN.

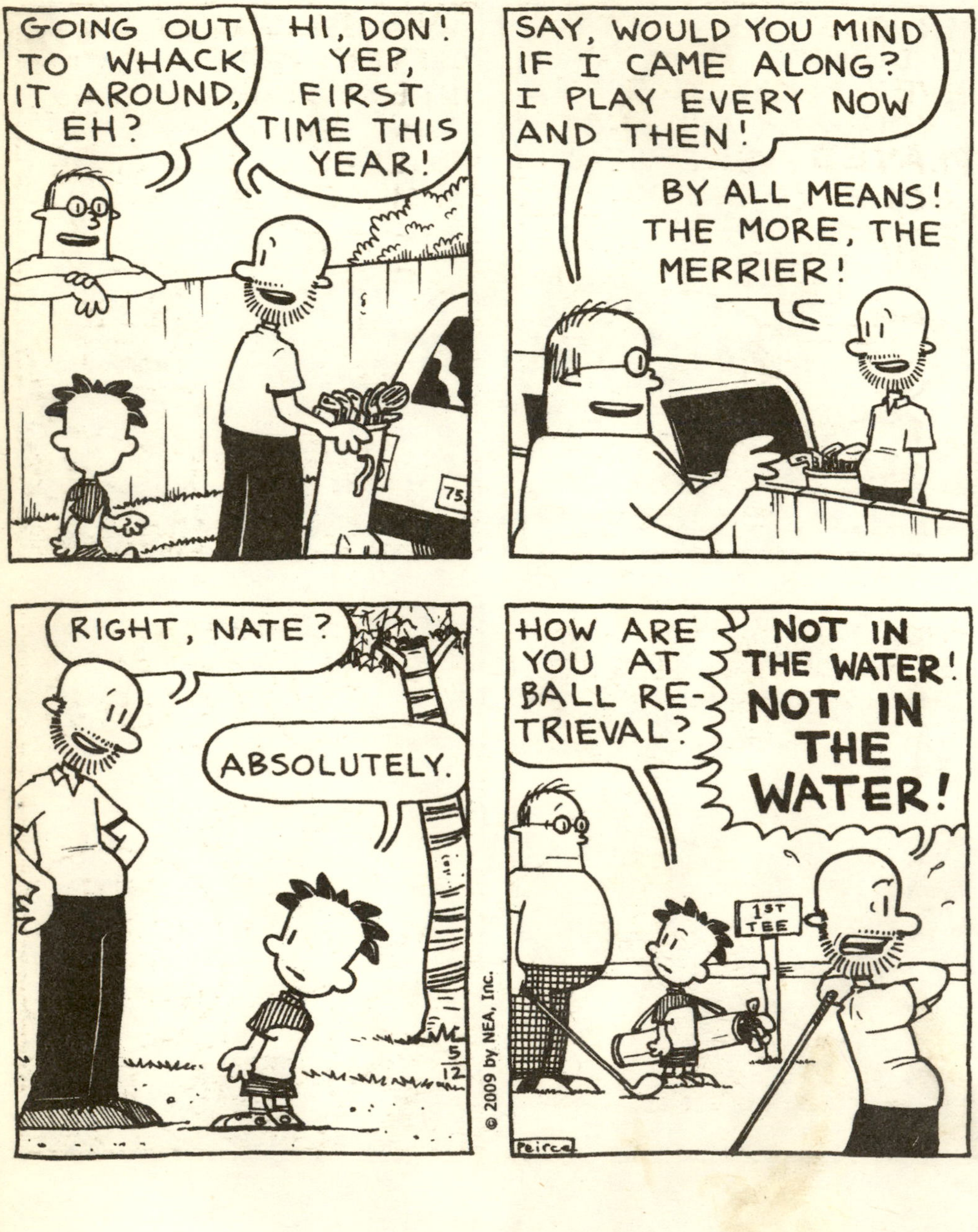
GOING OUT TO WHACK IT AROUND, EH?
HI, DON! YEP, FIRST TIME THIS YEAR!
75
SAY, WOULD YOU MIND IF I CAME ALONG? I PLAY EVERY NOW AND THEN!
BY ALL MEANS! THE MORE, THE MERRIER!
RIGHT, NATE?
ABSOLUTELY.
5/12
© 2009 by NEA, Inc.
HOW ARE YOU AT BALL RE-TRIEVAL?
NOT IN THE WATER! NOT IN THE WATER!
1ST TEE
Peirce

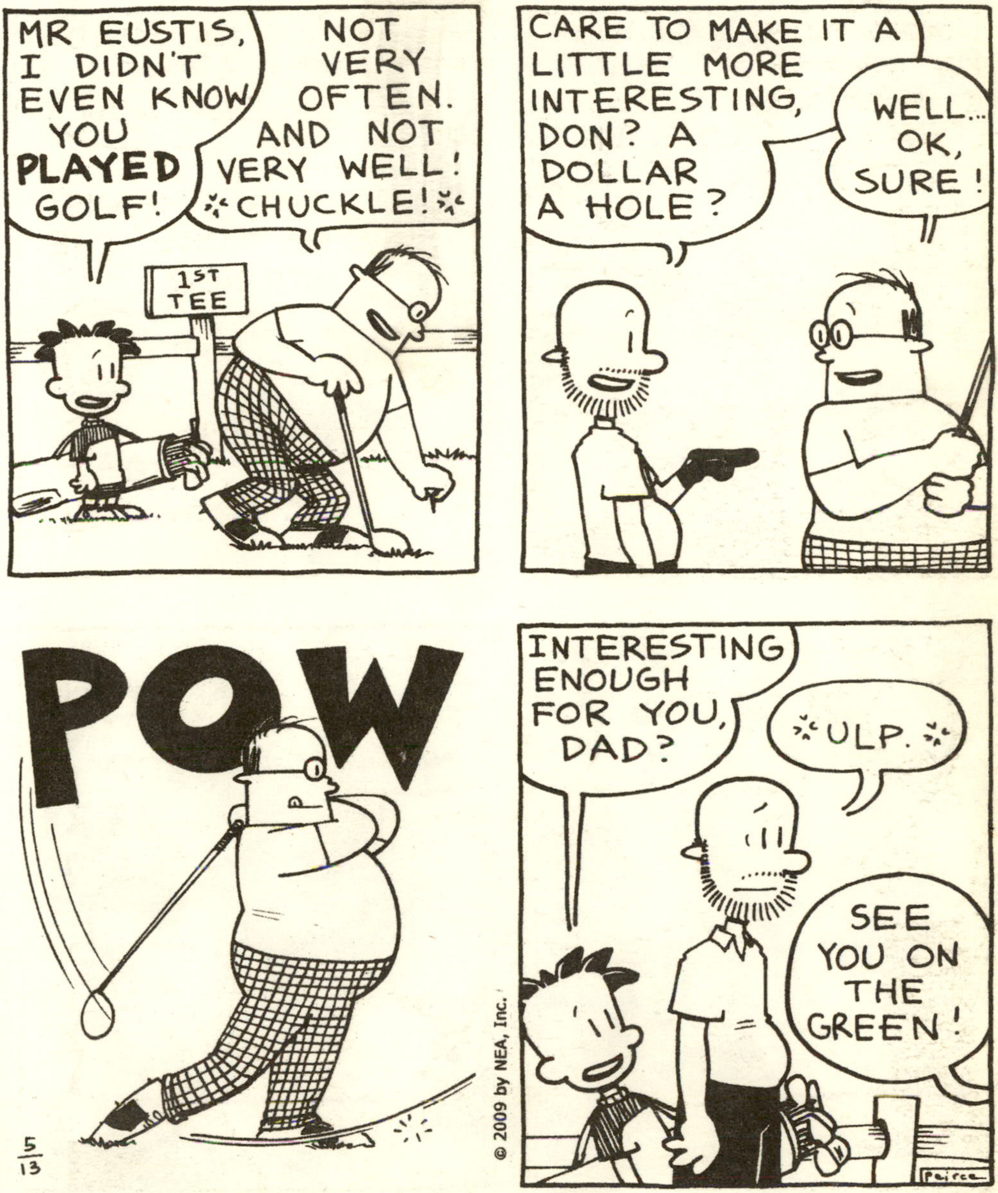
MR EUSTIS, I DIDN'T EVEN KNOW YOU **PLAYED** GOLF!
NOT VERY OFTEN. AND NOT VERY WELL! *CHUCKLE!*
1ST TEE
CARE TO MAKE IT A LITTLE MORE INTERESTING, DON? A DOLLAR A HOLE?
WELL... OK, SURE!
POW
5/13
© 2009 by NEA, Inc.
INTERESTING ENOUGH FOR YOU, DAD?
ULP.
SEE YOU ON THE GREEN!
Peirce

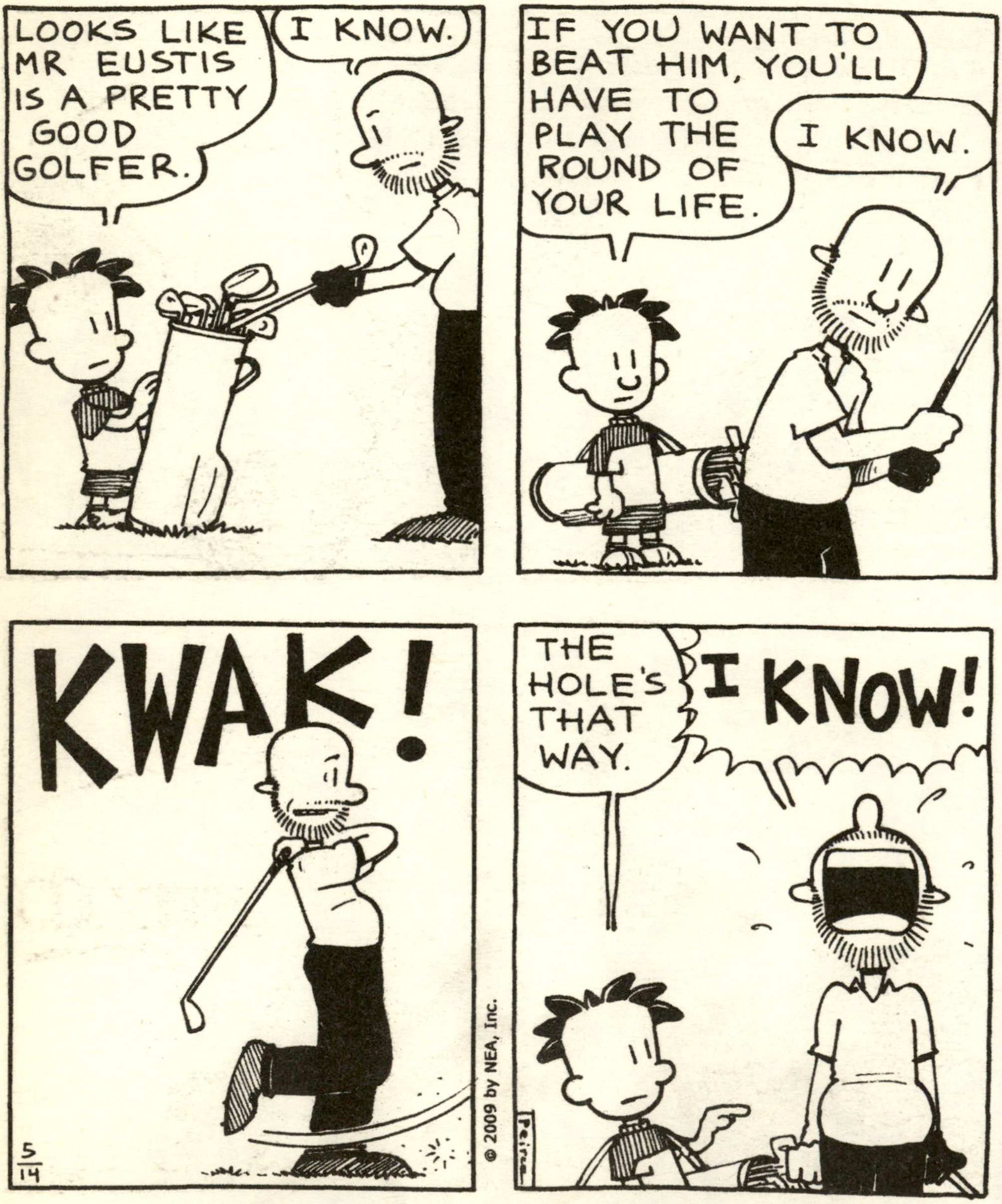
LOOKS LIKE MR EUSTIS IS A PRETTY GOOD GOLFER.
I KNOW.
IF YOU WANT TO BEAT HIM, YOU'LL HAVE TO PLAY THE ROUND OF YOUR LIFE.
I KNOW.
KWAK!
THE HOLE'S THAT WAY.
I KNOW!
5/14
© 2009 by NEA, Inc.
Peirce

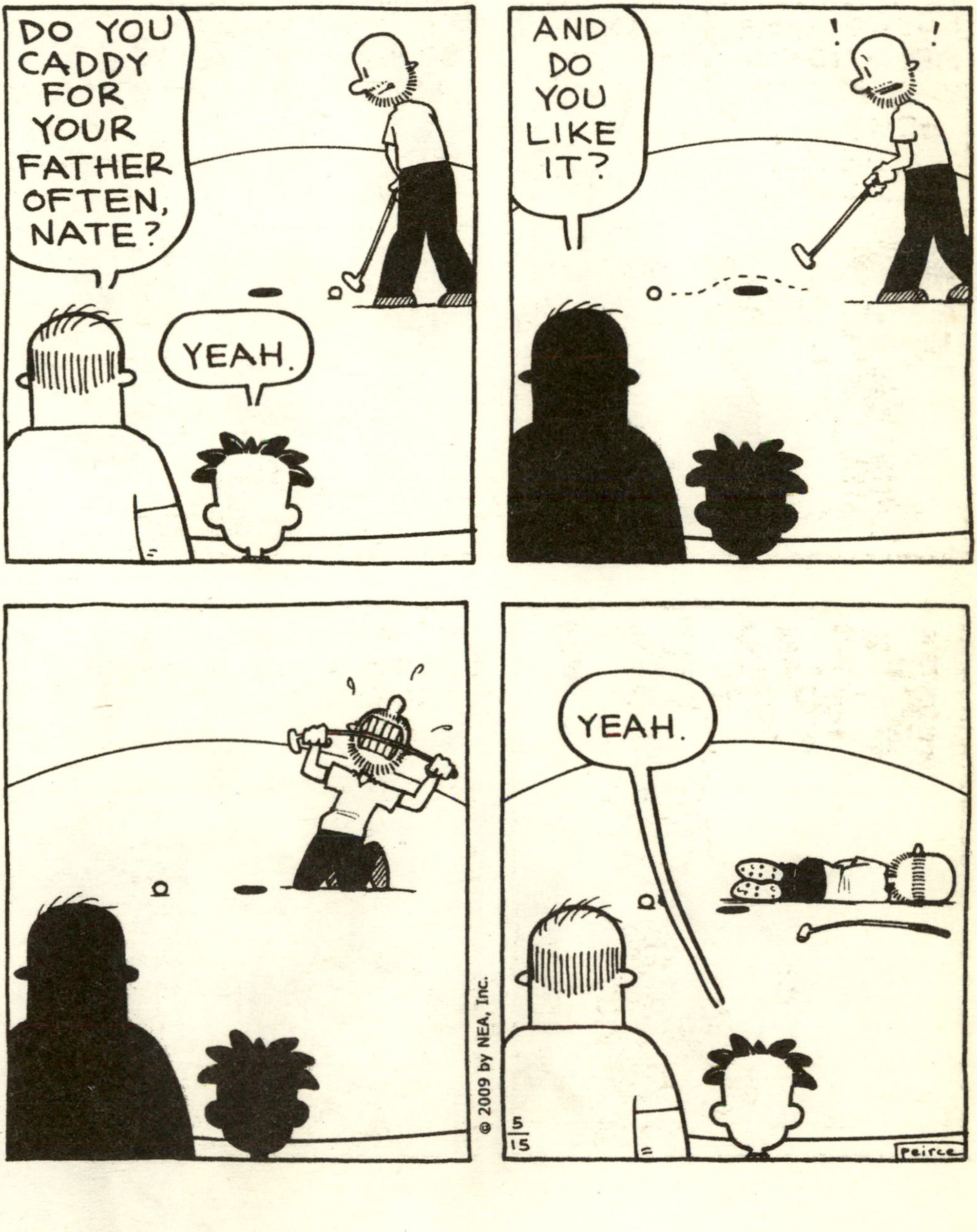
DO YOU CADDY FOR YOUR FATHER OFTEN, NATE?
YEAH.
AND DO YOU LIKE IT?
! !
YEAH.
© 2009 by NEA, Inc.
5/15
Peirce

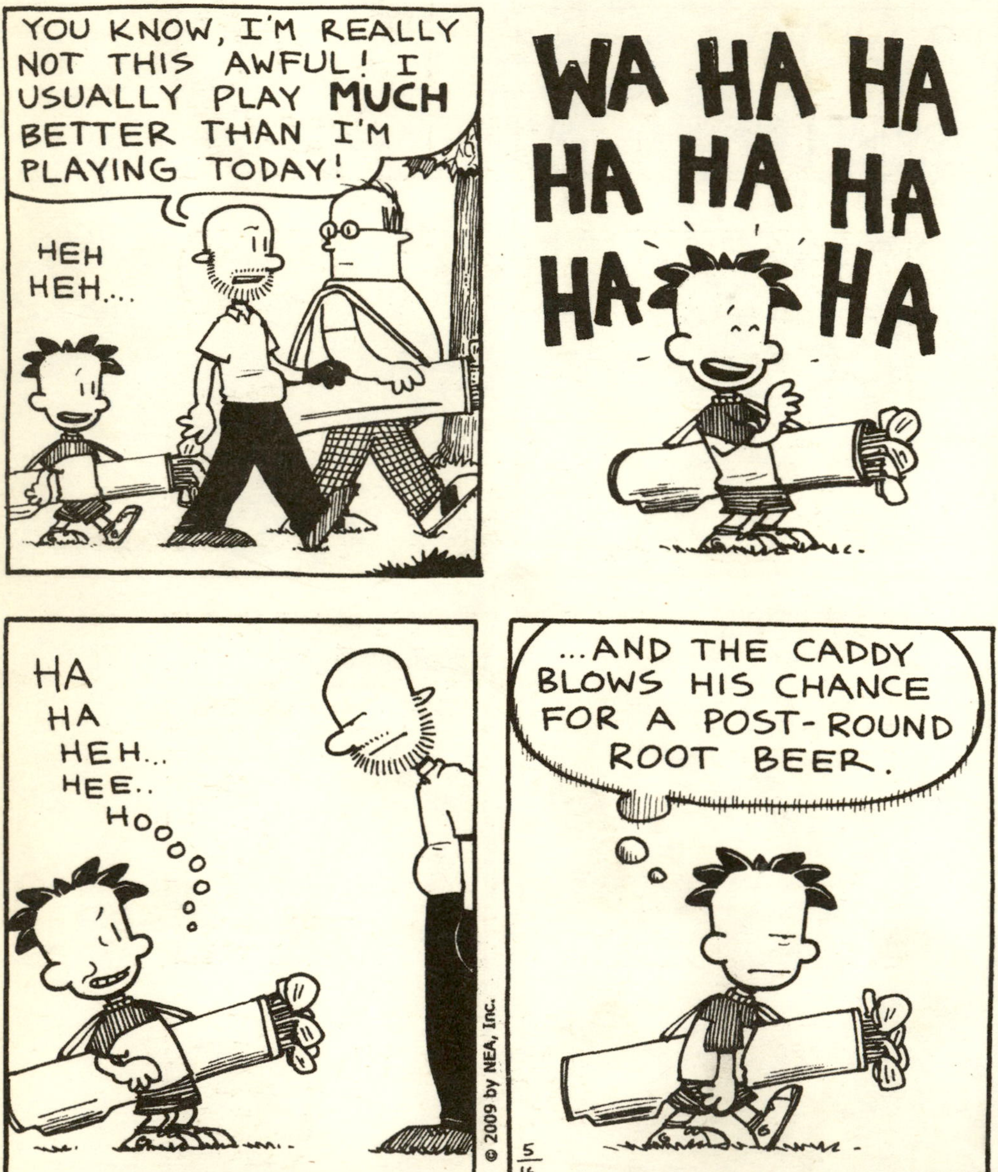
YOU KNOW, I'M REALLY NOT THIS AWFUL! I USUALLY PLAY MUCH BETTER THAN I'M PLAYING TODAY!
HEH HEH....
WA HA HA HA HA HA HA HA HA
HA HA HEH... HEE.. HOOOOOOO
...AND THE CADDY BLOWS HIS CHANCE FOR A POST-ROUND ROOT BEER.
© 2009 by NEA, Inc.
5/16
Peirce

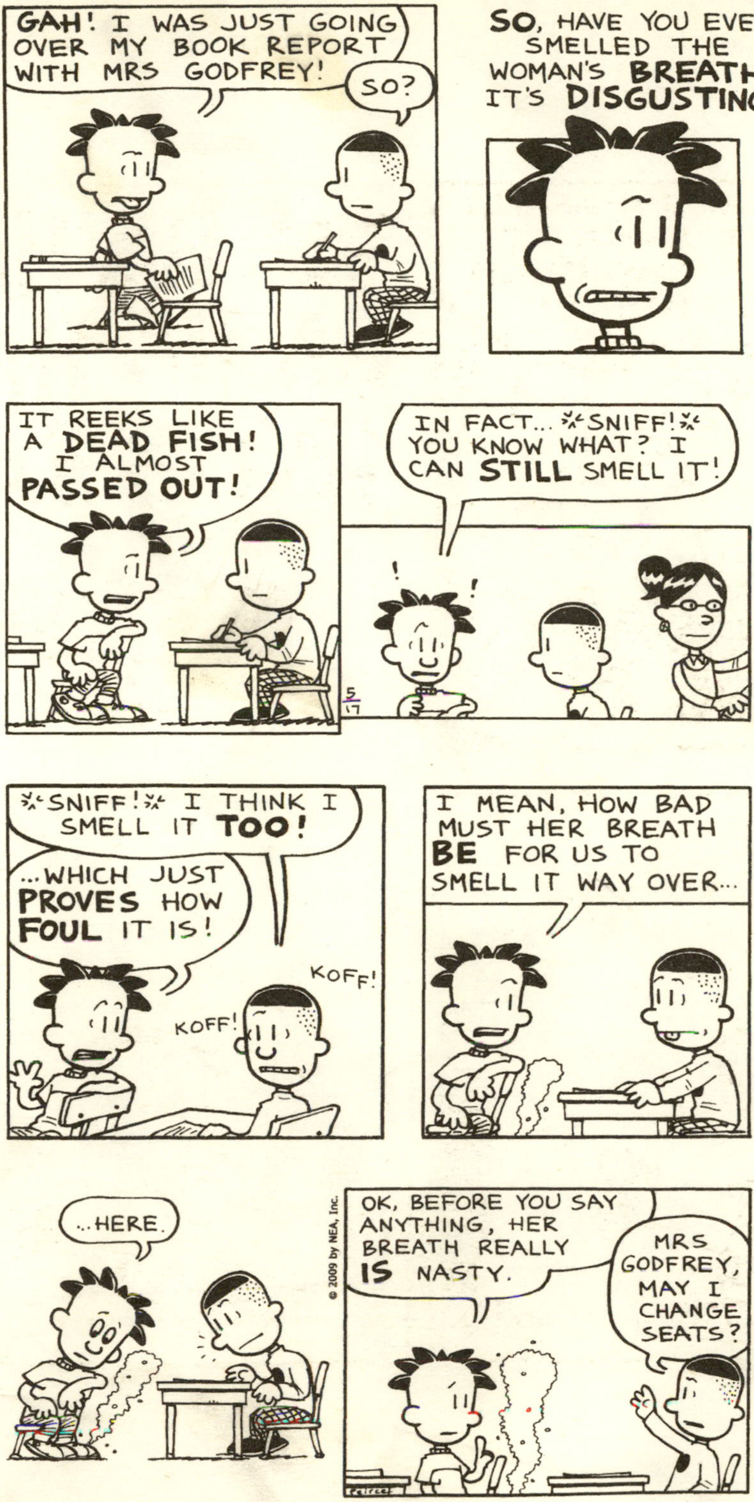
GAH! I WAS JUST GOING OVER MY BOOK REPORT WITH MRS GODFREY!
SO?
SO, HAVE YOU EVER SMELLED THE WOMAN'S BREATH? IT'S DISGUSTING!
IT REEKS LIKE A DEAD FISH! I ALMOST PASSED OUT!
IN FACT... *SNIFF!* YOU KNOW WHAT? I CAN STILL SMELL IT!
!
!
SNIFF! I THINK I SMELL IT TOO!
...WHICH JUST PROVES HOW FOUL IT IS!
KOFF!
KOFF!
I MEAN, HOW BAD MUST HER BREATH BE FOR US TO SMELL IT WAY OVER...
...HERE.
OK, BEFORE YOU SAY ANYTHING, HER BREATH REALLY IS NASTY.
MRS GODFREY, MAY I CHANGE SEATS?
© 2009 by NEA, Inc.

25 . . . AND COUNTING

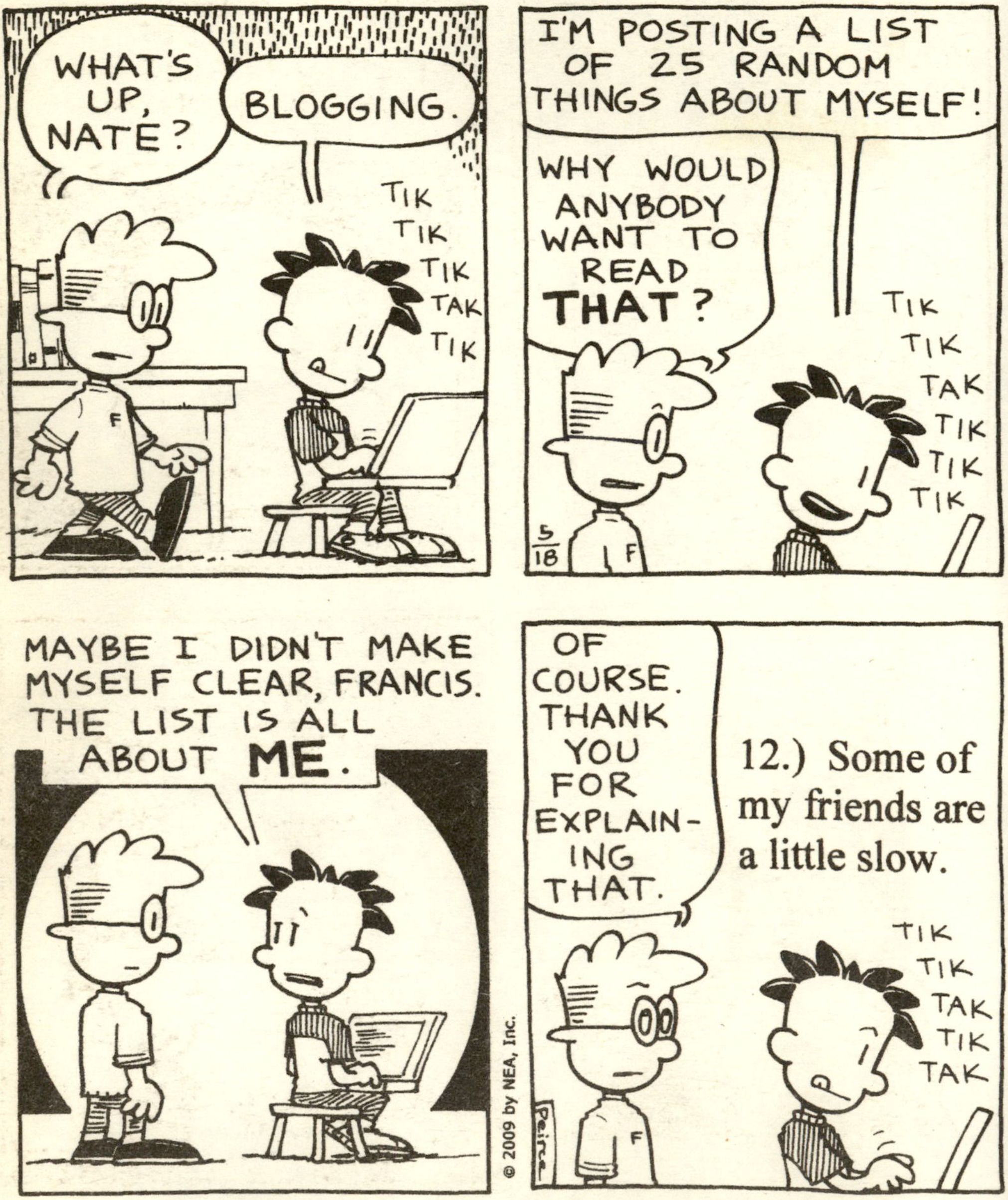
WHAT'S UP, NATE?
BLOGGING.
TIK TIK TIK TAK TIK
I'M POSTING A LIST OF 25 RANDOM THINGS ABOUT MYSELF!
WHY WOULD ANYBODY WANT TO READ **THAT**?
TIK TIK TAK TIK TIK TIK
5/18
MAYBE I DIDN'T MAKE MYSELF CLEAR, FRANCIS. THE LIST IS ALL ABOUT **ME**.
© 2009 by NEA, Inc.
OF COURSE. THANK YOU FOR EXPLAINING THAT.
12.) Some of my friends are a little slow.
TIK TIK TAK TIK TAK
Peirce

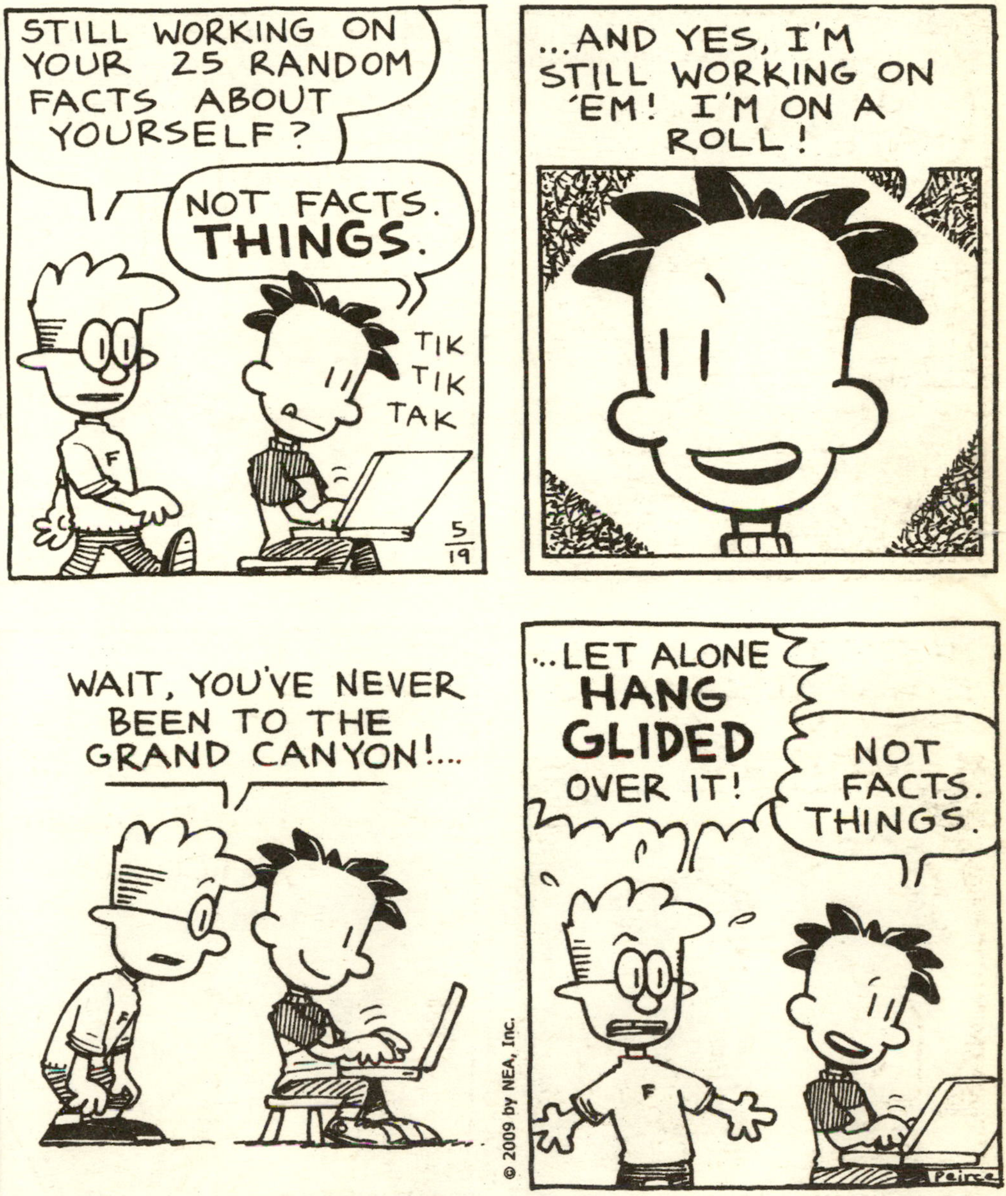
STILL WORKING ON YOUR 25 RANDOM FACTS ABOUT YOURSELF?
NOT FACTS. THINGS.
TIK TIK TAK
5/19
...AND YES, I'M STILL WORKING ON 'EM! I'M ON A ROLL!
WAIT, YOU'VE NEVER BEEN TO THE GRAND CANYON!...
© 2009 by NEA, Inc.
...LET ALONE HANG GLIDED OVER IT!
NOT FACTS. THINGS.
Peirce

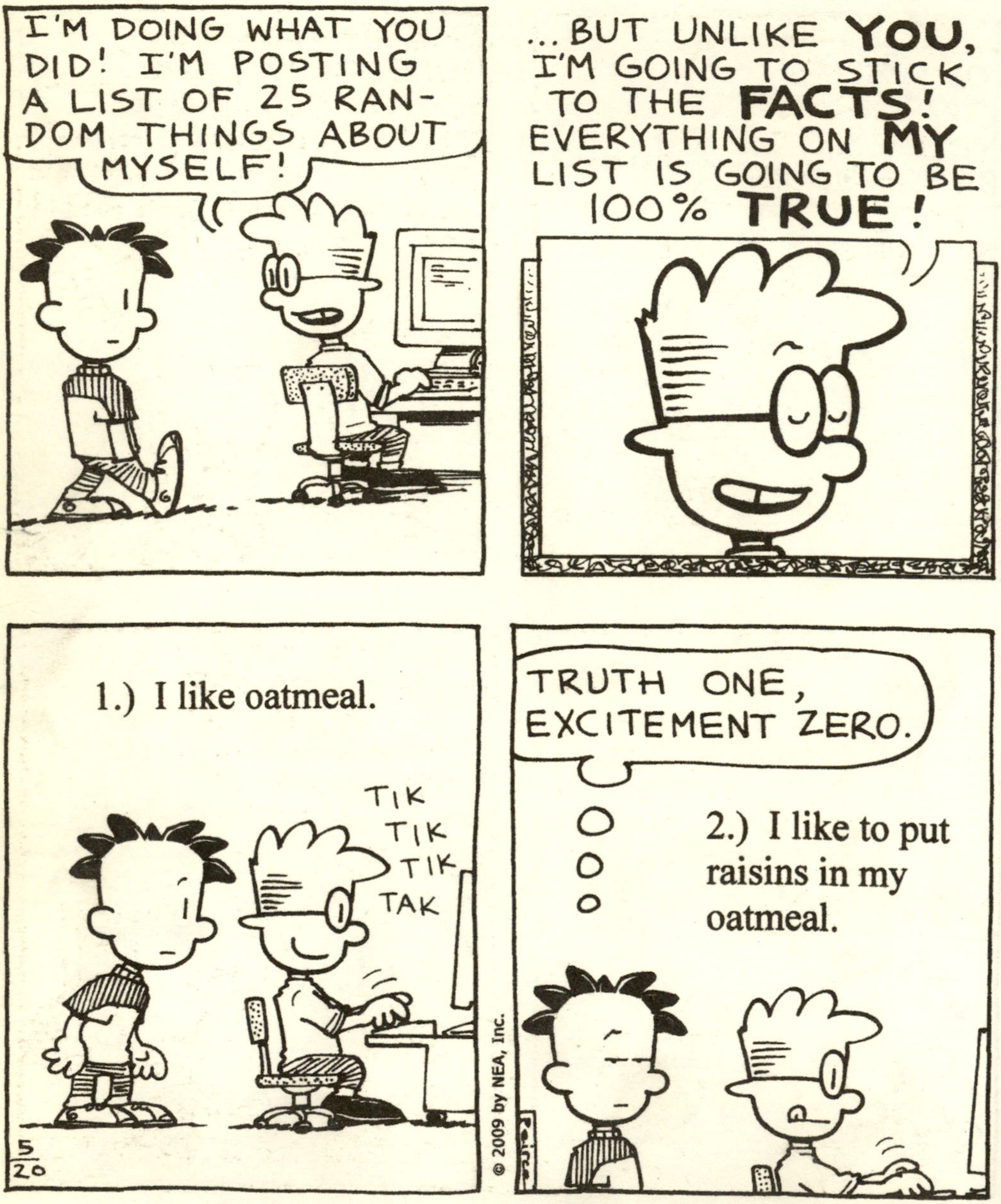
I'M DOING WHAT YOU DID! I'M POSTING A LIST OF 25 RANDOM THINGS ABOUT MYSELF!
...BUT UNLIKE YOU, I'M GOING TO STICK TO THE FACTS! EVERYTHING ON MY LIST IS GOING TO BE 100% TRUE!
1.) I like oatmeal.
TIK TIK TIK TAK
5/20
© 2009 by NEA, Inc.
TRUTH ONE, EXCITEMENT ZERO.
2.) I like to put raisins in my oatmeal.

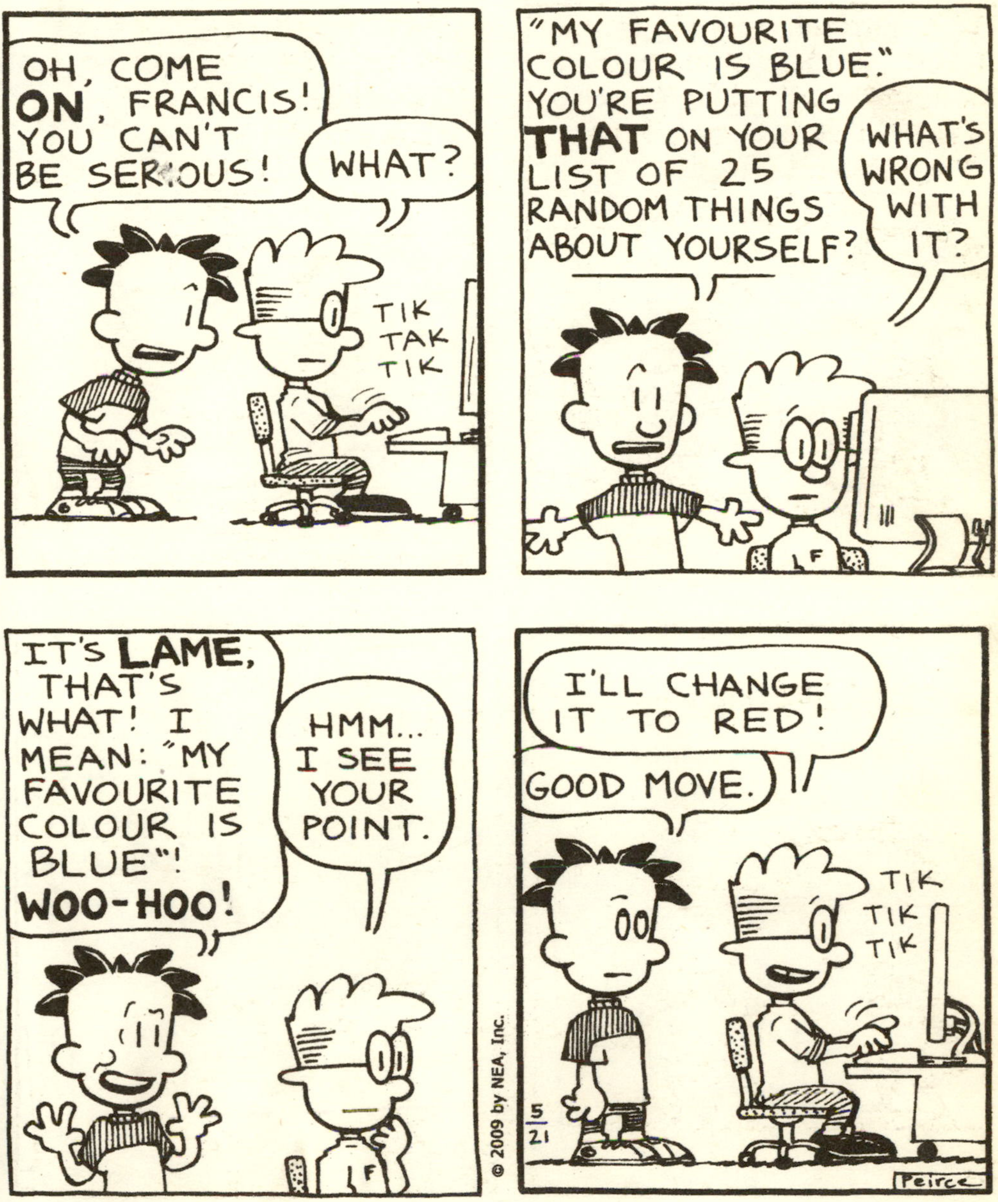
OH, COME **ON**, FRANCIS! YOU CAN'T BE SERIOUS!
WHAT?
TIK TAK TIK
"MY FAVOURITE COLOUR IS BLUE." YOU'RE PUTTING **THAT** ON YOUR LIST OF 25 RANDOM THINGS ABOUT YOURSELF?
WHAT'S WRONG WITH IT?
IT'S **LAME**, THAT'S WHAT! I MEAN: "MY FAVOURITE COLOUR IS BLUE"! **WOO-HOO**!
HMM... I SEE YOUR POINT.
I'LL CHANGE IT TO RED!
GOOD MOVE.
TIK TIK TIK
© 2009 by NEA, Inc.
5/21
Peirce

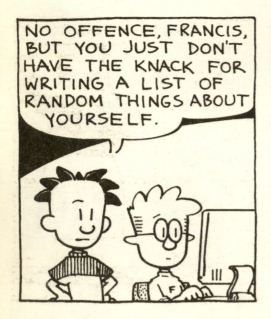

NO OFFENCE, FRANCIS, BUT YOU JUST DON'T HAVE THE KNACK FOR WRITING A LIST OF RANDOM THINGS ABOUT YOURSELF.

STEP ASIDE! **I** CAN DO A BETTER JOB OF SUMMING YOU UP THAN **YOU** CAN!

1.) I'm so lame, my friend has to write my list of 25 random things about myself.

TIK TIK
TAK TIK

THAT **IS** PRETTY LAME.

2.) Plus, I still haven't realised that he's charging me by the word.

TIK TIK TIK

© 2009 by NEA, Inc.

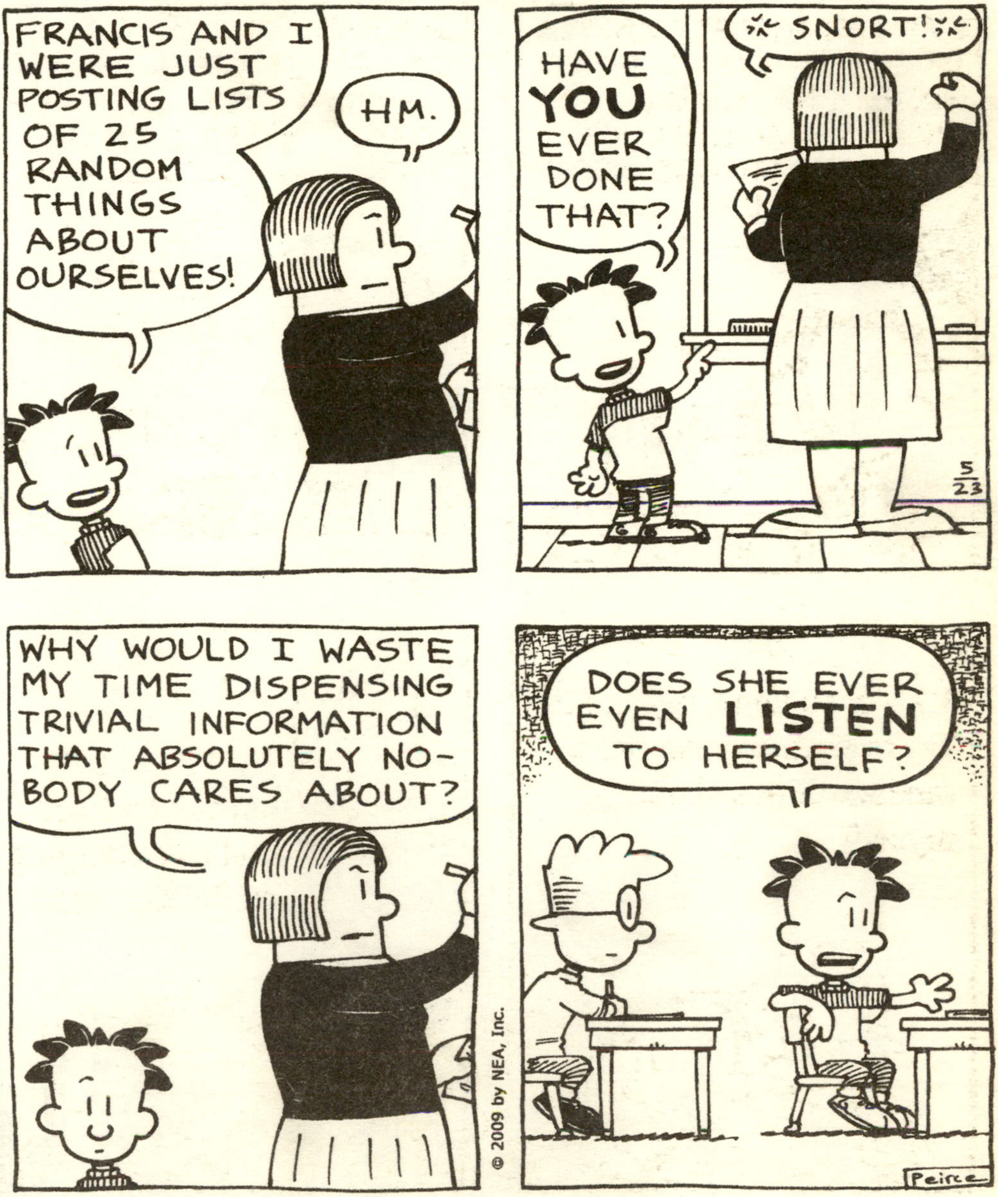
FRANCIS AND I WERE JUST POSTING LISTS OF 25 RANDOM THINGS ABOUT OURSELVES!
HM.
HAVE YOU EVER DONE THAT?
SNORT!
5/23
WHY WOULD I WASTE MY TIME DISPENSING TRIVIAL INFORMATION THAT ABSOLUTELY NOBODY CARES ABOUT?
© 2009 by NEA, Inc.
DOES SHE EVER EVEN LISTEN TO HERSELF?
Peirce

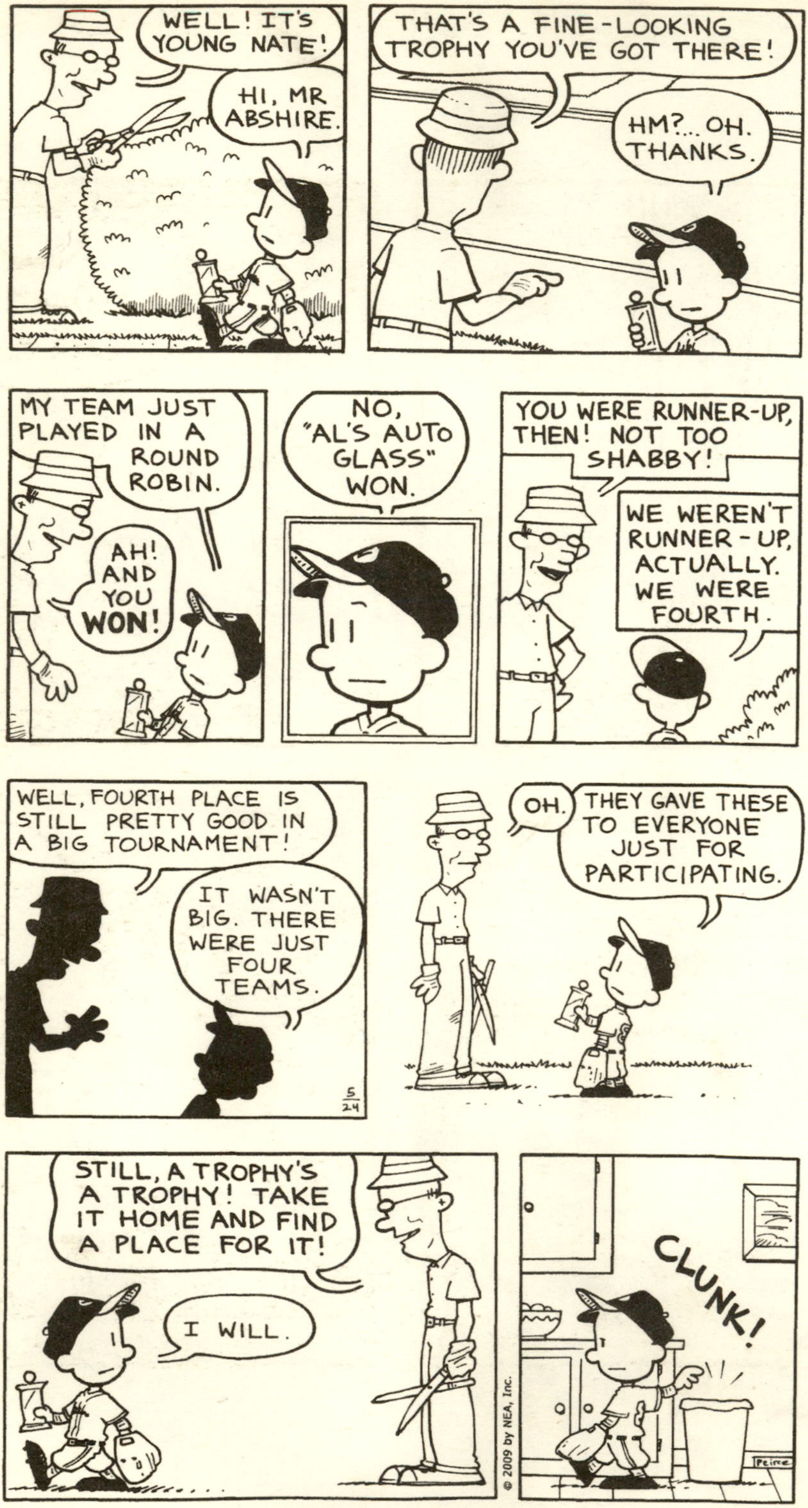
WELL! IT'S YOUNG NATE!
HI, MR ABSHIRE.
THAT'S A FINE-LOOKING TROPHY YOU'VE GOT THERE!
HM?... OH. THANKS.
MY TEAM JUST PLAYED IN A ROUND ROBIN.
AH! AND YOU WON!
NO, "AL'S AUTO GLASS" WON.
YOU WERE RUNNER-UP, THEN! NOT TOO SHABBY!
WE WEREN'T RUNNER-UP, ACTUALLY. WE WERE FOURTH.
WELL, FOURTH PLACE IS STILL PRETTY GOOD IN A BIG TOURNAMENT!
IT WASN'T BIG. THERE WERE JUST FOUR TEAMS.
5/24
OH.
THEY GAVE THESE TO EVERYONE JUST FOR PARTICIPATING.
STILL, A TROPHY'S A TROPHY! TAKE IT HOME AND FIND A PLACE FOR IT!
I WILL.
© 2009 by NEA, Inc.
CLUNK!
Peirce

HELLO, GORGEOUS!

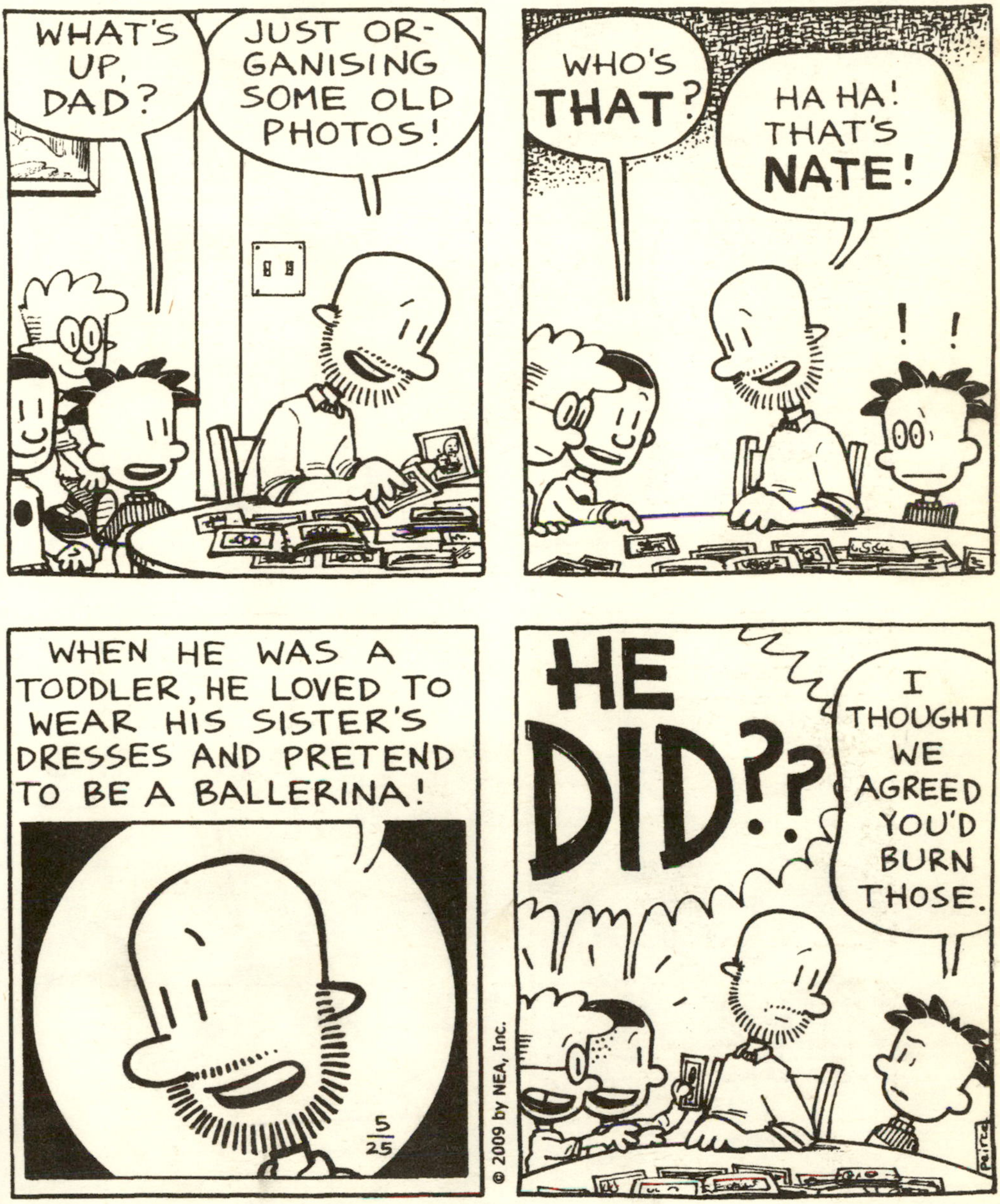
WHAT'S UP, DAD?
JUST OR-GANISING SOME OLD PHOTOS!
WHO'S **THAT**?
HA HA! THAT'S **NATE**!
! !
WHEN HE WAS A TODDLER, HE LOVED TO WEAR HIS SISTER'S DRESSES AND PRETEND TO BE A BALLERINA!
5/25
HE DID??
I THOUGHT WE AGREED YOU'D BURN THOSE.
© 2009 by NEA, Inc.
Peirce

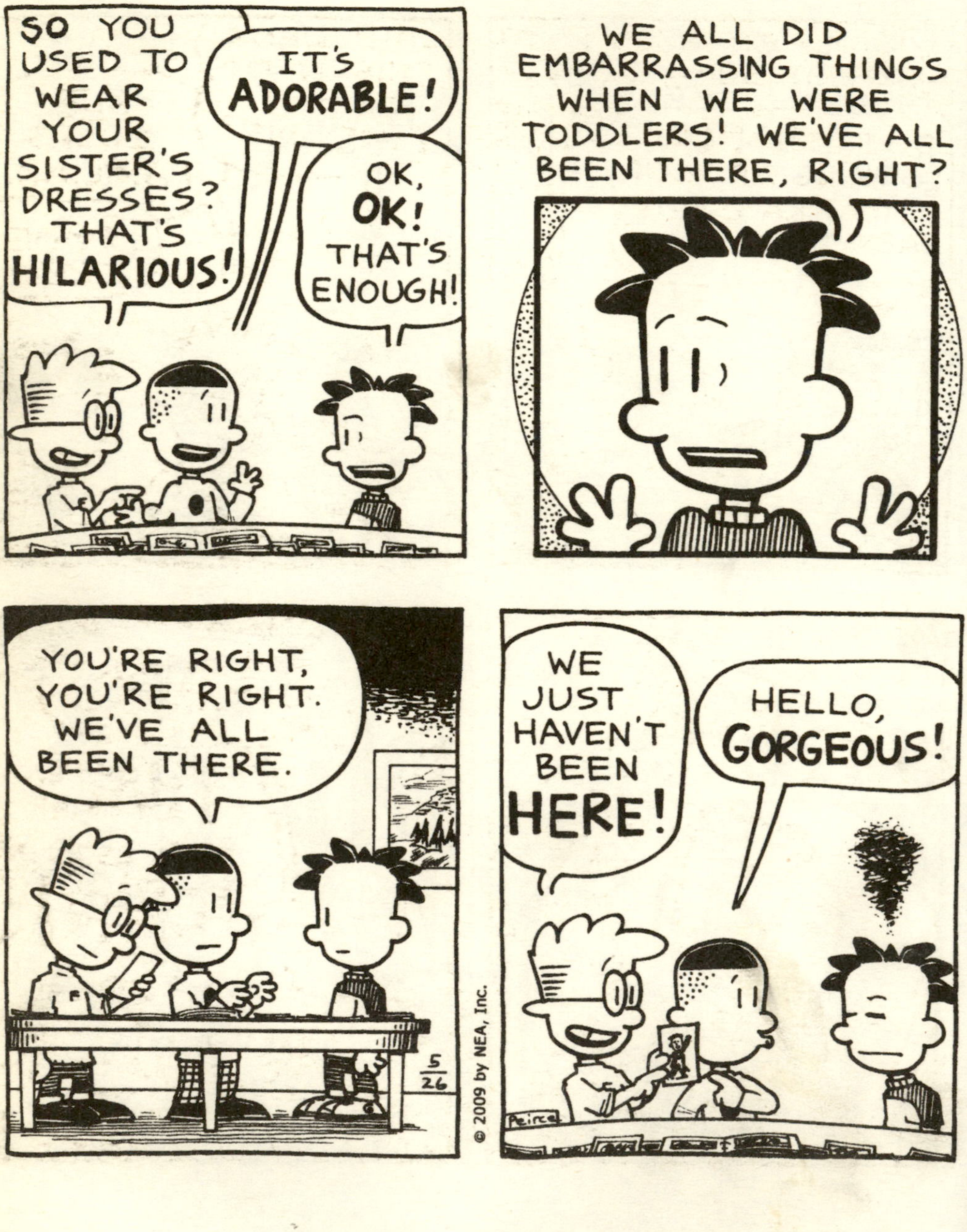
SO YOU USED TO WEAR YOUR SISTER'S DRESSES? THAT'S HILARIOUS!
IT'S ADORABLE!
OK, OK! THAT'S ENOUGH!
WE ALL DID EMBARRASSING THINGS WHEN WE WERE TODDLERS! WE'VE ALL BEEN THERE, RIGHT?
YOU'RE RIGHT, YOU'RE RIGHT. WE'VE ALL BEEN THERE.
5/26
© 2009 by NEA, Inc.
WE JUST HAVEN'T BEEN HERE!
HELLO, GORGEOUS!
Peirce

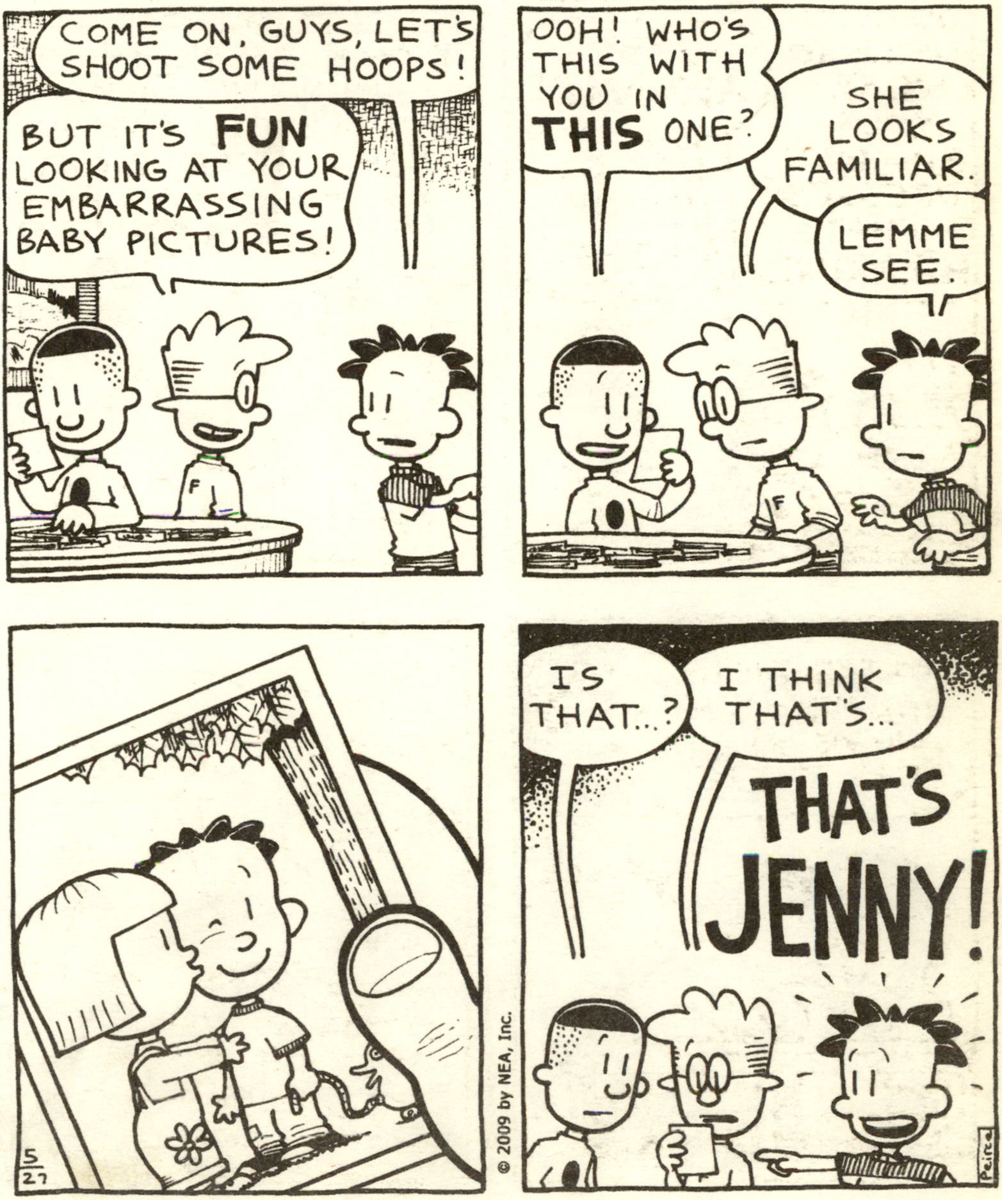
COME ON, GUYS, LET'S SHOOT SOME HOOPS!
BUT IT'S FUN LOOKING AT YOUR EMBARRASSING BABY PICTURES!
OOH! WHO'S THIS WITH YOU IN THIS ONE?
SHE LOOKS FAMILIAR.
LEMME SEE.
5/27
© 2009 by NEA, Inc.
IS THAT...?
I THINK THAT'S...
THAT'S JENNY!
Peirce

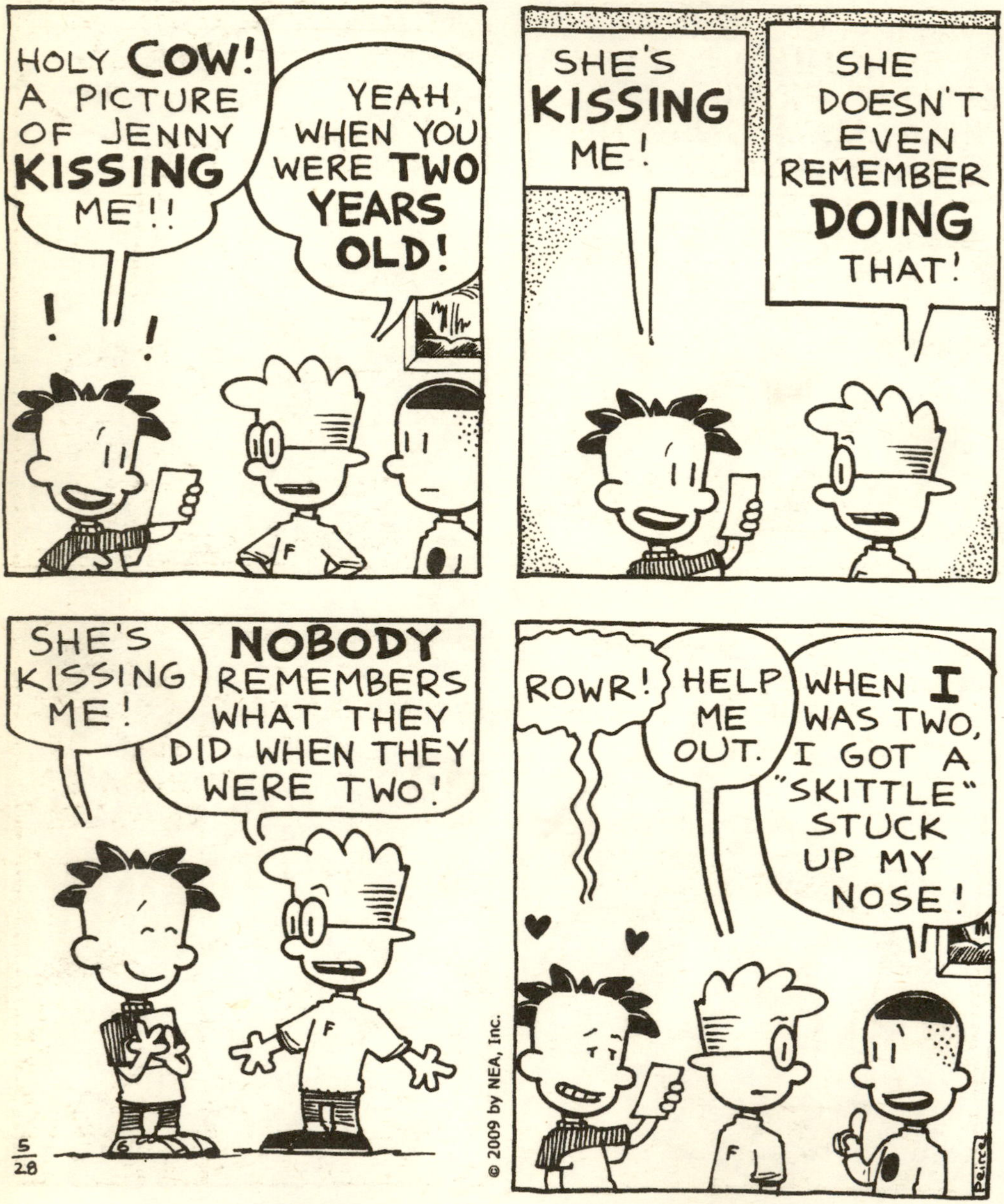
HOLY COW! A PICTURE OF JENNY KISSING ME!!
YEAH, WHEN YOU WERE TWO YEARS OLD!
! !
SHE'S KISSING ME!
SHE DOESN'T EVEN REMEMBER DOING THAT!
SHE'S KISSING ME!
NOBODY REMEMBERS WHAT THEY DID WHEN THEY WERE TWO!
5/28
© 2009 by NEA, Inc.
ROWR!
HELP ME OUT.
WHEN I WAS TWO, I GOT A "SKITTLE" STUCK UP MY NOSE!
Peirce

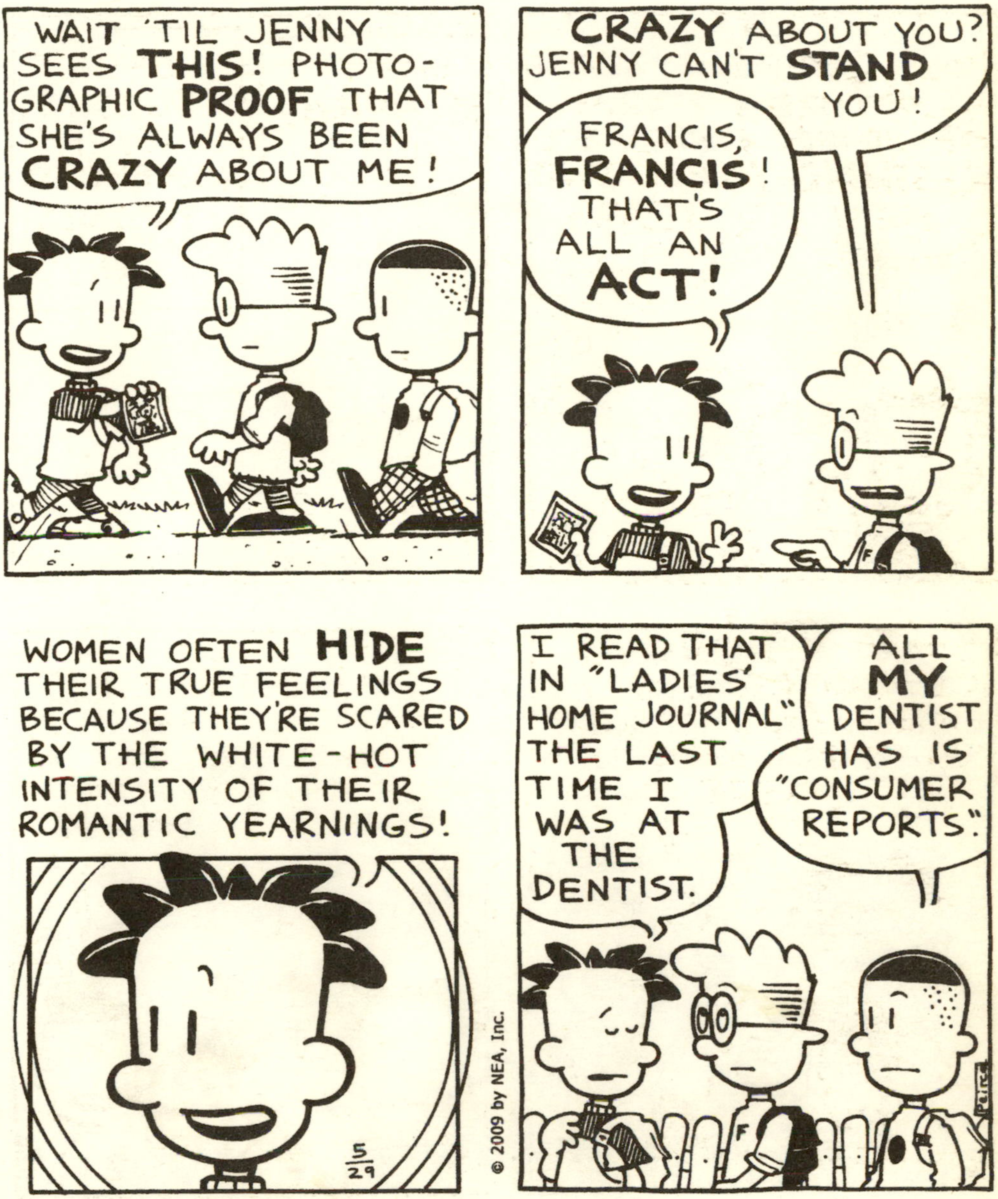
WAIT 'TIL JENNY SEES THIS! PHOTO-GRAPHIC PROOF THAT SHE'S ALWAYS BEEN CRAZY ABOUT ME!
CRAZY ABOUT YOU? JENNY CAN'T STAND YOU!
FRANCIS, FRANCIS! THAT'S ALL AN ACT!
WOMEN OFTEN HIDE THEIR TRUE FEELINGS BECAUSE THEY'RE SCARED BY THE WHITE-HOT INTENSITY OF THEIR ROMANTIC YEARNINGS!
5/29
I READ THAT IN "LADIES' HOME JOURNAL" THE LAST TIME I WAS AT THE DENTIST.
ALL MY DENTIST HAS IS "CONSUMER REPORTS".
© 2009 by NEA, Inc.
PEIRCE

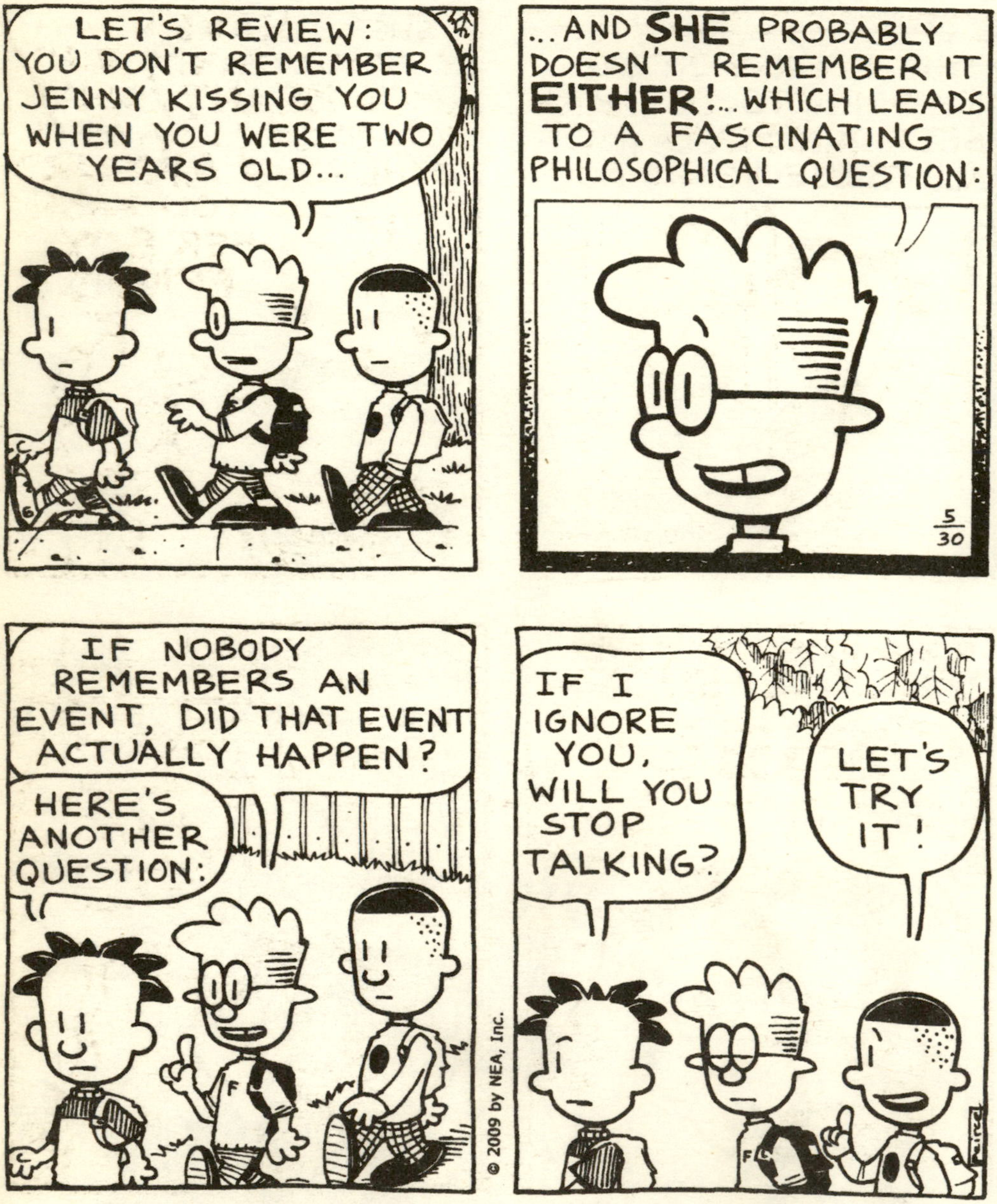
LET'S REVIEW: YOU DON'T REMEMBER JENNY KISSING YOU WHEN YOU WERE TWO YEARS OLD...
...AND SHE PROBABLY DOESN'T REMEMBER IT EITHER!...WHICH LEADS TO A FASCINATING PHILOSOPHICAL QUESTION:
5/30
IF NOBODY REMEMBERS AN EVENT, DID THAT EVENT ACTUALLY HAPPEN?
HERE'S ANOTHER QUESTION:
IF I IGNORE YOU, WILL YOU STOP TALKING?
LET'S TRY IT!
© 2009 by NEA, Inc.

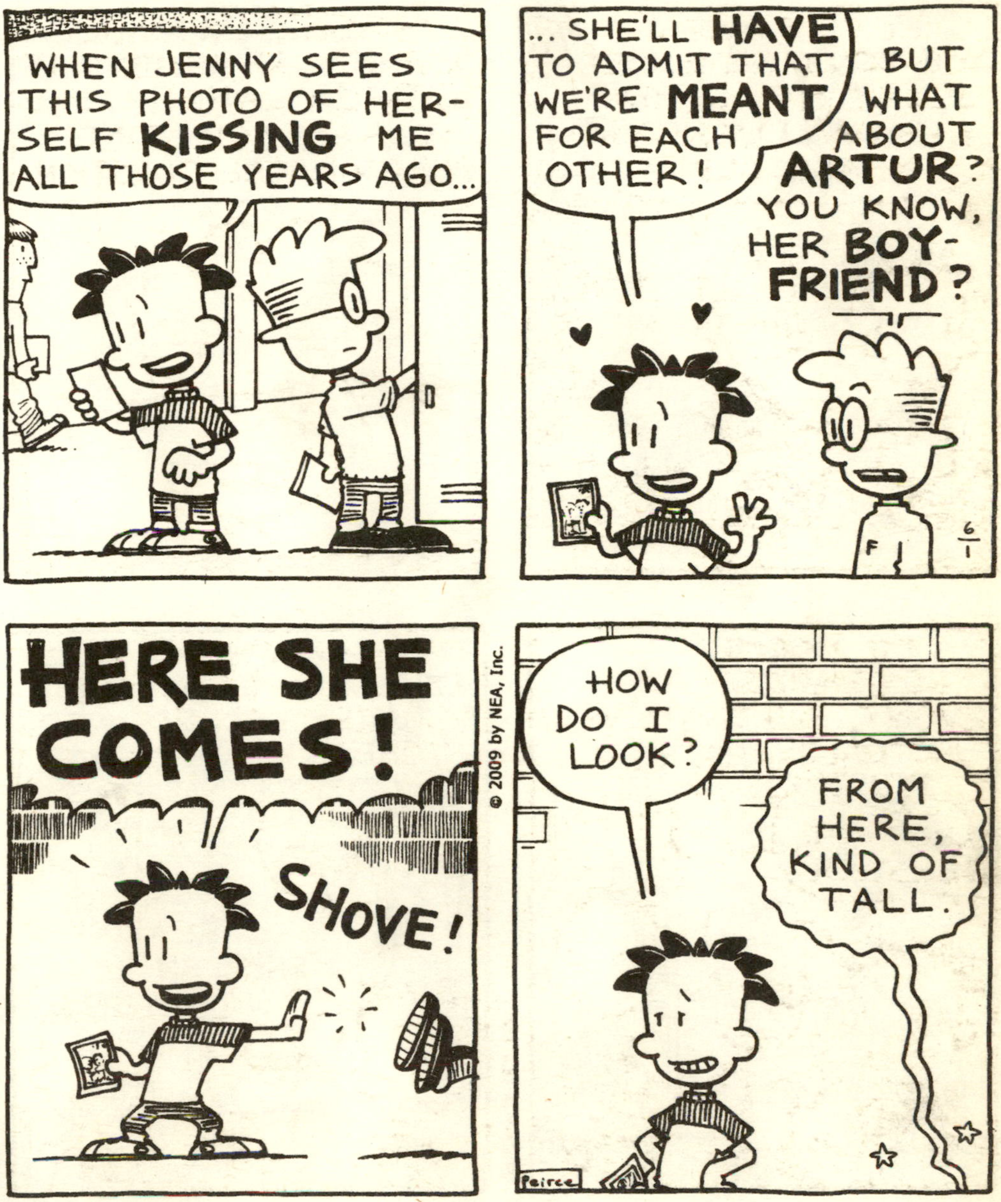
WHEN JENNY SEES THIS PHOTO OF HER-SELF KISSING ME ALL THOSE YEARS AGO...
... SHE'LL HAVE TO ADMIT THAT WE'RE MEANT FOR EACH OTHER!
BUT WHAT ABOUT ARTUR? YOU KNOW, HER BOY-FRIEND?
HERE SHE COMES!
SHOVE!
HOW DO I LOOK?
FROM HERE, KIND OF TALL.
© 2009 by NEA, Inc.
Peirce

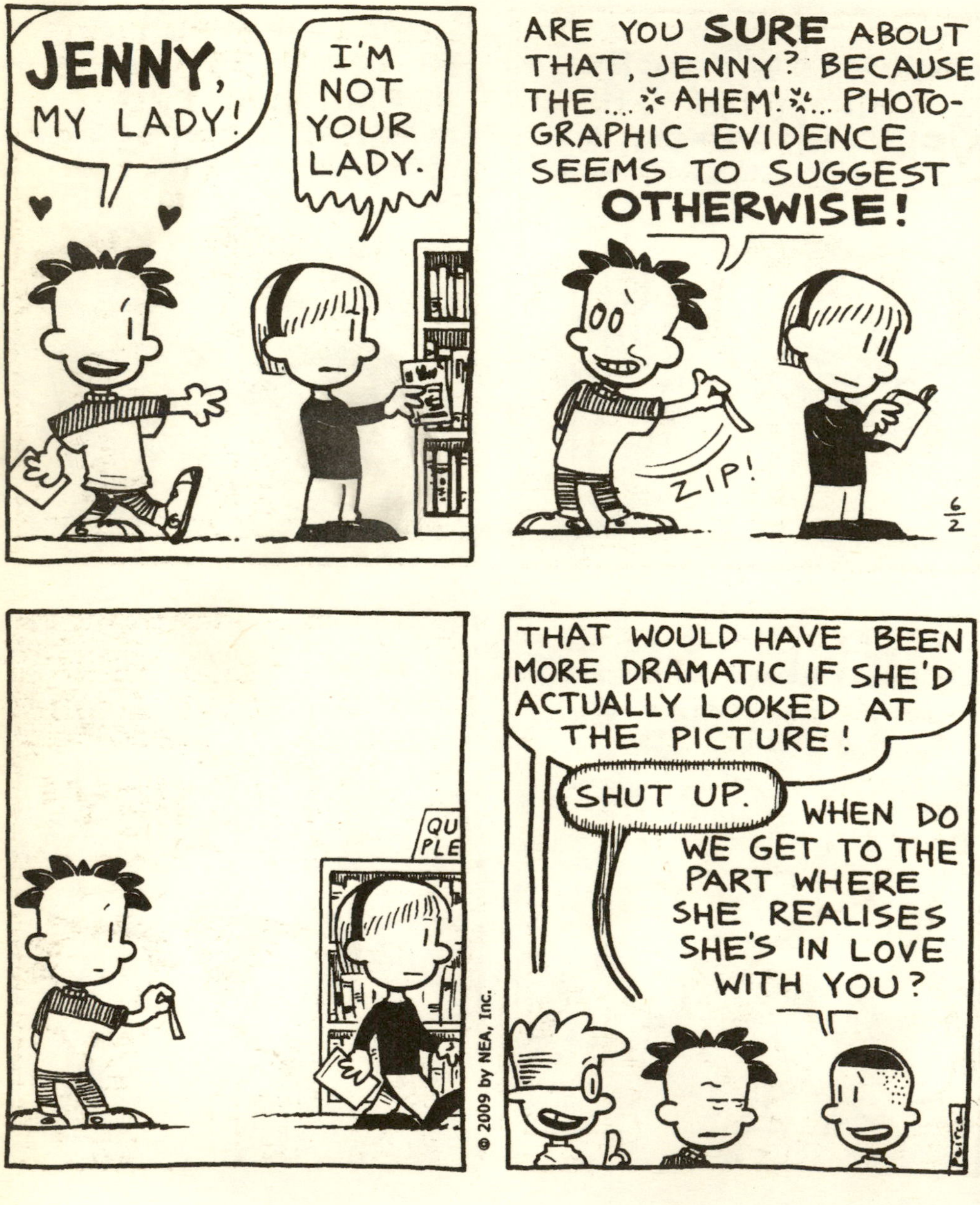
JENNY, MY LADY!
I'M NOT YOUR LADY.
ARE YOU SURE ABOUT THAT, JENNY? BECAUSE THE.... *AHEM!*... PHOTOGRAPHIC EVIDENCE SEEMS TO SUGGEST OTHERWISE!
ZIP!
6/2
QU PLE
© 2009 by NEA, Inc.
THAT WOULD HAVE BEEN MORE DRAMATIC IF SHE'D ACTUALLY LOOKED AT THE PICTURE!
SHUT UP.
WHEN DO WE GET TO THE PART WHERE SHE REALISES SHE'S IN LOVE WITH YOU?

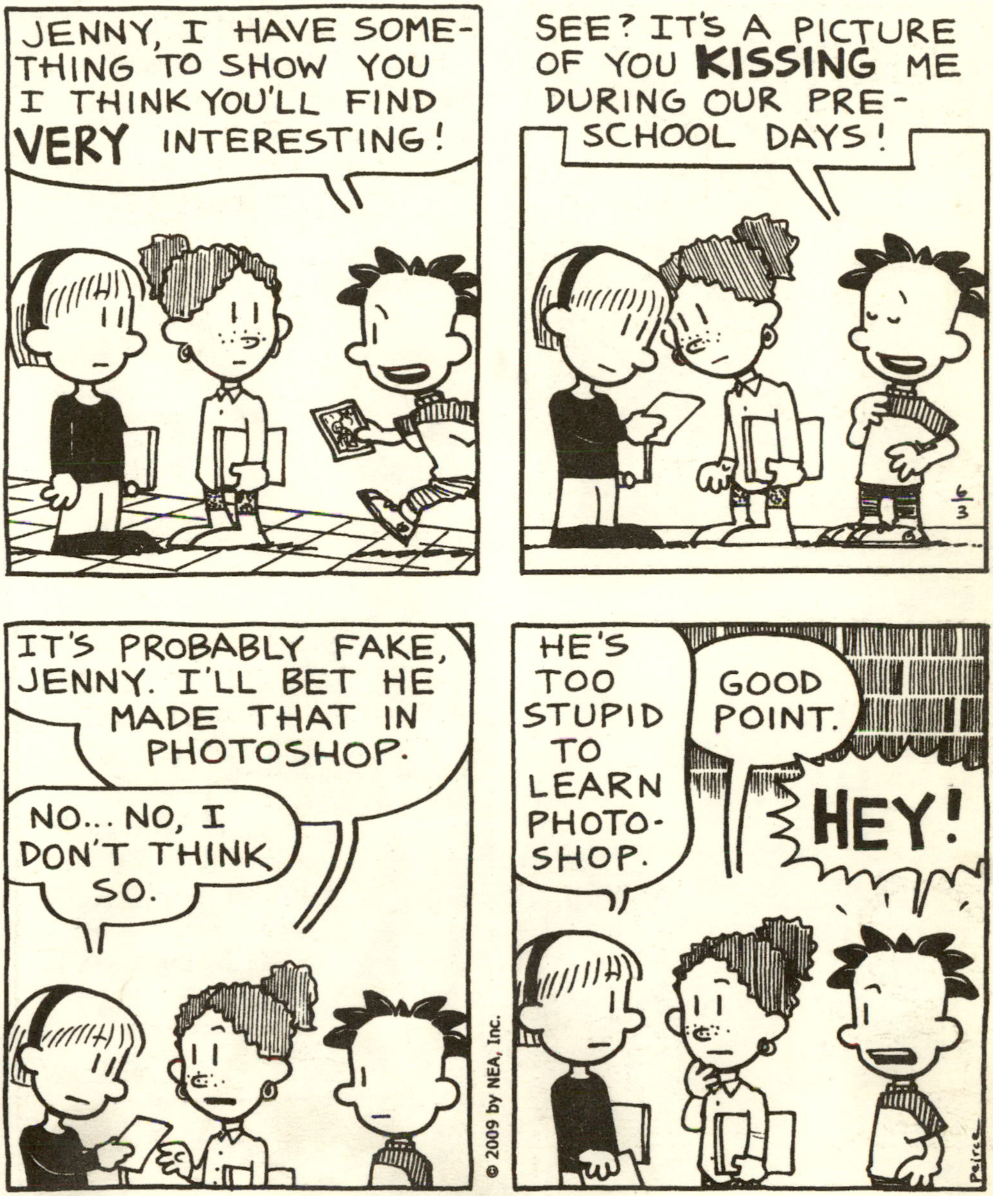
JENNY, I HAVE SOMETHING TO SHOW YOU I THINK YOU'LL FIND VERY INTERESTING!
SEE? IT'S A PICTURE OF YOU KISSING ME DURING OUR PRE-SCHOOL DAYS!
6/3
IT'S PROBABLY FAKE, JENNY. I'LL BET HE MADE THAT IN PHOTOSHOP.
NO... NO, I DON'T THINK SO.
© 2009 by NEA, Inc.
HE'S TOO STUPID TO LEARN PHOTO-SHOP.
GOOD POINT.
HEY!
Peirce

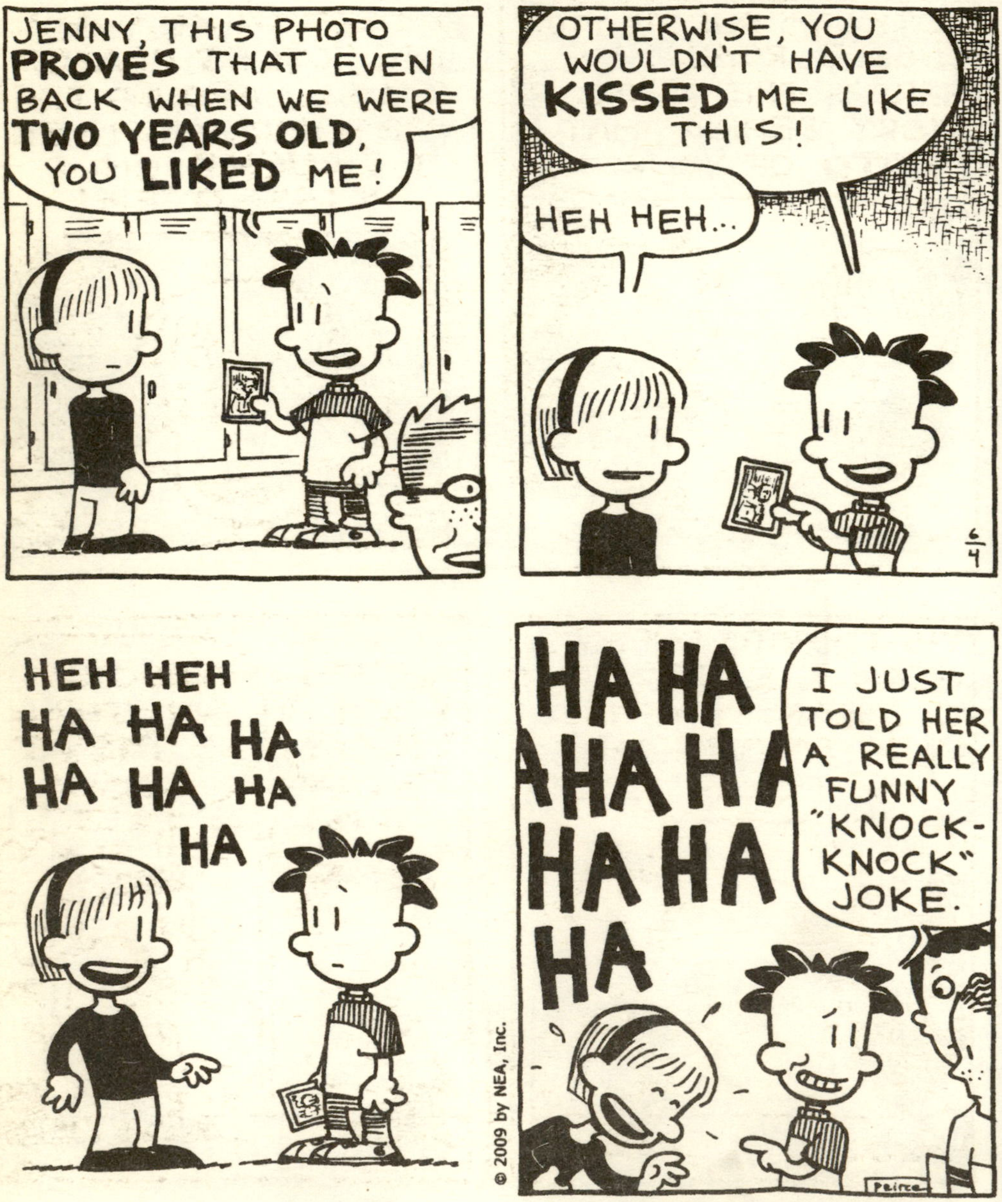
JENNY, THIS PHOTO **PROVES** THAT EVEN BACK WHEN WE WERE **TWO YEARS OLD**, YOU **LIKED** ME!
OTHERWISE, YOU WOULDN'T HAVE **KISSED** ME LIKE THIS!
HEH HEH...
HEH HEH HA HA HA HA HA HA HA
HA HA AHAHA HAHA HA HA HA
I JUST TOLD HER A REALLY FUNNY "KNOCK-KNOCK" JOKE.

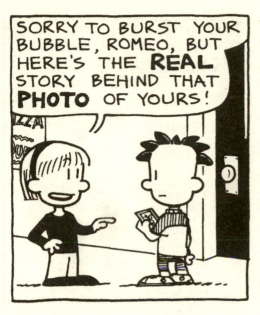

SORRY TO BURST YOUR BUBBLE, ROMEO, BUT HERE'S THE **REAL** STORY BEHIND THAT **PHOTO** OF YOURS!

I USED TO KISS **ALL** THE BOYS! I CHASED 'EM ALL AROUND THE PRESCHOOL, AND WHEN I **CAUGHT** 'EM, I **KISSED** 'EM!

THAT PHOTO DOESN'T MEAN I **LIKED** YOU! IT MEANS I COULD **RUN** FASTER THAN YOU COULD!

I'M SLOW.

TELL US SOMETHING WE **DIDN'T** KNOW!

© 2009 by NEA, Inc.

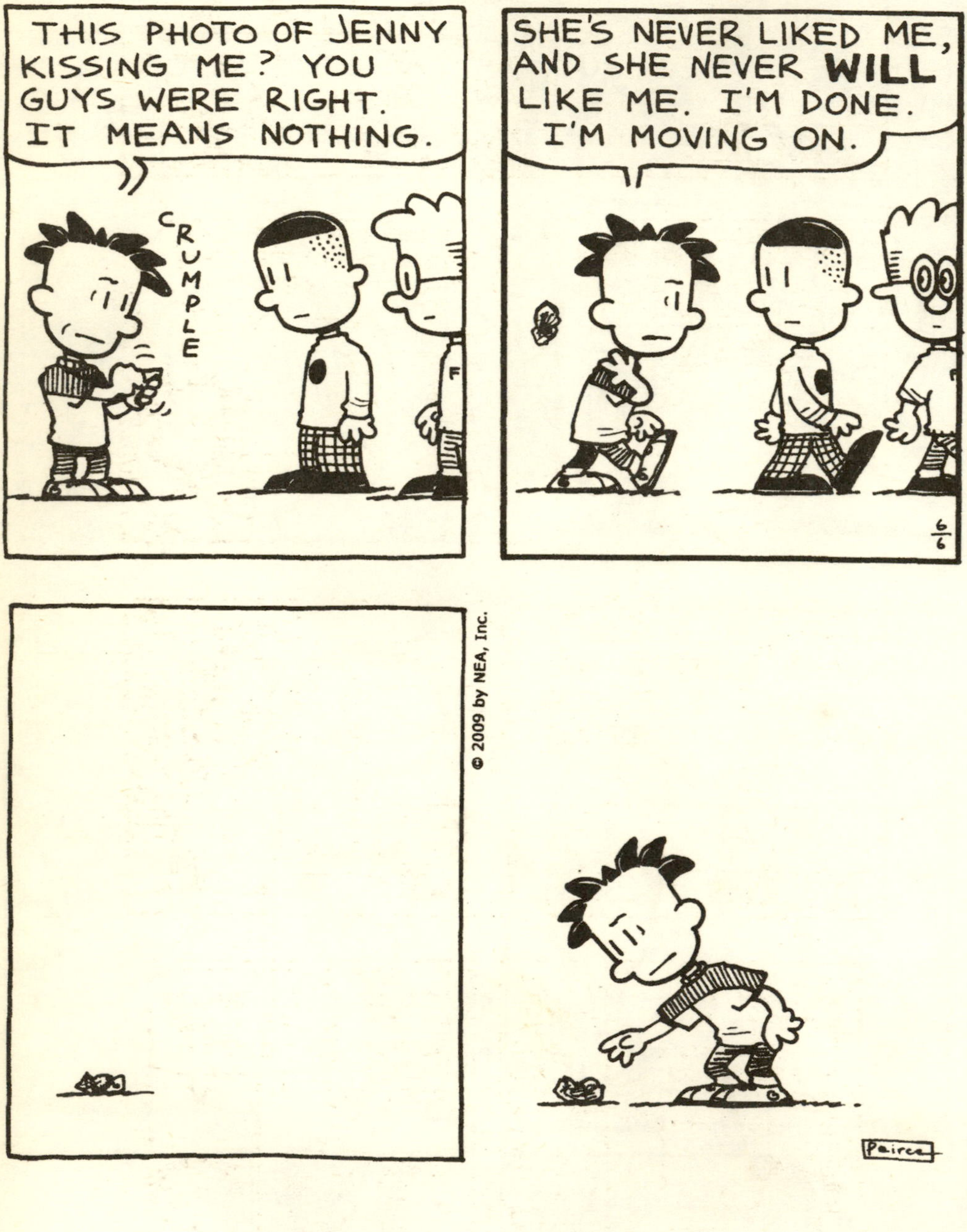
THIS PHOTO OF JENNY KISSING ME? YOU GUYS WERE RIGHT. IT MEANS NOTHING.
CRUMPLE
SHE'S NEVER LIKED ME, AND SHE NEVER **WILL** LIKE ME. I'M DONE. I'M MOVING ON.
6/6
Peirce

HEY, THERE'S NATE!

NATE!

DUDES!

WHAT'S WITH THE TROMBONE?

CA

50

JUST CONDUCTING A LITTLE BUSINESS, BOYS! A LITTLE FREE ENTERPRISE!

5/31

TURNS OUT THIS LI'L BABY IS QUITE THE MONEYMAKER!

MONEY-MAKER?

PEOPLE PAY YOU?

BUT YOU STINK AT THE TROM-BONE!

exACTLY!

EXCUSE ME, MA'AM!...

OPEN

COME

Bo

R

HOW MUCH WILL YOU PAY ME NOT TO PLAY THIS TROMBONE IN FRONT OF YOUR STORE?

PAT PAT

© 2009 by NEA, Inc.

I CAN'T DECIDE IF IT'S GENIUS OR EX-TORTION.

IT'S GENIUS. THE CASE IS EMPTY.

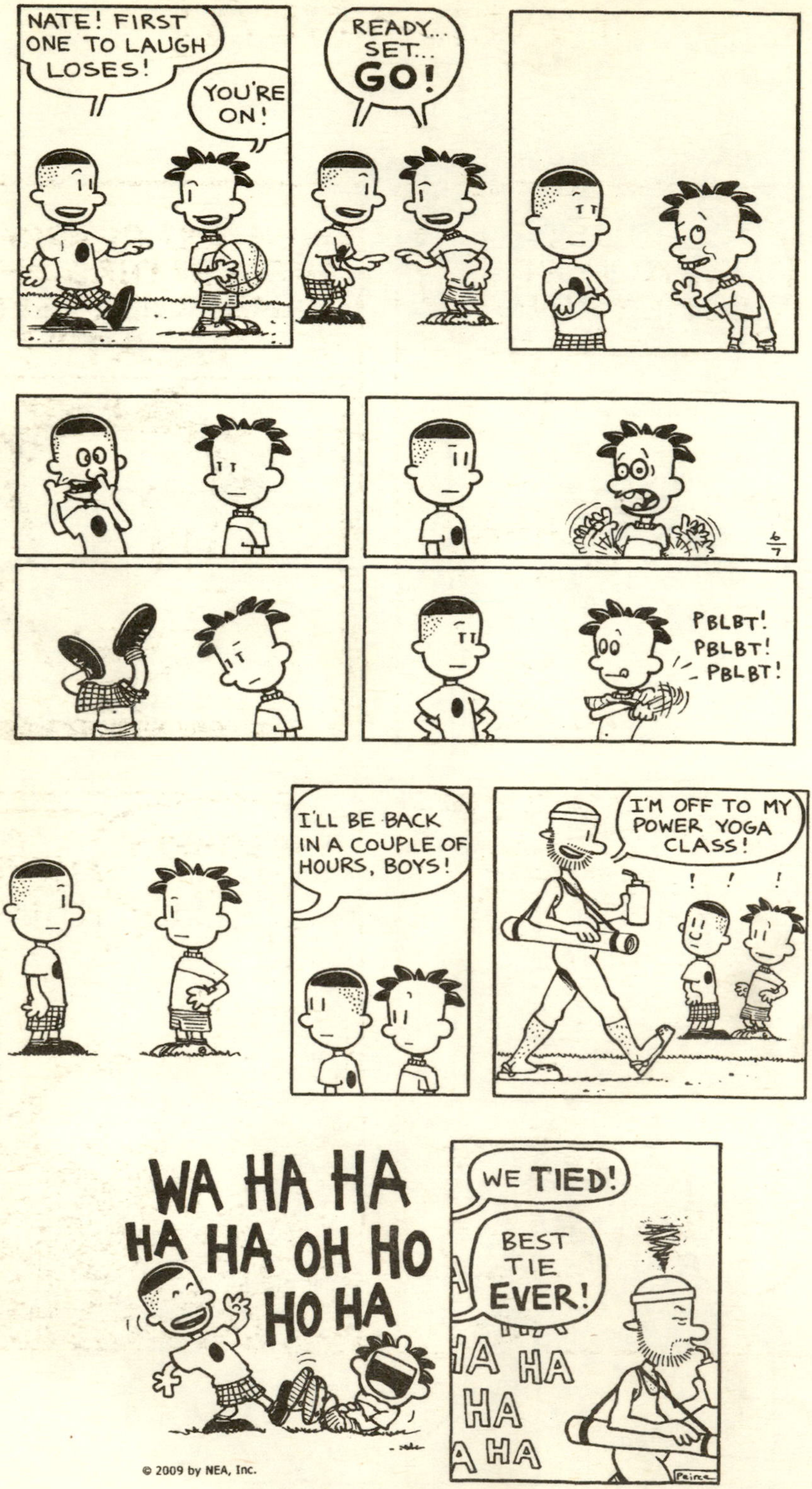
NATE! FIRST ONE TO LAUGH LOSES!
YOU'RE ON!
READY... SET... GO!
PBLBT! PBLBT! PBLBT!
I'LL BE BACK IN A COUPLE OF HOURS, BOYS!
I'M OFF TO MY POWER YOGA CLASS!
! ! !
WA HA HA HA HA OH HO HO HA
WE TIED!
BEST TIE EVER!
HA HA HA HA
Peirce

NATE ≠ NEAT

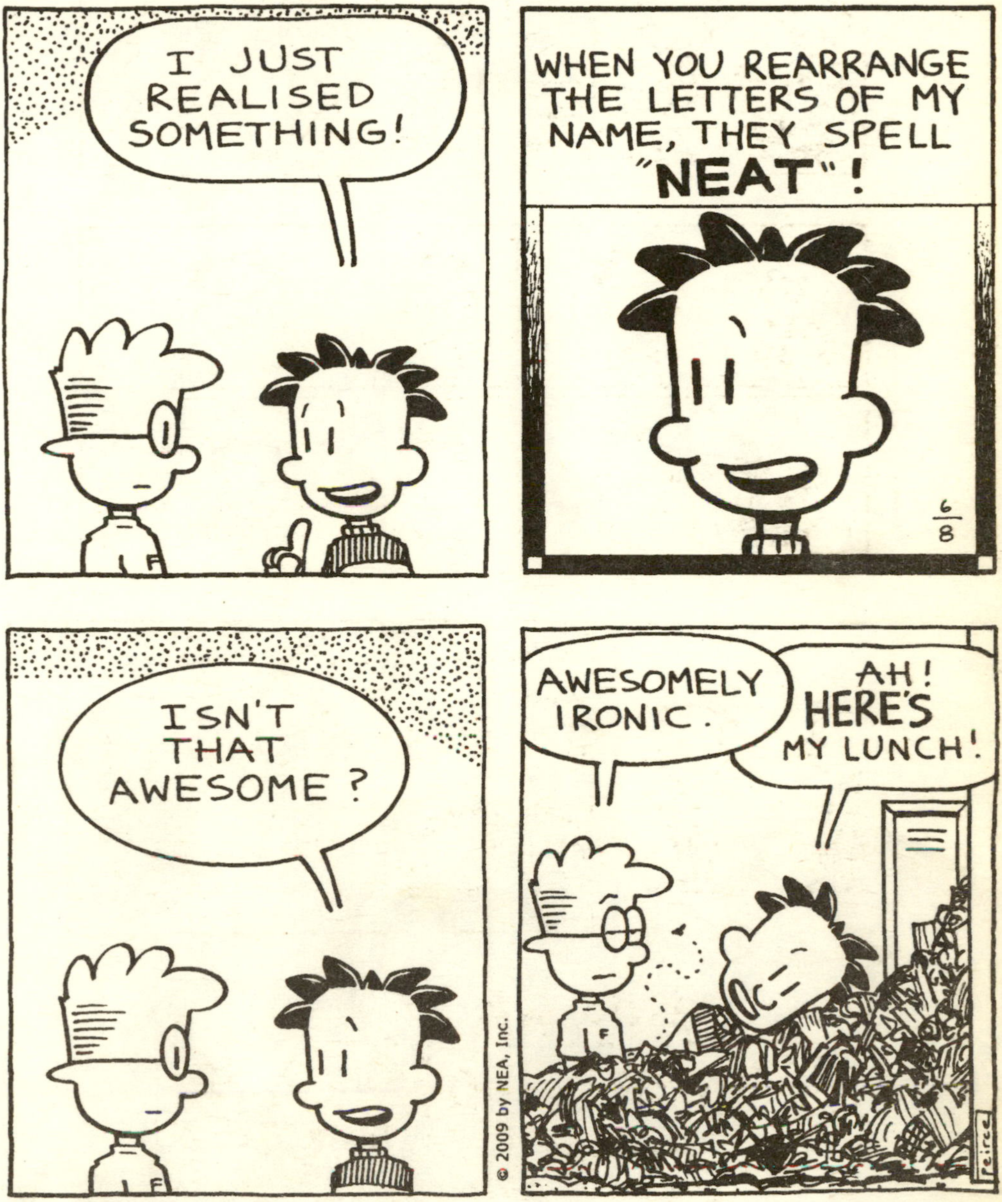
I JUST REALISED SOMETHING!
WHEN YOU REARRANGE THE LETTERS OF MY NAME, THEY SPELL "NEAT"!
6/8
ISN'T THAT AWESOME?
AWESOMELY IRONIC.
AH! HERE'S MY LUNCH!
© 2009 by NEA, Inc.
Peirce

KLIK!
FOOM!
MY LAPTOP CRASHED.
© 2009 by NEA, Inc.
6/9
Peirce

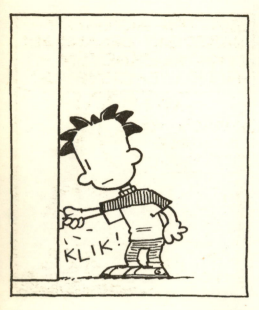

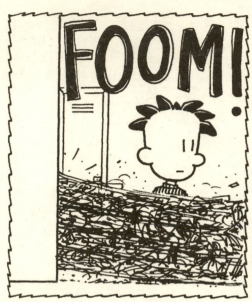

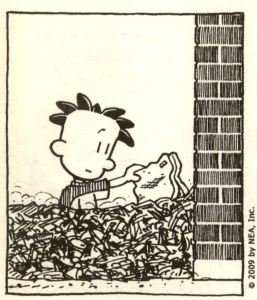

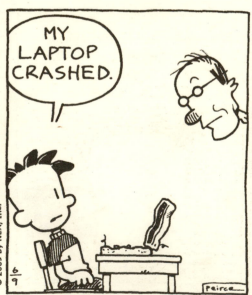

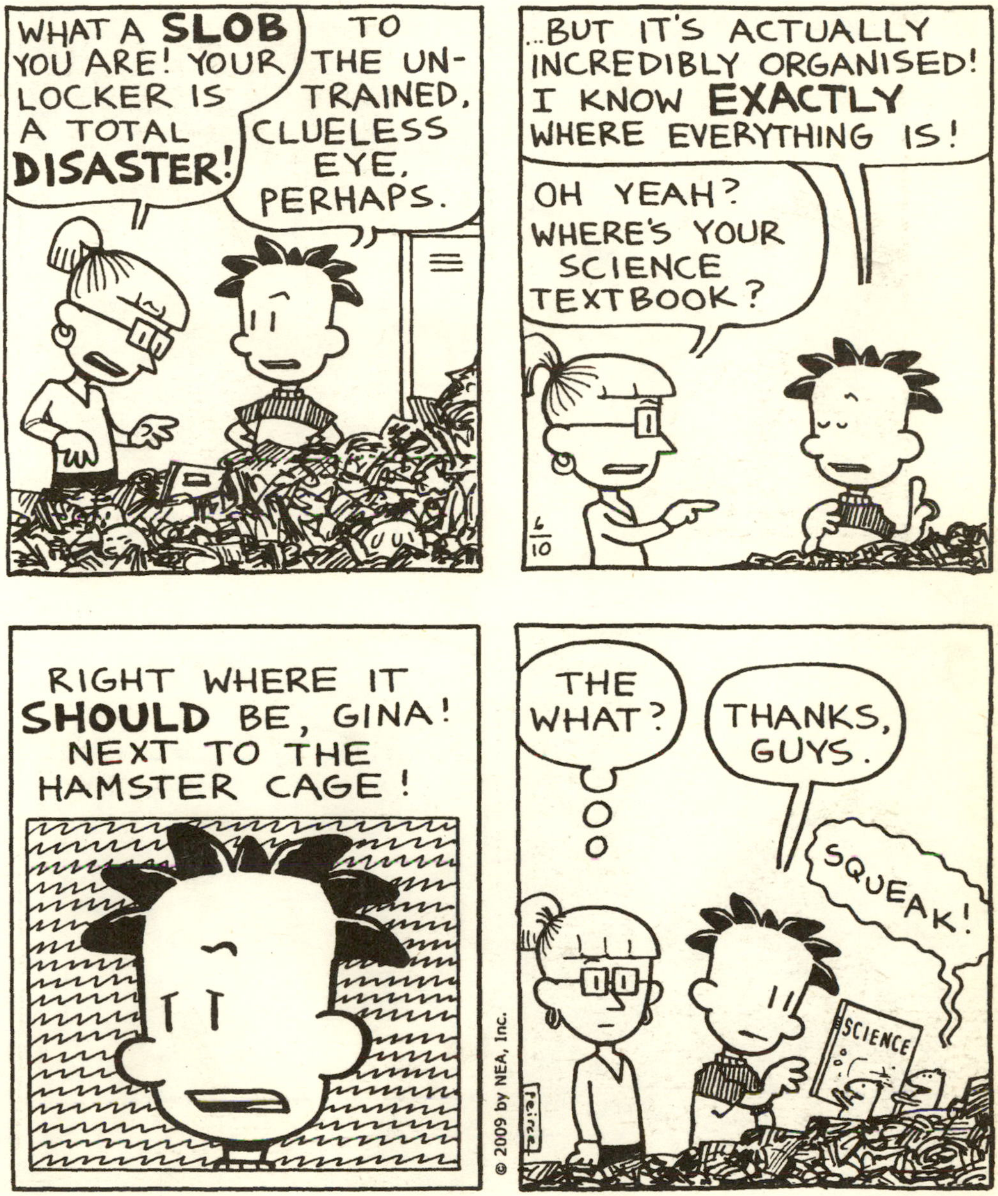
WHAT A SLOB YOU ARE! YOUR LOCKER IS A TOTAL DISASTER!
TO THE UNTRAINED, CLUELESS EYE, PERHAPS.
...BUT IT'S ACTUALLY INCREDIBLY ORGANISED! I KNOW EXACTLY WHERE EVERYTHING IS!
OH YEAH? WHERE'S YOUR SCIENCE TEXTBOOK?
RIGHT WHERE IT SHOULD BE, GINA! NEXT TO THE HAMSTER CAGE!
THE WHAT?
THANKS, GUYS.
SQUEAK!
SCIENCE
© 2009 by NEA, Inc.

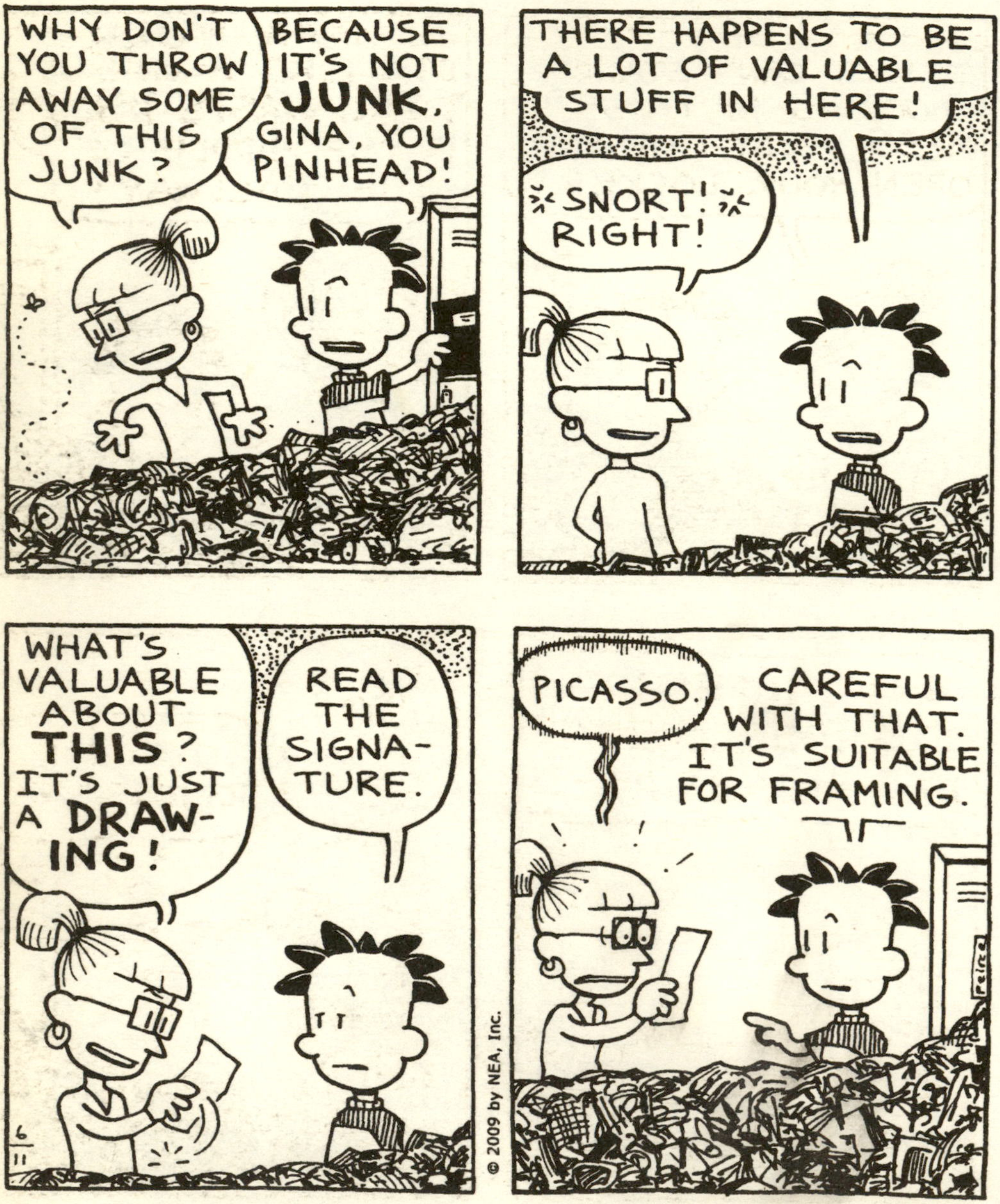
WHY DON'T YOU THROW AWAY SOME OF THIS JUNK?
BECAUSE IT'S NOT JUNK, GINA, YOU PINHEAD!
THERE HAPPENS TO BE A LOT OF VALUABLE STUFF IN HERE!
SNORT! RIGHT!
WHAT'S VALUABLE ABOUT THIS? IT'S JUST A DRAWING!
READ THE SIGNATURE.
PICASSO.
CAREFUL WITH THAT. IT'S SUITABLE FOR FRAMING.
© 2009 by NEA, Inc.

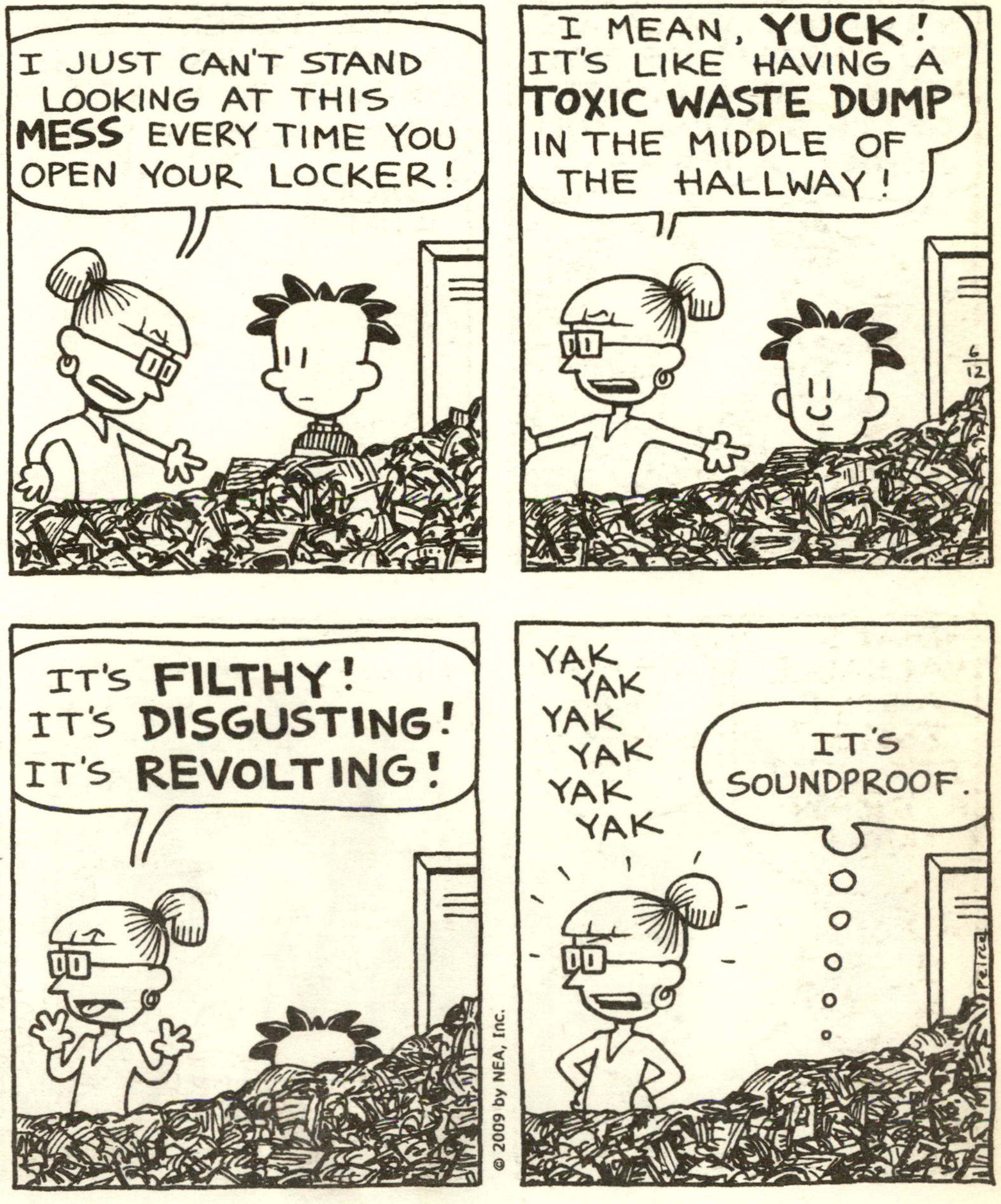
I JUST CAN'T STAND LOOKING AT THIS **MESS** EVERY TIME YOU OPEN YOUR LOCKER!
I MEAN, **YUCK**! IT'S LIKE HAVING A **TOXIC WASTE DUMP** IN THE MIDDLE OF THE HALLWAY!
6/12
IT'S **FILTHY**! IT'S **DISGUSTING**! IT'S **REVOLTING**!
YAK YAK YAK YAK YAK YAK
IT'S SOUNDPROOF.
PEIRCE

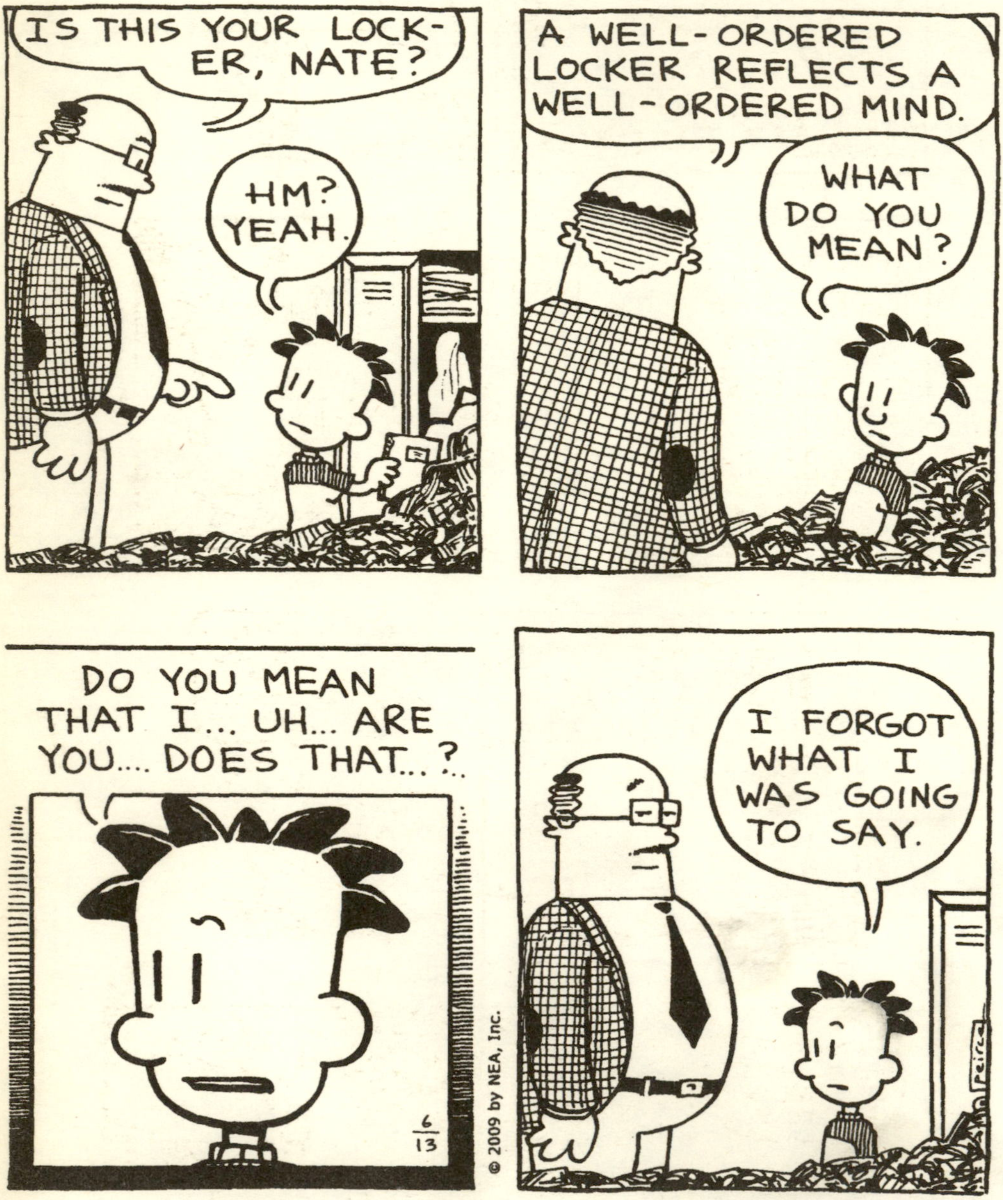
IS THIS YOUR LOCK-ER, NATE?
HM? YEAH.
A WELL-ORDERED LOCKER REFLECTS A WELL-ORDERED MIND.
WHAT DO YOU MEAN?
DO YOU MEAN THAT I... UH... ARE YOU.... DOES THAT... ?
6/13
© 2009 by NEA, Inc.
I FORGOT WHAT I WAS GOING TO SAY.

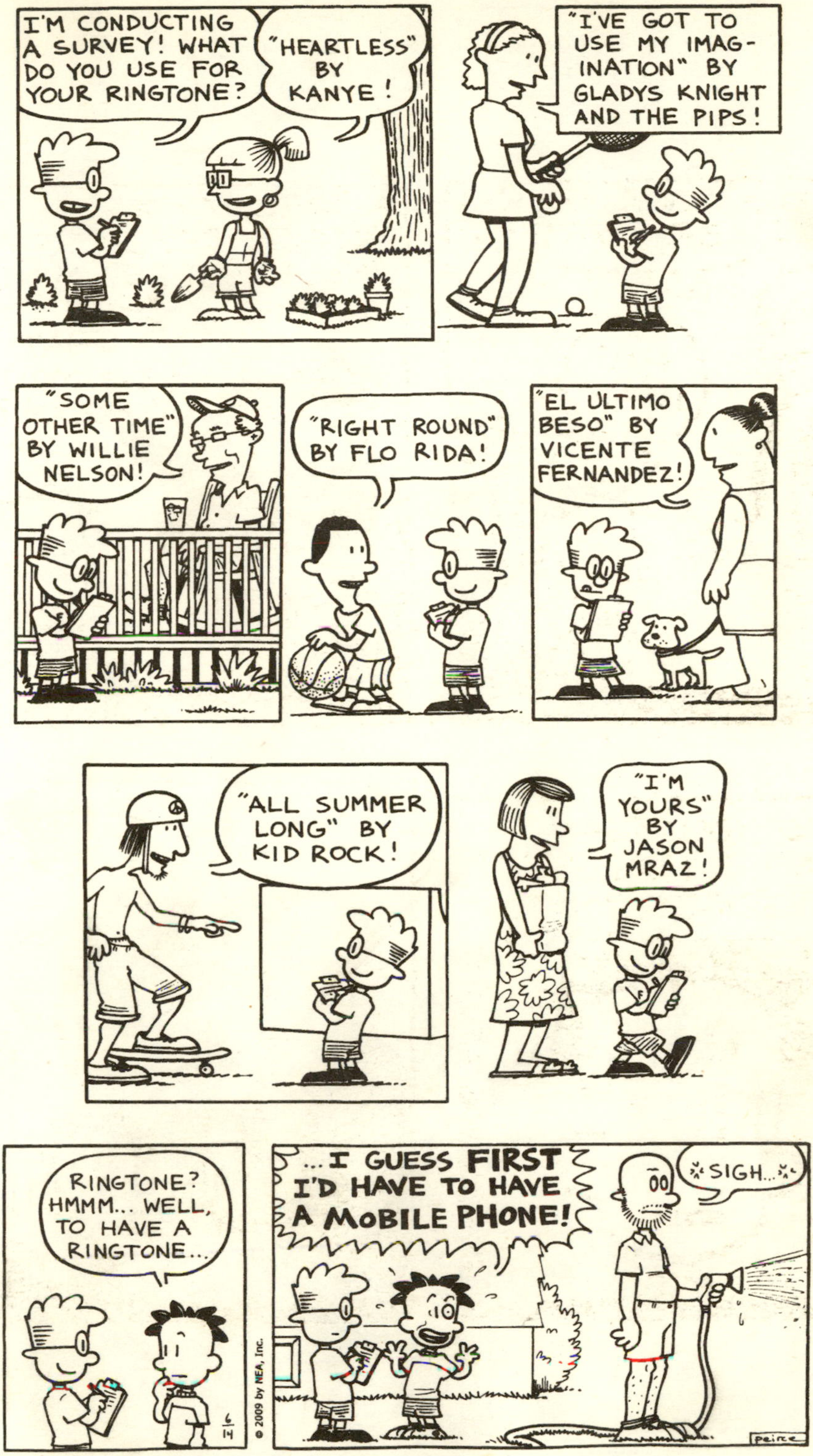
I'M CONDUCTING A SURVEY! WHAT DO YOU USE FOR YOUR RINGTONE?
"HEARTLESS" BY KANYE!
"I'VE GOT TO USE MY IMAGINATION" BY GLADYS KNIGHT AND THE PIPS!
"SOME OTHER TIME" BY WILLIE NELSON!
"RIGHT ROUND" BY FLO RIDA!
"EL ULTIMO BESO" BY VICENTE FERNANDEZ!
"ALL SUMMER LONG" BY KID ROCK!
"I'M YOURS" BY JASON MRAZ!
RINGTONE? HMMM... WELL, TO HAVE A RINGTONE...
...I GUESS FIRST I'D HAVE TO HAVE A MOBILE PHONE!
SIGH...
6/14
© 2009 by NEA, Inc.
peirce

THANK YOU!

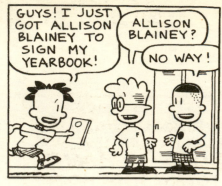

GUYS! I JUST GOT ALLISON BLAINEY TO SIGN MY YEARBOOK!

ALLISON BLAINEY?

NO WAY!

SHE'S AN A-LISTER! SHE'S, LIKE, MISS POPULARITY!

AND SHE'S AN 8TH GRADER! DUDE! HOW'D YOU DO IT?

I JUST WALKED UP AND ASKED HER!

WOW!

WHAT DID SHE WRITE?

I HAVEN'T EVEN LOOKED YET!

WHAT A COUP! ALLISON BLAINEY DOESN'T SIGN JUST ANYONE'S YEARBOOK!

"I HAVE NO IDEA WHO YOU ARE, AND I DON'T REALLY CARE."

ON THE BRIGHT SIDE, IT'S MORE MEMORABLE THAN "HAVE A GREAT SUMMER"!

I LIKE THE WAY SHE DOTS HER I'S WITH LITTLE SMILEY FACES!

© 2009 by NEA, Inc. 6/21

BEAT THE HEAT

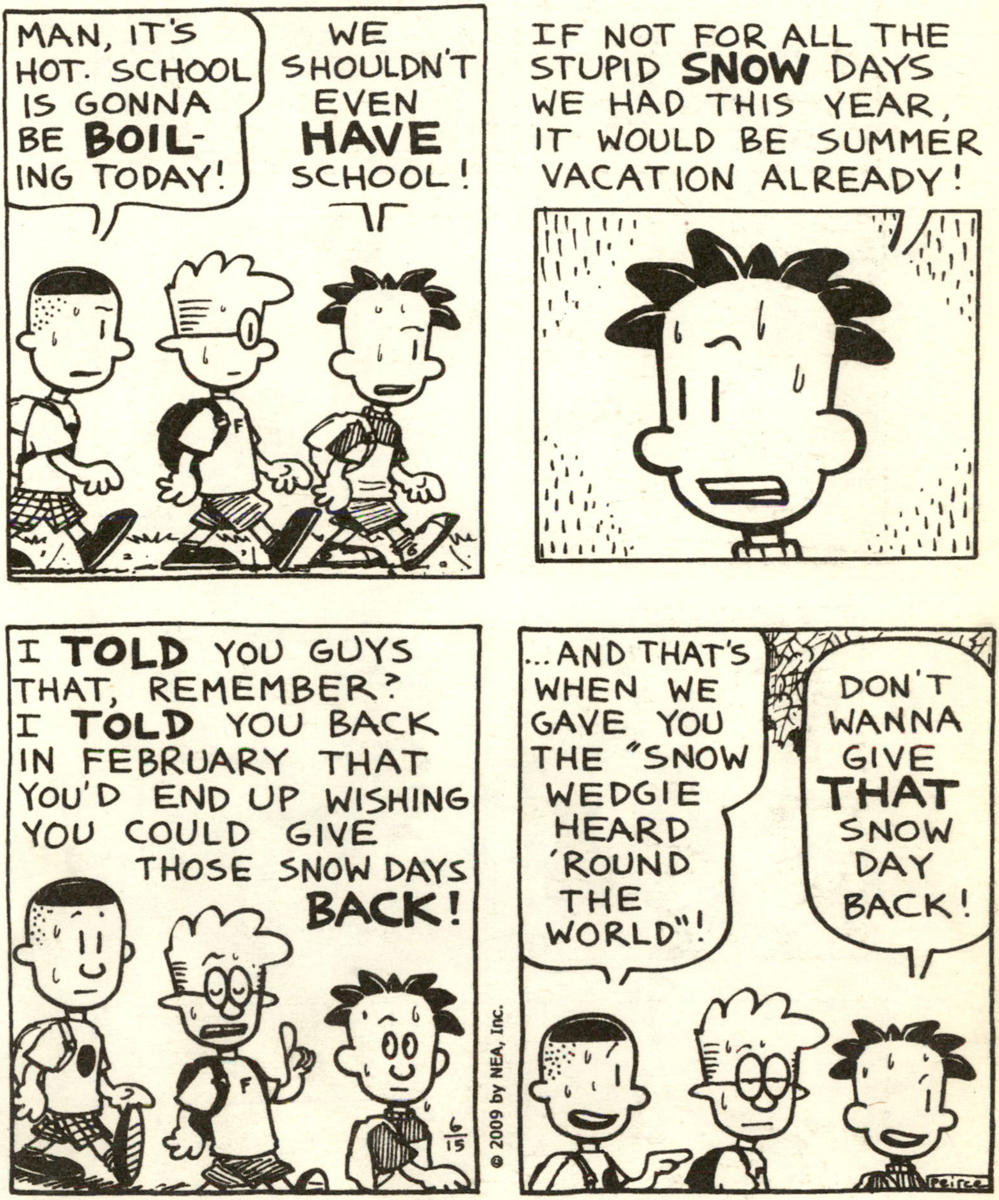
MAN, IT'S HOT. SCHOOL IS GONNA BE BOILING TODAY!
WE SHOULDN'T EVEN HAVE SCHOOL!
IF NOT FOR ALL THE STUPID SNOW DAYS WE HAD THIS YEAR, IT WOULD BE SUMMER VACATION ALREADY!
I TOLD YOU GUYS THAT, REMEMBER? I TOLD YOU BACK IN FEBRUARY THAT YOU'D END UP WISHING YOU COULD GIVE THOSE SNOW DAYS BACK!
6/15
© 2009 by NEA, Inc.
...AND THAT'S WHEN WE GAVE YOU THE "SNOW WEDGIE HEARD 'ROUND THE WORLD"!
DON'T WANNA GIVE THAT SNOW DAY BACK!
peirce

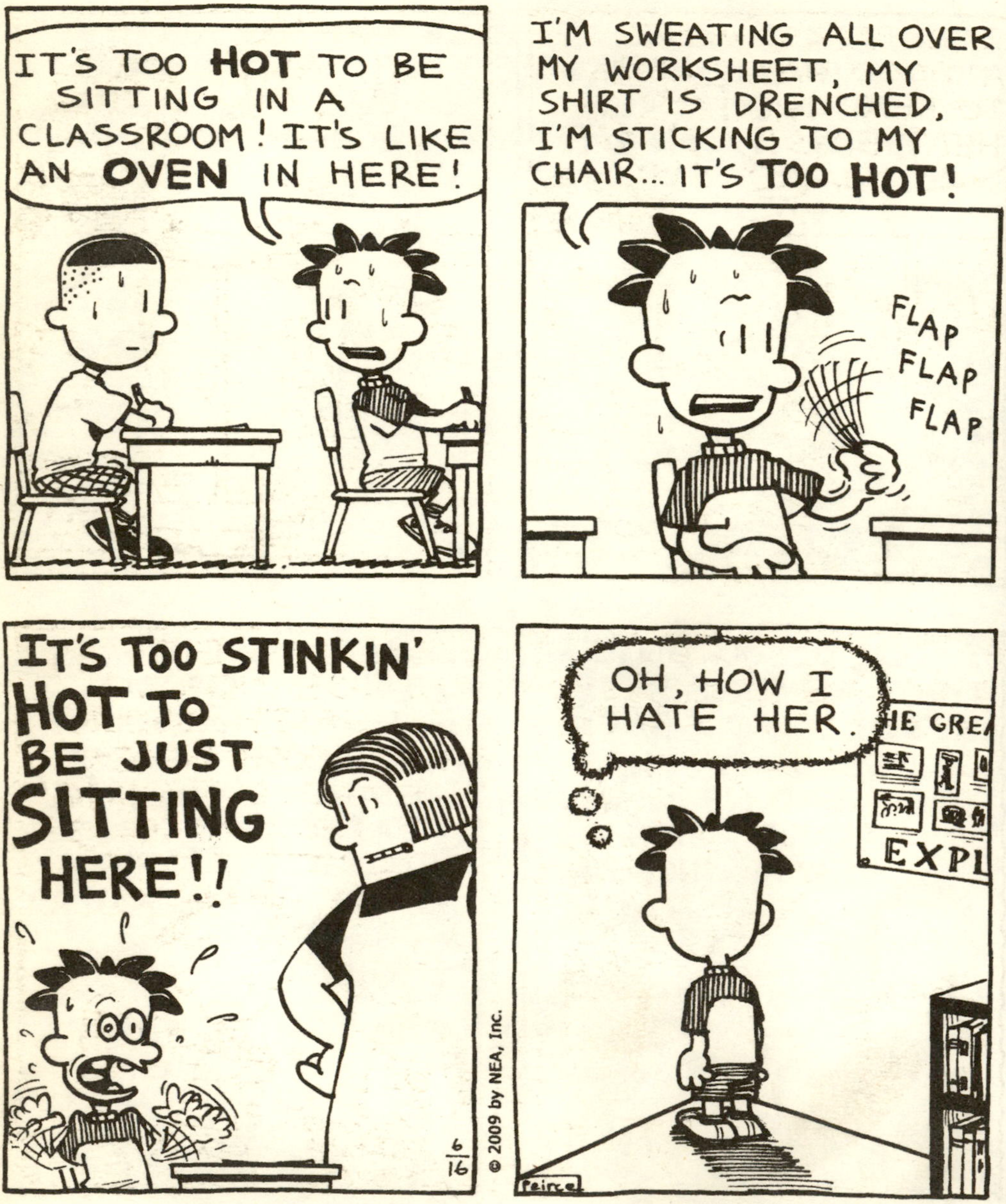
IT'S TOO HOT TO BE SITTING IN A CLASSROOM! IT'S LIKE AN OVEN IN HERE!
I'M SWEATING ALL OVER MY WORKSHEET, MY SHIRT IS DRENCHED, I'M STICKING TO MY CHAIR... IT'S TOO HOT!
FLAP
FLAP
FLAP
IT'S TOO STINKIN' HOT TO BE JUST SITTING HERE!!
6/16
© 2009 by NEA, Inc.
OH, HOW I HATE HER.
HE GRE
EXPL
Peirce

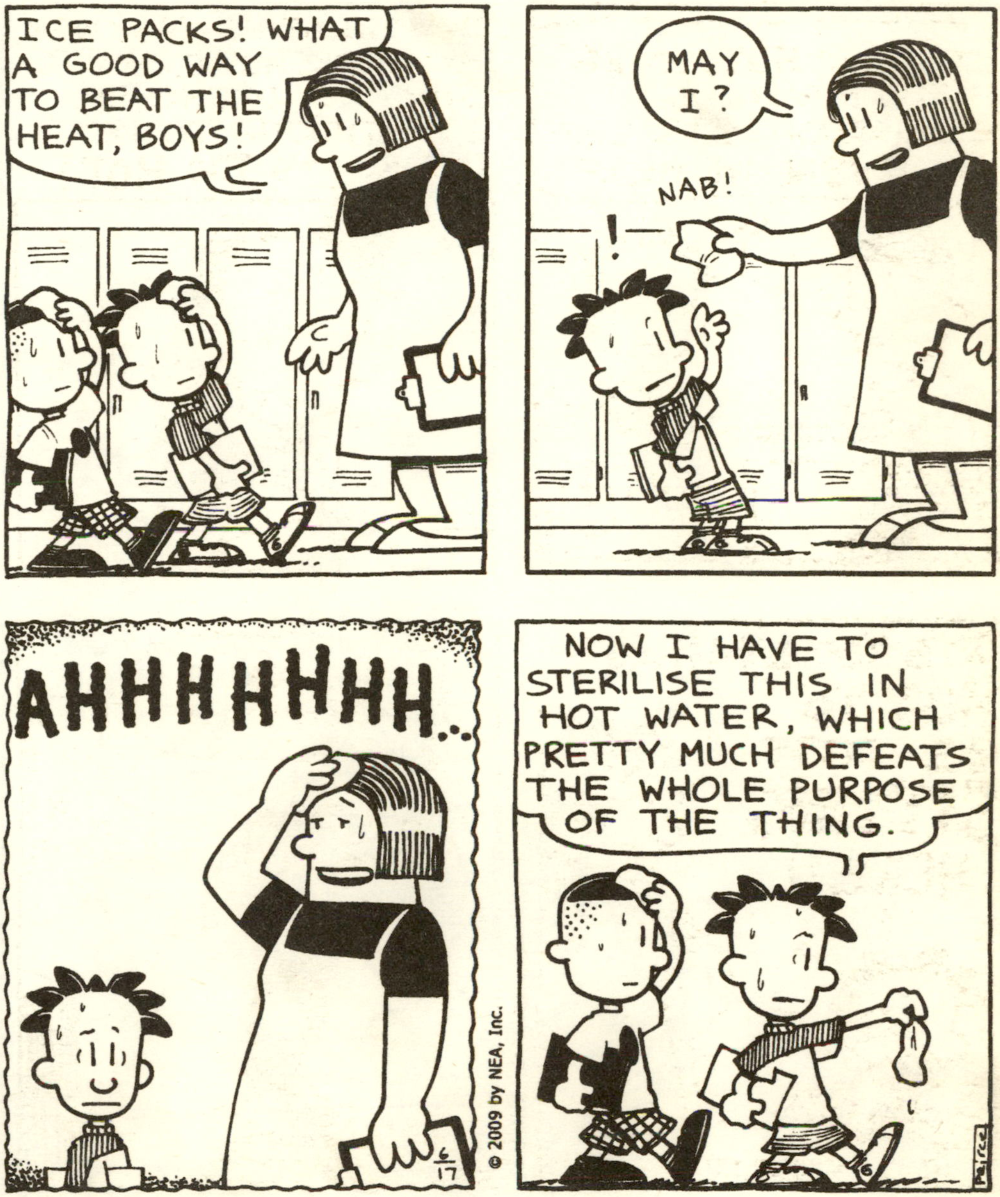
ICE PACKS! WHAT A GOOD WAY TO BEAT THE HEAT, BOYS!
MAY I?
NAB!
!
AHHHHHHH...
6/17
NOW I HAVE TO STERILISE THIS IN HOT WATER, WHICH PRETTY MUCH DEFEATS THE WHOLE PURPOSE OF THE THING.
Peirce

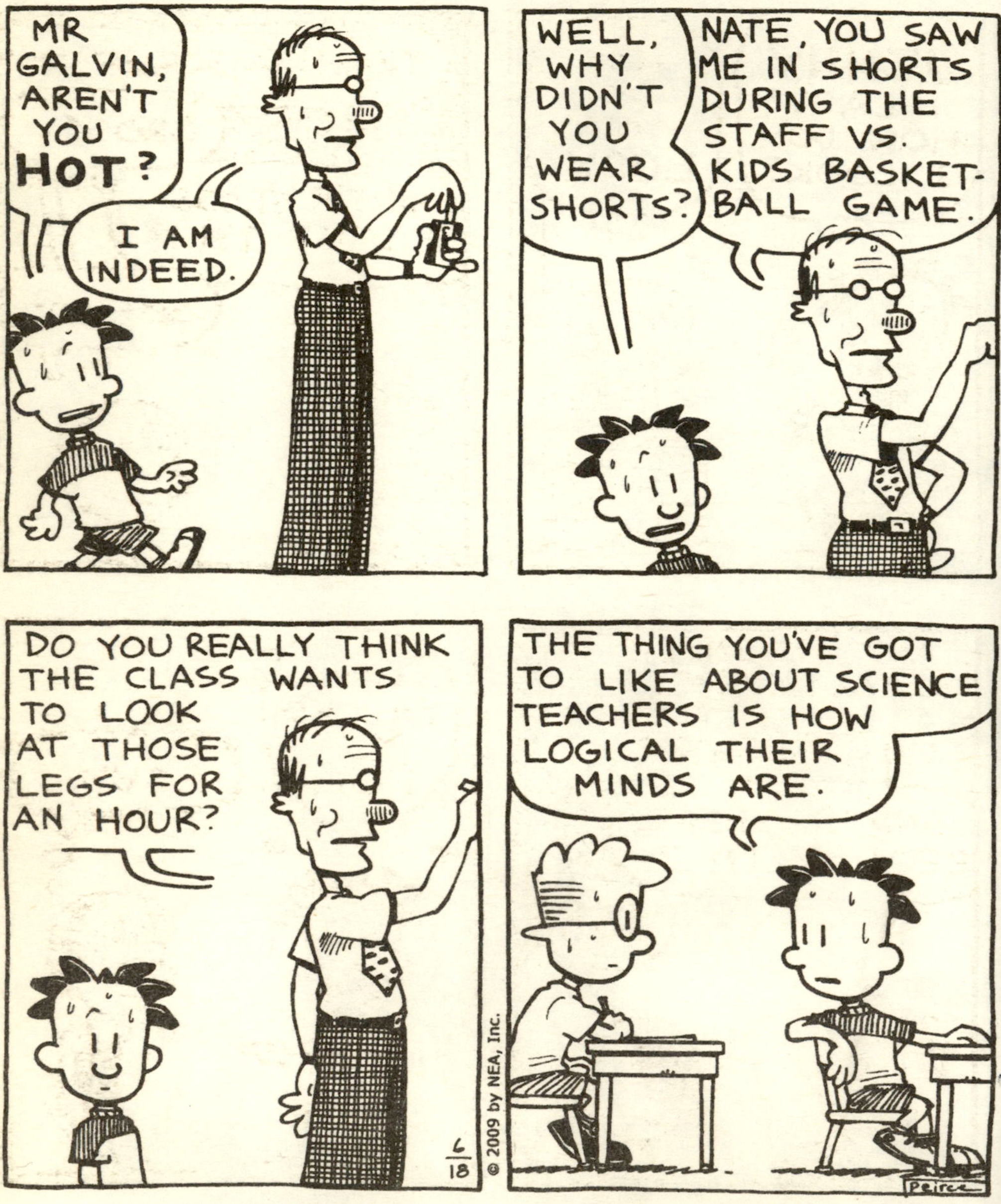
MR GALVIN, AREN'T YOU **HOT**?
I AM INDEED.
NATE, YOU SAW ME IN SHORTS DURING THE STAFF VS. KIDS BASKETBALL GAME.
WELL, WHY DIDN'T YOU WEAR SHORTS?
DO YOU REALLY THINK THE CLASS WANTS TO LOOK AT THOSE LEGS FOR AN HOUR?
6/18
© 2009 by NEA, Inc.
THE THING YOU'VE GOT TO LIKE ABOUT SCIENCE TEACHERS IS HOW LOGICAL THEIR MINDS ARE.
Peirce

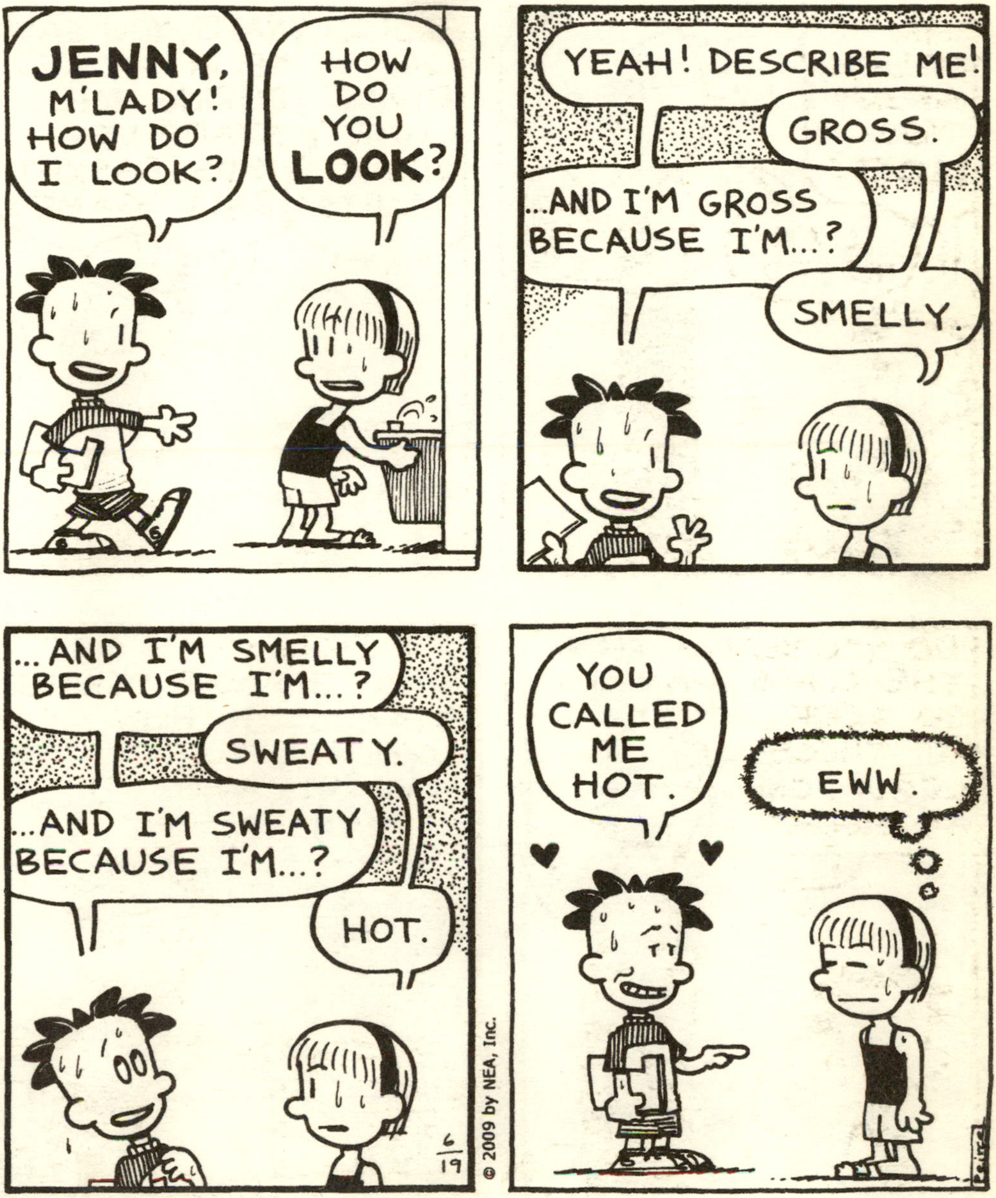
JENNY, M'LADY! HOW DO I LOOK?
HOW DO YOU LOOK?
YEAH! DESCRIBE ME!
GROSS.
...AND I'M GROSS BECAUSE I'M...?
SMELLY.
...AND I'M SMELLY BECAUSE I'M...?
SWEATY.
...AND I'M SWEATY BECAUSE I'M...?
HOT.
6/19
© 2009 by NEA, Inc.
YOU CALLED ME HOT.
EWW.

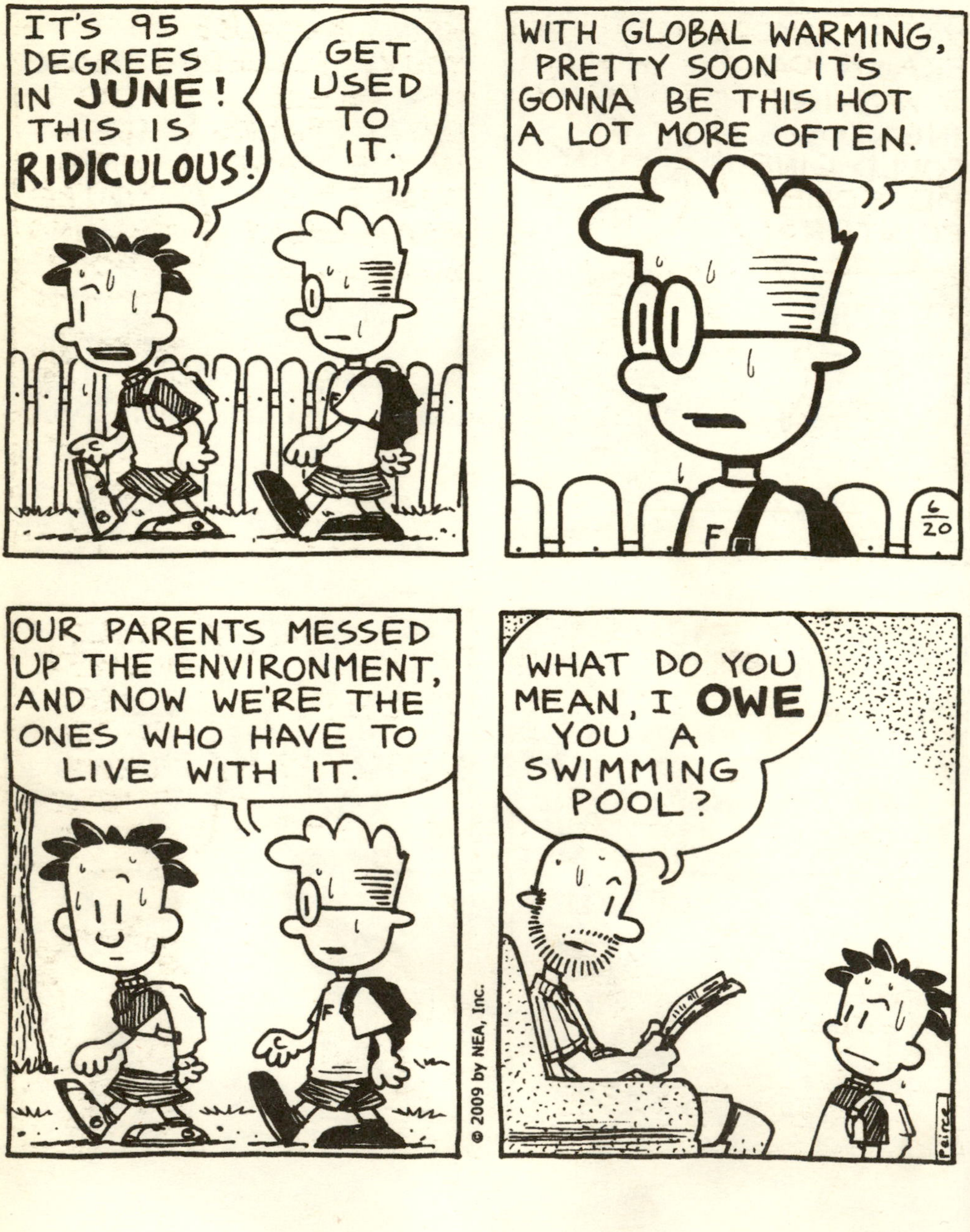
IT'S 95 DEGREES IN **JUNE**! THIS IS **RIDICULOUS**!
GET USED TO IT.
WITH GLOBAL WARMING, PRETTY SOON IT'S GONNA BE THIS HOT A LOT MORE OFTEN.
6/20
OUR PARENTS MESSED UP THE ENVIRONMENT, AND NOW WE'RE THE ONES WHO HAVE TO LIVE WITH IT.
© 2009 by NEA, Inc.
WHAT DO YOU MEAN, I **OWE** YOU A SWIMMING POOL?
Peirce

WATCH AND LEARN

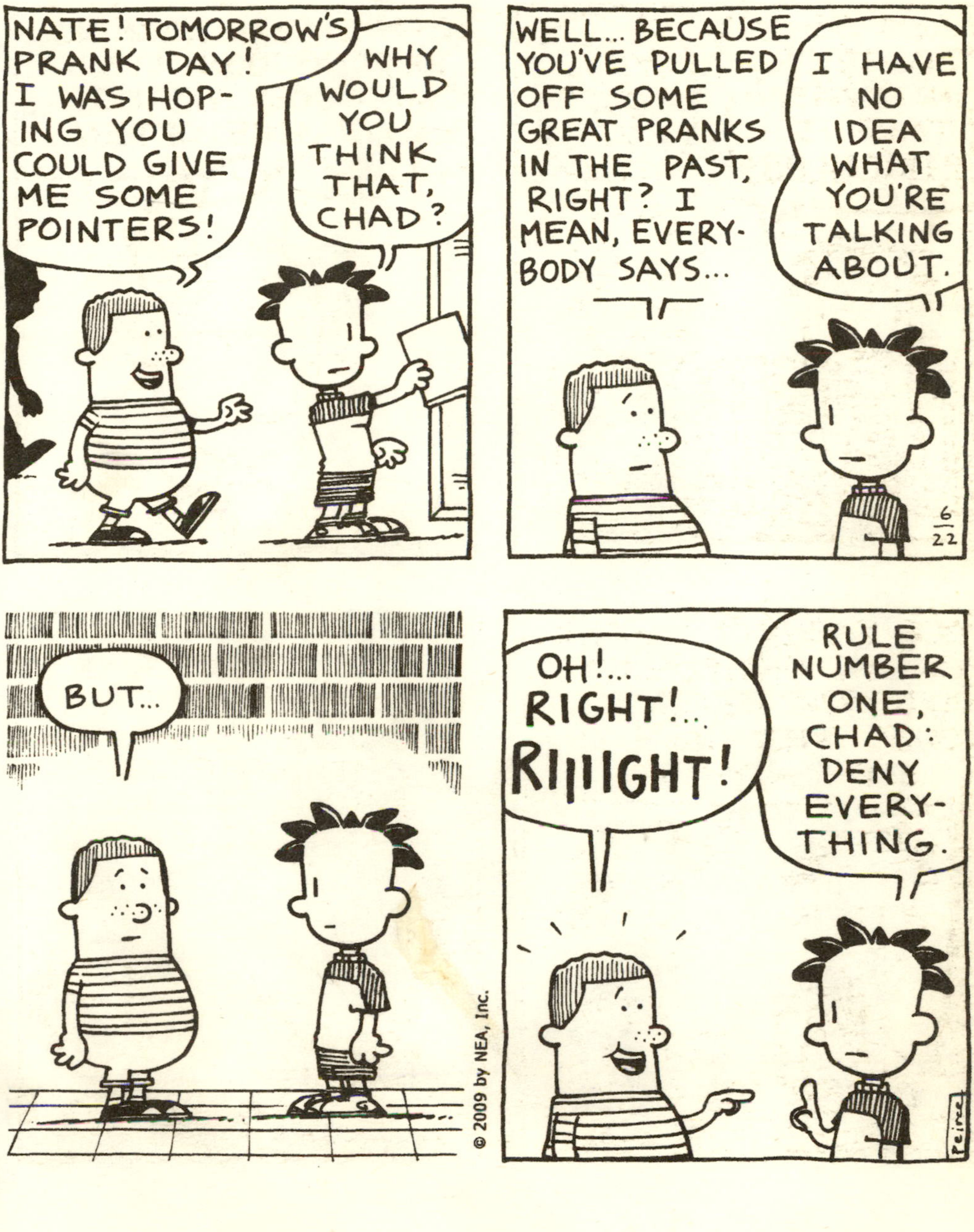
NATE! TOMORROW'S PRANK DAY! I WAS HOPING YOU COULD GIVE ME SOME POINTERS!
WHY WOULD YOU THINK THAT, CHAD?
WELL... BECAUSE YOU'VE PULLED OFF SOME GREAT PRANKS IN THE PAST, RIGHT? I MEAN, EVERYBODY SAYS...
I HAVE NO IDEA WHAT YOU'RE TALKING ABOUT.
6/22
BUT...
OH!... RIGHT!... RIIIIGHT!
RULE NUMBER ONE, CHAD: DENY EVERYTHING.
© 2009 by NEA, Inc.
Peirce

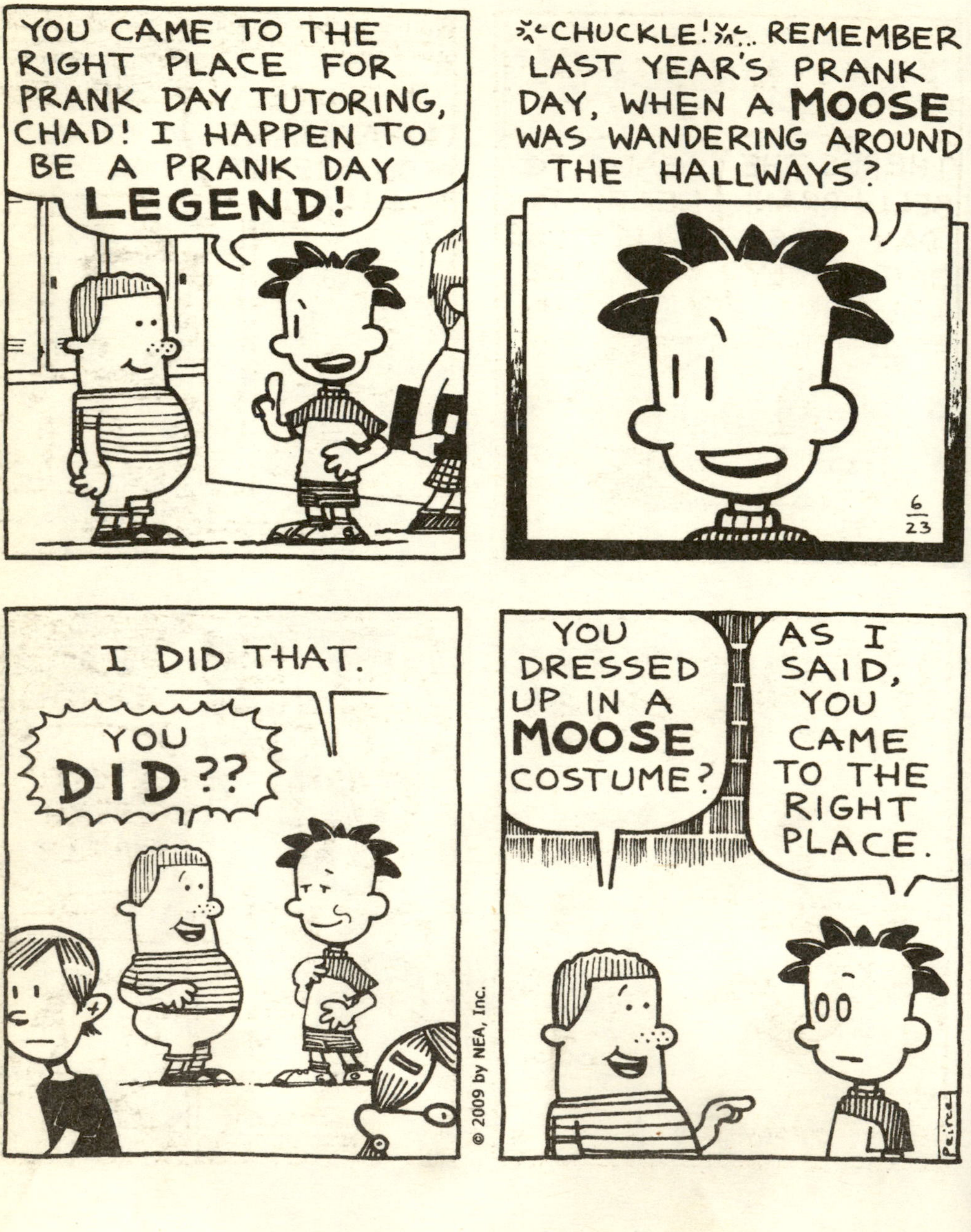
YOU CAME TO THE RIGHT PLACE FOR PRANK DAY TUTORING, CHAD! I HAPPEN TO BE A PRANK DAY LEGEND!
CHUCKLE! REMEMBER LAST YEAR'S PRANK DAY, WHEN A MOOSE WAS WANDERING AROUND THE HALLWAYS?
6/23
I DID THAT.
YOU DID??
YOU DRESSED UP IN A MOOSE COSTUME?
AS I SAID, YOU CAME TO THE RIGHT PLACE.
© 2009 by NEA, Inc.
Peirce

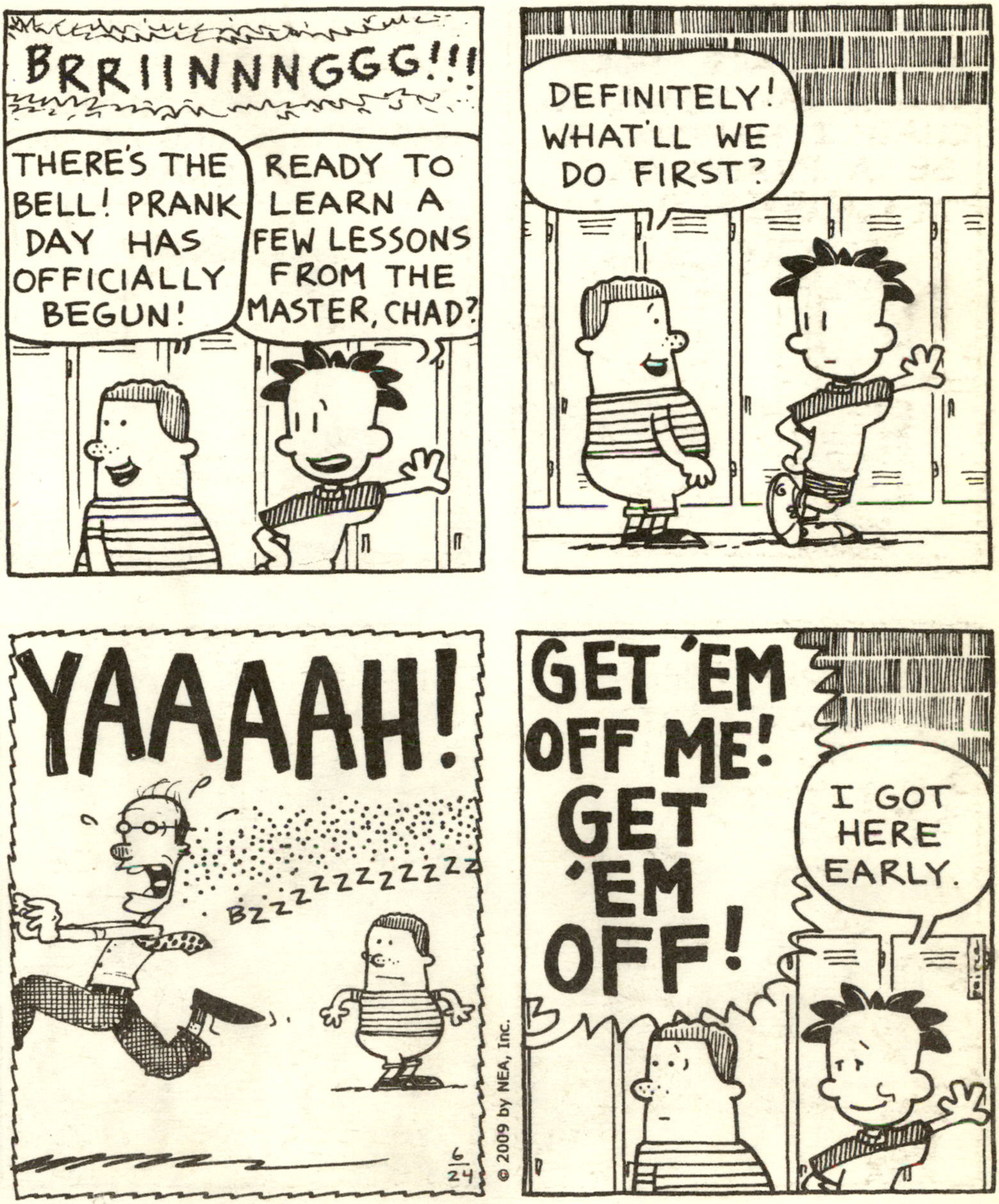
BRRIINNNGGG!!!
THERE'S THE BELL! PRANK DAY HAS OFFICIALLY BEGUN!
READY TO LEARN A FEW LESSONS FROM THE MASTER, CHAD?
DEFINITELY! WHAT'LL WE DO FIRST?
YAAAAH!
BZZZZZZZZZZZZ
GET 'EM OFF ME! GET 'EM OFF!
I GOT HERE EARLY.
© 2009 by NEA, Inc.
6/24

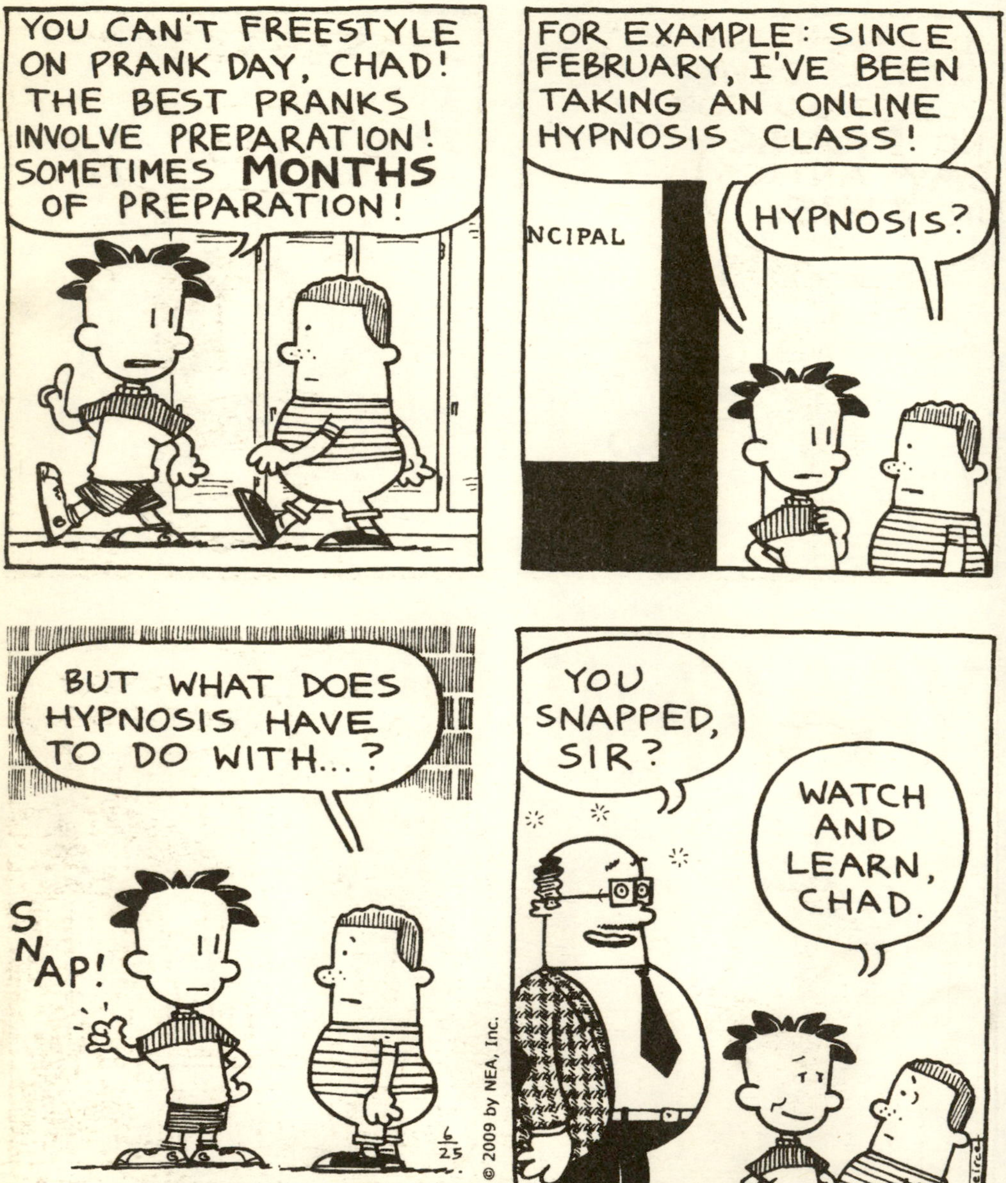
YOU CAN'T FREESTYLE ON PRANK DAY, CHAD! THE BEST PRANKS INVOLVE PREPARATION! SOMETIMES **MONTHS** OF PREPARATION!
FOR EXAMPLE: SINCE FEBRUARY, I'VE BEEN TAKING AN ONLINE HYPNOSIS CLASS!
NCIPAL
HYPNOSIS?
BUT WHAT DOES HYPNOSIS HAVE TO DO WITH...?
SNAP!
6/25
© 2009 by NEA, Inc.
YOU SNAPPED, SIR?
WATCH AND LEARN, CHAD.

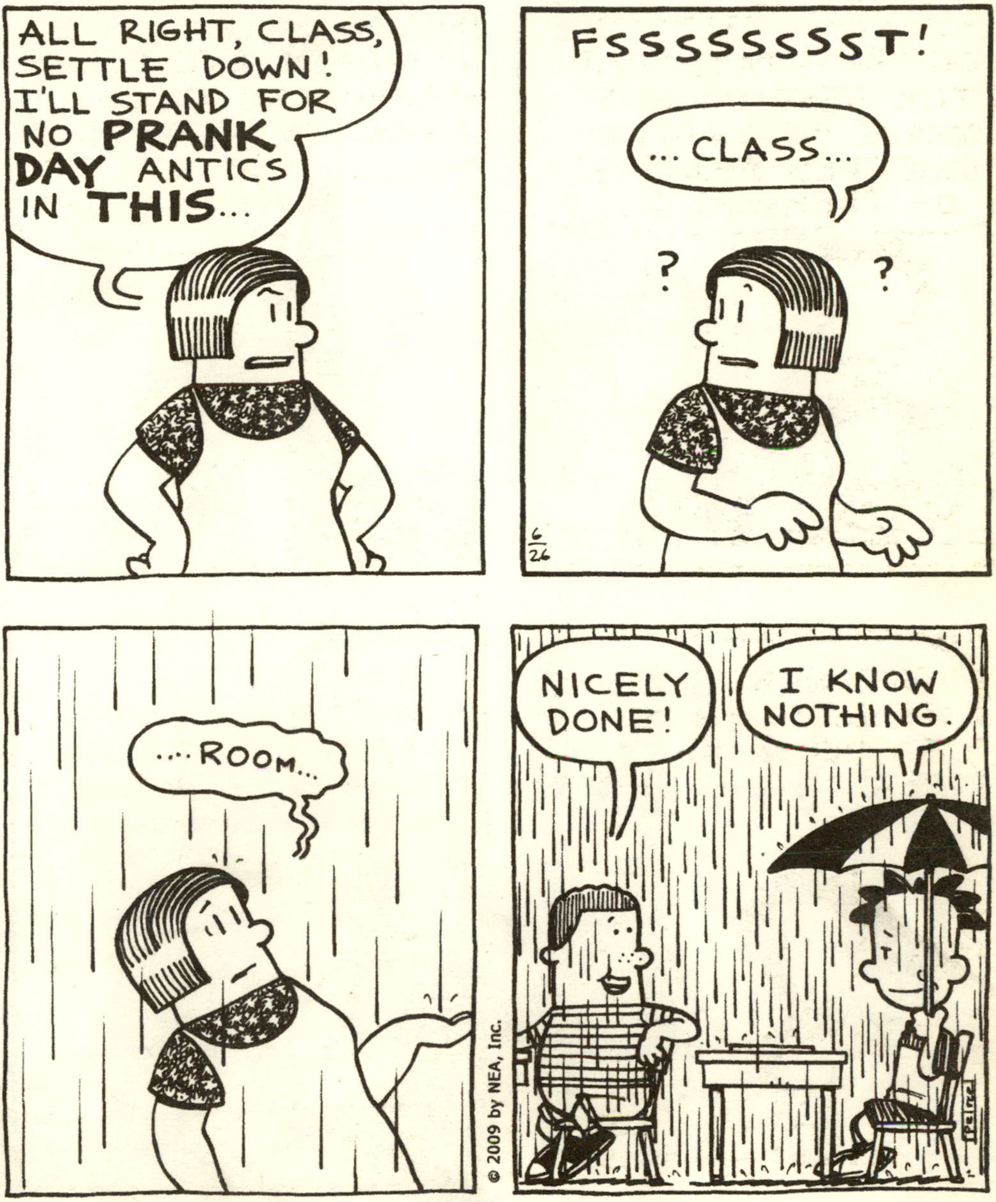
ALL RIGHT, CLASS, SETTLE DOWN! I'LL STAND FOR NO PRANK DAY ANTICS IN THIS...
FSSSSSSSST!
... CLASS...
? ?
6/26
.... ROOM...
NICELY DONE!
I KNOW NOTHING.
© 2009 by NEA, Inc.

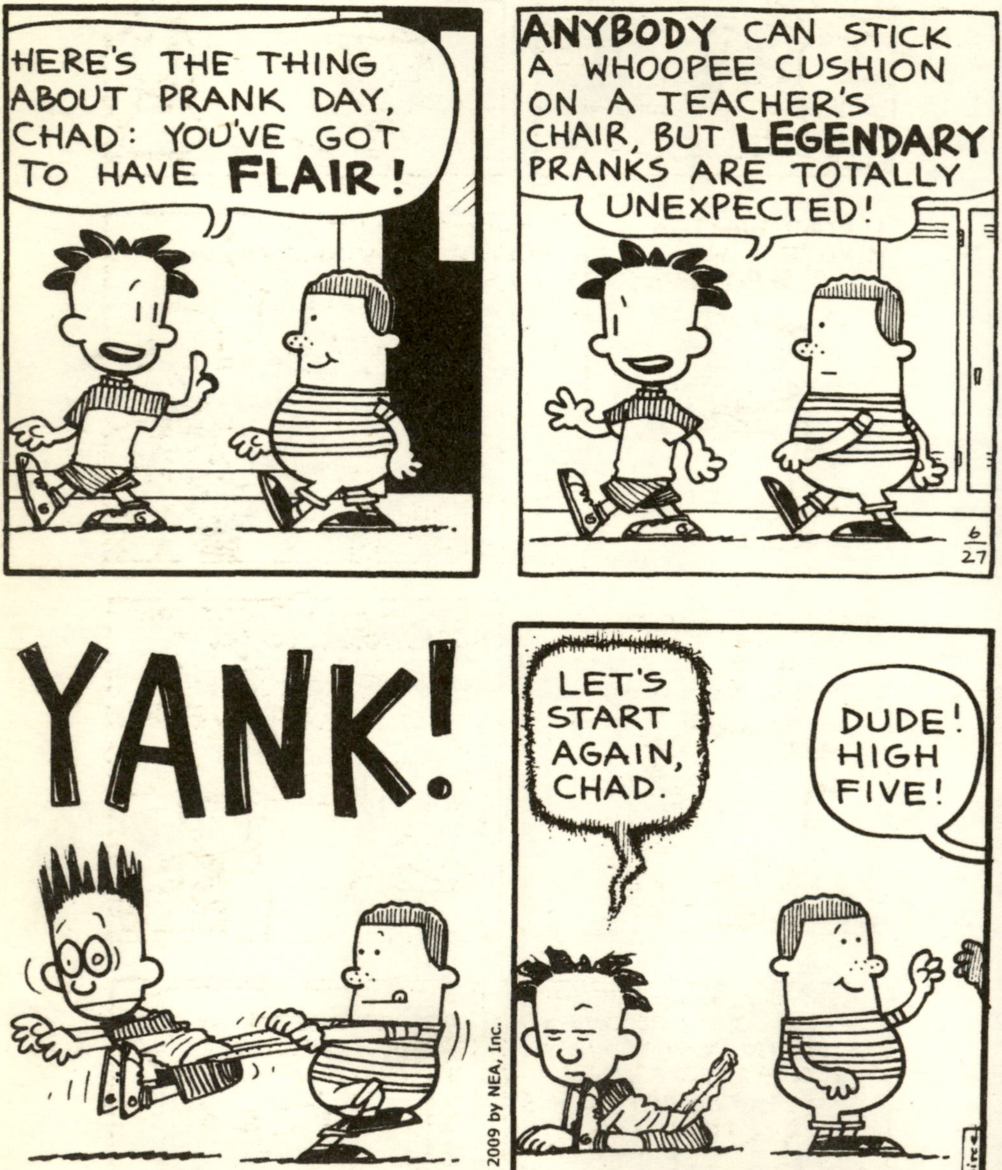
HERE'S THE THING ABOUT PRANK DAY, CHAD: YOU'VE GOT TO HAVE FLAIR!
ANYBODY CAN STICK A WHOOPEE CUSHION ON A TEACHER'S CHAIR, BUT LEGENDARY PRANKS ARE TOTALLY UNEXPECTED!
YANK!
LET'S START AGAIN, CHAD.
DUDE! HIGH FIVE!

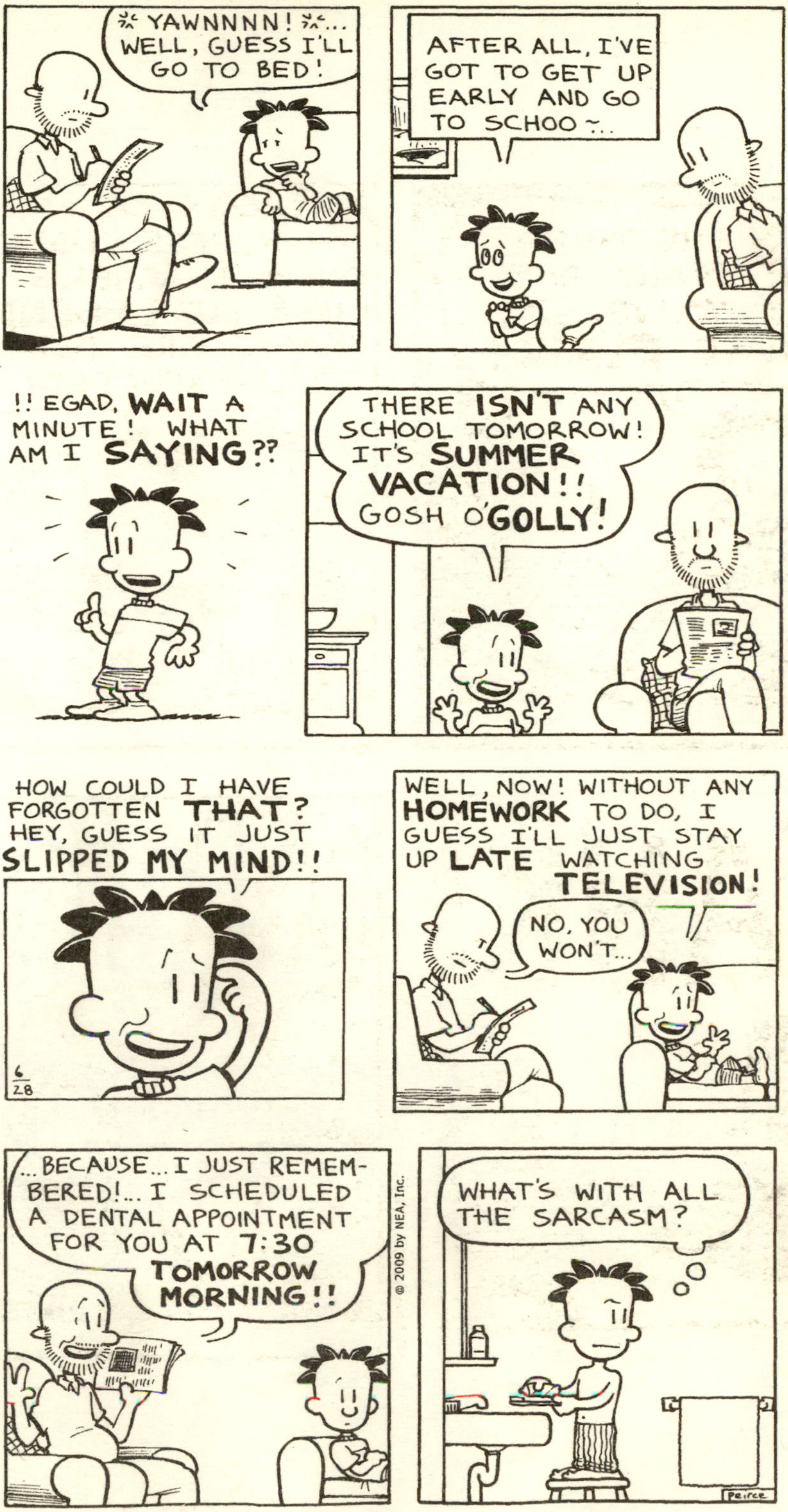
※ YAWNNNN! ※... WELL, GUESS I'LL GO TO BED!
AFTER ALL, I'VE GOT TO GET UP EARLY AND GO TO SCHOO~...
!! EGAD, WAIT A MINUTE! WHAT AM I SAYING??
THERE ISN'T ANY SCHOOL TOMORROW! IT'S SUMMER VACATION!! GOSH O'GOLLY!
HOW COULD I HAVE FORGOTTEN THAT? HEY, GUESS IT JUST SLIPPED MY MIND!!
6/28
WELL, NOW! WITHOUT ANY HOMEWORK TO DO, I GUESS I'LL JUST STAY UP LATE WATCHING TELEVISION!
NO, YOU WON'T...
...BECAUSE... I JUST REMEMBERED!... I SCHEDULED A DENTAL APPOINTMENT FOR YOU AT 7:30 TOMORROW MORNING!!
© 2009 by NEA, Inc.
WHAT'S WITH ALL THE SARCASM?
Peirce

THREE IN A TREE

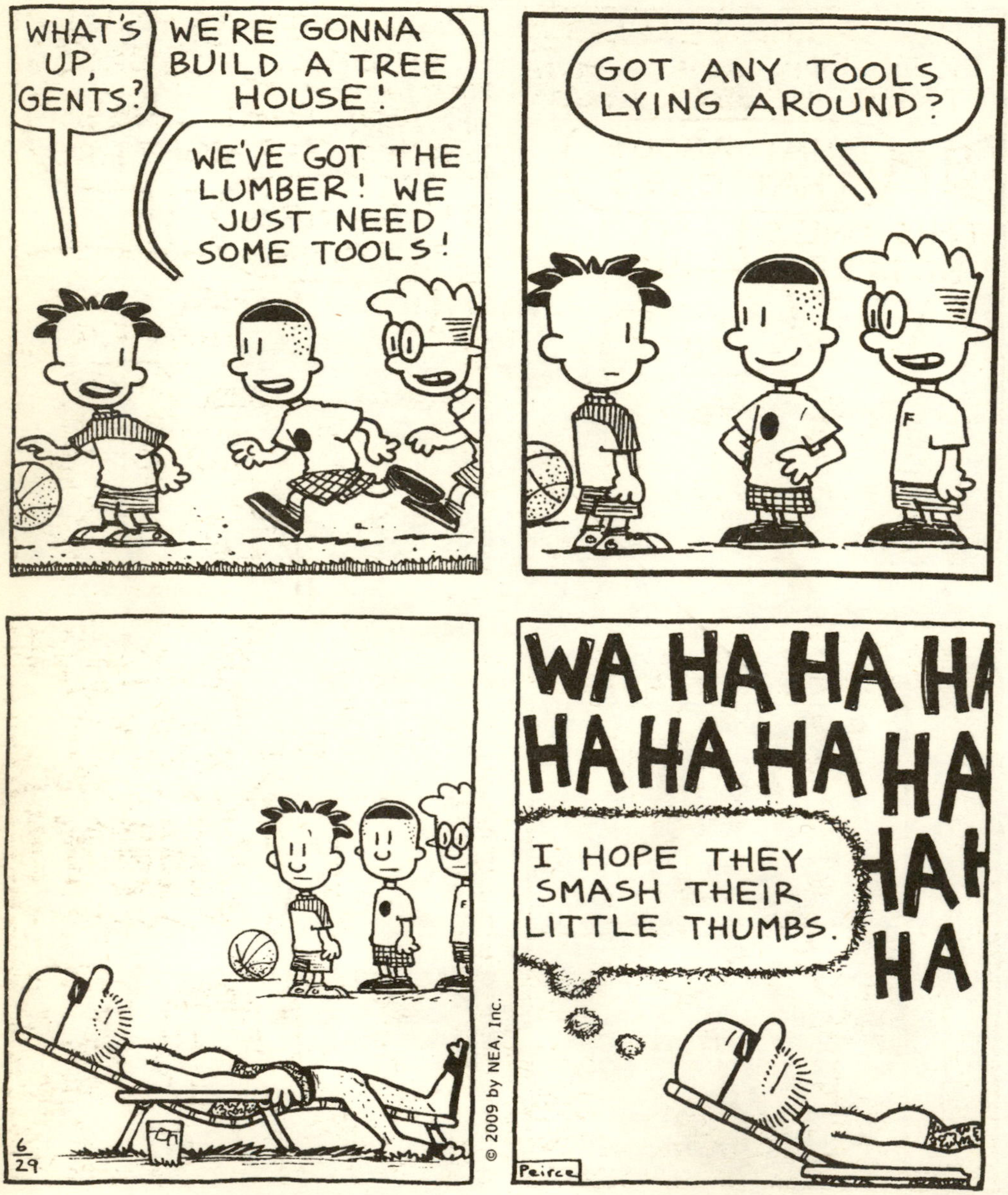
WHAT'S UP, GENTS?
WE'RE GONNA BUILD A TREE HOUSE!
WE'VE GOT THE LUMBER! WE JUST NEED SOME TOOLS!
GOT ANY TOOLS LYING AROUND?
6/29
WA HA HA HA HA HA HA HA HA HA HA HA HA
I HOPE THEY SMASH THEIR LITTLE THUMBS.
Peirce

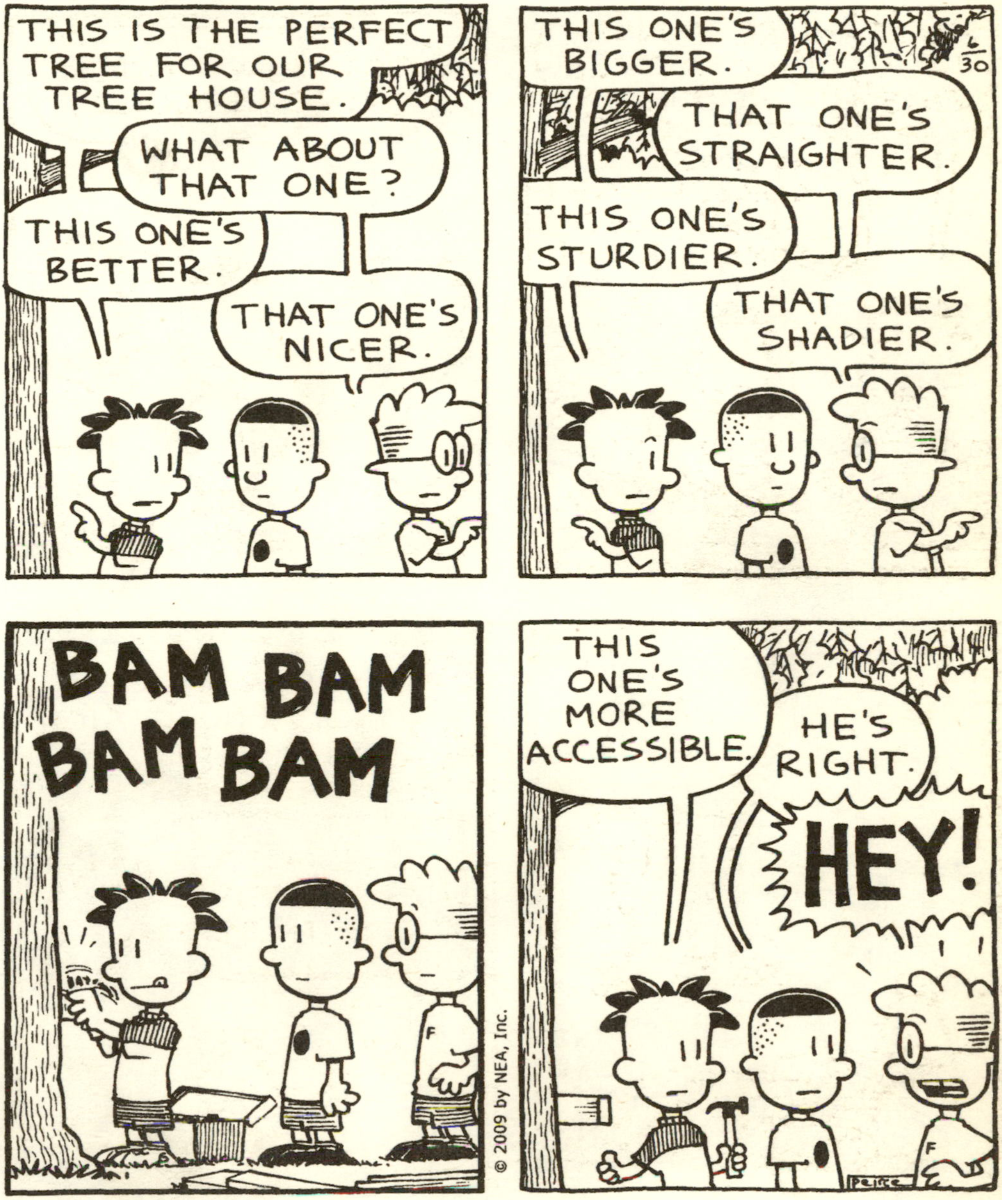
THIS IS THE PERFECT TREE FOR OUR TREE HOUSE.
WHAT ABOUT THAT ONE?
THIS ONE'S BETTER.
THAT ONE'S NICER.
THIS ONE'S BIGGER.
6/30
THAT ONE'S STRAIGHTER.
THIS ONE'S STURDIER.
THAT ONE'S SHADIER.
BAM BAM BAM BAM
© 2009 by NEA, Inc.
THIS ONE'S MORE ACCESSIBLE.
HE'S RIGHT.
HEY!
PEIRCE

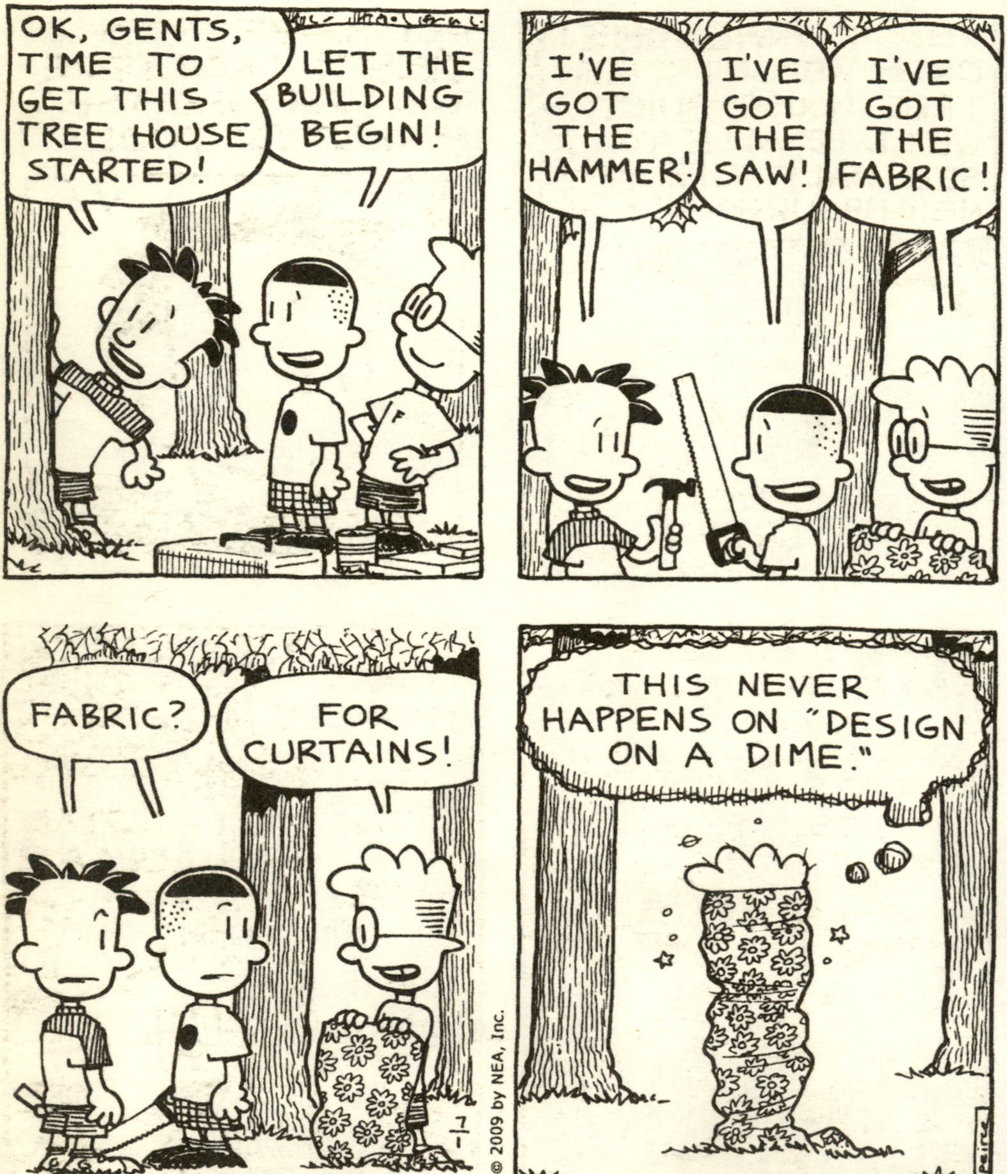
OK, GENTS, TIME TO GET THIS TREE HOUSE STARTED!
LET THE BUILDING BEGIN!
I'VE GOT THE HAMMER!
I'VE GOT THE SAW!
I'VE GOT THE FABRIC!
FABRIC?
FOR CURTAINS!
© 2009 by NEA, Inc.
THIS NEVER HAPPENS ON "DESIGN ON A DIME."

THIS IS **AWESOME**! ONCE WE GET THIS TREE HOUSE BUILT, WE'LL BE ABLE TO SEE HALF THE NEIGHBOURHOOD!

HEY, MAYBE... **YES**!... **YES**!! FROM HERE YOU CAN SEE THE McNULTYS' POOL!

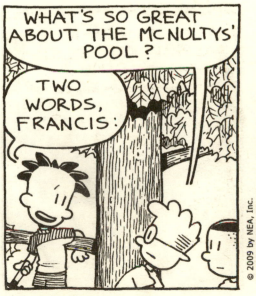

WHAT'S SO GREAT ABOUT THE McNULTYS' POOL?

TWO WORDS, FRANCIS:

...MRS McNULTY.

ROWR!

TOTAL COUGAR!

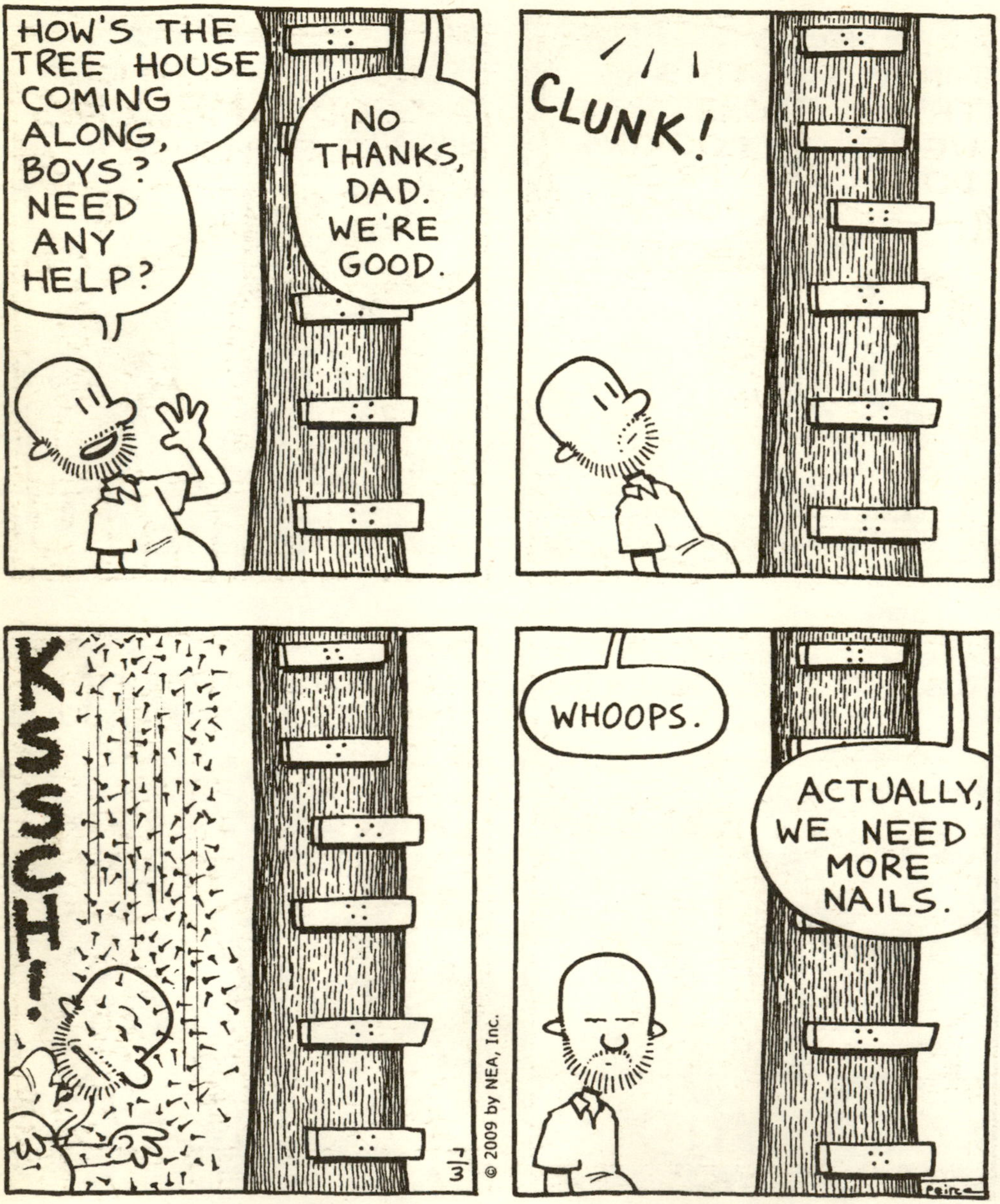
HOW'S THE TREE HOUSE COMING ALONG, BOYS? NEED ANY HELP?
NO THANKS, DAD. WE'RE GOOD.
CLUNK!
KSSCH!
WHOOPS.
ACTUALLY, WE NEED MORE NAILS.
7/3
© 2009 by NEA, Inc.
peirce

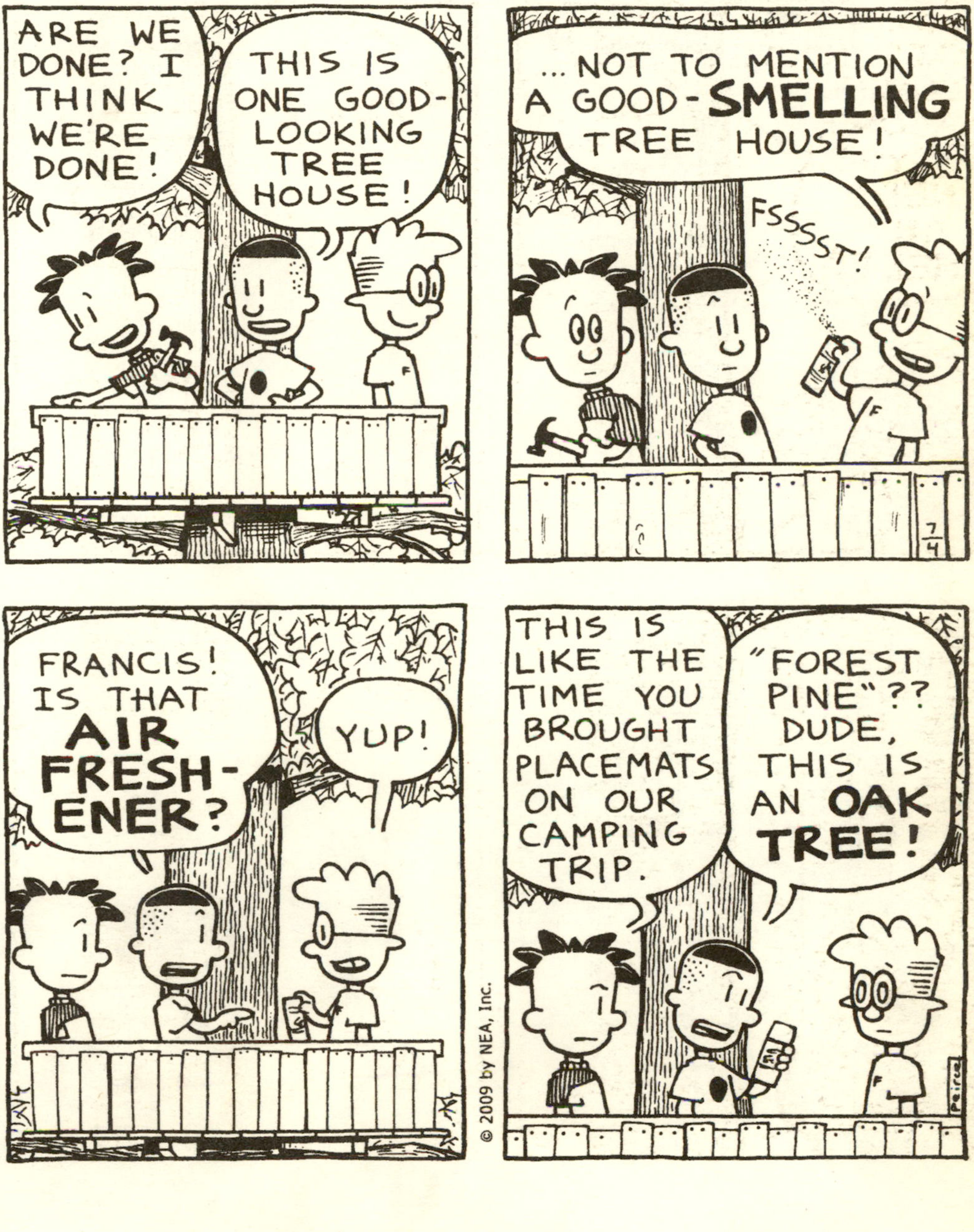
ARE WE DONE? I THINK WE'RE DONE!
THIS IS ONE GOOD-LOOKING TREE HOUSE!
...NOT TO MENTION A GOOD-SMELLING TREE HOUSE!
FSSSSST!
7/4
FRANCIS! IS THAT AIR FRESHENER?
YUP!
THIS IS LIKE THE TIME YOU BROUGHT PLACEMATS ON OUR CAMPING TRIP.
"FOREST PINE"?? DUDE, THIS IS AN OAK TREE!
Peirce

LET'S HEAD OVER TO TEDDY'S HOUSE AND...
WURF!
OH, HEY, SPITSY.
WOOF! WURF! WURF! WORF! WROWF! WOOF!
GEEZ, SPITSY, CHILL OUT! WHAT'S YOUR PROBLEM?
DUH, FRANCIS! HE'S TRYING TO TELL US SOMETHING!
WURF! ARF! WO
WHAT IS IT, BOY? WHAT'S GOING ON? IS SOMEONE IN TROUBLE?
ARF! WURF! WURF!
WE'D BETTER FOLLOW HIM! SOMEBODY MIGHT NEED HELP! SOMEBODY MIGHT NEED TO BE RESCUED!
WURF!
!
WURF!
© 2009 by NEA, Inc.
REMIND ME NEVER TO GET TRAPPED IN A BURNING BUILDING WITH YOU AROUND.

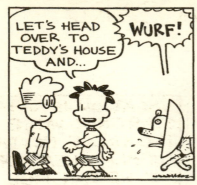

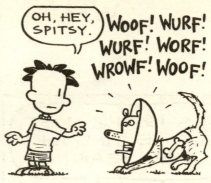

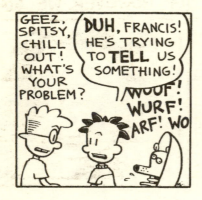

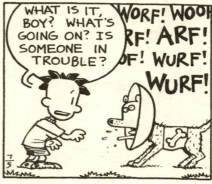

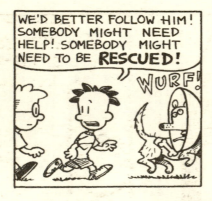

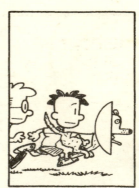

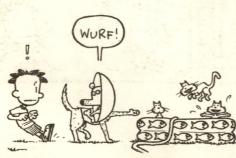

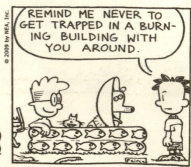

WHAT A CARD

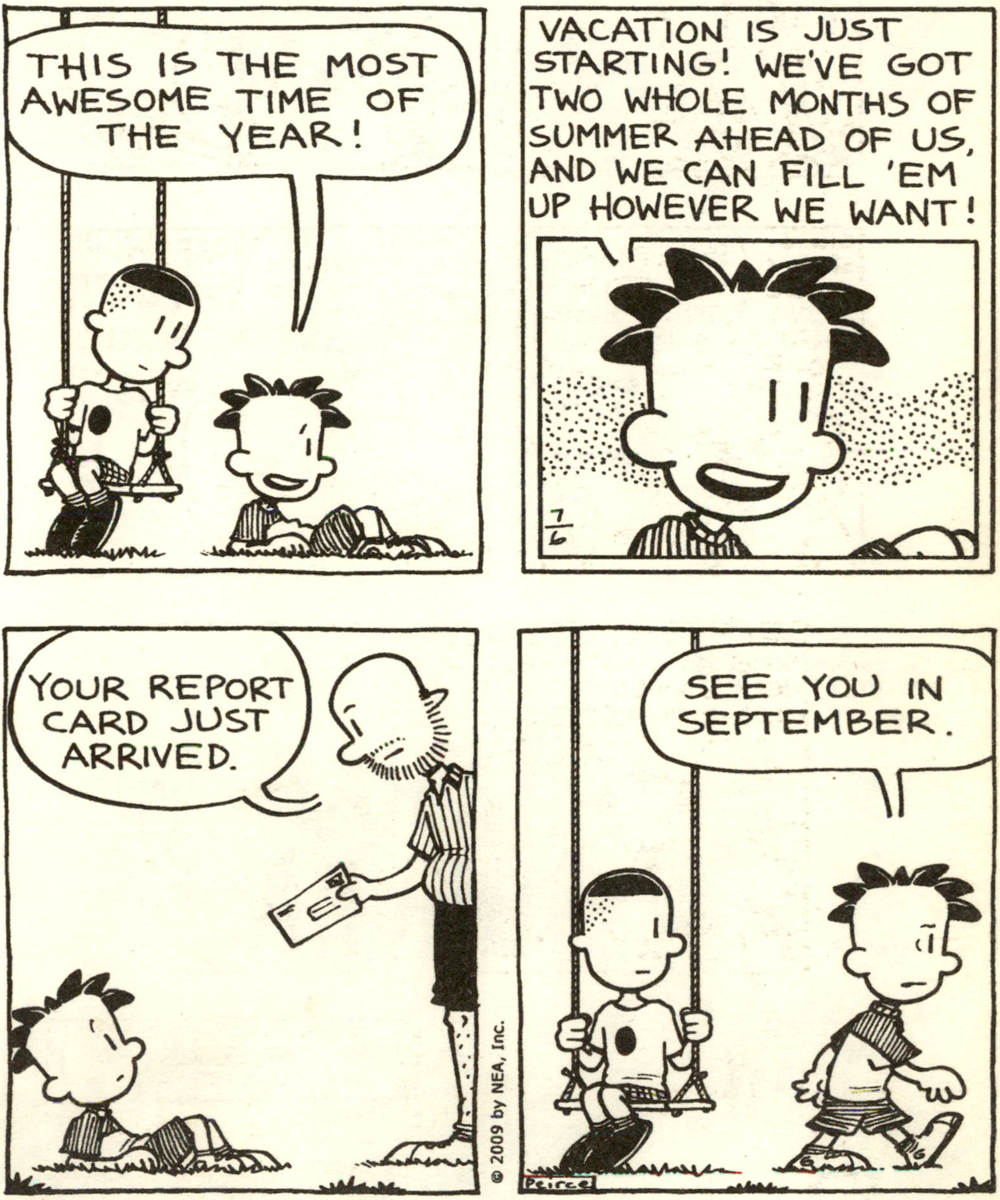
THIS IS THE MOST AWESOME TIME OF THE YEAR!
VACATION IS JUST STARTING! WE'VE GOT TWO WHOLE MONTHS OF SUMMER AHEAD OF US, AND WE CAN FILL 'EM UP HOWEVER WE WANT!
YOUR REPORT CARD JUST ARRIVED.
SEE YOU IN SEPTEMBER.
© 2009 by NEA, Inc.
Peirce

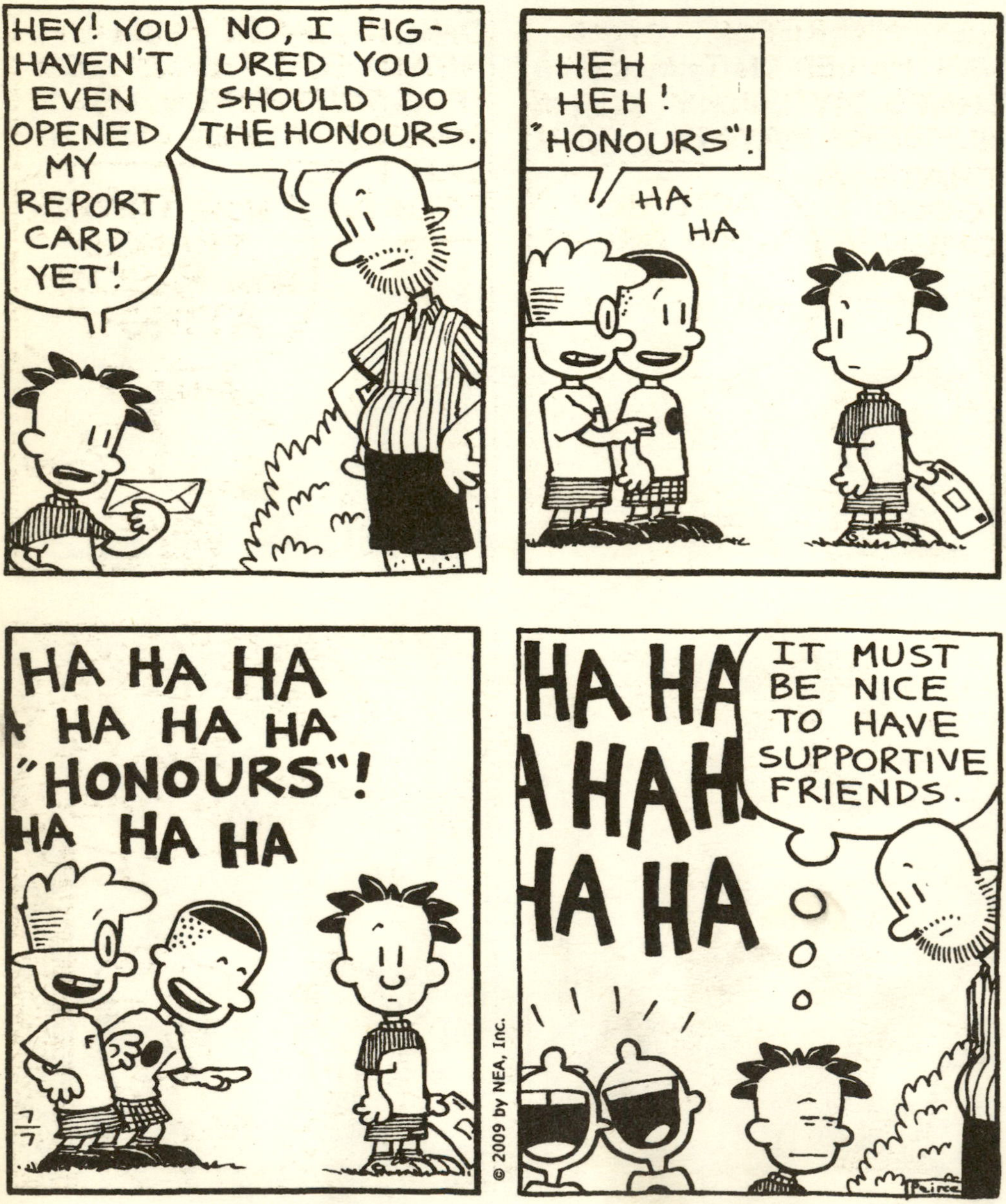
HEY! YOU HAVEN'T EVEN OPENED MY REPORT CARD YET!
NO, I FIGURED YOU SHOULD DO THE HONOURS.
HEH HEH! "HONOURS"!
HA HA
HA HA HA HA HA HA "HONOURS"! HA HA HA
HA HA HA HA HA HA
IT MUST BE NICE TO HAVE SUPPORTIVE FRIENDS.
7/7
© 2009 by NEA, Inc.
Peirce

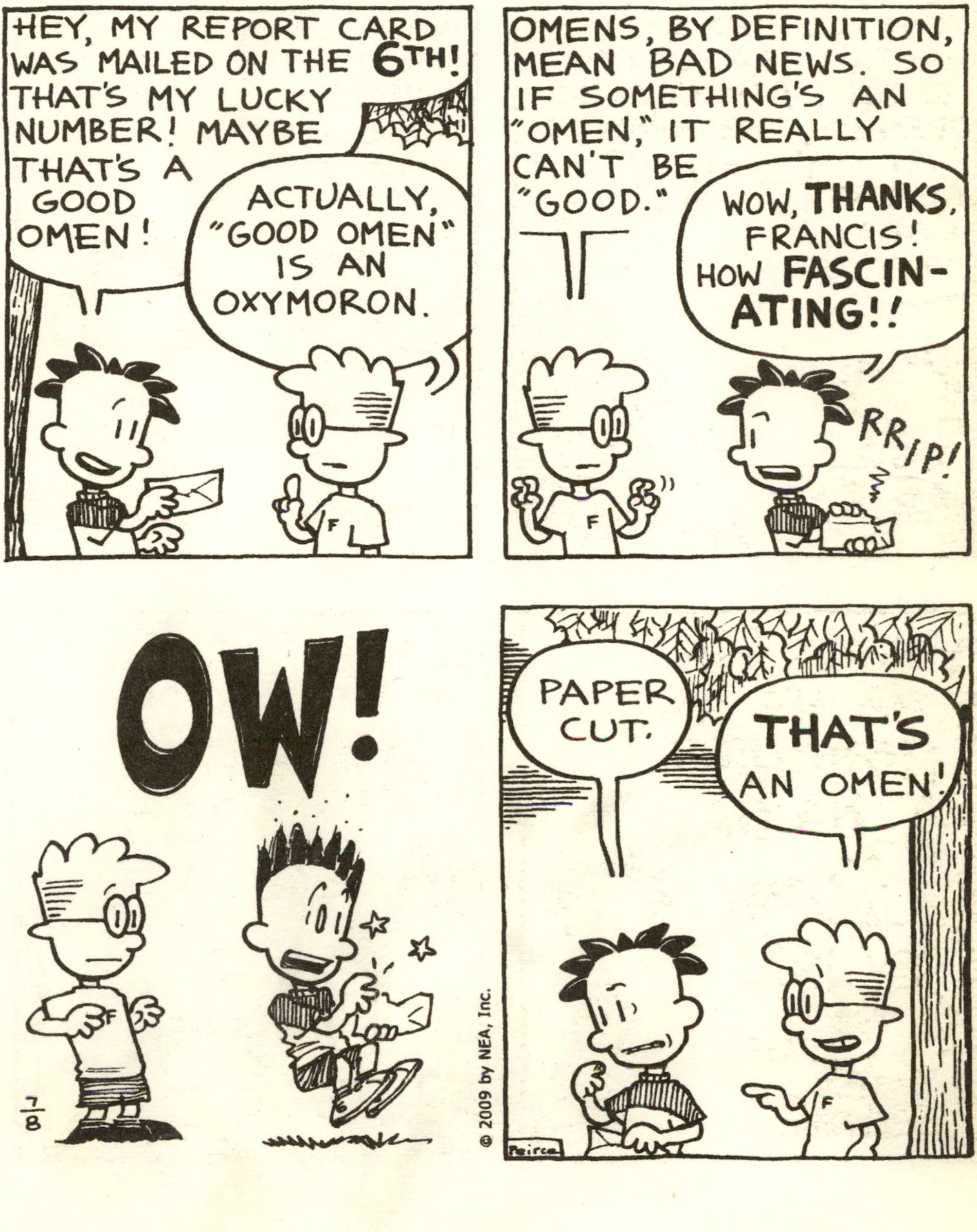
HEY, MY REPORT CARD WAS MAILED ON THE 6TH! THAT'S MY LUCKY NUMBER! MAYBE THAT'S A GOOD OMEN!
ACTUALLY, "GOOD OMEN" IS AN OXYMORON.
OMENS, BY DEFINITION, MEAN BAD NEWS. SO IF SOMETHING'S AN "OMEN," IT REALLY CAN'T BE "GOOD."
WOW, THANKS, FRANCIS! HOW FASCINATING!!
RRIP!
OW!
7/8
© 2009 by NEA, Inc.
PAPER CUT.
THAT'S AN OMEN!
Peirce

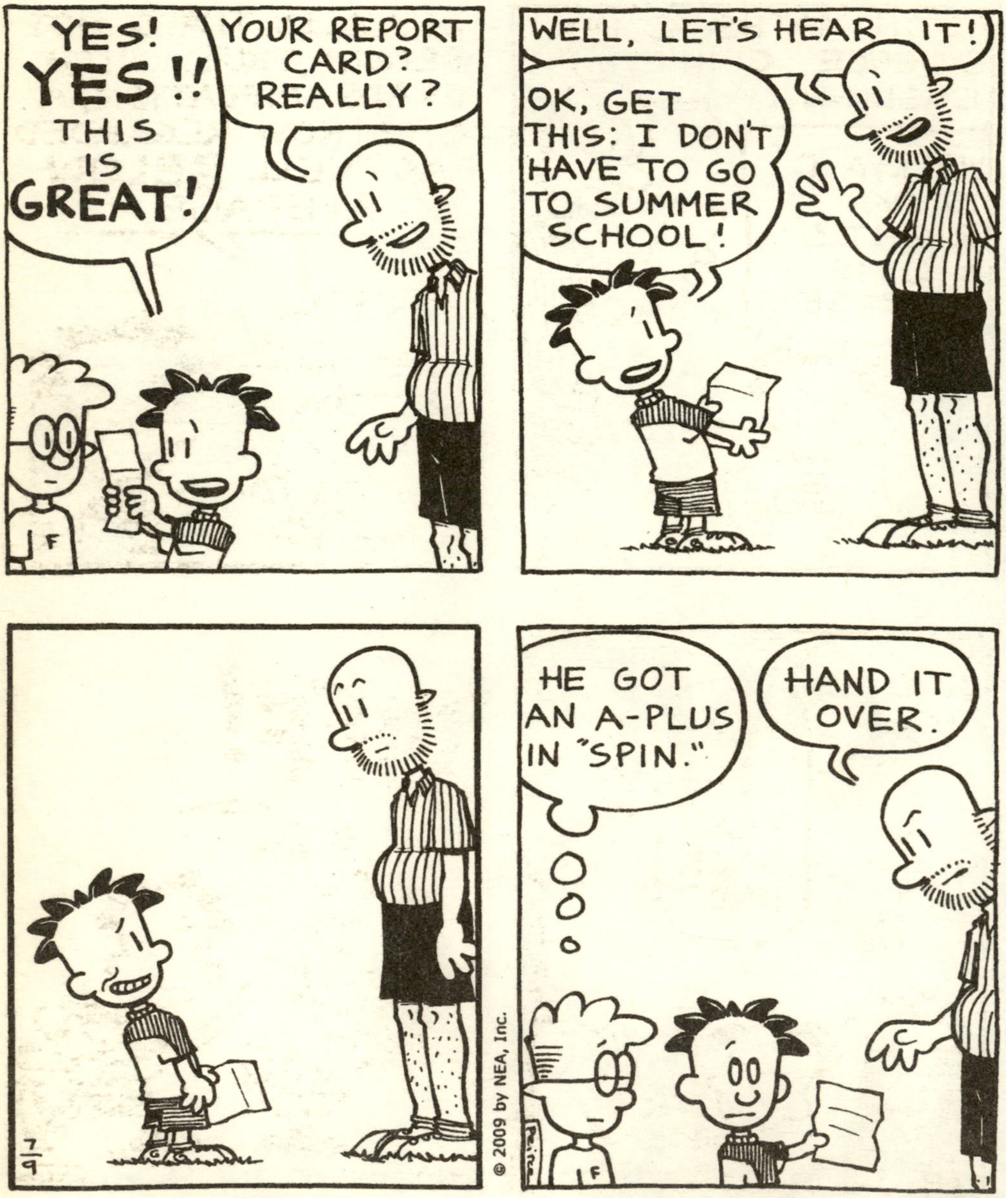
YES! YES!! THIS IS GREAT!
YOUR REPORT CARD? REALLY?
F
WELL, LET'S HEAR IT!
OK, GET THIS: I DON'T HAVE TO GO TO SUMMER SCHOOL!
7/9
© 2009 by NEA, Inc.
HE GOT AN A-PLUS IN "SPIN."
HAND IT OVER.
F

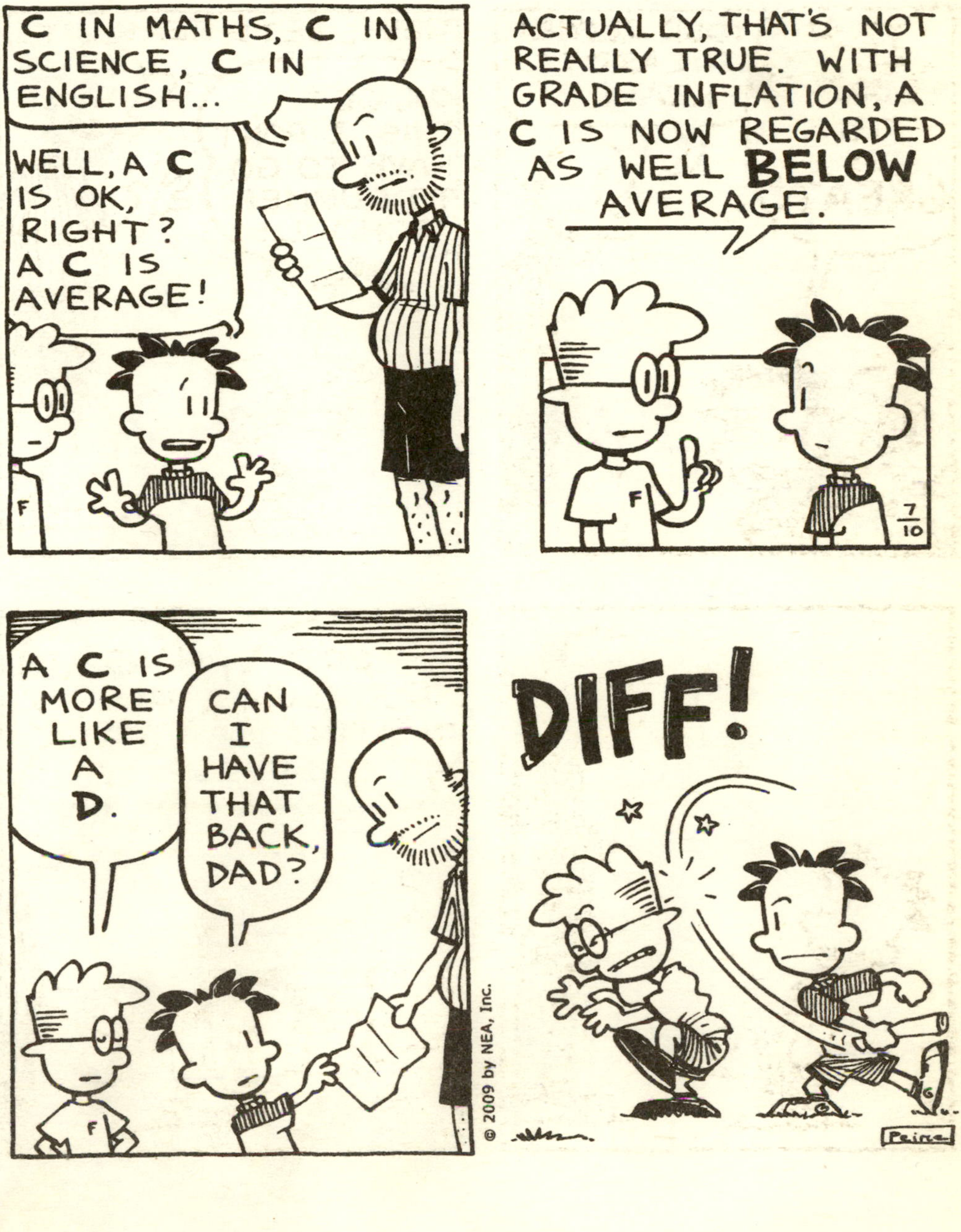
C IN MATHS, C IN SCIENCE, C IN ENGLISH...
WELL, A C IS OK, RIGHT? A C IS AVERAGE!
ACTUALLY, THAT'S NOT REALLY TRUE. WITH GRADE INFLATION, A C IS NOW REGARDED AS WELL BELOW AVERAGE.
7/10
A C IS MORE LIKE A D.
CAN I HAVE THAT BACK, DAD?
© 2009 by NEA, Inc.
DIFF!
Peirce

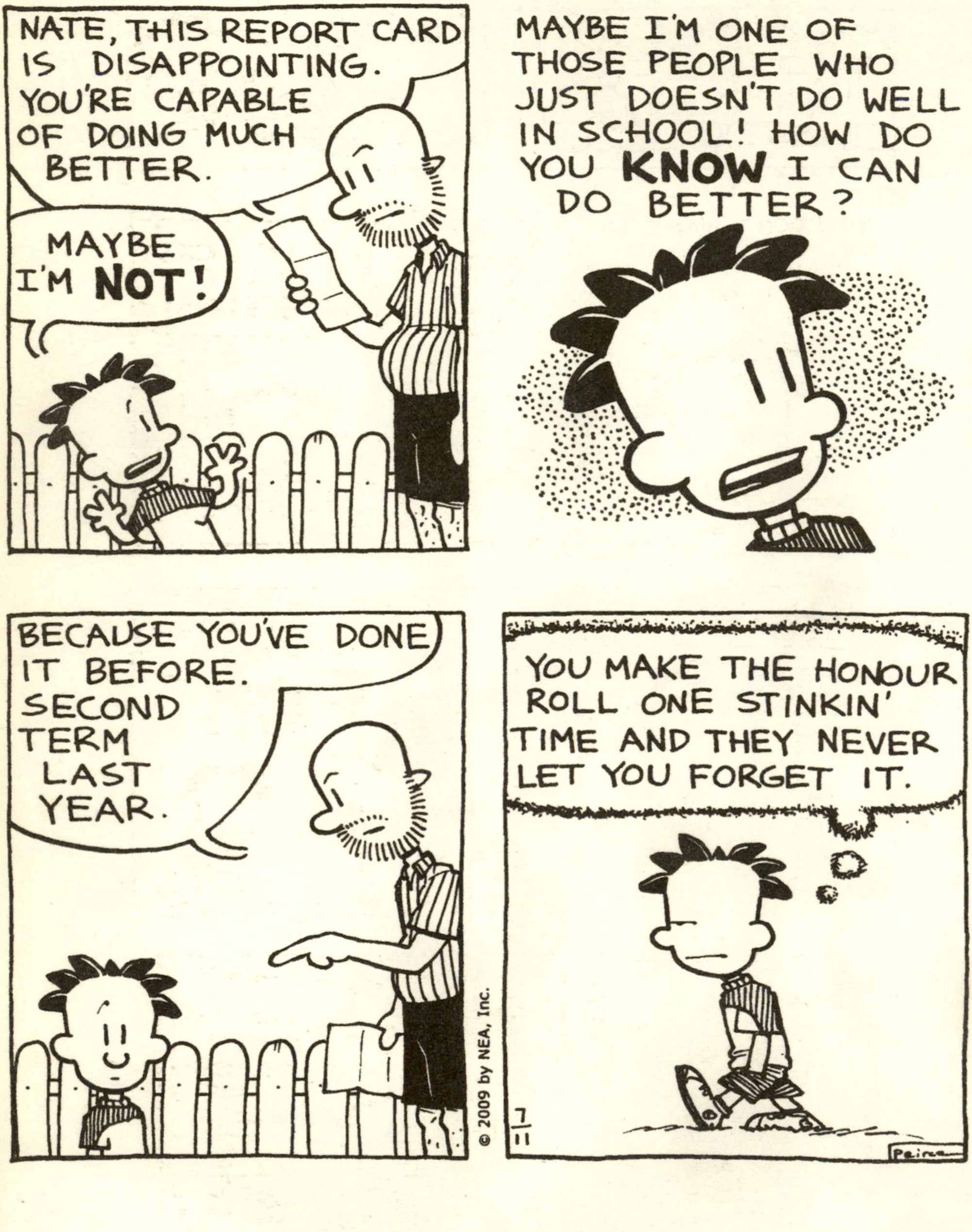
NATE, THIS REPORT CARD IS DISAPPOINTING. YOU'RE CAPABLE OF DOING MUCH BETTER.
MAYBE I'M NOT!
MAYBE I'M ONE OF THOSE PEOPLE WHO JUST DOESN'T DO WELL IN SCHOOL! HOW DO YOU KNOW I CAN DO BETTER?
BECAUSE YOU'VE DONE IT BEFORE. SECOND TERM LAST YEAR.
YOU MAKE THE HONOUR ROLL ONE STINKIN' TIME AND THEY NEVER LET YOU FORGET IT.
© 2009 by NEA, Inc.
7/11

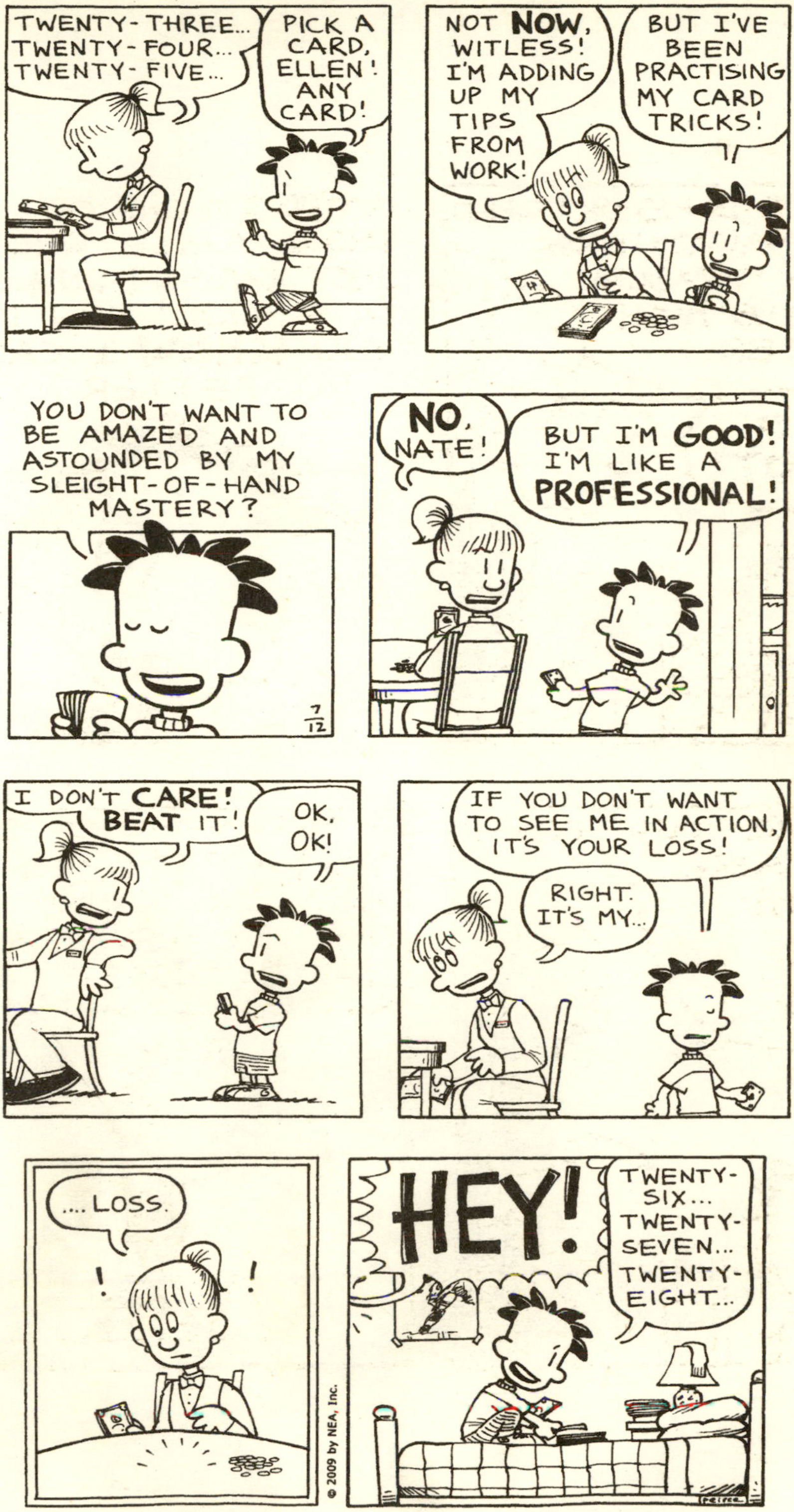
TWENTY-THREE... TWENTY-FOUR... TWENTY-FIVE...
PICK A CARD, ELLEN! ANY CARD!
NOT NOW, WITLESS! I'M ADDING UP MY TIPS FROM WORK!
BUT I'VE BEEN PRACTISING MY CARD TRICKS!
YOU DON'T WANT TO BE AMAZED AND ASTOUNDED BY MY SLEIGHT-OF-HAND MASTERY?
7/12
NO, NATE!
BUT I'M GOOD! I'M LIKE A PROFESSIONAL!
I DON'T CARE! BEAT IT!
OK, OK!
IF YOU DON'T WANT TO SEE ME IN ACTION, IT'S YOUR LOSS!
RIGHT. IT'S MY...
.... LOSS.
! !
HEY!
TWENTY-SIX... TWENTY-SEVEN... TWENTY-EIGHT...

THE JOY OF READING

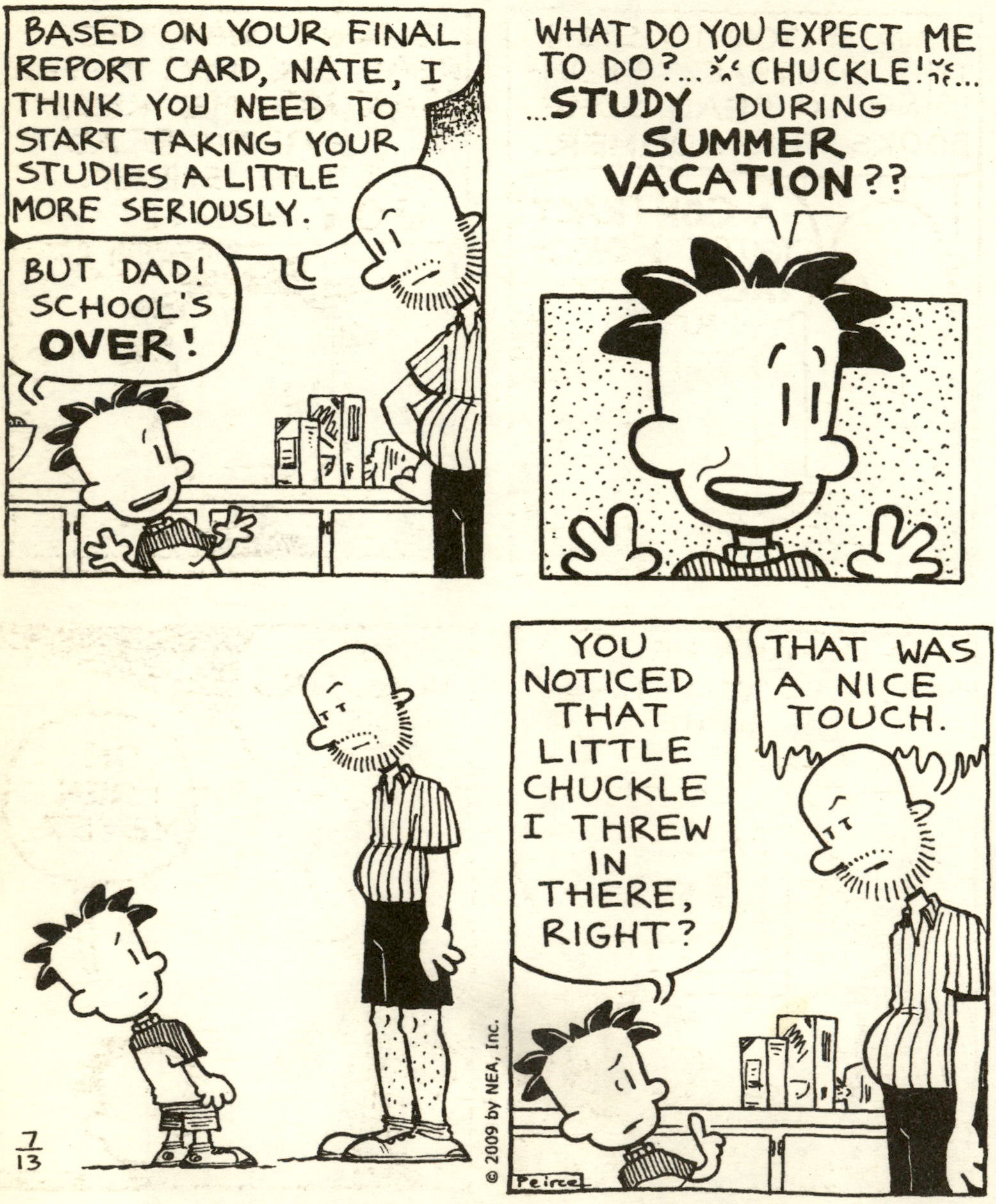
BASED ON YOUR FINAL REPORT CARD, NATE, I THINK YOU NEED TO START TAKING YOUR STUDIES A LITTLE MORE SERIOUSLY.
BUT DAD! SCHOOL'S **OVER**!
WHAT DO YOU EXPECT ME TO DO?... CHUCKLE!... ...**STUDY** DURING **SUMMER VACATION**??
YOU NOTICED THAT LITTLE CHUCKLE I THREW IN THERE, RIGHT?
THAT WAS A NICE TOUCH.
7/13
© 2009 by NEA, Inc.
Peirce

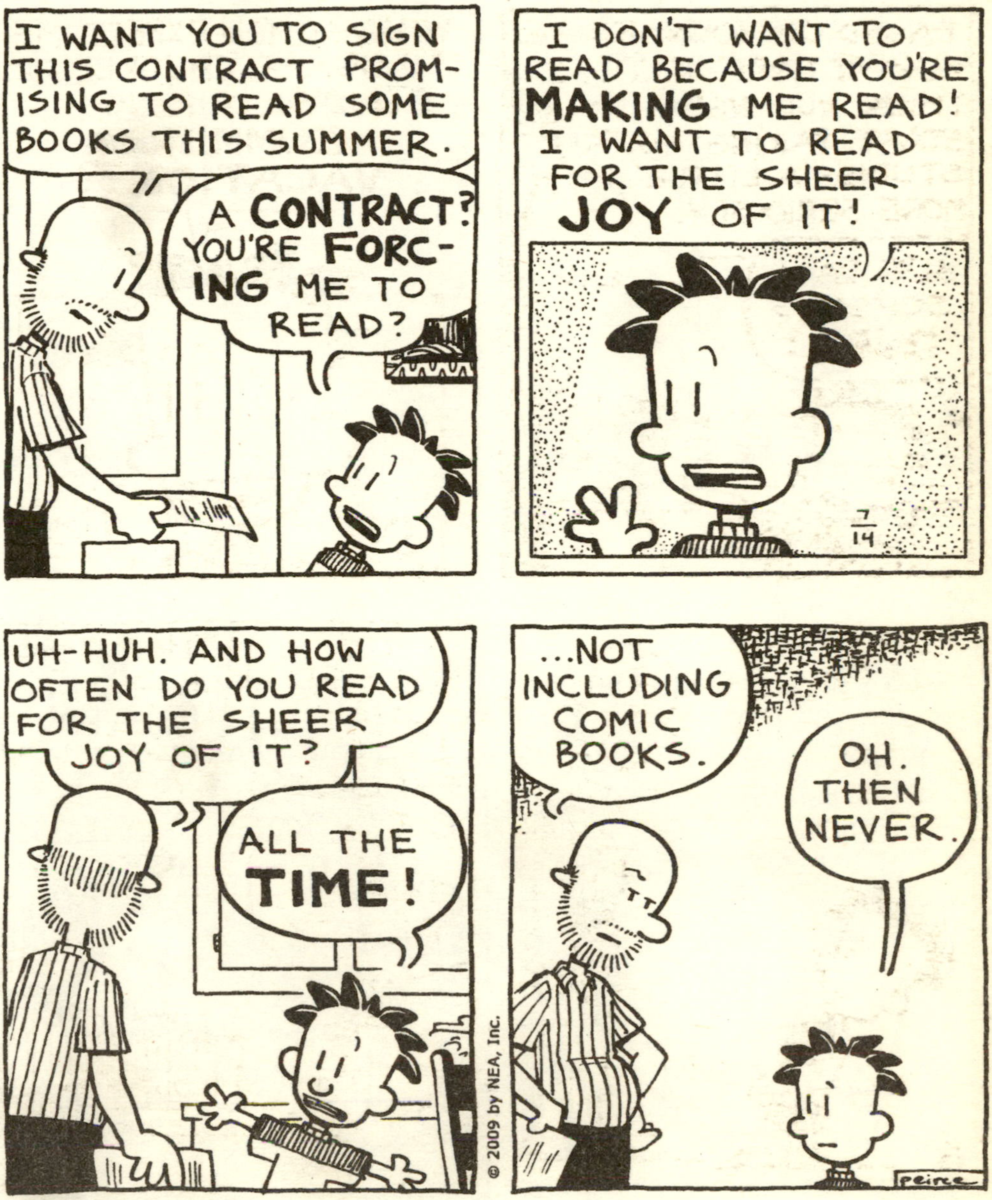
I WANT YOU TO SIGN THIS CONTRACT PROMISING TO READ SOME BOOKS THIS SUMMER.
A **CONTRACT**? YOU'RE **FORCING** ME TO READ?
I DON'T WANT TO READ BECAUSE YOU'RE **MAKING** ME READ! I WANT TO READ FOR THE SHEER **JOY** OF IT!
7/14
UH-HUH. AND HOW OFTEN DO YOU READ FOR THE SHEER JOY OF IT?
ALL THE **TIME**!
© 2009 by NEA, Inc.
...NOT INCLUDING COMIC BOOKS.
OH. THEN NEVER.
peirce

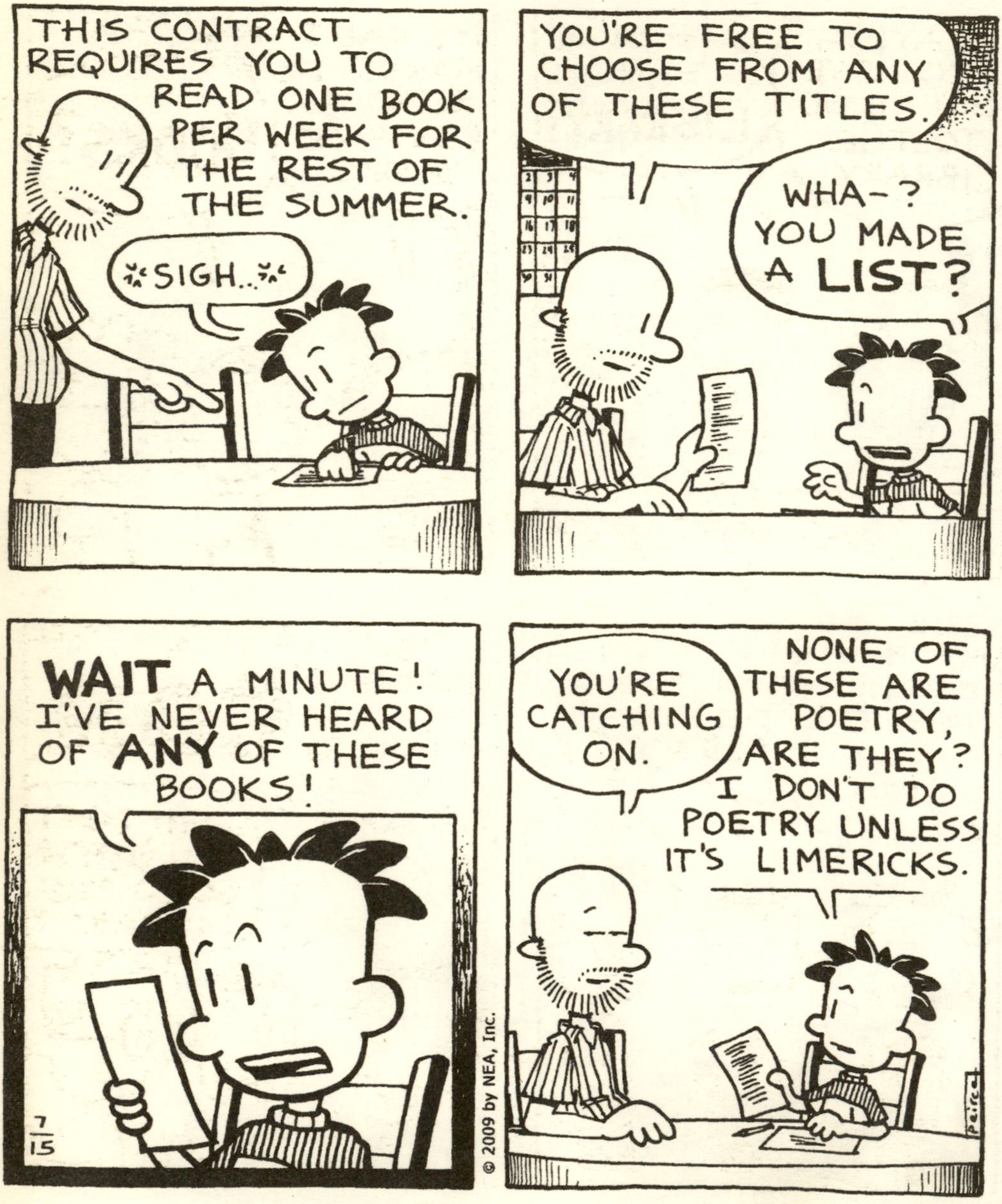
THIS CONTRACT REQUIRES YOU TO READ ONE BOOK PER WEEK FOR THE REST OF THE SUMMER.
SIGH...
YOU'RE FREE TO CHOOSE FROM ANY OF THESE TITLES.
WHA-? YOU MADE A LIST?
WAIT A MINUTE! I'VE NEVER HEARD OF ANY OF THESE BOOKS!
7/15
© 2009 by NEA, Inc.
NONE OF THESE ARE POETRY, ARE THEY? I DON'T DO POETRY UNLESS IT'S LIMERICKS.
YOU'RE CATCHING ON.
Peirce

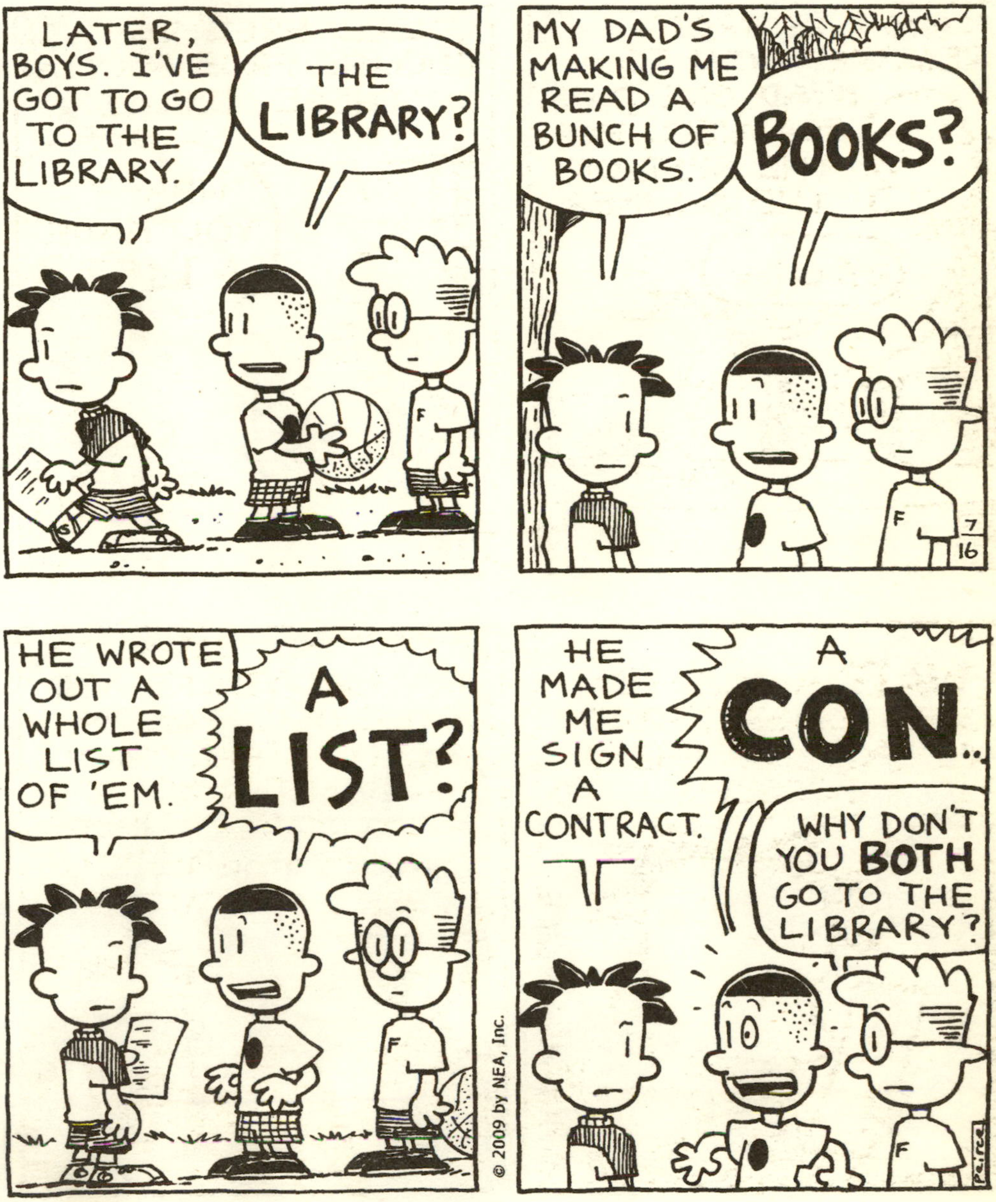
LATER, BOYS. I'VE GOT TO GO TO THE LIBRARY.
THE LIBRARY?
MY DAD'S MAKING ME READ A BUNCH OF BOOKS.
BOOKS?
7/16
HE WROTE OUT A WHOLE LIST OF 'EM.
A LIST?
HE MADE ME SIGN A CONTRACT.
A CON...
WHY DON'T YOU BOTH GO TO THE LIBRARY?
© 2009 by NEA, Inc.
Peirce

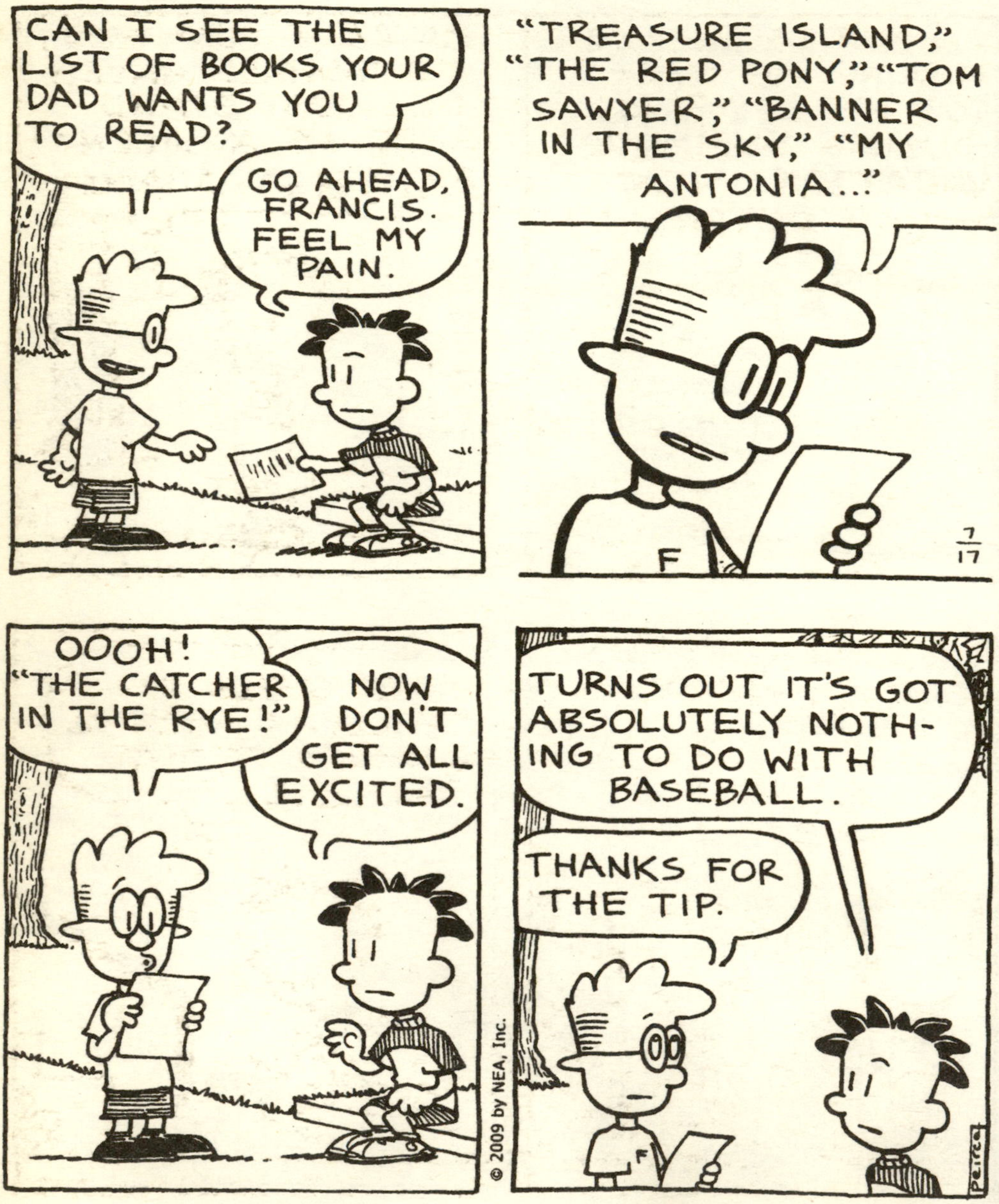
CAN I SEE THE LIST OF BOOKS YOUR DAD WANTS YOU TO READ?
GO AHEAD, FRANCIS. FEEL MY PAIN.
"TREASURE ISLAND," "THE RED PONY," "TOM SAWYER," "BANNER IN THE SKY," "MY ANTONIA..."
7/17
OOOH! "THE CATCHER IN THE RYE!"
NOW DON'T GET ALL EXCITED.
© 2009 by NEA, Inc.
TURNS OUT IT'S GOT ABSOLUTELY NOTHING TO DO WITH BASEBALL.
THANKS FOR THE TIP.
PEIRCE
F

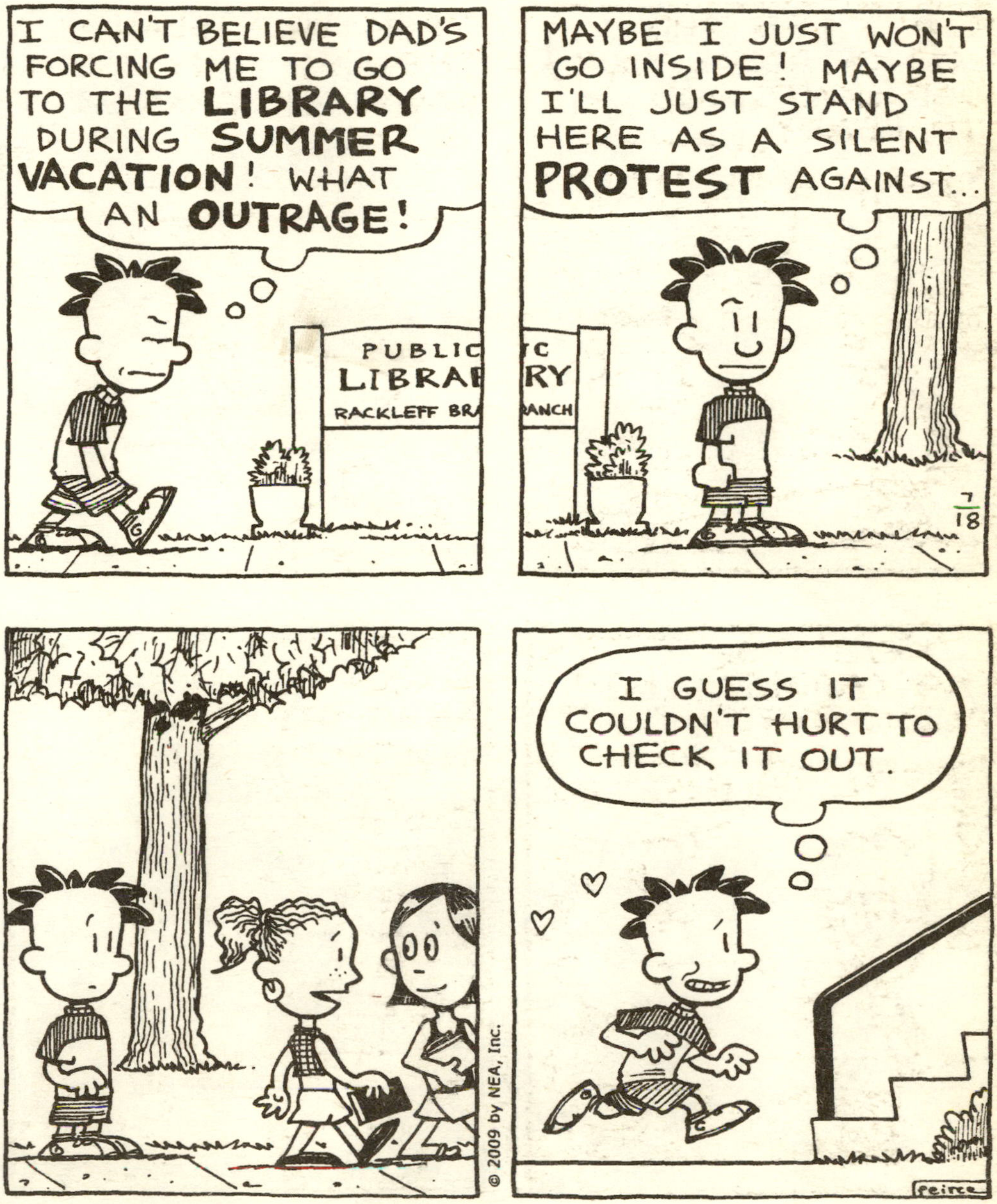
I CAN'T BELIEVE DAD'S FORCING ME TO GO TO THE **LIBRARY** DURING **SUMMER VACATION**! WHAT AN **OUTRAGE**!
PUBLIC LIBRARY RACKLEFF BRANCH
MAYBE I JUST WON'T GO INSIDE! MAYBE I'LL JUST STAND HERE AS A SILENT **PROTEST** AGAINST...
7/18
I GUESS IT COULDN'T HURT TO CHECK IT OUT.
© 2009 by NEA, Inc.
peirce

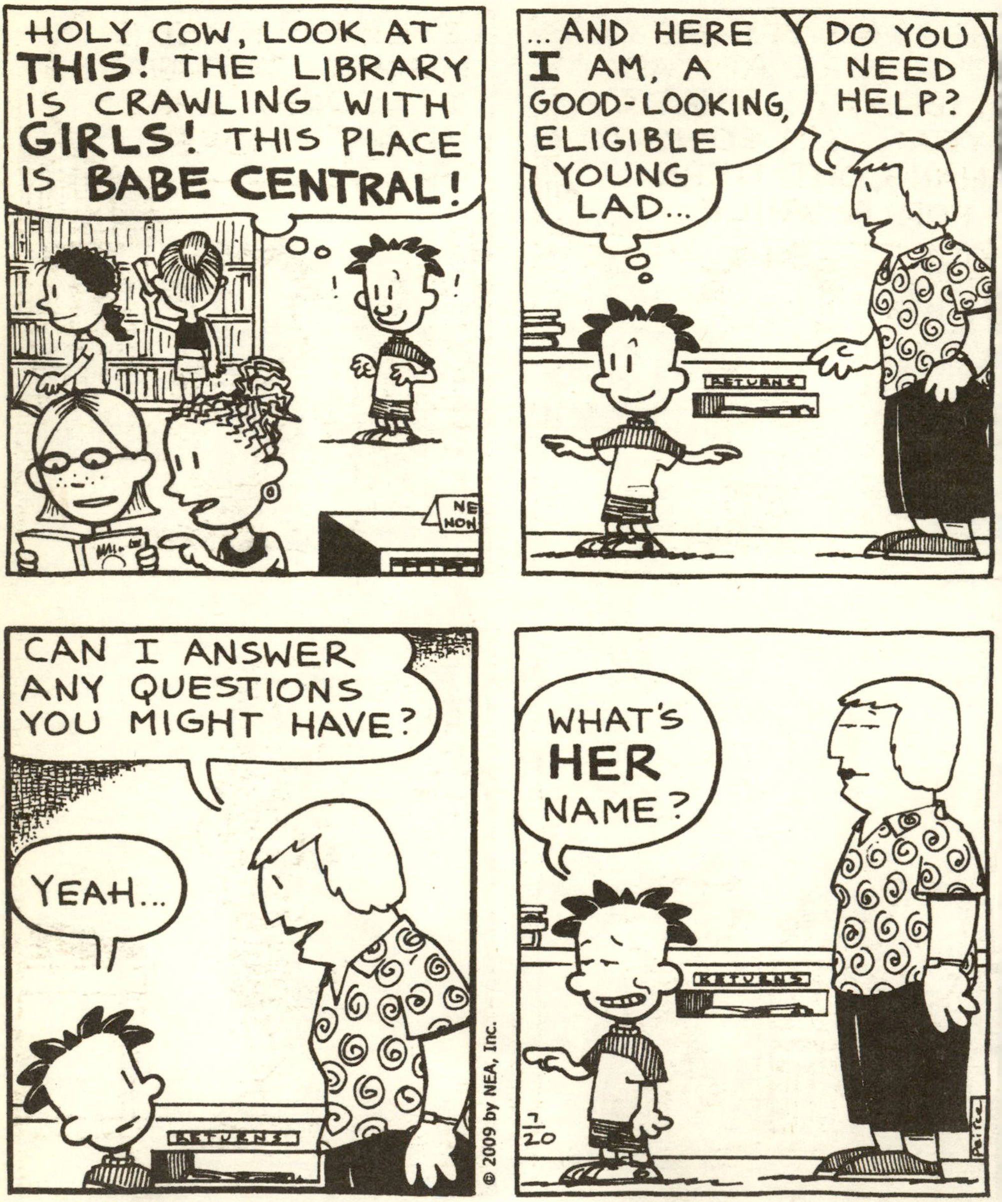
HOLY COW, LOOK AT THIS! THE LIBRARY IS CRAWLING WITH GIRLS! THIS PLACE IS BABE CENTRAL!
...AND HERE I AM, A GOOD-LOOKING, ELIGIBLE YOUNG LAD...
DO YOU NEED HELP?
CAN I ANSWER ANY QUESTIONS YOU MIGHT HAVE?
YEAH...
WHAT'S HER NAME?
© 2009 by NEA, Inc.

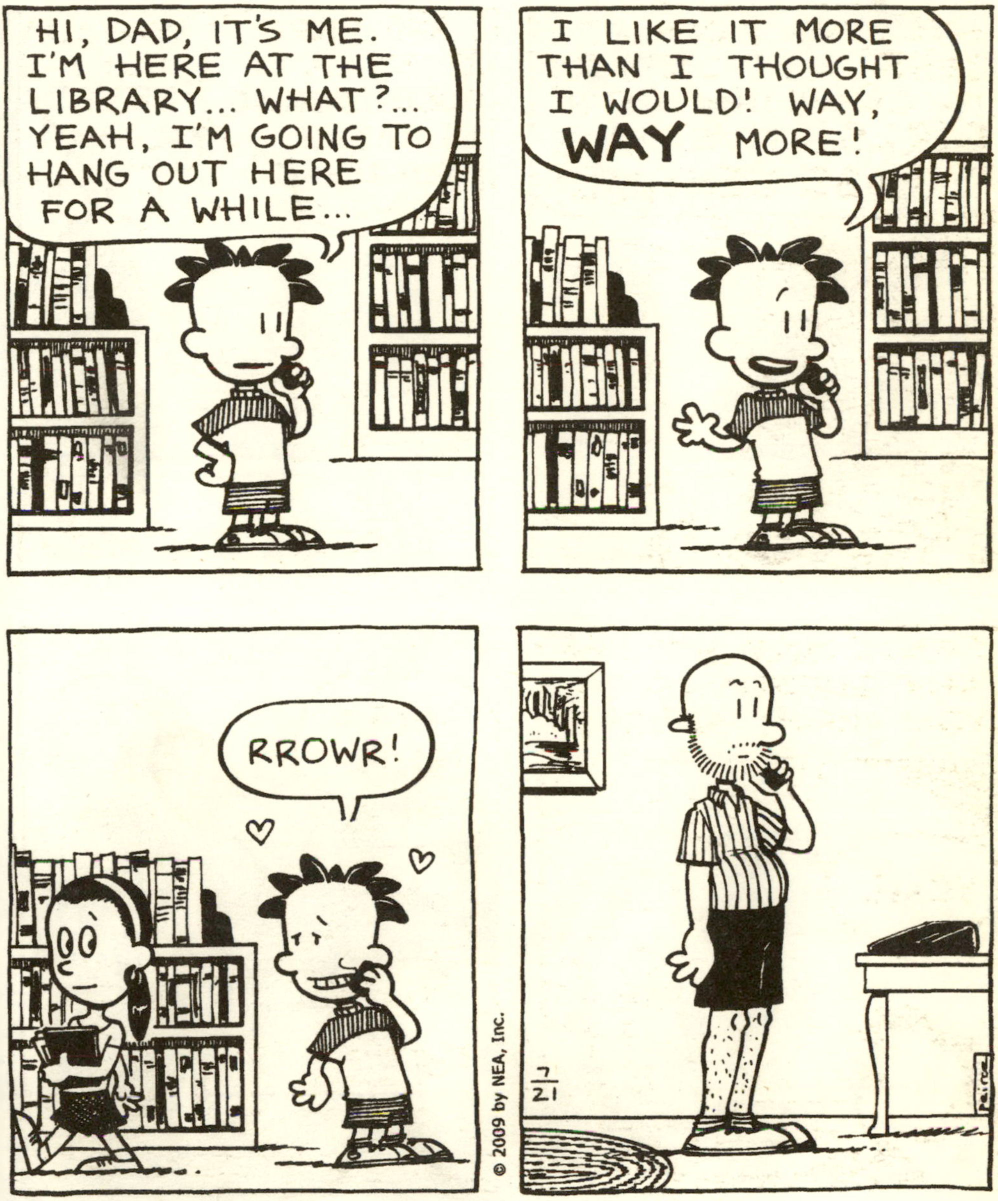
HI, DAD, IT'S ME. I'M HERE AT THE LIBRARY... WHAT?... YEAH, I'M GOING TO HANG OUT HERE FOR A WHILE...
I LIKE IT MORE THAN I THOUGHT I WOULD! WAY, **WAY** MORE!
RROWR!
© 2009 by NEA, Inc.
7/21
PEIRCE

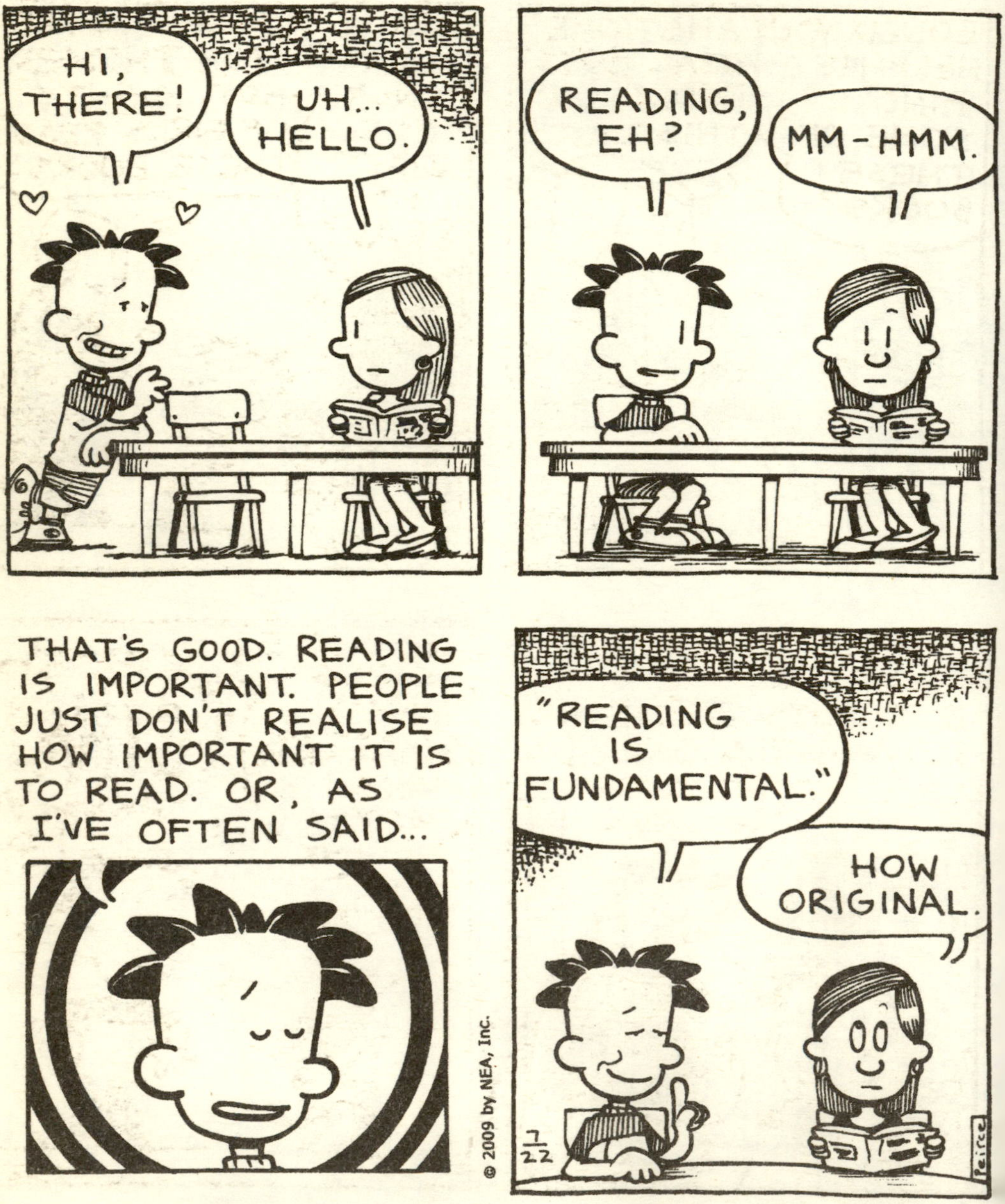
HI, THERE!
UH... HELLO.
READING, EH?
MM-HMM.
THAT'S GOOD. READING IS IMPORTANT. PEOPLE JUST DON'T REALISE HOW IMPORTANT IT IS TO READ. OR, AS I'VE OFTEN SAID...
"READING IS FUNDAMENTAL."
HOW ORIGINAL.
7/22
Peirce

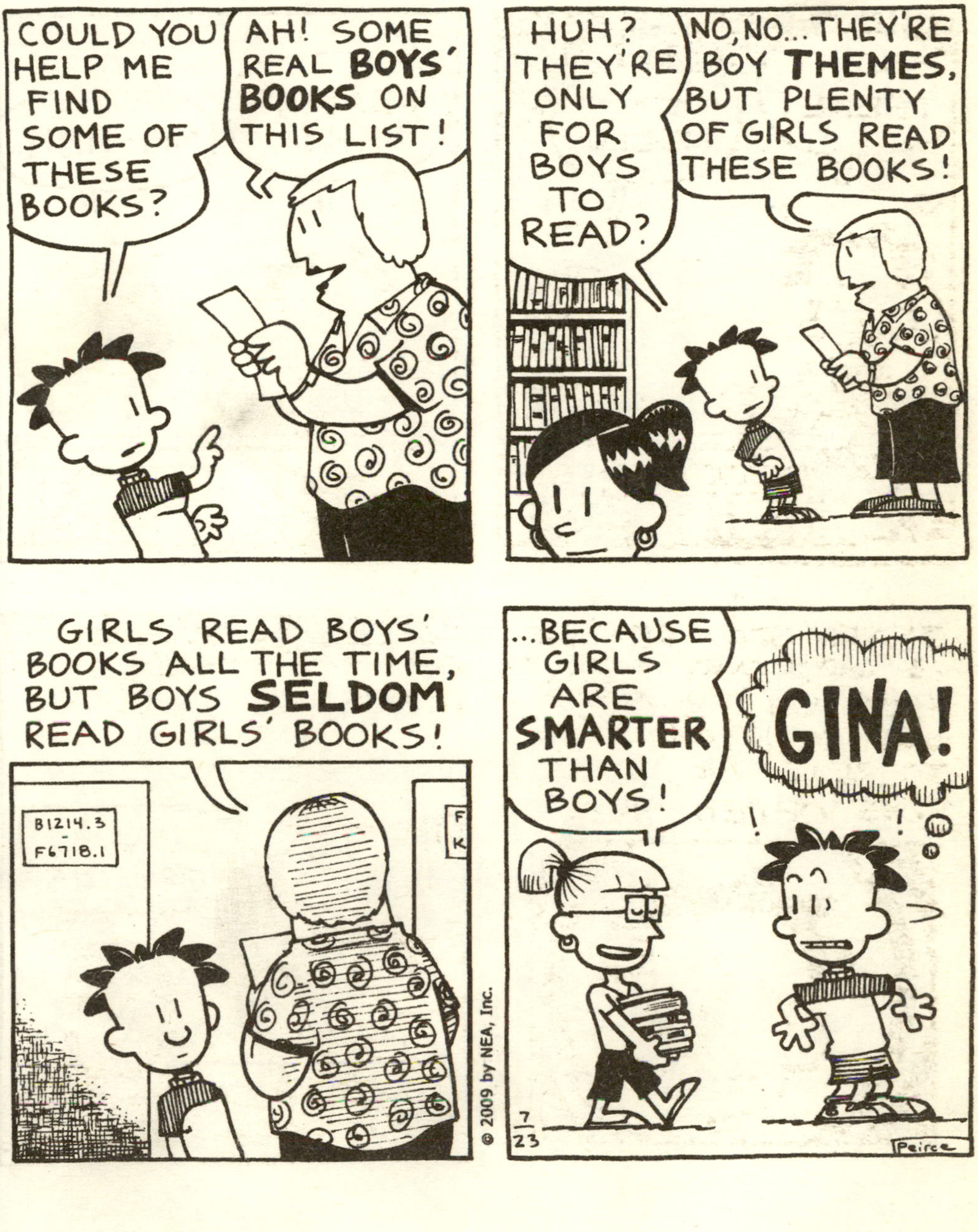
COULD YOU HELP ME FIND SOME OF THESE BOOKS?
AH! SOME REAL BOYS' BOOKS ON THIS LIST!
HUH? THEY'RE ONLY FOR BOYS TO READ?
NO, NO... THEY'RE BOY THEMES, BUT PLENTY OF GIRLS READ THESE BOOKS!
GIRLS READ BOYS' BOOKS ALL THE TIME, BUT BOYS SELDOM READ GIRLS' BOOKS!
B1214.3 - F6718.1
...BECAUSE GIRLS ARE SMARTER THAN BOYS!
GINA!
! !
© 2009 by NEA, Inc.
7/23
Peirce

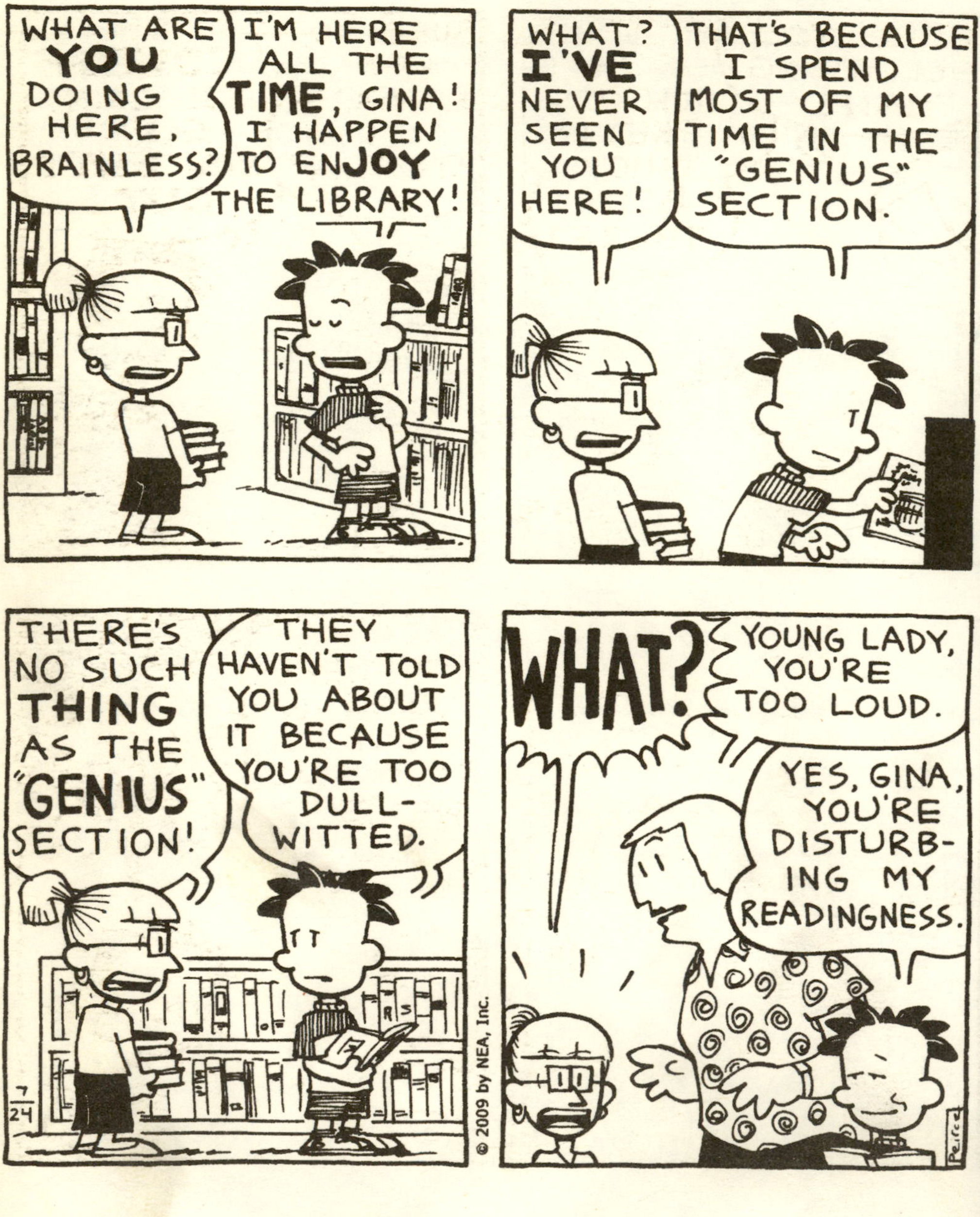
WHAT ARE YOU DOING HERE, BRAINLESS?
I'M HERE ALL THE TIME, GINA! I HAPPEN TO ENJOY THE LIBRARY!
WHAT? I'VE NEVER SEEN YOU HERE!
THAT'S BECAUSE I SPEND MOST OF MY TIME IN THE "GENIUS" SECTION.
THERE'S NO SUCH THING AS THE "GENIUS" SECTION!
THEY HAVEN'T TOLD YOU ABOUT IT BECAUSE YOU'RE TOO DULL-WITTED.
7/24
© 2009 by NEA, Inc.
WHAT?
YOUNG LADY, YOU'RE TOO LOUD.
YES, GINA, YOU'RE DISTURBING MY READINGNESS.
Peirce

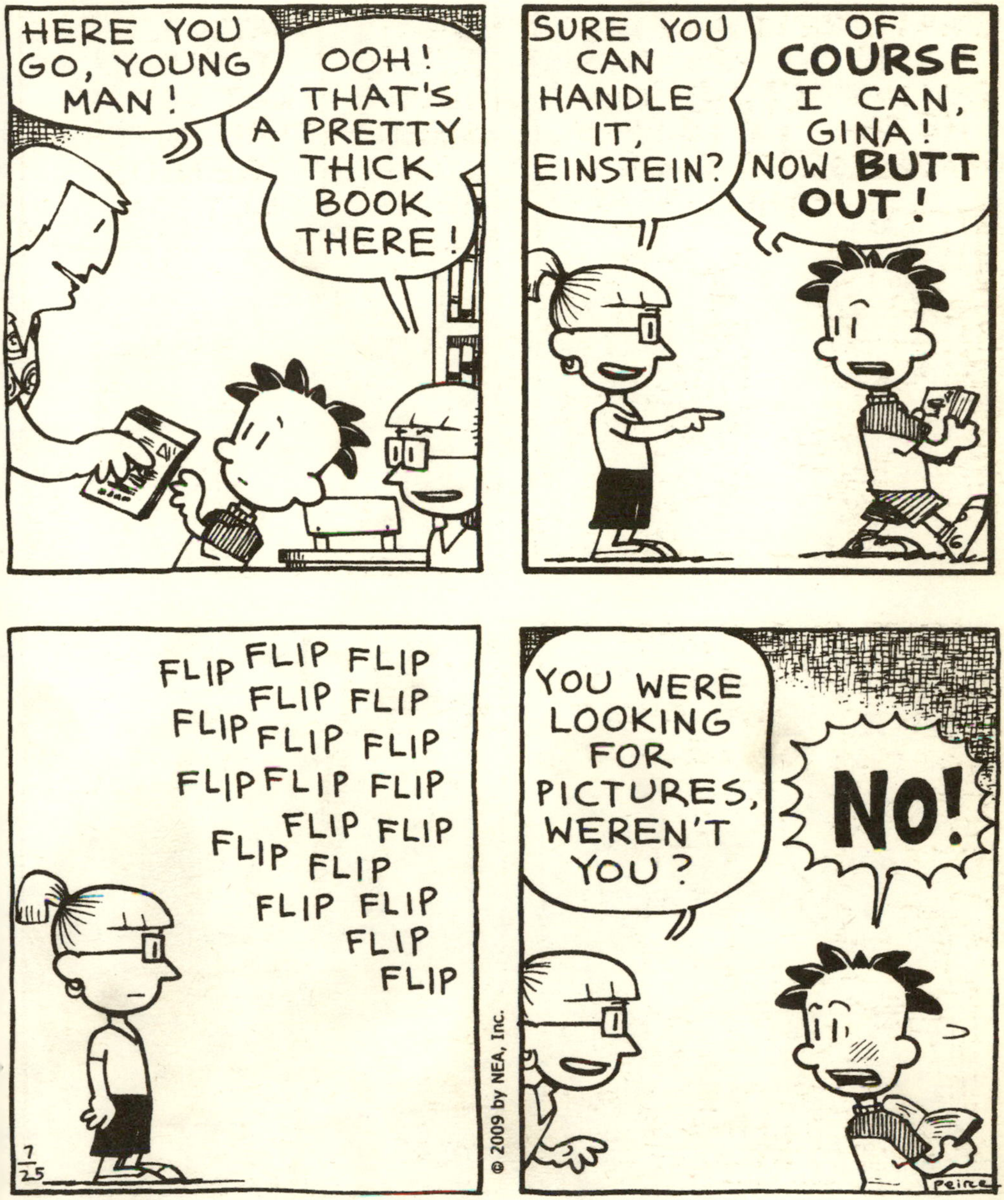
HERE YOU GO, YOUNG MAN!
OOH! THAT'S A PRETTY THICK BOOK THERE!
SURE YOU CAN HANDLE IT, EINSTEIN?
OF COURSE I CAN, GINA! NOW BUTT OUT!
FLIP FLIP FLIP FLIP FLIP FLIP FLIP FLIP FLIP FLIP FLIP FLIP FLIP FLIP FLIP FLIP FLIP FLIP FLIP
7/25
© 2009 by NEA, Inc.
YOU WERE LOOKING FOR PICTURES, WEREN'T YOU?
NO!
Peirce

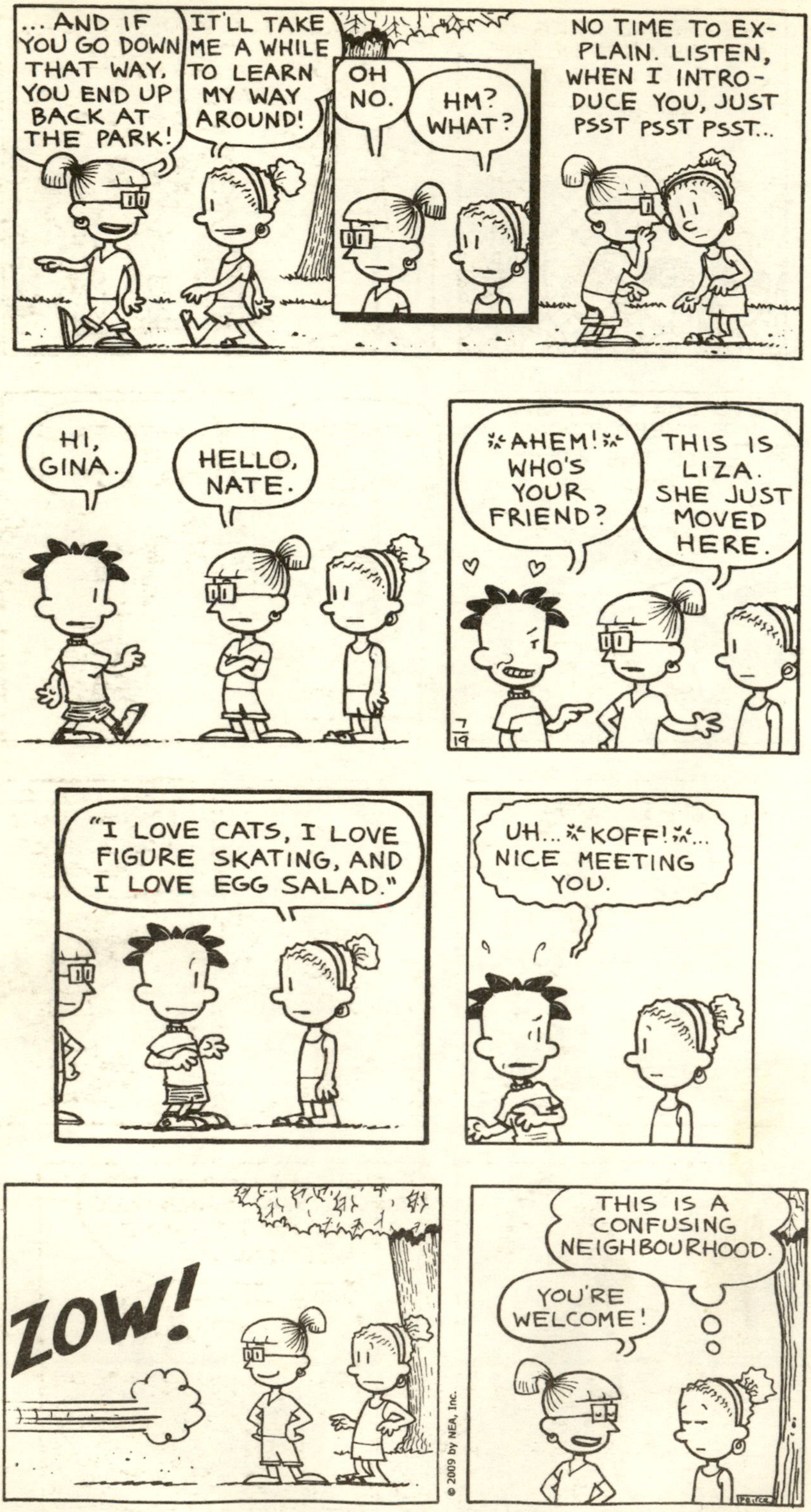
... AND IF YOU GO DOWN THAT WAY, YOU END UP BACK AT THE PARK!
IT'LL TAKE ME A WHILE TO LEARN MY WAY AROUND!
OH NO.
HM? WHAT?
NO TIME TO EXPLAIN. LISTEN, WHEN I INTRODUCE YOU, JUST PSST PSST PSST...
HI, GINA.
HELLO, NATE.
AHEM! WHO'S YOUR FRIEND?
THIS IS LIZA. SHE JUST MOVED HERE.
7/19
"I LOVE CATS, I LOVE FIGURE SKATING, AND I LOVE EGG SALAD."
UH... *KOFF!*... NICE MEETING YOU.
ZOW!
© 2009 by NEA, Inc.
THIS IS A CONFUSING NEIGHBOURHOOD.
YOU'RE WELCOME!

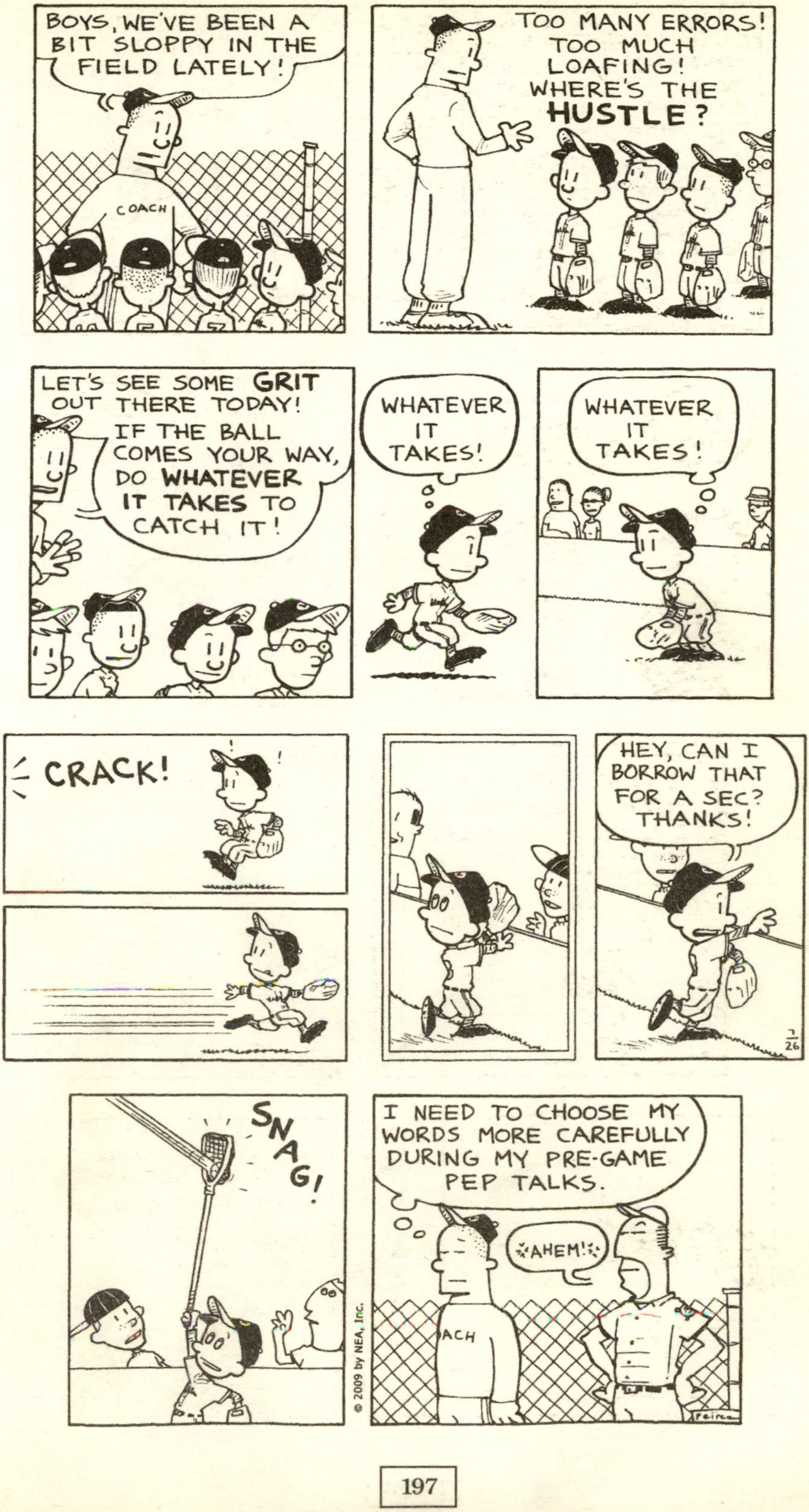
BOYS, WE'VE BEEN A BIT SLOPPY IN THE FIELD LATELY!
COACH
TOO MANY ERRORS! TOO MUCH LOAFING! WHERE'S THE HUSTLE?
LET'S SEE SOME GRIT OUT THERE TODAY!
IF THE BALL COMES YOUR WAY, DO WHATEVER IT TAKES TO CATCH IT!
WHATEVER IT TAKES!
WHATEVER IT TAKES!
CRACK!
HEY, CAN I BORROW THAT FOR A SEC? THANKS!
7/26
SNAG!
© 2009 by NEA, Inc.
I NEED TO CHOOSE MY WORDS MORE CAREFULLY DURING MY PRE-GAME PEP TALKS.
AHEM!
ACH
Peirce

GAME ON!

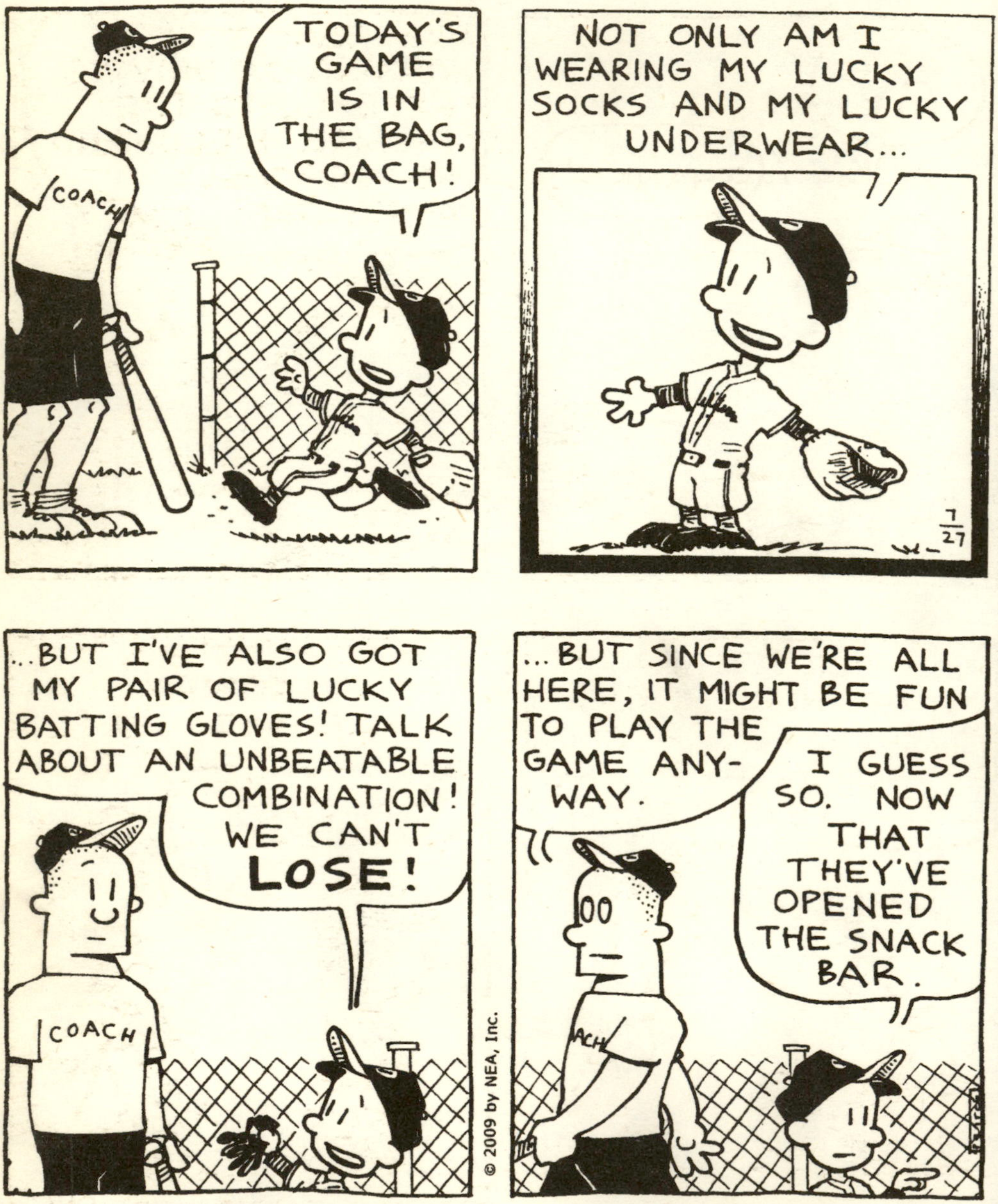
TODAY'S GAME IS IN THE BAG, COACH!
COACH
NOT ONLY AM I WEARING MY LUCKY SOCKS AND MY LUCKY UNDERWEAR...
7/27
...BUT I'VE ALSO GOT MY PAIR OF LUCKY BATTING GLOVES! TALK ABOUT AN UNBEATABLE COMBINATION! WE CAN'T **LOSE**!
COACH
© 2009 by NEA, Inc.
...BUT SINCE WE'RE ALL HERE, IT MIGHT BE FUN TO PLAY THE GAME ANYWAY.
I GUESS SO. NOW THAT THEY'VE OPENED THE SNACK BAR.
ACH

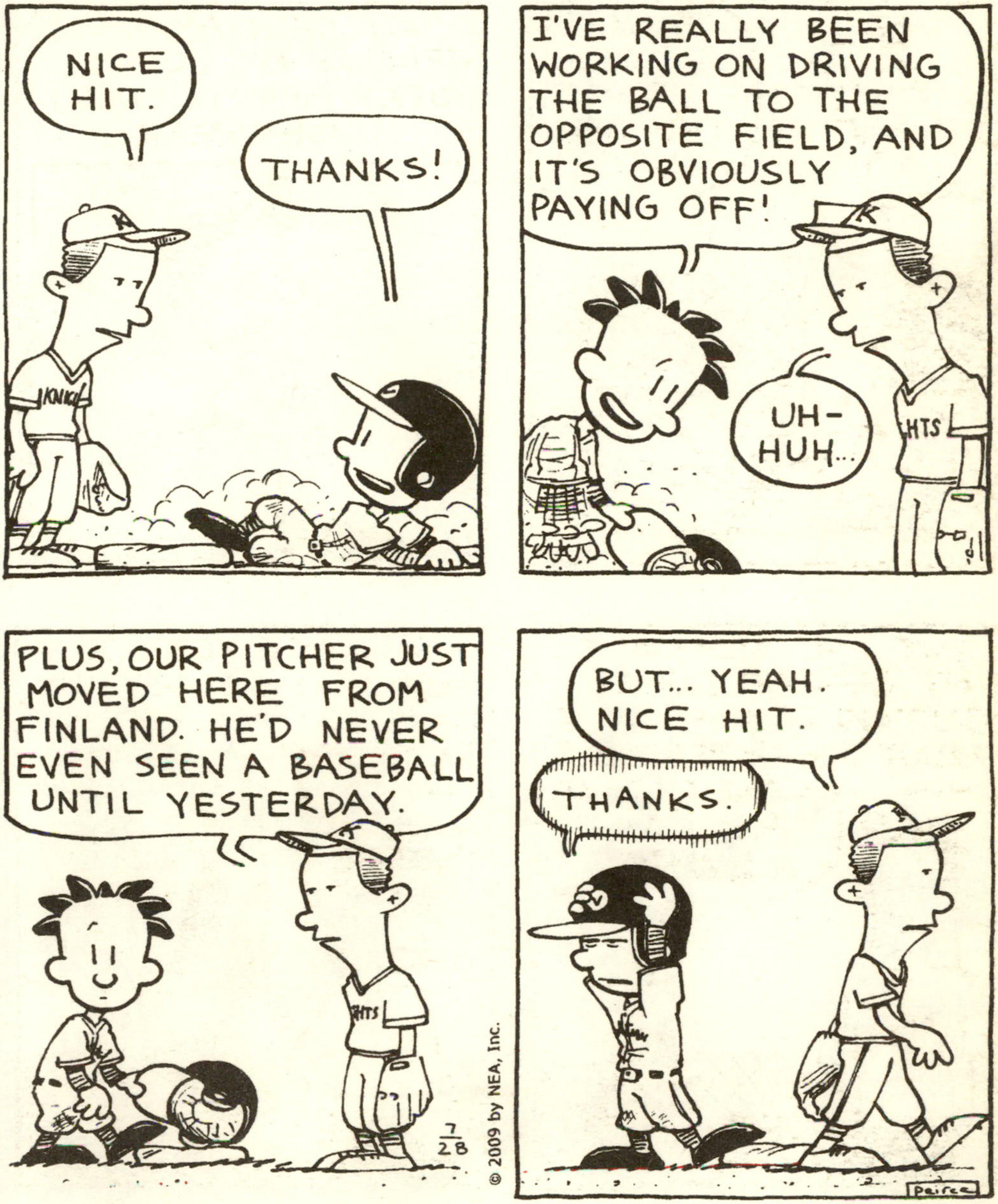
NICE HIT.
THANKS!
I'VE REALLY BEEN WORKING ON DRIVING THE BALL TO THE OPPOSITE FIELD, AND IT'S OBVIOUSLY PAYING OFF!
UH-HUH...
PLUS, OUR PITCHER JUST MOVED HERE FROM FINLAND. HE'D NEVER EVEN SEEN A BASEBALL UNTIL YESTERDAY.
7/28
BUT... YEAH. NICE HIT.
THANKS.
Peirce

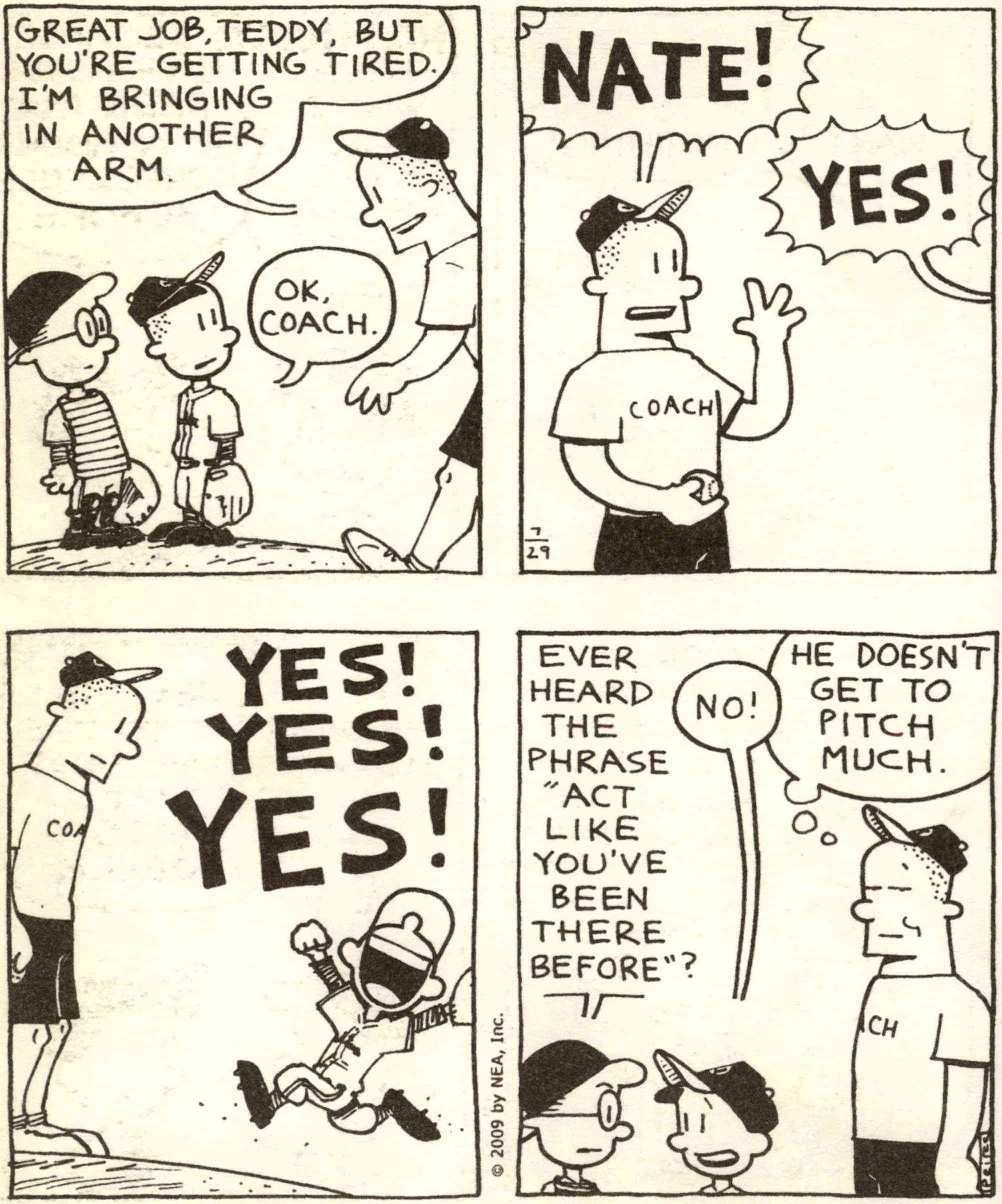
GREAT JOB, TEDDY, BUT YOU'RE GETTING TIRED. I'M BRINGING IN ANOTHER ARM.
OK, COACH.
NATE!
YES!
COACH
7/29
YES! YES! YES!
COA
© 2009 by NEA, Inc.
EVER HEARD THE PHRASE "ACT LIKE YOU'VE BEEN THERE BEFORE"?
NO!
HE DOESN'T GET TO PITCH MUCH.
CH

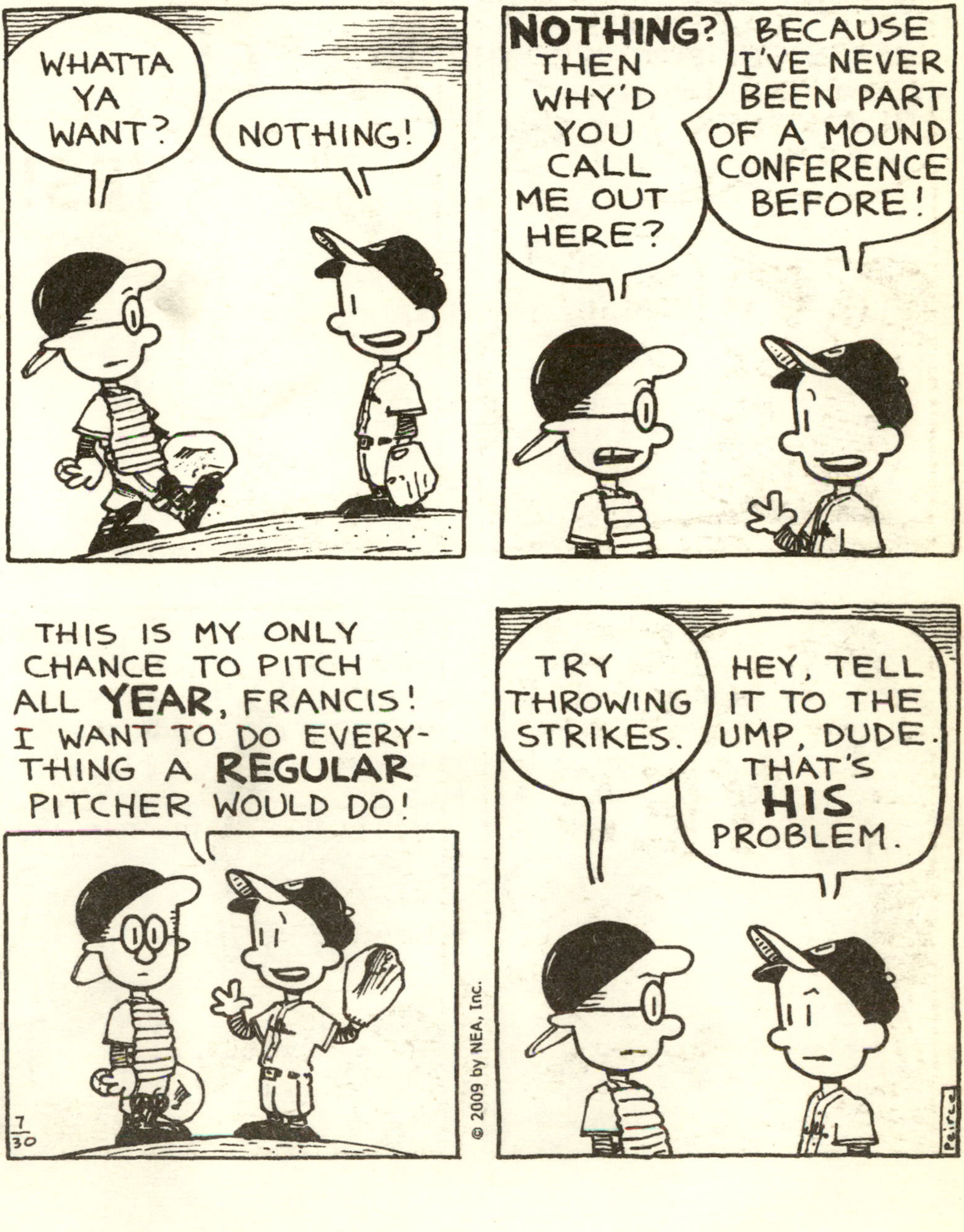
WHATTA YA WANT?
NOTHING!
NOTHING? THEN WHY'D YOU CALL ME OUT HERE?
BECAUSE I'VE NEVER BEEN PART OF A MOUND CONFERENCE BEFORE!
THIS IS MY ONLY CHANCE TO PITCH ALL YEAR, FRANCIS! I WANT TO DO EVERY-THING A REGULAR PITCHER WOULD DO!
7/30
© 2009 by NEA, Inc.
TRY THROWING STRIKES.
HEY, TELL IT TO THE UMP, DUDE. THAT'S HIS PROBLEM.
Peirce

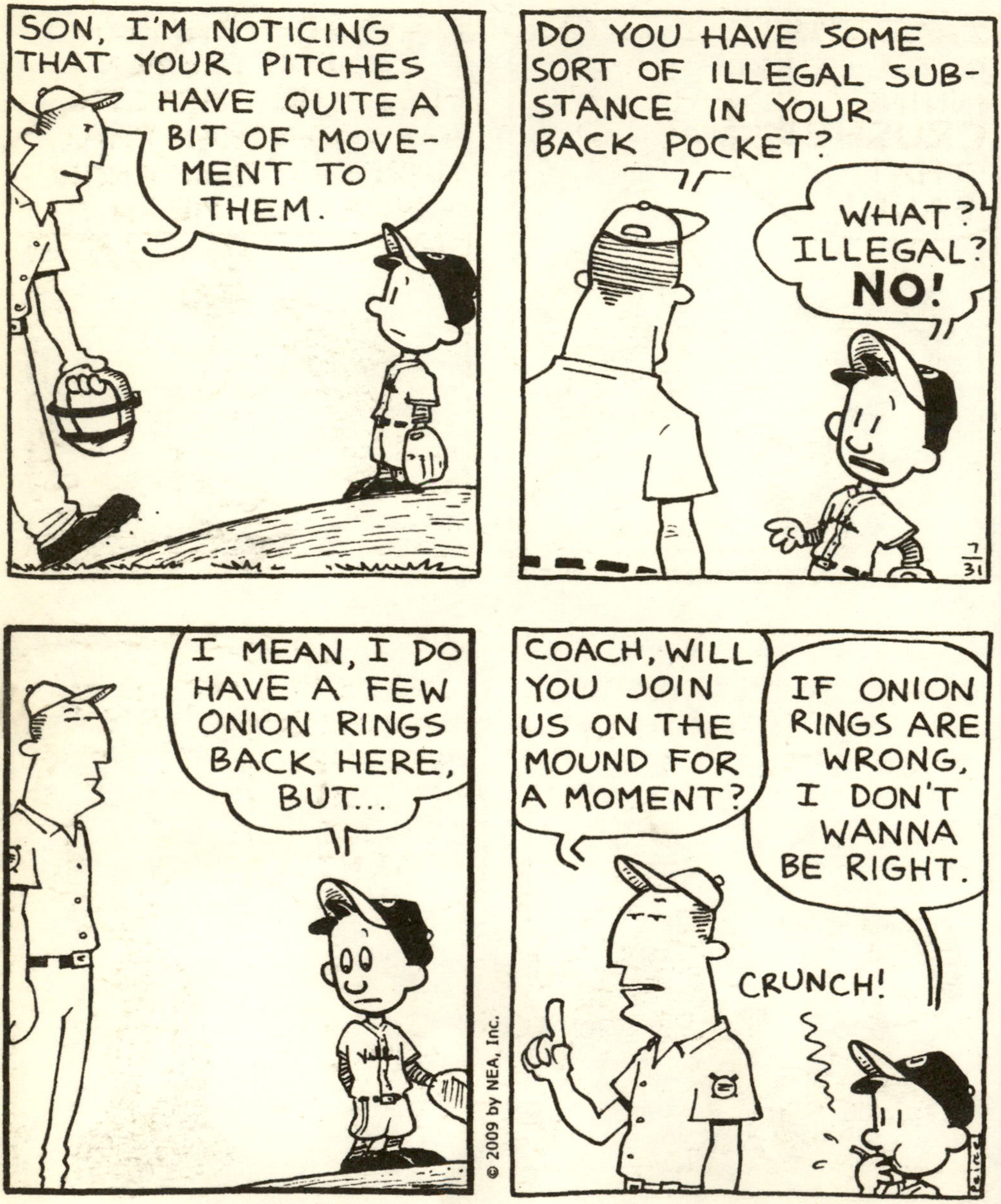
SON, I'M NOTICING THAT YOUR PITCHES HAVE QUITE A BIT OF MOVEMENT TO THEM.
DO YOU HAVE SOME SORT OF ILLEGAL SUBSTANCE IN YOUR BACK POCKET?
WHAT? ILLEGAL? NO!
7/31
I MEAN, I DO HAVE A FEW ONION RINGS BACK HERE, BUT...
© 2009 by NEA, Inc.
COACH, WILL YOU JOIN US ON THE MOUND FOR A MOMENT?
IF ONION RINGS ARE WRONG, I DON'T WANNA BE RIGHT.
CRUNCH!

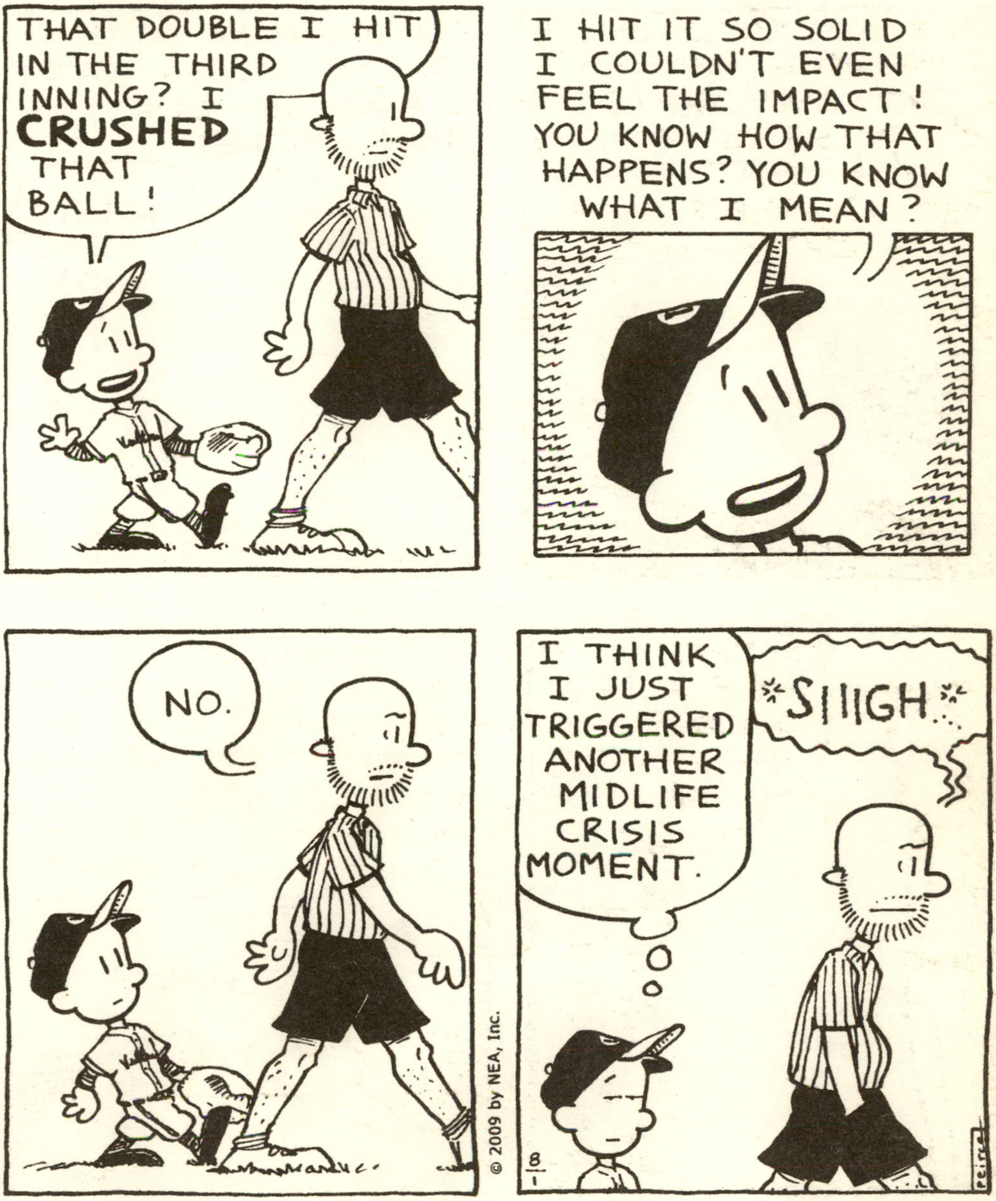
THAT DOUBLE I HIT IN THE THIRD INNING? I **CRUSHED** THAT BALL!
I HIT IT SO SOLID I COULDN'T EVEN FEEL THE IMPACT! YOU KNOW HOW THAT HAPPENS? YOU KNOW WHAT I MEAN?
NO.
I THINK I JUST TRIGGERED ANOTHER MIDLIFE CRISIS MOMENT.
SIIIGH
© 2009 by NEA, Inc.
8/1
PEIRCE

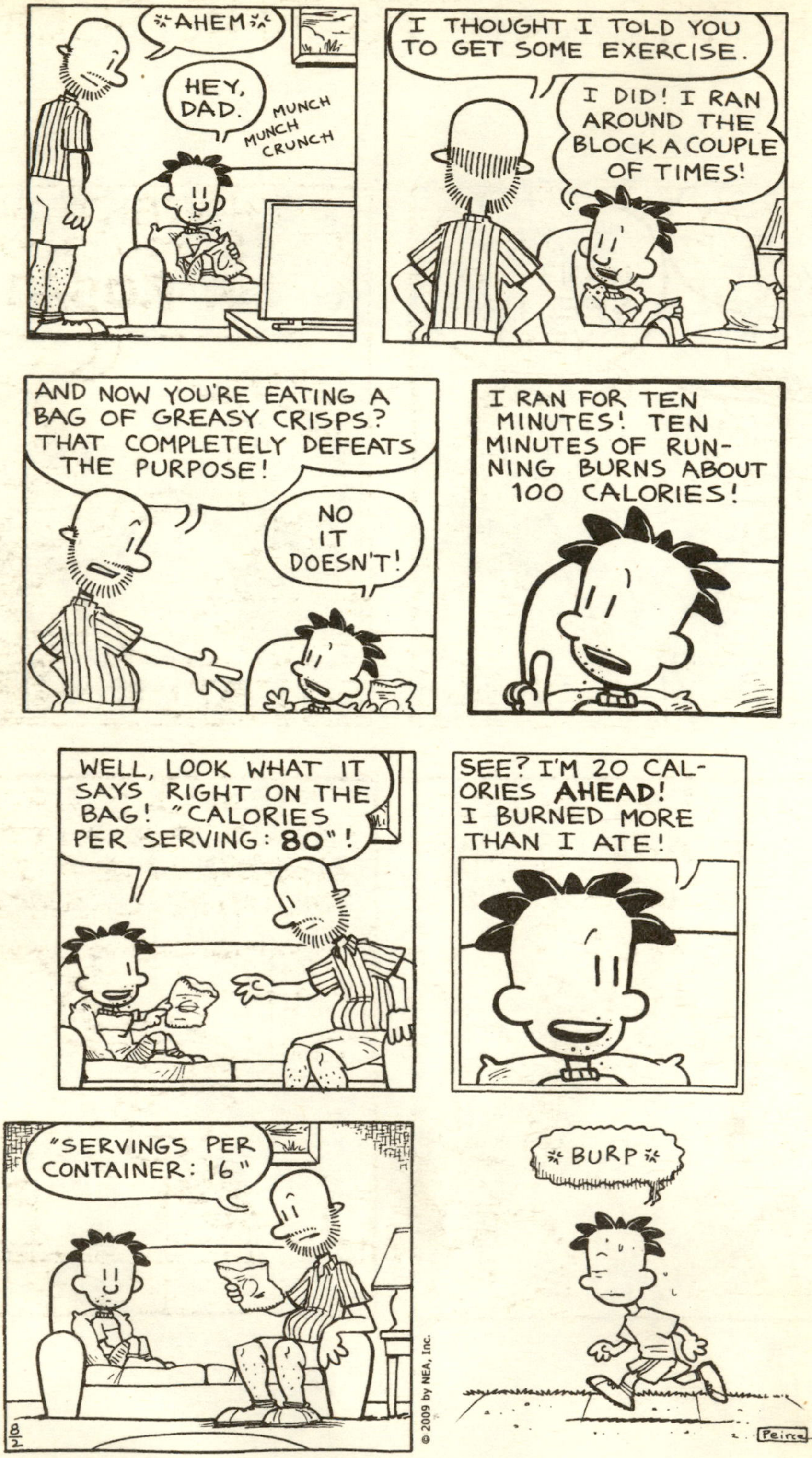

AHEM
HEY, DAD.
MUNCH MUNCH CRUNCH
I THOUGHT I TOLD YOU TO GET SOME EXERCISE.
I DID! I RAN AROUND THE BLOCK A COUPLE OF TIMES!
AND NOW YOU'RE EATING A BAG OF GREASY CRISPS? THAT COMPLETELY DEFEATS THE PURPOSE!
NO IT DOESN'T!
I RAN FOR TEN MINUTES! TEN MINUTES OF RUN-NING BURNS ABOUT 100 CALORIES!
WELL, LOOK WHAT IT SAYS RIGHT ON THE BAG! "CALORIES PER SERVING: 80"!
SEE? I'M 20 CAL-ORIES AHEAD! I BURNED MORE THAN I ATE!
"SERVINGS PER CONTAINER: 16"
BURP
8/2
© 2009 by NEA, Inc.
Peirce

MR ROSA GETS THE SCOOP

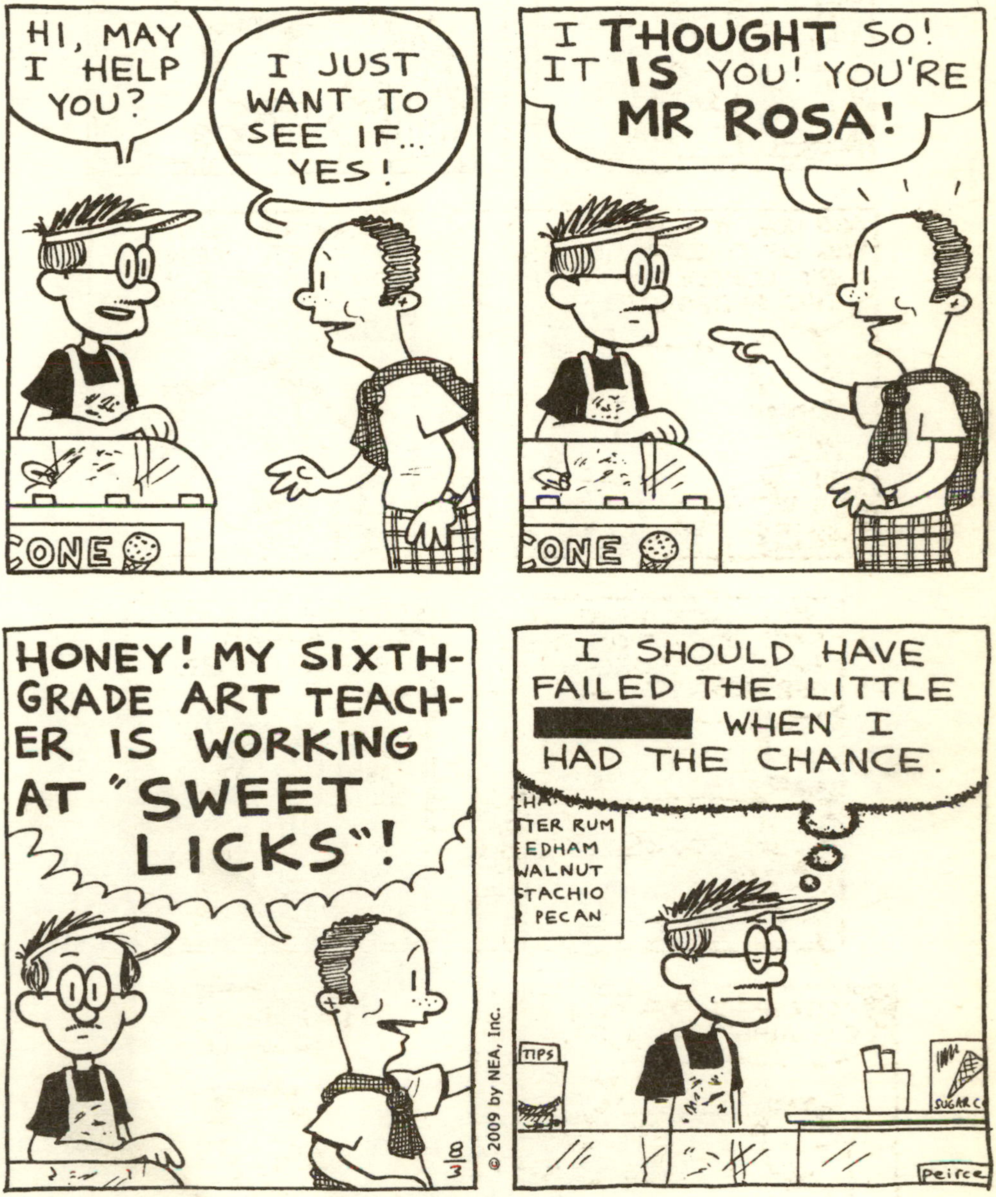

HI, MAY I HELP YOU?
I JUST WANT TO SEE IF... YES!
CONE
I THOUGHT SO! IT IS YOU! YOU'RE MR ROSA!
CONE
HONEY! MY SIXTH-GRADE ART TEACHER IS WORKING AT "SWEET LICKS"!
© 2009 by NEA, Inc.
I SHOULD HAVE FAILED THE LITTLE [redacted] WHEN I HAD THE CHANCE.
TIPS
peirce

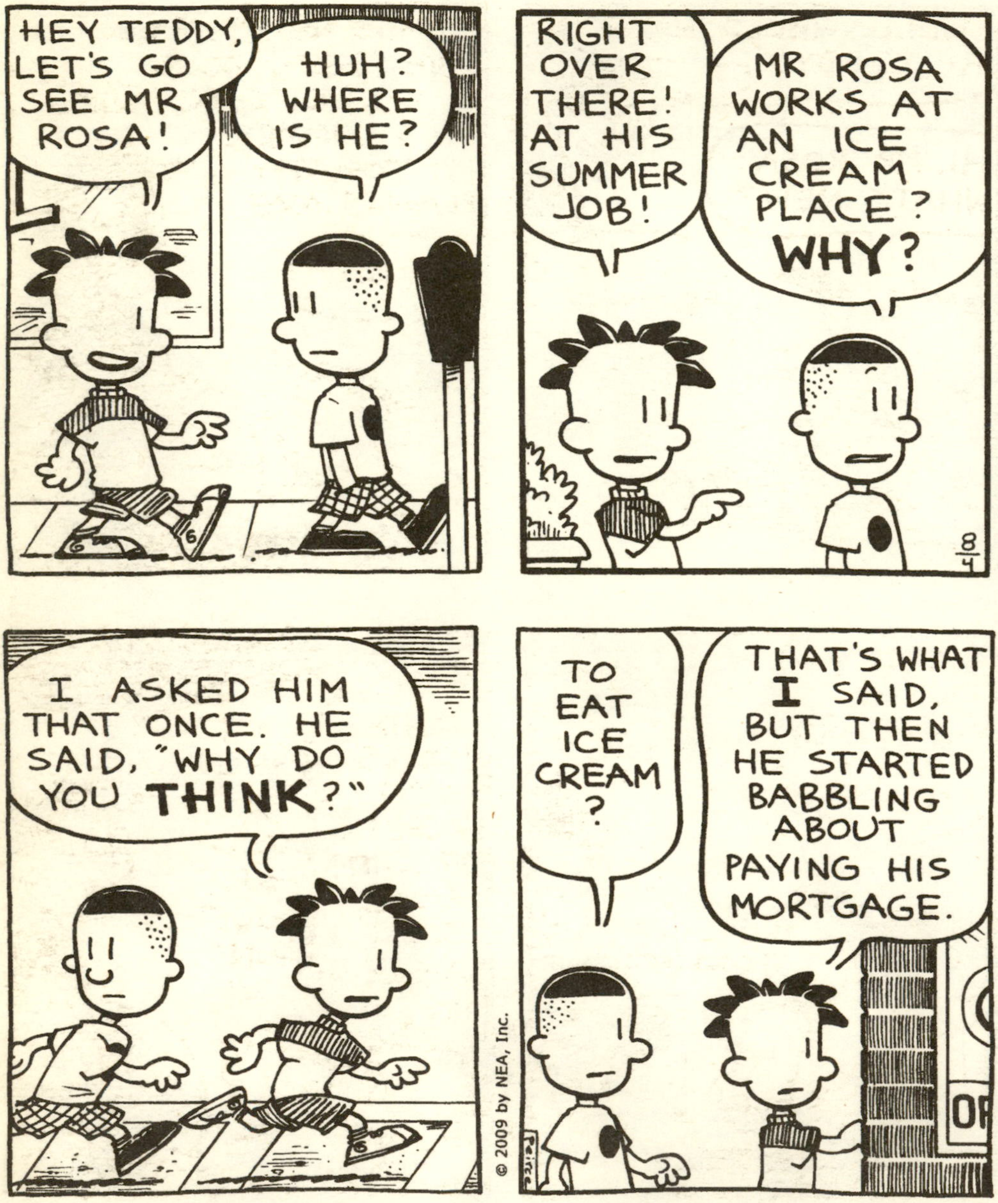
HEY TEDDY, LET'S GO SEE MR ROSA!
HUH? WHERE IS HE?
RIGHT OVER THERE! AT HIS SUMMER JOB!
MR ROSA WORKS AT AN ICE CREAM PLACE? WHY?
8/4
I ASKED HIM THAT ONCE. HE SAID, "WHY DO YOU THINK?"
TO EAT ICE CREAM?
THAT'S WHAT I SAID, BUT THEN HE STARTED BABBLING ABOUT PAYING HIS MORTGAGE.

WELL! HELLO, NATE! HI, TEDDY!
HI, MR ROSA! WHAT'S NEW?
TRY DEL W
WHAT'S NEW? WELL, I'VE BEEN DOING A LOT OF GARDENING THIS SUMMER! MY TOMATO PLANTS ARE...
NO, NO...
TRY DEL
I MEANT WHAT **FLAVOURS** ARE NEW.
TRY DEL W
8 5
© 2009 by NEA, Inc.
AH.
... AND COULD YOU HOOK US UP WITH SOME FREE SAMPLES?
IT'S A TWO-PART QUEST-ION!
Peirce

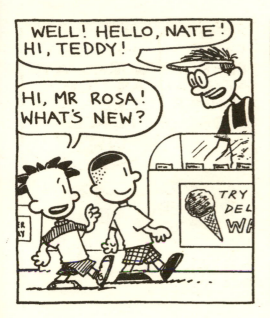

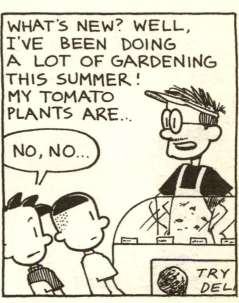

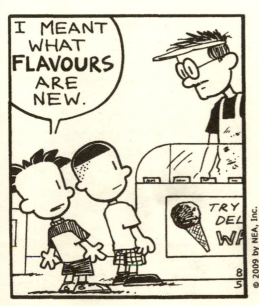

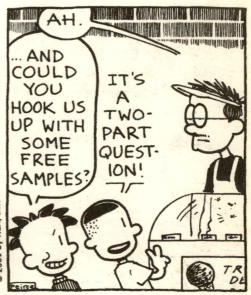

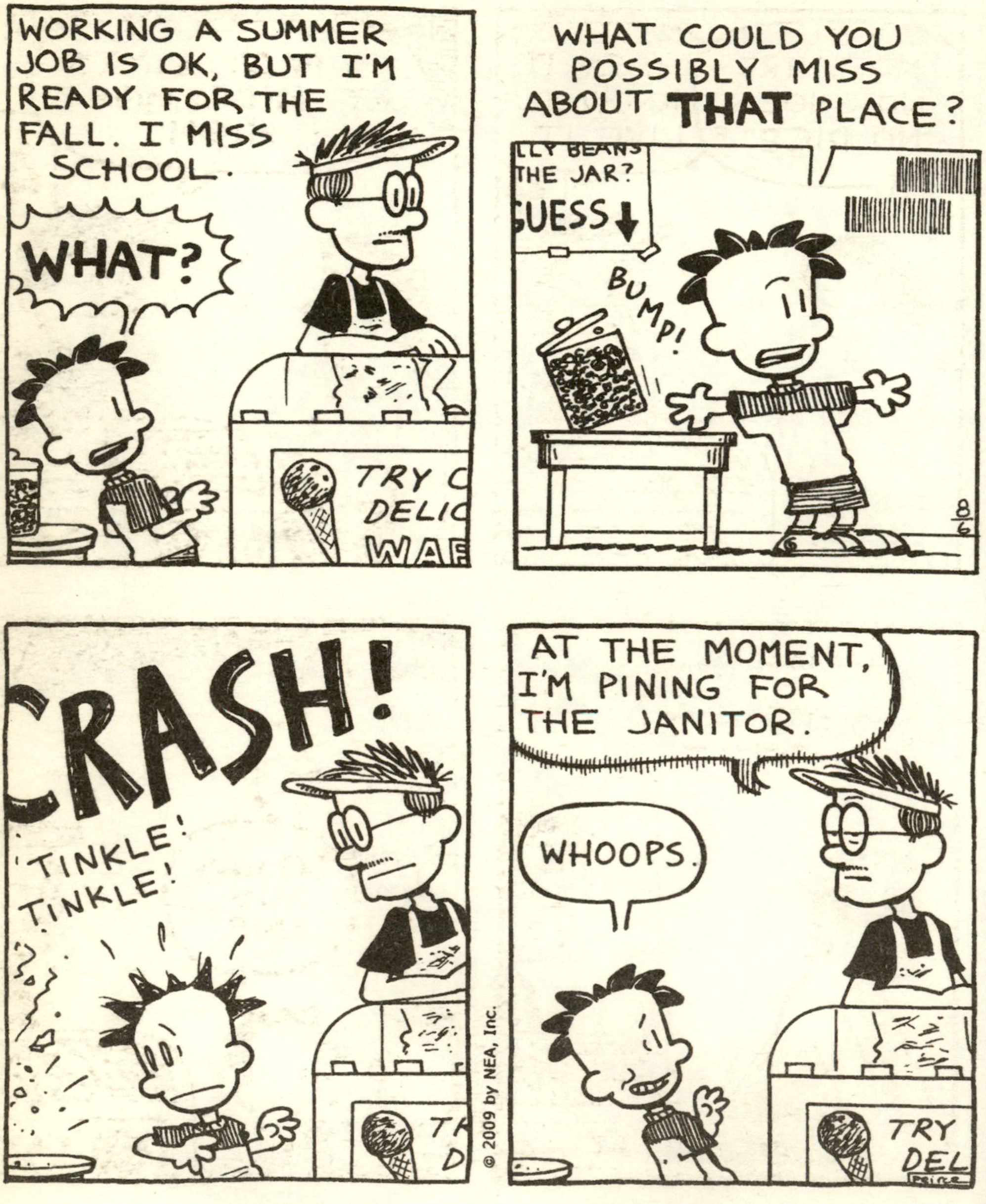
WORKING A SUMMER JOB IS OK, BUT I'M READY FOR THE FALL. I MISS SCHOOL.
WHAT?
TRY DELIC WAF
WHAT COULD YOU POSSIBLY MISS ABOUT **THAT** PLACE?
LLY BEANS THE JAR? GUESS
BUMP!
8/6
CRASH!
TINKLE! TINKLE!
© 2009 by NEA, Inc.
AT THE MOMENT, I'M PINING FOR THE JANITOR.
WHOOPS.
TRY DEL

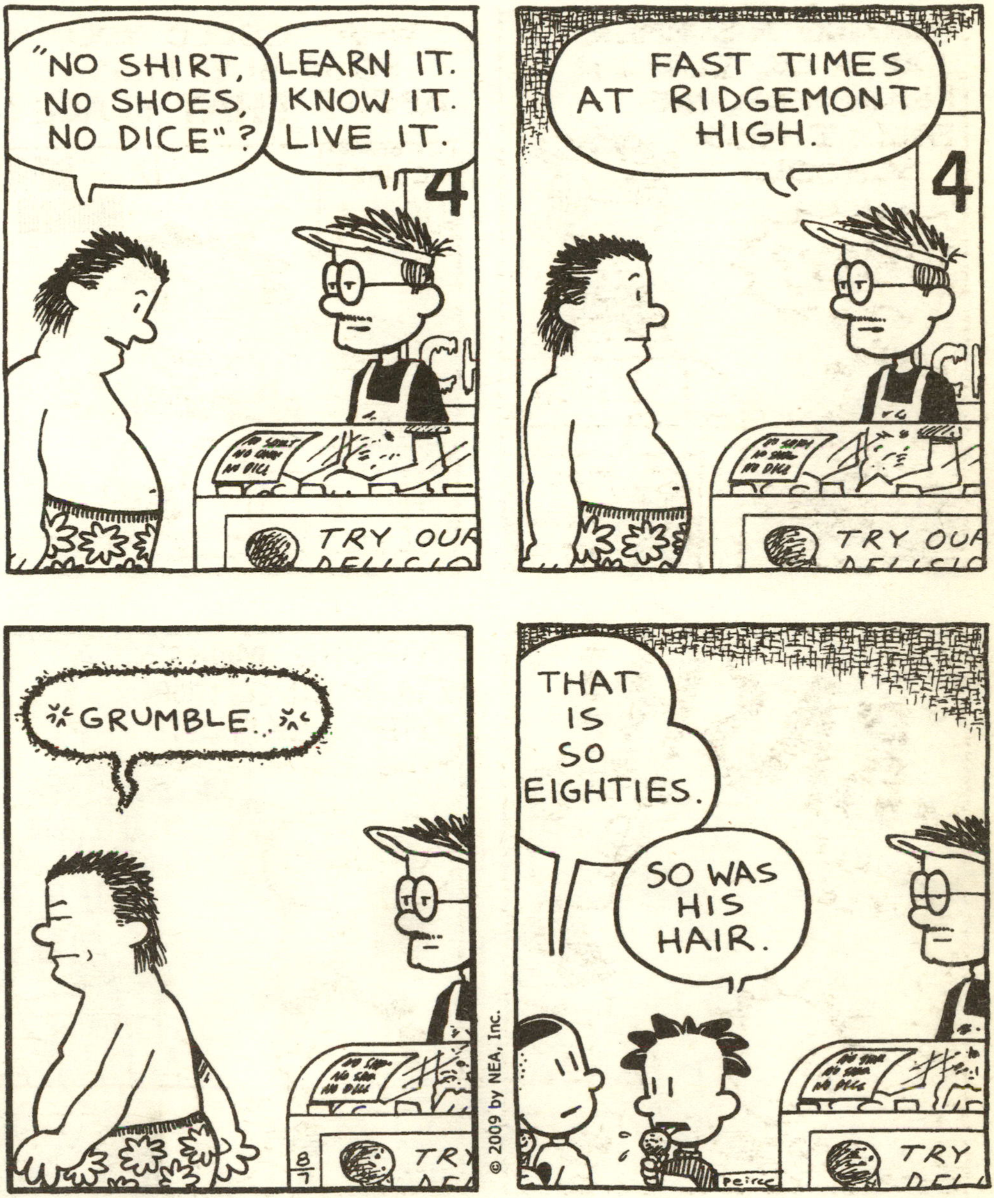
"NO SHIRT, NO SHOES, NO DICE"?
LEARN IT. KNOW IT. LIVE IT.
FAST TIMES AT RIDGEMONT HIGH.
GRUMBLE..
THAT IS SO EIGHTIES.
SO WAS HIS HAIR.

SEEING MR ROSA SERVING ICE CREAM AT HIS SUMMER JOB WAS... WELL, FRANKLY, I FOUND IT DEPRESSING!
DEPRESSING BECAUSE HE CAN'T MAKE ENOUGH MONEY TO LIVE ON AS AN ART TEACHER?
NO, BECAUSE HE MADE US PAY FULL PRICE FOR THESE CONES.
IT JUST MADE ME SAD.
WELL, THAT'S YOUR SENSITIVE SIDE.
8/8
PEIRCE

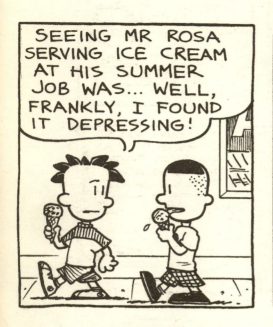

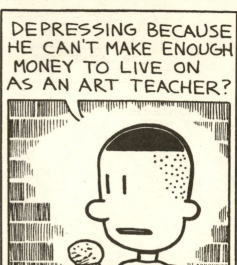

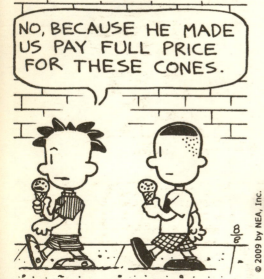

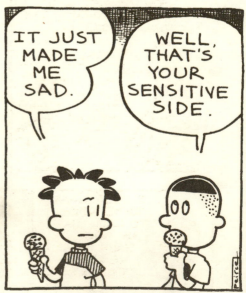

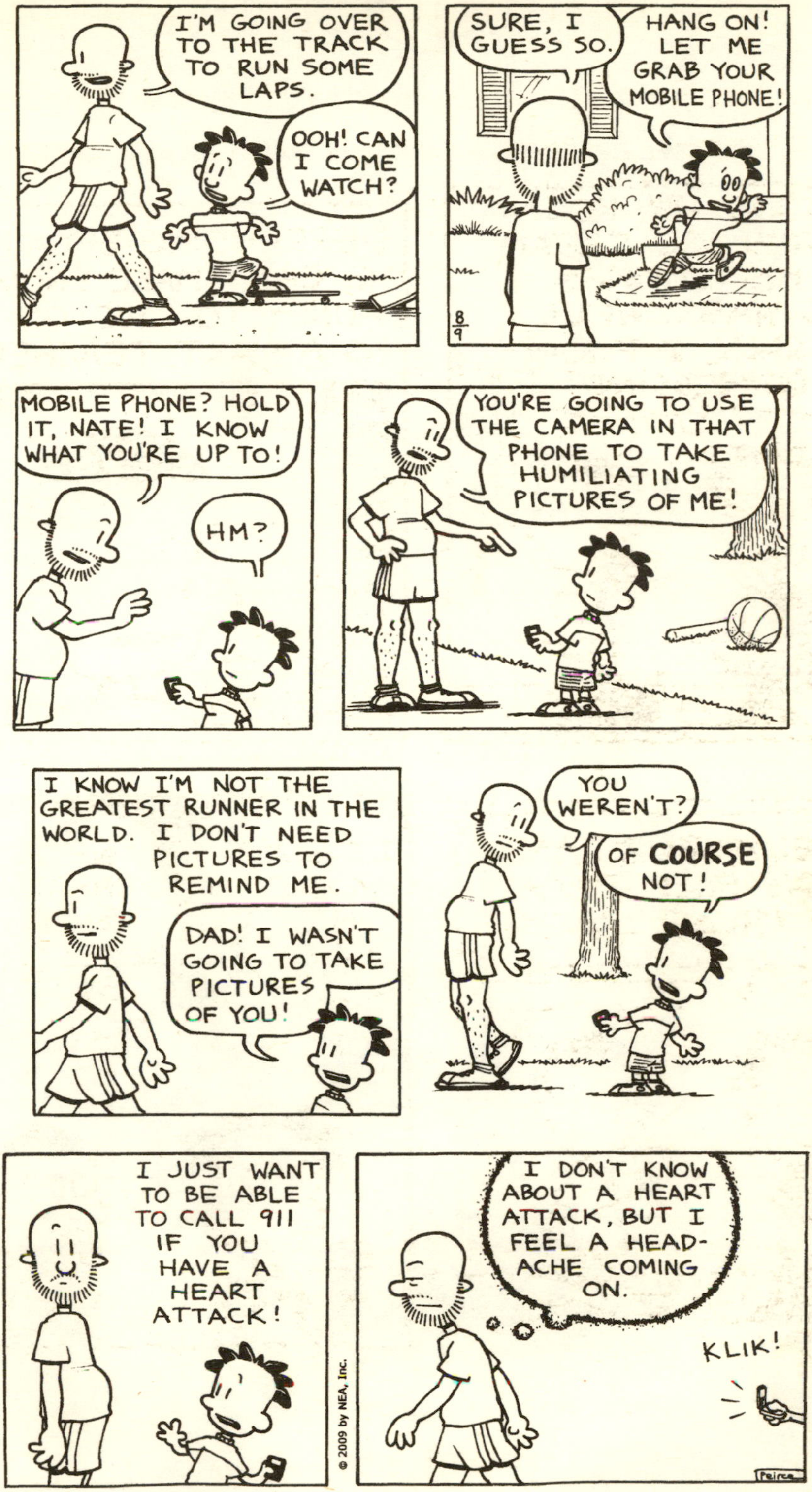
I'M GOING OVER TO THE TRACK TO RUN SOME LAPS.
OOH! CAN I COME WATCH?
SURE, I GUESS SO.
HANG ON! LET ME GRAB YOUR MOBILE PHONE!
8/9
MOBILE PHONE? HOLD IT, NATE! I KNOW WHAT YOU'RE UP TO!
HM?
YOU'RE GOING TO USE THE CAMERA IN THAT PHONE TO TAKE HUMILIATING PICTURES OF ME!
I KNOW I'M NOT THE GREATEST RUNNER IN THE WORLD. I DON'T NEED PICTURES TO REMIND ME.
DAD! I WASN'T GOING TO TAKE PICTURES OF YOU!
YOU WEREN'T?
OF COURSE NOT!
I JUST WANT TO BE ABLE TO CALL 911 IF YOU HAVE A HEART ATTACK!
© 2009 by NEA, Inc.
I DON'T KNOW ABOUT A HEART ATTACK, BUT I FEEL A HEAD-ACHE COMING ON.
KLIK!
Peirce

THIS JUST IN!

Everything Nate does is newsworthy – at least in his mind!
Write your own headlines for some of Nate's all-star moments!

(A)

TOP PLAYS
6
5
4
3
2
1

(B)

Hello?
HelLO?

(C)

(D)

$

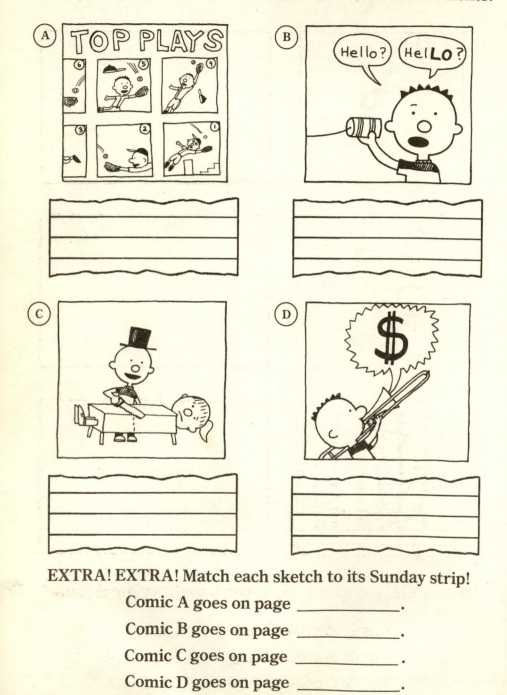

EXTRA! EXTRA! Match each sketch to its Sunday strip!

Comic A goes on page __________.

Comic B goes on page __________.

Comic C goes on page __________.

Comic D goes on page __________.

Answers: A: p. 99; B: p. 155; C: p. 183; D: p. 147.

WHAT HAPPENS NEXT?

Come up with the next scene using Nate's Sunday strip sketches as inspiration!

(A)

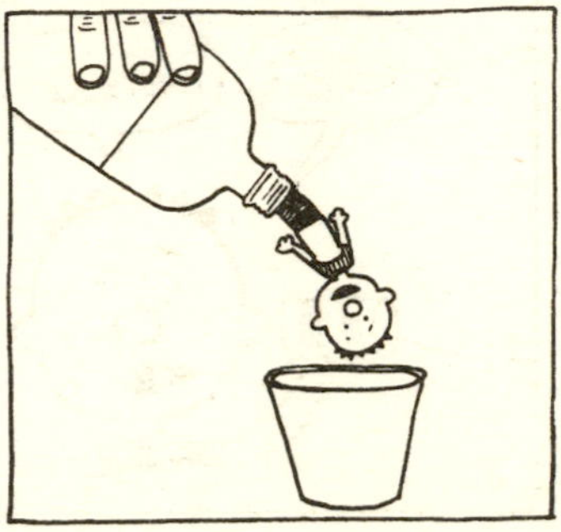

(B)

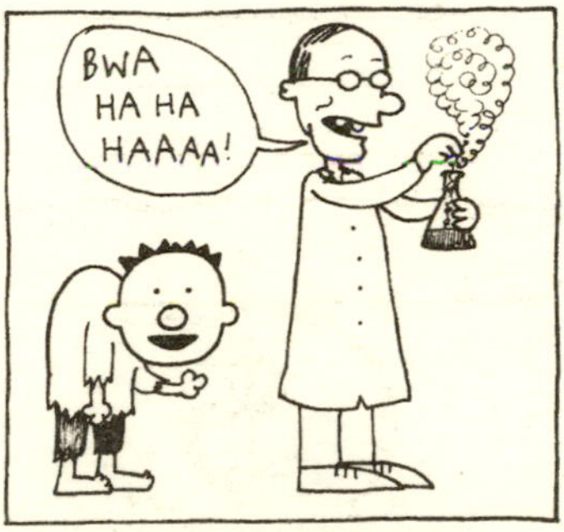
BWA HA HA HAAAA!

(C)

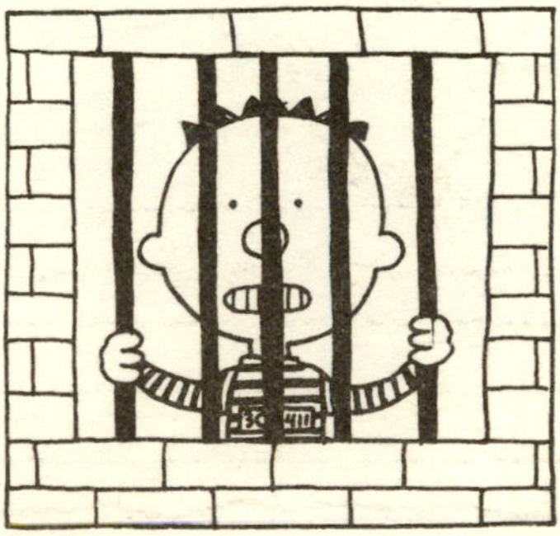

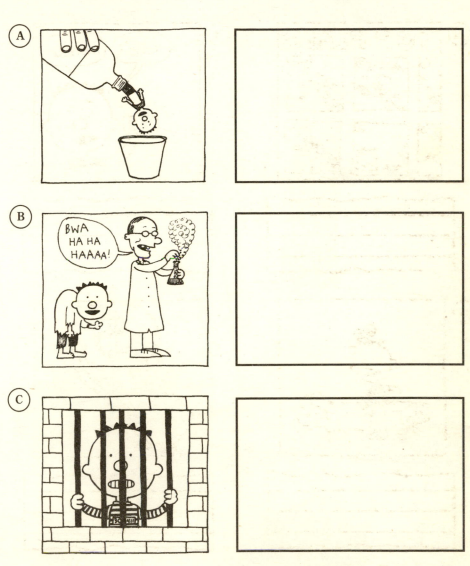

Bonus: Can you match each sketch to the original comic?

Comic A goes on page ______________.

Comic B goes on page ______________.

Comic C goes on page ______________.

Answers: A: p. 1; B: p. 8; C: p. 15.

WHAT A ________!

(YOU FILL IN THE BLANK)

Can you make up an awesome and hilarious story based on Nate's drawings below?

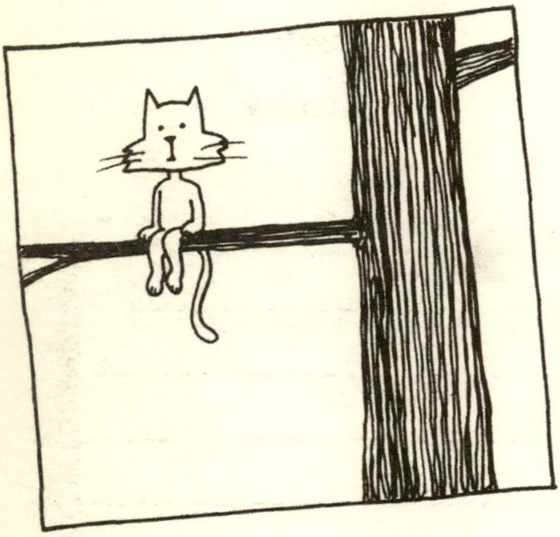

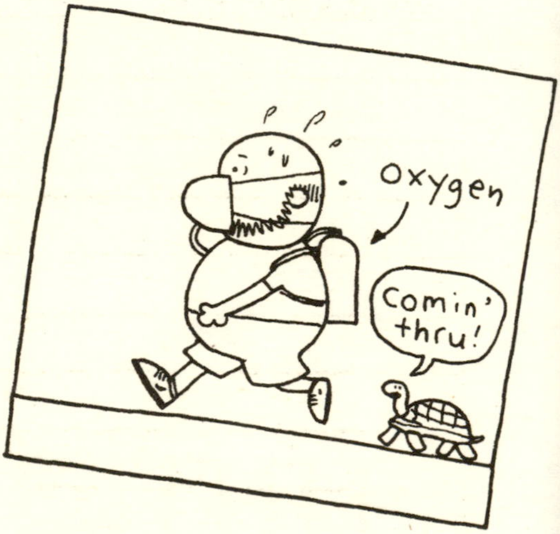
oxygen
comin' thru!

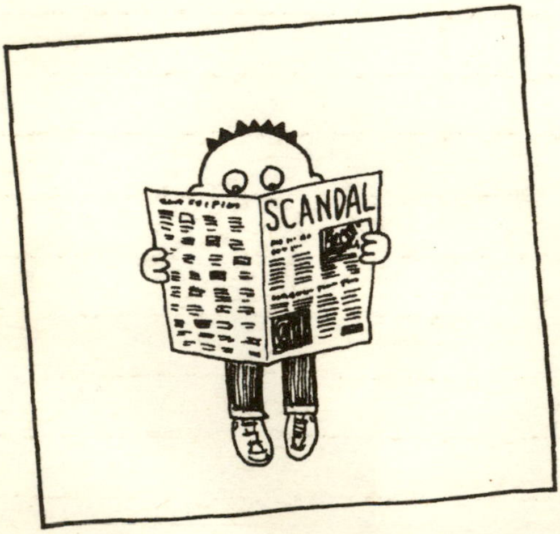
SCANDAL

For added silliness, use these words in your story!

fence	tomato
parachute	emergency
headline	turtle
marshmallow	cat
faint	crazy
firefighter	lightning

What a day! First, Nate . . .

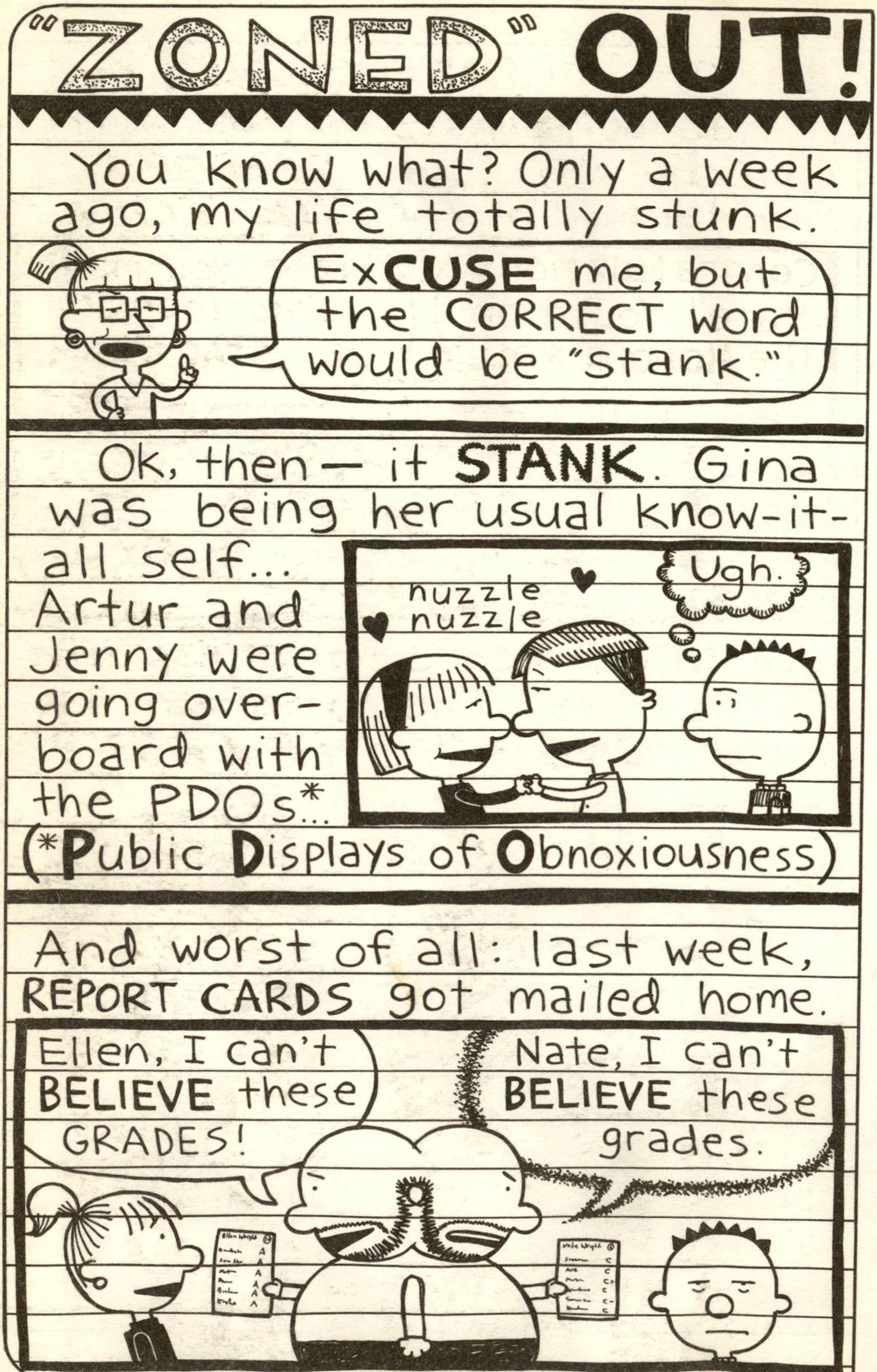
"ZONED" OUT!
You know what? Only a week ago, my life totally stunk.
ExCUSE me, but the CORRECT word would be "stank."
Ok, then — it STANK. Gina was being her usual know-it-all self...
Artur and Jenny were going over-board with the PDOs*...
nuzzle nuzzle
Ugh.
(*Public Displays of Obnoxiousness)
And worst of all: last week, REPORT CARDS got mailed home.
Ellen, I can't BELIEVE these GRADES!
Nate, I can't BELIEVE these grades.

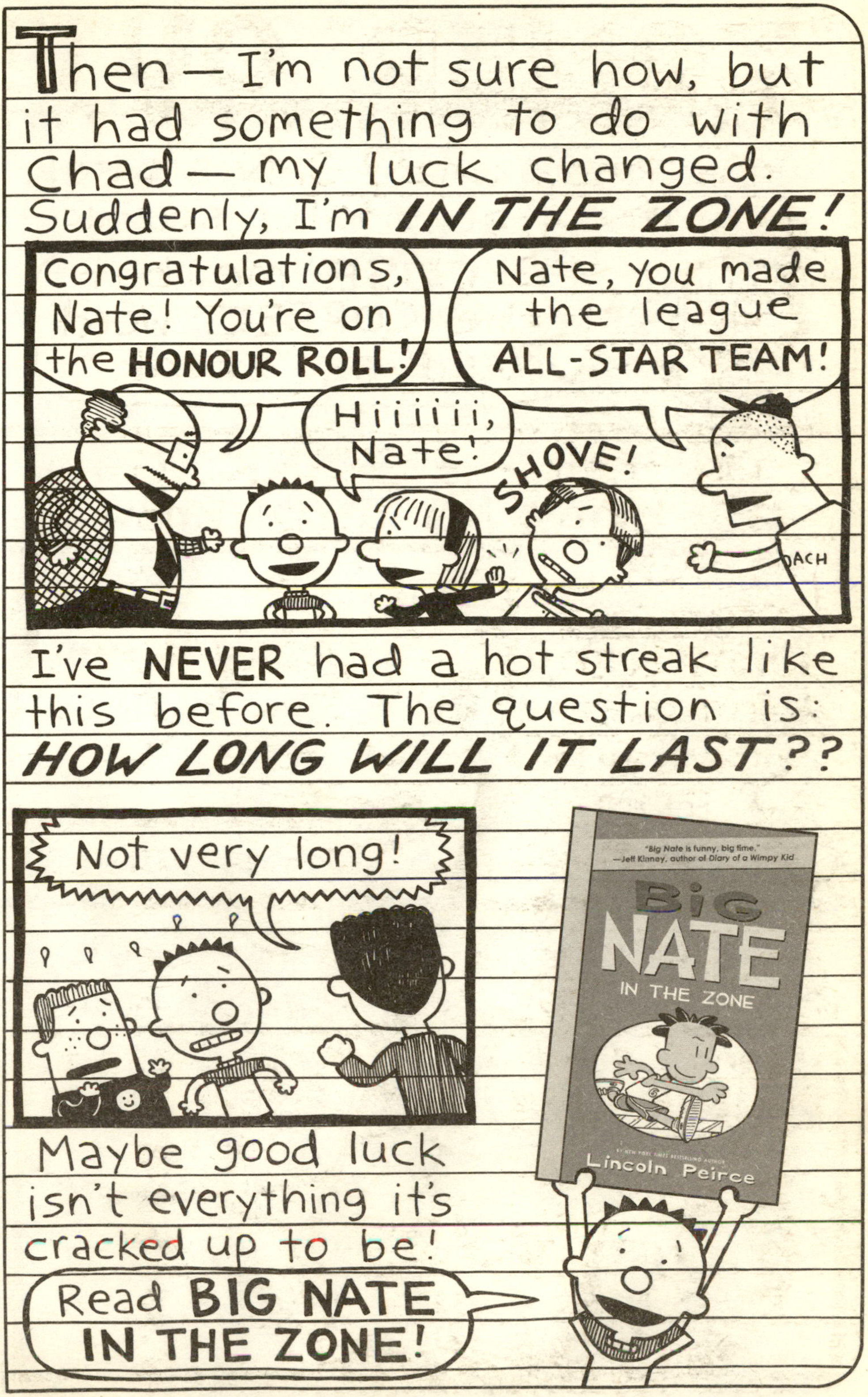
Then — I'm not sure how, but it had something to do with Chad — my luck changed. Suddenly, I'm *IN THE ZONE!*
Congratulations, Nate! You're on the **HONOUR ROLL!**
Nate, you made the league **ALL-STAR TEAM!**
Hiiiiii, Nate!
SHOVE!
I've **NEVER** had a hot streak like this before. The question is: ***HOW LONG WILL IT LAST??***
Not very long!
"Big Nate is funny, big time." —Jeff Kinney, author of Diary of a Wimpy Kid
BIG NATE IN THE ZONE
Lincoln Peirce
Maybe good luck isn't everything it's cracked up to be!
Read **BIG NATE IN THE ZONE!**

Lincoln Peirce

(pronounced "purse") is a cartoonist/writer and author of the *New York Times* bestselling Big Nate series, now published in twenty-five countries. He is also the creator of the comic strip *Big Nate*, which appears in more than 250 U.S. newspapers and online daily at www.bignate.com.

Lincoln loves comics, ice hockey, and Cheez Doodles (and dislikes cats, figure skating, and egg salad). Just like Nate.

Check out Big Nate Island at www.poptropica.com. And link to www.bignatebooks.com for more information about the author and the Big Nate series, app, audio, and ebooks. Lincoln Peirce lives with his wife and two children in Portland, Maine.

BIG NATE IN THE ZONE IS COMING RIGHT UP!

BiG NATE
Comix by U! App

Create your own comix with art from BIG NATE! With your favourite characters, cool backgrounds, and fun props and sound effects, you can design your very own Nate-inspired comic strip.

The number of different comix you can make is infinite, so the possibilities are endless. As Nate says, your comix will "surpass all others"!

Includes five original app comix created by Lincoln Peirce himself!

Available on the Apple App store NOW - Search 'Big Nate Comix'.

CHECK OUT MORE BIG NATE

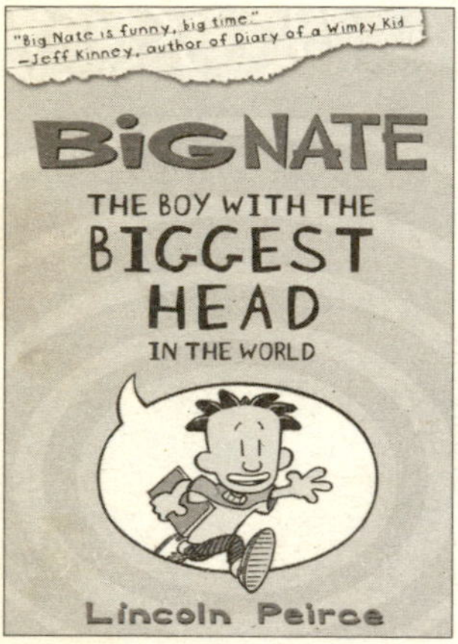
"Big Nate is funny, big time." —Jeff Kinney, author of Diary of a Wimpy Kid
BIG NATE
THE BOY WITH THE BIGGEST HEAD IN THE WORLD
Lincoln Peirce

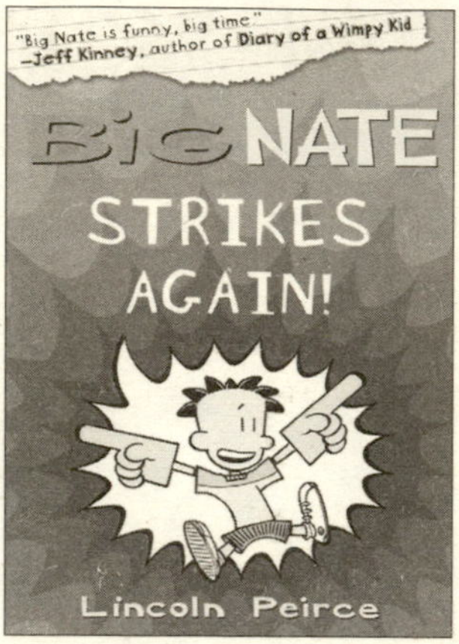
"Big Nate is funny, big time." —Jeff Kinney, author of Diary of a Wimpy Kid
BIG NATE
STRIKES AGAIN!
Lincoln Peirce

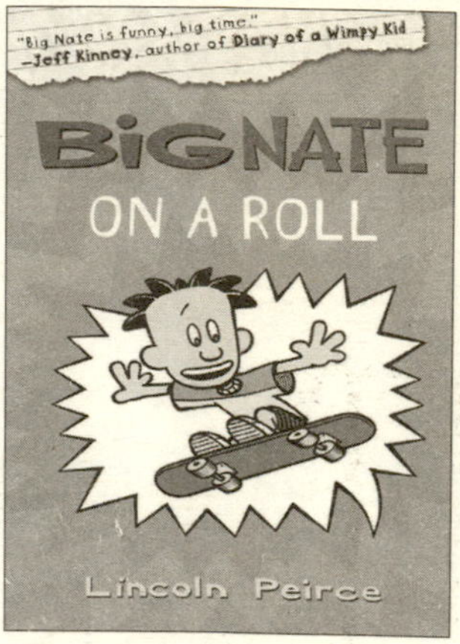
"Big Nate is funny, big time." —Jeff Kinney, author of Diary of a Wimpy Kid
BIG NATE
ON A ROLL
Lincoln Peirce

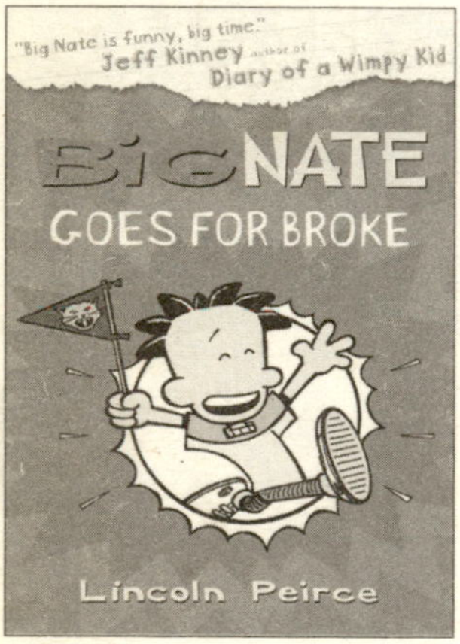
"Big Nate is funny, big time." Jeff Kinney author of Diary of a Wimpy Kid
BIG NATE
GOES FOR BROKE
Lincoln Peirce

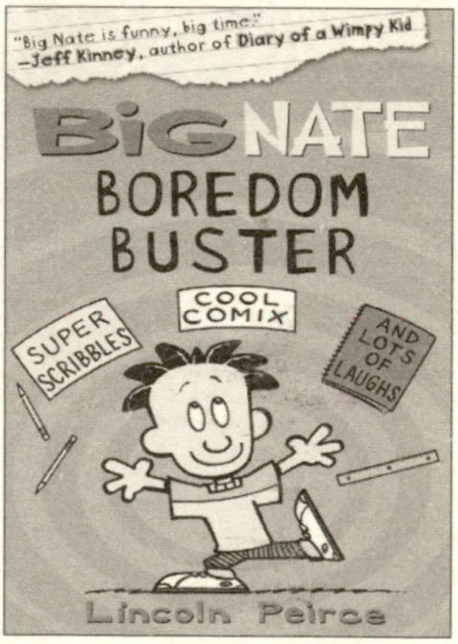
"Big Nate is funny, big time." —Jeff Kinney, author of Diary of a Wimpy Kid
BIG NATE
BOREDOM BUSTER
COOL COMIX
SUPER SCRIBBLES
AND LOTS OF LAUGHS
Lincoln Peirce

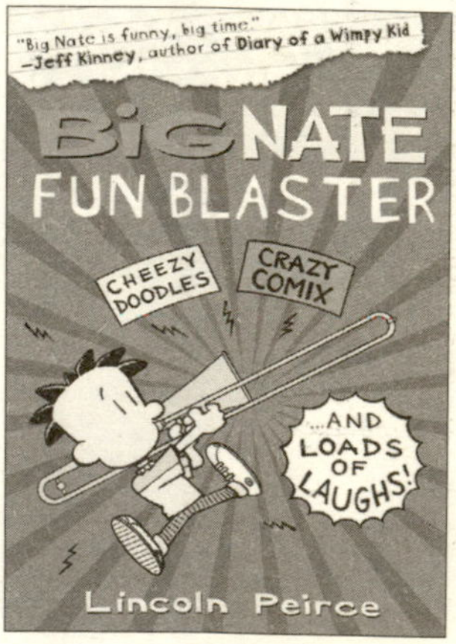
"Big Nate is funny, big time." —Jeff Kinney, author of Diary of a Wimpy Kid
BIG NATE
FUN BLASTER
CHEEZY DOODLES
CRAZY COMIX
...AND LOADS OF LAUGHS!
Lincoln Peirce

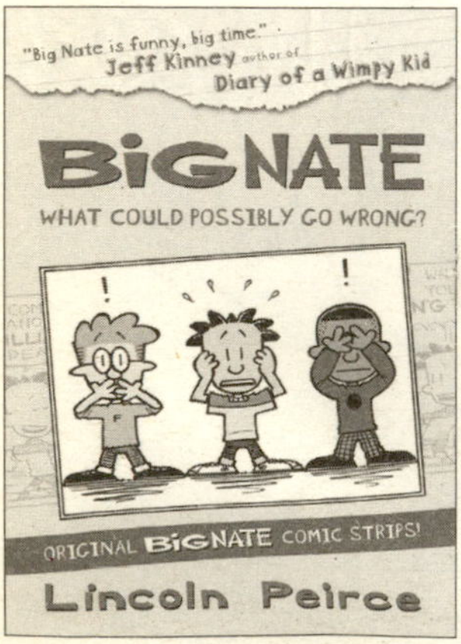
"Big Nate is funny, big time." Jeff Kinney author of Diary of a Wimpy Kid
BIG NATE
WHAT COULD POSSIBLY GO WRONG?
ORIGINAL BIG NATE COMIC STRIPS!
Lincoln Peirce

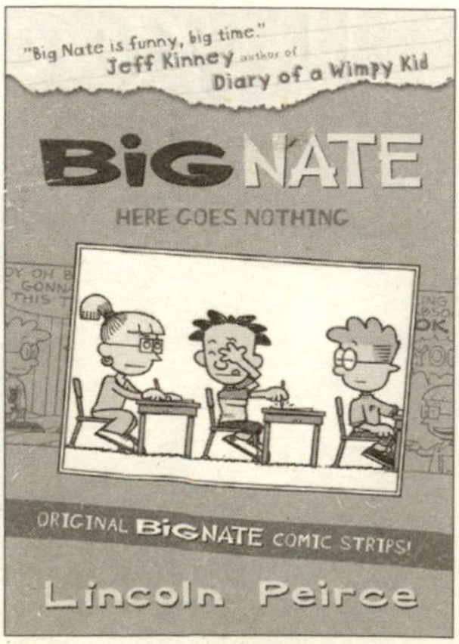
"Big Nate is funny, big time." Jeff Kinney author of Diary of a Wimpy Kid
BIG NATE
HERE GOES NOTHING
ORIGINAL BIG NATE COMIC STRIPS!
Lincoln Peirce

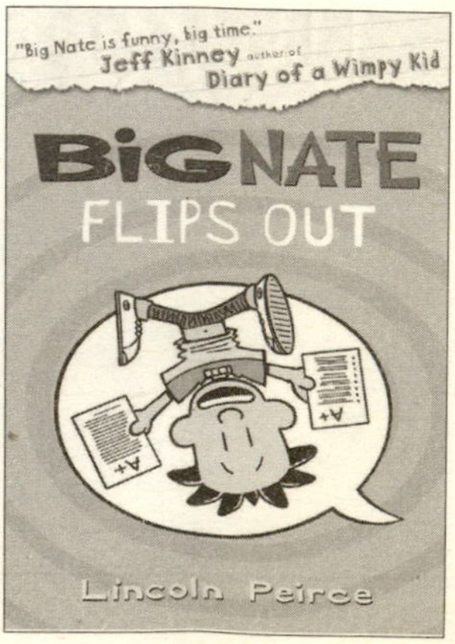
"Big Nate is funny, big time." Jeff Kinney author of Diary of a Wimpy Kid
BIG NATE
FLIPS OUT
Lincoln Peirce